Unlikely Attraction
Delaney's Story

d. w. cee

Unlikely Attraction – Delaney's Story

D. W. CEE

Ebook Edition
Chickygirl Publishing

ISBN-13: 9780615913346
ISBN-10: 0615913342

Hell-o Madamoiselle Delaney!
You bring habitual joy and shiitake-mushroom laughter.
For that I say gracias!

Author's Note

When I first wrote *Indelible Love – Emily's Story*, Laney was a minor character I never thought to bring to life. Even when she appeared in *Indelible Lovin' – Max & Jane's Story*, she was not a part of the big picture, and never did I see her with Donovan Taylor.

In all honesty, the more I developed Donovan, I fell in love with him and considered pairing Jane up with Donovan rather than Max. But, I knew Donovan needed a spunky girl who would keep him on his toes and the most (un)likely match was Delaney Reid.

This book is separated into three sections. Mo(u)rning chronicles their initial "relationship," where Laney sees more heartache than happiness. In (New) Day, we see Laney in a different setting, surrounding herself with new friends and a possible new happiness. But of course, her (K) Night will come after her in the last section and the true courtship begins.

This book is the fourth volume of the Indelible Love series and if you haven't read *Indelible Lovin' – Max & Jane's Story*, I *highly recommend* you read those volumes first, before starting this one. This book contains a lot of information that will answer questions from Max & Jane's blog. If you aren't familiar with the Reid family, you may get lost.

This book has become my absolute favorite story and I can't wait to hear what you think!

Prologue

"What are you doing with this?" I couldn't believe I was holding my diary again, months after it'd been lost. "And where did you find it?"

"Well..."

"DONOVAN TAYLOR! WHY DO YOU HAVE MY DIARY?"

"This is going to sound bizarre, but it was mailed to my house. I got it in the mail with a typed note that said, 'FYI.'"

"Please tell me you are joking. How did my diary get mailed to *your* house of all places and who would do that? And why you?"

"I'm a bit unsure as to why me, but it was, and now here it is."

"Well, I suppose I should thank you. I've been looking for this for months. I tried to remember where I last used it by remembering the last entry, but none of it would come to me."

"Oh, you wrote about being sad about leaving your home in LA, in your last entry."

"YOU READ MY DIARY?" I went a bit ballistic at this point. "HOW COULD YOU READ MY DIARY?"

"Well...I only opened it up, first to see what it was. Then I flipped through the pages to find the owner's name. Then...I read the first few pages to see if I could get a sense of who wrote the journal. And then..."

"Yes? And then...?"

"I got a little sucked into the journal entries."

I started convulsing.

"You're a really good writer, I must say."

"Is that *all* you have to say?"

"I enjoyed your writing?"

"Oh my gosh, oh my gosh, oh my gosh..." I walked in circles while hyperventilating.

This diary-stealing, diary-reading rat, stopped me dead in my circle, put his hand around the back of my neck and kissed me hard! I'd been kissed before, but never this completely.

"Mr. Taylor! Donovan Taylor! What are you doing?"

"You, Miss Delaney, are adorable!"

And then he grabbed me again and kissed me senseless. I gave up my fight...for now.

Mo(u)rning

It all started with a diary that my friend Alice Hancock gave me at my 9th birthday party. It was pink and sparkly and came with a lock and key. Of course, I quickly attached the key to my bracelet and starting August 7, 1999, I wrote in my diary daily. There was not a day that went by when I didn't record what happened to me. Looking back, most of the entries were boring, of course, but this is what got me writing and interested in a possible future career as a scriptwriter. And who would have known, that a wee bitty diary would lead me to the wedding of my dreams. But...I'm getting ahead of myself. The following are just highlights of what led to this beautiful Christmas Day.

Age 9—Summer Vacation

"Laney, where are you? We're all loaded and ready to leave. Please don't lag behind. Your cousins and brother are waiting for you in the RV," Mom yelled while I searched for my diary. I had to take it on my trip since I was going to write about all the details of Yellowstone National Park.

"I'm looking for my diary," I yelled back. Of course, I didn't really yell at my mother, but I was getting a bit worried.

"If it's that pink book with a lock, I think I saw Doug with it in the RV."

"What?" I ran down the steps and hurried into the RV. Doug was holding my diary on a table and Nick had a hammer in his hand, raised up to the roof of the RV. He was about to swing down on my treasured book.

"NO!" I yelled as loudly as my nine-year old body would let me.

My scream freaked out both boys and the hammer ended up hitting Nick on his thigh on its way down, and Doug on the chin on its way up. Lucky for me, the diary was safe! The boys weren't too badly injured, either.

"What'd you do that for?" Doug and Nick yelled back at me. They looked so funny hopping around the RV trying not to cry from the pain.

After laughing as much as I wanted to at them, I argued back, "Serves you right for being nosy. I hope you both suffer the entire trip." With that, I ran out of our RV and into Jake and Jane's RV.

Jake is the coolest, smartest and best-looking boy cousin a girl could ask for. All my friends have a crush on him. He is going to be a senior in high school and he always dates the prettiest cheerleaders. I'm going into 4th grade, Doug is going into 6th grade, Nick is going into 7th grade, and my cousin Jane is going into 8th grade. We all go to the same school and Jake is the only one who says hi to me if he sees me on the playground. Of course, he isn't playing handball or tetherball like me and my friends. When he sometimes walks across the field and sees me, he'll rub the top of my head and call me *Squirt*. All my friends get so jealous because he only talks to me.

Jane is sometimes mean and ignores me. She is only nice when she wants something from me. But, since she is in the junior high campus, I don't see too much of her. My brother for sure ignores me. Nick generally says hi, but he is also on the other campus so I don't see much of him either.

"Why are you in our RV?" Jane was not nice today. Maybe she is on her period. I don't know exactly what a period is but that's what I hear the boys giggling about whenever she is in a foul mood.

"Nick and Doug tried to break open my diary, so I came here to get away from them."

"You and your silly diary. Why do you always write in that thing?"

"'Cuz I like it. Why do you always talk on the phone whenever I come over to your house?"

"'Cuz I like it," she said in the same way I did. I think she was making fun of me.

"Are you on your period?" I asked.

Jane screamed louder than I did when I saw my diary about to be hammered open. Maybe a period is something you don't want destroyed. Who knows?!?

Age 10–He's The One!

I saw my future husband today—the man I'm going to marry. He is sooooooo handsome! He's even more handsome than Jake. He's the brother of Jake's girlfriend, Kelley (I love Kelley!), and Doug tells me that he's also Jake's best friend. When I asked Doug why I hadn't seen him before, he says it's because I'm stupid and I never notice anyone since I'm always either reading or daydreaming. Well, yes...I read a lot and daydream a lot, but NO! I'm not stupid! Why, I just got better grades on my 5th grade report card than Doug did when he was in 5th grade. You see! I'm NOT stupid! Anyways, my future husband's name is Donovan Taylor, and he's soooooooo dreamy. How can anyone be sooooo handsome? Today, Auntie Sandy was girlsitting me (not babysitting, but girlsitting) and Jake, Kelley and Donovan came home from school to pick up snorkeling gear before going to some place called Cabol? They kept saying Cabol this, Cabol that, and I didn't want to sound stupid so I just sat and stared at Donovan.

"Who's this pretty little girl?" my future husband asked.

"I'm Delaney Reid, but everyone calls me Lane or Laney."

"Hello Delaney Reid. Can I call you Delaney? I don't want to be like everyone else and call you by the same name. I'd like to be someone special to you." He winked at me.

"Stop flirting with my ten-year-old cousin. She's seeing stars right now between your smooth talking and 'dizzying good looks.' All women must be blind if they think you're 'devastatingly handsome.'"

"Oh, but he is..." Oh my gosh, oh my gosh, oh my gosh! Did I just say that? Aaaahhh! I wanted to scream and die of embarrassment right in my auntie's kitchen.

"You see...Delaney agrees, so it must be a fact that I'm 'devastatingly handsome!' I'll see you around, Delaney Reid." Donovan touched me. He really, really touched me. He patted the top of my head and told me he'd see me again. This was the best day evahhh!

Age 10 (After Cabol)— I Hate Neon!

The front door opened and I heard Donovan say hello to my father. *Whaaaa?* What was he doing in my house? Oh! My! Gosh! I wanted to die! My night retainers were on—you know the kind with the metal-wrap around the head? I was in my Cinderella "nightgown" and my hair was a mess in pigtails. And I had my neon green underwear that showed through my WHITE nightgown! Why, oh why, does Mom always have to buy me such bright and colorful underwear? And why, oh why, do I always forget that I'm not supposed to wear bright underwear with something white? I'm going to burn all my underwear next time Mom buys any more of them for me!

"How was your Christmas, Little Girl?"

"Why are you here?" I asked in a snippier way than I wanted to ask. Mom was always scolding me these days about sounding "snippy."

"Jake needs to talk to your dad and I'm tagging along."

"Are you going to be a doctor like my dad?"

"No way! I don't have any interest in being a doctor. I suck at science. What about you, Little Girl? You going to be a doctor like your dad?"

"Maybe. I'm good in science and I'm smart, too. I heard my mommy and daddy say I was way smarter than my brother. I don't think they wanted me to hear that, but I heard it."

"I'm sure you are, Cutie-pie. You're definitely cuter than your brother." He patted my cheek with his hand. I was NOT going to wash my face tonight. I'd even lie to Mom when she asked me later if I'd brushed my teeth and washed my face. "You must have lots of boys chasing after you, or maybe you have a boyfriend?"

"What? NO! I don't have a boyfriend…" I shot up from my belly-on-the-floor position and kinda ran around in circles. "I DO NOT HAVE A BOYFRIEND!" I yelled.

Donovan laughed and laughed at me.

"What in heaven's name are you doing?" Daddy asked as he walked in the family room with Jake and Doug.

"Nothing, Daddy." I stopped running, embarrassed I'd acted like a dummy, again.

"Well, whatever you were doing, you might want to know we can all see your neon green underwear!" my brother announced *REALLY* loudly.

"AAAAAHHHHH!!!" I screamed and ran up to my room as I heard all the guys laughing at me.

Age 10—Valentine's Day!

I made Valentine's Day cards for everyone in my class. When I say I made cards, I mean, I REALLY drew, colored, and wrote personal messages to everyone—even the kids who bugged me! Of course, I made an extra big one for Donovan. I didn't know whether or not he'd stop by our house, but I hoped he would because Mom threw the coolest, craziest parties. She's the BEST party planner, evaaaaahhhh! She decided to throw a Valentine's Day party this year and the theme was PINK, my favorite color. Mom is the absolute best in every way. When I woke up this morning, the entire house was pink and filled with hearts and balloons. My room had streamers all over and on my desk sat a big box, bigger than my head—and trust me, my entire family tells me that I have a big head.

"What's this, Mom?"

"A present." *Did my momma think I was stupid?* Of course it was a present. "Don't give me that snippy look, young lady." *How on earth did she know what I was thinking?* "I know 'cuz I'm your momma." *Aaaahhh! She's psycho.* Or is it psychic? Whatever.

"Who's this from?"

"Open it," Daddy suggested.

I did open it, and it was the most fantabulous dress in PINK! "Thank you, thank you, thank you! It's so pretty. Do you think Dono..." I turned

PINK myself and ran into the bathroom with the dress. I think my parents were laughing at me, but I ignored them.

School was soooooo boring and it lasted soooooo long. As soon as it was done, I ran home with Doug and helped Mom wherever she'd let me help. The party started at 6:00pm with a wonderful dinner that Mom did NOT cook. Mom is a great party planner, but not the best cook. Lucky for all of us, she catered the meal. Now, I'm not trying to be mean. She just doesn't cook. However, she does a lot of other cool things, so it's all good.

I quickly ate my dinner with my cousins at the children's table. Jane was pouting because she had to sit with us even though she said she was almost 15 years old. Jane looked gorgeous in her soft pink dress (it helped that Auntie Sandy let her put on blush and lipstick tonight—something my own mom would not let me do). I felt like an ugly duckling! Even worse, my dress was big and poofy; something a little three-year-old would wear. What ten-year-old wears a big, poofy, pale pink dress? Jane was in a long, slinky, pink dress. With her black hair, blue eyes, and the pale pink dress, she looked like a high schooler. With my blonde hair and the big poofy pink dress, I looked like cotton candy with a curly yellow bow on top. Ugh! I was going to have to stay away from my really pretty cousin.

"Hi Donovan!" Jane stood up and greeted him with a great big hug.

"Hello, Beautiful." He answered her with a kiss to her forehead. "Happy Valentine's Day."

"Same to you. Did you just get here?"

"Yeah. Your brother, Kelley, and I just popped in to say hello before heading over to the frat house."

Donovan chatted away with my cousin, and I don't know why, but my heart hurt so much to see him with Jane. And I felt so inadequate next to her. Quietly getting up from my seat, I went up to my room, found the card I'd made for Donovan and threw it in the trashcan. I also tried to take off this stupid dress but of course the complicated buttons in the back made it impossible for me to take it off. This was probably the stupidest thing I've ever done, and I knew Mom was going to yell at me till next Valentine's Day, but I got out the hugest pair of scissors I could find and searched for a way to get this dress off me. *Should I start cutting from the top, or the bottom?* I couldn't make up my mind. *What the hell, I mean heck.* Mom would be furious with my snippiness now...but she wasn't here to see it or hear it...ha! ha! ha!

"What the hell?"

I jumped back at the real *"what the hell"* and the scissor landed right between my big toe and the one right next to it. Would that be called the fore-toe? Second toe? The one right after the big toe? Who! The! Hell! cares what the toe is called when my foot hurts so badly? OW! OW! OW! I hopped around my room but held back the tears because Jake and Donovan had come in my room.

"I'll go get the first aid kit. You stay here with Laney."

"Jake! Please don't tell Mom! I'll be in big trouble!"

He laughed at me (again!). "All right. I'll clean and bandage you up myself," he answered and walked away.

"Why the hell did you have a pair of scissors the size of Jaw's mouth on your dress?"

"I couldn't unbutton the dress so the only way out was to cut it off."

I think Donovan thought I was coo coo for cocoa puffs—and by the way, isn't that a great saying? Daddy says that about some of his patients, though I don't think he means for me to hear it.

"Do you normally cut off all your dresses if you can't wait for your mom to help you take them off?" He was trying really hard not to laugh at me. WHY oh WHY do these people always laugh at me? WHY can't he just give me a hug and kiss on my head like he did to Jane? Instead, this boy, man, college student—whatever!—was always laughing at me. *Aaaarrrggghhh!*

"No." There was so much blood coming out and it hurt so badly, that's about all I could say.

"Laney." Uncle Bobby was here. Thank GOD! "Let's see what's happening."

Uncle Bobby is a doctor like Dad, but in a different part of the body. He must be much smarter than Daddy because Daddy only knows about the heart, but Uncle Bobby practices something called general medicine, which means he takes care of the whole body. I'd never tell Daddy I thought Uncle Bobby was smarter, but I think I'm right.

"It's bleeding so much." I croaked so I wouldn't cry.

"Ooh, this looks pretty deep. I'm going to have to suture the wound. Jake, give me my kit." My cousin did just that. "This might sting a bit. I'm going to have to clean it first."

As soon as Uncle Bobby put the cotton pad with antiseptic on me, I yelped, "SHIT," then added very quickly when I saw the look on all of their faces, "-take mushroom!" Uncle Bobby's body started convulsing, and he couldn't stop laughing at me. Then, Jake and Donovan joined in. I was probably redder than the red balloons in my room.

"You want me to hold your hand when your uncle starts with the stitches?" Donovan offered, and I was no dummy. The offer was taken even before the question was finished.

Getting stitches is not for the weakling. It hurt! But, I didn't cry in front of Donovan and this crazy weird feeling in my stomach that came on after Donovan started holding my hand, helped take my mind off the needle tying my two toes together.

"What do you keep muttering?" Donovan asked.

"Huh? I'm not saying anything."

"Yes you are. You keep saying all these words that don't have any meaning when stated together."

"Oh." *Shiit*ake mushroom! I didn't realize I was saying any words aloud.

"Say them louder, Laney."

"Do I have to, Uncle Bobby? I'd prefer to keep them to myself. It's just my private collection of words."

"I'd like to hear them," he said with a nice smile.

"Oh, OK. Here goes....*shiit*ake mushroom, Hoover *Damn*, *hell*-o, *as*-*s*inine, ha*bitch*ual and there are a couple more but I think I'll stop before I get into any more trouble." My head went down. I waited for Uncle Bobby to have a "word" with me.

"Where did these words come from, Laney?"

"I make them up. And I promise I only use them in my head whenever the situation is extreme, like it is now. I don't use these words on anyone else. It's just my private collection of words, Uncle Bobby."

"So, it's like a substitute word for the actual bad word itself?" Jake was snickering at me. And so was Donovan.

It wasn't cool of them to make fun of me. I got mad! "Um, *HELL*-o, I think that's called a euphemism...," answered the girl who was in a lot of pain, and with a lot of snarkiness. After getting cut with a pair of scissors, I never wanted to use the word snip(py), ever again! Donovan and Jake were practically on the floor, shaking with laughter. Uncle Bobby was too. "Have I put you all in *stitches?* Can we finish up *my stitches* once yours are contained?"

"Where on earth did you get such a large vocabulary, Delaney? Who teaches you all this stuff?"

"Nobody teaches me. I read, unlike some people in this household." I pretended to cough and say Doug's name at the same time.

"I don't think we need to go anywhere for entertainment tonight. I could hang out with your cousin all night and be perfectly happy."

Really? Meeeee toooooo!

"I think you're all set, young lady. It will be up to you to explain to your parents what happened here."

"Thank you, Uncle Bobby. When you're too old to take care of your-self, I'll help you." Maybe that wasn't the best thing to say?!?

"Why thank you, Laney. Not even my own kids have offered help in my dotage. I'll keep it in mind."

"Bye." I called out to my uncle and expected the other two guys to leave. "Good-bye?" I said to the both of them.

"Before I leave, I want to know why there's a handmade Valentine's Day card in your trashcan."

Oh! My! Gosh! Donovan was almost at my trashcan picking out his card.

"NO!" I screamed. And that helped. He stopped long enough for me to grab the card out from under him.

"Is that for your boyfriend?" Donovan teased. "He must have the same initials as mine as I see a huge D in the front and a T in the back."

Mortification with a capital M—thy name is Delaney! I could be a bit melodramatic at times, but at this very moment, I should be nothing less. Donovan almost guessed my secret.

"Stop harassing a ten-year-old and let's get going. Kelley's going to be waiting."

"I can't leave till Delaney tells me who she made the card for and why it's in the trashcan."

"I made it for a boy. But I got mad at the boy for paying attention to another girl. So I trashed it." I looked him dead in the eye and dared him to challenge me. But inside, I was sooooo nervous he may challenge me. "Satisfied?"

He smiled his one-million megawatt smile and said, "Happy Valentine's Day, Little Girl. See you again, soon."

This was the best Valentine's Day evahhh!

Age 10—Easter

$\mathcal{E}$aster is always on Uncle Billy's boat in San Diego. His boat isn't that big, but somehow we all make it work. Today, with the weather being so nice, I was told we were sailing somewhere deep into the ocean. I love water! And when I make this statement, I mean what I say. I LOVE WATER! I can surf, much better than my brother, of course. I swim well enough to be on a swim team, and I love to jump off the high, high diving boards. I haven't learned to water ski yet, but I figure that's coming up soon—like maybe this summer in Hawaii.

"When did you get that dress, and with what money?" Mom was commenting on my Easter outfit. After that cotton candy dress fiasco, I asked Mom to get me a non-poofy dress. Her answer to my plea—a Lilly Pulitzer dress that would be great...if I were FIVE years old. I'm TEN now and can NOT wear a dress that makes me look like a baby. Plus, Jake is coming to Easter brunch with Kelley, and where they are, Donovan isn't far behind.

"I bought it." My proud announcement didn't sit well with Mom. If Valentine's Day taught me anything, I learned I didn't want to look like a baby, I didn't want any more pastels (sorry, RL and Lilly Pulitzer), and I didn't want to look like everyone else. I wanted to POP, and my orange dress POPPED! "Isn't it pretty?"

"It's beautiful, Baby." Daddy finally came out to the car, ready to leave. "Did your mother buy it for you?"

"No, I didn't. She must have taken my credit card and made another online purchase. Young lady," uh-oh…here came the scolding. "You are not to use my card…"

"Let her be, Babs. It's Easter, she looks gorgeous—in fact, that dress is much sweeter than the one you picked out for her. Maybe you should let her buy her own clothes from now on. Then we won't have this issue."

"Thank you, Daddy." I kissed him on the cheek and jumped in the car before Mom could continue her lecture.

Our ride to San Diego was boring, and as expected, Uncle Billy took the boat out to sea. Right before we left, Jake, Kelley and Donovan hopped aboard, and I knew today was going to be fantastic! But the water was choppier than usual, so I stood, holding the railing, hoping to ease my rioting stomach.

"Hey there, Little Girl. Whatcha doing here by yourself?"

"I'm feeling a little queasy so I thought I'd come here and calm my stomach."

"Laney," Doug yelled. "You want to jump in the ocean with us?"

Between feeling like I was going to throw-up and not wanting to take off my POP-orange dress, I didn't want to go in, but everyone was doing it and I didn't want to look like a chicken. I thought I should follow along.

"You going to jump in with all of us?" I hoped Donovan would join us, but I doubted it since he was wearing the most handsome suit, *evahhh!*

"You're not scared to jump in? You need me to hold your hand, again?" Donovan was teasing me and I liked it. I probably had on my dorky smile but all was good because Donovan was with me and not Jane.

"I'm happy to hold *your* hand, Donovan, if *you're* too scared to jump in," I teased back. Before he could get a word in, I grabbed his hand and pulled us both into the water.

"I can't believe you did that," he said while rubbing the water out of his face. "I'm fully clothed," he complained and started splashing water on my face, then swam over to dunk me in the ocean. We were both fully clothed. My bright orange dress floated in the water with me, but since I had a bathing suit underneath, it was a-OK.

"Race you back to the boat," I hollered getting away from Donovan. He swam after me, grabbed my right foot and pulled me under. He swam ahead, laughing away until I caught his jacket that trailed behind him. Hanging on, I let him pull me as he struggled back toward the boat. When he slowed, I took my chance and jumped on his back. He swam with me on his back over to the boat, up the ladder, and onto the deck. I couldn't let go because I didn't want to let go. That was so much fun!

"All right, Little Girl, let's get you dried up." Leaning back gently, he made sure my feet were on the deck and he placed the large towel around my body. I knew for sure, right then and there, that I loved Donovan Taylor!

Age 10—Spring Break

Can you believe my luck? Daddy says we are going to Hawaii—the Big Island this time—when we could be camping with Jake's family and Donovan's family! I begged and begged, but Daddy says he doesn't camp. Who wants to go to the Big Island and stay at some place with a weird name like Four Seasons Hulahula, or something like that, when you can sleep in tents and see a bear in Yosemite?

"But Dad!" Jane had her own complaints. "Why are we going camping instead of Paris this spring? I don't want to sleep on the ground. I don't want to shower in a public place. And I don't want to take all these long hikes you keep mentioning."

"Sweetheart, it'll be a lot of fun. I promise! This will probably be the last time the entire family can get together, both for us and for the Taylors. We will rent two large RVs and spend ten days in nature."

TEN days with Donovan? Why Jane and not me? *WAAAHHHH!* I really wanted to cry.

It was a bummer to be in Hawaii with just the four of us, but I had to admit, it was fun. I got to parasail, and surf and take water skiing lessons. We went to a luau and saw the big volcano. Doug bugged me so much on this trip I thought I was going to go coo coo for cocoa puffs.

But overall, it was fun to be in Hawaii, again. I hope Jane won't brag about her trip to Yosemite when I see her. I so don't want to hear about her and Donovan!

Age 10—Summer Break

I believe I mentioned that I love the water!?! We swim a lot in the summer time. We usually go to Gram's backyard to swim because she has the biggest pool and because my daddy and uncles put in a humongo slide in Gram's pool. There are actually three slides built in a crazy, curvy, swurvy way that criss-cross above and below each other, and eventually straighten out to a side-by-side-by-side slide. Sammy, who is my age, and I are on the slide, daily. Today, almost every cousin on the block decided to join us and we had a gigantic party. The water guns were out, all the floaties were blown up and we lounged, played water tag, cannonballed into the pool, and had water slide races. I love summer. What about no homework, no school, and no mom nagging me about studying wouldn't I like? Doug and I are going to some camp in a few weeks, but for now life is good. And of course, it got better the moment Donovan stepped into the backyard with Jake and cannonballed into the pool. We all gave them a wide berth and Donovan popped up right next to me!

"Hello, Little Girl. How have you been?"

"I'm good. How are you, Donovan?"

"Great now that I see you!" *Gaaawwwddd!* Could he be anymore perfect? "Whatcha' got planned for the summer?"

"I'm going to swim every day till Mom ships us off to the East Coast for three weeks for some summer camp. Then I'll be right back here, swimming again."

"I'll be on the East Coast as well doing an internship. What state are you going to be in?"

"Um...Michigan? Minnesota? Montana? Dunno. Can't remember which state, but it starts with an M."

Donovan started guffawing. "None of those states are on the East Coast. Those are more Midwestern states. Maybe Maine?"

"Maybe. Who knows? I just know that Mom and Dad are getting rid of us so they can take a vacation without us. I heard they're going to be all over Europe. Dad's taking a few weeks off from the hospital and vacationing 'in peace.'" I curled my two forefingers and two middle fingers and made the quotation marks while saying the words, "in peace." Donovan laughed even harder. "What's an internship?" I asked.

"It's where you work, but don't get paid."

"Why would you or anyone want to do that?" Maybe Donovan wasn't as smart as I thought he was. Why would anyone be tricked into working for no dinero? Even I knew that wasn't a smart thing to do.

"It's so I can get experience in a certain field to determine whether or not I want to work in that field."

"Are you going to be gone the whole summer?"

"I am, Little Girl. I'll miss your smiling face and genius-sized vocabulary." Oh my gosh! He would miss me! Maybe he likes me like I like him? "Hop on my back, Little Girl. Let's go challenge your cousin Jake to a water slide contest."

Of course I got on his back and stayed on his back as long as I could. Donovan's younger sisters were so lucky to have such a great big brother. He was so much fun to be with. I doubt he bugged them like Doug bugged me. After beating both Donovan and Jake on the slide three out of five times, I hopped up on his back, and Donovan started spinning me like crazy. Sammy was on Jake's back and both of them started spinning us in the pool.

"Donovan, stop! I'm really dizzy."

"Just hold on a little bit longer, Delaney. We have to beat Jake and Sammy. We need to be the last two standing in this dizzy contest."

Being the competitor that I was, I wanted to win and I didn't want to let Donovan down. I held on, closed my eyes and tried to think of something that would make me less dizzy. Finally, Donovan stopped and we both collapsed into the water. Immediately, I could feel the throw-up coming up my throat. I walked/ran as fast as I could in the pool to try to get to a restroom.

"What's the matter?" Donovan stopped me as I got up on the first step. I did my best to get my wrist out of his hand, but he held it tighter the more I fought it. "You OK?"

I turned around quickly to tell him that I was sick and that I needed to throw up, but as I started saying those words, the most horrifying thing happened to me. I threw up on myself, first. And if that didn't make me want to die right then and there, as Donovan tried to step back and get away from me, I let out the most God-awful projectile throw-up right on his head and face.

I ran away from everybody, leaving a trail of throw-up, all the way to the pool house. God, just kill me now!

Age 11—My Birthday!

$\mathcal{M}$om threw me the craziest water-themed birthday party today! It was soooo much fun. We had water slide contests on Gram's slide, a crazy tall blow-up water slide that was maybe 50 feet high (OK, I may be exaggerating a bit...), water gun fights, who can make the biggest cannonball challenge, and a Slip 'N Slide on blocks of ice. I could tell Mom was praying none of us would get hurt on those blocks. I invited my entire class and all my cousins to join in the fun. Everyone came except for the person I most wanted to see. He was still on the East Coast somewhere working for free. Doug won the hot dog eating contest with eight hot dogs and ten glasses of lemonade. I am not getting anywhere near his room tonight. He isn't going to be a happy camper when the hot dogs decide they need to leave his stomach—and fast! Nick won the cannonballing contest. That's because Nick is a lot heavier than all of us. Most of my friends are my height (OK, maybe a bit shorter because right now, I am even taller than my brother—but don't tell him I told you so), but Nick is taller and much, much heavier. I heard Auntie Sandy telling Mom one day that Nick's waistline is larger than Uncle Bobby's, and he is only fourteen going on fifteen. I think he might need to DIET one day.

"Laney, this has got to be the coolest party I've ever attended." Kelley came over to me and gave me a huge birthday present.

"Thanks, Kelley. Did you and Jake have a good time visiting your brother?"

"We did. And my brother sends you a very happy birthday kiss." She kissed me on the cheek and I swear it felt like it was Donovan kissing me for real.

I giggled and gave Kelley a huge hug and got her clothes all wet.

"Kelley, I hope you marry my cousin Jake. He's the best guy any girl could wish for in the whole wide world!"

"I agree. Then we can be cousins by marriage. Or maybe, if you married my only brother, we could be sisters!" she exclaimed.

How on earth did she know? I love Kelley! I love Jake! But most of all, I love DONOVAN!

Age 11—Christmas

We always celebrate Christmas dinner at Uncle Bobby and Aunt Sandy's house but this year, we had to have a Christmas Eve dinner. Mom told me why, but I can't remember. I think it has something to do with someone going somewhere and...who knows...who the *hell*-o cares? I get to open my Christmas presents very, very soon, and that's all I care about!

"Laney? Are you finished getting dressed? We need to walk over to Uncle Bobby's now."

"I'll meet you there, Mom. I'm not quite ready."

"All right. Hurry up."

"OK." *Phew!* I got out of that argument. You see, I bought another dress pretending to be Barbara Reid. Mom bought me this green, red and black plaid Christmas outfit. I know Christmas was all about green and red, but outfits with those color combination should be banned! I'd walk into Uncle Bobby's house after most everyone arrived, then Mom wouldn't be able to make a huge deal about me using her credit card...again!

At age 11, it isn't customary for girls to order their own clothes. Mom is a genius at decorations and party planning, but she needs a wee bit of help in the clothes department. Take for instance today. She is wearing a red long pencil skirt with a green fluffy teacher-style Christmas cardigan that has Santa and his elves all over the knit sweater. It's really the type of sweater you see on your elementary school teachers. You know the ones with bells for Rudolph's nose, type of cardigans? My mom's a beautiful lady but the way she dresses diminishes her looks. I am not going to let her taste in clothes ruin my chances of being noticed by a certain someone whose family had been invited to spend Christmas with us.

"Delaney Grace Reid!" *Uh-oh!* Why oh why did I have to run into Mom the moment I stepped into Uncle Bobby's house?

"Hi Aunt Sandy!" I turned my attention to my aunt and another lady who was standing next to Mom. "Hello." I brought the other lady into our conversation.

"Hi Laney. Beautiful dress." Aunt Sandy winked at me. She was so smart and helpful. She already *ass*umed the trouble I was in with my mother.

"Who are you?" The stranger asked. "Is she yours, Babs?"

"She is..." The way Mom said that wasn't good...I was so busted!

"What's so funny, Sandy?" The stranger wanted answers and she was about to get them.

"Hey, Little Girl!" My savior! Donovan would save me from this mess.

"Hi Donovan! Hi Jake! Hi Kelley!"

"Hey, Cousin. Don't you look pretty, tonight!"

"Nice dress, Laney." Did I tell you how much I loved Kelley? "You pick it out yourself?"

"Um yeah, and my generous mom bought it for me. Isn't she nice? It wasn't even on sale but I was able to purchase it."

Mom's face crinkled like a french fry. "And how generous was I, Delaney Grace Reid?"

"Um...generous...?"

"Give me a ballpark figure."

"Well..."

While I was doing this song and dance with Mom, Aunt Sandy whispered to everyone in the room about my "identity theft" habits. The stranger, who turned out to be Mrs. Taylor, laughed aloud. The three collegians, laughed almost as loudly as Mrs. Taylor. I, for one, was hoping Dad would walk in and save me if Donovan Taylor wasn't going to jump in.

"Please tell me this dress was south of $100."

I let out a weak, *"Hahaha..."* and tried to walk out of the kitchen.

"You may not leave here till you give me a clear answer, young lady."

"Oh, all right!" In my bravest voice I said, "With tax and delivery it cost $300." Mom gasped—like, loudly! "But, I have $200 saved up from doing all my chores. I'll pay for $200 of it, and if you'll let me put it on lay-away, I'll pay it off in less than a year. I'll still do all my chores and you don't have to give me my $10 allowance."

Mom had her hand on her forehead. Everyone else just outright laughed at me. I had no idea why any of this was funny!

"And by the way, Mom...I do most of the chores in the house, but get paid the same as Doug. There's something wrong with this system. In addition, how is a girl supposed to buy anything when she only gets paid $10 a month? I'd have to save up for almost three years before I could buy a dress. And what about shoes? I'd be in college before I could save up for a pretty dress *and* a pair of decent dress shoes."

Mom's head titled back and all I heard was a sigh.

"You know, Delaney," my dream man spoke up, "I haven't bought you a Christmas present yet. Why don't I pay for the rest of your dress?" *Gaaawwwddd!* Did I ever tell you I love this man?

"No." What a party-pooper that Barbara Reid was! "That's way too much for Donovan to be paying for your irresponsibility."

Come on, Mom! Can't I just accept and move on?

"How about if I chip in with Donovan?" I love Jake!

"I'll chip in, too. Then it's only $33 a person." Kelley smiled at me.

I ran over and hugged all three of my saviors—of course, Donovan got the last and longest hug.

What a fantastic Christmas!

Age 11—New Year's Day

New Year's Day is always a long, long day. It starts way too early for my liking. Our whole family meets at the end of the cul-de-sac and walks far, far away to watch the parade. The great thing about the parade—the cool floats; the bad thing about the parade—the porta-potty. Those are so gross. I always make sure I don't drink anything so I can hold my pee all morning.

"Where are the donuts?" Donovan said as we picked up the Taylor family on our way to the parade. They live very close to us and every year, we walk to the parade together.

"Mom has them in the rolling cooler with hot cocoa."

"Happy New Year, Little Girl."

"Same to you, Donovan."

"Did you make a New Year's resolution?"

"I sure did!" *My resolution is to get married to you at exactly double my age, today.*

"What is it?"

"It's for me to know and for you to find out...maybe..." I smiled and tried to walk ahead so I wouldn't have to explain myself.

"Get back here," he pulled me right back to his side and had his arms around me.

"Give me a hint."

"Nope!"

"What's the big deal? Why can't you tell me?"

The big deal is…I want to marry you.

"Can't a girl have any secrets around here?"

"You are too funny, Little Girl. One day, I hope I'll end up with a girl who'll keep me laughing like you do."

And one day, I hope I'll end up with you!

When Donovan was busy hanging out with Jake, I wrote a note and slipped it into his coat pocket. The note read, *Donovan, I truly hope you will one day help my New Year's resolution come true. See you again in 11 years.*

Age 11—Valentine's Day

$\mathcal{M}$om didn't throw a Valentine's Day party this year, but I was determined to give Donovan a card and tell him how I feel. I was old enough to know who I wanted to marry, and if I didn't let Donovan know that he was the perfect man for me, someone else might steal him from me. Today was it. I was going to confess and get this over with. Now, I just needed somehow to find Donovan.

"Hi Jake. Happy Valentine's Day!"

"Same to you, Squirt."

"Did you get a nice gift for Kelley?"

"Well...Kelley and I decided to call it quits."

"Again? Why do you and Kelley break-up so much?"

Jake laughed at me. "It's complicated, Squirt. I don't know if I want to marry Kelley, and if that's the case, there's no reason for us to go on."

Now after having dated for this long, how could you not want to marry each other? What was I missing? "Who do you want to marry, then?"

"Dunno, Squirt. Maybe I'll meet her one day in the dead of the night at some random place like the grocery store."

Now it was my turn to laugh. "You've been reading way too many of those Harlequin novels my mom likes to read." Jake laughed and messed up my hair. "Don't tell Mom, but I read one the other day and there were a lot of things in that book I didn't understand."

"Yeah? Like what?"

"What's an orgasm?" I don't know why, but Jake started choking on his drink when I asked him this question. "Are you OK?"

It took him a while to calm down, and he wheezed out an answer. "Well...it's um...why do you ask?"

"Because the heroine in the book kept having one. The book always had her screaming the hero's name and yelling out, 'I'm coming!' I don't get where she was coming to and why she had to yell that out. He was always right there on top of her...or was it behind her...or were they upside down? Oh, I don't know. The two were always in strange positions."

"Uh, maybe you should stick to your books rather than reading your mom's?"

"I think I will. Anyways..." I kind of beat around the bush and tried to slyly ask about Donovan. "How come Donovan hasn't been around lately?"

Jake held back initially, then told me, "He's been busy."

"Doing what?"

"Well, he has a new girlfriend and they've been spending a lot of time together."

"Oh!" was all I could say.

I guess what I felt right now was what those Harlequin heroines felt when their heroes left them mid-way through the book. Just like these women, my heart hurt, I wanted to cry, and I didn't know what to do with myself.

"He'll be around, again. Don't worry, Laney. He won't forget you."

For the first time, I knew Jake was wrong. Donovan had already forgotten me.

Age 11—Summer

om is shipping us off to that camp again on the East Coast, and I'm bummed to report I haven't seen Donovan in ages. He stopped coming by. I have no idea what he is doing other than hanging out with his girlfriend, and why he's forgotten me. Whenever Jake is around, I ask him about Donovan, but Jake never gives me a clear answer. Either he doesn't want me to know, or he himself doesn't know.

"Are you all packed for your trip?"

"Yes, Daddy. Doug and I are ready to leave."

"I'll miss you, Baby! Three weeks is a long time to be away from your family."

"Then why do you send us away if you'll miss us?"

Daddy chuckled. "We want you to experience life away from home. It's a privilege to be going to a summer school at a prestigious university, not a punishment. Didn't you enjoy it last year?"

"I did." *But I don't want to miss seeing Donovan if he stops by.*

"And plus, you're my genius in the family. I know you'll be well challenged by the classes at this program."

"OK, Daddy. But if anything happens at home, or if anyone is looking for me, can you let him...or her know where I'll be and how he can contact me?"

Daddy chuckled again. "I'll be sure to let *him*...or her know."

"Thank you, Daddy. You're the greatest!"

Age 12—New Year's Day

It's been so long since I've seen Donovan; I almost forget what he looks like. He never came to my birthday party, he didn't stop by our Thanksgiving dinner, and he was absent at Christmas. I was about to give up on him when I finally saw him today!

"Hello, Delaney! Made any New Year's resolutions, lately?"

"Donovan!" I was so happy to see him; I embarrassingly threw my body at him and hugged him. "Where've you been?"

"You missed me?"

"Of course I mi..." And then, I saw her. The woman who eventually walked right next to Donovan looked like a supermodel. She was so beautiful I couldn't even be mad at her for holding Donovan's hand. All I did was stare at her. I was so stupid at times.

"Hello," she said to me.

"Uh, hi?" I questioned and answered at the same time. "Who are you?" What another stupid question.

This woman and Donovan laughed at me. "She's cute. Did you say her name was Delaney?"

"Um, it's Laney, to you. Only Donovan calls me Delaney." I almost bit her head off. What was wrong with me? Instead of embarrassing myself anymore, I walked ahead of those two and hung out with my cousin, Sam.

"What's wrong, Laney?"

"Sam...so many things are wrong, I think I might just become a nun!"

"You're so melo all the time." She laughed at me, too. "Did you see that crazy pretty woman Donovan came with? Who is she?"

"Who the hell knows!"

"Laney!" Sam was shocked to hear my language.

"Um, I mean, hell-o, Sam. How are you?"

"Yeah, good one. As if I don't know you just said a bad word? Where's Jane, today?"

"Who knows...who cares?"

What a way to start the New Year. This year is going to suck!

Age 12 Spring—I Asked Him To Marry Me Today, But...

Today I did it! I made sure that Donovan and I were going to get married. I was sick of waiting for him to come to me. So when I saw the chance, I took it and proposed! Of course, I am only twelve and I need to finish middle school, high school, college, and (my mom says) graduate school. But I am going to marry Donovan. This is how it happened. I asked Donovan to marry me on a sheet of paper scribbled in my messiest handwriting. The instruction on the sheet said for him to meet me on the swing of my front porch at 11:00 pm, when I knew the entire family would be asleep. It's 10:59pm right now and I'm on the swing waiting for Donovan to appear. But while I am waiting, let me explain how I proposed and how I am going to become Mrs. Donovan Taylor.

Nick, Jane, Doug and I were swimming at Jane's house and Jake, Kelley and Donovan came home. All is right in Jake and Kelley's world again and they are happily dating. When Donovan came out in his swimsuit, I snuck over to his clothes and shoved my proposal letter in his front pocket. Then I jumped back in the pool

"Donovan, you're splashing water all over my hair!" I complained as I purposely got close to him while he was doing the backstroke. I hadn't seen Donovan since New Year's Day and I'd missed him.

"Sorry, Little Girl. Did I get any in your eyes?" He was so nice checking that my eyes weren't hurt.

"I'm all right," I answered. "Are you done with school? Are you and Jake and Kelley home for good?"

"No, Little Girl. We are here for the afternoon, cooling off, and then we are going to a frat party. It'll be our last one before we all head off for our summer trips before graduate school."

"What graduate school are you going to?"

"I'm off to law school in New York. Jake will still be around here for med school, and my sister Kelley is off to business school in Chicago."

New York? How was I going to see him again if he went to New York? How were we going to get married if he lived all the way in New York? Last time I went to New York, we had to ride the airplane for a super long time.

"Hey." Jake interrupted our conversation. "Are we going down to Kate's tonight after the party? I need to pack an overnight bag if we're staying with her."

"Yeah, Jake. I'm spending the night with her. She says her guest room is ready for you and Kelley if you want to come."

"Who's Kate?" Like I didn't know...

"My girlfriend."

"Girlfriend? When did you get a girlfriend?" Shoot! He was still with this woman. What was I going to do with the letter? I had already shoved it in the pocket of his pants. Should I go through with this? Did I need to surreptitiously get out of the pool and take that letter out of his pocket? Would he die laughing at me when he read the letter? Why did no one in this family tell me that Donovan still had a girlfriend? *Aaargh!* I wanted to shout, cry, throw a fit...*why me?*

"Kate and I have been dating for a little while. Remember, you met her on New Year's Day?"

Yeah, I remember meeting that grotesquely beautiful woman! "Are you going to marry her?" Now why did I need to ask him that and give him ideas? This man was to marry me, not Kate!

Donovan looked at me super surprised. "How did you know I was going to propose to Kate?"

You are? NO! "I..." I stuttered. "I didn't know. I was only asking." I had to leave, like NOW! *Don't cry, don't cry, don't cry,* I kept telling myself.

Jumping out of the pool as fast as I could, I ran home and cried on my bed. Why did this have to happen to me? I thought Donovan and I were perfect for each other. Why, oh why, was he planning on marrying someone else?

"Laney," Mom sat on my bed and woke me up. "It's time for dinner. Do you want to eat with us, or would you like to go back to sleep?"

"I'll stay asleep, if that's all right with you."

"Sure, Baby. See you in the morning."

Why was I asleep at this time of the day? I thought through what happened today and...oh *shiit*ake mushroom! I proposed to Donovan Taylor through a letter, and it was still in his pocket! Jumping out of bed as fast I could, I ran to Jake's house but no one was home. It was dark outside and everyone had gone to wherever they were going.

I remembered sadly that Donovan was going to propose to his girlfriend, Kate, tonight.

Regardless, I decided to wait for him on my swing because I knew Donovan loved me, in his own way, and we would get married. We couldn't get married for a long time, but I knew it was meant to be for us!

"Young lady, what the hell are you doing out on the swing at this hour?"

"Daddy..." I said getting up, wiping the drool off my face. "What time is it?"

"It's morning!" Dad was upset. "The whole house was in an upheaval looking for you. Why are you asleep on the front porch?"

Shoot! I didn't think I'd fall asleep out here. "Do I have to explain? Would you believe me if I told you that my room was hot and that I needed some fresh air?"

Dad looked at me as though I was coo coo for cocoa puffs. "Explain!"

"Oh, all right! Someone was supposed to meet me here but this some-one never showed up. That's all I'm going to say, and that's that!" I came on strong, and this made Dad actually laugh rather than scowl.

"Don't ever do this again, young lady. We were scared somebody made off with our beautiful daughter. It's not safe to sleep outside, even on our cul-de-sac."

"Sorry." I showed penance. "I won't ever do this again because no one is ever coming for me."

And that's what became of my proposal—absolutely NOTHING!

Age 18—Senior Prom

*W*ho at this age can say that she has never really been out on a real date? Even more inconceivable, who would keep herself from dating because she was waiting for some guy, ten years her senior, to notice her? I can raise my hand to both questions. Who is a moron? Yep, I raise both hands really high to that last question.

"Laney, why did you turn down Brad for the senior prom? He seems like such a nice guy."

"He is Mom and he's a great friend, but..."

"He's not Donovan?"

Mom and I started talking about Donovan Taylor when I got asked to the junior prom last year and didn't go. She asked me point blank if he was the reason I never went out on dates—not that either of my parents minded that I didn't get friendly with boys.

"I know you think I'm ridiculous for holding onto this childhood crush, but I can't help what I feel. If I could, I would have let it go a long time ago. Really, I don't want to have these feelings for a man who doesn't even remember me."

"You're being melo again!" Melo was short for melodramatic, according to Mom. "You just saw him at Uncle Bobby's birthday. Didn't you talk to him?"

"No. He didn't even notice me. He only stopped by briefly and he was with that crazy beautiful woman. She's so old! Why would a young guy like Donovan want to date an old woman?"

Mom started cracking up. "She's not *that* old. I'm sure a woman in her late 30s has some uses."

"Yeah? Like what? What could she possibly do for him?"

Mom choked on her coffee. This Kate lady was gorgeous, but she stuck out like a sore thumb at Uncle Bobby's birthday party. She didn't say much to anyone except Jake and Donovan, and she was dressed like she was going to some movie premiere. Who wore a Valentino gown to a simple birthday dinner? I wished Jane could've been there so I could ask her questions about Kate, but Jane arrived after Kate left.

"There's nothing wrong with crushing on a boy, but don't let him stop your life. Go out, enjoy yourself, and meet new friends. You're going to be in college in a few months, and I don't want you to stop living life, waiting for someone who may never materialize into anything more than a childhood crush."

Mom was right, but her comment crushed my hope. I guess I should listen to Mom and go find myself a prom date.

January 7, 2013
It's Nice To Meet You, Donovan Taylor

My life took an unexpected turn when I went to Jane's work to drop off her Kindle. I saw my "future husband" again for the first time since I was in grade school. Well, I suppose I'd seen him a few times in between, but those didn't count since he never came up and talked to me. Case in point, Jake and Emily's wedding. I know he was busy as a groomsman, but it wouldn't have killed him to talk to me, or maybe to even ask me to dance. But like a stranger in the night, he pretended not to know who I was, so today, I turned the table and pretended not to remember him. In fact, I had done a good job forgetting him for a while. He disappeared from my life sometime when I was in junior high school and he reappeared again, today, at Jane's law firm. When William asked me out on a date on a Monday night, I thought he was crazy. I almost turned him down, but was happy that I didn't. Why you ask? Because I looked *GOOD* when I ran into my "future husband." LOL! I shouldn't call him that anymore, especially since he infuriated me that last time we spoke. He was just

Donovan. Donovan Taylor, age 31, Capricorn, lawyer, middle child, my true love...when I was younger. He still looked wonderfully handsome—so rascally, and so debonair, all combined in one package. His eyes were shiny blue-green-gray, his hair was unruly wavy and brown, and his smile was knock 'em dead gorgeous. He was one of those men that caught the eye of every woman walking down the street; the kind of guy who dressed like a male model for Armani or Calvin Klein. He'd always been this way, for as long as I could remember, and so many years later, nothing had changed. Emily had lent me her special Chanel outfit and I spent a little extra time curling my hair and placing my hat, just right, on my head. Boy was I happy I did that. Jane looked a bit peeved that I was wearing Emily's outfit but I didn't care. Jane always got what she wanted, anyhow.

"Hello, Miss Delaney Reid. My, you've grown up. How old are you now," was how he started our conversation.

He remembered! He remembered that he was the only one who called me Delaney. He said he wanted to be someone special in my life (a long, long, time ago) and he asked for my permission to call me Delaney. He's been the only one to call me by that name since then, and no one has called me Delaney in a very long time. I guess I wasn't that special to him if he could blow me off so easily.

"Do I know you?" I asked just to be rude. I didn't want to give him the satisfaction of knowing that he had been in my thoughts, all these years later. Even though I knew he wouldn't show up to answer my proposal, he could've had the common courtesy to call and say he wouldn't be there. I waited the entire night for him and could've been seriously busted by my parents for sleeping on the front porch.

He chuckled at me and asked me to lunch with him and Jane, but I turned him down and walked away. My heart was pumping hard as I walked down the block. I prayed they weren't behind me and I prayed I wouldn't fall in these high patent leather boots. I wanted to turn around and get one more glimpse of him, but I couldn't do it. In the end it didn't matter. He wouldn't come after me and he could care less where I was going and what I was doing. Nothing had changed between us. We were acquainted strangers...yeah, that's what we were.

January 11, 2013
Your Date's Name Is William, Not Donovan

I never made it to our date a few days ago. The day I ran into Donovan, I was so nervous and so freaked-out I couldn't function. To be completely honest, I didn't want to go out with William after having seen Donovan again. He took my breath away, made my heart beat again, and brought back all the ugly feelings of does-he-love-me, does-he-not. It was silly to think this and even sillier to feel it since he didn't love me—never had and never will.

"Are you feeling better, Laney? I was worried about you when you canceled our date."

"Sorry, William. I feel well now. I was on my way to meeting you and came down with...some weird illness. I went straight home." Weird illness, my left foot! That was an *ass*inine explanation but what could I say, *"I ran into the love of my life since I was ten and hyperventilated after I saw him?"*

"I chose this Japanese restaurant because I remembered you saying you liked sushi. Was this a good choice?"

"Yes. Anything is fine, William."

"So, what classes are you taking second semester? I'm taking a senior English class that's..."

I saw William's mouth move and heard noises coming from his mouth, but couldn't focus on what he was saying. This took me back to the time a large group of us went out for sushi. Donovan was there when I was trying raw fish for the first time. I loved fish, but I never liked the idea of eating a fish that just died.

"Just try it, Laney."

"But Dad. This shrimp just died and I don't want to eat its flesh. I saw it still move when the sushi chef took it out of the tank."

"That's why this dish is called live shrimp, Dummy!"

"Gross! Do I eat the head too? Its beady eyes are begging me not to eat it."

"No. The head will come separately in your miso soup."

"Dad! Doug's being a butthead and trying to freak me out!"

"Laney, stick to your California rolls if you don't want to try the shrimp."

"I promise this is really good. Close your eyes and I'll feed it to you. If you don't like it, I have a napkin ready for you to spit it out."

"Thank you, Donovan! You're the best."

I nodded my consent and Donovan fed me my first raw fish. It was the yummiest thing I'd ever eaten in my life! I opened my smiling eyes and Donovan winked at me before going back to sit with Jake.

"What's your favorite fish, Laney? I don't eat anything raw. I think I'll stick to the rolls." I should have paid more attention to my date, but as I savored my piece of live shrimp, I couldn't help longing for Donovan to feed me my next piece of sushi.

January 12, 2013
Really? Jane Is Who You Want?

*S*topping by Emily's today was probably the single worse decision I've made this year—though I know it's only twelve days into the new year. What I heard pissed me off, made me sad, and made me even more resolute that I would forget Donovan Taylor, again.

"I'm so glad you're here, Max."

"Where's the fire, Emily? What's wrong?"

"I don't mean to scare you, but I think you should go up to San Francisco right now and see Jane this weekend."

"Em, I'm in the middle of exams. I haven't slept much all week, and I have one more to go. I can't go see Jane—no matter how much I'd like to be with her."

"But you don't understand." Emily sounded a bit frantic. "Gram called and told me she was seeing Jane at a ball tonight, and Jane is going with Donovan."

Donovan and Jane?

Max looked disgruntled and a bit sad. I was sad for him. He was such a great guy who adored my cousin. Why would she look anywhere but at him? And what the hell was wrong with Donovan? Why would he look at a woman who already had a boyfriend? I didn't know what bothered me more—the fact that he had no scruples, or the fact that he preferred my cousin over me. *UGH!*

"I trust Jane. I know we've only been back together a month, but I don't think Donovan poses any threat."

"Please go," Emily pleaded again. "I know Jane will stay faithful to you and your relationship, but she's going to a Regency ball and she may get swept away by the whole mystique of the night and romanticize Donovan as her true love. She loves this era and the ambiance of the ball will be her perfect romance novel. You have to walk into that ball, be her knight in shining armor and end up the hero in this story."

"Em..."

"Please Max. Just do this for Jane. She'll love seeing you when your name is called out. And you'll enjoy your time with her. It'll be a great respite from exams." She handed him a printout and started pushing him out the door. "This is the plane ticket. The name and address of the place where you'll rent your clothes has been emailed to you, along with the Regency romance glossary."

"Is this truly necessary? Are you that worried about Jane?"

"Yes and no. I know Jane's in love with you, but I think you need to be up in San Francisco as soon as possible. Just do as I say and *don't* forget to read over the glossary or you'll be completely lost at the ball. Have a great time." Emily literally pushed him out the door.

"Do you believe something will happen between Jane and Donovan?" I asked when I knew the coast was clear.

"No. I don't. Max and Jane love each other and they'll be fine."

"Do you think Donovan is in love with Jane?" It broke my heart to ask this question and Emily somehow knew it broke my heart.

She gave me a tentative smile. "I can't answer for Donovan, but I can tell you that I don't think Donovan and Jane are meant to be. They have been good friends for a long time and sometimes you can mistake friendship for something more. Is there a reason why you're asking me this question?"

It wasn't that I didn't feel comfortable enough with Emily to tell her about my once-feelings for Donovan. It was the fact that I felt like a loser for having crushed on him for so long. Today was not the day for confessions.

"Nope," was my final answer.

January 24, 2013
A Night With Mr. Taylor

Jake and Emily are the ideal couple. They not only are beautiful as man and wife, but add the twins to their portrait and it doesn't get any better. I was always happy to help them whenever they needed a night out because Emily, of all people, deserved some time away from the babies.

"The twins are sleeping, already?" I was truly disappointed that I wouldn't get to play with the babies. Though they were a lot of work, I enjoyed those two so much. It was almost like practice before I got married and had babies of my own. *Bummer!*

"Laney, you mean to tell me you actually prefer the kids to be up when you babysit?" Jake asked this ridiculous question.

"Of course! You know how much I'm in love with your babies. I can't wait to have kids of my own. I need all the practice I can get with your two. I know most people gravitate toward Ellie, but I have to say, James has an extra special place in my heart."

"And I think James feels the same way about you, Laney. His whole demeanor lights up when you enter the room. Why I think he's almost as happy to see you as he is to see me," Emily kidded.

"I highly doubt that. Everyone lights up when you enter the room, my love." Jake, the epitome of a perfect husband, never ceased to amaze me with his love for his wife. "Laney, you said you needed some help with statistics?"

"Yeah. I don't seem to have a head for numbers. I have an exam tomorrow and I'm so lost. Can you help me a little before you leave?"

"Bring it out. Let's see what you have."

Jake was kind enough to unravel the mysteries of statistics when a beautiful surprise walked into the kitchen.

"Look who's here..." Emily said with a big grin on her face.

"Hey. What brings you to our neck of the woods?" Jake said while shaking his best friend's hand.

"The office needed to get Roland's signature on a few documents so I volunteered. I figured I could bum off dinner from Emily while I was at it. It's been a while since I've had her culinary delights."

"Sorry to disappoint you, Man. We're going out tonight. That's why we have Laney here."

"Hello, Delaney!" He flashed his brilliant smile.

"Hello, Mr. Taylor." I nodded as nonchalantly as possible.

"Mr. Taylor? What's with the Mr., Laney? He sounds ancient. And if Donovan sounds ancient, so do I. You know we're the same age?"

"Jake, you're not old. I just call him that because...I don't know...it's just because I'm not on friendly terms with him..." I sounded totally lame!

"What do you mean not on friendly terms? Don't you remember I saved your life at the swimming pool that one summer?" Donovan flashed his brilliance again. "Remember, Jake threw that volleyball at your head and knocked you out? Who pulled you out of the pool before you drowned, and saved your life?" He and Jake started laughing.

"It wasn't *that* dramatic. It wasn't as though I was drowning. I just had a bump on the head."

"Whatever! You need to be grateful to me because you might not be here if not for me."

"Donovan, could you help Laney with her statistics test and keep her company during dinner? I have food made ready to be heated. Or, you can always order take-out." Emily and Jake got up to go out. "We have to meet Jane and Max in half an hour."

"Jane and Max?" Donovan had a weird expression on his face. It was a bitter, somewhat unhappy expression.

"Things didn't go as planned up north?" Jake laughed. "I gave you my opinion already. You're barking up the wrong tree. Focus your energy elsewhere." What did that mean? Was Donovan interested in Jane?

"Whatever...just leave. I'll help Delaney with her stats test and be the guardian of our godchildren until you get back. I was the fool for giving up a tasting menu at Spago tonight and for wanting to dine with my best friend and his wife. Not exactly the fun night I'd imagined."

I know Donovan didn't say this to hurt me, but...it hurt...way more than it should have. No one asked him to stay here with me. I've never needed his help babysitting, and no one invited him to have dinner with me. He made me feel like a little child who needed help with her homework.

"Bye, Laney. Thank you for watching the kids tonight." Emily whispered and kissed me on the cheek.

I waved good-bye.

"Mr. Taylor, you don't have to stay here with me. I'm used to watching the kids by myself, and Jake helped me with my stats test already, so please don't let me or the kids keep you from dining with your friends." I couldn't look at him while saying this. Like a fool, I felt my heart break. It was more than ten years ago when I fell "in love" with him and asked him to marry me. He had no idea what he meant to me. But it was time to let him go, again.

"Delaney..." he pulled me toward him and he kind of rubbed my head like I was some five year old. "I only said that to make Jake feel guilty. I didn't mean any offense. Let's order dinner. I'm starved. Where are the menus?"

I just stared at him.

"Did anyone tell you, you look like a doll?"

"Um, yes...Jane tells me that all the time."

"Well, Jane is correct. Especially when you stare at me with those big blue eyes of yours, I feel like I'm looking at one of those American Baby dolls."

"You mean American Girl dolls?"

"Yeah, American Baby, American Girl...whatever."

"Thank you, I guess?" I took out the menus from one of the kitchen drawers and handed it to Donovan.

"What do you mean, I guess? Those dolls are adorable."

"I think those dolls look like the girls from Poltergeist. I guess I could audition for a horror film."

Donovan almost fell off the stool, laughing. "You could not audition for a horror film and how do you know Poltergeist?"

"I've watched it."

"You like horror films? I would have never pegged you for a girl who likes scary movies. You look like you'd like Disney movies."

I stopped what I was doing and gave him my nastiest look. Of course I did like Disney films, but he didn't need make fun of my movie choices.

"You don't scare me with your attempt at an ugly look. You wanna have Chinese tonight?" He proceeded to ignore me and ordered what he wanted to eat. I didn't have issues since I liked all his choices.

We sat at the island and had Chinese food with one of Jake's expensive bottles of wine. How did I know it was expensive? Because my father taught us to appreciate good wine, and also because when Donovan found it in the wine cellar, he let out an evil chuckle, took a picture of the opened bottle, then texted the picture to Jake. Jake sent back a text threatening to send Donovan a bill for that bottle of wine. Donovan took a picture of me drinking a glass and told Jake to charge me instead.

"You and my cousin have a great relationship, huh?" It was delightful to watch Donovan and Jake in action.

"Yeah. We've been buddies since our sandcastle-in-the-park days. It also helped that we went to the same school up until professional school. When he dated my sister Kelley, I was so psyched I'd have him as a real brother."

"You don't like Kelley's husband?"

"I like him, but we're not buddy/buddy like Jake and I are."

"Is that why you're interested in Jane...?" Donovan looked surprised that I knew anything about them. Maybe I shouldn't have asked such personal questions. It was possible that he didn't want me to know, and the possibility was even greater that *I* didn't want to know.

"Jane and I...it's complicated..."

So he *was* attracted to Jane. *Donovan...why my cousin and not me?*

"You do know that she's in love with Max, and Max loves her just as much?" His silence said it all. "I'll clean up here if you need to leave. You don't have to stay till Jake and Emily get home."

"I can't leave a young lady here by herself with our godchildren. Who will be your protector, Lady Delaney?"

I blushed at the thought of Donovan finally being my protector.

"I don't need a protector. I'm fine on my own. You can go now."

"Are you dismissing me?" He grabbed me in a headlock. Just what I wanted...for the man I'd been obsessed with, to put me in a headlock like I was one of the guys. *Ugh!* "Let's go stream a scary movie on that theater-sized TV."

Donovan streamed Chainsaw Massacre in 3D and I didn't know where he found 3D glasses, but he made me sit next to him and watch this terrifying movie.

"What's the point of watching a scary movie if you're going to cover your face the whole time?" he teased.

"I'm only covering my face when I think it's going to be scary."

"Is this how you watch a scary movie?"

"Uh-huh..." I answered in a nasally voice, then jumped at the scary scene.

"Come here." He pulled me right next to him and put his arm around me to keep me from getting too scared and I instantly melted. I melted right into his arm and his body. It was a perfect fit. I didn't ever want to leave this position.

"Laney..." Someone whispered my name.

I opened my eyes to find Emily and Jake waking both Donovan and me up. Somehow, our bodies got tangled on the oversized sofa, and we were both sprawled out against one another, with Donovan's arms around my body. A bit flustered, but happy to have been in this position, I got up and apologized to Donovan.

"I'm sorry. I didn't mean to fall asleep on you."

"No worries." Donovan passed it off as if he fell asleep like this with women all the time. "I guess the movie wasn't as scary as I thought it would be. It put us both to sleep. Can I walk you home, Delaney?"

"No. It's all right. It's just next door. Thank you for a fun evening, Mr. Taylor." I turned my face not wanting to show this man how much this night meant to me. I wished I could've been awake when Donovan put his arms around me. I wished he would find me interesting rather than my cousin, Jane. I wished...I wished...there were always so many wishes with this man.

"Good night Emily. Good night Jake. Please give the twins a kiss for me when they wake up."

"We will. I really wish you'd let us pay you for watching the kids," Emily said. "I can't keep asking you to be with the kids if you won't let me do something for you."

"Emily, you and Jake do so much for me all the time. Why the trip to New York alone was enough to earn you a year of babysitting services. I love being with the twins. Please call me whenever you need me. I'm happy to help."

"Thank you!" Emily hugged me hard.

"You're like the sister I never had, Emily..." With that admission, I walked along the pathway and headed down the steps when Donovan caught up with me.

"That was a bit heavy over there with Emily. You all right?"

Do you really care if I'm all right, Donovan?

"I'm fine, Mr. Taylor. Once again, thank you."

"Hey." He stopped the both of us right in front of my door. "After bonding over Chinese take-out and a scary movie, you think you can stop with the Mr. Taylor? Like Jake said, I feel like your father's friend whenever you call me Mr. I'm not that much older than you."

I smiled. I guess I half-laughed. "Mr. Taylor, you are a decade older than I am. When I was eleven, you were of legal drinking age, and in college, dating someone a decade older than you." *You proposed to another woman the day I proposed to you but didn't have the courtesy to answer my proposal, ever.* "Let's stick to our usual M.O."

"Delaney." He stopped me again before I could walk into the house. "Did I wrong you somewhere along the way? I remember you being spunky and happy whenever we hung out. Somehow, I lost that with you. Shit, you didn't even recognize me the other day. When did we become strangers?"

"Were we ever anything but? Good night, Mr. Taylor." *Donovan.* "I'll see you again."

And that's how my night ended.

January 27, 2013
Decisions, Decisions

*A*fter much thinking and researching, I decided to go away for a year after graduation and live abroad. Regardless of what I would eventually decide concerning graduate school, I wanted to experience life away from home and in a foreign land. I hoped this decision would go over well with Mom and Dad.

"What's the family meeting about, Laney-Babaney?"

"I've made an important decision, and I'm hoping Mom and Dad will be supportive and happy for me, Doug-the-Bug"

"This doesn't sound good, Henry." Mom whispered, but not so quietly.

"It never is when she wonders whether or not we will support her decision," Dad grumbled.

"I can hear you," I grumbled, myself.

"You were supposed to hear it." Dad laughed.

I laughed with my wonderful father who found reasons to laugh no matter the situation. "I'd like to go away for a year after I graduate from college."

"No...!" Mom complained. "Not again. You already did that just a year ago."

"Mom, that was two years ago, and I only want to go away for one year. Once I go to grad school, I'll get a job, and I don't know when I'll have this opportunity again."

"Where is it you want to go, Baby?"

"Well, Dad, if it's OK with everyone, I'd like to stay at Gram's home in London. If I base myself there, I can travel around Europe and get in a fantastic year of learning and living other cultures."

Dad considered it. Mom rejected it.

"Come on, Mom. You've always said if you hadn't gotten married right out of undergrad, you would've traveled the world. That's been your only regret, getting married so young. You can live vicariously through me." I put up a perky smile.

"How can you go away for a year without missing your family? What about the twins? You love those twins, and Emily is having another baby. You won't see the baby for a year."

That fact did give me pause. "Of course I'll miss you, and I'll miss the entire family, but I'd like to do this and I can't unless you and Dad approve."

"Mom, let her go. You know she'll mope until you approve."

"I do not mope!"

"Whatever. Is this discussion over?"

"Babs, she'll live at Mom's, they speak English there, she'll be fine. Let's give her our blessing." Dad spoke to a hesitant Mom. "But young lady, I'm not supporting you while you gallivant around Europe next year. I'm only paying for school now. You'll have to get a job and earn your own spending money."

That was as good as an approval. It would probably take till I was in London for Mom to accept me leaving for another year. "Thank you, Daddy! I have a lot of money saved up already, and I'll get a job when I get to London. I won't waste the year away. There's a chance I may do a little studying at Cambridge or Oxford."

"That's my girl. Go, enjoy life, but be productive."

"You agree with my decision, Mom?"

"No, but the decision's been made, already, hasn't it, you stubborn girl," Mom sighed.

"Thank you, Mom. I love you." I kissed her on her cheek and walked away with a smile.

I'd leave as soon as I graduated, and nothing would hold me back. What an exciting year this will be!

January 31, 2013
A 60-Year-Old Proposal

*H*ow romantic is my future grandfather! Sir Roland Hugh Ascot III proposed to my grandmother for the second time during their sixty-year friendship. He'd been in love with her from the start and continued to love her after his wife passed away. Both Gram and Sir Roland could live the rest of their lives being in love again. The tears were falling heavily when I heard his romantic confession and proposal. It appeared the entire Reid family was blissfully in love with a mate, but me.

"Hello?" Someone's hand kept making circles around my face in an annoying way. "Anybody home?"

"Mr. Taylor!" He was standing so close to me, I took a step back. "Can I help you?"

"You were in such a daze. I saw your face go from smiles, to tears, to something that looked close to sadness. You don't approve of your Gram marrying Roland?"

"Don't be ridiculous! Of course I approve. In fact, I adore Sir Roland and can't wait to call him Grandfather. Plus, it doesn't matter whether or not I approve. Gram is a grown woman; she can make her own decisions."

"Then why the long face? My heart did this weird-ass somersault when I saw you go from tears of joy to tears of sadness."

"I didn't know you had a degree in facial expression. There were only tears of happiness."

"Tell me one thing, Delaney. Why are you so hostile toward me?"

Why? Did I want to tell him the truth? "I'm..."

"Yes?"

"I apologize if I come off gruff. That's not my intention. I guess I need to work on my interpersonal skills."

"There's not one thing wrong with your interpersonal skills. You are beautifully lively and comical with everyone, but me. I want to know why." He was serious.

With no way out, I gave him a partial truth. "I like Max. He's genuine, kind, and he loves my cousin. You...I'm unsure if I like so much." *(Well, it was more of a love than a like but...)* "You're hard to read, only nice on the surface, and you only love yourself."

The partial truth turned into much more than I intended. Scared he might be upset with me, I kept looking for a diversion, or someone to shield me from the wrath headed my way. He stayed quiet; he stayed thinking. Hoping he was done with me, I started taking minor steps to the side, edging my way toward someone else's conversation.

"Stay," he commanded and stopped me dead in my track. "Repeat what you just said."

"I forgot?" I squeaked out those two words and literally gave a cheeky smile.

"What makes you think you know me so well? 'Hard to read, only nice on the surface, and you only love yourself,' is what I believe you said."

"I plead the fifth?!?" This time, the smile was more of an uncomfortable, *uh-oh, I'm in trouble,* kind of smile.

"So that's why you're hostile toward me? You think I'm fake and narcissistic?"

"Now you're putting words in my mouth. I don't believe I used such negative words."

He laughed at my defense. "I'm going to give you a few days to come up with an explanation to your accusations. Next time I see you, you had better be able to explain why you think I'm a phony, egotistical man."

Damn! Why couldn't I keep my thoughts to myself?

February 6, 2013
Co-ed Softball

My girlfriend Elle accosted me at school and would not let me go till I agreed to join her and her boyfriend in a co-ed softball league. Eric and Elle started dating a few months ago, and they were the cutest couple. Elle and I became good friends this year while working on a senior English project together. Elle was an English major going into the Peace Corps for a few years, while Eric was going off to grad school somewhere in middle-America. It was unclear where Elle would be once she joined the Peace Corps, but I was secretly hoping she'd be somewhere near London so we could still hang out from time to time.

"Come on, Laney! If you don't join, I'll be the only girl on the team. Puleez!"

"Elle. I don't want to play. I haven't played softball since high school."

"Eric is playing and he wants me to join. Come on. It's a co-ed team, and Eric says there are plenty of single guys for you to choose from, not that that's ever been your issue. Or we can ask William and see if he wants to play, too. Laney! Please. Help me spend more time with my boyfriend. Be a good friend."

She took out her phone, texted, received a text and gave me a splendid smile and two thumbs up.

"What was that?"

"William wants to play."

"Elle...! I don't want to see him every Wednesday. We've been out on one date. We're not a super-couple like you and Eric. And you know I've decided to leave after graduation. I can only play till late May."

"That's perfect. The season ends in late May." Elle gave me the biggest hug known to womankind. "You won't regret it. I'm told there are many hot guys on this team every year, but most girls can't join because they aren't good enough to play with the men."

"You and Eric are too cute together. He's always looking for ways to be with you. I hope one day I'll meet a man who wants to be with me all the time, too."

"Eric and I will be apart come this summer. That's why we look for every which way to be together. I wish we'd met sooner, but oh well. We have to make the most of what we have." She pulled me toward the softball field. "And you, Miss Reid, have a long line of wanna-be suitors. You just need to let them get a little closer than the 10-foot ring of fire you have around yourself." We both laughed. "Let's go sign up right now. Then we have a few days to get our gear together for tryouts."

Eric met us on the intramural field and confirmed that we were the only two girls to sign up, though many were lurking around the team, already.

"I assume you know how to play softball?" Eric nervously asked. "The men are pretty competitive."

"I played up through high school, then gave it up. I wasn't good enough to play in college."

"What position did you play?"

"I was a pitcher."

"Fantastic! Elle's a pitcher too. It'll be a perfect matchup since most guys don't like pitching underhand—makes 'em feel like they're throwing like a girl," he said with a chuckle.

"I'm not very good and I haven't played in four years. I don't think I'll be much help to..."

"Hello, Delaney Reid." Only one person in the world called me Delaney, and only one person would so confidently cut off my conversation with my friends and call my attention. I turned around to face this one person—my favorite person. "What are you doing here?"

"Hi," I stuttered while saying this one-syllable word. "I go to school here. What are *you* doing here?"

"I came down to hang with my buddy who is the new coach for the softball team. And you are here because...?"

"Because my girlfriend Elle convinced me to join the co-ed, IM softball team. Since she was going to have a blast playing with her *boyfriend*, she thought I may enjoy it just as much playing with a bunch of *strange men*." I added sarcastically.

Elle looked a bit awe-struck as she *gently* demanded, "Are you going to introduce us?"

"This is Elle and Eric."

Eric put out his hand as a greeting, and Elle coyly waved hello to Donovan.

"And this is...?" Elle was inquiring of Donovan's name.

Shoot! I saw the smirk on Donovan's face as I was going to have to say his name if I was going to introduce him to my friends. He thought he was soooo smart with that stupid-ass grin of his.

"And this is Mr. Taylor," I announced.

"Mr. Taylor?" Elle asked a bit dumbfounded. "Does Mr. Taylor have a first name? Or is Taylor his first name?"

"Ask him," I answered with a smile.

A once disgruntled Donovan cracked a huge smile and started laughing when I stuck my tongue out at him. *You think you're so smart. I will forever call you Mr. Taylor just to bug the crap out of you.*

"Hey, Kevin. Can anyone join this IM team?"

"Nooooooo!" I thought I was just saying this in my head, but apparently I'd said it aloud, and very out loud. Elle, Eric, and Kevin all jumped back. Donovan now held an evil grin.

"Anyone can play. It's not a school team. There have been alums in the past. In fact, I thought about joining the team as well. We have two beautiful pitchers, and all the guys returning are good guys. It should be a fun team."

"Count me in. I played catcher back in the day. I'll play if I can catch for this particular beautiful pitcher," he put his arms tightly around me, but it wasn't the most affectionate hold. It was more of a *gotcha now* kind of hold.

"Great!" Elle clapped her hand. "Laney and I will be here on Friday for tryouts. This is going to be so much fun!"

FUN...?!? I didn't need to see this man on any regular basis. I didn't want old feelings resurfacing—or more honestly, I didn't want to obsess anymore. I'd done it for too long.

"I'll take you home, Delaney."

"Thank you, but Elle is my ride. We carpool."

Disgruntled-Donovan came back. "So carpool another day. I'm sure she won't mind if she doesn't drop you off at home. You and I—the fake and narcissistic one—have a little unfinished business. Let's go grab some dinner."

Shit. I was in trouble now. "I thought you were grabbing dinner with Kevin."

"I'll see you on Friday?" He turned to Kevin and got out of whatever their original plans were.

"See you tomorrow," Elle whispered. "Damn! He's hot! He's hotter than hot! Forget William; hold onto this one, instead."

I rolled my eyes while being pulled away by Donovan Taylor.

"When did you play softball?"

"From age five till about age eighteen."

"How come I never knew this?"

I shrugged my shoulders and cut into my steak rather than answering him. There were lots of things he didn't know about me. What made him think that he was an expert on Delaney Reid?

"What other sports do you play I don't know about?"

"I play lots of sports you don't know about, Mr. Taylor. You don't have the 411 on me."

He laughed. "You want a glass of wine? Are you even old enough to have a glass of wine? Shit, did I give alcohol to a minor the other night at your cousin's?"

"Yes I'm old enough to drink, and yes, thank you, I'd love a glass of Cabernet."

"Where did you learn to drink wine?" Donovan was unnecessarily baffled. "I'm sure you've had your share of beer at frat parties, but I can't see you as a wine drinker." Now that comment just pissed me off. Where did this man get off thinking I went to frat parties, I drank beer—and lots of it—and I didn't know anything about wine? I thought about rebutting all of his statements, but decided not to. Who was I kidding? What would make me think he had complimentary thoughts of me? "Well?" He asked again after he ordered both of us a glass of wine.

"I learned to drink wine from my dad, who gave me a small cupful since I was fourteen. My father, the heart surgeon, is an oenophile. He believed everybody should know a little something about wine. Doug and I have probably been on more wine tasting jaunts than most people double our age."

"Impressive. Though, I don't know about Mr. Heart Surgeon, Chief of Staff, letting his fourteen-year-old girl drink."

"It was only at home and on special occasions, like birthdays and holidays, or when he got a great bottle of wine. He would share it with all of us. Don't go getting judgmental on my father. This Cab that you ordered is terrible, by the way."

He only laughed as he called our server and changed the glass of wine.

"And as for the beer and frat party statement, I don't drink beer and I've attended only a small handful of frat parties during my four years at school so…think what you like."

"OK, my bad on making assumptions about you. Let's talk about your assumptions about me."

I immediately got defensive. "I never said you were narcissistic and I did not call you fake. Those were your words."

"Those may have not been your exact words, but that's pretty much what you meant. I'd like for you to explain yourself. I apologized for my incorrect assumptions about you."

"And I apologize for my incorrect assumptions about you as well."

"Oh no, you're not getting out of this that easily. I know you just said that. That's not what you meant."

"Mr. Taylor," I sighed. "I don't really know what I meant." He looked up at me as though he did not believe me. "I swear! What I said the other day was not the kindest thing to say to anybody. I don't know if I can take it back, but I also can't pinpoint why I said those things." Though deep inside, I knew why I said every one of those words.

It was unfair of me to call him selfish. Just because he paid more attention to Jane, who already had a boyfriend, than to me, who was single and dying for him to be my boyfriend—that did not make him selfish.

After dinner was done Donovan took me home, and I was sad to see this date end. It wasn't a true date, but it was nice to be with him.

"You want me to pick you up from home before tryouts on Friday?"

No doubt, I wanted to be with him again. However, I didn't think spending so much time with him was a wise choice. What meant nothing to him meant the world to me. Spending time with him always had.

"Thank you, but that's OK. I'm going to stay at school and finish up some projects and then head straight over to the IM field."

"Is it your carpool day again?"

"Yeah. It's Elle's turn to drive again."

"Then I'll bring you home after practice." I was going to contest his offer, but he quickly added, "And I won't take no for an answer."

Thinking back on tonight, I realized this was the first night I'd ever been out with Donovan. To one of us, it was dinner, to the other of us, it was a dream.

February 8, 2013
Try-Outs And Scrimmage

*A*fter a long day of school and finishing all the editing for my clients, I seriously considered not showing up for tryouts. I'd been at school since 8:00am, which meant Elle picked me up at 7:00am. I met with a professor, went to three classes, and met up with potential clients every chance I got. Since deciding to leave for London, I thought I should earn as much money as possible. Dad and Mom told me I wouldn't be receiving an allowance once I graduated, and I didn't think they were kidding. I needed a nest egg to last me an entire year, so I met with students who wanted me to edit their school papers. Maybe going away for an entire year wasn't the best idea, but I wanted this change and was looking forward to living away.

Where are you? A text from an unknown number came in.
Who is this?
Donovan, or Mr. Taylor to you.
I'm sitting on a bench trying to figure out how to get home.
Get your ass over to the IM field. Everyone is waiting for you.

I'm tired. I've had a long day, and I haven't had a bite to eat. Please apologize to everyone for me.

Get your ass over here! After tryouts, I'll take you out to eat.

I don't want you to.

Why not?

Because...

Because why?

Just because!

Are you coming here or do I need to search all over campus for the bench you are sitting on?

Oh, all right! You're a despot! I'll be there in a few minutes.

"You're quite good!" Kevin came over and patted me on the back after I pitched an inning. "Why haven't you tried out for the college team?"

"Yeah, Laney. I didn't realize you were such a good athlete," William chimed in.

"I'm not that good."

"You wouldn't have made the starting team, but you would've made the team."

"Are we done here?" Donovan asked while taking off his catcher's uniform. Donovan caught for me, and though I was a bit rusty, we played well together.

"No," Kevin, who ended up being the "coach" on our team, said, "we're going to play a quick scrimmage against the other team."

That quick scrimmage lasted till 9:30 at night. I thought I'd collapse from fatigue. Before I could get called back for anymore pitching, I grabbed my bag and hurried off with Elle.

Where the hell did you go?

Home with Elle.

Are you on the road already?

No. We are walking to the parking lot.

Which parking lot?

Lot 6

Stay right there at the entrance. I'm coming to get you.
You don't have to come. I'll go home with Elle.
STAY!

"Damn man! He thinks I'll ask how high if he tells me to jump." I grumbled.

"Damn, is right! Where have you been hiding him, Laney? I'm in love with Eric, but in lust with your man."

"He's not my man. He's just a family friend."

"He doesn't look like any of my family friends. Shit, he can be my family friend, any time!" I slapped her on the arm and started laughing.

"I'm going to tell on you next time I see Eric."

"I already told Eric I'd give him a bye if Donovan asked for a night with me."

I rolled my eyes at that incredulous statement. "Shut up and go home. Drive safely." We hugged good-bye.

"Get in!" I heard the damn man yell from the other side of the parking lot.

"See ya," Elle winked. "I say do whatever he wants. Let loose and go for it!"

"Go home!"

Donovan honked a few more times to get my attention so I walked as slowly as humanly possible to his car.

That pissed him off enough for him to get out of his car, carry me over his shoulder, and plop me onto his convertible.

"Seriously?" I yelled.

"Seriously! Let's go eat." He smiled

"Mr. Taylor. I'm exhausted and dirty. Can you just take me home?"

"I'm hungry too," he whined. The moron that I was, I found his whining adorable. "I haven't had dinner either and I don't want to eat alone." Who could possibly resist this man?

"I tell you what. Let's go back to my house. Let me shower, then I'll fix us something to eat."

"Can I shower, too?"

"You are more than welcome to use Doug's bathroom. You can even borrow some of his clothes if you need them."

"Naw. I brought a change of clothes with me. Hey, I have a great idea." He called his voice-person in his car and had her dial Jake's number.

"Hello?" My cousin answered.

"Hey. It's me. Can Delaney and I bum off a meal from Emily tonight, in about half an hour?"

"You do know food makes my wife ill?"

"So did she starve you and the kids today?"

"Of course not."

"Jake. I'm sorry to bother you. Forget what Mr. Taylor just said." I then turned my attention to Donovan. "What a stupid request. You know she has morning sickness all day. Don't bother her."

"What are you two doing together?" my cousin inquired. "Come over. I'll order a pizza for you."

"I knew there was a reason why I kept you around as a best friend. We both need to shower and change at Delaney's. We'll come over after."

"Delaney's parents are out tonight and so is Doug. Why don't you shower and change at *our place,* and she'll meet you here for pizza after she's done grooming at *her house.*" The way Jake said those few sentences made me blush.

The pizza had just arrived when I got to Jake's; it smelled heavenly.

"What is this delicious smell?"

"Hi Emily!" I gave her a hug. "The pizza smells good to you, too?"

"Oh my gosh, those sausages smell divine. Let's eat."

The three of us stared in wonder as we saw Emily polish off half a box of an extra large pizza. Good thing Jake had no idea how to order a pizza for two, because Emily went to town.

"You think it's wise to eat so much, Love?"

"I'm starving. I haven't eaten a complete meal in weeks. This is so..." She suddenly got up and ran upstairs.

"Shit! I knew I shouldn't have let her eat so much." Jake ran after her.

"You think we can eat the rest, now?" Donovan whispered with a laugh. "I had to stop eating for fear Emily might chop off my hand for taking her slice."

I laughed with him. I, too, had stopped eating and just stared at Emily.

Jake came down, without Emily, and joined us in a slice of pizza.

"She'll be all right?"

"She'll be fine, Laney. This seems to be de rigueur with her. Neither of you told me how you ended up together."

"We are on a co-ed softball team at the University," Donovan answered because I was too busy eating.

"How'd that happen? Was it planned?"

"Nope. I went to visit Kevin, and there Delaney was, signing up to play IM softball."

"Kevin doing well?"

"He's married, with a kid on the way. He's happy."

"Good to know."

I watched two of my favorite men conversing, and I couldn't help thinking that Donovan would fit perfectly in our family.

February 13, 2013
First Game, Another Argument

Our first game was against a local junior college team not far from our school. We all got matching "uniforms"—white pants, maroon shirt, and a maroon baseball visor. I arrived on the field and found Donovan, already there, strategizing with Kevin. I'd never seen fitted white pants look so good on any man as they did on this man. Standing next to Kevin was a beautiful blonde with a slight bump on her stomach. It didn't take a genius to figure out that she was Kevin's wife.

"Hello." I called out to everyone.

"Hey, Laney." Kevin patted me on the back. "How's my star pitcher feeling today?"

"Um...I'm OK, I suppose."

"Have you met my wife, Isabella?"

"No. Nice to meet you," I said with a smile. "If you'll excuse me, I'm going to go put my stuff down and get ready for the game."

Donovan had that disgruntled face, again. This was becoming commonplace with him. "Would it kill you to say hello to me as well?"

"Hello, Mr. Taylor. How are you today?" I asked as formally as possible. To the best of my ability, I tried not to fraternize with this man. He had no idea how much I wanted to be his friend, his best friend, his girlfriend. I couldn't just be an acquaintance, so it was better I didn't get friendly, lest I fall back in love with the man I've wanted to marry since I was ten-years-old.

"Are you majoring in pissing me off?"

"Sorry." Anytime Donovan got upset with me, that feeling of hurt resurfaced, and I didn't need to go there again. "I'll just go get ready." I couldn't do anything right where this man was concerned.

Throughout the six innings, I saw Donovan with a myriad of women who kept coming up to him during our time in the dugout. He greeted all of them, laughed with them, and charmed them to the utmost.

"I'm glad Elle told me about this co-ed league. This is fun getting to hang out with you weekly." William enthusiastically said.

"I'm glad to be here, too. This is more fun than I expected, and everyone on the team is super nice."

"I have to thank you for pitching for us because had you not, the guys would have forced me to pitch."

"You played ball?"

"I was a pitcher for my baseball team in high school, and these guys think it all translates. No matter how hard I try to explain to people that it's not the same, they don't understand. I think it's especially harder for a male pitcher to change to underhand pitching. You want to grab a bite to eat after this?" That was a weird transition, but I suppose I should've expected it.

"Um..."

"She can't." Donovan came out of nowhere and answered for me.

"Why not?"

"Because, Miss Reid, I told your dad I'd take you straight home after this."

"You've got to be kidding me. I drove today so you don't have to take me anywhere." I wanted to see how he was going to work around this one.

He took out his phone and texted someone, then waited...

His phone buzzed, and upon reading the text he proudly announced, "Your brother's on campus, and he's dropping by the game right now. We can all go out to dinner after this is done."

Why? I didn't ask. I'd let him know in private that I didn't need another older brother in my life.

"Would you like to join us, William? My brother went to undergrad here, and now he's in business school. You might know him." Donovan was peeved. "In fact, let's invite Elle, Eric, Kevin and Isabella, too."

We ended up at dinner with a large group of players, both from our team and the opposing team. I made it a point to sit as far away from Donovan as humanly possible.

"You play pool?" William asked and challenged.

"I'm afraid not. That's one of those games I've always wanted to learn, but never got around to it."

"Come on. I'll teach you." He put out his hand and helped me out of my seat. We walked over to the pool table and after teaching me the gist of the game, he began showing me ways to hold the cue stick and to sink a ball into the pocket. It was harder than it looked. Either I missed the ball entirely or I kept sinking the wrong ball. This was not my game, but it was fun learning. "You're not bad for a first timer."

"And you're a terrible liar. I sucked. I think I'll stick to softball."

"How come I've never seen you on campus before this year?"

"Um, because there are like 30,000 students here on campus?"

"What will you do after you graduate?"

"I'm going to..."

"Time to go," Donovan rudely interrupted us.

"No it's not."

"It is. Doug says he needs to leave and he's catching a ride home with you. We'll see you next week, William."

With his hand on my wrist, Donovan pulled me away from the pool table and took me outside. He didn't even give me a chance to say a proper good-bye to everyone.

"What the hell? Why'd you do that?"

"Your brother says he needs a ride and he needs to leave, now."

"Next time, I'd like for my brother to tell me. And next time, I'd like for you to stop acting like *my* older brother. One big brother is enough, Mr. Taylor!"

"Can you please stop calling me that? It's damn embarrassing when you call me that on the diamond."

"Then stop acting like a Mr. Taylor!" I walked off and hoped I wouldn't see him again, any time soon. OK, that was a lie. I was pissed, but if he wanted to see me, I'd make time for him again in the next minute. *Gaaawwwddd!* I was so pathetic.

February 14, 2013
A Day of Love

I have to be the only girl alive who has never had a date on Valentine's Day. No, I guess the more correct way to say this would be, I've never gone out with a boyfriend on Valentine's Day. But then again, I was a loser all around—always dating, but never finding the right man. William asked me to go out with him tonight, but I thought it'd be too serious to go out with a guy on a night like this when we weren't together. Plus, Jake had asked me to babysit tonight, months ago. I couldn't turn him down when I knew he went through so much trouble to get Emily a spot at a charity event where she was one of four people cooking with Mario Batali.

"Are you ready to go to bed now, my sleepy heads? You're both rubbing your eyes and yawning." I said to the twins, whose eyes had turned red. "Which book shall we read tonight?" I went to pick up James, then attempted to pick up Ellie, but didn't quite know how to hold both. This motherhood stuff wasn't easy. Then of course, there was a knock at the door.

"Don...Mr. Taylor." He was busy finishing a call, so he didn't hear me slip and almost call him by his first name.

"...all right, I'll call you when I get there. See you. Bye." He ended the phone call and without thinking, kissed Ellie—who was in her chair, James—who was in my arm, and me—who was...just a part of the package, I suppose. "Oh!" He even surprised himself with that kiss to my cheek, quite close to the edge of my lips. In all honesty, that's where he had kissed both kids, and he was working his way down the "assembly line" without any thought or meaning. "Sorry. I didn't mean to do that. I just thought of you as one of the kids." Of course he did!

"No worries. I didn't take it any other way. What would possess you to kiss me, otherwise?" Now, why did I have to say that? I had a serious case of diarrhea of the mouth where one Donovan Taylor was concerned.

"Hmmm. I don't know. Have you been thinking about what would get me to kiss you?"

I stammered for an answer while he grinned. "Well, I...of course not! Why would I think about that? It's not as though..."

"Easy, Delaney. It was just a joke."

"Oh." That ended that awkward conversation. "What brings you by? Jake and Emily aren't home."

"I know. Jake called me earlier and told me to stop by and make sure you and the kids were doing well. Plus, I still have a bone to pick with you."

"And what could you do if the kids and I were not doing well?" As though I had trained them, both kids started crying. They were tired, and they wanted their mother. "You want to pick up Ellie and show me what you can do?"

He could do absolutely NOTHING! He made Ellie cry even harder by over-stimulating her with his crazy "let's see Ellie fly" antics. Ellie sat perched on his shoulders and he zoomed around the house pretending to be an airplane. She enjoyed it for about two minutes, then started howling, which made James unhappy.

"Bring her to me," I commanded while sitting on the rocking chair in the kids' room. He obeyed immediately and put her on my lap.

While I started on *One Fish, Two Fish, Red Fish, Blue Fish,* Donovan tried several times to ingratiate himself into our comfy position. He sat on one arm of the rocking chair and almost flipped us all back and got the kids crying again in fright. "Obviously, you've never been in a rocking chair, before?" I whispered an admonishment. "Sit over on the couch."

"It's too far from you three," he whispered back while I was calming the twins.

"Then sit on the floor," I answered.

"Are you crazy? Do you know how much this Dolce & Gabbana suit costs? I'm not plopping on this rug. Who knows what kind of shit" he whispered really softly, "is on this thing." I choked up in the middle of, "*Some are sad. And some are glad. And some are very, very bad,*" and added, "that's you," staring straight at him, since I had no fingers left to point as they were holding two very cuddly little ones, plus a book.

"Not I, said the fly," he whispered while deliberately pulling us off the rocking chair and seating all of us on the couch. We fell together like a group of kids cannonballing into a swimming pool together.

"*Why are they sad and glad and bad?*" I kept reading.

"*I do not know. Go ask your dad,*" Donovan finished without skipping a beat. "I think they're down, even with the Chinese fire-drill," he said, gingerly prying Ellie from my arm.

We laid both kids down, took turns kissing each one, turned off the light and scampered away fast.

"Man, those buggers are a lot of work. Thank God for women like Emily, who choose to stay home and take care of them. I, for one, could not do it. And I know Jake agrees."

"It is hard work, but when you look at them and they look back at you with those trusting eyes, you know it's all worth it. There's no way I'd want anyone else raising my children, but me."

"So you won't be one of those corporate ladder climbing women? No high-powered job in your future?"

"I doubt it. That's not my thing. I want to be happy, not stressed."

"But many women are happy in their big offices, bossing men around."

"And more power to them...that's just not me. I want to create a family and a home, not a fancy office." Donovan stopped and stared. He probably thought I was acting naive again. He was so used to working with high-powered, genius women, my idea most likely sounded lame and very 1950's. "Must sound pretty stupid to you..." I left it at an open-ended statement and walked into the kitchen.

"Sounds..." He stammered for the right word. I knew I came off like some idealistic collegian living in the throwback days of June Cleaver. "...refreshing..."

The clock struck seven, and it dawned on me that today was Valentine's Day. Donovan was here with me and we'd spend Valentine's Day together. Emily had made a wonderful roast chicken—which she didn't get to eat because she had no idea Jake was taking her out. Donovan and I could bake a red velvet cake together—my personal favorite, and while the cake was baking, maybe we could sit and talk, or watch another scary movie. What a surprisingly fun night this was turning out to be. Never in my craziest dreams did I think I'd spend this day of love with him.

Remembering the beautiful flowers Emily received earlier; I brought them out from the bay window and refreshed the water, then placed them in a prominent location on the large kitchen island. I turned off the oven, which was keeping the chicken warm, and brought out the delicious smelling dinner. Taking out two plates, I started placing vegetables and rice on both plates and began carving the chicken while Donovan was in the other room taking a phone call. Donovan's footsteps neared the kitchen as I was almost done plating our dinner.

"OK. I'm off. I have a dinner date in half an hour. I'll see you again, soon." He spoke those words as he entered the kitchen and the only thing I could think of was how to hide the second plate I'd prepared for him. How moronic was I, thinking Donovan was dateless tonight. How stupid of me to think he'd want to spend the evening together. I quickly put his plate in the sink and threw a dishtowel on top of it.

"Um...yeah...sure...I'll see you again..." The words came out in a jumbled mess. I was a mess, but I wasn't going to show him how much he affected me. "Have a great time." I put on a big smile and opened the kitchen door for him.

He said nothing of the plate he saw on the kitchen counter, or the plate he might have seen me throw into the sink. He left with nothing more than a good-bye.

I sat on the breakfast table and held back the tears. Yes, my heart broke, but I wasn't going to cry over some idiotic misunderstanding, solely on my part. Rather than crying over spilt milk, or more aptly stated, an unnecessarily plated dinner, I took out a bowl and started mixing ingredients for a cake. I'd be damned if Donovan Taylor was going to ruin my night.

2 1/2 cups of cake flour—measured and in

1 1/2 cups of sugar—also in the bowl

1 tsp. baking soda—added

I went down the dry ingredient list, sifted everything together, and then I mixed all the wet ingredients together. I was perfectly fine till I tried to mix the dry ingredients into the wet and the hand blender went psychotic and splattered batter all over me, the cabinets, the floor, the counter—and this is where I lost it. The tears rolled down out of frustration. Frustrated with my cake, frustrated with him, and frustrated with myself, I cleaned up the mess and started over again.

The cleaning took forever, but the cake turned out beautifully. I cut out all different-sized heart shapes of the red velvet cake, sliced them in half, and filled them with the cream cheese frosting. After sprinkling them with powdered sugar, they looked picture-perfect. Most of them sat on Emily's antique cake platter, but I took two for myself and poured water in the coffee maker so I could feast on these beauties.

"Hey!" I jumped when I heard a man's voice. "Why didn't you lock the door behind me?"

"Hey..." I don't know why, but my broken heart felt like it was breaking some more. "Give me a sec?" I ran to the upstairs' bathroom and calmed my racing heart. Gawwwd! I was such a loser! Why couldn't I act nonchalant whenever he was around? Why couldn't I be cool like Jane? Those two had such a great friendship.

"You're back," he said with a mouth full of a heart-shaped mini-cake. "These are delicious."

"Thanks," I answered while pouring him my cup of coffee before he choked on the cake. "Why are you here?"

"I came back for cake."

"But you didn't know I was baking a cake. How could you come back for it?"

He smiled and shoved the second piece of cake in his mouth. "Have you had dinner?" His gentle ways almost broke me again. Why'd he have to be so sweet when he didn't mean anything by it? "Have you?" he repeated.

"No, not really. I was going to fill my calories with cake, instead."

"Then let's eat." He got up and brought over a bag filled with boxes of food. Without me having to ask, he explained, "I had a dinner date with some friends, but after a drink, I thought I may enjoy having dinner with you instead."

He made that statement with enough hesitation to make me think he felt sorry for me. That's not what I wanted from Donovan Taylor. I'd rather he be out with other women, men, whatever—than feel sorry for me.

"You didn't have to come back. I would've been all right without you." I answered with a forced bravado.

"I know." He said with a genuine smile. "I wanted to come back."

That was all he was willing to say.

"You two are having a late dinner." Emily and Jake walked in and Emily looked worn out from her night out.

"Did you have a fun time?" I asked. "Is Mario Batali as amazing as he appears on TV?"

"He's even more fun and creative. I had a wonderful time, but I think it's past my bedtime. I'll see you in the morning?" She hugged and kissed Donovan on the cheek first, then came over and hugged and kissed me as well. "Thank you for taking care of my children." She waved good night with those words and left us.

"Emily did OK with all that food?"

"You know, Laney, in hindsight, a cooking lesson at this stage of her pregnancy wasn't the brightest idea."

"It's not as though you had any clue she was going to be pregnant when you bought this package."

"True." He laughed. "She kept getting green every time Mario brought out raw meat or fish, and she was trying so hard to cover up her nausea. Even in the car, she refused to admit she didn't have a good time."

"She doesn't want you worrying so much about her. Emily is incredibly grateful for everything you do for her. She's always talking about you as the most ideal husband."

"I don't come close to being ideal when compared to Emily. I don't know what I would have done had I not found her in Japan."

"All that matters is that you found her." I told Jake with mixed emotions. Of course I was happy for my cousin and his wife, but I was sad for myself because I couldn't envision this kind of happiness in my life—at least not while I was still pining away for Donovan Taylor.

"I'm going to go up and make sure my wife is OK. Can you two lock up behind you?"

"Sure, Jake. I'm going to leave soon, too. If you're done?" I asked Donovan and offered to take his plate to the sink.

Donovan walked me home in silence. It was a weird night that started out promising, then turned abysmal, only to be brightened again. I didn't appreciate these mood swings. I was trying so very hard not to fall for Donovan Taylor again, but it was impossible not to when he was in my life this often.

"What's on your mind, Delaney?"

"Nothing."

"The creases between your brows speak differently," he said while smoothing out these creases with his thumb.

"I was thinking about Jake and Emily."

"What about them?"

"Just how perfect they are for one another, and whether or not I'll find that kind of perfection in my own life." I'd offered too much information, but I couldn't help it. So many of these "days of love" passed me by and through every one of them, I'd wondered whether I'd ever spend this day with Donovan. This year I had, but it was just as lonely as all the other ones I'd spent alone.

His face gentled. I'd seen and memorized all his looks, but this was a new one. Was this a look he gave to that special woman in his life, or was this a look he gave his little sisters when they were heartbroken over some guy?

"Who could possibly resist loving you?" His thumbs moved over my eyebrows and were now caressing my cheekbone. "You are damn near perfect yourself, Miss Delaney Reid. Any man who doesn't recognize this would be a fool."

Then what does that make you, Donovan?

February 18, 2013
Dr. Delaney Reid?

I got it! I got a regular business-sized envelope from my first choice medical school—the only medical school I applied to—and my hands were shaking from excitement. Running to Emily's, I wanted to share the news with someone.

"I got it!"

"What is that?" Emily asked, carrying both babies in her arms while holding one in the belly.

"James. Come to me." I held out my arms for him so I could give Emily a hand. Surprisingly, Ellie jumped into my arms.

"James just took a spill on the kitchen floor, so he needs a little extra attention from his mama. He still adores you, Laney."

"Did you fall?" I asked James, and made him cry again. "Don't cry, big boy. You'll be all right." I kissed him on his forehead.

Ellie patted my cheeks with her chubby hands and screamed, "Me!" so I kissed her chubby cheeks many times over. She giggled in glee.

"What's in that envelope, Laney?"

"It's either an acceptance or rejection letter to the one med school I applied to last fall."

"Med school? I didn't know you applied to med school!"

"No one knows. Everyone thinks I only applied to film school, but I thought I'd take my chances and do both."

"Why haven't you told anyone?"

"I didn't want the pressure from the family. I'm double majoring in English and chemistry, and I didn't want to let Dad down if I didn't get in. It was a long shot."

"Well? What are you waiting for? Open it!" Emily was as excited as I was.

I ripped open the envelope, and sure enough, it was an acceptance letter! I jumped up and down—as much as I could with a baby in my hands. "I got in." I announced and gave Emily and the kids a big hug.

"I'm so proud of you, Laney! You are such a remarkable woman." Emily continued to hug me and said, "Now are you going to tell everyone?"

"No. I'm going to wait a bit. I don't want any pressure. If the school will allow me to defer, I'm going to sit on it for about a year and decide which graduate program I want to attend. This is a decision I'll have to live with the rest of my life. And as much as I love and respect my parents, I can't let them decide for me."

"Good for you. So when will you tell them?"

"Maybe on graduation day. I have a chance at graduating summa cum laude if I keep my grades up second semester. I'm going to surprise my parents on both accounts."

"Wow! I hope my little girl will be as bright and confident as you are, Laney Reid. Congratulations!"

"Thank you. I'm off to talk to the Dean and see if he'll allow me to defer for one year, and I also have to beg him not to tell Dad."

"You do that."

"Can I ask you to keep this secret from Jake?"

"Your secret is safe with me." She hugged and kissed me one last time.

Wow! Dr. Delaney Reid. I'm kinda digging that moniker!

February 20, 2013
Alone on the Diamond

*I*t was pathetic how lonely I was on the diamond without Donovan Taylor catching for me. He was on a business trip and I couldn't believe how alone I felt. William did a great job as catcher, and we soundly beat the IM team from across town, our biggest nemesis, but nothing about this evening felt right.

"Good game," Eric said to us after Elle pitched the last inning. "You both pitched beautifully! We beat the toughest team, and this is only our second game. You ladies are going to win this season for us."

"Thanks," I answered with a laugh. "I guess you guys take this game pretty seriously, huh? And here I thought it was just an IM game. It's not like we win anything."

"It's the pride factor, Laney. We don't like to lose, and to lose to our cross-town rival is the worst!"

"Hey guys. Thanks to you and Elle, we had our best game, yet!" Kevin, too, was a little more excited than necessary.

"Thanks," we both answered as we got our belongings together to head home.

"You want to go and have dinner?" William came out of nowhere and asked.

"I can't tonight, but thank you for asking."

"Is it because your keeper won't let you go out with me?"

"Who's my keeper?"

All the people answered at once. "Donovan Taylor."

Much laughter ensued. "You guys are exaggerating. Donovan is a close friend of the family and he feels the need to act like my older brother when I am outside of the family wings. He is not my keeper, and he does not control my actions."

"Then dinner...?"

"I really can't tonight. I have work to do and a quiz to study for once I get home. Next game?"

"That's a date!" Shoot! I wasn't meaning for it to turn into a date. "See you next Wednesday?"

"Sure. See you next week."

As we walked to Eric's car, Elle had many opinions on who I should and should not "date."

"Why would you go out with William when you have Donovan?"

"First of all, I'm not going out with William. We've had *one* date. And second of all, Donovan is not mine."

"Uh-huh. You keep telling yourself that, and maybe one day you'll believe your own words."

"Whatever, Elle." She had no clue how much I wanted Donovan to be "mine," but that was only in my dreams.

"Your phone's buzzing." Eric chimed in.

I took out my phone to find the text that quenched my loneliness.

Did you pitch well today?
Yes. I had a good catcher for a change, so I did very well.
Just to piss him off, I had to add that part.
And who caught for you?
Not saying...
WHO WAS YOUR CATCHER?
Where are you and why are you bothering me?

NYC and you still haven't answered me.

WILLIAM. Now go to bed, Mr. Taylor. I'm sure it's past your bedtime! Good night.

Are you going straight home?

Yes

Good. See you soon, Little Girl.

Whatever! I didn't answer him, but I did have a huge smile on my face after I put my phone away—a smile Elle and Eric did not miss as they commented, "Uh-huh!"

February 23, 2013
Surprise!

*T*hanks to Jane's generosity, the Reid ladies all got a fabulous weekend away at the Montage Hotel in Laguna Beach. I don't think I was on the original invite list, but Jane asked me to tag along, and I was grateful. Mom and Dad were away for the weekend, Doug went up to the ranch with all the Reid men, and I missed Donovan. I knew I had no right to miss him, but I did.

What are you up to, today? This was an unfamiliar number, which made me wonder...Donovan?

I'm down at the Montage for the night, thanks to Jane. What are you up to?

Who's Jane? Montage at the beach or in Beverly Hills?

Who's this? Who the hell was I texting if this wasn't Donovan?

William. William?

Uh, hi.

Hey. I'm headed to OC myself today. I'm coming to see you if you're at Montage in Laguna. I'll be at there around four. See you then?

Shit. What was I going to say? I didn't want to introduce him to the family.

Hello? Laney? You there?

Yeah. Um...I'm not sure about seeing you today. I'm here with my family and it's a girls' weekend.

Just an hour or so, Laney. I'll buy you a cup of coffee, an iced tea, an ice cream cone—whatever. Let's hang.

William, let's just see each other tomorrow. I don't think it's cool of me to step out on a girls' retreat. I'll call you later? I need to go in for my first treatment.

Talk later...

"Wasn't that wonderful, Gram? They really know how to spoil a girl at this resort."

"You're right, Laney. They do know how to spoil you."

Gram and I were almost comatose after the massage.

"Gram, will you excuse me? I've got a voicemail on my phone."

"Sure."

This voicemail I retrieved left me with mixed emotions, leading more toward annoyance. William told me with no qualms that he was coming down to see me around 4:00pm and that we could stay right here and have a drink together. Since our last date, I'd been trying to distance myself from him. He wanted a relationship and didn't listen to my protest of wanting to get to know him better. He was coming on stronger than I'd wished.

Even earlier than stated, William showed up at the pool before the male faction of my family surprised us with their appearance. After all the introductions were made we hung out a bit longer, but I dreaded the alone time with William. Sensing my discomfort, Doug suggested we all go out and Nick joined us for drinks in the lounge area. There actually was an upside to having an older brother who watched over me like a hawk. I'd have to thank Doug, later.

"Will you excuse me?" I was happy for the intrusion when my phone rang.

All the guys nodded, and I got up and went out to the large veranda for a breath of fresh air.

"Hey, Laney." Surprisingly, Max called. "Any chance I can ask you for a huge favor?"

"Of course. Anything."

"Since both Nick and Doug will not be staying tonight, could I ask you to switch rooms with me?"

Silly Max. He asked that question with way more hesitation than necessary. "Max, of course I'll switch with you. I'm sorry. I should have offered to room with my brother and cousin to begin with when they showed up. I'll be down right now to move my stuff."

"Thanks, Laney. You're fantastic."

This was my chance to leave William until dinner. Without asking my opinion, Jake had asked him to join us, and William accepted. My wonderful brother and Nick offered to hang out with William while I went and settled into my own room. My mind was cluttered with more jumbled-up emotions than I cared to admit. I dreaded dinner with the six of us, I dreaded the eventual conversation with William, and I missed Donovan. This was the longest I'd gone without seeing him since we started playing softball together. On the one hand, I despised these longings, again. I'd done well all throughout undergrad controlling the want, but it was back. On the other hand, my heart rejoiced every time I knew I'd be with him. This kind of whimsical happiness had left me a long time ago. Even if it was only a fairytale, I always saw myself as the princess to my handsome prince.

"Hello Miss Delaney. Don't you look stunning tonight! What brings you to the Montage?" *What?* There was the voice that made my heart skip too many beats. What was he doing here? He was dressed so sharp, wearing a suit that made him look like he was a runway model for Armani. This man stepped out of my dreams and made me hold my breath many, many seconds longer than necessary.

He was standing right before me, and I wanted to run to him and feel his arms around me. I 'd dressed for dinner early and walked up to the gorgeous lounge area so I could stare at the beach and dream about the man who probably never thought about me. And here he was... "Hello Mr. Taylor. You look very nice tonight as well. It's nice to see you again." *I'm so happy to see you, Donovan. I missed you.*

"What brings you here?"

"My family, as well as a date."

"A date?" He cocked his head slightly looking surprised, and maybe slightly disappointed? *No...that couldn't be.* "Who's the lucky fellow? You never told me you were dating someone. Is it William?"

"Yes, it's William, but we're not dating. He happened to be in Orange County and..." I started to answer, "I'm sure you're not interested in the fine details." I left it at that.

"Where is he? Are you meeting him here?"

"He's here somewhere. We separated for a bit so I could get dressed for dinner. What brings you here, tonight?"

"A...date..." He was slow in getting those words out, but I was quick to feel devastated. It became awkward between us once those two words appeared.

Did I have any right to feel this crushed knowing he was on a date with someone? How hypocritical of me when I was on a "date" myself. This crazy elated excitement of running into Donovan took a nosedive and drowned in the Orange County Sea as soon as I learned of this plans.

"Well, I guess I shouldn't keep you. It was nice seeing you. I...miss..." My heart sped up and almost crashed when I almost blurted that I'd missed him while he was gone.

"What was that?" The smile on this man's face told me he wasn't going to let my misstep go.

"Nothing. I've got to go." I started walking away. "I have to get to my dinner."

"He's a lucky man, Delaney..." he pulled me back to him and almost admired me. That made my heart melt, and I started to panic a little. My heart was up, down, to the right, to the left—aargh! I didn't like feeling so crazed every time I saw this man. "You look beautiful tonight, and I'm sure your date will find you almost as enchanting as I do."

Do you really find me enchanting? Do you think I look pretty tonight? My mind and heart were in such disarray, I stopped listening, or at least I thought I'd stopped listening, until of course he asked his next question. "Can I walk you to your destination? Are you dining at Studio?"

He put out his arm, like a Hollywood leading man, and dared me to hold onto it. I curled my hand into the crook of his elbow and we looked like Hollywood royalty walking through the hotel, by the pool, and onto the ground level to the restaurant that faced the ocean. What would it feel like to be on a date with this man? How would it really be if he were to show interest in me and I told him about my love for him since I was ten?

"Do you see your date?"

"Yes. He's over there." I pointed in William's direction.

"Well, I see that you're not the only surprise here for me tonight."

I had no idea what he was talking about. He walked me to our table and I saw that glamorous woman from earlier—the same woman who knew Jake—give Donovan a blinding smile. I slowly let go of his elbow, not that he noticed. Then it dawned on me. The truth stabbed me like a battering ram. This was Kate. The same Kate, Donovan dated back in college, the same Kate, Donovan had asked to marry him, the same Kate, who usurped my proposal ten years ago.

"Donovan..." The unspoken words from this Kate said a lot more than the spoken one. He walked over and lightly, but sensually embraced her—not enough so it would look casual to the nonchalant observer, but just enough for it to suggest a past, a history, and possibly a future to those like me who cared. They were still together...

I couldn't express the heartbreak that just occurred with their embrace. If I could, I would have walked right back to my room and cried an ocean. After believing that he found me *enchanting*, stunning, and *beautiful*, he went off to his woman who was the true symbol of beauty. Rather than enchanting, stunning, and beautiful, I was silly, nothing special, and cute. I knew at this very moment, that I'd "lost" Donovan, again.

Everyone greeted one another in surprise and we all sat to a long meal. Jake appeared to have a knowing look of what would happen even before dinner began.

I had a hard time eating. William was overly attentive and close to overbearing—sitting next to me, taking care of me every which way he could. He asked me if he should get me more water, more bread, was I hot, was I cold, was I OK with the tasting menu...aahhh! *Just leave me alone!* I knew he was only trying to be nice, but all the coddling was annoying.

"These boys, or at least at the time they were boys, stayed at my place," Kate said as she explained that she, Donovan and Jake spent every weekend together. I didn't want to hear that.

"Are you not hungry?" William hovered, again.

"I'll eat, William. You enjoy your meal." I answered softly, but looked up to see Donovan and Kate in a serious discussion. They looked so beautiful together, so intimate, so...perfect. I felt numb. No matter how hard I tried to make Donovan a nobody in my life, he persistently stayed a somebody. Who was I kidding? In the short month he'd reappeared in my life, I'd let him become everything to me again. How stupid was I to let a man control my emotions? I had to leave the room.

"Laney, you don't look good," William repeated for the tenth time.

"I'm OK William. I think I'll go outside for some fresh air."

"I'll go with you," was what I think he answered, but I didn't stay to reply. To my chagrin, I'd brought too much attention to myself as I abruptly got up and left the room.

"Laney..." Emily came outside and found me. "Is everything all right?"

"No..."

"Does it have anything to do with Donovan?" I must have given her a *how did you know* look because Emily uncharacteristically laughed at me. "Have you liked him long?"

"Oh my gosh, is it that obvious?"

"No, it's not obvious to most. Laney, I find myself drawn to you more than the other cousins because we are similar in many ways. There are times where I catch you looking at Donovan, and you have that same look of longing that I had when Jake and I were separated. It was so painful knowing that he was right there, but that he didn't want me. Is that how you feel?"

"I don't know how I feel, Emily. I've been in 'love' with him since I was ten. I saw him for the first time in Aunt Sandy's kitchen, and I knew that he was the one I wanted to marry. You know, I actually asked him to marry me when I was twelve years old." I started laughing and was about to tell Emily the entire story when William walked our way.

"I'll take him back in," Emily said. "Do you want to join us or are you done for the night?"

"I think I'll go to my room. Will you make up an excuse for me?"

"Definitely." Emily gave me a quick hug and kiss on the cheek and met William before he could reach me.

It was going to be a long night for me.

February 24, 2013
The Morning After

I'm unsure if I slept last night after that debacle of a dinner. Emily told me that dinner went well and William left after the meal. I woke up to texts, and a couple of voicemails from William that I've yet to return. Sitting on the grass with James, and listening to the waters crashing, soothed a broken heart that wouldn't mend anytime soon.

"Can we join you two on the grass?" My dream man who had found his dream woman last night came over with Ellie, and plopped down next to me and James. "You feeling OK? You left the dinner table early last night."

"I'm well today, thank you." I pretended to help James gather his toys because the sight of Donovan all sweaty and gorgeous after his workout was making me flustered.

"What are you up to today, Delaney?"

"I'll be going home with Gram and Sir Ascot after brunch. What will you be doing?" I asked out of courtesy. It's not like I didn't know what he and that stunning woman would be up to once they got back to her residence.

"I think I may go surfing or paddle boarding. It's a beautiful day. I'd like to jump in the water. Why don't you stick around and join me? I'll drive you back home later if you can't catch a ride with anyone else."

That was a very tempting offer, but did I want to be a third wheel? Did I have that much of a masochistic side to me? "Won't Kate mind if I stick around? It looked as though you two were getting *reacquainted* last night." My more than snarky remark coincided with Donovan's chuckle.

"Reacquainted..." the jerk thought on that word. Did he need to rub it in? "That's about as apt a word as any. Did you see William again after you left?"

I shook my head no.

"He didn't stop by your room last night?"

This time, I looked at him in horror. "*Hell*-o, why would he stop by my room?"

Donovan chuckled again. "Never mind. Stick around. Kate's not much into water sports. I'd like to see if you're as good in the water as you are on the mound."

"Buddy, I could whip your ass in the water. *That's* my sport."

"Is that right, Little Girl? You can whip my ass? Let's see you try."

That damn '*little girl*' moniker would stay with me for life. "I think your Kate will mind if I stick around. I prefer not to force a bicycle into a tricycle."

"What?" He looked thoroughly confused.

"I prefer not to tagalong."

"Kate won't mind a sweet young girl like you tagging along. Why you're younger than my youngest sister. Kate's an only child. I'm sure she'd love to get to know you."

*...sweet young girl tagging along... That's me...*Whatever!

"Thank you for the fun offer, but I think I'll go back home. I still have some stuff to do for school and I'm sure you and Kate need time to get *reacquainted*. You two make a beautiful couple. I guess you're over my cousin, Jane?"

Now what had possessed me to ask that question? I didn't need to know about his private life, and I especially didn't need to know if his private life concerned Jane.

Donovan, of course, didn't answer my questions concerning him, Kate, or Jane. I figured he wouldn't.

James called out to me and took my attention back to him. He pointed toward the family, so I figured he wanted his mother.

"You want to go back to Mama?" I asked, picking him up.

"Mamamama," he muttered.

"Excuse me, I think I'll take James back to Emily."

Donovan grabbed my arm and said, "Would it kill you to address me by my name?"

"Not at all. I'll see you later, Mr. Taylor." I addressed him by his name as he'd asked and walked away.

February 27, 2013
Play Ball

I dreaded another game without Donovan. I'd overheard Jane and Jake talking about Donovan staying down at the beach this week with the oh-so glamorous Kate, so I knew I was in for another lonely time up on the mound. William and I were done. I felt bad calling him after I got back home, rather than the morning of, but the hovering at the dinner table put me over the edge. One of my biggest no-no's was anyone who babied me or tried to take care of my every need. I liked my man strong, but not overbearing (though I'd never really been with a man, so perhaps that was what I thought I liked). William was weak and motherly—NOT for me! Today, I'd let him know.

"What's the nightmare about? Your face looks completely disgruntled."

Donovan! "What are you doing here?"

"I'm here for the same reason you're here—to play ball."

"Jake said you were staying down at the beach this whole week."

Donovan had a weird smile on his face all of a sudden. "You checking up on me, Little Girl?"

"Get a life!" I pretended the best I could to feel flabbergasted. "You are not the focal point of my life," *LIAR*, "and I did not ask about you. Jake said it in passing."

"Yeah, sure!" This conceited man didn't believe me. With the way he was looking at me, I'd swear he was seeing right through me. *Shit!* Was I that transparent? "Let's go play ball, Little Girl."

Our game was phenomenal! I pitched well, batted well, and hung out with Donovan the entire game. We sat next to one another in the dugout, joked around, and I'd forgotten that he had a woman who was waiting for him back at her home on the beach.

"You ready?" William approached me once the game was done.

"Huh?" I had no clue what he was talking about.

"You promised me a date." I was still drawing a blank. "Last week? When I asked you to dinner, you said you couldn't, but today was OK."

Shoot! Had I really done this? I guess I had. This was my chance to end the little we started. "Where shall we go?" I asked with a smile.

"Whatever strikes your fancy, my lady. I'm just happy to have a meal with you."

"Jake told me you and William weren't dating anymore."

What the hell? Donovan just outed me in front of half the softball team.

"Laney?" William looked surprised.

Damn Donovan Taylor! I spoke in a pissed-off manner. "Don't you have a woman and a beach to get back to?"

"Are you dismissing me?"

There was a look of shock on Donovan's face, and I'd put it there. That made me smile. "Yes, Mr. Taylor. You're dismissed." I stuck my tongue out at him like I used to do when I was ten years old. "Let's go, William."

Date with William? Productive.

The look on Donovan's face when I stuck my tongue out at him? Priceless!

March 8, 2013
Cinderella
At The Ball

*G*ram and Sir Ascot decided to move up their wedding date to this weekend, which threw Mom into an absolute tizzy! She put me on decorating duty, though I didn't know much about decorating. Actually, I was in charge of sending men and women to their correct locations. We were transforming Aunt Sandy's backyard into an English garden. To my utter surprise, by the end of the day, I thought we had all been transported back to old-England.

"Laney! I need your help over here."

"Mom. The caterers are here, and I need to show them where to set up."

Mom ran around like a chicken with its head cut off.

"Should I get Mom a stiff drink?"

"Doug! You know that'll make her go straight to sleep. She's needed here."

"Dude. I'm eloping if Mom goes this psycho every time there's a family wedding."

I laughed. "You can't do that. You're her only son. She'll want to throw you a grand wedding."

"No thanks. Nick and I've already decided we're eloping to Vegas. This isn't for us."

"A wedding is for the bride, not for the groom. Trust me. Your wife is not going to want a Vegas wedding, and you'd break Mom's heart if you eloped."

"Damn! I guess I just won't get married."

"Whatever."

The entire day was happily spent getting the house ready for a rehearsal tea and an English wedding tomorrow morning.

"Don't you look dapper, Master James." I picked up James and kissed him all over his cheek. Emily had dressed him to look like a little English boy from back in the olden days. He had a white button down shirt, knickers, matching suspenders, bowtie and a hat. His sister Ellie looked beautiful in her dress and matching hair-bow, but it was James that made me squeal. I couldn't wait to have little kids of my own.

"Emily, the kids look incredible."

"I think they look sweet, too. I couldn't stop kissing these two once they were dressed." Emily herself was so cute, talking about the babies.

"Me too. I think James is afraid to come anywhere near me because I attacked him the moment I saw him."

"Laney, can I ask you and Nick to be in charge of the twins today?" Jake was always putting his wife's needs first and the depth of his love for his wife always put a smile on my face.

"Jake, don't do that. Let them enjoy the day. I'll be with the kids." Emily was quick not to inconvenience any of us.

Without hesitation, Nick and I agreed to watch the kids.

Nick, the kids, and I happily hung out together till dinner was over, then our soon-to-be grandfather went up and continued our fun Reid tradition of "something old, something new, something borrowed, something blue." Our family loves tradition and each time anyone gets married, the soon-to-be groom has to follow the tradition his predecessor set. The last person to get married was Jake, and since Grandfather was in a class of his own, we were all wondering what he might do to continue our Reid tradition.

He did not disappoint!

"When I approached Estelle's five sons a few months back," my future grandfather started his speech, "and told them about my intention to marry their mother, they told me about the long-standing tradition you have in the Reid family. Though I'm not a Reid, I was told that I couldn't marry Estelle unless I agreed to honor and continue this tradition. Now, I don't quite fit into any category since I'm not the first child to get married, of any of your generations. Jerry picked the tradition of something old and started with a pearl necklace. Henry, the cheap bastard, picked something blue, and gave his wife a blue garter." Everyone would always pick on Dad for his gag gift. What most people didn't know was that he'd also bought Mom a set of emeralds, sapphires and rubies—ring, bracelet, necklace, and earrings—as her wedding present. Those stunning sets would become our personal heirlooms. "Jake, with the help of his gracious grandmother, gave his lovely wife not only the prize ring, but also something old and something new, with a pair of diamond earrings. Since I needed to *best* the young man who robbed the Reid family coffers, I brought the Ascot family jewels to refill what's been plundered."

The atmosphere changed from curious to absolute wonder when the large chest was opened and the jewels sparkled brighter than the heavenly night. I'd never seen so many jewels in one place!

Our little Ellie was the first one to go up and pick her gift. She "walked" away with a tiara. Sir Ascot proclaimed this was the greatest treasure in the chest. Her gummy grin sparkled brighter than the tiara. The look on her face when Jake put the crown on her head was precious. The entire family got a picture of that smile.

Next up was Auntie Sandy, and she picked a beautiful Tahitian pearl ring. Mom chose a bracelet, her jewel of choice, Emily picked a very small and understated broach, Jane picked a cute pendant, and when it was my turn, I knew immediately what I wanted.

Sitting beautifully on the bottom of the chest were a pair of glass slippers, and in my size. These were *tailor*-made for me and quite possibly, may turn me into Cinderella at the ball one day. With a silly smile, I picked the glass slippers and hugged my future grandfather.

"Thank you, Grandfather. You're too generous."

"I hope those shoes will make all your fairytale dreams come true, Laney."

"Even if they don't, I'll always remember the sweet man who gave them to me." I kissed him on the cheek, and let Sam have her turn.

What a magical night for all the Reid women.

March 9, 2013
Cinderella After Midnight

*T*oday was a perfect day for a wedding. Gram and Grandfather looked lovely together and would live a good many more years together as man and wife. Last night's revelry rolled right into today. All the guests came dressed in their English wedding best—even Donovan and Kate. When they both walked in, they looked like English royalty. Donovan looked every bit the English gentleman attending a society wedding, and with glamorous Kate on his arm, I finally felt like the little girl moniker Donovan continually accused me of being. How could I compete with that kind of sophistication?

"You've done a beautiful job here, helping your mom." Jake came up and kissed me on the cheek as I watched Mr. and Ms. Royalty walk in. "And you look beautiful today—almost as beautiful as my wife and the bride."

"Thank you," I answered glumly. "I think she ran away with the beautiful title today." I pointed my head toward Kate. "How can any one person get everything?"

Jake flashed a comforting smile. "Kate has always been beautiful and she's a nice person, too. But, you know everyone has their strengths and weaknesses. No one has everything."

"Who is she, and why is she here?" I knew the answer, but wanted confirmation from my cousin. "I take it she's the one Donovan wanted to marry when he was in college?"

Jake was surprised I knew so much. "You still keeping tabs on my buddy?" he kidded.

"No..." My heart broke. "I try not to...but sometimes I can't help myself."

Jake gave me one of those side-hugs and kissed the top of my head like I was ten, again. "She's going to be working at our grandfather's law firm, and as for her status with Donovan, you'll have to ask him."

I chuckled cynically. "Yeah. Next time we're together, I'll do that."

"You going to be all right?"

"I'll be fine, Jake." I answered with false bravado. "I'm not going to be sad today of all days. It's not every day a granddaughter gets to see her grandmother married." I smiled and walked with my head high and my heart pushed into a corner where no one could find it and break it.

"Laney." Nick called with a voice of desperation. "I can't dance with both the kids anymore. Can you take one?"

With pleasure! "Come on, Master James. Let's dance." I took hold of my favorite little boy and we danced in circles and enjoyed ourselves on this happy occasion.

"May I cut in?" Max already had Ellie in one arm, and he wanted James as well, so I handed him my little man and walked over to get the twins some food.

I tried desperately to walk away from the table where Donovan and Jane were in an intimate conversation, but I just couldn't help myself. How desperate did I have to be to want to be near him every chance I got?

Nonchalantly walking near their table, I focused on my goal of the food area, and couldn't help but overhear part of their conversation. Why oh why did I have to be such a masochist? This day would've been per-fectly fine had I not heard what Donovan was declaring to Jane. *"She came back to ask me to marry her, if you must know, my curious Jane. I don't love her anymore, though the attraction is still there. Maybe what I felt for her back in college was a young buck's fascination, adulation, obsession. I don't know if it was love. Plus, there's somebody holding me back from wanting to explore anything with anyone new. I know you're with another man. I'm not going to take what's not mine. But I can't help but wonder what it would be like to be with you...to laugh with you...to love with you.... A chance with you is what's holding me back from moving on.... There's my confession for the day. And now, I better get out of your boyfriend's seat."*

This confession devastated, overwhelmed, and destroyed me. It was one thing to think I couldn't compete against a glamorous older woman, but it was another to know that my cousin, who was already committed to an ideal man, held the heart of my ideal man.

"You look like you're about to cry. What the matter?"

Why was God so cruel to me that he had to send Donovan right here and now, to notice my dejection?

"I guess I'm just happy to see Grandfather find his true love, again."

"Are you sure? Your mouth tells me these are happy tears, but your face says otherwise. What's got you so sad?"

"I'm not sad." Simultaneously, the distress in my voice broke through and I had to wipe the tears that fell. I was such an idiot.

"Well, tears or not, you really do get prettier every time I see you."

"Thank you, Mr. Taylor." I decided to change the mood and turn this into a lighter situation. "You don't look half-bad, yourself." *Half-bad?* OMG! He looked striking. I'd never seen a more handsome man in my life. I had to stop and control my breathing—to control the tears that wanted to flow, and to control my ogling eyes that wondered how someone could be so breathtaking.

"I heard you ladies all had a grand time with Roland's treasure chest."

"Yes, we did. That was really kind of him to give us all a gift. He only needed to gift my grandmother but we all got blessed as well."

"What'd you pick?"

"I picked..." I hesitated because I knew he'd laugh at me. I knew my choice would solidify my little girl status.

"Yes?" He quirked his eyebrows in a really cute way. How, even after plundering my heart, could I find this man so irresistible?

"I don't think I want to tell you. You're going to make fun of me."

"Now why would I do that?" He laughed. No matter the pretense, we both knew he had his answer already. He just wanted an admission from me.

"You already know what I picked, don't you?"

He shook his head no, coupled by laughter that only grew with my silence.

I walked away from him, hurt. *Shoot!* I was getting seriously tired of this (in)significant man hurting my feelings at every turn. Something needed to be done...and fast! After what I'd heard between him and Jane, I was sick of being hurt.

I stopped, turned around and yelled at him. "I picked a pair of Swarovski crusted glass slippers! Go ahead and laugh at me. I'm sick of you treating me like a ten-year-old. Go back to your sugar-mama or who-ever else is holding you back from your sugar-mama and leave me alone!"

By the shocked look on his face—POINT MADE! I was so over him!

March 13, 2013
Heartbroken? You Have No Idea!

I could not face Donovan at softball today, so I told Elle I had too much schoolwork and bailed on the game. William had also been leaving me messages since I ended our "relationship" so not showing up to softball was a double blessing. Sitting at the library, I'd read and reread the same paragraph of my literature book. There was really no point in sitting here, pretending to study since nothing was being accomplished. I packed up my bags to leave.

"Where do you think you're going?"

Donovan!

"How'd you find me?"

"Elle thought you might be here. She said this is the only library you go to." He gallantly took my heavy book bag and carried it over his shoulder. "You haven't answered me. Where are you off to?"

"Home. I have much to do. Nothing got accomplished this weekend so I need to get to work."

"About this weekend...should we talk?"

"Nope!" I cut him off before anything else could be said.

"I think I need to explain a few things to you."

"Nope, nope, and more nope. You and I owe each other nothing. You have your life, I have mine—and our lives do not intersect like a Venn diagram."

"Delaney, I think..."

"Seriously, Mr. Taylor. I don't need to know, I'm not interested in knowing, and I have no right to know. What you choose to do as a grown adult is not for me to judge. What I will say is that Max is a great guy. He loves my cousin and I believe she loves him in return. Whatever the hell is going on in her mind and heart as well as yours, I just hope you'll consider the collateral damage of both your selfishness."

Shit. That was way too much talking. I just confessed that I'd heard everything that was spoken at the wedding between him and Jane.

"Yeah, I thought you might have heard all that." He had some sense of modesty and stopped talking...but not for long. "Let me ask you this..." he started again, "does my conversation with Jane have anything to do with why you looked so heartbroken at the wedding?"

Heartbroken? Mr. Taylor, grief-stricken, hopeless, crushed would be much better words for how I felt on Saturday. Naturally, I had to lie. "I've told you in the past, I like Max. He was sacrificing enough to let the love of his life go so she could find Jake. He deserves happiness...." I left it at that and took my bag back from Donovan.

Surprisingly, he didn't stop me from leaving. Stupid me was more hurt that he let me go, than relieved that this conversation was over.

March 30, 2013
Hawaii?

I made a fine mess of my "relationship" with Donovan. He didn't show up to the last two games and I received no texts this time asking how I played. Somehow, I made myself believe this was the best thing for me, and the less of one Donovan Taylor, the better. Why would he keep in touch with me on any regular basis, and why should I wonder where he was and who he was with? I wasn't anyone important in his life. This was the break we needed, or better stated, I needed. Emily had texted a few minutes earlier asking me to stop by, and when I got to her home, practically the entire cul-de-sac, ages thirty-five and under, was here.

"Since Jane will be working, maybe Laney can room with you two? It would be sad if we were all away and she was here alone during spring break. Doug, will you buy her a ticket?" My kind-hearted cousin-in-law was always looking out for my welfare.

"Heck no!" My cheap brother looked out for me *only* when it was convenient. "She has more money than I do. I'm a poor MBA student."

I was tired of my brother acting like an older brother only when he saw fit. "Quit your whining! I don't need you to buy me anything. I'll buy my own ticket," I said walking into the middle of this conversation. *How much could a ticket cost?* "By the way, Emily, what am I buying tickets to...a show? The movies? What are we all watching?"

"Hawaii!" Everyone cried out.

Shit! What had I gotten myself into? I didn't have that kind of money to spare. Every dime I made needed to be saved up for a yearlong trip to London.

"Um...I can't go to Hawaii. I don't have money to buy a ticket."

Jake and Emily immediately stepped in. "We'll take you."

"Thank you, but no. I mean, I have the money, but I can't spend it on a vacation to Hawaii. My dad says he's not supporting me outside of school, so I need to save up all my money for the next year. You guys have a great time."

"Come on, Laney. We'll all chip in and buy you a ticket." Nick, my good-natured cousin, smiled at me. I wondered why Nick never dated anyone. With his good looks and easy-going nature, what woman could resist him?

"I'll be fine at home. I can't do everything I want. My parents think I'm taking a year-long vacation, anyhow."

"Delaney Reid." I turned around looking for that voice, but didn't see anyone matching the masculine sound. "Get on the phone."

Jake pointed to the phone I was to pick up.

"Hi Mr. Taylor."

"How are you, Little Girl?"

"I've been good. How are you? We've missed you at the games." Shit, shit, shit! Now why did I have to go and say that?

"You have?" At first Donovan sounded surprised, then he sounded like he was smiling when he said, "I knew you'd miss me when I didn't show up to the game."

"I didn't say I have, I said we have, as in the collective group. And plus, you've missed two games."

"So you've noticed..." The smile was still there.

"Yeah, I've noticed. How can I not when there's no one to catch for me? We lost the last two games."

"We can talk about softball later. What's this about you not joining us next week?"

"It would be fun, but I need to save up my money for London. Some of us aren't high-powered lawyers charging ridiculous amounts of money per hour."

"I'll buy you a ticket. Show up with the group."

"No."

"Why not?"

"Because you have no reason to buy me a ticket."

"My plane ticket, my lodging and all my meals will be paid for by the firm. I want you to join us. I'll pick up your ticket."

"Don't."

"Just did. It's in your inbox."

"Mr. Taylor...!" I groaned.

"See you tomorrow, Little Girl. I'm glad you missed me." He hung up.

"I take it you're coming with us?" An astute Jake whispered in my ear while everyone else was oohing and aahing over the property we were staying at in Hawaii. "Did my buddy pull through?"

"I'll go and pack. See you tomorrow, bright and early."

"We'll all have a blast!" Jake sent me off with those encouraging words.

Hawaii. One week. Me + Donovan Taylor.

I smiled.

April 1, 2013
Hawaii!

What the hell was I thinking?

"Hello, Laney," was the sultry voice that greeted me as I arrived at our gate.

Hawaii. One week. Me + Donovan Taylor?

Ha! It was more like, Hawaii. One week. Kate +Donovan + Jane!

Last night, the excitement of Donovan wanting me to join him in Hawaii was too much for me. Sleep wouldn't come so I packed, repacked, and thought about the copious activities I'd like to do with him. This morning—REALITY check! Kate stood next to Donovan in all her splendor, and she greeted us with her stunning smile and knockout, fitted couture suit. It made me and my maxi dress look like some hick, billowy, out-of-fashion LOSER.

It was at this moment I hated everyone. I hated myself for living in la-la land. I hated Donovan for getting my hopes up. I hated Jane for being front and center on Donovan's radar. And I hated Kate for being nice to me. Well...I didn't really hate anyone, but I felt like a fool. To add to my foolishness, through Kate's unexpected kindness and an unexpected business meeting, I ended up sitting in her seat with Jake, Emily and Donovan, in first class. The flight attendant offered me a mimosa, and I gladly accepted the drink while calming myself before the flight began.

I also looked for ways to change seats—to sit next to Emily, rather than Donovan, because after throwing a rant at Gram's wedding, I was embarrassed to be with him. Why, oh why, did I get myself into such predicaments?

"Are you going to go dark on me this entire plane ride?" He was so handsome this morning in his casual pants and button down shirt-look. How could a man look this good?

"I don't know. Do you have anything stimulating to talk about, Mr. Taylor?"

"I won't if you keep calling me by my dad's name."

"I guess we'll practice the AMC rules." He gave me a blank look. "Silence is golden?" He still gave me a blank look. "Don't you watch movies? You know...silence is golden is strewn across the movie screen at AMC theaters?"

He smiled. "I guess it's been a while since I've been to the movies. What have you watched, lately?"

"Well, I've seen a lot of movies."

"Such as? Do these movies have a name?"

"I saw *The Last Exorcism Part 2*..." I paused after this because I thought about how we ended up asleep and tangled on the sofa the last time Donovan and I saw a movie together. "And I saw *Oz, Burt Wonderstone, G.I. Joe*, and *The Host*."

"You saw *all* those movies recently? How do you possibly see so many movies in the course of a few weeks?"

"I..." Should I tell him?

"I...?" He expected an answer.

"I went on a few dates last month and we ended up watching movies before or after dinner."

"With this William guy?"

"No! I had to end things with him."

"Why?" Donovan laughed at me.

I gave him an ugly look and turned away to talk to Emily instead. I was embarrassed enough with this man; I didn't need him making fun of my life.

"No matter what kind of funny face you make, you're adorable, Delaney Reid," he said as he put his thumb and forefinger on my chin and turned me back around to face him. "Now finish your story."

I thought about it for a while, then concluded he wasn't going anywhere. There weren't too many other options but to speak with my dream man.

"William was too clingy."

"How was he *too clingy*?" He imitated my last two words.

"He just was…" I dared him to ask again. Of course, Donovan asked again so I had to explain. "He just hovered all the time and I don't like guys…girls…people who hover. I need my freedom." There. I was done with my explanation.

"Then why date anyone, if you need your freedom?"

"Because I want to find my happily-ever-after, my soul mate, my love…" I hated that I sounded so sappy. "You probably think I'm being foolish, but I'll find my knight in shining armor, and I plan to live a fairytale life."

"Boy, you don't make it easy on any man, do you?"

"Now why would you say that? Why can't I expect a happily-ever-after? Look at Emily. She found her dream man in Jake. That's what I want—a guy just like Jake!"

"Great…" Donovan was now as sarcastic as could be. "He's not as *wonderful* as he appears on the outside. Trust me. I've known him all my life."

"So have I, and yes, he is as *wonderful* as he appears to be—in fact, he's even better. Right, Emily?"

Jake and Emily only laughed at our silly argument.

"Laney, you will find your perfect man who will love you, cherish you, and do a mad dash to keep up with the spunky you. And I know for a fact that when you find this man, he will fall head over heels in love with you and you two will have an even better courtship story to tell your grandchildren than Jake and I had, because you are *that* special."

I looked at Donovan and gave him a *you see* look! He raised up both hands in concession.

The Big Island was gorgeous. This was not my first time on this island, but it always shocked me to see all the lava rocks that surrounded the airport. The airport was like an outdoor hut. Literally, we landed on a strip, got off the plane and walked a few steps to baggage claim. Everything was outdoors, the weather was perfect, and the ocean was super inviting. We all got into the cars that came to pick us up from the hotel. Donovan, Jane, Jake and Emily got into one car, and the three of us got into the other. When we arrived at the hotel, O...M...G...! It was DROP DEAD GORGEOUS!!! I remembered coming here when Doug and I were younger, but I never thought it was this beautiful. We were probably too young to remember any of this luxury. Nick and Doug were speechless as well.

"How'd we get this lucky?" I heard my brother ask. "Are you sure this place is paid for, Nick?"

"I don't know now. Let's confirm with Donovan before checking in. I don't think I can afford this kind of hotel on my dime, ever."

Once Donovan confirmed that his room was our room, Doug, Nick, and I unpacked our clothes for the week. This hotel boasted six pools, eight tennis courts, a golf course, its own beach (though I was told that technically it was a public one, even if the beach sat on their property), and the most stunning view. I had died and gone to heaven.

We got a nice ocean front room with two double beds and one rollaway. Since I was the odd-woman out, I offered to stay on the rollaway. Nick told me he'd sleep on the rollaway, but I didn't care. I was just happy to be here. Jane's room looked no different than ours, except there was only one of her and three of us. Jake and Emily were staying in a suite/bungalow with a huge bedroom, living area, a private lanai with an amazing view of the Pacific Ocean, and a massive fruit arrangement that we three helped ourselves to while visiting their quarters.

When we got to Kate and Donovan's villa, the three of us almost died of shock. We'd never seen anything so massive and palatial. This villa was bigger than my house—literally. And I don't live in a small house. It looked like someone's plantation home on a large resort. We Reids don't exactly bum it on our vacays, but this place was by far the nicest place we'd ever seen. We were in awe...!

"How'd Kate score this place? Man, it's huge!"

"Dude, Nick...it's bigger than huge. This must be the Presidential villa. Did the company actually pony up money for a place this extravagant?" Doug went around checking out the whole place.

"I'm not sure what Kate did for this place, but when I went to check in for the both of us, she started with a room just like yours, but when I gave them her hotel identification card, they immediately upgraded her to the best room in the house." Donovan sounded like a proud papa.

Normally, I'd be irked that Donovan was sharing a villa, and obviously a bed, with Kate, but the place was so magnificent, I didn't care. I chose to go outdoors to the wrap-around lanai and laid on the chaise lounge.

"Let's go to the beach," Nick said. "You all have your bathing suits on? Can you come out and play for a while, Donovan?"

"Yep! The clients haven't arrived yet. They don't come in till later this afternoon, and I'm sure we won't start until tomorrow morning at the earliest. Let's go."

At the beach we saw Emily and Jake sipping pineapple-infused water and reclining on the lounge chairs. Jane thought about coming into the water, but chose instead to hang out with Emily. The guys decided to get information on the outrigger canoes that the hotel offered, and I chose to jump into a fitness challenge that was just about to begin.

"Aloha," this cute guy said when I walked over to their group.

"Aloha," I answered back.

"My name is Nolan. I'm the golf pro here at the hotel."

"I'm Laney. I'm just your average guest." I smiled. "You here for the challenge?"

"Yeah. Are you here for the swim and run as well?" He looked surprised.

I tend to get this reaction often, as I don't look like the athletic-type. It's not that I'm good at any sport, but I enjoy every sport I pick up.

"I am. See you at the finish line," I giggled and raced into the water to start swimming.

Oh my gosh, oh my gosh, oh my gosh...! I thought my lungs would collapse on me during the swim. Swimming in the ocean was no lap in the backyard pool. *Just kill me now!* I toughed it out and finished the 1,000-yard swim then *SHOOT!* the 2.2 mile run was next. There was no finer sight than the finish line as I finished respectably. I didn't win the race, but I stayed with the first third of the pack. *YES!* It was over. Why I did this kind of stuff to my body, I didn't know. It did feel good to get rid of the grogginess from the plane ride.

"You were fantastic out there." Nolan congratulated me with a high-five.

"How would you know? Didn't you compete?"

"I did but I was behind you the whole time. I tried to catch up, but you were too fast. Do you normally compete in triathlons and biathlons?"

"Nope. Never done them before in my life. I didn't think it would be so hard. Otherwise, I wouldn't have done it."

"My friends and I are going paddle boarding in a few minutes. Would you like to join us?"

"Sure." That sounded like a lot of fun, but I needed to catch my breath.

I got back to where my family was hanging out, and immediately wished I hadn't. My brother got all huffy-puffy with me for the rash guard and bikini bottom I was wearing. What did he expect me to wear on a beach swim and sand run? He was irritating me so much, I decided to get back at him and take off my rash guard and go on the beach in my super cute teal bikini top and bottom. Normally, I wouldn't paddle board in so little clothing, but just to annoy my brother, I decided to go for it.

"Hey Laney." Jake was calling me back to the family.

"Yeah, Jake?" I reluctantly came back.

"I told Donovan here that you could whip his ass in golf. You want to challenge him?"

I had to laugh. *Did I want to spend an entire day playing one of my favorite sports with him? Yes? No?* How would I answer this question in the most honest way? Like the fool that I was, I challenged him—no, I taunted him—to a game of golf. We even had a bet going. If I lost, I'd give up the Mr. Taylor name and if he lost, he'd have to take me hiking to see the lava flows at the volcanoes. Either way, I suppose I couldn't lose.

"Who turned on the damn alarm?" Nick groaned. "We're on vacation. Turn it off...PLEASE!" He begged.

"Sorry Nick," I apologized.

Why oh why did I agree to this stupid golf challenge against Donovan Taylor? It's not as though I needed to spend more time with him. And I definitely couldn't look my best when I was getting up at 4:30am for a 5:00am tee time. Thank goodness Nolan would be there as a buffer between the two of us. Truly, I didn't want to keep obsessing over a man who barely knew I existed. But when he was practically a part of the family, it was hard to find that space to let go.

"Good morning!" I tried to sound chipper, though it was hard when I hadn't had my morning cup-o-joe.

"Good morning, Delaney. You ready for the big challenge?" Donovan asked as he handed me a delicious smelling cup of coffee. "I was told you need a cup of strong coffee with a splash of hazelnut creamer?" *Goodness!* He looked incredible even at this hour and that smile...

"Thank you, Mr. Taylor. How do you know about my coffee habits?"

"I know a lot more about you, Delaney Reid, than you think I do." His eyebrows quirked.

I quirked my own eyebrows in response. "I doubt that, but thank you for the coffee. You know, you're giving ammunition to the enemy."

"Bring it on Little Girl! I welcome the challenge." *Little Girl, Little Girl, Little Girl!* What else would I be? "Before we start, I wanted you to be aware that our clients wanted to golf with us so it'll be a fivesome. Is that all right with you?"

"Sure."

The game got started, and I hit a series of lucky shots to start me off at 1-under on the first hole.

"Very nice shot, Miss Reid," Mr. Weston Hong called out after my drive on the second hole.

"Why thank you, Mr. Hong. And please, call me Laney."

"Then you must call me Weston."

The two clients we were golfing with were both from Taiwan, but spoke perfect English. They were about the same age as Donovan, but mega wealthy.

"When did you learn to golf, Laney?" Weston walked with me on one side while Nolan walked on the other. Donovan kept the other client occupied.

"I've been golfing practically all my life. My dad loves to golf, and he used me and my brother as an excuse to golf at the club all the time. My poor mother would sit at home, alone all weekend long, while my dad played in tournament after tournament. A lot of the times, he'd partner up with me or my brother, Doug."

"Is Doug as skilled as you are?"

I only laughed. "You'll have to ask him. We all have differing opinions."

"Stop the chatter, Little Girl, and hit your iron shot."

"My...isn't someone a bit pissy at 5:30 in the morning? Coffee wear off? You need some of mine?" I teased Donovan.

He yanked my arm and pulled me into the crook of his arm and it was almost as though he had his arms around me. I wasn't too much shorter than Donovan so it was a most perfect fit.

"You sassing me, young'un? Just get ready to call me by my given name," he said and actually kissed my temple. I know that meant nothing to him, but it meant the world to me. I wanted to say one of those silly school girl sayings like, *"I'll never wash my temple again!"*

"Is Laney related to you, Donovan?" The other client, Brad Wang asked.

"She might as well be. We all grew up together. Her cousin is my best friend, so Delaney is like a cousin to me too."

"You are lucky to have such good friends, Donovan – and such good looking ones, too. Isn't Jane related to you all somehow?"

I explained to Brad, and then again to Weston when he joined us, how we were all related.

Throughout the morning, I hit some great shots, and Donovan hit some spectacular ones. Nolan was our scorekeeper and he gave me pointers on each hole as he saw fit, without giving me too much help. I enjoyed hanging out with everyone. It helped make this whole competitive game much more relaxing and fun.

After being up one, down one, throughout all 17 holes, it came down to the last hole. I shot 1-over, Donovan shot 1-under and we were tied. We tied two more times and on the third try, I shot 1-under and won the round. It was exhilarating!

Then, it wasn't exhilarating anymore. We got around to telling my family about the match and at first, I thought Donovan was pretending to be surly about losing. Once he called me a cheater and told Jake his side of the story, it dawned on me he probably didn't want to take me to the volcano. He was looking for ways to back out of the bet.

Defeated, I told him, "All right, Mr. Taylor. You win. You don't have to take me to the volcano. I'll see it next time." I'd find my own way to the volcano. I didn't need Donovan Taylor taking me on any field trips. Saying good-bye to everyone, I left before anyone could see my broken heart.

"Laney?" Emily followed me.

"Yes?" I answered trying to mask my hurt.

"I don't think Donovan was trying to get out of going to the volcano with you. He seemed really proud of the fact that you were so good out there today."

"Thanks, Emily. You always have a way of making me feel better, no matter the situation. It's OK. It's not as if I thought we were going on a date or something. I'll catch the volcano by myself or on a tour group. Please go back in and eat. Jake will worry."

"Do you really have a lunch date, or was that an excuse to get away from us?" My sweet cousin-in-law, who felt more like a sister, sounded very worried.

"I'm having lunch with Nolan. I'll see you in there soon." I rushed off trying not to feel so brokenhearted. This, too, was just another get-my-hopes-up-only-to-be-shot-down, moment.

April 2, 2013
Volcanoes & A Pseudonym

$\mathcal{N}$ot once had I felt uncomfortable with the two gentlemen while golfing, yesterday, but today was another story. Weston, the more outspoken of the two, paid more attention to me than I cared for, and he kept finding reasons to touch me. They were innocent pats, here and there that I did not appreciate. I did my best to stay away from both of them, but when there were only five of us on a very long hike, that wasn't as easily done. Today was the first of many days that made me think that my heart was definitely in too deep with Donovan Taylor, again, and I needed a respite from him. The closer I got, the uglier we were to one another, and the more Donovan showed me that we didn't suit.

"Delaney," Donovan yelled at me, "don't walk so close to the ledge!" He found too many reasons to be upset with me today, and I was getting pissed.

"What the hell is the matter with you?" I yelled back in a whisper. "Why are you so pissy this morning? I know this isn't what you wanted to do today, and I know you don't want to be with me. I'm sorry I ever made that bet with you!"

"What's wrong is that you're flirting with my clients, and I don't like it. You could jeopardize our relationship with them once they realize you're just playing games."

Did this man really say that? He thought I played games with men, and was upset because he didn't want to lose these men as clients?

"I'm not flirting with anybody," I quietly insisted. The accusation and the lack of concern for me were beyond a knife to my heart.

"Yeah you are. My clients' heads are spinning every time you smile at them and touch them."

"How can you say that?" I asked, broken. "I haven't done anything to warrant this kind of censure and criticism. I can't believe you just said that to me."

All my life I'd saved myself for Donovan. Of course he never asked me to, and there was no guarantee he'd appreciate what I did. In fact, what I did was stupid! I almost missed my high school prom because he was the man I wanted as a date, and throughout my four years in college, I dated but never got serious because none of the men were as great as Donovan, or so I thought. Why the hell had I put him up in heaven with God? This man was being an absolute bear, and I hated the way he was treating me. I deserved better than this and dammit, I wasn't going to stand for it.

"I came on this excursion because your clients asked me to, and I believed I was *helping you* with your clients. Don't you dare accuse me of doing something I did NOT do! I did NOT flirt with these men, I did NOT touch these men, and if my actions bother you so much, I'll just leave."

And I did just that. I turned myself around and walked straight back the way I came. Donovan Taylor was being the biggest asshole on this side of the island. I didn't need him, or his attitude.

With a pissed-off demeanor, Donovan chased after me and pulled me back on our hike without a word, an apology, or an explanation. I fought his grip and turned the other way, again.

"Let's just finish this hike, and then we can stay as far away from one another as possible. Let me remind you that *you* are the one who wanted to come here, and *you* accepted my clients' offer. You can't leave just because you feel like it."

What a jerk! Why oh why did I ever find this man attractive? He was about as attractive as a grizzly bear.

I decided to trail behind our tour guide, Donovan, and his two clients. If Donovan had any clue how much I adored him, just how long I had loved him, he could never accuse me of paying attention to any other man. Not only did he have no idea, he just didn't care. *ASSinine!*

"We will stop here for a quick lunch," the tour guide explained. All the men were ready to break for a meal. It had been a long morning, and I, too, was hungry. But I really had no place to be. I couldn't be next to Donovan's clients for fear that I would be accused of flirting with them, nor did I want to be next to them. And Donovan paired himself with our tour guide and didn't look twice at me. I felt so alone.

"If it's OK with you, I'm going to walk ahead just a little bit and I'll be back by the time you guys are done with your lunch."

Before I heard any protest, I walked off. My feelings were hurt and I was surely pissed, but I decided not to let Donovan break my spirit, and I would not shed any tears for this man.

The hike was super long, and would have been phenomenal if someone hadn't ruined it for me. However, I felt a hundred times better once we got to the beach and I let out my aggressions in the water. Our tour guide offered to take us to a secluded beach that only locals were familiar with, so we called my brother and cousins to join us there.

I grabbed the surfboard my brother brought from the hotel, and swam as far out as I could. Surfing made me so happy, but I guess anything water-related made me happy.

I was doing fine until I lost my footing on the board and wiped out. That would not have been a big deal except the leash on my board loosened and the board came crashing on my head. For a split second, my eyes couldn't focus and fainting was nearby. My breathing was labored and I was taking in water by the gulps.

"Delaney." A worried Donovan held me in his arms just a few seconds longer than anyone would consider friendly, and began taking me back to shore. "How do you feel?" His genuine concern erased the ugliness of this morning.

"My head hurts and I feel dizzy. Why are you in here helping me?"

"What the hell kind of question is that? Why the fuck do you think I'm in here...because I want to be rescuing you from your crazy daredevil antics? What were you thinking when you got on this surfboard with waves that huge? Are you showing-off, or do you not have any sense of self-preservation?"

Donovan, why can't you just let me be? Why do you need to constantly remind me that you don't love me? I get it. I really do. Please...I beg you...just stop playing with my heart.

"Please put me down." He wouldn't let go of me. "PUT ME DOWN!"

I tried to jump off but he pinched me in the back and told me, "Stay still, Brat!" Then he had the gall to add, "You have been a pain in my ass all day today."

Every damn person on the beach heard what he said and it was mortifying. I felt like a five-year-old being scolded by her older brother. Who the fuck did he think he was?

I pinched him back, HARD and flipped myself off him when he flinched in pain. "I didn't ask you to come into the ocean and save me." That first statement came out in a torrent of anger. But the next statement couldn't hide the flood of pain. "I get it. You don't want me anywhere near you. I'll stay away." Before a flood of tears came, I ran back up to the car.

The ride back to the hotel wasn't a fun one. I waited to see which car Donovan was getting in to so I could ride in the other car. Josh kept asking questions, and but I wasn't in the mood to answer. Josh, the youngest of the Davis brothers, was fun, hilarious, and sweet. Today just wasn't the best day for socializing.

"You want to have dinner together?" I didn't think I had a way out of not having dinner with everyone.

"Sure. We'll probably all do dinner together somewhere on the resort. Maybe we can sit together and we can talk more then?" That probably wasn't the smartest suggestion, but I just needed a breather from Josh's questions.

"Great idea. I'll see you soon."

We parted ways and I quickly showered, dressed, and left our room so I wouldn't bother Jane and Max. Jane generously brought out the Davis brothers to join our vacation. My brother and Nick were having a grand time with Josh and Garret, and Jane and Max were equally enjoying themselves.

"Where are you off to when the luau isn't for another hour?"

"I'm off so you and Jane can have some privacy," I smiled at this great man who was perfect for my cousin Jane. I hoped Jane knew what a treasure she had in him. As Max and I became better friends, I wondered where I could find someone so genuine, and so in love with his woman, that he'd overlook her straying eyes.

"You don't have to leave. Hang out here with us."

"I think my cousin would prefer I leave. And to be honest, I'd like to walk off my headache. That bump on the head was a bit harder than I thought."

"Then you should definitely stay here and let me keep an eye on you."

Shoot! Not the right thing to say... "I'll be all right. The beach is too inviting. I'd like to take a walk before dinner."

"Come right back if you feel any nausea or more pain."

"I will."

Donovan and Kate's large villa appeared along my path, and the two of them were laughing and having a drink out in their lanai. They looked so beautiful and so right for each other. What could I possibly offer a man like Donovan Taylor when he had a sophisticated woman who suited his every need? Jake and Emily lived in wedded bliss, Max and Jane, if they kept going strong, would be right behind Jake and Emily in the bliss department, and Donovan and Kate had been together and in love for the past ten years. That was longer than the first two couples combined, times two. Why was I such a dreamer?

Sitting on the sand, watching the sun begin its descent, I regretted coming to this beautiful island. This week was a time for lovers, not loners.

"Laney?" I heard Jake call my name, but didn't fully register. Physically, I was at the luau, but mentally I was back at the beach, sitting on the sand, watching the sunset. "Laney?"

"Hey!" Donovan called out.

Ignoring Donovan, I only faced my cousin and listened to what he had to say.

"I think you should stay with us tonight. You have a bump on your head and I'd like to make sure you are OK." Bothering Jake and a very pregnant Emily was not my idea of caring for my family.

"Jake, I'm totally fine. I don't need anybody waking me up."

My cousin wouldn't take no for an answer and as much as I dreaded bothering them, the idea of staying with anyone else made my stomach churn. I was about to give in when Donovan came up with the stupidest idea yet.

"Why don't Kate and I take Delaney tonight? We have two extra bedrooms and I can check up on her throughout the night."

Good Gaaawwwddd! Was he kidding me? Could he possibly come up with more ways of torturing me? *Please, Jake. No! Anything, I'll do anything you ask. Please don't send me to their love villa.*

For some *Gaaawwwddd* forsaken reason, Emily and Jake both saw fit to send me to hell tonight. I was told to pack my bags and Josh was to be my escort to the love-shack. *Aargh!* Why does crazy, stupid shit like this happen only to me?

"Hello." I barely squeaked as I saw an enormously unhappy Kate. "If you'll show me where I'm to stay, I'll go there now and not bother you."

Donovan led me to a room around the bend from their room.

"Thank you," I whispered again. "You don't need to check up on me tonight. There's nothing wrong with me." He gave me a dubious and disapproving look. "I promise. I'm fine and I'll be out of your way first thing in the morning."

"I'll be here in about an hour so go to sleep now."

"Who the hell died and made you God?" Where that idiotic boldness came from, I could not say.

"Do you have to be a bitch about everything? Why can't you just take what I say as fact and follow the program?"

"Because you can't program me. I'm not a part of this crazy harem-thing you have going on here. You accuse me of flirting with men, but you're the man-whore!"

"What the hell are you mouthing off about? How did we get into talking about me, and how the hell did I become a man-whore?" He was about as flabbergasted as I was about this whole man-whore business. I couldn't say where that really came from and why I decided to speak my mind at this very moment. The frustration of the day must have been bubbling in this cauldron of mine because I was seriously in *double, double, toil and trouble*, right now.

"You think we don't see you flirting with my cousin Jane, a woman with a *boyfriend*, when you have a *girlfriend* of your own? You're physically with one woman, mentally thinking about another woman, but don't have the fucking guts to emotionally love the right woman! You can accuse me all you like of *flirting* with other men, but when I find that right man, he will not doubt my love for him. Go back to your *woman*. She didn't look happy to have me here."

Oh my gosh! Oh my gosh! Oh my gosh! I didn't know where all that came from and who had stolen my mouth and spewed out all those absurdly perfect words! I was so on...so right...so sublime! But thank God Donovan left the room as abruptly as I chewed him out, or else he would have heard my nerves shatter the moment I finished realizing what I had just "mouthed-off."

"Where did we go so wrong, today," was the last, rhetorical question he asked before leaving me to my own device.

Who the hell knew where we went so wrong today? Where I went wrong in life was my early-aged infatuation with this man!

I milled around the room and turned on the television to fill the time, but couldn't sit long enough to watch it. Then I opened up a book and got depressed once the romance novel started heading in the happily ever after stage. I didn't want to read about anyone else's happily ever after, and I for sure didn't want to be in the same villa with the happily-ever-after couple.

"I don't understand why you had to insist on bringing her here." Kate had no qualms about voicing her opinion of my stay here. Perhaps they were not as happily ever after as I'd imagined?!?

"It's just for a night. We have two empty rooms. What's the big deal?"

"We have no privacy, is what's the big deal. We can't talk, we can't argue, we can't have sex with her next door to us." Shit! Did she just say that? She was accusing *me* of disrupting her sex life?

"What's the matter with you? It's one fucking night. She's injured, we have a room, and she's Jake's cousin."

"Jake wanted to take her with them but no, you had to bring her here. Do you know when the last time was when we were intimate?"

Damn. This was not a conversation I wanted to hear! It pissed me off that she was accusing me of ruining their sex life. *I didn't ask to sleep here!* Rather than getting more and more pissed by the second, I left. With a quick note for Donovan and my belongings in tow, I went to the front desk and got myself my own room where no one could bother me. No Jane giving me the annoyed-eye for bothering her time with Max, no Kate for accusing me of stupid things, and no brother and cousin who considered me one of the guys when sharing a room.

This room was *way* beyond my price range, but it was all mine for the night. I could wear pajamas without a bra and wouldn't have to be self-conscious of the men in the room. Everything could just hang loose. It was wonderful! But as much as I wanted to enjoy the room, I was physically exhausted from the hike, and mentally and emotionally exhausted from Donovan Taylor.

Oh. My. Gosh! What the hell is that noise outside my door? The noise wouldn't stop. *Go away!*

I had no choice but to get up and figure out how to get rid of this annoyance.

In a less than brilliant move, I opened the door to find a mob of people standing, waiting for me. *How did they find me? So much for my clever pseudonym.*

"Laney," Emily hugged me for dear life and closed the door behind us. "I thought something bad had happened to you. Don't go missing like that, again. You scared me to death!"

Not once did I consider my family would find out I'd left the villa. Damn Donovan Taylor! "I'm sorry, Emily. No one was supposed to know what happened. I just wanted some peace and quiet. I wasn't trying to upset you, or anyone else. I feel terrible."

"It's all fine now that we know you're safe. Maybe you'd like to put something on and tell everyone you're OK?"

Shit! I'd forgotten I had no bra on and with my size boobs, it wasn't a pretty sight to be bra-less. I put a sweatshirt over my t-shirt and opened the door.

"Delaney, are you OK?" Donovan got that in before I could apologize. He looked like hell—and even that was gorgeous. I was so doomed!

"Yes, I'm fine. I'm sorry to have caused you guys any worry." I apologized to the rest of my family. Then I added, "I told you not to tell my family that I left." All of this could have been avoided had he kept his mouth shut.

"Jake, can I have a word with Delaney, alone?"

Shit, shit, shit! No Jake!

He was about to say no, but something in Donovan's plea made him change his mind. Emily gave me a nod of encouragement as Donovan walked in my door and shut it behind him.

"You!" Uh-oh! He was not happy with me. "Don't you ever, ever scare me like that, *ever again!*" He didn't yell loudly enough for the people outside to hear, but it was loud enough for me to understand. "I lost at least ten years of my life when I couldn't find you. What the fuck were you thinking, disappearing on this island like that? How irresponsible can you be to scare all of us, especially your pregnant cousin..."

That did it! I was going to listen quietly and let him rant because he did look like I'd scared the shit out of him, and also because I enjoyed this frazzled look, but bringing Emily into this was a low blow!

"Do NOT accuse me of being irresponsible, and do NOT give me guilt about scaring Emily. I don't give a rat's-ass whether or not you 'lost ten years of your life.'" And yes, I put up my fingers air-marking the quotations. That really pissed him off! "I left you a letter asking you not to tell my family. I told you in that letter that I would see you tomorrow, or in another lifetime, if I was lucky enough!"

It was at this point, the craziest, most bizarre, but a most phenomenal thing happened. Donovan—who up until two seconds ago, was some ways away from me—rushed me, grabbed me by the face with both his hands, and KISSED ME! My initial thought—*Oh. My. Gaaawwwddd! Donovan is kissing me.* My second thought—*Shit! I have morning breath. Just kill me now. Donovan Taylor is kissing me for the first time and I have bad breath.*

Gaaawwwddd! My third thought—*I hope I'm doing this correctly. Damn! Why'd my first real kiss have to be with Donovan?*

"Don't ever do that to me again or I'm going to spank your ass till you can't sit for a good long time. You got it?" That was it. He kissed me, threatened me, then left me reeling in my room.

That kiss, that pressure on my mouth, and that image of Donovan so up close and personal, stayed with me the entire night. I didn't sleep, but adrenaline kept me going till the next day.

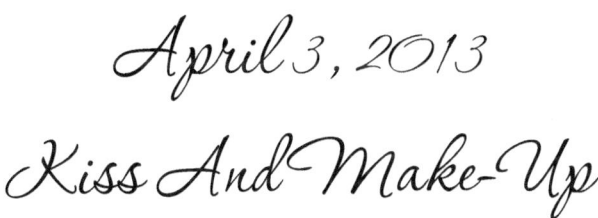

April 3, 2013
Kiss And Make-Up

Since I didn't sleep a wink last night after the kiss, I got my workout clothes on and ran along the beach as the sun rose. Our next to last day in paradise brought a mixture of sadness, relief, and bliss. In full (embarrassing) disclosure, I'd never been properly kissed until Donovan kissed me last night. Part of the reason for this was the fact that I'd never seriously dated anyone. Another part of the reason was that I never liked anyone enough to want them to kiss me.

"Hey." A beautiful voice called out softly, tenderly.

He came and sat next to me on the sand, and we watched the sun rise little by little.

"Hi." I felt self-conscious and shy about talking to him, but eventually broke the silence. What do you say to a guy who doesn't like you, but kissed you passionately the night before? Was there a Miss Manners guide to a situation like mine?

"You ran?"

"Yeah. Couldn't sleep so I thought I'd be productive and exercise."

"...a beautiful sight!" I wasn't clear what Donovan was talking about. I wanted his 'beautiful sight,' to be me, but most likely, it was the gorgeous sunrise. How could I compete with a Hawaiian sunrise? "Why couldn't you sleep?"

Was he really asking me this question? "Oh, I don't know..."

He gave me a *seriously?* look that made me laugh. "What brought you out here at five o'clock in the morning?"

"Maybe it had something to do with an intruding girl in a large villa, a frantic family looking for this same girl with a poorly attempted disguise as Briar Rose, and this same ratty-haired, frightening-looking, woken-up-in-the-middle-of-the-night girl who had a kiss stolen from her amidst all the mayhem and drama."

This beautiful man laughed with me at the frivolity of my statement. "Yeah..." he sighed, "I guess we should talk about that kiss, huh?"

I shook my head no. "Not necessary. I'll consider it a bad dream, a crazy passer-byer, a figment of my convoluted imagination—in short, I won't cause any more trouble with you and Kate." I hugged my knees even tighter into my body and only stared off into the ocean.

"When I realized you had left last night, and couldn't find you, I didn't know what to do. I was wholly lost." The sincerity in his voice was sweet. Everything he said, I believed. "When we found you and you went off on me..."

It was at this point, I had to interrupt and say, "After you went off on me..."

He chuckled. "You can't let me win an argument, can you?" He put his arm around my shoulder and brought me closer to him. "Yes, after I went off on you, *first*, I was in a state of distress and somehow that translated into a stolen kiss. I'm sorry. It shouldn't have happened. I didn't mean for any of this to happen."

He still had me in his hold. "I know that kiss meant nothing to you, and I won't say anything to Kate. I heard part of your argument last night with Kate, and I hope you were able to explain to her that I don't mean anything to you other than being '*a pain in your ass.*'"

He brought me even closer to him and kissed me on the head. "You mean more to me than I think even I understand. Don't worry about Kate. I'm sorry about last night. I hope you'll forget any of this ever happened?"

I stared at this beautiful man. *You can forget since it meant nothing to you, but your kiss—even done in a state of distress—was what made my fairytale dream come true. I love you, Donovan.*

April 4, 2013
To Each His Own

Today was our last full day on the island so we all decided to do our own thing. Since the fiasco I caused trying to be Briar Rose on this resort, several changes happened. The first big change—Kate left. Donovan didn't say much other than that she had meetings to attend in London so she was flying all the way from Hawaii to London. That was going to be a helluva long trip! I was told to give up my very expensive room and take over Donovan's original room. Max moved in with Jane, and Donovan opened up the villa to the four single men. It was a serious frat party in the villa.

Where did you go off to so early in the morning?
I'm golfing.

Of course my brother had to check up on me even though we said we were off on our own today. Though his attention irked me at times, I was grateful he took care of me in his bizarre way.

You want to go to the northern-most point and swim at a black sand beach?

Thanks, but I can't. I'm already in a foursome and can't get out.

You playing with Nolan?

No. I just grouped with a random threesome. I've got to go. Have a great time.

Bye.

Purposely, I set out for a 5:07am tee time, so I wouldn't have to hang out with anyone. I didn't want to bother Max and Jane, who were definitely in a zone of their own. Jake and Emily needed their rest. Josh, as nice as he was, showed a wee-bit too much interest in me, and that made me uncomfortable. The rest of the guys could go do guy stuff without having me hold them back, and as for Donovan...I stayed away all together from him. He didn't explain why Kate left, but I felt responsible. It wasn't as if I was important enough in his life to cause any serious rift between them, but it was no secret she didn't like me in her room the other night.

The golf course was fairly empty so our foursome finished a little past noon. The three elderly players invited me to have lunch with them, but with a polite decline, I dined alone at a restaurant on the beach. The surroundings were incredible, and knowing this was my last day, I wanted to enjoy all that the resort had to offer.

To my annoyance, a random hand grabbed a bunch of my french fries and said, "You eating all that food by yourself?"

"Yes, Mr. Taylor. I've expended a lot of energy this morning."

"Golf is hardly a strenuous sport. I don't think you've expended that much energy." He noshed on more of my fries and the other half of my burger I'd cut up.

"I just played 18-holes, I walked the entire course, and carried my own bag." I started on my salad before he gunned for that as well.

"What idiot walks the entire 18-holes when you can ride a golf cart? Any why the hell would you carry your clubs?"

I shrugged my shoulders. "The course is beautiful, and I wanted to walk through it and experience it. And though they had golf clubs to lend, they didn't have any push carts—so I carried them the entire way."

"Why didn't you just buy a cart?"

"Mr. Taylor, unlike you, I don't have $200 to throw around. Plus, it'll cost me another $100 in baggage fees to take it back with me." He looked at me as though I was a nut. "Why aren't you out with everyone?"

"I should've had you room with me instead of those frat boys. They had a serious all-night party. The noise kept me awake till dawn. I told them they were sleeping on the lanai tonight if they woke me up this morning."

I laughed as I finished off the salad.

"Are you done? I need to shower, change, then catch the shuttle."

"Where are you going?"

"I'm going to do some window shopping at the shops in Waikoloa. The hotel shuttle leaves every hour. I need to hurry."

Donovan gave his characteristic quirking of the head when he didn't understand something. "You're going to get on a hotel *shuttle* and go *window* shopping?"

"Yes. See you later." With a nervous gait, I practically ran back to my room. Donovan Taylor was the last person I expected to see today. After the other morning, I just wasn't ready to talk to him.

I changed into a cute Hawaiian sarong and walked over to the valet area to catch the shuttle. I waved to the elderly golf-threesome and walked toward the open door of my ride when I heard, "Delaney." Donovan, Jake and Emily rode up in a jeep convertible. "Get in."

I followed his directions and sat next to Emily, who gave me a kiss on the cheek.

"What have you been up to? I haven't seen you all day." Emily greeted me.

"I played golf with an elderly threesome and had lunch."

"By yourself? Nolan wasn't available?"

"I didn't ask."

"Why didn't you go with everyone to the black sand beach? Didn't you get invited?" Emily sounded slightly upset.

"Doug asked but I was almost 9-holes into my game already. Plus, I needed my..." I didn't need to divulge further information so I changed the topic. "What did you and Jake do? And please, I only want the rated G version." I grinned.

"We slept, ate a late breakfast, then sat on our lanai and drank lemon-ade and watched the waves crashing into the ocean. Exciting, huh?"

"That's about as exciting as my day. Where are we going, by the way?"

"Didn't you say you wanted to go shopping? I thought it'd be a good idea to get these two out of their room and see other parts of the Big Island. Emily also needs to buy gifts for the family."

So Donovan Taylor rented a car to take me shopping? *Noooooo!* He rented a car, or perhaps Jake rented a car, but Donovan was driving it, and we were all tagging along. That latter idea sounded more plausible.

We started at a jewelry store where Jake bought Emily a new watch when he spotted the perfect watch in a window. Then we walked into the Louis Vuitton store and to Emily's huge protest, Jake bought her a darling pink diaper bag. I'd never seen anything so cute in my life. It was hideously expensive, but he bought it regardless of Emily's threats and refusal of the gift. Then Jake led us to a shoe store, and he bought Emily another pair of walking shoes because her feet had swollen, and he didn't want her to be uncomfortable in the shoes she was currently wearing. Emily sat on a bench while Jake was down on his knees, pulling out the holder in the new shoes, and gently tugging at her ankles to replace the old ones with the new pair.

This beautiful sight made me grapple with that funny, heart-splitting feel—that one where it tingled, pinched, poked, pressed, and made a girl sad enough to tear up without warning. I walked out for air, hoping to discover a way to stop this unwanted sensation. As happy as I was for my cousin and his wife, I couldn't help wondering when I'd find a man—any man—who'd care for my every well-being. Who would worry about my swollen feet and change out the shoes of my sand-ridden feet? My feelings for Donovan aside, that kind of love didn't loom anywhere on my horizon.

"Why'd you leave the shoe store?" Donovan followed me out.

"I saw a cute bathing suit. I thought I'd take a look." I lied.

"You going to buy it?"

I shook my head no.

"Why not? Aren't you the original shopaholic on your cul-de-sac? You don't shop pretending to be Barbara Reid anymore?"

We got a good chuckle out of my younger-year misdemeanors.

"No. Mom was quite relieved when I stopped doing that. I still shop more than I should. I need to save up all the money I can before going to London."

"One bathing suit going to set you back that much? Doug said you earn good money from your part-time job."

"Even with your kindness—buying me a plane ticket and allowing me to use your room—I've spent way more money on this trip than I should. And I don't need any more bathing suits." Donovan stayed unusually quiet. "Would it be all right if I strayed a bit and looked at some stores on my own? I'll meet you at that coffee shop," I pointed to the one at the back of the mall, "in about thirty minutes?"

He nodded his head yes, and let me go without a fight. This was nothing new, but it still hurt the same.

April 12, 2013
Beeautiful!

*D*onovan had called in the morning asking if I'd do him and Jane a favor. He explained the situation and told me—apologetically, I might add—that his Taiwanese clients wanted one last dinner and they had requested I attend. After what happened at the volcanoes, I wasn't thrilled about having dinner with the two guys, or with Donovan. But since I wouldn't have been in Hawaii without the generosity of all three men, I thought this was the least I could do. As it turned out, it was indeed the worst night ever. Josh stopped by to see Doug as I was about to leave, and convinced me to ride with him to the Westside. The entire ride was me avoiding Josh's invitations to hang out with him. I didn't know how many more ways I could say no without being an outright bitch. The dinner, too, was a disaster! After saying no to Josh for the past hour, I thought I was done with that word. Weston could give Josh lessons on aggressive behavior.

"If I sent you my plane, would you come visit me in Hong Kong?"
Seriously?

"Thank you for the invitation, Weston, but I'm going to London as soon as I graduate."

"Why London? What's in London?" Even before I could come up with a proper answer, he added, "I do actually have a home in London because business takes me there often. Where are you staying? If you don't have a place to stay, I'd be happy to let out a room to you."

Seriously? I was so close to telling this guy off but didn't want to ruin anything for Donovan and Jane. I politely explained the what, where, why, how, and when's of my plans, and stayed as quiet as possible.

"Then, can I come see you in London?"

This Weston just wouldn't go away. I looked to Donovan, and though he didn't have a happy expression, he didn't step in to protect me from this predator. It was stupid of me to expect any sort of buffer from Donovan, but I did...and when it didn't come, I felt a splinter in my heart. It didn't hurt severely but the pain was constant. I needed to get away and just... just...I didn't know what but I needed to get away from here and these men. Without thinking, I moved the chair back right as the servers were bringing our pasta course, and I caused the server to spill the bowl on my dress.

The pasta was piping hot, my right thigh burned, and I simply didn't know how to get away from this mess.

It was at this point Donovan came over and quickly brushed the pasta with a napkin, into the empty plate. "You OK?"

No...where've you been all this time? Physically, you're right next to me, but emotionally, you're not even in the same state.

This was my chance to leave and regroup. Once the management headed our way, I excused myself to the ladies' room, and stayed there as long as possible. Deciding eventually that this was not the end of the world, my courage came back and I headed to my table. I had no idea what had happened, but to my relief, both men decided not to speak to me anymore.

Until, of course, it was time to go home. "Ms. Reid, may I offer you a ride home?" Weston offered me a ride in the black limousine that pulled up.

"Hell NO!" was on the tip of my tongue, but I seized hold of that tongue, smiled kindly and uttered, "No thank you."

"Josh is coming to pick us both up," Jane announced with the biggest smile that annoyed me. After the harassment tonight, I didn't need to try and get out of another date.

"Thanks, but I'm calling a cab."

"Who the hell calls a cab in LA? I'll take you home." Donovan never asked, he commanded. "I live right by your parents' home. I can drop you off."

"I'd really like some time to myself, and to be myself. I don't like it when I have to pretend to be happy." There I went again—diarrhea of the mouth. "...Ok, I'll go with you if we can leave now, and if you promise *NOT* to talk to me in the car."

"What the..." My annoyed look stopped him from finishing his statement. I took out my phone and searched for a cab company. "All right. Get in. Valet is waiting for us."

After apologizing to Jane for leaving her before Josh arrived, I ran to the car and let out a sigh of relief that this night was OVER.

Donovan looked over at me a few times before he broke his only promise to me for the night.

"I'm really sorry about your pretty dress, Delaney." Donovan broke the silence after exactly three minutes into the ride. How did I know? I timed him from the moment he got in the car. I knew he couldn't and wouldn't keep his promise. I looked at him, but didn't answer. "Are we really going to be silent the entire ride back home?"

I nodded yes.

"OK...suit yourself...I'm a really fun person to talk to when you get to know me. I've been told many times that I'm a stimulating conversationalist. Why, women flock over and talk to me at any gathering I attend. Nobody has ever been this silent with me for this long at any point in my life." He was babbling on and on, but I kept to my guns and didn't say a word. However, I did want to laugh at him. "You are one tough audience, Little Girl."

I just stared. Then I looked over to the other side and out the window.

"Aww come on Delaney. I can't go silent the entire ride home. Show me some mercy and let's have a little conversation." I still looked the other way. "You want to go have dessert and a cup of coffee with me somewhere?" He was relentless. I could see why women could not and would not resist him.

I shook my head no.

"Did you get new shoes and a purse? A little above your budget there, no? What happened to saving money for London?"

This question almost broke my code of silence. I desperately wanted to ask him, though it was a retarded question, whether he was the one who bought me these very expensive Louis Vuitton shoes, purse, and a charm. Oddly, after the four of us came back from our Waikoloa shopping trip, Emily dropped off a bag of goodies saying this was from her and Jake. In it was a small charm in the form of a letter "D," a beautiful patent leather clutch, and these ridiculously sexy suede peep-toe ankle boots with criss-cross leather straps near the ankle—to die for! No matter how hard I refused these three gifts, Emily wouldn't take no for an answer. She dropped them off and practically ran back to her room.

As soon as she left, I tried on the shoes and fell in LOVE! Somehow, she knew my shoe size and preference, and picked the hottest shoes in that store. I didn't even see these three items when I was in the store, but I sure was glad I'd received them. Inevitably, the guilt ate at me, so I went back to return the gifts to Emily and Jake, but they would not open their door for me. Without much of a choice, I accepted their generosity. Still, something didn't feel right. It made no sense that my cousin would buy these items for me, but it made even crazier sense to think Donovan would have bought these for me. I decided to accept, be grateful, and enjoy. This was my lotto ticket for the year.

"Damn you're a tough cookie. How about…" He was coming up with his next plan of attack. "I know!" He brightened up at his latest idea and flashed his killer smile. "I know what's going to get you to talk. You just wait and see, Delaney Reid."

He made a quick phone call to somebody and asked about some sample and he drove for the next 10 minutes with a smile on his face, but not a word from his lips. He stopped in a building somewhere and told me to get out. I didn't think this was his home, and I had no idea where I was, but I didn't want to ask, so I just kept quiet.

Donovan and some woman enthusiastically greeted each other with a very friendly hug. "I haven't seen you in months. What brings you here at this late hour? And who is this pretty, but *very young* lady?" She emphasized the *very young* heavily.

"Bee, Delaney Reid. Delaney, Bee Taylor, technically my aunt, but we call each other cousins."

This is how he was forcing me to talk. He brought me to a cool loft in downtown LA and this Bee Taylor appeared to be a clothes designer. There were rolling racks of dresses, shirts, pants, jackets, coats, men's clothes, women's clothes, all lined up to sell, or to show. I wasn't quite sure what it was for, but they all looked beautiful.

"Hi Bee. It's very nice to meet you," I said pleasantly to Bee, but gave Donovan a grudging stare. He in turn gave me a smug look knowing he had won this battle.

"Hey Cuz," he answered with a loud chuckle bordering on a guffaw, "you have some samples I can buy off of you?"

"For...?"

"For this pretty girl here whose dress got ruined because of me."

"Some new Donovan Taylor dating tactic? Ruin a dress so it comes off easier?"

I was floored at what she said, but it didn't faze either one of them. They busted up and had a good laugh at my expense.

"This girl here is younger than Rachel."

"So? What does it matter whether she's older or younger than your youngest sister? You tend to like extremes. First a cougar and now you're robbing the cradle. Sounds like classic Donovan Taylor to me."

"Funny Bee. You always were the comedian in the family." And Donovan really did find his aunt, cousin, whatever – funny!

I'm glad somebody was finding this conversation funny because I didn't find it funny at all. It always bugged me that Donovan saw me as a little girl, and now that he referenced it with the fact that I was younger than his youngest sister; I suppose I had absolutely no chance with him.

Why was I thinking there was any chance to begin with, where this man was concerned?

"Delaney here is Doug's younger sister and Jake's cousin."

"That's right, Donovan mentioned that you were a Reid. I don't see the resemblance between you and Jake. What happened?"

Since she asked, I had to answer. "That part of the family got all the looks…and the brains…and…I suppose they got everything." I sounded so juvenile. Bee probably thought I was an absolute moron and it didn't help that I was a blonde with big boobs. Crap! I was your blonde Betty Boop!

"You don't think you got any of the looks?" That sounded more like a statement than a question.

"No…" I agreed with her. "My cousin Jane is stunning. Jake and Nick are very handsome as well."

"I remember your handsome cousin very well." She did a weird twisting of the mouth that made me think I didn't want to know what she was talking about, or which brother she was referring to. Jake looked more her age, but who knew with couples nowadays. Case in point, Donovan had or has a girlfriend almost 10 years older than he.

"Delaney is wondering which Reid you're salivating over," Donovan guessed on the nose. I wondered how he knew. "It's written all over your face." He laughed, but didn't bother to enlighten me on which Reid they were talking about. "Delaney was helping me and Jane with a client, he came onto her too strong, she got a bit antsy, the waiter dropped the pasta onto her lap, and here we are."

"That's why we're here? Because of this mess?" I pointed to the bottom of my dress. "I don't need a new dress, Mr. Taylor. Just take me home, and I'll put some Spray n Wash on and throw it into the wash. It's no big deal. This dress doesn't even look good on me." Now I was babbling because I didn't want Donovan Taylor buying me a dress out of guilt.

"Do you have low self-esteem issues or do you just not get it?" Bee asked.

"Get what?"

"That you're tall, striking, beautifully figured, and gorgeous enough to model! I'd love it if you'd wear all my clothes because you'd make them look so good. If you need a job after you finish school, you could model for me and a host of other designers. We'd fight over you."

These people were so odd. Why would they want someone like me?

"She doesn't believe you." Donovan guessed correctly again.

"Here. Go try this on." She pointed to a makeshift dressing area, almost commanding I do as she said. This Taylor was as bossy as the other Taylor.

The dress she handed me was soft, comfortable and uniquely designed. I loved the feel of the fabric under my hand, and I easily put it over my head and slipped it on. It was casual enough to wear to a lunch, but just dressy enough to last through a nice dinner.

"What's with the Mr. Taylor moniker?"

Donovan didn't say anything, so I assumed he shrugged his shoulders.

"You two have an odd relationship."

"Um..." I called over the partition, "we don't have any relationship. We are barely friends." I walked out of the "room" and said, "Your creation is wonderful. I love the dress. Can I buy it from you?"

"Wow!" Bee exclaimed. "That dress was made for your body. You make that dress come alive. And those shoes only add to the effect. Where'd you get them? Who's the designer?"

"I..." How would I explain these shoes? "They're from Hawaii and they're LV."

"You Reids are high-rollers."

"Um...well..." I looked over at Donovan who only had smiles for me. "In any case, I don't think it's me that brings your creation alive, Bee. You're obviously a talented designer. How much can I pay you for the dress?"

"Delaney, I've got it." Donovan butted into our conversation.

"What do you mean, 'you've got it?'" I asked.

"I mean, I will pay for the dress. So put your wallet away."

"Why would you pay for my dress?" I had no idea what would possess Donovan Taylor to buy me a dress.

"Did you not hear me telling my cousin that I ruined your dress, and that's why we are here? I'm going to replace it for you."

"First of all, my dress is not ruined. It just needs to go in the wash. Second of all, I don't need you buying me a dress."

"Why are you so damn stubborn?" He yelled in frustration. "I'm offering to buy you a dress, I want to buy you a dress, so can't you just say thank you and be done?"

"I don't want a dress from you," I yelled in frustration, too. "I don't want anything from you, I don't want to feel like I'm a part of your…"

"Yes, yes, I know. You don't want to feel like a part of my harem. I understood what you said back in Hawaii." Now he sounded upset. "For your information Little Girl, you are not a part of my harem, I never asked you to join my harem, and I never will. You are not my type, you are not my age, and you're definitely not in my league."

His comment shocked me, pained me, and put me in my place. I had no ready answer. *What can I say to you when you tell me you'll never be attracted to me and I'm not what you're looking for in a woman? Will I ever be good enough for you?* I felt that ugly heartbreak one more time. This was something I felt way too often when I was around this man. The best thing to do was to be as far away from him as possible.

"I'm sorry," was all I could say. Then I turned to Bee and asked, "May I use your restroom, please?"

"Sure," she answered. "The one downstairs is being fixed, but you're more than welcome to go up to the loft and use the master bathroom in my bedroom."

"Thank you," I said with a manufactured smile and walked away as quickly as possible without seeming obvious.

I heard Bee whisper to Donovan, "You're such an asshole. I don't know why women find you attractive. You were about as smooth as that snakeskin dress over there."

"You heard what she said." Donovan defended himself. "She was getting bitchy with me and I was just trying to be a nice guy and replace a dress for her. It's just a damn dress. It's not like I offered her an engagement ring."

"Incredible! Did you not hear yourself tell her that she wasn't good enough for you and that you'd never be attracted to her?"

"Bee, look at her age and lack of experience. Do you think we fit?"

"I think you fit better than you realize."

"Whatever."

I sat up in Bee's room a bit longer and only came out when their conversation died—all the while, my heart attempted to resuscitate itself.

"Donovan said that he would wait for you in his car. Let me walk you out."

"Thank you, but you don't have to do that. I'm sure I can find my way out."

"You know…my nephew seems worldly, and I know he may seem like a womanizer, but he's always been true to the woman he's with. He just needs a little guidance, and he's not quite as mature as you may think he is."

I didn't know why she was bothering to tell me all this stuff. It didn't concern me since I wasn't ever going to date Donovan Taylor.

"Thank you for the information, but I think your breath is wasted on me. You can let his girlfriend know next time he brings her over."

She muttered something under her breath about "letting me know" or "being the one for him," something like that, but I didn't bother to have her clarify.

"Hi," Donovan said with a guilty look. "You ready to go home?"

"Yes, please. It's been a long day and I still have a lot to do when I get home."

We rode in an awkward silence, but Bee didn't live far from my home so it was a short awkward silence. I was actually glad that Donovan wasn't speaking to me.

We got to my street and Donovan parked somewhere in between my house and Jake's house. "I'm sorry, Delaney. I don't know what came over me when I got angry with you back at Bee's place."

"There's no need for an apology, Mr. Taylor. I understand, and I'm sorry I jumped to the wrong conclusion. I know you could never be attracted to somebody like me." My voice actually cracked a little and my heart skipped multiple beats when I said this to him. There was no way Donovan Taylor could ever understand or comprehend the number of tears I'd shed deep inside my heart. I refused to shed these tears on the outside, so my heart was an ocean filled with unshed tears. Even now, I was adding to the ocean.

"I wasn't saying that you aren't an attractive girl. I was just saying that you and I couldn't work. I know that guys find you attractive. In fact, I've seen you work your magic on just about every man who's crossed your path. Why look at..."

I walked out in the middle of his sentence. I didn't want to hear his patronizing consolation speech. "Thank you for the ride home." Shutting his door, I sprinted to my door.

Quickly shutting the front door behind me, I ran up to my room and closed my door. Donovan's words hurt me so much I just stared at the wall. There was no point in crying, and I was tired of being sad, but those words killed. In my mind, I knew Donovan Taylor was an impossible dream, but my heart still dreamed a million dreams that one day he'd notice me. Tonight, he actualized this dream into a nightmare.

"Whatcha doing? Am I bothering you?" That familiar voice was back, and this time, in my room.

"I'm editing some essays. I didn't do any work in Hawaii so I'm a bit backlogged." In a desperate attempt to distract myself, I had opened up my computer, but not gotten anything done.

"How much money do you make off each paper?"

"It depends on the length. I charge one cent per word so it can be anywhere from $200 to $500 per paper. It's been a decent side job."

"That's not bad. How many papers do you edit per week?"

"Anywhere from 1-10. Obviously, there's more to do during midterms and finals, but the rest of the semester is fairly consistent. I've developed a nice clientele."

"How do you correct without actually writing someone's paper for them?"

"I don't take on a tone or a voice. I just correct spelling, grammar, and sentence structure. If a paper is really bad, I'll make suggestions on how to improve it, but I won't rewrite it for them. Also, I'm careful who I help. I won't take on a poor writer, because it's too much work, and they tend to want you to write their papers for them."

"Is this what you want to do when you grow up?" He asked with the gentlest smile I'd ever seen on Donovan Taylor.

"I have a lot of things I want to do, when I *grow up*," I emphasized that last part since he made a point to state it. "But for now I think I'd like to be a writer."

He looked at the screen that had the paper I was correcting. "Have you ever written anything?"

I wondered if I should share such an intimate secret. "Yeah, I've finished a couple of screenplays for fun."

"Would you let me read them?"

I laughed. "No way! No one's ever read my writing. You're the first person I've even told, and if you go off spilling my secret, I'll deny it." We both laughed.

At times, the rapport between us was beautiful and easy. And his alpha-male confidence made him utterly irresistible.

"All right. I'll keep your secret."

"Is that why you haven't left? You wanted to know my deepest darkest secret?"

He thought about my statement for a second. "I couldn't leave because I felt I'd put us in an awkward situation, and somehow hurt you."

Why, oh why, couldn't he have just left after telling me there was no chance between us? Why did he have to come back and try to be nice and apologetic?

"I'm all right, Mr. Taylor. We are no better, no less, a friend to one another than we were just a few hours ago."

He didn't look happy to hear what was just said, but didn't voice what his face explained.

"I wanted to say I'm sorry if I hurt your feelings in any way, and I'm sorry for stealing a kiss from you in Hawaii. I'm not quite sure what came over me."

I stepped over to the small sofa in my room so I wouldn't be in such close proximity with Donovan.

I gave him a flat smile and didn't explain that his was my first real kiss. I must be the *ONLY* girl on this earth who'd never been kissed by a boy her entire life. How embarrassing and unbelievable. *Who had virgin lips at twenty-two?*

"You have a funny look on your face. What's that all about?"

There was no way I was going to explain my thought. "You sure have a way with words, Mr. Taylor. First, you tell a girl she's not good enough for you. Second, you tell her you could never ever be attracted to her. Then you go for the kill and tell her she's funny looking. I know I'm not the prettiest girl out there, and I know I'm nothing when compared to Jane, but golly-geez..." Those tears were there again filling up in my heart.

"Do you really believe what you just said?" He asked with a tender look on his face.

"Yes..?" I answered mid-croak.

"I believe I meant to say that you and I run in different circles, you and I have birthdays in different decades, and in your own way, you are much more beautiful than your cousin Jane."

That made me break out into a fit of laughter.

"What's so funny? No, let me rephrase that, lest you twist my words around again," he said while seating himself next to me on the couch. "Why are you laughing?"

I shook my head back and forth and rolled my eyes. "You really get as many girls as you're purported to get? You're about as smooth as a prickly pear."

"Damn! Why do I keep getting that metaphor today? You don't think I'm smooth, either?"

I shook my head no almost as severely as Ellie shakes her head no.

"I'm going to have to work on that," he answered with a chuckle. "Are we good about everything?"

I nodded yes this time. "We are good about me not being attractive enough, old enough, or experienced enough for you. You may leave in good conscience, Mr. Taylor."

This time, he shook his head in mirth. "We OK with the unintended kiss?"

"We are OK with you kissing me while 'in a state of distress' because I was lost. And we are OK with it being a terrible kiss." I gave him a matter-of-fact look while he looked stupefied. "You can go home now. This little girl is all right. I'm not as emotionally unstable as you believe."

"You thought it was terrible?"

He quickly got over being flabbergasted, slid over so close we were almost thigh to thigh, and his mouth did an even smoother slide over my mouth. His kiss was warm, wet, and softer than all the silk in China. It started with only our lips touching. Next thing I knew, he had his right arm around my neck, left arm around my back and it appeared that he was intent in swallowing my mouth. I could do little more than mimic his style. As his mouth put more pressure on mine, his tongue touched mine and some unnamed endorphin released because my hormones went buck wild. I'd never felt such arousal.

I itched to wrap my arms around him, and stay this way all night. My mind went back and forth, back and forth, on whether or not I should put my arms around him, and just as I'd decided to make my move, Donovan saved me the embarrassment and broke off abruptly.

"Sorry," he said again.

He was sorry that he kissed me again.

"I should be the one saying sorry. I'm not anywhere in the same league as the women you normally kiss."

"Delaney..."

"Why don't we call it a night, before we make any more mistakes?" I gave him an out.

He surprisingly gave me another light kiss on the lips, said good night, and left my room.

April 17, 2013
Bittersweet

Softball had been on a two-week spring break hiatus, and today, it was back. I arrived at the softball field to a very nice surprise. Jake and Emily had brought the kids to watch our game, and Mom and Dad had brought Gram and Grandfather to watch the game. This was going to be an extra fun day.

"How did you end up coming here? Who told you I was playing softball?"

"It should've been you who told me that you were playing softball, but I had to hear it from my hubby's best friend. And Donovan suggested since it was an early game today, we stop by with the family."

"I'm glad you're here." I took over James-carrying duties as my darling little cousin was reaching out for me. Donovan came in out of nowhere and swept Ellie out of Jake's hands to her utter delight. "Shall we go sit in the dugout James?" Of course he nodded his head yes, though I didn't think he understood what I was asking.

"Who are these adorable little kids? Are they twins?" Elle was enam-ored. She and Eric coaxed Ellie and James out of our hands. Soon all the players took turns playing with the twins and several times Coach Kevin had to yell into the dugout for the next batter.

"If you and Donovan had kids they would be just as adorable as your cousin's kids," Elle whispered into my ear.

I shot her a nasty look and said, "We are not together. He has no interest in me."

"By the way you phrased that statement, I assume you have an interest in him?"

"I think it's your turn to bat, Elle. You better get up there before coach Kevin yells at you."

I had the loudest and largest cheering crowd thus far of anybody at our game. Mom could be pretty loud when she wanted to be. What was I saying? She was usually pretty loud.

"Young lady," Mom said, "how come I didn't know you were playing again?" And then she directed her attention to Donovan. "How did you end up on this team?"

I answered for the both of us. "I signed up because Elle forced me to sign up and as for Mr. Taylor, he just happened to be there when I was signing up. He and Kevin, our coach, were college fraternity buddies."

"So you two have been spending every Wednesday together since February?" Emily had a sly smile on her face when asking this question. I didn't know Emily owned anything sly.

"No. There are times when Mr. Taylor is out of town, and even when he is in town, it's not like we're spending every Wednesday together. We just play a game together." No one in my family needed to think there was any existence of a weekly get-together between us.

"Well I, for one, am glad that Donovan is here with you."

"For what reason are you glad, Daddy?"

"Most of the time these games run late and I'm glad to know he will bring you home and take care of you."

Once again, I had to deny any "relationship."

"Daddy, Donovan does not take care of me, and most of the times Elle and I carpool."

"Hey, Donovan?"

"Yes, Chief?"

"Can I ask you to bring my daughter home every Wednesday after the game?"

"Sure Chief. I'd be happy to bring her home."

"Daddy, that's not necessary, and that's not going to work. Elle can't carpool for a few weeks so I need to drive to school every Wednesday, now. I'll have a car so there's no need for anyone to drive me home."

"Donovan?"

"Yes, Gram?"

"Would you be a gentleman enough to pick up our Laney in the morning on Wednesdays? None of us like seeing her coming home late at night by herself. Perhaps you could drop her off at school, go to work, then bring her home after your game?"

Incredible! What was my family up to? It was as though they were in matchmaking cahoots with one another, but it couldn't be since they had no idea that I had an interest in Donovan.

"What a great idea," Emily joined in the conversation.

I saw my grandfather smile and nod in agreement.

"I would be honored to take your granddaughter to school and back home. You hear that Little Girl?" He turned to me, "I guess you and I will be Wednesday carpooling buddies for a while."

Was this good news or bad? I couldn't decide whether I liked this change of events masterminded by my family.

When dinner was done, I tried to catch a ride home with my family, but once again, they thwarted me.

"How did you all fit in this car, and why would you come together?" Incredibly all eight of them came in Emily's minivan. My only way home was to ride in Donovan's Porsche.

"Get in, Little Girl." Donovan commanded. I could've sworn I saw everyone in the minivan smirking at me while it passed us. This was one strange night.

"You mind if we stop somewhere and grab a cup of coffee? Those ribs aren't sitting very well with me. I need a strong espresso."

"Not at all. You're the driver. I'm just grateful to have a ride home since my family didn't see fit to bring me home with them."

Donovan laughed at my comment. "Who would've thought that such sarcasm would drip from such a sweet looking face? You definitely have a way with words. I guess you've always had a way with words."

"Speaking of words, I don't know quite what to say about the bag of dresses you left in my room."

"You finally found them, huh?" He had on a cute grin. "I expected at least a thank you text the moment you found them. Most women would've done that or come over and said thank you in person."

I was at a loss for words. How did I reply to a statement like that? Should I have just been happy that he bought me dresses? Should I have been sad that he lumped me with a group women he casually purchased clothes for? What was the right response in a situation like this?

After a bit of silence I answered, "I didn't respond because I didn't think you would like my response via text."

"What does that mean?"

"When you drop me off at home, if you could wait a little bit I'd like to return the dresses to you."

"Dammit Delaney. Why is everything so difficult with you? Think of it as a gift, as an apology for what happened between us in Hawaii. Think of it as me supporting my aunt. Think of it in any damn way it makes you comfortable. Or just stop thinking." He was frustrated, he rushed his hand through his unruly hair several times, and stupid me found it adorable. I was such a goner where this man was concerned!

In all seriousness, though, how would I explain to this man that him giving me gifts out of pity, or as an apology, or flippantly, did me no good? Who would understand that those kinds of gifts were unwanted, no matter the type, size or price?

I thought very carefully through my answer before giving it. "I… there's no reason to accept so many generous gifts from you. The ticket to Hawaii alone was over the top. You didn't ruin my dress, and I'm not upset about what happened at Spago the other night." *And I really want to ask you about the three Louis Vuitton gifts I received in Hawaii* but that was such a ridiculous thought, I couldn't bring it up—no matter how much I wanted to.

"Could you just accept the dresses without any complaints? Just think of it as Doug giving you a present. I'm definitely old enough to be your older brother." A rebuttal was on the tip of my tongue, but he cut me off. "Just know that this will be the end of our friendship if you return those dresses to me or to Bee. You got it?" He smiled his devastating smile. What could I say? "Let's go grab some dessert and a cup of espresso."

Ounces of sweet and cups of bitter—a fitting description for our "relationship."

April 19, 2013
Happy Birthday, James & Ellie!

For the twins, it was a perfect day until they wigged out at the very end from utter fatigue. For me, the day didn't start too well, but ended in a promising way. It all started with the beautiful dresses Donovan had left for me. I put the prettiest one on, knowing I was going to see Donovan later today at Ellie and James' birthday party. Since I wasn't successful in returning them, I decided to enjoy them and show Donovan that I appreciated his gift.

"I see you chose to wear the dress?" Donovan surprisingly stopped by to wish the twins a happy birthday, first thing in the morning. We spoke while each entertaining a twin.

"I did. Thank you very much. It really wasn't necessary for you to have given me all these dresses, but in any case, I won't complain anymore and am very happy to have them. Dare I ask one more time if I can pay you?" His surly look was answer enough.

"Are we good? And I'm not talking about the dresses...you know, with what happened again the other night? Though, I do still have one more question," Donovan whispered.

"All is good. No need to mention what happened the other night, or better yet, Hawaii." I gave him a bit of an exasperated look. I didn't want to talk about this anymore. I was done with what had happened a few nights ago since I knew it meant absolutely nothing to him. "But if you must ask…"

"I just want to hear from your lips that I am not a terrible kisser."

That made me crack-up. He thought I had accused him of being a bad kisser when I was only blaming my own kissing abilities, or lack thereof. "All right Mr. Taylor, I'm going to blow up your ego this morning. Yours was the best kiss I've ever had, hands down! There's no comparison."

"Really?" He had the grandest, most ridiculous smile on his face.

"Truly," I answered with a wink and walked away. I couldn't stop chuckling at the fact that what I said was meant in the most literal sense, since I had no one to compare him to.

Roland, my new grandfather, convinced me to catch a ride to school with him, Jane and Donovan after we were done loving the twins this morning. I absolutely adored Grandpa Jerry, but Grandpa Roland was something else. He'd been in love with my Gram since he was twenty-something, and his love only grew with the years. Grandfather Roland was as brilliant and charming as Grandpa Jerry, and I loved the fact that he would be with Gram the rest of their lives.

"Young lady, let me know when you plan on leaving. I'll get the plane ready for you."

"Grandfather, I already purchased my ticket. You and Gram should use your plane allotment, not me."

"Your mother and grandmother are planning to travel with you and get you settled, so you need to take my plane. You can use the ticket you purchased, next time."

"Grandfather," I paused and thought through what I wanted to say. "I'm leaving very soon, and as much as I love Mom and Gram, I don't want them to come with me in the beginning. It's a large inconvenience to them, and I need to stand on my own two feet. I'd like to try and do this on my own."

"Young lady, has anyone ever told you your appearances are deceiving?" That comment brought a smile to my face.

"Thank you. I've never been thrilled with the way people perceived me."

Once our private conversation finished, the four of us had a nice chat about the twins' birthday party and about my move when the first spoiler of the day happened. Donovan asked me a very personal question about whether or not I'd ever been in a serious relationship. I told him I hadn't, and that's when he made this condescending remark. "No man has swept you off your feet and wooed you like a fairy princess from a Disney movie? No glass slipper at midnight...Prince kissing Sleeping Beauty awake from slumber...Beauty kissing the Beast into a prince...?" Donovan couldn't hold back his guffaw as he said this.

If that remark didn't hurt enough, Jane joined in the snickering, and made me feel like a moron for never having had a relationship before. Was it my fault that I hadn't found the man I wanted to share my life with? Did I want my first real kiss to be with Donovan at age twenty-two? Well... Donovan—yes. At age twenty-two—no. I was mad that they were laughing at me, but I was pissed that I'd waited and waited this long to get into a relationship with any man because I'd put Donovan Taylor on such a pedestal. If I was a moron for any reason, waiting for Donovan to notice me would be it.

The rest of the morning passed without anyone else upsetting me, and when I got to the party, I noticed Josh on the other side of the tent. Josh was sweet and funny and perfectly my age. Why couldn't I find him more desirable? Maybe Josh was right. I hadn't given him enough time. We needed to get to know each other better before I could make a decision.

"You're here." Emily greeted me with a hug and kiss. "Everything all right?"

"Yeah. I was just thinking about Josh."

Emily gave me a funny look. "Really?" She giggled soon after. "You think about men whose initials don't start with DT?" Now she was just plain making fun of me.

"Donovan is not the only man I think about. In fact, I've decided not to think about him anymore. As of today, I'm going to make a concerted effort to get to know Josh, and see if I can learn to like him." There. I said it. I meant it.

Emily outright laughed at me. "Laney. This is only the 100th time you've given up on Donovan Taylor, and I don't want you leading poor Josh on if you're not truly interested. He's a sweet boy and he's smitten with you. Don't encourage him if you don't have feelings for him."

"But how will I know if I have feelings for him if I don't hang out with him and get to know him? I may grow to like Josh. Right? Didn't you grow to like someone...ever?"

"Nope. I was smitten with Max the moment I saw him, and I was blown away with Jake's attention when we met at the supermarket. Your cousin was mesmerizing."

"Did I hear my name being called?" Jake walked over with each kid in hand, and gave his wife a kiss on the lips and me a kiss on the cheek. "Hello, Cousin. Want a child?" He handed James to me.

"Hello, Handsome!" I kissed my beloved cousin, once removed. "Hi Beautiful!" I gave Ellie a kiss as well before she yelled at me. She only had one setting—LOUD!

"I think I'll take James over to Josh and see if we can convince Nick to get into the dunk tank."

"Josh, huh?" Jake gave me a dubious look. "My buddy just walked in the tent. You don't want to go say hi?"

"You can tell him I said he and his insensitive words can go to h-e-l-l!" I had to spell that last word because I didn't want to curse in front of the babies.

Jake and Emily busted up, and I beelined for Josh as I saw Donovan walking toward us. It wasn't that I was scared of talking to Donovan. What I was feeling was pure—ANGER! I was still angry from this morning.

"Can we join you?" I asked Josh, who was watching the contortionist do her weird...contortions.

Josh smiled a sinful smile. This man looked so much like Max, but with delinquent twist. I loved it. He had fun written all over him.

"Of course you can join me. Does this mean we can hang out?" He asked with uncertainty.

I decided to be upfront with him and see where this might take me. "Josh, I'll be honest with you. I'm not attracted to you, but I'd like to get to know you. If you're OK with that, and you're OK knowing this may turn into nothing more than a great friendship, let's hang out."

"Shit! You just made my day. I never thought you'd give me a chance." Josh breathed a sigh of relief and stole a quick kiss from me. That kiss so startled me, I actually had to laugh. Josh laughed too, after he got over looking like a frightened bunny, wondering about my reaction.

"This must be steal-a-kiss-from-Laney week. I've been kissed more times this week than..." I stopped myself from revealing my lack of experience. Josh didn't seem like the type to make fun of a girl because she was inexperienced, but after this morning, I didn't need to find out.

"Who the hell's been kissing you this week aside from me?"

"No one of importance." I moved Josh along. "James is expecting to be entertained, and all he's done is stand here staring at us."

"Master James, what shall we entertain you with? How about the bottle toss? Maybe I can win you both a prize."

Josh tried his toss at the bottle, I took a turn, and even James threw some rings, but that was a difficult game. We all came out losers. Next we moved onto the "throw a ping pong ball into a fishbowl," and it was James who ended up winning a fish. Of course, he didn't exactly throw a ball into a fishbowl. Josh held him out and he accidentally dropped the ball into the bowl. Whatever...he won! I held onto the stuffed animal for him, and we went to face my father in the "shoot water into a clown's mouth and pop a balloon" game. James watched as I did my best to beat my dad and brother. No such luck. Dad, who shot rifles as a second hobby, beat us by several seconds.

"Here you go, Grandnephew. I don't think I need a SpongeBob stuffed doll in my bed. Your grandaunt may get jealous," Dad laughed at his own joke, and handed James the doll. "You having a good time?" Dad asked James while relieving me from kid duty. "Let's go grab a beer together, Grandnephew."

"Your dad is cool," Josh spoke.

"He is," I answered. "He's always been a lot of fun. All the kids used to love coming over to our house. Between the crazy parties Mom threw and Dad's lively personality, my friends and Doug's friends had a ball whenever they came over."

"Delaney?" I stopped and made myself refocus so I could go another round with Donovan. Life was a battle with Donovan Taylor.

Turning around, I saw the man who hurt me this morning. I expected him to show penitence but instead, he had the gall to emanate anger. What the hell did he have to be angry about?

"Yes?" I answered, gritting my teeth.

"Can we talk?"

"Again? Haven't we talked enough?" I stared back at his beautiful blue-green-gray eyes. He expressed his dissatisfaction with tight lips formed into a semi-pout. If I weren't so perturbed with him, I would've smiled because he looked as darling as James when he didn't get what he wanted.

"We need to talk, NOW!"

Did he really believe he ruled the universe? He was under the assumption that all he had to do was crook his finger and I'd obey his every word. Well, he had a hell of a surprise coming to him.

If I read his demeanor correctly, he was still upset, but he knew yelling at me was not going to get him what he wanted. He was about to say another word when I simply walked away. Josh walked in step with me, and we left a flabbergasted Donovan standing in the same spot.

"You want to go eat?" I asked Josh as though nothing had happened. "I haven't eaten all day. I'm starving and I know for a fact Mom brought in a corn dog vendor. She batters and fries these huge corn dogs, like the ones you get at Disneyland. Let's get one of those with fries and wash it down with a Diet Coke."

"Sounds good to me." Josh and I were getting along well and it was an enjoyable time for the both of us.

"Delaney." This time it was a plea more than a demand.

"Can I meet you in line? I'll be only a few minutes."

"Sure," Josh answered with a squeeze to my shoulders and a glare to Donovan.

"How can I help you, Mr. Taylor?"

"Why the hell..." he started off angry again, but decided to change tactics. "Why is Josh kissing you on the lips?"

I rolled my eyes and walked away from him again. Perhaps it should have pleased me that Donovan wasn't happy with another man's lips being on mine, but after all the words that were spoken this morning, and the laughing at my expense between him and Jane, I didn't feel one bit pleased with his "jealousy."

"OK. I'm sorry. I shouldn't have said that."

"Mr. Taylor..." I felt my heart split so I took a second to control my emotions. "You couldn't begin to understand the truth to those last five words. You've made your intentions clear to me. I know I don't mean anything to you, but I'm tired of being your punching bag. Just because I don't show it on the outside, doesn't mean I'm not black and blue on the inside."

With those truths spoken, I hurried over to the picnic table where Josh had our meals waiting for us.

"Everything OK?" He asked carefully.

"All good!" I smiled the best smile I could give under the circumstances.

"Should we go pick up James again after lunch?"

"Nick," I asked. "Will you go in the dunk tank, and Josh and I'll bring the twins over?"

"Aw, come on! Why me?"

"Because you're their uncle, and they'll love seeing you fall into the tank."

"They'll love watching anyone fall in."

"You start, then Doug will be next up."

"Hell no! You go in, little sis, if you're that intent on watching the twins laugh."

"Fine!" I got upset with both guys. "I'll do it."

Josh stepped in and tried to help. "If you lend me a suit, I'll go in. You don't have to do it, Laney." This guy was truly a nice guy, and I appreciated him trying to help me.

"How about if you get a suit on, I'll join you. It's big enough for the both of us." I figured what the hell? I'd do it for my favorite twins.

"Love it! Let's do it. Which one of you can lend me a suit?"

Nick motioned for Josh to follow him, and they walked over to Nick's home to get suited up.

"So you giving Josh a chance?"

I shrugged my shoulders. "I'm not interested in him. He knows it, but I told him today I wouldn't mind getting to know him. He appears to be a nice guy."

"I think if you get to know him, you could grow to like him." Doug was actually giving me advice. "Open your eyes and let others in. The guy you're looking for may be right next to you but you can't see him because you're always looking in the wrong direction."

"Thanks, Dr. Phil. Same to you," I laughed and waved him off.

After I changed, we brought the twins with us to the dunk tank and as expected, they could not stop laughing when they saw a still reluctant Nick plopping into the pool every time someone hit the bullseye with the ball. Soon, both kids wanted to take turns pushing the bullseye with their hands. They always required a little help, but they loved it.

"Jake, Emily. Can you hold the twins? Laney and I are going into the dunk tank. You can let both kids push us in." Josh and I gave the twins back to their parents and we carefully climbed onto the ledge-like seat.

"You think this seat will hold the both of us?" I asked nervously.

"I guess we'll find out soon enough. In any case, we'll end up wet, and the twins will end up happy."

After several failed attempts at throwing the ball to the bullseye, Nick brought both kids over, and the three of them dunked us into the tank. The twins loved it, and Ellie kept calling out, "Mo!" We went up several more times and did as she asked. Emily calling for cake-time was our saving grace. I was feeling awfully gross after being dunked in water that had been sitting there since this morning, with many visitors before me.

"That was fun. Thank you for helping, Josh."

"For you, sweet Laney, anything," he said with a wink, and went to grab us a towel.

For the twins, who had not taken a nap today because they were so excited about all that was going on in their backyard, they were done! They both lost it and Jake and Emily took them inside for the night.

"Mom," I said while giving her a kiss. "Another fantastic party. It's not too late to do this for a living. You may allow Dad to retire with your income."

"You were a good sport getting in that dunk tank."

"Didn't you see how much the twins enjoyed it?"

Doug came and spoiled my fun again with his statement, "I think every man who isn't related to you enjoyed seeing you bob up and down in that tank. Must you wear swimming suits that can't hold all your body parts?"

"Shut up, Doug. I wore my rash guard, and I'm still waiting for those long board shorts someone promised to buy for me."

"I can't believe that even at age twenty-four and twenty-two, you two still fight like you're twelve and ten. Some things will never change, huh Babs?"

"But Dad, Doug's always complaining about what I wear. What guy even notices what his sister is wearing?"

"Sweetheart, he only does it because he cares. Why don't you go shower and put something on that shows a little less legs?" Dad's chagrin was apparent.

"Oh, all right." I answered with my own chagrin.

The party was slowly dying down with the stars of the circus close to being fast asleep. Walking out of the tent, I noticed Donovan in a serious conversation with none other than his girlfriend, Kate. I did a wide circle around them. After Hawaii, I didn't want to be a part of their argument in any shape or form, not that they even noticed me.

The party wore me out almost as much as it did the twins. I stopped back at Emily's to make sure she didn't need my help, refused a dinner invite from Josh, and then from Max and Jane—who were going out with Josh, Garret, Nick and Doug. I told them I was turning in for the night and I walked back home to find Donovan sitting in the kitchen, having a beer with my dad.

"Hey," Donovan called out. "You want a beer?"

"No. That'll put me straight to sleep. As it is, I'm halfway there. What brings you here?"

"I invited him in to have a drink with me. Your brother went out, your mom's asleep already, and I found that this young man had no place to be. So I thought I'd see if he wanted to catch a game and do what men do."

"Are you drunk, already? You sound like you've had one too many beers, Dad."

"De, honey. What time is it?"

"Only 7:00pm. Why?"

"Shit! I've got to get some shut eye. I've got an early meeting with the board of directors, tomorrow." He dumped the rest of his beer in the sink and turned to Donovan. "Stick around, Son, and keep De company for a while. Sorry to skip out on you. Beer and basketball another night?"

"Sure, Chief."

"That was so bizarre! Did you ask him to leave so you could harass me again?"

All that got me was a disgruntled look. "No, I didn't ask your father to leave, and yes, he did invite me in."

"I thought you were leaving with your girlfriend? Why are you still here, and where's Kate?"

Donovan laughed like he was a patient in the looney bin. "That was a smooth move, walking all the way around the tent to try and avoid us. I don't think more than the entire tent noticed what you were doing in that bathing suit of yours."

Damn! I was trying so hard to be inconspicuous. Obviously I failed, and failed badly!

"If you're done with your beer, I'd be happy to walk you out. I sure am tired," I emphasized those last words.

"Why do I feel so lost when I'm around you?" *What on earth did that mean?* "Usually, I'm this self-assured guy who's been known to be suave around women and say outrageously flirtatious comments. Around you, I get tongue-tied, I say the stupidest things that end up hurting your feelings, and yet I don't want to be away from you. Why is that, Delaney Reid?"

Now I was tongue-tied. "I'm unsure, Mr. Taylor. But what I am sure of is that you're involved with another woman. A woman who was not happy when she mistakenly thought I was getting between you two, and a woman who will not be happy to know that her man is sitting in my kitchen hanging out with a girl who is not his woman. As you pointed out this morning, I don't know anything about men and relationships, but I do know that I'm worth a lot more than being someone's curiosity. Mr. Taylor, your life is too complicated. A friend of mine once lamented that her boyfriend wanted to 'have his cake and eat the whole damn bakery, too.' That's you, and I will not be a part of that. When I finally have a relationship, I'll be with someone whose eyes, mind, heart, and body are wholly with me."

April 20, 2013
Golf

_N_olan, from Hawaii, called last night and asked if I'd like to join him in a round of golf today. He explained that part of his job was to go around the world and play on different golf courses. Once the shock of his awesome job description wore off, I accepted his fun offer.

"Baby!" Dad sounded a little stressed.

"Hold on a moment, Nolan."

"Sure," he answered.

"What's up, Daddy?"

"Two out of four of our guys are out with a stomach bug. They think they got food poisoning. Can you fill in, Baby? I really need you and one more person or we have to forfeit."

"Daddy, I just made plans."

"Baby, this is the annual golf tournament at the club." Dad pleaded. "I can't forfeit, and I don't know if there's enough time to find two more players. Everyone's already paired up into foursomes."

I felt bad for my father, but I wasn't keen on playing with him and his friends. Competitive was an understatement for what was to come tomorrow at the golf tourney.

"Laney?" Nolan called out.

"Yes?"

"How about if we play with your father tomorrow, and I can take you golfing on Sunday, instead?"

"Are you sure? You'd be willing to do that? This gets really competitive and sometimes kinda ugly."

Nolan laughed. "Yeah, I'm sure. Are all these guys your father's age?"

"It'll probably be two-thirds my dad's age and one-third young married guys."

"Any women?"

"Very few to possibly none."

"Tell your dad I'd like to play."

"All right...I'll send you all the info via text. See you bright and early."

Dad could care less about Nolan until I told him what his job was and why he was here, and next thing I knew, my father was whooping for joy. Even before he left my room, he started group messaging all his friends telling them to watch out because his team was going to kick everyone's ass. I shook my head and smiled. It didn't take much to make my father happy.

Today was an absolutely perfect day to golf! I took out my favorite golf outfit and drove to the club with a very happy Henry Reid.

"We're going to kick everyone's ass, aren't we, Baby? We're going to take first place this year!"

"Let's not count our golf balls before they're in the hole, Daddy. We have 18-holes to play before claiming any prize."

"I can feel the weight of the trophy in my hands." My father was literally pretending to carry a trophy over his head, and declaring himself the champion.

Nolan was already at the course when Daddy and I got there, and he was chatting with our golf pro. Daddy was ecstatic to meet Nolan, and even more ecstatic that Nolan and our golf pro, Rick, were friends.

"You get any tips from Rick?"

"Of course, Dr. Reid. I asked him all the pertinent questions. The three of us can sweep! Your daughter and I will help you earn that first place trophy."

Dad's lips were about to split because he had such a huge smile. He was just about to answer Nolan but got distracted by his buddy passing by. Dad went over to brag about his situation.

"Your dad is great. He must have been fun to be around growing up."

"You think he's fun, you should see my mother."

"Delaney."

That voice...that unmistakable, undeniable voice. "Good morning." I smiled.

"Nolan." He greeted him coolly. "What brings you to the mainland?"

"My job brought me to Southern California this weekend to golf."

Donovan handed me a cup of coffee to hold and said, "I thought you weren't playing today."

"I wasn't but Dad's two partners got food poisoning, so here I am."

"Here you are...together?" Donovan looked at me then at Nolan.

"Yeah." I didn't know how to explain this situation without going into a long-winded one.

Nolan helped me out. "I asked Laney to golf with me this weekend and we ended up here."

"I see," he added casually.

"Are you playing with your father?"

"No. He and Ma are on a cruise somewhere in the Mediterranean. I'm golfing for the firm. They sponsored several teams in this tournament." I nodded my head in acknowledgement. "Why aren't you drinking your coffee? It's getting cold."

Oh! "It's for me? I thought you wanted me to hold it for you." Donovan gave me another one of his classic *are you stupid or something?* looks—which made me giggle. "Well...since you had no idea I was going to be here, what would make me think you brought this cup of coffee for me?"

"I saw you through the window from the restaurant and ordered you a cup. Are you complaining because I got you a cup of coffee?" He sounded incredulous.

"No...no...thank you. I guess I can always count on two things when I'm on a golf course with you—a perfect cup of coffee and your loss to me at the end of 18-holes." I cackled and carefully "ran" away with a piping hot cup of coffee before Donovan took my drink away from me for jabbing at his Hawaiian loss.

A stupid cup of coffee that burned my tongue because it was so damn hot gave me a new burst of energy this morning. Of course it wasn't the coffee, but the purchaser of the caffeine that jolted my system to happiness. He actually remembered how I liked my coffee and brought it out for me. That gave me *way* too much happiness. I was a serious loser!

"Hello, Laney." Damn! There was *that* sultry voice and there went *that* happiness.

"Hello, Kate. What brings you out to the golf course?"

"I'm here to play with the firm."

"Oh, how nice." The way my voice went puberty-high, outed me as a liar. "Do you golf?"

Kate gave a confident smile with her silky-smooth voice. "I've been known to play a little golf." She obviously believed she rocked on the golf course. I'd show her a thing or two. Shit, I was going to make her eat her slimy-ass words that had all the men staring at her in her couture golf outfit. Who the hell wore Fendi golf apparel? Who the hell knew Fendi made golf apparel? Who the hell wore Fendi but middle-aged women?

It took me longer than even I thought it would to calm myself down. After Hawaii, this woman pissed me off. However, I was here with my father, I was here to spend a day with a friend, and I was here to kick-ass!

"See you back at the club house after we win." Kate actually had the gall to call out to us as she and Donovan rode away on their cart. Donovan had a stupid grin to add to that catty remark.

"Daddy, we're going to destroy them! We're going to destroy everyone!"

"That's the spirit!" My father was pumped!

And destroy we did. In all fairness, Kate wasn't bad. But she'd pissed me off enough to get me on a lucky streak. We were the team right behind Donovan and Kate's team, and we nipped at their heels the whole day with our fast playing.

"You're seriously kicking our ass, Little Girl. What's got you on such a hot streak?"

I shrugged my shoulders and sunk my last putt. Donovan had waited around at the 18th hole for our group to see our scorecard. Once Dad showed it to him, he shook his head in misery and conceded a loss.

"I guess I can't beat you out here. Damn! And I thought I was the best one out here."

"You are one of the best ones out there. But today, I was better." Donovan looked haggard and low in spirit. He definitely wasn't the Donovan who brought me a cup of coffee. "What's the matter?"

"It's been a long day," was all he'd say. "You staying for dinner?"

"I don't think so. I don't know. Nolan wanted to go grab a bite to eat, but I'm unsure Daddy will let us leave."

"You and Nolan dating?" Donovan's voice kinda went high-pitch with that question.

I shook my head no in answer. "He's just here to play golf. We were supposed to go play elsewhere today but since Daddy needed two more people on his team; we decided to join him instead. We'll go play at his 'work' course, tomorrow."

"You seeing him again?"

I nodded my head yes this time. "We're just friends, and he enjoys golf even more than you or I."

Donovan didn't have a response and his questions went silent. His moods swung on a pendulum and I was afraid to bring up the subject of Kate—as curious as I was about their status. They did not portray the happy couple today.

"I'm going in. Stick around for dinner." He walked off to the dining room and left me to wonder why he was in such a bad mood.

Our foursome stayed out and watched the rest of the players come in from their rounds, and we let my father and his partner go up to the podium to accept their first place trophy. After all the awards were done, Nolan apologetically went back to his hotel as he wasn't feeling well, and I went inside the dining area, excited to possibly sit with Donovan at dinner.

I walked in to Donovan and Jane enjoying themselves at a table for two, drinking. They were laughing and having the time of their lives. Deciding I didn't need to sit and watch their intimate camaraderie, I chose to go home and enjoy a quiet evening with my mother.

April 21, 2013
A Long, but Fun Day

This entire weekend was a draining one, and I was glad to have nothing going on today. Nolan still wasn't feeling well, so he decided to head back home early and thus canceled our golf outing. My family got up late and all decided to skip breakfast, but meet up for lunch and a movie.

"Emily, our family is going out for lunch and a movie. You and Jake want to join us?"

"I'd love to, but the kids are still cranky from their party. We're going to have a very low-key day today."

"How about lunch? You can bring the kids, can't you?"

"I'll talk to Jake, but most likely we will stay home."

"OK, you let me know. We can always bring something back for you."

"Thanks, Laney."

We went to our favorite sandwich shop down the street from us. We actually decided to take a leisurely walk to lunch, even though it was rare for anyone in Southern California to walk anywhere. My dad was still on a natural high from winning the golf tournament. He was still all smiles.

"Lunch is on me today," he announced.

"Hon, lunch was going to be your treat whether or not you liked it, or knew it." Mom answered and we all laughed. "It's a once in a blue moon kind of day when we are all in the house with nothing to do."

As we walked in to the tiny sandwich shop, Donovan was on his way out.

"Hey, Son. You picking up lunch?"

"Hello Reid family," he answered and kissed Mom on the cheek. I didn't know why but I expected the same treatment. It almost seemed as if he wavered between giving me a kiss...or not. "Yes. I picked up a sandwich and I'm heading to the office. I've played too much this weekend."

"Come join us. Work can wait. I'll talk to your boss if he gets mad. I happen to be on excellent terms with him." Dad had on his signature grin.

"Yeah? You'll pay my missed hourly wages, too?" Donovan asked with a smirk.

"What do you do with all the money you make? You have neither woman nor child. Where's all your money going?"

Donovan showed us his beautiful grin. "Well, this month has been harder on the wallet thanks to a certain someone, but you're right, Chief. I have neither woman nor child, so I guess I can ease up on the billing. What are you all up to today?"

Mom spoke, "We are having lunch, then going to a movie. Why don't you join us, Donovan? I don't ever get a chance to speak with you."

"I'd like to, but I'm quite behind with this one client. I need to draft some proposals."

Mom spoke again. "Why don't you come back and work at our place? It's beautiful today. I know Laney's behind in her editing. You both can sit outside, I'll make some iced tea and lemonade, and I promise I won't bother you too much. Say you'll come spend an afternoon with us."

"How can I refuse such an offer?" His smile was melting every female in the shop. "Am I going to bother you if we work side by side?"

I shrugged my shoulders in answer. After the conversation I heard last night between him and Jane, Donovan wasn't high on my list of favorite people right now. Some days...like today...it hurt even to be near him.

Mom caught a ride in Donovan's convertible while the rest of us walked home.

"Daddy, would it be all right if I stopped by somewhere before going home?"

"Sure. Where are you stopping by?"

"Just a few places. I need to walk off all this food."

"But you hardly ate. You only picked at your food. Is everything OK, Baby?"

"I'm fine. I'd just like to take the long way home."

My dad let me go and I walked to the park, not so close to my house. Sitting on the swing, I tried to shake this not-so-happy feeling. I despised the fact that my moods rode the waves of Donovan Taylor's whims. I also despised the fact that I had to work to control my feelings whenever he was around. This was not who I wanted to be, and I was tired of myself!

"Finally, you're home." Donovan looked up from his laptop when I came in from my walk.

I nodded yes.

"You want some iced tea, Laney? It's beautiful outside. Why don't you bring your laptop and join us?" Mom motioned her hand furiously and had me join them.

I grabbed my laptop from my bedroom and sat next to Mom, as far away from Donovan as possible. As soon as I sat, Mom got a phone call and left us.

"Everything good?" Without looking into his eyes, I nodded yes. "What's the matter? What's with the silent treatment? I hate it when you girls do that. Rachel and Becky used to do that kind of shit all the time just to drive me crazy."

How did I explain to this guy that last night I heard him tell Jane he wanted her and he wanted Kate? How did I explain this without having to explain that I wished for him to want me and only me? How did I do this without sounding pathetic and desperate and having him laugh at me? Simply stated, I didn't.

"Here." I put an envelope on the table. "This is your earnings from the golf pool yesterday. Dad says you're the big winner. That's a lot of cash to add to your depleted pile for this month. I'm sure buying gifts for Kate is not an easy undertaking."

"Thanks." He casually looked through the bundle. "Why do you have this?"

"Dad asked me to give it to you yesterday, but I couldn't approach you so I kept it and figured I'd give it to Jake."

"Why couldn't you approach me yesterday?" I shrugged my shoulders, again. "Shit, Delaney. Finish the conversation." He was frustrated.

"You and my cousin looked to be in such a deep and personal conversation I thought it was best not to bother you."

"Is that what you're pissed about?" He gave me a challenging stare.

"I'm not pissed about anything. I just don't have much to say to you." That came out more defensively than I'd planned.

Donovan scratched his head like crazy with both hands and declared, "You women all drive me insane! Grab a bathing suit. Let's go for a drive!" He commanded in his usual domineering way. With pursed lips and raised eyebrows, I let my displeasure in his tone be apparent. "Sorry. If you'll get a suit on, there's some place I'd like to take you. I haven't taken anyone there, yet, and I'd really love for you to see it." Now why couldn't he have said this to begin with?

By the time I came down with a bikini under my tunic dress, Donovan had cleaned up what was on the patio table, and had told my parents we were going out for the afternoon. Mom and Dad waved a silent good-bye from the kitchen table as we left for our excursion.

"Where are we going?"

"A surprise."

He placed two plastic cups of ice tea Mom had packed in to-go cups in his cup holder, and set us out for our drive.

"How far?"

"About 90 minutes."

"North, South or East?"

"North. Do you know how I won all that money yesterday?"

I shook my head no because I really didn't understand how and why these men gambled so much over a game of golf.

"We all had to pick who we thought would be the top three finishers in yesterday's tournament. As soon as I saw you and Nolan, I changed my original entry and I put Nolan as third-place finisher, me as second-place finisher, and you as the top finisher." Now that put a smile on my face. "I knew you'd be happy to hear my confession."

"Why would you pick me as the top place finisher when you're a much better golfer?"

"I am a great golfer, but never when you are around. Thanks to you, I believe I made over a thousand dollars yesterday."

"No way!"

"Yes way!" He laughed. "After we have some fun, I'll take you out to dinner. It's only fair I spend this money on you, since you helped me win it."

While talking about this and that, it was a short hour plus ride up to the beach, and to a tiny little shack of a home right on the beach. There was actually a cluster of homes across from the water in all different shapes and sizes, but all very tiny. Donovan unlocked the door to one of these shacks.

"Where are we?"

"My new home."

"What do you mean your new home?"

"I mean I just purchased this beach house a couple of weeks ago, and it's actually my first time here since I bought it."

He gave me the grand tour of the two bedrooms, one bathroom and really small living room, kitchen and dining room all combined in one. I noticed the bedroom had a tiny fireplace and a magnificent view of the beach. It was perfect.

"Give me a second, and I'll get my suit and some towels. I want to go try something with you."

This shack was sparsely furnished, but when I looked through the kitchen, every cupboard was bare. "Where did some of this furniture come from if you just bought the place?" I asked while nosing around the place and opening all the drawers and cupboards.

"The guy I bought it from; he had to leave for another job immediately. So I bought the house and pretty much everything in it."

"You know there's nothing in the kitchen but major appliances?"

"Yeah. I suppose I'll get around to buying kitchen ware but I don't have a clue where to begin."

"This is your first time coming here?"

"Yes. The deal went through while we were in Hawaii. And I haven't had a chance to come here till today."

"It's really nice here—perfect for a young married couple. You and your wife will have a great time here together." That last statement was so unnecessary. It was stupid of me to bring up Donovan and his future wife. It also made me sad to think he and I would not have much of a friendship once he got married. Donovan didn't answer.

"There are kiteboards outside in the locker. Have you ever been kiteboarding before?"

"No. I've never done that before. What is it? "

"I think it's also called kitesurfing. It's a combination of surfing, windsurfing, wakeboarding, and paragliding. It doesn't look easy, but since you're such a strong surfer, I think you can do it. Last time I was here, I saw a guy on the beach giving lessons. Let's go try it."

Kiteboarding, or kite surfing, was exactly what it sounded like—a short surfboard + a kite. Our instructor had us blow up the kites with a manual pump, harness the kite to our bodies, and once we understood how to control the handle, he demonstrated what to do. It was harder than it looked. We followed the instructor into the ocean, and let the kite drag us far in. The hardest part of this entire activity was getting both feet into the slipper-looking feet holders on the board. My feet continually slipped out as I tried to stand.

Finally, we both got up and the ride was thrilling! Our instructor told us that due to the mild winds, we'd be able to ride longer than beginners can usually hang on. I did well for a while till I slipped and the board came loose. Donovan was surfing beautifully and every time he flexed, I got a gorgeous view of his muscular chest. He waved and gave me his iconic smile. I waved back with a silly grin and of course wiped out entirely. It was utterly embarrassing how badly I wiped out in front of Donovan!

Our two-hour lesson flew by. We both had so much fun learning a new sport.

"You want to kiteboard some more or do you want to give it a rest for now?" Donovan came over to me and asked when we got back on the sand.

"Let's stop for now. I'm starving. Let's go eat."

"What do you want to eat?"

"Let's go to that little restaurant over there," I pointed to the beach shack that looked like it had good seafood, lively music, and a rowdy crowd.

After deflating the kites and rinsing everything off, we put the equipment back in the locker, quickly "showered" outside, and roughly dried ourselves clean. I put my tunic back on, and we walked over to the restaurant.

"What would you like to eat, Little Girl?"

"Oysters, raw and deep-fried, clam strips, crab, fish tacos, any or all sound good."

"We'll order a dozen Hama Hama oysters, a small basket of clam strips, a whole Dungeness crab steamed and shelled, and clam chowder in a bread bowl." While I looked at him in wonder he asked, "Beer or wine?"

"Pinot blanc."

"There you go." He finished his order with the server then turned to me. "There's laughter in your eyes. What's so funny?" *Shoot!* My eyes betrayed me. Did I want to tell him? "Speak!" He was so bossy!

"Back in December when we were all in New York, my brother, Nick, Jane, Max and I went to an all-you-can-eat crab place and at this place, I had mentioned that I wanted to find a man who would shell an entire crab for me and hand it to me on a silver platter." I laughed and took a sip of my wine. "Doug then proceeded to burst my bubble and tell me I'd be lucky to find a man who could buy me crabs, let alone shell them for me."

"So I'm your knight in shining armor who will hand you a mound of crab on a silver platter?" He kidded while drinking his beer.

I shook my head no. "When you placed the order, I thought maybe I should lower my standards and look for a man who might order it shelled, instead. At this point in my life, I am beginning to think Emily found the only knight in shining armor in America."

"Trust me. Jake is not as much of a prince as you've conjured him up to be in your head. He can be an asshole, too—just like the rest of us."

"I think you're wrong. Didn't you see him changing out Emily's shoes for her because her feet began to swell? The way he tenderly replaced the shoes from her pregnant feet was the most beautiful sight I'd ever seen in my twenty-two-years of life. You tell me that wasn't chivalrous and indulgent." Donovan showed a bit of caprice in his smile as he listened to me drone on about my cousin.

"Your knight will come, Delaney. No need to give up hope already. You're only twenty-two."

Our soup came first, and we shared from one big bread bowl. Then the oysters came and I was in heaven. Between the smell of the ocean, the crashing of the waves, and the delicious oysters, I was in my element. It didn't hurt that Donovan Taylor was a part of this element.

"You know what's the best way to eat oysters?"

"What, Little Girl?"

"Hama Hama oysters with a slab of uni, a dollop of caviar, a sprig of cilantro, and a squeeze of lemon—now that's the best way to eat an oyster."

"Damn, Little Girl! No knight is that rich. He's a working class man, not royalty. You better make your own fortune, then look for your knight."

"Why Mr. Taylor...I think I will do just that." I winked at him and ate the last oyster.

The mound of crab came just as I got a phone call.

"Hey, Doug."

"Where are you? You still with Donovan?"

"We are at the beach. What's up?"

"We decided to go to a later movie, and Jake and Emily decided to join us. You guys up for it? It's a 7:00pm showing."

"I don't know. I can join but..."

"What's up?" Donovan asked when I stepped away from the conversation with my brother.

"The Reids are going to a 7:00pm movie. They want to know if we're game."

"What the hell? I've played all weekend. Might as well finish it off with a bang. We're in."

"You heard that?"

"We're going to that fancy theater with the reclining chairs and dinner service. Buy your tickets online."

"You're not buying them for me?" I kidded. There was no way my brother was buying me an expensive movie ticket.

"Hell no! You've got a rich date sitting across from you at dinner. Have him pay for your movie." There was no hesitation in that statement.

"Good-bye."

"See ya."

"What are you doing?" Donovan looked over my phone.

"Searching for the movie so I can purchase tickets. Everyone has seats already. They want us to get seats right now."

"Give me that," he took over my phone, and punched in his information along with his credit card info. He handed the phone back to me when he was done. "I told you I won a lot of money yesterday, thanks to you."

"It wasn't thanks to me. It was thanks to your gambling skills."

"We should get going if we're going to make it back for the movies."

Having done good damage to the meal, Donovan changed back into his clothes, and took the dirty towels and bathing suit back with us. I was pretty grubby, but I put one of Donovan's college sweatshirts over my tunic, made sure I had no more sand on me, then hopped into the car.

"Should I put up the top?"

"Naw. It's gorgeous out. Why drive a convertible if you're going to keep the top on?"

"My sentiment exactly, Ms. Reid."

The ride back home was a quick one only because—I fell asleep! I woke up to Donovan opening my side of the door and putting his hand on my head.

"Princess, we're here," he whispered in my ear, and almost carried me out.

"I'm sorry. What a friend I turned out to be today. You helped me learn a new sport, bought me dinner, and are taking me to the movies, and here I am falling asleep the second we get in the car."

He still had his arm around my shoulder as I was a bit dazed getting out of the car. Two hours of an extreme water sport, and a glass of wine put me in a deep sleep.

"I've had more fun with you today than I've had on any date in a very long time."

Of course he didn't consider what we did today a date, but it was nice to hear.

"Laney. Over here." Emily called us to their seats.

Originally, our seats were behind Jake and Emily, but we traded with my brother and Nick, and I sat next to Emily.

"You kids have a good time today?" Jake asked with a quizzical smile—quizzical only to me. "You take our Laney to the hut?"

"I did. We learned to kiteboard, we had an all seafood dinner, and here we are watching a movie with you. Does that meet with your approval?" Donovan asked with sarcasm.

Emily and I decided to recline our seats while the men talked around us. This heavenly theater offered fully reclining seats, in-theater dining, pillows, and a plush blanket. Next thing I knew, both Emily and I were being woken up as the credits rolled. I remembered seeing absolutely none of the movie.

"Princess," Donovan whispered in my ear. "You'll never know if the guy you're with is your knight in shining armor if you keep falling asleep on him." He let out a deep masculine chuckle.

"Damn! I fell asleep again. Sorry! What an expensive nap. I owe you a movie."

He chuckled again. "I'm holding you to that." He pulled me up, and we walked out of the theater with his arm around me again. I could get used to this kind of attention.

"Laney," Doug spoiled my dream. "What did you do today? You look like hell."

"I do?" I asked Donovan whose face gentled upon looking me over.

"You look adorable," he declared and walked next to me.

After the kind of day we had, and after that statement and sweet look he gave me, I was tempted to link my fingers with his and hold his hand, had my cousins and brother not been with us. Donovan's words made me feel bolder by the second, but as our fingers accidentally brushed, I woke up to the realization that Donovan's feelings did not equal mine. As much as my heart was already his, I clearly heard him tell Jane last night that he was confused because his heart belonged to both Kate and Jane. These were words I couldn't and shouldn't forget—no matter how wonderful the day with Donovan Taylor.

April 26, 2013
Donovan's Date

*O*ur Wednesday carpool and softball game was cut short even before my alarm went off. Donovan called to tell me he would be in Las Vegas all day meeting with a client and didn't think he'd get back in time for the game. He made sure I had a ride, told me to have a nice day, and went off to earn his pay. Since I had spent almost the entire weekend with Donovan, I did feel his absence even more profoundly than usual. On Friday, Jake and Emily were going out, so I rushed home as soon as classes were over to watch my favorite twins.

"What do you mean they're sleeping already? It's only 5:30." I complained.

"They are both trying to drop their afternoon nap, and they are tired and cranky by four. They're knocked out, so you have the whole place to yourself. Dinner's warming in the oven, and feel free to download any movies."

"Will do."

While walking them to the back door, I wanted to ask where they were going for the night, but since they didn't offer the information, I didn't want to pry. Usually, Emily and or Jake offered information on their whereabouts, but tonight they were silent.

"Have a great time." I waved good-bye and closed the door behind them.

Being so early in the evening, I twiddled my thumbs trying to figure out the best course for the evening. Finally, I pulled out my laptop and decided to work on all that was backlogged from the eventful weekend.

"Laney?" Emily popped her head back in the door.

"Did you forget something?"

"No. I couldn't leave because I felt so guilty not telling you that we will be meeting Donovan and Jane for dinner and a Laker game."

"Oh..." My heart sank in my chest and stayed there like dead weight. *Why, oh why, did that news hurt so much?* "Have a great time." I put on a brave front, and Emily waited for me to say more. "I'm all right. We are only friends, at best."

"And Donovan and Jane are only friends as well. He invited her because..."

"It's really fine. He doesn't live in my pocket, and he doesn't need my permission for anything. Please go and have a great time and don't worry about me."

She hugged me, and reluctantly left.

As much as that news hurt, I decided not to dwell on what Donovan was doing tonight and forced myself to work. I could spend the entire night correcting papers and I wouldn't be done. Mom popped in to say hello and to make sure all was right with the twins, and a few hours later, Aunt Sandy did the same. I was proud of the way I forged ahead with my plans and wasn't derailed by Mr. Donovan Taylor.

All is good at home?

Yes, Jake. All is good.

What are you doing?

Editing papers. My mom and yours stopped by earlier.

If I can get one of them to relieve you, would you like to meet us for dessert?

No thank you. Enjoy.

I knew Jake and Emily felt sorry for me, so they did what they could to include me. That wasn't necessary. I would be fine.

They came home earlier than expected, and as they didn't offer any more information on their night, I didn't ask. No one was home when I got in, so I sat on the front porch swing and began making mental notes of what I wanted to accomplish while out in London. After seeing all the major sites, I thought about auditing a class or two at Oxford or Cambridge. Perhaps starting fall, I'd take some classes, find a part-time job, and join some sort of intramural-type sports team so I could make some friends.

"Hey." That voice was calling my name.

"Hi." I answered softly.

"Why are you out here by yourself?"

"Jake and Emily came home early, and no one is home right now so I'm hanging out. Did you have a good time at the game? Did the Lakers win?" Like the glutton that I was, I courted the punishment.

"Yes and no."

I nodded my head to explain I understood his terse answer.

"You upset with me, again?" he asked cautiously.

I was surprised he asked this question. "Why would I be upset with you, and what do you mean, again?"

"You're never happy when I spend time with Jane."

"It's not jealousy." I was too quick to add. "I just feel for Max the way Jane tows the line with you, and I think it sucks you keep dangling a golden apple at her. Either you both should give up the people you're with and date, or walk away from one another." My head shook at the absurdity of my admonishment. Who was I to tell these people what to do? And of course it was jealousy. I was jealous as hell that Donovan found my cousin attractive, but not me.

"Tonight was just friends going out to a game. Jane and I..."

"Mr. Taylor, I've told you this before. Your life is too complicated. Pick a woman and love her."

"What if I don't know which woman is the right one to love?"

"Then stay away from all of them, and you'll figure out the right one for you. It's not that hard."

"What if I can't stay away from her?"

I could tell Donovan was still looking at me, but I kept my head up-top my perched-up knees and stared at my feet.

"Maybe if there's one woman you *have to* be with, then she's the woman for you. I just hope there aren't too many collateral damages that come with your decision." I started to get up. "Good night."

He grabbed my hand and pulled me into his body. The movement was so quick and yet so beautiful I could feel my unguarded emotion flaring. We were perfectly and intimately connected. From my head that lay in the crook of his neck, we were chest to chest, hip to hip, toe to toe. "I'm sorry I'm always disappointing you and hurting you. Those are never my intentions, but in the end, you become my only collateral damage." Unable to decipher what he meant, but cherishing this time together, I didn't have any more to say. "Good night," he uttered while he brought his hands that were once snugly around my back to cup my face. Silently, I wished for him to kiss me, but that wasn't meant to be. He let go all together and walked to his car. I went back to the swing and sat back at my original position with my knees against my body, arms around the knees, and now my cheek resting atop the knees.

Donovan Taylor, why do you make me love you so?

May 1, 2013
Collateral Damage

I've had a hard time concentrating since Donovan and I last spoke. His final words and actions made me hope. Perhaps I was the woman he couldn't stay away from, though deep in my heart, I knew I wasn't the one. School was winding down and I had so much work piled up—but I couldn't get my head in this game called school.

My car only seats two and I have two beautiful Reid women to shuttle to school and work. Who else will drive?

Donovan sent a group text this morning, and I didn't want to be a part of this or any other threesome.

I don't need a ride. You and Jane go ahead without me.

Why don't you need a ride, Delaney?

I can drive on my own. Have a nice day.

Donovan quickly sent me an individual text.

I'll see you later?

I don't know. I have too much work. I will see.

You upset about Jane...again? We have a meeting to attend together.

We are not each other's keeper. No need to worry about what I think and feel. Bye.

Delaney! I'll see you at softball.

School was seriously kicking my ass. My senior thesis professor returned my work with enough red corrections to make it look like someone had died on my thesis. Shit. I wasn't expecting it to be that bad. Without a doubt, I had a few all-nighters ahead of me. It was getting close to softball time and I had so much work to do, but I still wanted to be in Donovan's vicinity. Lame. I knew I was being lame! But I wanted to see him. Of course I got to the game, changed, and waited for my catcher who never showed up. There was no message on my cell phone, and Kevin substituted William as my catcher. I played, we won, and two hours later, I drove home.

I drove past a Porsche parked in front of Jane's house, and my cousin stepping out of this car. My house being further down the cul-de-sac, afforded me this unwanted view of Donovan dropping Jane off at home. Quickly pulling into my garage, I sat in the car for a long while, controlling my emotions. Stupid me! *Stupid, stupid, stupid* me. Regardless of what Donovan might have said the other night, his actions spoke an entirely different tune. Deciding I was being stupid for every reason under the sun, I got out of the car and chose not to dwell on actions I couldn't control.

"Hey." That voice startled me enough to make me drop all the crap in my hands.

"What brings you here?" We both got on the floor to pick up all the scattered books and papers.

"What took you so long to get in?"

"I was organizing my car and junk." I pointed to the evidence, though that was a total lie. "What brings you by?"

"Have you had dinner?"

I shook my head no.

"You want to go eat?"

I shook my head no, again.

"Why not?" he asked quietly, guardedly.

"Too much work. As it is, I'm going to be up a good part of the night." I pointed back to all the junk in my hands.

"I have a long night ahead of me, too. I see you played?"

I nodded yes, but didn't ask where he was and why he didn't let me know he wasn't coming.

"Go shower. I'll order a pizza in the meanwhile and we can eat here."

He took my pile of papers, I skipped up the steps two-by-two, and my world was all right again. My rollercoaster emotions were too idiotic for words.

"You think that pizza's big enough for the both of us?" Donovan had pulled a Jake and ordered a pizza the size of my door.

Donovan chuckled. "We're walking next door. Prego mama wants some too."

"Well, in that case, lead the way."

I stopped at our door, and waited for Donovan to open it for me while carrying an extra large box of pizza. Trying hard not to giggle, I turned and stared, expectantly.

"Don't be a smart ass!" he growled. "Open the damn door."

"A knight in shining armor, you are not," I quipped, opening the door and motioning for him to go out before me. Donovan in turn lightly "kicked" me in the ass and chuckled. "You're seriously cutting into my work time, Mr. Taylor."

"You've got to eat. I haven't had anything since a late breakfast. I'm starving."

"Knowing I had more work than hours in a night, I went to softball not wanting to let you down, only to find out that you had let..." *Shit! Diarrhea of the mouth, again!*

Donovan went quiet as Emily greeted us at the door. "Pizza!" She gave a huge smile.

"Should we wait and see how much Emily eats, first?" Donovan whispered in my ear. *Damn!* Why did his breath in my ear feel so good?

"Mr. Taylor, I'm hungry, too. If I wait for my cousin to finish, there may be none left."

"Good point, Little Girl."

"Emily," I asked, mid-bite, "did you see any stars at the Laker game the other night?"

"Who did you say I was sitting next to, Donovan?"

"Justin Bieber."

"Eew. Not my cup of tea."

"Who is your cup of tea?" Jake asked with a knowing grin.

"If we're talking teenybopper stars, I'm more a fan of Harry Styles or Rpatz." I could tell Donovan had no clue who these guys were.

"You been on any dates lately?" Jake asked.

"I got asked to watch the Clippers' playoff game, and I'm thinking about whether or not I want to go."

"Why wouldn't you want to go?" Emily asked while finishing off her third slice. Donovan and I waited to see if she'd take one more.

"I have so much work to do before I graduate, and also the seats are in a box. I don't like sitting in a box."

"Why not?"

"Because, Mr. Taylor, it feels impersonal all the way up there. I like being closer to the game. Maybe I'll meet CP3 or Blake Griffin if I'm right there. I've also been invited to a Kings' playoff game the next night. Most likely I won't go to either—too much schoolwork. And speaking of school work, I've must leave." I got up and held out my hand to all three people who tried to get up with me. "Don't get up. Thank you for dinner," I told Donovan, "and the stimulating conversation. I can find my way home, blindfolded. See ya!"

In the end, this night didn't turn out too badly, after all.

May 11, 2013
Mother's Day Celebration!

My mom is absolutely the greatest Mom created by God. She's funny, she's smart, she throws the best parties, and she's always been my best friend. Both my parents try to listen to me and treat me with respect. They help me make smart choices, and encourage me to push myself to become a better person. With that said, I love my mother with all my heart and can't wait to show her what Doug and I created for her Mother's Day gag gift.

"Laney, Mom and Dad have walked over to Jake's. Let's get the shower curtain up. Mom's going to flip when she sees this gift. That was a brilliant last minute idea on your part."

"Thanks. I think Mom will be pleasantly surprised, or horrified." I laughed.

"At first I was annoyed they brought this tradition back. It's not easy coming up with a gag gift for Mom. She's the ultimate party planner. What could we possibly do to top her?" Doug said while carrying the shower curtain upstairs.

"But it's fun. I've always liked this tradition of coming up with the best gag gift, though the $100 buy-in is a little steep for my blood. I don't know how all the cousins are coming up with the entry fee. Do you know what anyone else has created?"

"They're all keeping mum. Even Nick has kept his mouth shut, but it sounded like they had a good one, too."

"Did Mom tell you we could split the money pot if she wins?"

"No shit? Seriously? Damn! Let's get this thing up and be the winning family!"

Normally, this brunch was held down at the beach, but since Emily was so pregnant, and since we brought our tradition back, it was held on the cul-de-sac. I supposed now that we were competing again, maybe this holiday would stay at Jake and Emily's. Uncle Dave and Aunt Deb would have to pick up another holiday to host at their fabulous beach house.

"Good morning, Reids."

"Hey Donovan." Doug gave him a fist bump. "Becky. I didn't know you were in town." Doug walked over to her and gave her a hug.

"Al and I came in last minute. We didn't know we were coming, either." She giggled.

Becky and I couldn't be called friends. She and Jane were always too old for me to hang out with them and too cool for them to hang out with me. Becky looked very much like Donovan, but not nearly as good looking. She had the brunette, hazel/blue eye combo similar to her brother, but while Donovan's face was chiseled like a model's, Becky's was rounder. Still, she was a beautiful woman.

"Hi, I'm Al. I'll introduce myself since no one here will show us the courtesy."

"Hello. I'm Laney Reid, younger sister to Doug, first cousins with Jake and his siblings." I shook the hand that was out for me. "Hi Becky," I called out tentatively.

Becky was never overly friendly to me. It wasn't that she was mean... she just wasn't ever nice. Fast-forward ten years, I didn't know what to make of her and me.

"Hey, Laney. Long time no see. What are you up to these days?"

"I'm finishing up undergrad."

"And will be living as a wastrel in London for a year after she graduates," Donovan added. Though it was said as a joke, it didn't feel like one. I didn't have an answer for Donovan's wisecrack, so I ignored it.

"I'll see you all inside." I waved politely and headed for safety.

"Ne Ne!" James *and* Ellie came running to me. I was surprised Ellie greeted me along with her brother.

"Hi James! Hi Ellie!" Crouching to their level, I gave them a group hug and part-kissed, part-blew raspberries on their cheeks.

"Mor!" Ellie declared and James followed suit by also asking for "Mo!"

With each cheek and each giggle more delicious than the one before, I was soon seated on the floor with the twins on top of me.

"Someone's having too much fun here." Donovan swung Ellie up into his arm and into the air. Once she got over the shock of the motion, she yelled, "Mor!"

"Yes, Your Highness!" He answered and threw her up several more times.

James, too, called out, "Mo," to Donovan and put out his hand so Donovan passed Ellie off to Al who continued the motion, and Donovan gave his godson the attention he craved.

"Oh my gosh! These two are even cuter than the last time I saw them." Becky pinched Ellie's adorable cheeks and she got a stern, "NO!" from Ellie. Our darling was not in the mood to be Becky's plaything. She wanted "mor" from Al, only. "You can be a brat, just like your Auntie Jane," Becky teased.

With the twins in good hands, and having wished every mother in the backyard a very happy Mother's Day, I grabbed a plate of food and sat with my mom.

"I didn't know Donovan and Becky were attending. Are Jamie Lynn and Scott coming, too?"

"Unsure."

"Donovan," Mom called out to him. "Come sit with us."

"Happy Mother's Day to you." He kissed my mom on the cheek and sat next to me.

"Are your parents coming?"

"They should be. I went and picked up Becky and Al from the airport. Mom and Dad should be here soon."

"What did you do for your mother today, Donovan?"

"Um...nothing, yet?"

"Donovan! Shame on you. Your mother carried you for nine months, went through severe labor pains for you because of your gigantic-sized head, and treated you like a king all your life since you were the only son. I can't believe you got your mother nothing." Mom laid it on thick.

"All right, all right! I'll send her something soon."

"Send her something?" Mom used her most horrified voice. "You can't just send her an Amazon package. You need to put your heart into it."

"I thought women loved any gift." Donovan gave Mom a playful smile.

Mom couldn't help but smile with him. "*You* are too charming for your own good!"

"What a compliment coming from a woman married to the ultimate charmer." Donovan turned his attention to me. "What did *you* get for your mom?"

Mom answered instead. "Laney wrote me a book of poems...or was it short stories?"

I cracked-up. "They're called vignettes, Mom. Something between a poem and a short story."

"Really? About what?"

"She captured significant moments of my life in these vignettes. It's beautiful. You want to read them, Donovan?"

"I'd love to read them." He was actually genuine in his answer.

"Everyone!" Dad got all of our attention. "Let the games begin!"

That was our signal to move to the first house on the block. At this first house, we saw what the Reid men had been working on all week. My father and his brothers had built a "throne" for their mother in honor of this special day.

"Is that what I think it is?" Donovan whispered in my ear.

I nodded yes. "I think they copied Joffrey Baratheon's chair."

"Who?"

"Joffrey Baratheon?" He shook his head no. "House Lannister?" Still, the head shook no. *"Game of Thrones?"*

"Is that a board game?"

"It started as a series of novels and now it's an HBO show. You've never watched it?"

"No. Is it good?"

"It's fantastic! There's only a few more shows left of Season 3; you should quickly catch up."

"When school's over for you, and I get a break from this case, you're going to sit and watch all three seasons with me," he stated as a fact.

"Why do you need me to watch it with you?"

"I'll need someone to explain the storyline to me."

"You'll get it as the story progresses. It isn't rocket science."

"Can you for once just agree to one of my ideas rather than fighting me every step of the way? You sure you don't want to go to law school, instead? You are one litigious girl."

I ignored him and watched Gram sit on her literal and figurative throne and unroll the toilet paper roll. We all roared when the tune of *God Save the Queen* blared. My father, his brothers, and grandfather had done a clever job of turning a regular toilet into a throne fit for a queen. Next, we moved on to Aunt Sandy's backyard. What we saw didn't disappoint the high expectations we all had.

Jake, Jane and Nick got Aunt Sandy a clock-shaped coffin. Being a clock lover, Aunt Sandy collected clocks from all over the world. Now, she not only had a coffin ready for her burial, she also had a clock to take with her when she left. Her gift read, *Counting down your mortality, Sandra Jane Reid*, but the eerie part about this coffin was that like a real clock, it had a working hour, minute, and second hand.

"Freaky!" Donovan whispered again, for my ears only.

"Uh-huh!" I whispered back. "And with no litigious undertone...you see, I agree with you from time to time."

"Smartass!" He "kicked" me in the ass again like the other night.

The next house was Jake's, and he uncovered a panoramic-sized frame that held an incredibly sweet caricature of the twins. The artist had accentuated all the darling features of both kids. Ellie's big blue eyes were even bigger and more sparkling than her normal self. James' beautifully rounded forehead was the focal point of his drawing and the picture depicted him as the Road Runner, wreaking havoc every which way.

The second frame, which hung in Jake's office, was a montage of his stunning wife, chronicling their every moment of love—from their short dating period, up to their special day commemorating the twins' birthdays. Though there were pictures of the kids, Jake and Emily, and the family, Jake chose to highlight mostly his wife. There were pictures of her smiling while eating sushi in Japan, laughing while throwing the bouquet at their wedding, crying with joy with the birth of the twins, and even crying with sadness at her parents' gravesite. Somehow, Jake had captured the essence of his wife, and the thought that went into this gift was infinitely more beautiful than even his breathtaking wife.

I felt that sad yearning again.

The last frame hung in Emily's sitting room and it was one of the Reid and Logan families. Instead of names, Jake had all of our pictures on the tree. I glanced over at Emily and Jake with a baby in each arm; the four of them fit into each other's embrace, so perfectly, so wholly.

"What's with the sigh," was Donovan's whisper this time. "Shouldn't you be tearing up with the rest of the women?"

I shook my head no. "They're perfect, aren't they?"

Donovan looked over at the joyous family. "They are," he answered with something that resembled a sigh, himself. "And I'm going to kick my best friend's ass if he keeps showing us all up like that."

"The bar is set pretty high. I don't know where I'll find any man even half as loving as my cousin."

"Oh, brother..." Donovan rolled his eyes and pushed me ahead of him.

When we got to our house, Doug called everyone's attention. "We have a little poem for our dear mother before we present her gift to her. The poem, recited to the tune of *Hermy the Worm*, is entitled, *Laying in My Bathtub, Drinking My Vino.*"

"Laying in my bathtub, drinking my vino," I started the reading.

"Gulp, gulp, gulp, gulp," Doug made the sound effects.

"Reading from my Kindle,"

"Yawn, Yawn," Everyone who knew my mother laughed because they knew she wasn't a reader.

"Along came Henry the Chief,"

"And he was *shivvverrring*," Doug exaggerated how cold he was.

"I said, 'Henry, what happened?'"

"I lost all my clothes!" Doug spread open the clear vinyl shower curtain on Mom's clawfoot bathtub so they could get a look at Dad in his birthday suit, with only a handkerchief strategically placed on his front side.

Once the laughter died down, Doug began again, except now we reversed roles.

"Laying in my bathtub, drinking my vino,"

"Laney, bring up another bottle of pinot!" I yelled like Mom would have had she been upstairs, while I was downstairs.

"Looking through my design magazines,"

"Fabulous! Fabulous! I have to try this at my next party!" I had practiced Mom's intonation for this line, and I think I hit it when Mom died laughing at my impression of her.

"Along came Henry, the Chief,"

"And he was laughing! *Hahahahaha!*"

"I said, 'Henry, what happened?'"

"I lost my underwear." This time I did an impression of my father.

"...for the pièce de résistance..." Doug said right before flipping over the shower curtain and showing everyone my father's *backside*—in the buff!

Everyone was bent over, howling with laughter. Mom declared she would never use her favorite bathtub again, Dad got a Sharpie and autographed the shower curtain, and Uncle David declared us the winner even before we finished seeing all the mothers' gifts.

Doug and I had done it! We had made our mother laugh, father proud, and ourselves $2100 / 2 richer. Giving each other a high-five wasn't enough, so we hugged one another, too.

"That was an ingenious idea, Little Girl." Donovan didn't whisper in my ear this time.

"Why, thank you, Mr. Taylor." I answered with equal enthusiasm.

"Is someone calling me?" In front of me stood Donovan, thirty-five years older. This gentleman cut a handsome grandfather figure, with a little less hair, a little more belly, but a killer smile nonetheless.

"No, Dad." Donovan lamented to his father about me calling him by his last name, rather than his given name.

Next thing I knew, a highly energetic and striking woman took over our conversation. This lady was none other than Jamie Lynn Taylor, Donovan's mother. Of all my aunts and my mom's friends, I always thought Mrs. Taylor was the most beautiful lady. As I looked at her today, she reminded me of an older Kate Beauvais. Mrs. Taylor had a regal, old-world classy and elegant look...until she talked!

"He's my stud, aren't you, Scottie?" Jamie Lynn was describing her husband.

"Mom, please don't start." Donovan sounded like a cute teenage boy embarrassed by his mother.

"Don't start what, Donny? I was just agreeing with this gorgeous young lady. Which Reid are you?"

I didn't register that Jamie Lynn was talking to me. I assumed she was asking Jane since she called out a 'gorgeous young lady.' It was only when Donovan whispered, "Are you ignoring my mother or have you forgotten your name?" that I understood what was happening.

I quickly answered, "I'm Laney, daughter of Henry and Barbara."

"My Gawwwwd!" Oh! My! God! was right. Once her New York, Italian accent started, I had to step back, lest she knock me down with one of her hand gestures while talking. Her decibel was along the same range as Ellie's. "Last time I saw you, you were in pigtails." Great. I'd never lose that pigtail-and-braces images. "When did you grow up to this?"

"Shit." Donovan whispered. "Now you got her all excited. Soon she'll go into one of her monologues."

"Not my fault. The way I see it, it was you who got her excited." I whispered back.

"What happened to working on not being litigious?"

"Made like a parking meter and expired." I got another "kick" in the ass from the side of his Louis Vuitton loafers.

"What kind of man wears white suede Louis Vuitton loafers? It's not Memorial Day yet. You can't wear white, already." We were still whispering while Jamie Lynn was reacquainting herself with all my cousins.

"First of all, it's not white. It's more of a taupe, so unless you're color blind, you can see that I'm not committing any fashion faux pas. And secondly, I'm the same kind of man who knows that *you're* wearing a pair of suede Louis Vuitton ankle boots. I think ours *soles* match perfectly today." He laughed at his own not-so-*pun*ny joke.

While we were both laughing at our inside joke, Jamie Lynn pushed me aside and started telling Donovan about wanting grandbabies, and his father Scott had a word or two to say about Kate, and how she was too old to have babies. I stepped aside and tried to walk away until the real Mr. Taylor asked me, "Laney, you married?"

"No, Sir."

"What do you think about my son? Isn't he handsome?"

"I think there's no one more handsome in this world, Mr. Taylor," was NOT what I said. What came out of my mouth instead was, "I guess he's all right." I said this as a joke but Donovan, his mom and his dad all had a conniption, or better stated in Italian, an *attaco di cuore.*

"My son is gorgeous!" Jamie Lynn defended her son.

Um...you're preaching to the choir...

"I was told I was even better looking than Henry Cavill." Donovan jumped on his own bandwagon. "You know, the new Superman?"

I'd be faster than a speeding bullet, more powerful than a locomotive, and able to leap all kinds of tall buildings in a single bound, to become your Lois Lane.

Since I'd put my foot in my mouth already, I decided to poke fun at Donovan Taylor as much as I could. "Mr. Taylor, I think you look like a mousy Harry Styles."

"A mousy Harry Styles? Who, me or my father?"

Donovan Taylor was UPSET. "This is *solely* about you!" I used his pun back at him.

"So if my son's not good looking enough for you, then who is?" Scott Taylor, who had that same rascally smile, cornered me.

I returned Scott Taylor's impish smile and answered, "Donovan Taylor is plenty good looking, but I prefer a bit more of a manly look."

It was here that Mrs. Taylor fanned her face with both her hands so she wouldn't faint, Jake choked on his own saliva because he was laughing so hard, and Donovan Taylor roared, "Explain, Delaney Reid!"

I shrugged my shoulder with a devil-may-care attitude and answered, "I like the weathered look." I decided to describe to Donovan my ideal fictional man. Little did he know that he was my absolute ideal man—in the fiction and the non-fiction world. "You know...the Harley Davidson, beautiful tattoo, five o'clock shadow, mussed-up hair, look? You, Mr. Taylor, look a little too cleaned up. You're the James Bond when he's at the casino. I prefer the James Bond when he's firing his Walther PPK, all cut up, with dirt on his face."

With the sweetest look I'd seen on his face, Donovan almost whispered, "You truly are full of surprises. No Prince Charming from Cinderella?"

"Prince Charming from Cinderella with a few tats, riding a Harley," I half-whispered back.

Mr. Scott Taylor gave me a different kind of smile this time—a tender, affectionate, and knowing-kind of smile. I, in turn, gave him a fond grin.

"This is the girl for you, Donny my boy! You need to marry this girl so she can help get rid of that metrosexual side of you..."

I briefly listened to what Scott Taylor was telling his son, but tuned him out to talk to Max. I didn't need to get my hopes up any higher than they already were. It hurt too much every time I fell in notches.

"Babs!" I heard Jamie Lynn call out to Mom. "Whatcha gonna do with all the money your kids earned you?"

"Jamie!" I didn't realize these two ladies were that close. "You look phenomenal. How'd you lose so much weight?"

"Pole dancing."

Talk about Oh. My. Gawwwwd! I couldn't believe what I'd just heard, and neither could Donovan. He started choking on his drink and spit up half of it on my dress. Jake and I sprung to action, and while I pounded on his back, Jake got ready to give him the Heimlich maneuver. Mrs. Taylor paused her conversation till Donovan was breathing normally, then continued.

"I got a pole in my bedroom and started getting private lessons. My Scottie loves it!"

"Maaa!" Donovan half-choked, half-begged. He still couldn't talk properly. Mumbling something to his mother, he pushed me along, and we walked to the opposite side of the backyard.

"You all right?" I rubbed his back.

Even now, his cough hadn't abated. "Damn! How do I get rid of this image of my 60+ year-old mother pole dancing? I'll never enjoy another pole dancing girl, ever again."

"Then I guess your mother's plan of pulling you out of those skanky *gentleman's* clubs, worked."

"You think I visit those types of places?" His voice went up a few octaves.

"Where else would you see a girl pole dancing if not at one of *those* places?"

"Lots of girls have poles in their bed..."

This was the last thing I needed to hear from the man whom I believed was my ideal. Waving both hands and walking away, now it was me who couldn't get rid of this image of Donovan Taylor with another woman.

"Wait," he pulled me back to him. "Sorry. TMI," he let out an apologetic laugh.

"It seems as though that magic hour between you and me has passed. I think we'd best be going our separate ways."

"What the hell are you talking about? You talk in riddles all the time, Delaney Reid. Is this some form of generation gap between us?"

I waved both my hands, again and said good-bye for the day, lest he hurt me again.

May 11, 2013
Mother's Day Continued

*G*randfather surprised all the mothers in our family, and sent all seven of them on a day of rest and relaxation. Soon after the unveiling of our gag gifts and lunch, a stretch limo came to pick up all seven mothers. They were whisked off to a secret get-away where they'd be wined, dined, and pampered. Only Jake had a difficult time letting his wife go. But once the good-byes were done, all the men and cousins disbanded quietly and quickly.

"I can stay and help you with the kids, Jake."

"Roland pulled a fast one on all of us. I didn't expect Emi to be gone tonight. Will you help? Can you help? Don't you have a lot of work to do?"

"I can help. I'll bring my laptop and work over here, and help you where I can."

"Hey, Donovan." Jake yelled over to the godfather of his children. "I'm going to need your help as well."

"Are we having problems parting with your other half?" Donovan teased.

"Hey, let's go up to your hut."

"With your kids?"

"Yeah. We can take the minivan up. The kids will love the beach and it'll kill the rest of the day."

"Like I don't know your scheming and desperate mind. You just want to be near your wife. You're looking for any way to not sleep alone."

Jake smiled a devious smile. "Have we been friends that long? Give me a few minutes and I'll get the kids' bags together. I trust you can entertain them till then?"

Donovan had that impish look again. "I don't think I agreed to go anywhere."

"Don't be an asshole." Jake grumbled and went upstairs to pack.

"You want to go play in the water with Uncle Donovan?" he asked both kids. Ellie jumped into his arms and James followed his sister. "I guess it's a done deal. Go get a bathing suit on, Godmother Delaney."

"I don't know if I have time to go frolicking on the beach. I really have a lot of work to do."

"Oh, and I don't have a lot of work to do? You heard your cousin. Once he gets his mind on something, especially where his wife is concerned, you know you can't change his mind."

That was true. Shit. When would I do all the backlogged work? Left without a choice, I put on a bathing suit and packed a bag with a change of clothes.

The kids both slept on the way up to Donovan's beach house, Jake and Donovan chatted up in the front, and I got some work done in the third row. Once at the beach, there was no work that was going to get done. Both kids loved the water and the sand. They quickly learned not to put any sand in their mouths, and they found the texture of sand—wet or dry—fascinating. It took all three of us to do what Emily did by herself on a daily basis.

"These buggers are a lot of work, aren't they?" Donovan was talking to me, but keeping a sharp eye on both kids who chose to sit on the wet sand and splash the water whenever the low tide came in.

"They are, but they're so sweet. Look at how much they're enjoying themselves, and look at how well they play together. I hope I'll end up with two sets of twins when I decide to have kids."

"Two sets of twins?" Donovan sounded shocked. "Why the hell would you want that kind of torture?"

His face of horror was cute. "I want a set of twin girls, then a set of twin boys. They can be each other's best friends and never need to rely on anyone else."

"Shit. You are a glutton for punishment. Your knight in shining armor definitely needs to come with his own castle and a chest full of gold if you want four kids." He shook his head at me.

"Not necessary, Mr. Taylor. We could live in a little hut like your beach house, and as long as we have each other, we'll be all right. Kids don't need to grow up in luxury, and though I enjoy the perks of money, I don't need it. I just need...love..."

Damn! I sounded like a sentimental fool again. I always hated showing Donovan my idealistic dreamer side. In his world of glamour and power, I came off sounding like a damn fool.

Afraid to look up to a disapproving face, I kept building mounds of sand so the kids could knock them over.

"You truly are an enigma, Delaney Reid. I've never met anyone who wants her fairytale prince, but is willing to live the life of a pauper, as long as she has her true love."

"Hey," Jake rushed back to us after getting his phone call.

"Hey, I think I've got to go check on Emi. I just spoke with her and she says she's not feeling well."

"You're so full of shit, Jake. You planned this whole thing, didn't you? Dump the kids on their unsuspecting godparents and go off and rendezvous with the wife?"

Jake only grinned. "I swear I didn't. Shit, you think Emi would lie and say she didn't feel well so we could meet?"

"It's not your wife I'm accusing." Donovan gave into my cousin's weak plea. "Just go. I'm thankful you had the foresight to bring Delaney."

"We'll take care of the kids, Jake. I hope Emily feels better, soon." I added my two cents to this conversation.

As soon as we gave our blessings, Jake kissed the babies and he was off. The kids were still so completely entranced with the concept of sand that they barely registered their father gone.

"I guess I owe you $50," I lamented. "I totally thought I'd win this bet." Right before we left, Donovan and I had made a bet to see how long it would take Jake to go searching for his wife. I thought Jake would want to make a pit stop at their spa right before we went home. Donovan believed Jake would leave us within an hour of our arrival at the beach. Forty-five minutes into our "fun," Jake was off to see his wife.

Fearing that the kids would get sunburned, we "hosed" them down the best we could and walked to the nearby restaurant to have some dinner. The kids feasted on soup, crab and bread. Between the dirt, the sand, and a messy dinner, I needed a bath as much as the kids did.

"How the hell do we clean up these two?"

"I don't know. I've been trying to come up with an answer, but can't think of anything. They're also dog-tired. Look at their eyes."

"That bastard of a cousin of yours is probably in bed with his wife while I'm here putting his kids to bed."

Most likely, that was a perfect assessment of the situation here. We got back to the house and I opted to jump in the tub in my bathing suit with James, while Donovan entertained Ellie. Washing him wasn't as difficult as I'd imagined since he was wiped-out. As soon as I was done, I got a new tub filed with clean water and did the same for Ellie. Donovan had no idea what to do with a naked child, so when I got out of the tub and put a gigantic robe on the both of us, I found him rocking a sleeping James.

The sight of Donovan rocking a baby and humming a tune struck me. If ever there was a doubt I loved this man, I doubted no more. A vision of him rocking his own baby hit me so hard, I was left speechless and heartbroken—because I knew this imaginary baby wouldn't be our baby. How would I bear to see this man at family functions watching him with his wife and kids, laughing and loving one another? How would I stand it if in addition to hearing their joys fill the air, I was still alone, searching for my prince? I wished I didn't know this man. I wished I didn't like this man. And more than anything one earth, I wished I didn't love this man.

"I think James is asleep, but I didn't put his pajamas and diaper on him. What do I do?"

Donovan's question brought me to the present. "I'll try and get him dressed if you'll do the same for Ellie and put her to sleep."

"All right," he whispered and we swapped kids.

Very soon, we had both kids sleeping in the second bedroom with every pillow and cushion laid around the bed just in case these critters fell.

"Shit! I am wiped! How the hell does any woman do this on a daily basis?"

"I'm tired, too. But, they're down. You want to make another bet on whether or not Jake's coming back tonight?" I grinned.

"Trust me when I say, he's not coming back. You have a change of clothes?"

I nodded yes. "I need to call Mom and tell her where I am."

"While you do that, I'm going to call my ex-best friend," Donovan chuckled.

I took a quick shower in Donovan's bathroom and got ready for the night. Since I wasn't planning to spend the night outside of my own bed, Donovan lent me some clothes as substitute pjs.

"You want to take my bed while I take the couch?"

"No Jake?"

"Asshole tells me Emily had indigestion, and she fell asleep in his arms. Now he can't bear to wake her up. So he'll come pick us up early in the morning, to take us home so we can get to work and school."

"That's fine. I have no more formal classes. I just need to meet a study group."

"Delaney, I have a mound of work to do. Why don't you sleep on my bed?"

"I have tons of work, too. I probably won't sleep much tonight."

We both got to work and didn't communicate for hours. Every so often, I looked up at him when I thought he wasn't paying attention, and wondered if this was what he did with his girlfriends in the past. Did he take care of them? Did he promise them the world? How much did he love them?

"What's your question?" Donovan caught me staring at him, and asked. I shook my head no. I didn't want to tell him. "I'll go pick up some coffee for us if you ask the question."

"How do you know I have a question for you?"

"It's written all over your face. Speak, Delaney Reid. What's on your mind?"

With more hesitation than Donovan could withstand, I asked, "How come you haven't married, yet?"

Now he was the one who hesitated in giving me an answer. "Well..."

"I didn't mean to pry." I gave him a way out. "I'll go get coffee. Why don't you stay and watch the kids?" I got up to grab my wallet.

"I'll go." Donovan reached out for my arm but ended up with my hand. Using me as leverage, he held my hand and pulled himself off the ground. "I'll grab our drinks and I'll tell you why I'm not married, in exchange for info on your relationship status."

"There's no info to give."

"That's exactly the info I'm interested in." He gave my hand a firm squeeze and added, "I want to know why there's never been a man in your life."

His interested glint gave me shivers. While Donovan was out getting our caffeinated beverages, my stomach did a gymnastic floor routine. What would I tell him? Why did he care to know? Why the hell did I pry into his life?

"Your coffee will get cold if you don't drink it very soon," a delicious whisper breathed into my ear.

"How long have I been asleep?"

In his still hovering state, he put one arm around my back, one hand against the top of the sofa, and pulled me up while seating himself right next to me.

"Here." He picked up my cup from the nearby table and I took a big sip.

"I thought about carrying you inside, but you said you have work to do, so it seemed prudent to wake you up."

"Thanks. I do need to get up. I have work I *have to* finish tonight."

"Is that your way of getting out of our unfinished discussion?"

"Ever since I was a little girl, I've had this illusion of my ideal man, and I've yet to actualize this ideal man—simple as that." I confessed and decided to lay this conversation to rest.

"How the hell are you going to get married if you're looking for an ideal man?" Donovan's bug-eye was cute. I wanted to put my hand on his face and lightly kiss his lips.

"I'm searching for *my* ideal man, not *the* ideal man."

"Isn't that one in the same?" I shook my head no. "So what does *your* ideal man look like?"

You...

"I want..." this was where I went into my dreamer mode. "I want a best friend, a lover, a protector...someone who is strong, but not dominating, kind, but not weak, and loving, but not overbearing. Is that asking too much?"

Donovan didn't respond for a very long time—he eventually never responded. Feeling stupid again, I got back to my work and brushed off his brush-off.

"Rise and shine!" Jake called out as he and Emily walked in with coffee, bagels and juice. "You both slept on the sofa?"

I woke up to find myself curled into a fetal position in the armchair, and Donovan "sprawled" out on the tiny couch.

"What time is it and how'd you get in here?" Donovan asked.

"5:00a.m., you're door was unlocked, and it's time to get back to reality."

"Yeah," Donovan snorted. "Delaney and I never left reality since you saddled us with the kids."

"I'm so sorry!" Emily answered the both of us. "I told you to come back and pick everyone up. You should have gone home last night."

"And miss the chance of having you sleep in my arms?" Jake smiled and kissed his wife's lips. "These two were earning their titles as godparents last night."

"Laney, you look so tired. You'll be fine at school today?"

I did feel like crap, but what could I say to a heavily pregnant woman?

"I'll be fine. I just have study sessions. It's Mr. Taylor you should worry about."

"He's a big boy. He'll be fine." Jake shrugged off the situation and pulled Emily toward the kids' room.

"What did you do to these two? They're wiped out." Emily was amazed as she and Jake transferred two sleeping kids from the bed to their car seats. "I've never been able to transfer these two without waking them up, ever."

Once the kids were situated, Donovan and I sat in the third row and I put my head back and tried to sleep more. Last night, Donovan never answered my question as to why he wasn't married, and he never responded to my comment on what I wanted in a man.

Placing his palm over the top of my hand, he squeezed it and asked, "You going to be all right today?" I opened my eyes to find his beautiful face looking only at me. I would miss this face...this voice...this attention.

"I'm ok. What about you? Did you get your work done?"

"I finished it up after you fell asleep. You want me to drive you to school this morning?"

His beautiful eyes gazed sweetly into mine. What I would do to experience his love for a day.

I shook my head no, and brazenly traced his five o'clock shadow with my index finger. With a desperation I'd not known before, I wished to lean into this man and place my lips over his. But of course, common sense won out, and I stopped my unreturned desires and action. "I have only a half day today."

"Stop by my office after you're done?" He whispered and carefully followed my finger that just left his face. "I'll take you to lunch."

I smiled and shook my head no again. "I don't want to bother you. I'll see you next time."

With almost a pleading he said, "Stop by when you're done. I'll be expecting you."

I didn't answer because the more time I spent with this man, the deeper I fell in love, the harder it was to leave, the more desperate I became to see my love returned. Only I could exercise the self-preservation of my heart.

As the study session ended, I naturally found myself having a mental war on whether or not to visit Donovan. I told myself no, but my heart kept asking why I couldn't stop by, especially when I knew he was waiting for me. During a moment of weakness, I picked up a pastrami and mustard sandwich—his favorite lunch—and walked up to his firm.

I regretted my actions the second I stepped onto the twenty-ninth floor.

"Hello. Can I help you?"

"Hi." I addressed Donovan's assistant. "I'm here to see Donovan Taylor."

"I believe he's having lunch with Jane Reid. Did you want to wait or shall I lead you to them?"

"No..." I trailed feeling utterly foolish again. "Never mind, thank you." I quickly retraced my steps and walked up to Grandfather's office, instead.

"Laney!" He gave me a brilliant smile and a warm hug. "What brings you by?"

"Have you eaten, yet? I have a sandwich here if you'd like to eat with me."

"And you brought this sandwich for me?" He questioned with much doubt.

I gave Grandfather an apologetic smile. "Well...I thought I'd surprise a certain someone who asked me to stop by with the promise of lunch, but I guess I was the one surprised."

"And where is this certain someone?"

"Having lunch with Jane." My shoulders slumped, defeated.

Grandfather stepped closer and hugged me, but made no mention of my pathetic status. He was kind to let me sulk without any judgment or unsolicited advice.

"My darling granddaughter. As much as I'd love to have a meal with you, I'm afraid I have to step into a meeting."

Now Grandfather was the one giving me an apologetic smile. "Your gram and I would like to have a meal with you before you leave—perhaps in a few days?"

"Sure." I got up without hesitation. "Have you had lunch?"

"I haven't. I was going to send out for something."

"Why don't you take the sandwiches, Grandfather? I'll eat when I get home."

"You sure?"

"I'm positive. I'll see you later?"

"Without a doubt." Grandfather walked me to the door and gave me another loving hug and kiss on my forehead.

"I know this certain someone will regret having missed a meal with you, Laney."

"I doubt it, Grandfather...but it's not the end of the world."

I never saw this certain someone who was full of promises this morning.

I knew it was unwise to follow my heart.

May 16, 2013
Diamond In The Rough

*J*ane started a new Reid tradition of playing softball—Reids vs. The Others. It was a great idea to get all the family members involved, and since I loved softball, everything would have been perfect, had I not already had plans.

"Bye, guys. See you on Monday. It's almost over." I sighed in relief.

"See ya," my classmate said as she walked me to my car.

I turned on my phone to a horrific number of messages in my inbox. Reading through, I was bummed I'd miss a family event, but I had this golf weekend planned for a while and I felt bad flaking.

I replied all to the baseball game recipients.

To: Jane Reid, et al
From: Delaney Reid
Subject: I won't be in town this weekend
Sorry, but I can't play. Have a great time.

As soon as I sent this off, I got a reply from Donovan asking for all the particulars. I wasn't in the mood to answer him after he blew me off the other day, so I sent back a snarky reply and drove home. Once home, I got an email telling me to head straight to Jake's.

The kitchen was filled with a mass of people.

"Hey, Laney." Jake greeted me with a side-hug.

"Hi Jake. Babies sleeping?"

"Is it past six-thirty?"

"Thought I'd ask."

I walked in a bit and was happy to see Bee. I never got a chance to thank her in person for all the clothes and was headed right for her when my troubles began.

Josh started the whole debacle. "Jane has a cool double date planned for us, although it's turned into the whole world joining our date." I didn't know how to respond to this. Last thing I wanted to do was go out with Josh. He was a great guy and I enjoyed our friendship, but my plane ticket was purchased, my mind was made-up. I didn't need to lead anyone on. After being in love with Donovan Taylor for so long, I hated the idea of anyone liking me when I couldn't return the sentiment.

"How was your date?" my idiotic brother asked with a stupid grin on his face. He knew he was about to get me into trouble.

Then, of course, Mr. Donovan Taylor joined in the conversation and ruined my entire night! "Why the hell do you date so much?" Did this gigolo actually have the nerve to ask me this question? "I don't get why so many guys ask you out." What the hell did he care if guys asked me out? Just because he wasn't interested in me didn't make the entire male population adverse to me as a woman.

I told off all three guys at once. "First of all, it wasn't a date. A group of us stayed to finish our project, then went out for a bite to eat. Secondly, I don't go out with everyone. And finally," I needed to get this off my chest, so I could go home, put the blanket over my head and hide. Two minutes was all it took to ruin this day. "Maybe I date so I can one day have a meaningful relationship rather than just a meeting of the bodies. And what the hell do you care why guys ask me out? If you're that curious, why don't you do a Q&A with Josh and see how many times I've gone out with him."

That did it. Josh and Donovan stammered for words, while the members in this kitchen laughed. I heard Donovan's sister, Becky, comment to Bee, "Wow! I've never seen any girl tell my brother off the way Laney just told him off."

"Isn't she great?" Bee responded to Becky while giving me two thumbs up. I had to leave quickly before I lost it and started laughing. Knowing the little I did of Bee, she'd probably take a crack at her nephew and make me laugh.

Why was I so childish where Donovan Taylor was concerned? Why couldn't I have just ignored the three guys and walked away? Now, I felt so stupid for having lashed out at everyone. I changed out of Bee's beautiful dress, which had soon become my favorite, and put on my rattiest sweats. I didn't want to bother with anyone. I just wanted to be comfortable and finish my schoolwork.

"Delaney?" I heard that whisper. Only one person in the world called me by my given name. And this was the one person I didn't want to see at this moment. So what did I do? I pretended not to hear him. That's right. I acted like a ten-year-old, and ignored him.

Of course, he knew what I was up to and spun my wheeled-chair around till I was so dizzy, I had to beg him to stop. Then, the jerk stopped my chair abruptly and I practically fell out of it. I would've fallen out had it not been for Donovan grabbing on to both sides of the chair when he halted it.

"So, now you'll notice me?" he said with an evil laugh.

"I may throw up on you first, if you don't get out of my way." That did the trick. He let me go and I contemplated leaving the room and locking myself in the bathroom. I didn't want to deal with the conversation that would follow.

Donovan caught on to my plan. "Oh, no you don't. We're going to have a little chat." He grabbed me by the waist and had me sit next to him. "First of all, why can't you play this weekend?"

"Seriously? You came here to ask why I can't play baseball with you?" Damn this man! I thought he might be here to apologize, but he was here to push his cause.

"I need you to play. It'll be just like our league. I'll catch, you pitch."

"You know I'm a Reid and you're The Other?"

"So? I'll figure something out so you and I can play together. Why can't you be there?"

"Maybe I don't want to play with you?"

"Why the hell can't you play this weekend?" He ground out every word. His abrasiveness was starting to bug...just a little. Truly, nothing about this man irked me, except for the fact that he didn't love me. It wouldn't surprise me if one morning I woke up to find a capital L stamped to my forehead—L for LOSER.

"I'm going to Scottsdale. Nolan got a room for me and a friend to play a round of golf and enjoy the spa facilities." I almost stuck my tongue out at him.

Donovan gave me the scary big brother scowl. "Nolan going to be there?"

"Um, yeah. That's his job."

"You like this guy?"

"No. We're just friends."

"Does he know you're just friends?"

"Yes. I made it clear to him I wasn't interested in him in that way. He understands and...why the hell am I explaining all this to you? When did my father give up his paternal rights to you?"

"I see the Reid spirit is coming out. All right. You said he got a weekend for you and a friend?"

Where was he going with this? "Yeah..."

He stepped outside for a brief moment, and walked in with my dad. "Chief. Delaney says she's going away for the weekend with that guy she met in Hawaii." That rat made me sound like a slut!

"I did not!"

"You did!" He spoke over me. "But she also said she could take a friend with her, so if it's all right with you, Chief, I'll be that friend and go on this weekend golf 'outing' with the two lovebirds."

I was so pissed he put me in this position. Now, I was determined to go. "Daddy! You cannot allow..."

My father cut me off, and spoke over me as well. "Thanks, Donovan. I'm happy to have you go with my daughter so you can watch over her. If she'd prefer to be with a boy, rather than her family this weekend, at least I'll sleep easy knowing you'll be there."

I wanted to scream! "Why?" was all I could ask. "Why are you doing this?"

"We only want what's best for you." My father and Donovan were in collusion.

I knew why my father was going through the trouble of joining forces with this rat. He and Mom were having a tough time accepting that I'd be leaving in a couple of weeks. I understood, and I was actually going to see if my parents wanted to go with me this weekend. Obviously, my dad would prefer to stay here and play baseball with the family. I didn't give either one of them an answer, though the decision was pretty much made for me at this point.

I texted Nolan while Dad and Donovan were having a meeting of the minds in the corner of my room, and I went back to ignoring Donovan Taylor.

"I'm going to spin your chair again if you don't look at me," he warned.

"I think I'll go back downstairs and leave you two to work out the particulars," Dad mumbled, not able to look at me.

"I just want it noted that I don't like you undermining and underestimating me."

"And how did I do either one?"

"That was a sneaky move bringing my dad into this argument. What I choose to do with my time is no concern of yours, Mr. Taylor."

Donovan smiled brilliantly. "I know! Wasn't that a great move on my part?" He now had the gall to laugh at me.

"Also," I raised my voice to talk over the chuckle. "Don't ever put into question my virtue. That pisses me off!"

Now I got his attention. Horrified, he stammered, "How the fuck did your virtue get into this conversation? When the hell did I ever question that?"

"You had the nerve to tell my dad I was going away with a guy for the weekend—my dad of all people!" I was so upset, now my hands were going in all directions with crazy gestures to get my point across. "And earlier, you told a room full of people that I dated all the time, and you had no idea why anyone would want to date me!" Shit! Now I felt the tears coming. I willed myself to cry on the inside, only. I didn't need to have to explain to this man why his every word affected me so much. "Am I that much of a pariah to you, where you can't understand why any guy would ask me out? I know I'm not glamorous like your girlfriend Kate, and my cousin Jane, but..." I had to stop. "Fine. You win. Let's go back to Jake's and let everyone know I'm playing." Before he could defend himself or give me the customary, *of course you're not a pariah*, answer, I headed for Jake's.

"You're back!" Josh was quick to come over with a hug to boot. I wasn't in the mood for him or anyone else. I dodged his hug and went straight to Bee to thank her for the clothes.

"You're a popular lady." I joined Bee and Donovan's sister, Becky, at the kitchen table.

"Not really, Bee. If I were popular, I'd have a nice man defending me from these men who only think about themselves. Speaking of nice guys, Nick?" I left that as an open-ended question.

"Don't ask. That's as open-ended as your question. I think all the nice guys are married." Bee lamented. "Guys don't get any better than Jake or Al, and they're both married."

Becky responded. "There are many more nice guys left in this world. You will both find your men. And speaking of nice guys, I like the way you handled my brother," she congratulated me without having any idea how manhandled I was just a few minutes ago.

"Your brother is *not* a nice guy. He can be an ass," I started saying when I heard my name called.

It was the ass himself making me a part of his team. If it wasn't bad enough that I couldn't go away this weekend with my parents, it only got worse as Donovan forced me to play with him. Though, we did make a good catcher / pitcher team.

Practice on Friday went long. Donovan made us play a scrimmage with five players each since Mr. Taylor and Mr. Davis decided to join our group. Mr. Taylor was a hoot. He was the funnier, more easy-going version of Donovan Taylor. And Mr. Davis, in his own quiet way, was quite funny as well.

"Laney Reid, you better not strike me out. I could be your future father-in-law and hold a grudge the rest of my life." Mr. Taylor warned with an aw-shucks smile. I could only wish that he would be my future father-in-law. Just because, I struck him out, and in three pitches. Mr. Taylor walked up to the mound, gave me a surprising kiss on the forehead, and walked away with a smile.

Mr. Davis gave me a slightly different version of the same riot act. "Laney Reid, you better not strike me out. I could be your future father-in-law, but I won't hold a grudge against you the rest of my life even if you do strike me out." Once again, just because, I struck him out, and in three pitches. He too came on the mound but decided to kiss me on both cheeks, instead.

"Enough with the damn kisses, old men, let's get some hits," Donovan yelled from behind his catcher's mask.

Josh was up next, and I struck him out as well, and he was about to walk up to the mound when Donovan stopped him. Finally, long after the sun went down, we all collapsed and told Donovan that we were exhausted. We needed sustenance.

"Your father's hilarious," I told Max, who sat next to me at dinner. "He's not what I imagined him to be."

"I don't know who has taken over my parents' bodies, but the both of them have changed lately. They have become the parents the three of us have always wanted in a mother and a father."

"This is great isn't it?"

Max scratched his head, and thought over his answer. "It is, if it'll continue this way. I don't want to get my hopes up, and I don't want my brothers to get their hopes up if my parents are going to revert back to their old ways."

"I hope everything works out well for your family. You and your brothers deserve it."

"Thanks, Laney." Max said with a kind smile. Jane was truly blessed to have such an amazing boyfriend. Max was such a sweet person, and madly in love with my cousin.

"Your arm sore?" Josh asked. "You pitched a lot today."

"It's a bit sore, but I'll be OK."

"You want another beer?" Max brought the pitcher our way.

Donovan stopped Max from pouring. "She needs to be alert tomorrow. No more drinking, Little Girl." That damn little girl moniker would stay with me for life. Just to piss him off, I poured myself more beer, and drank it all in one gigantic gulp. If he weren't staring at me, I would've run into the bathroom and thrown it all up. This wasn't a smart move on my part. Donovan got pissed, and he poured me another glass with a challenging stare. I took that glass, gulped that one down as well, and stared back.

"Laney, why don't you join us over here?" Bee said with a chuckle. "That was impressive," she whispered. Becky and Al laughed at me.

"Stupid is more like it. Now I'll be up all night going pee. And I don't even like beer."

Becky and Al laughed even harder. "I think your brother has finally met his match." Al said.

"But I think he's too stupid to understand this." Becky added.

Whatever. They had no clue Donovan Taylor's interest lay elsewhere.

"It was great hanging out with you today, but I think I'll go home." As soon as I said that, I realized I needed a ride home. "Shoot! Bee, can I ask you for a ride? My car is in the shop."

"I'll give you a ride," Josh quickly jumped into the conversation. "How about if I ask my brother for his bike and we can take a long ride back home?" Was it mean of me not to want to be on a bike with a man I wasn't in love with? Was it too much to ask that the man I loved would return this affection, rather than a man I didn't have feelings for showering me with affection?

"I'll take you if you'll stop by my house and model a few new outfits for me?" Bee was giving me my out.

God bless Bee! "I'd love to try on more of your clothes." Then I whispered, "Thanks, Bee. I owe you one."

Bee's loft was littered with clothes. She said she was in the middle of all new designs for next spring so there were not only patterns everywhere, but also beautiful fabrics thrown about all over the tables, chairs and floor. This time, there was an excess amount of lace everywhere. The fabrics were so exquisite; I went about touching all of them.

"What do you need me to try on? And by the way, I get loads of compliments on all your dresses. I never got to thank you for the dresses you sent me."

"No need to thank me. Thank Mr. Taylor."

"Why would I thank him?"

"Because he paid me retail for all those clothes."

I must have had a super surprised look on my face. "What? Are you in shock that I charged him retail, rather than wholesale? I tried to give it to him at wholesale, but he insisted on paying what was on the price tag."

"It's just...never mind, Bee. I'll thank Donovan next time I see him."

Bee had a sly smile on her face as she said, "So you can say his first name."

I laughed. "Yes, I know it and can pronounce it."

"Then what's the deal with you calling him Mr. Taylor?"

I had to think about that for a bit. "It's along the same line as him calling me 'little girl.'" She handed me a slip of an outfit she wanted me to try as I was trying to explain myself to her. "What's this?"

"I'm trying my hand at lingerie. This is a first attempt, so I'd love to see how it would look on someone with an amazing body."

"These are beautiful and so delicate."

"I handmade each piece. These are a labor of love."

"You want me to try on everything?"

"Would you mind? Can I take some photos of you wearing them? I won't take any face shots. I just need to know what it looks like on a real body, so I can make the appropriate tweaks."

I went behind her screen and first rolled up the ultra sheer thigh-high stockings. Then I realized that maybe the stockings were the last items I was supposed to put on. This whole outfit had a 60's feel with soft pink silk and creamy yellow lace all around the edges. The underwear was all pink, with a cute yellow bow in the front, and French yellow lace all around the sides. The bra was made of the same concept with French lace on the top outer part of the bra. The belt or suspender looked like an upside down tank cami cut in half with sweet French lace all around the edge. I stepped out as soon as I snapped the suspenders onto the thigh-highs.

"Do women really wear these kinds of beautiful lingerie?"

"Damn! My creation looks beeaauutiifuulll! I need you to model my entire line. Do a 360."

Bee was not wrong when she exaggerated the word, beautiful. That's exactly how I felt wearing such upscale lingerie.

"What the fuck are you wearing?" An angry man's voice boomed in the small loft.

"Ahhh!" I screamed and ran back into the screen wall.

"What are you doing wearing...that?"

"Chill out, Nephew. Your friend here is helping me."

"When did you start making lingerie? And why Delaney? She's too young to be modeling lingerie."

Bee laughed in sincerity. I laughed in mockery. "You mean you've never seen a twenty-two-year-old in lingerie?" She had him there with that question.

I answered for him. "No, he hasn't because when he was twenty-two, the woman in lingerie was thirty-two, and when the woman was twenty-two, he was twelve." Bee and I both cracked-up at my stupid logic.

"Very funny. Take that off, now!"

"I need pictures. You," I assumed she was pointing at Donovan, "go sit over there and watch TV while I finish here with my model."

I could hear him grudgingly walk over. How did I know he grudgingly walked over? I heard his boots stomp.

"Come on out."

Carefully, I stepped out and peeked over at Donovan. He was trying hard to stare out at the city lights. "Let's get this done, quickly. I feel self-conscious."

Bee started clicking away.

"What the hell are you going to do with those pictures?" Donovan asked, still looking away. "You're not going to use them in your ads, are you?" He sounded horrified.

"Relax, Mr. Taylor." That was Bee talking, not me. "It's for personal use only. My creation needs improvement and these pictures will help me figure out what I've done well, and what needs changing."

"It looks pretty damn near perfect." Donovan muttered the last few words, but I heard them and felt pretty damn near perfect, myself.

"Why are you here, Mr. Taylor?" This time, it was me asking.

"I'm here to take my star pitcher home. When are you going to be done?"

"I don't know. Plus, Bee said she'd take me home. You can get going. I'm sure you're tired after bossing us all around today."

Bee and another woman started laughing. Then, I heard a man's whistle, which made me run behind the screen again.

"Don't look!" I heard Donovan yell.

"Damn, bro'. I get it. No worries. I have your sister keeping me warm at night; I'm not here to steal your lady."

"What the hell are you two doing here?"

"Um...we're staying with Bee for another couple of days till we go back home." Becky reminded her brother. "Hey Bee. What's up with you using Laney as a model? You could have asked me. I'm feeling offended you didn't ask me."

"I don't want a prego body, and I need someone who can give me more than a B cup."

Becky stammered. "I am NOT a B cup. Why I'll be close to a DD in a few months when my milk comes in." Becky put both her hands on her breasts and cupped them together to make them look fuller.

"Beck, I need a real D cup, not a wannabe from a soon-to-be mother." Bee then turned to me. "We're not done. I have a few more you need to try on. There's the black one and the fire engine red one. I also need you to try on the leopard print one. That's my personal favorite."

"I don't think it's a good idea. Maybe tomorrow, when there isn't an audience."

Bee looked around and saw an uncomfortable Donovan and a curious Al and Becky. "How about after I get back from Paris, early June?"

"I won't be here, Bee. I'd love to help, but..."

"What do you mean? Where are you going?"

"I'm leaving for London soon, Bee."

"What for?"

"So she can waste away a year of her life doing nothing productive," was Donovan's answer to his family.

Donovan had no clue all that I'd accomplished in my four years in undergrad, and why I needed this break from school. His belittling hurt. Sure, I wasn't some mega-wealthy, semi-retired forty-year-old, but I had accomplished enough, where I thought I deserved a break. I hated that he could break my spirit so easily and readily.

"Bee, could you give me a lift home?" I went back into the screen to grab my jacket and purse.

"You're such an asshole," I heard Becky whisper.

"I'll take you home." Mr. Gruff Taylor appeared again before waltzing off to the garage.

Seriously not wanting a ride from Donovan, and not wanting to bother anyone else, I did a little research on my phone and figured out how to call a cab. Everyone in the loft protested and offered me a ride home once they figured out what I was doing, but I decided not to put anyone out, or to put anyone on Donovan's shit list for taking me home. He could sit in his car the entire night waiting for me to come down, for all I cared.

The cab arrived sooner than I'd expected. "I'll see you all, tomorrow?" I waved good-bye.

"Donovan's going to kick my ass if I let you get into that cab by yourself at this hour. I'm going with you." Al followed.

"Please...I'll be fine." I left before they could protest much more.

What a night...

Saturday morning was gorgeous, despite the crappy night of sleep I got. What a great day to play a ball game. The sun was shining, but it was just cool enough to play ball in the morning, and possibly swim in the afternoon. I'd have to take James in the pool today. I vowed to spend as much time with my little man before I left. Too few days were left to spend with him, and that made me sad. He would be the one, besides Mom and Dad, I'd miss the most.

"Good morning," I said to my father.

"Sleep well?"

"Not really, but I'm ready to play." I started our coffee.

"You going to go easy on your old man?"

"Why would I do that when I know what an athletic stud he is on the baseball diamond?"

Dad only laughed at my comment. "Your mom's at Bobby's getting the field ready."

"I figured." I took out a frying pan and asked, "You want some eggs?"

"Only if they're scrambled."

"Do you eat them any other way?"

"Who will make my scrambled eggs when you're gone, Baby?"

"How about you learn to make scrambled eggs till I get back? Then, I'll make them for you till I get my own place, or till I get married?"

"Must you leave? You can stay here. No one will get on your case about lounging around for a year."

I guess it was only natural everyone would believe I had no right to take a year off. I wasn't going to let that bother me. This year off was something I needed and wanted. Of course I didn't deserve it. Who deserved to travel for a year with no care in the world?

Mom had done her usual splendid job creating something out of nothing. She took a plot of land and turned it into a softball field. The bases were freshly spray-painted white, the chalk lines were dusted on, and the mound had a huge L spray painted in the middle, and in pink! My mother was so cute. I was really going to miss my parents, and the entire Reid family.

There was a meeting on the mound when I got to the field, and I was told by Jane that I'd have to pitch for both teams. In my ideal world, I'd like to have played second base or shortstop, but I'd do as I was told. As soon as Emily helped Jake into his catcher's gear, Jake came up to the mound to talk to me.

"Donovan tells me you took a cab home last night from Bee's. Everything all right?"

"Yeah. Everything's OK," I answered with a sigh.

"You want me to have a talk with him before you leave?"

I shook my head no.

"*You* want to talk to him before you leave?"

I shook my head even more so, no.

"You want me to tie him up so you can kick his ass, before you leave?"
That made me crack-up, badly.

"I think you may be pleasantly surprised with Donovan if you choose to reveal your feelings to him."

"I don't know Jake. I'm tired of being hurt. I want to make a clean break and find something new for myself."

"Let's get the game going before the sun goes down!" Mr. Taylor yelled at the both of us.

"Let's strike him out Laney and make him eat shit today," were Jake's last words before going back to his position as catcher.

The first inning went well for both teams. When I was on, I struck out several players at a time, but Donovan and Max hit triples off my fast pitch. I'd have to try to get my off-speed pitch back in play.

Once the inning was done, Donovan was my catcher, and he came up to talk to me on the mound. He probably did this more to retaliate against his buddy. I wasn't happy being forced to talk to him.

"You got home OK, last night?" I nodded yes. "I'm not even going to get into how pissed I was last night when I found out you left in a cab, by yourself, at that late hour. I didn't know whether to strangle you, or my moronic family for letting you go by yourself."

Donovan pissed me off too, but I kept my mouth shut and just made random shapes on the mound with my feet crossing back and forth.

"Do not ever scare me like that again, you got it?"

I looked him dead in the eye and saw that he had been worried for me. He did care, in his own bizarre way. I kind of nodded yes, but looked down at the mound and made my shapes again.

"I'm sorry, Delaney." Now the voice in which he said those words shook my determined *I will not let this man rattle my heart, I will not let this man rattle my heart,* stance. But it actually sounded like he really did care for me... which couldn't possibly be true. I'd be a fool to believe this with only two weeks left before my new life began. "I keep saying things I don't fully mean, when I'm with you. I don't know why I do this, but I do know I was an asshole, and I need to know that we're OK."

I gave him another brief nod, without looking at him.

"Hey," his tone was so gentle, stance be damned! My heart was going into a tizzy. "Can you look at me?" Briefly giving him what he wanted, he was satisfied enough to say, "I'll make this up to you. OK?"

Jake was always the wisest among the cousins. Somehow he sensed my fear, and broke up our conversation by complaining to Grandfather, our umpire, that Donovan was taking too long on the mound. The ump agreed and threatened to penalize Donovan if he didn't get in the catcher's box. That broke up our "happy" reunion.

The rest of the game went well till the very last play. The Reids were up, 10-9 and of course, my favorite man was up to bat. Jake called a meeting on the mound and basically told me to take out Donovan by scaring his chances at reproducing.

"No way, Jake!" I complained. "I can't control my pitches to that degree and I will NOT be responsible for his posterity." (Especially if I had any chance to be a part of this posterity!)

My dad was even worse, fully encouraging this kind of shenanigan.

I had no choice but to try since my entire family was counting on me. I *soooo* didn't want to do this. The first ball was just that—a ball. The next pitch was a perfect fast pitch that went way on the inside. Donovan had to do a serious concave curve of the body to help save his posterity. The third pitch had the exact same effect. I turned back around once my giggling was contained, only to find one Donovan Taylor, in my face.

"You going to nurse me back to health, if you hit me where I think you're aiming?" That was all he said. Shit! I was so rattled. What the hell was I thinking trying to take him out?

I couldn't do much with the next two pitches, but on the last pitch, with a full count, I got lucky and caught Donovan unaware in the batter's box. He stepped in, but wasn't ready to swing. Softball rules stated that I could pitch the ball to anyone who was in the batter's box, ready or not, unless he called a time-out. And so, that was what I did. I pitched a fastball, then struck him out. The jubilation from the outfield overflowed. The Others were disappointed, but not by much. We all had a wonderful time together.

"Did you even eat?" Bee asked, as she cannonballed into the pool splashing an already happy James and Ellie.

"Nope! I chose swimming with my little man here over eating with the mamas."

"Donovan apologize about last night?"

"Yeah. That was the long discussion on the mound. He started by telling me how pissed he was, and that he didn't know whether to strangle me or the Taylor family. He told me *all* that before apologizing."

Bee laughed while doing backstrokes near us. I took James by the arms and swung him around the pool. When I saw Ellie and Max swimming toward us, I put James on my back and we did breaststrokes over to meet them.

"You pitched well, today. Thanks for pitching for both teams."

"It was nothing. I had a good time doing it."

"When do you leave, Laney?"

"In two weeks."

"Seriously? You leave that soon? Why didn't I know this earlier?"

"Nobody but my parents, Jake and Emily know. And my parents are still in denial, even though the ticket has been purchased."

"Can I tell Josh?"

"I'd prefer you didn't." I brought James around to the front so he and Ellie could talk and play with one another for a bit. "I'm sorry, Max, but you know I don't have feelings for your brother other than friendship?"

"Yeah, I know. I wish you did. You'd make an awesome younger sister."

Why couldn't I love someone as genuine as Max? Why did I pick a man who was more a playboy than a boy scout?

"I wish you and Jane all the happiness in the world. You are as ideal as my cousin, Jake. I'd be honored to call you my big brother—but that doesn't seem to be in the cards for us. Can we just be cousins? That's about the same thing, isn't it?"

"It sure is," he answered with a smile, and swam off to meet Jane.

Talking to Max, and watching him and Jane love and laugh with one another brought on another bout of sadness. I'd miss them very much too.

"Whatcha staring at?"

"Hey, Nick. I'm just tired, I guess. Can I give James to you? I'd like to go lay down for a bit, before I come back here to watch the kids overnight."

"Bring my nephew over here." He took James and started on the SpongeBob imitation and James' beautiful face broke into a cackle. I loved watching him smile. Before leaving the pool, I stopped to give him one last kiss on the cheek, then I snuck out of Emily's backyard before getting accosted by anyone else.

There was so much to do before I left, I didn't have time for this nonsensical sadness. I wasn't going away for good and it was my choice to leave. Little by little, all the clutter was either thrown away or placed in its rightful location. Ever since I was young, I was your typical packrat. I'd accumulated so much stuff. It was time to purge and rid most of this junk.

"Can I come in?" That voice was in my room again.

I put on my best smile and answered, "Sure."

"What's with all this mess?"

"I'm purging, spring cleaning, getting rid of years of hoarding—take your pick..."

"Why'd you leave so soon?"

"I have a ton of things to do before I leave for London and there's still some school work left, too. I thought I'd make good use of the rest of today, before Jake whisks Emily off on her birthday surprise. Plus I'm tired. It's been a long morning."

Donovan came closer to me, and put his hand on my head and caressed it. I don't know what came over him but he pulled me into his body and held me. *Please don't do this to me now. I can't take you going hot and cold on me. It hurts too much, Donovan.*

"I need to drop by work, but I'll be there later to help you. Then you and I need to have a little talk, OK?"

With my head still stuck between his chest and neck, I could hear his heart beating fast, just like mine.

"All right." It didn't matter what this man wanted to talk to me about—I'd go anywhere, do just about anything, if I could spend a little more time with him.

May 19, 2013
Before Midnight

There was truly no more a romantic husband than Jake. He planned a beautiful weekend for him and his wife and asked me to help. What started as a night with the twins, ended in a date night with one Donovan Taylor. This weekend was truly a fairytale dream come true for me.

"We'll be home right after dinner. The kids are exhausted from today so they should go down even earlier," Emily kept talking while Jake stood behind her and kept repeating *no* to me, just in case I might have forgotten I was spending the night with the kids here, while their parents had a much needed night away.

"OK, Emily. Enjoy. Don't worry about the kids. There will be four of us. We should be able to watch two kids?"

Jake pulled her out of the house before Emily could give out any more instructions. "Max will be here with Laney so don't worry. Jane and Donovan can...I don't know what the hell they can do, but the babies are in good hands, so stop worrying."

"Bye!" The twins and I waved. It was shocking that they didn't cry with both parents gone. It may have had something to do with the new *One Fish, Two Fish, Red Fish, Blue Fish* video, Emily kept up her sleeve for an emergency like this. This book was definitely on James' most-read list, and Ellie liked it because her brother liked it.

I was able to heat up dinner and cook the pasta while the kids happily sat in their high chairs watching the monitor. Normally, I wouldn't have left the kids in front of a television monitor, but today was an exhausting day. To add to my long day, my mind kept running circles around what Donovan and I might talk about tonight. Would it be about us? Was he going to tell me to stop perving on him? Did he even know that I perved on him? Was he running away with Kate and living his happily ever after? It was anyone's guess what he needed to say to me after such a tender hug.

"Hello, big boy, beautiful girl!" Donovan was first to greet the kids, as they were finishing up their dinner. Jane, too, went over and kissed her niece and nephew. While both left for a while to change out of their work clothes, I got both kids into their bath chairs and once again, turned on the movie. I felt horrible for being such a lazy sitter today. No books, no engaging toys—a movie was all I could muster.

Ellie was first to be done, and I had her dressed in the cutest Hello Kitty bathrobe and slipper combo, and Jane adored her. James got no less attention from both Jane and Donovan, and lucky for me, they took the kids up and wanted to get them changed into their jammies. Hopefully, Donovan or Jane would read them a book to finish the night.

The kitchen was a mess, and as much as I didn't want to, I started sweeping up the floor. It was unreal how much spaghetti was on the floor. For every bite that went into their mouths, they must have dropped another three bites on the floor. In the middle of sweeping up the floor, I heard James crying, so I ran upstairs and was horrified to see him about to fall off the changing table. Only by God's grace did I get to James in time before he hit his head on the hard, wooden floor.

Both Donovan and Jane started yelling at one another, so I picked up the kids, calmed them down, and read them their most comforting book.

Even after having cried hysterically, they were both so tired from the softball game and swimming, they both conked out immediately. It didn't make me feel good to hear them still hiccup-crying in their sleep, but this afforded me some time to sit. We all needed the rest.

"I'm not the girl you want to marry if you need a mother for your kids." Jane was lamenting to Donovan as I stayed on the rocking chair with both kids, while they headed downstairs. "Go talk to Laney, instead."

"I think I prefer a woman to a little girl, when I decide I need to procreate," was his answer to my cousin.

A little girl—that's all I ever was, and all I'll ever be to him.

I couldn't leave the rocking chair. I'd tried to show him how grown up I was, how responsible I was, how much of a woman I was. Nothing about me impressed Donovan Taylor. My body was tired from the day, my head was filled with images of Donovan consoling Jane, and my heart was crying from the knowledge that any affection from this man was only that of an older brother. I needed to stop believing otherwise.

"Laney," I heard a gentle whisper. It was Max, rather than Donovan, helping me with the kids. Max took each kid, put him and her in their respective beds and helped me off the chair. I should have gone straight to bed myself, but since Max led me toward the kitchen, I followed and the four of us began reheating dinner.

Dazed, I watched the pasta boil when Josh made a visit. He was a welcome distraction as we started talking about both our pending trips. Josh gave me his tentative itinerary, and I told him some of the places I wanted to visit when I got to London. We were having an info exchange when Donovan made another crack at me being lazy and not wanting to live in the real world and get work experience. I thought about responding, but decided not to let it bother me. There weren't enough words for me if I was going to have it out with Donovan Taylor.

"Laney?" Max interrupted my thought. I'd been mostly a space cadet this evening since I'd come down from the kids' room. "Everyone's gone. I'd like to stay and hang out with you till you're ready to go to sleep. Do you mind?"

Where was I when everyone left?

"I don't mind, Max, but it's OK. You can go and hang out with Jane instead. The twins and I will be all right by ourselves. I've babysat them many times before."

"I know, but it would make me feel much better if I stayed with you little bit."

"Would you like some coffee and a slice of cake? I saw a coconut cake sitting in the fridge."

"That Em has such a sweet tooth this pregnancy." Max started the coffee himself while I took out the cake. "I think every time I come here she has a different cake in the fridge."

I agreed. "I think Jake's been feeding her habit by bringing home cake every chance he gets."

"Well, I know I've enjoyed this habit of hers."

When we got to the table, I hesitated wondering if I should ask him the question that's been on my mind.

"You look like you have something you want to ask me."

"How did you know?"

"You have a very expressive face, Laney. I don't think you could ever lie, because it will show up right on your face."

"That's not good." I worried.

"You afraid Donovan might catch on to your big secret?"

My face must have blanched because Max choked on his coffee trying to keep himself from laughing. *Damn!* This was seriously not good.

"You Reid girls all have a crush on him at some point in your lives?"

"Is it that obvious?" What a nightmare! If Max caught on this easily, who else knew?

Max tousled my hair. He would've made such a neat older brother. I could see why Emily had loved him so much, and why Jane was so crazy about him now.

"I don't think anyone else knows. I only noticed when Josh took a liking to you. I watched you a little bit more carefully, wondering where my brother was going wrong. And that's when I noticed the obvious answer. How long have you liked him?"

"May I ask you to keep this confidential, even from Jane? Would it make things difficult for you if I asked you to hold a secret from her?"

"Not at all, Laney. If you tell me something in confidence, it's just between you and me. It has nothing to do with Jane."

"I've had a crush on him since I was ten." I put my head down on the table and put my hands over my head because I was so embarrassed. "I'm so pathetic, huh?"

"Since you were ten?" Max was in shock. "Wow. That's half your life."

"Pathetic!"

"I think it's wonderful Laney. I think you two suit nicely."

"You do? You're probably the only one who thinks that way. *I* don't even think we suit. I'm too young and definitely not cosmopolitan enough."

"I think you're a beautiful young lady with a lot going for her. In my opinion, he's not good enough for you."

"That's sweet of you to say. But, no matter—I leave soon and all should be back to normal."

"What does that mean?"

"This is probably something you won't understand, but my heart is so bruised from years of 'loving' someone without being loved in return, I needed a clean break. I had that break when I didn't see Donovan for years, but since he's come back into my life, the pain's been inescapable. You must think I'm such a loser—running away. Initially, this trip to London started as a getaway from reality, but now, it's turned into a getaway from Donovan."

"I wish you wouldn't do that, but I can't say I don't understand what you're feeling. When Emily and I first broke up, I wished I had a place to go and not have any contact with her. The first time I saw her a year and a half after our break-up was almost as bad as the break-up itself."

"How did you do it? You were both so much in love. How did you let her go?"

"Em meant that much to me. I didn't see any other way but to allow her to find her happiness. And look who she found. She and Jake are perfect for one another."

"They are, and so are you and Jane. I know she isn't the easiest person to please, but Jane's one of the best people I know." I didn't know if I should reassure Max that Jane's harmless flirting with Donovan was nothing more than fun banter. I desperately wanted to give Max the same comfort he afforded me, but I thought I might be overstepping what's proper. "You are lucky to have Jane as your girlfriend, and she's more than lucky to be with you. Right after Jake, I think you are the best fish in the pond."

Deciding we'd had enough of this maudlin conversation, I gave Max a wide smile, and he smiled right back at me. I hoped Jane understood what a prize she had in this man.

"What are you still doing here?" Donovan questioned, mildly irritated.

"Taking care of someone who needed a little taking care of," Max said with a wink and a grin. "You want me to kick him out?" he whispered and hugged me good night. "Or you could try letting him know how you feel before you leave." I pulled away shocked at the suggestion. Max nodded his head in encouragement. "Try it. You may be surprised at the result."

"Don't you have a girlfriend to tend to?"

"I surely do!" Max kissed my head and patted me on the back as a farewell.

"What was that all about?"

"Nothing. If you're here for your bag, I left it by the kitchen door."

"What bag?"

I pointed to his overnight bag by the door and walked away. I was too worn out for good-byes with this man. I went up to the guest room, went under the blanket and turned on the television.

"What was that?"

"What was what?" I asked the man who wouldn't go away when I needed him to go away, and stay when I wanted him to stay. "What have I done wrong, this time?"

"You just left me back there."

"Mr. Taylor, I'm tired. Thanks to you, it's been a long day for me physically, mentally and..." Once again, diarrhea of the mouth. "Can I please be myself without being judged, compared or belittled? I can only take so much." Damn! Why couldn't I just shut up?

"I can understand the physical part; I am sorry about that. You are such a good athlete, it would've been unfair to your family to have someone else try and be their pitcher."

"Fair enough. Apology accepted. Good night." I turned off the TV and the light – thank God for universal remotes!

Donovan wouldn't be pushed away. He came and sat upon the bed, and on my side. "What did I do to you mentally?" I shut my eyes and kept quiet. "I'm not leaving, and we've got a lot to talk about."

"You can sit there all you want. I'm going to sleep." I opened one eye a few seconds later and he hadn't moved. "You and Jane..." I didn't want to throw my cousin under the bus so I stopped talking.

"Jane and I, what?"

Fine! If this is what he really wanted, I'd give him a piece of my mind. "I fed the kids, bathed the kids, caught a kid who was about to fall on his head, put crying kids to bed by myself, only to discover Jane upset with me for who knows what reason, and you belittling all my efforts by telling Jane that I was only a little girl and could be dismissed because of my age." Donovan stupidly tried to get a word in, to no success. "Then you and Jane have the nerve to accuse Josh and me of not wanting to work in the real world or have any responsibilities?" I was pissed at this point. "Do you know that Josh day trades his money and has made enough to buy a small home and finance this art trip?"

Donovan looked surprised and showed a little remorse for thinking so little of Josh.

"And do you know that I worked my ass off the last four years in school? I made the Dean's list every semester, and I've had a job since my junior year in high school. You may not think very highly of me, but I have many interests and goals that you have no idea about, Mr. Taylor. Yes, I'm going to enjoy myself next year, but dammit, I deserve it."

"I'm sorry if you thought I was belittling you, but I'm not afraid to tell you, everyone goes through four years of college and most people have a job during those years. That's nothing special. I guess I'm old school where education is concerned. Not too many people just drop everything to go travel for a year. Then, to come back and..." He stopped knowing he was about to dismiss film school as well.

"Let's just forget it. I don't need to justify anything I do to you. My parents are fine with my decision, and my grandparents think it's a fine decision as well. In your eyes, girls like me will always be frivolous and not good enough. You stick to what you believe is the correct path to *success.*"

"Delaney, you're now being unfair to me. Just because I said..."

My cell phone rang, *hallelujah*, and I was spared the lecture. "Hey Jake."

"The house is still standing and the babies are asleep?"

"Yes and yes. Both are well. How are you and Emily?"

"My wife ate well and now she's sleeping. She was upset when I told her we were spending the night here, but once she embraced the idea, she was grateful for the rest. We are both thankful to you for taking care of the kids."

"It's my pleasure, Jake."

"Laney, I keep hearing an interesting rumor at the hospital these days. Care to confirm or deny?"

Jake had finally figured out my secret. "I can confirm only that I've been allowed the privilege of figuring out what I want next year."

"So you got into med school and deferred it?"

"Yes."

"You are one phenomenal young lady." Making Jake this proud wiped away any anger from today. All was right again. "Do your parents know?"

"Not yet, but they will at graduation. Can you keep this info to yourself for a bit longer? It's been hard enough with my parents accepting my decision to move, I can't take any more coercion—and you know Dad's going to go nuts when he hears."

"All right. I'll keep my mouth sealed for just a bit longer."

"Thank you, Jake, and have a good night."

"Same to you, Laney."

Once again, I'd said too much in front of Donovan. Briefly, I wondered who I could call to get out of this mess! Deciding to go back to "sleep," I closed my eyes and waited for the questions to begin. There was no sound initially, then I heard a buzzing, a gargling, a rinsing, and I saw a light turn off. What the hell was going on?

The blanket lifted on the other side. Arghh! What the hell? "What do you think you are doing, Mr. Taylor?"

"It's going to be a long night of explanations after that phone call, so I decided to get ready for bed."

Abruptly sitting up, I saw Donovan in a low-hanging pajama bottom and a white nightshirt. And he was actually hopping into bed with me.

"This is not your bed," I stammered.

"It's not yours, either," he laughed. "I'm tired too so let me get in, let's talk, then let's sleep."

"We can't sleep in the same bed."

"Then you can move to another room. I called this room when I first got here. You rudely moved my stuff out of the way."

"Who said you could spend the night here?"

"Jake."

"But I thought you had left with Jane, earlier. You didn't even say good-bye when you left so I thought you were gone for the night."

He got himself comfortable and turned my way. "You were wrong. I let Jane know I was going home to pick up some clothes for tomorrow, and that I'd be back. If she never told you that, then blame her." I had nothing to say after that explanation. "So you want to start with your explanation, or do I need to start with my defense against your accusations?"

Always the lawyer! "Where do you want me to begin?" I figured since he was right next to me in bed, I had no choice but to give him what he wanted.

"First of all, what the hell are you wearing to bed? Is that considered pjs?"

That was a funny question. I was in really ugly, baggy pants, and an even baggier shirt that covered the baggy pants. Hey, it was comfortable and I wasn't exactly thinking of entertaining in bed. I was extremely grateful I hadn't taken off my bra, yet. That could've been a scary sight.

"I'm in my boyfriend sweats, and a boyfriend tee."

"Uh-huh...is your boyfriend a sumo-wrestler? That outfit is like four sizes too large for you." He was looking me up and down making me feel uncomfortable.

"I wasn't planning on having a party in this bed tonight, so excuse me!"

"Forget the clothes—start with the conversation with my buddy. What was that all about?"

"Can you promise to keep my secret? No one in my family knows yet except for Emily, and now Jake."

Donovan made a rolling of the hand gesture urging me to continue with the story. "I applied to two graduate school programs and got into both, and was given the opportunity to defer both."

"Film school and...?"

"Med school."

"Shit! Are you fucking with me?"

Now I was offended. "This is why I didn't want to tell you or anyone else. Why is it so hard to believe that I got into med school? Do I come off as that much of a dumb blonde? Is it so difficult to..."

"Shut up, Delaney and keep going with the confessions." Now that was just rude. I wasn't going to let anyone talk to me that way, no matter how much I was in love with him.

I got back into bed, turned myself around and faced the other way.

"Dammit all to hell," he muttered, "this is worse than getting Rachel to talk." He tried to pry my body around but I was a lot stronger than I looked. I didn't budge, much. "Turn around or I'm going to go over to your side and lay on top of you." I didn't turn, and he did as he threatened. He got out of bed and walked over to my side, but I quickly turned over to his side and moved. Donovan was just fast enough to catch me as I turned, and he forced me to face him. "I've never questioned your brain power. When you mentioned med school, it took me off guard because you never mentioned even taking a science class, much less excelling in them."

"Well, I double majored in English and chemistry. I enjoy both subjects, and I worked hard all four years getting my degree and fulfilling the requirements to apply to both schools."

"Shit-yeah, you did. You must have kicked-ass in undergrad."

I gave him a sly smile. "I did kick-ass. My GPA could probably kick your GPA's ass to the curb."

"Uh...I don't think so. Your cousin and I both graduated cum laude. Beat that, Little Girl."

"Well, I'm graduating with summa cum laude honors, Old Man. Did I beat that?"

"You're a fucking genius! Does Jake know this?"

"No. You're the only one. That's my Father's Day surprise for Dad. He's going to be so happy to hear my name called at graduation. I worked super hard to make Mom and Dad proud of me."

I sat back up in bed because it was too weird laying in bed together with Donovan.

"So that's why you're going off to London for a year? You need to cool your Mensa-sized brain?"

"That, among other reasons."

"And those reasons are...?"

Now this part, I couldn't tell him the truth. "I just want a break before going back to school, especially med school, if that's what I end up choosing."

"Well, I guess I owe you and Josh an apology. I thought..."

"Oh, I know what you thought. There are so many thoughts you have about me that are incorrect. I'm not that little girl anymore, I don't date every guy who crosses my path, and there is a purpose to my life. You just don't care to see it. But that's OK. I know I don't mean much more to you than..." Who knew what I meant to this man?

"Let's get a few things clear," he started what I hoped would be a long apology. "When I tell you I'll drive you home, I mean for you to finish what you are doing and get in my damn car. That does NOT mean you call a cab in the middle of the night and get in by yourself. You got that?"

"Is this like a rerun of Tom Hank's *A League of their Own*? Are you going to now tell me that there's no crying in baseball?"

That brought out a gruff laugh from Mr. Taylor. "Stop being a smartass," he said and lightly pushed my head with the palm of his hand. "Secondly," he cleared his throat and tried to contain the laughter, "I have never questioned your virtue, and when I talked to your dad, I only said what I said because both of us know you are above reproach. Your dad and I were having a little fun at your expense. It was a joke!"

"Well, I don't like those kinds of jokes. This is another area where I have to work really hard to keep people from getting wrong ideas about me." I shot back.

"Understood." He nodded. "Now my turn." He looked me dead in the eye and wouldn't let my eyes roam away. "You've said several times now in the last twenty-four hours that you think I'm belittling you. I'm not. I don't know why you would take it that way. Sometimes things are said in jest. Can't you take a joke?"

"Most of what you say is not done in jest. *'Why the hell do you date so much? I don't get why so many guys ask you out. No more drinking, Little Girl. So she can waste away a year of her life doing nothing productive.'*" I didn't mention that last statement he said to Jane where he preferred a woman like Jane to a little girl like me. That one was too painful.

"You have a photographic memory too? I don't think I said even half those things." The grin on his face admitted his guilt.

"Why are we even having this conversation? What do you care how I feel? Don't pretend to care." *It hurts too much when I know it's not true.*

Donovan rubbed his face with both hands in frustration, multiple times. "Can we start all over and just be friends? I'll try not to usurp your father, or Doug, or Jake's place in your life. Please just treat me like a good friend—like you do with Max and his brothers."

What could I say? This man had no idea I could never be just friends with him. "Sure."

"Great!" He got comfortable in my bed. "Let's watch a movie until it's time to sleep."

"And where are you sleeping?"

"Right here. I told you I called this room and this bed."

"Fine!" Opening up the comforter on my side, I proceeded to get out. "I'll go sleep in the twins' room."

"There's no extra bed in there for you."

"I'll sleep with James. The bed is big enough for the both of us if we cuddle. I don't think he'll mind."

"No man would," he murmured, "but we have a movie to watch. Get back in bed and you can leave when the movie is done. I have a really scary one for you I downloaded when I first got here."

I wondered if I should be happy that he planned to watch a movie with me in bed, from the onset. It was probably not the smartest thing to do when I was doing my hardest to try to *FORGET* this man.

I got back in bed, and tried to leave several times within the first ten minutes because the movie was that scary. Donovan eventually laid his head on my thigh to stop me from moving. Though I tried my damned-est, I couldn't help from running my hand through his wavy hair. He had such beautiful hair. After a brief while, I brought myself back to reality and took my hand off his hair, only to have it brought back by Donovan. "That's relaxing. Do some more," was his only comment as he went back to the movie. Donovan eventually fell asleep on my lap and, even with the circulation in my right thigh cut off, I was at my happiest.

Lightly tracing my index finger around his eyes, and the bridge of his nose, and on the bottom of his lips, I knew this would be my only chance to touch him. What would it feel like to freely kiss those lips? How happy would a woman be to be touched by this man? How much love did this man have to give the woman he chose to be his future bride? I wanted to stay and lay with him, holding him—and hoping he would hold me back. But I didn't need any more deceit in my life. I didn't need him holding me while thinking of another woman. Painfully, I pulled away without waking him up. The kids were sleeping soundly on their beds and I didn't want to wake them with any commotion, so I pulled a blanket out of the kids' closet and crawled onto their couch. Drawing into a fetal position, I went to sleep, content that Donovan was only a wall away from me.

James and Ellie chatting away in their beds got me up to start this day. Feeling disoriented, I tried to get myself out of bed, only to find the circulation in my leg cut off again. Unbeknownst to me, I was somehow back in Donovan's bed and his arms and legs were draped around my body. We were both facing each other and my heart embraced the image of the both of us so effortlessly tangled. I was also mortified that somehow I'd gotten myself back in bed with Donovan. I guess even in my sleepy state, I couldn't resist being close to him.

While it was a mystery as to how my body ended up so close to this man's, I couldn't help staring again. Donovan's five o'clock shadow was beautiful. Once again, I sketched a small pattern while touching his stub-bly hair. It tickled, pricked, and felt amazing. Though I shouldn't, my in-dex finger followed the gorgeous arch in his eyebrow from start to finish, several times. His side burns, his overgrown bangs, and curls at the back were all unchartered territory to this novice explorer. I didn't think I could ever get my fill.

"Donovan, I love you. And I wish you only the best. I hope you'll find your special lady and live a happily-ever-after life with her. And I truly hope in a year's time, I'll be happy to see you happy." I whispered these words and got out of bed before Donovan got up to see a pathetic me mooning over him.

"Good morning, James. Good morning, my beautiful Ellie." I greeted both kids once I did a quick wash and changing of my ugly pajamas.

"Ne Ne!" James was happy to see me, but Ellie was upset.

"Mama!" She didn't want me first thing in the morning.

"Mama and Daddy will be back soon. But for now, you have me. How about if we change your diapers, then go have some breakfast? I'm told you two like oatmeal with blueberries?"

Everything took so long with two kids. After somewhat successfully changing both diapers and putting on a pair of shorts and a t-shirt for James, and a dress for Ellie, I held both hands and we walked down the stairs together. Well, James walked down the steps and Ellie scooted down the steps on her rear end. Once downstairs, both kids knew the drill. They climbed up their high chairs, which were set on the lowest levels for the kids to climb into easily, and "read" their favorite books, while patiently waiting for their oatmeal to be ready.

"Hello, my favorite godchildren!" Donovan came down and greeted both kids with a kiss on their foreheads, since their cheeks were stained with oatmeal and blueberries. "What a mess you are." He tried to pick up the spoon to help feed them, only to be greeted with a stern, "NO!" from Ellie and a shaking of the head, no, from James.

"They like to feed themselves," I informed him. "It's no use trying to help them. They're trying to assert their independence."

"What a mess."

"I know."

We had an entertaining time at the breakfast table watching Ellie try to feed herself, then try to feed James. These two always insisted their high chairs be right next to each other, and Ellie fed James' nose, his chin, and almost his eyes, before making a spoonful into his mouth.

"Good morning." Jane and Max walked in with coffee and pastries for us.

"Hi Jane. Hi Max." I greeted, happy to break-up our alone time.

Max looked at me, then looked over Donovan for a bit and asked, "I trust all went well last night?"

I didn't say anything, but nodded yes and Donovan went to get his coffee from Jane. I noticed whenever Jane or anyone else was around, Donovan barely noticed that I was in the same room. He could have easily reached for my coffee from Jane's other hand and given it to me, but he took his and walked away. Not wanting to be hurt by something so silly, I thanked Jane for the coffee and didn't know where to go. Max and Jane stood almost attached at the hips, the twins were also seated almost attached at the hips, and I...well, there was no hip to attach myself to, so I went over to the babies and checked to see if I could refill their milk cups.

"So, we were thinking," Jane started to say, but was interrupted by Donovan's cell phone. She stopped talking and let Donovan answer his call.

"Hello?" Donovan took a sip of his coffee. "Hey, Kate."

Jane listened attentively as well, and it sounded like something wasn't going well with one of their clients.

Donovan continued his conversation and said, "I'm at Jake's right now, but why don't you meet me at my place and we'll figure out what to do with the proposal. I can be there in 15 minutes. If you get there before I do, just use your key and make yourself comfortable."

"Just use your key..." Those were definitely words I didn't need to hear. Taken aback at how close Kate and Donovan still were, even after having broken up, I tried not to show my disappointment and started cleaning up after the kids. Picking up a roll of paper towels, I got on my knees and began picking up the dropped oatmeal. It was a mess on the floor, and this was the perfect excuse for me to forget what was going on in the real world. The real world hurt so, so much.

"Laney?" Max got down on the floor, helped me clean up, then pulled me up. "Jane and I were thinking we'd take over and watch the kids today. Why don't you go enjoy your Sunday?"

"I can stay if you and Jane have things to do."

"No. We'd like to spend some time with the babies. You go and have a fun time."

I looked at Jane and she encouraged me with her smile. The twins were in good hands with both Max and Jane, so I decided to take them up on their offer and gather my stuff to leave.

Kissing both kids good-bye, I tried to leave before Donovan came out with his overnight bag.

"Laney?" Max asked. "I have my bike here. You want a ride sometime before you leave?"

Did I? I would have loved a ride, but from the look on Jane's face, it wasn't the proper thing to do. I couldn't blame Jane for not wanting me on the back of her boyfriend's bike. That was an intimate place to be, and it wasn't the place for me. I agreed and understood.

"Thanks, Max. I think I'm all right. I'll get my own bike soon. Maybe you can go to the dealer with me when I'm ready to buy? You can show me the ropes when I get back in a year."

Taking another peak at Jane, my answer made her happy.

"Bye." I said, opening the door.

"Laney?" Max called out one more time while searching for something in his laptop bag. "Here," he said and threw me a set of keys. "It's yours for today. Enjoy."

"Max, no. I couldn't take your bike."

"You can, and I insist. The ride will help you feel a hundred times better than what you're feeling now."

I was grateful beyond words. Max caught on to my defeated spirit after hearing about Kate, and he was doing his best to help me. "Thank you," I whispered. "I take back what I said last night. I think you surpass my cousin in one area."

"Yeah?" Max said with a surprisingly huge grin. "And what would that be?"

"Selflessness!" I whispered. "Thank you."

I practically ran home to get my leather jacket and motorcycle helmet, and hopped on the bike to take it for a ride. It had been a long time since I'd been able to ride a motorcycle, and I didn't want to waste any time. After spending a few minutes to get myself acclimated with the gears and controls, I started the bike and felt it purr under me. I didn't know what it was about being on a motorcycle that gave me such a sense of freedom, but it did. This would also help alleviate the restlessness I couldn't control.

I was about to take off when I felt my phone vibrate. It was a message from Bee.

Brunch today? If so, meet us at the divey Mexican joint across the street from my loft.

I texted back.

Cool! See you there.

Before taking off, I felt a tap on my shoulder and was forced to pause one more time. I lifted up the face shield on my helmet to respond to whatever Donovan wanted to say.

"Do you really know how to ride this?"

I shook my head yes.

"Where are you off to, and in such a hurry? You didn't even say good-bye."

"I have a lunch date."

"With whom?"

Hell if I was going to tell him after making me suffer through his conversation with Kate.

"Wouldn't you like to know!" Simply stated, I put my foot on the metal and left. I was giggling under my helmet at the stupid, but effective comment. I so wished I could've turned around to see the look on Mr. Taylor's face after I left him eating my dust!

"Sweet bike! Yours?" Al inspected the bike inch by inch.

"Naw. It belongs to Max. He was nice enough to let me borrow it."

"You see, Beck. Jane's OK with Max riding a bike. Why won't you let me get one?"

"The bike came with Max, and they are not expecting a baby in half a year." Becky rolled her eyes and pulled Al back into the curb. "You so don't look like a Harley girl. When did you learn to ride?"

"I had a friend my freshman year who lived in the same dorm as I, and he'd take me on rides. I took such an interest, he eventually taught me how to ride and let me borrow his bike whenever I needed a car."

"Great friend. Boyfriend?"

"Naw. Just a friend."

"Where you coming from?" Bee asked. "If you're not busy after this, will you help me finish modeling the lingerie?"

"Sure I will."

"There's my baby!" A lady called out loudly from the parking lot area. Turning around, I saw Mr. and Mrs. Taylor walking our way. Apparently, they were joining us for brunch.

We all expected Mrs. Taylor to go and hug her daughter Becky, but instead she was referring to me when she called out her baby. Bee, Al and Becky started busting up when they saw Mrs. Taylor fawning all over me, while I mouthed to them, "Me?" They all nodded yes.

I answered with reservation, "Hello, Mr. and Mrs. Taylor. It's very nice to see you again."

"Why are you so formal with us, Baby? Call us Ma and Pa. That's what all the kids call us."

The three behind me were snickering at my predicament.

"Oh, I couldn't call you 'Ma and Pa.' I'm sure your children won't like it. I'll just call you..."

"Nope!" Mr. Taylor jumped in. "I insist you call us Ma and Pa. You're family, now."

'Ma and Pa' each took my arm and walked me into the restaurant. Before they sat me in between them, Becky sat next to me on the right, and Bee sat next to me to the left. "Thanks!" I whispered to each Taylor.

"You're welcome, Baby," Bee answered with a laugh.

"Becky, are your parents normally this...loving?" I don't know if 'loving' was the right word, but that's all I could think of synonymous to crazy, over-the-top, strange—all in a very good way, of course.

"Nope." She shook her head. "They've never approved of Kate, or any other girl. You are the final 'Baby' in their life, until you start popping out babies, yourself."

Happily confused, I didn't know where to go with this information. Of course, I wanted to be considered a part of the Taylor family, but everyone here was jumping the gun. Donovan didn't like me in that way.

"I think you are all way over-thinking my friendship with your brother. In fact, I know you are because your brother and I aren't even friends. He says that I'm a 'pain in his ass,' and I think he's..." *wonderful? handsome? the man of my dreams?* Of course, I didn't say aloud those last three words.

While the server came over and interrupted our conversation, Bee whispered in my ear, "How long?" I gave her a *how long, what?* look. "How long have you been in love with my nephew?" I slowly shook my head in denial. "The sooner you answer, the less chance there is of me asking this same question out loud in front of everyone at this table." I gave her a *you wouldn't dare,* look. "Oh yes, I would," she warned.

Dammit all to hell—why was I so transparent? Max asked me the same question last night. How many other people have kept my secret a secret to themselves? How did everyone know?

"How..." Bee said aloud. I glared at her with such a frightful and frightened look, Bee laughed and excused herself. "I don't know where that came from," she cleared her throat and went back to her menu.

"Since I was ten," I whispered purposely to her ear while she put the mimosa to her lips.

She choked on the mimosa badly enough that orange juice was coming out of her mouth, her nose—she was coughing, she was choking, she was sneezing—Bee didn't know what to do with herself and this information I'd given her.

"Not cool, little niece," she threatened, once she got herself together. "You and I will have a long talk once we get back to the loft."

"Look who's here!" 'Ma' Taylor's surprised cry was about as genuine as a three-dollar bill. "Donny. Heeya. Come ovah heeya."

"Excited-to-see-her-son-accent-alert," Al coughed out. We all chuckled.

'Ma and Pa' stood up to greet their son but were caught open-mouthed when they saw Kate walk in a few seconds later.

"What the hell is she still doing sniffing around my son?" 'Ma' said loudly enough for the entire restaurant to be privy to her thoughts.

"Uh-oh-possible-bitch-slapping-alert," Al coughed out again and Bee, Becky and I started dying of laughter now.

"Donny! Look who's having brunch with us? It's Baby!"

Damn! I stopped laughing out of sheer embarrassment that she called me Baby in front of Donovan.

"Hello, *Baby*." Jerk stressed the word, *Baby*, just to rattle me. "Long time no see. I see your life isn't as exciting as you portend."

"Ooh! Such big words, Mr. Big Bad Lawyer. What brings you here? I thought you had *work* to do?"

"Donny, sit," his mother literally pushed him into a chair next to her.

Kate finally caught up with Donovan, and greeted his parents. "Hello Scott, hello Jamie."

Mr. Taylor gave her a lukewarm greeting and Mrs. Taylor all but ignored her.

The greetings continued. "Hello Becky, Al, Bee..." She paused and didn't know how to respond to me sitting in the middle of this family affair. "Laney. I wasn't aware that you knew the Taylors."

I couldn't believe this woman. "You do know I'm a Reid?" I asked point blank.

"Well, yes. I was told you and Jake are cousins."

"If *you* knew anything about the Taylors, you'd know that 'Ma and Pa' knew me even before I was born, Ms. Beauvais."

"Bitch-slapping-happening-now!" Al coughed, again. I did my best to hold back the laugh. Bee and Becky quietly giggled until I couldn't hold it in any longer and I busted up. The three of us looked ridiculous and all took turns giving Al dirty looks. That gave me an excuse not to look at Donovan or Kate. I was mortified that I used the monikers 'Ma and Pa,' and I was even more mortified that I was so mean to Kate.

I just couldn't help myself.

"Are you drunk?" Donovan asked with a quizzical stare.

"Nope!" I answered matter-of-factly. "Haven't had anything to drink but coffee."

"Well, I must get going or I'll miss my plane." Kate announced to no one in particular. "I'll see you in London?" She gave him a sultry look. Damn her! She was sexy—I had to hand that to her.

"Yeah. I'll see you Wednesday morning." It was an awkward good-bye as she expected more—a kiss good-bye, a walk out to her car...who knew? But, 'Ma' had a stronghold on her son and he couldn't move. All he could do was wave.

"What the hell is she still doing with you?" Mrs. Taylor smacked her son on the head to show her displeasure. "I thought you said you two broke up?"

"Ow, Ma! You can't go around hitting your grown son."

"I'm your Ma! I can do anything I damn well please. Now answer me!"

"We are not together anymore, but she is a co-worker, and we had work to do. I see her in the office, Ma. That's not going to change."

Mrs. Taylor changed subjects as soon as she was pleased with Donovan's answer. "Donny, have you had anything to eat this morning? You want to eat with us?"

Before he could answer, I started getting up. "I can help you now, if you like." I addressed Bee only. "Otherwise, I need to get back and return the bike to Max. I also have school work to finish."

"No, Baby. You can't leave us, already. We didn't even get to talk and get to know one another." Mrs. Taylor cried.

Mr. Taylor joined in. "I need some golf lessons, Laney. I was hoping you would go to the club with me and give me some pointers."

"I really do have school work I must finish in the next few days," I answered Mrs. Taylor. Then, I said, "And Mr. Taylor, why would you want pointers from me when you're son is an excellent golfer? His handicap is much lower than mine."

"Yeah, Dad. Why would you ask Delaney, instead of your own son?"

"Because she kicked your ass the last two times you played against her. Plus, she's a lot prettier to look at."

Donovan put up both his hands in concession. "I've got no rebuttal for that one."

Mr. Taylor got out his phone and started talking, "Henry. I have your Laney here. She's going to give me pointers so I can kick your sorry ass next week when we meet at the club. What?" Mr. Taylor started bellowing and he put my dad on speakerphone.

"Baby! What are you doing, helping your dad's enemy? We have a club tournament next week. I thought you were going to work with your old man?"

When did I become everyone's *"Baby?"*

"Hi Daddy. I'm having brunch with the Taylors."

"PA!" Mr. Taylor called into the phone.

"The hell you are." My dad argued back. "I'm her only Daddy."

Now this conversation was getting absolutely ridiculous.

"OK!" I cut off both men. "I'll meet both you men at the club in exactly two hours. I can help you till 4:00pm, then I need to get some work done before I go out tonight."

"Where are you going?" Donovan asked, but I ignored him.

"Laney?" Dad asked. "Where are you going?" Same words, different intonation—which meant I didn't have a choice of answering or not answering.

Grudgingly I answered. "A group of us are going to a UFC fight tonight."

"And?" Dad continued the inquisition in front of the Taylor family as though I were a sixteen-year-old.

"And what?" I asked.

"Who's coming to pick you up?"

"No one. I'm meeting everyone at the fight."

"How many boys, how many girls?"

"Daddy," I complained, "this kind of questioning really necessary? I'm twenty-two."

"Until you're married, this kind of questioning is necessary," my dad answered back.

"That's right, Henry old buddy," Mr. Taylor jumped in. "You keep her under your nose until I can have her in my household as a Taylor."

I looked over at Mr. Taylor. Was he really trying to match-make me and Donovan?

"Pa!" Donovan was complaining of his father's matchmaking. "I tell you what," Donovan tried to come up with a brilliant idea, which I didn't consider too brilliant. "How about if the five of us go out and play 9 holes today? And after we're all done, we can have a family dinner before I take Al and Becky to the airport to catch their red-eye flight back to Chicago."

"Son," now my father was getting into this comedy act, "that's the most brilliant idea I've heard you say, yet."

"My son is a genius, isn't he, Henry, old buddy?"

"He sure is Scott. You raised a good one over there."

"Oh brother," I heard Becky lament. "Does this mean Al is golfing the rest of today as well?" Al nodded his head in a hopeful bid to play golf.

"Of course Al is playing golf, Becky. He's family isn't he?" Mr. Taylor stated in a way that told Becky she should know better.

"What was I thinking?" Becky concurred with her dad, sarcastically.

"You guys can play all the golf you like, but I'm going to this MMA fight." I stood my ground and wasn't going to let Donovan Taylor change my weekend plans, twice.

It royally pissed me off that Donovan could change my plans depending upon which way suited him best. It wasn't as if he would change his weekend for me. I didn't remember him asking me if he could go work with Kate while we were feeding the kids breakfast.

"You have to go with us," Donovan exclaimed as though he had a right to what I could and could not do. "Who's going to team up with your dad? You're the only other Reid."

"Why can't you team up with my dad? Why do we need to team up at all? Isn't it each man for himself?"

"Nope," Donovan answered matter-of-factly, again. "It's team play. It's not like you're going to be around much longer to play with your dad, so stop being selfish, and give your dad an afternoon of golf."

"Baby," my dad pleaded. "Donovan's right. You're leaving soon. I want to play as much golf with you as possible before you leave."

Donovan sat there smirking.

"How dare you call me selfish?" I was angry now. "I gave up an entire weekend in Scottsdale so I can play for my family. I want to go out one night and hang out with my friends. How is that so wrong?"

Mr. Taylor tried to calm me down. "Baby, it's not wrong to want to go out with your friends. We just want to spend some time with you too. Where are you going by the way?"

Before any more of the conversation was drawn out about where I was going, and why I was going, I gave in again.

I was mad. Donovan manipulated and guilted me again, using my family and his family as well. I got up to leave, but needed to get in one last word. "Why do you do this?" As this was a rhetorical question, I didn't wait for Donovan's answer. "It's not like you're ever going to take me out on a date," my voice weakened and my courage waned. I'd never shown him my hurt feelings before, but this weekend—after the ups and downs, the hot and the cold, playing "limb"-o in bed, only to see him run off to Kate—I couldn't stop the reveal. "Why do you stop anyone else from wanting to go out with me?" My shoulders dropped and I walked away embarrassed with myself. Fortunately, Donovan didn't come out to cross-examine my accusation.

"Heavy confession at the table, Miss Laney Reid," Bee spoke after I finished modeling and readied myself to leave.

"Aargh! I feel like such a moron. I can't wait to leave. I keep slipping up. It's time to go."

"How are you going to be away from my nephew for a year, if you've been in love with him for twelve years?"

"I'll survive." I muttered, and got myself back to the bike.

After thanking Max for the use of the Harley, I lay in bed thinking about last night. The talk we had in bed, the movie we watched, the night we spent together. Two weeks could not come soon enough.

I didn't say much during the few hours of golf. Mr. Taylor and Dad talked most of the time, and I made sure to sit with Dad on the golf cart, every time. After a surprisingly friendly game, Dad handed me a bag and said, "Change into this after you shower, Baby."

The bag had clothes with Bee's Beeautiful label. A gorgeous dress covered the beautiful black lingerie I modeled today. It would fit perfectly under the strapless dress, fitted up top, and A-lined on the bottom. Bee had also thoughtfully sent a large spring-colored scarf that doubled as a shawl and stunning black sling-back heels. The sexy lingerie made me feel bold and confident. I finished getting dressed and walked into the dining area so we could all have dinner.

Al let out a modest, but appreciative whistle, and jerked his brother-in-law's attention. "Dude. You're so lucky that I'm a married man, or you'd have serious competition from me for this beautiful woman." That was very sweet of Al to say. "We will probably not see each other again for awhile, so I'll say my good-byes, now?"

"It was very nice getting to know you this week, Al. Have a nice trip back, and hope all goes well with Becky's pregnancy. I'm sure I'll see you sometime after I get back from London."

"Take it easy on my brother-in-law." Al pleaded quietly, and with a smile. "He's never been in love before so it's taking him a while to figure things out. Once he figures it out, he'll be the best damn husband a girl can ever find."

I gave Al a bewildered look, and he smiled and kissed both my cheeks.

"Let's go," Donovan said and held out his arm. Unsure what to do with that arm, I walked away. He dismissed the distance and put his hand on the small of my back as we walked out.

"You taking me home? I thought we were all having dinner here."

"No and no. I'm taking you somewhere else."

"Why? And where?"

"After you lambast my chivalrous side, you ask why?" He chuckled.

Damn! He was taking me on a "date" because he felt sorry for me. I should've kept my mouth shut!

"You want me to put the top up? Is it messing up your hair?" It was weird that Donovan was acting like he was on a date with me.

I took out a clip from my clutch and pulled back my hair in answer.

Donovan pulled up to the observatory way up on top of the hill.

"Stay." He warned and I obeyed.

He walked around, opened my car door, and soon proceeded to grab a large blanket and picnic basket.

"Let's go." He said and offered a hand. I really had no idea what the hell to do with the hand he was offering. Rather than assume anything, I walked to the side of him that housed all our stuff.

He chuckled, and allowed me to walk in peace. "There's a star gazing event tonight. All the telescopes will be open, and you can look up at the stars and sky to your heart's content."

I gave him a shy but expressive smile. That sounded wonderful. Though, I could've stared at a smoggy sky with this man and I would've been content.

After we laid down our blanket and food, we walked around and saw stars, the star patterns, the dark sky, and the full moon. It looked so close and so clear.

"You hungry?" This was so weird how it seemed like a real date.

"Yes." I answered.

He held out his hand again, and I swear my heart beat so fast I thought I might have a heart attack right here. Like the moron that I was, I didn't know what to do with his hand. Do I hold it? Do I stare at it? Do I walk away from it? Donovan saw my contemplation, and his face broke into the most devilish smile. Knowing I was thrown the biggest question mark of my life, he left his hand out with his expression completely unguarded.

I admit, I wanted nothing more than to be intimately connected to this man whether by hand, foot or mouth. But knowing he was "gifting" me this date tonight, I didn't want to pretend, or worse yet, believe this was as special to Donovan as it was to me.

He continued to hold out his hand and gestured for me to take it. Sheepishly, I shook my head no, and with a mischievous smile, gave him a low-five, instead. He laughed and grabbed my hand without warning, and started walking us back to the blanket.

I didn't know that holding a man's hand would make my blood race the Indy 500. I wanted to pass out from a lack of air. Holding Donovan's hand was a dizzying, run to the top of the hill and shout from the top of my lungs, "I love everything and everybody," kind of feeling. His hand intertwined with mine was getting into med school, earning summa cum laude, knowing your parents will be proud of you – all rolled into one, but still better than all that, kind of feeling. It was like ice cream on a super hot day, a hot bath on a freezing cold day, and a can't-put-downable book on a dreary rainy day, kind of feeling. A BAM! POW! BOOM! WHAM! KRAKA-DOOM! feeling of power and strength superheroes experienced after beating up on the bad guys, kind of feeling. This feeling of him touching me with purpose was indescribable. It was only hands, but the intimacy confounded my entire senses. In short, I was happy.

"You have a smile on your face. What does that mean?"

Did I really need to explain all that raced through my mind right now? No way! I was not going to open myself up for rejection.

"It means I'm hungry."

"Smartass!"

We laughed together, and he brought out a dinner prepared by the golf club. He made me a plate, he made himself a plate, and we sat and listened to the orchestra get ready for their concert. The music began toward the end of dinner, and once Donovan got himself comfortable leaning against the tree, he brought me between his legs and had me leaning against his body. If I thought holding hands was confounding—I couldn't even begin to explain the feelings of euphoria that knotted up my stomach and wouldn't let my dinner digest.

At first, my body was tense when he pulled me into his chest and had me leaning into him, but once I got there, it was the perfect fit. I partially turned myself into him, and had one arm around his waist and one hand on his chest. Eventually, the side of my head completely laid on his chest. The rhythm of his heartbeat made beautiful music with the musicians on stage. Donovan's arm slowly traced around my back and curved into my waist, and his other hand continually caressed my hair. Lightning could have struck and I would have stayed in this exact spot and position.

Is this what Cinderella felt when she first danced with her Prince Charming at the ball? Did Sleeping Beauty wonder how she could have missed out on a hundred years of being without her Prince Phillip? Or was this the paramount feeling of love Snow White felt the instant her Prince kissed her back to life and they went off to live happily ever after? This was my fairytale and my dream. I was going to live it tonight—be the star of it for just one night—then go back to my reality when the clock struck twelve.

"Delaney," My Prince whispered. "Hey, Princess. It's time to go."

Peeling myself from him in slow motion, I regretted having molded my body so deeply into his. I felt an instant hollowness the moment his half of the imprint disjointed from my half.

"That was so beautiful! Thank you for the most wonderful night."

"Tonight was a wonderful night. I agree. Thanks for coming with me."

I helped get our stuff together, and we got back in the car and were almost home, to my chagrin.

"I'm sorry you were forced to take me out, after my big speech. But, I'm not sorry you did. Tonight was more special to me than you'll know." I leaned over and kissed him on his cheek. "Thank you," I said, getting out of the car.

Donovan was speechless, and unlike his chivalrous self, did not get out of the car. I waved good night and watched him leave. WHAT. A. NIGHT.

May 20, 2013
After Midnight

*E*very beautiful story must come to an end. And sometimes the ending is a happy one, and at other times, the author chooses to make the ending a sad one. In my case, my fairytale did not have a happily-ever-after. What started as the most incredible night of my life, soon turned back into my reality.

"Happy birthday, Emily." I greeted my favorite birthday girl. Emily was busy getting the twins ready for the dinner at her house. Jake had brought in a small staff to prepare food for the family to celebrate his wife's birthday. "How was your night at the SLS hotel?"

"It was fabulous. But, apparently not as fabulous as your night last night?" Emily grinned knowingly. "Details?"

"How did you know?"

"Uncle Henry told Jake, who told me. Though none of us have any details. Care to share?"

I went all dreamy on her. "Is it too high school if I say it was the best night of my life?"

Emily cracked-up.

"What's so funny, Love?" Jake walked in with a baby in each hand. James ran over to me and I picked him up and held him.

"ME!" Ellie wanted her turn. I handed James to Jake, and I picked up Ellie and spun her around as well.

"I'm going to miss these two so much." I got sad thinking about my pending trip. "These are the only two reasons holding me back from leaving for London."

"Only two? You counting the twins as one reason and my buddy as the other?" Jake teased. "Donovan tells me you had a fun night?"

"It was the best night of her life," Emily teased this time. "You sure you want to leave now? It looks like Donovan is waking from his slumber."

"Donovan only took me out because I made a big fuss and complained that he was sabotaging my efforts to date anyone. I didn't mean for him to feel guilty."

"Did you ask him for a dress and shoes as well?"

"What do you mean, Jake?"

"The outfit you wore last night, did you ask him to buy it for you?"

"No, of course not. He bought those?" My heart did that crazy thumping again.

"From the little I could get out of Donovan, it sounded like he rounded up a dress from Bee and stopped by a department store to buy you matching shoes. He's such a girl. What self-respecting man goes to the mall with a dress and looks for matching shoes?" Jake harrumphed.

"I think that's absolutely romantic. Have you ever done that for me?" Emily teasingly complained to her husband. "I'd love it if you put that much thought into an outfit for me. Maybe you can take Donovan with you so he can show you what to buy."

"Emi, there's no way I'm stepping into a department store with Donovan. You know you can buy whatever you want."

"That's not the point," she pressed.

"Forget it. Clothes shopping is not my forté."

"Lucky for you, you have many other fortés." She winked, and kissed Jake on the lips.

I was still freefalling from the revelation that Donovan purposefully went out and put together an outfit for me.

The birthday dinner was a simple, but elegant affair, and as soon as the birthday cake was done, I went up with Emily to help put the kids down, while Jake entertained the family.

"So you never finished telling me about last night."

"I don't know if I should relive it. I told myself last night that I'd pretend I was Cinderella at the ball, but when the clock struck midnight, I'd go back to my real life and not live in fantasy anymore. Look at tonight. He's barely acknowledged me. It hurts too much to pretend...I'll just live in the present." I wasn't trying to get out of not telling Emily what happened. All day long, I had relived last night. That was until I saw Donovan at dinner. He grunted a hello, then sat next to the guys, and never looked my way again.

"I think Donovan needs time to process all that's going on in his heart and mind."

I smiled to appease Emily, but I knew the truth. Donovan would have never spent the evening with me had I not been a brat about the whole dating thing. "It's all right Emily. I know he's not interested in me. There's no need to try and make me feel better."

Back at the party, I sat with my parents, then with Max and Jane for a while. I offered to walk Gram back home when she got tired and sat with her for a cup of tea.

"Laney, are you sure you want to be so far away from home?"

"Yes, Gram. I want to experience life in London and I want to be independent. My family life is ideal, but I desire to open myself up to new opportunities. Do you think I'm making a mistake?"

"No, Dear. It's not that I think you're making a mistake living abroad. There's a great deal to be learned when you're on your own—especially coming from such a close family. I just hope you're leaving for the right reasons. I don't want you to be running away."

How did Gram know I was running away?

"You know the story of your grandfather and me. I ran away to Paris, almost married Roland, and wouldn't have had any of you in my life."

"But Grandpa came after you and everything worked out well. And even if he hadn't chased after you, you would've married Grandfather Roland and lived a different, but no less a happy life. I might be running away, a bit, but I also want to spread my wings and fly independently. I hope you'll understand, Gram. I enjoy being completely immersed in a different culture."

"I wanted to make sure you were doing this because you wanted to move. Always know that you are welcomed back home, no matter if the year is fulfilled or not."

"I know, Gram. And thank you. I'm very happy you and Grandfather Roland decided to stay here on the cul-de-sac with us. I hope you'll see me get married and have kids as well."

"I believe those days aren't too far away." Gram had a knowing smile only she could decipher.

Laughter came from Emily's backyard when I crossed the street from Uncle Bobby's home, after my tea with Gram. I decided not to go back in, and slowly walked home. It was such a beautiful night; I sat on my swing and thought about what I'd like to do when I got to London. Last time I was there, I was a teenager and not very impressed with the gloomy city. Now as a twenty-something-er, I was sure I'd like the city much more.

"That looks comfortable. Why haven't you come back to Emily's party?"

"I was just sitting, contemplating the things I should do when I got to London."

"And what did you want to do, Delaney? I go there often enough. I could help you sort out your thoughts. In fact, I could probably help you find the places as well. When do you leave? I'll get there soon after and be your guide." He waited for me to answer, but I wasn't going to do so. "What?"

"Nothing." I said with a broken heart. "I'm going to go in. I'll see you around?"

I got up to leave, but he held my wrist.

"I asked when you leave so I can come visit you."

"You don't have to visit..." I lightly twisted my wrist so I could walk away.

"Why not? Why don't you want me to visit?"

"You don't have to come all the way to London to pretend to be my friend. I'll do OK finding new friends there."

"Delaney. What the hell is this? What do you mean, pretend to be your friend?"

"One day, you're my Prince Charming at the ball—holding my hand, paying court, and dancing with me. The next day, you're my wicked step-mother—ignoring me, embarrassed to be with me, and hurting me. I don't need that, so no thank you on the tour guide offer."

He let me go.

Tonight was definitely back to reality.

May 23, 2013
Matching Outfits

School work DONE! I turned in my last paper today, and I had exactly a week now to get my butt in gear to move. I'd shipped some of my belongings already, and I needed to make sure all the i's were dotted and the t's crossed. Mom was becoming more of a mess as the days went on, and I didn't know how to explain any further that I just needed this time away. At Bee's request, I dropped by once again to help her with her spring collection.

"What beautiful creations can I try on today?" I asked when she opened the door.

Bee looked haggard. "I've been up all night sewing this one gown, but something still isn't right. Maybe when I see it on an actual person, I'll know what I need to change."

Bee didn't even let me go behind the screen this time. She had me strip out of my shorts and t-shirt and try on this insanely gorgeous ball gown. The dress reminded me of Anne Hathaway's pink satin Academy Award's dress, except this one had small pearl beads and crystals sewn-in to the top part of the bodice and it was midnight blue. It shimmered from all angles, but not so much that I looked like a disco ball. It fit me like a glove.

"Did you make this for me? I feel like a movie star going to an awards ceremony. This is so stunning."

"Those are Swarovski crystals and beads on there. You can't comfortably put your arm to the side because of the crystals." She laughed. "Gorgeous, but not functional."

"I have a pair of Swarovski glass 'slippers' that would go perfectly with this dress. They're made of glass but the weird thing is, depending upon what you wear, they reflect that color, so if I wore this dress, the shoes would look a shade of dark blue."

"I need you to go home and bring the shoes. In the meanwhile, I'm going to fix what's wrong with this dress. I've figured it out."

"Nothing's wrong with this dress. It's perfect!"

"And while you're gone, I'll order some lunch for us. How long will it take you?"

"Half an hour?"

"Perfect. See you."

Bee was lost in her world again. She began taking apart the dress as I left. The dress looked perfect, but I guess she'd know better.

"Laney?" Emily called me from her house as I parked in my driveway. I walked over to her. "What are you doing this long weekend?"

"Packing?"

"You want to go to Texas with us? We weren't going to go to Ashley's wedding, but since it's so close to my parents' gravesite, I'd thought we'd go one more time before this baby came. I just got the approval to fly from my OB. Any chance I can ask you to come with us and help with the twins?"

"Sure. You know I'm always happy to help you."

"I'm sorry. I know it's a great imposition since you're leaving in a week."

"No it's all right. Mom and Dad are going as well. It'll give me a chance to spend more time with them. When do we leave?"

"Tomorrow?" Emily smiled apologetically. "We'd like to see my parents on Saturday, then attend the wedding on Sunday, and leisurely get home on Monday. Would that work?"

"Sure, Emily. I'll make sure to get all my packing done tonight."

"Thanks. You're a lifesaver." Emily hugged me and walked back in the house. "Oh, by the way," she mentioned, "we're having an impromptu barbecue tonight. Can you stop by?"

"I think so. I'll let you know later."

I got my shoes, my list of items to be purchased before leaving, and a shopping list from Emily. I offered to pick up supplies Emily might need for this trip.

I ran all my errands first, after getting an OK from Bee, and I left the rest of the afternoon to hang out with her. Though our friendship was young, we'd become fast friends and I really enjoyed her company.

"The dress is done." Bee was so excited when she saw me. "I need you to try it on before we sit down to eat lunch."

"All right," I said. She handed me the most insanely gorgeous lingerie to go underneath the dress. "Oh Bee, these are so beautiful," I stressed. "By looking at the lingerie, I take it it's supposed to peek out of the dress slightly?"

"Exactly," she said with a smile. "You understand the designer in me!"

"Wow!" I exclaimed when I saw the dress on me. I could not do the dress justice.

Bee had the same expression of wonder, amazement, and satisfaction when she saw the dress on me.

"I feel like a movie star." I said, "I wish there was some place I could go where it was fancy enough to wear something this gorgeous. I'd ask to borrow the dress."

"Aren't you all going to a wedding this weekend? I know Becky was talking about being in Texas this weekend for her best friend's wedding."

"I don't really know Ashley very well, though my parents will be there since they are good friends with her parents. Originally, I wasn't going, but Emily just asked me if I could come along and help with the two kids. So I guess I'm going."

"Then take the dress and the lingerie and model it for me at the wedding. You can tell me where this dress goes wrong when you have to be in it for five hours."

"Oh no, Bee. I'm not going to take the dress. I'll probably just stay in the hotel room with the twins during the wedding and reception. I highly doubt I'm attending anything. There's really no reason for me to be there."

"Regardless, take the dress and the shoes and borrow some jewelry from your grandmother. If you do end up at the black-tie reception, wear my dress."

"How do you know it's black tie?"

"Donovan told me. He needed a little adjusting on his suit, so he brought it by before he left for London. In fact, you think you can take this with you and give it to Donovan? I think he comes home tonight." She went over to where a stylish black suit was hanging and put it back in its Prada suit bag.

"Yeah. He looks as good in it as you are imagining right now." *How the hell did she know?* "It's written all over your face. If you continue to look like that every time my nephew's name is spoken, your secret's going to be headline news in the Reid and Taylor family."

"No!" I cried. "I've got to learn to school my emotions and expressions better. In any case, there's no reason for me to hold onto it. If he comes home tonight, I'm sure he'll stop by your place to pick up his suit."

"I won't be home tonight. I have a date." She gave a devilish grin.

"Any Reid I know?"

"Maybe," she was being cryptic.

"You don't get away with a maybe after making me confess that I had a secret crush on your nephew for the last twelve years."

"I'm having dinner with Nick." That's all she would divulge.

"Come on! I need more details." I begged. "Also, what's with the nephew, auntie business? Explain that one."

"That's easy. My dad, Donovan's grandfather, remarried after his first wife died, and had me very late in life. And thus, I'm the auntie."

"How old are you?"

"Twenty-nine."

"And my cousin, Nick? Where did you meet him? How long have you two been dating?"

She didn't give up this info easily. She sat on it till lunch was almost over. Only when I told her I wouldn't come over any longer to help her model, did she divulge.

"We met through friends. Initially, we didn't give any last names so it didn't register that our families were friends. We went out once and that's when we realized we were bosom buddies without knowing it. That's also when Nick never called for a second date, and I figured it wasn't going anywhere."

"So...you wanted it to go somewhere? You're interested in Nick?"

"Interested? I don't know. I wanted to see if it would go anywhere, but he obviously didn't feel the same way."

"And tonight?"

"Just two friends having dinner."

"Who asked whom?"

"It was mutual..." She was being coy. "Let's chat about something else."

"I want details when I get back from Texas, OK?"

"Only if I get details about your date with Donovan the other night."

"There isn't much to tell." All I could think about was our conversation in front of my house. "It was the most beautiful night of my life, and then he completely ignored me the next day at Emily's. The hot and cold from your nephew is something I need to get away from, and I'm mad at myself for being so affected by it. He's just a man, no different from any other man. My head needs to get on straight and I can't seem to do that when he's always around."

"Donovan has never had to work for a girl. He doesn't have his head on straight, either. Give him some time to come to terms with what he's feeling. I do believe he has feelings for you, but he doesn't know what to do with them."

This was the story the Taylor family kept feeding me, but I knew better than to believe it. "Bee. He doesn't have any other feeling than that of a protective older brother. And that's OK. That's how it's been all my life with him. I've accepted it. One day, I'll look back on these years and know it was just a phase in my life."

There was an unfinished look on Bee's face, but she didn't pursue the topic any longer.

I took an extra long time shopping. Donovan's smart suit inspired me, or maybe better stated—gave me the boldness—to do a little shopping for him. That crazy side of me pretended we were attending this wedding as a couple. To match my midnight blue gown, I bought button covers made with the same dark blue and clear Swarovski Crystal rounds, set to resemble a camellia. Since I purchased these, I had to get the matching cufflinks and I knew the exact piece of jewelry I was going to borrow from Gram. Perhaps I was setting myself up for a fall, but it was fun to dream.

I proceeded directly to Gram's house, showed her my dress and shoes and asked if I could borrow her camellia necklace. It was perfect for my dress. This high neckline dress needed a short necklace that dangled long in the back because the back pretty much was...backless. There were beautiful delicate white and platinum camellias sitting at the base of my neck and one at the very end of the long chain that dangled almost to the top of my lower back. Better described, the camellia landed directly on the small of my back. Gram thought it was gorgeous. I agreed with her. The entire outfit was perfection. The beautiful dress hung right next to Donovan's stylish suit, and as ridiculous as it sounded, it was the most impeccable pairing!

A phone call brought me back to reality.

"Hi Emily."

"Did you forget about the barbecue? You've been gone for a long time."

"I did a lot of little shopping for this weekend. Is Donovan there?"

"Uh-huh. You want to come over and see him?" she asked teasingly.

"His Aunt Bee asked me to give his suit to him. I just wanted to know if he was there so I can take it over."

"Come on over," she invited.

"Emily?" I hesitated to ask this question.

"Yes?"

"I bought a little something for Donovan to wear with his suit this weekend at the wedding. Do you think it was forward and unwise of me to have purchased a gift for him?"

"You did?" She sounded very surprised.

"Maybe I won't give it to him." Now I was having serious second thoughts.

"Come over, there's somebody who would like to see you." She added, "We can talk about it here. Oh and by the way," she said before she hung up, "have your bathing suit on."

Afraid that my brother Doug might be at this barbecue and not wanting to hear him yelling at me, I put on my most modest one-piece as well as a cover-up and walked over to Emily's.

"Hello, everyone," I said as I entered the backyard. James was dressed in the most adorable Superman swimsuit.

"Are you my man of steel?" I asked, and he answered with his adorable yes and nodded his head. He pointed to the water before I got into any conversations with anyone, so I picked him up and took him in the pool.

Ellie had her entourage of men swimming with her in the shallow end and I decided to jump in the deep end with James. James always enjoyed doing a piggyback ride on my back while I did the breaststroke, so I let him hang on me and listen to the commotion on the other end. It was hilarious once we all realized that Ellie had pooped on the other side and contaminated the pool. To James's chagrin, I had to pull him out.

Handing James back to his dad, I turned to Donovan and said, "Your aunt gave me your suit and it's hanging in my room. Before you leave please stop by and pick it up?"

He didn't say much other than OK, and that was the extent of our conversation.

So much for swimming and a barbecue, I went home to take a shower.

"Hey," that familiar voice opened my door and called out at the same time. "Emily was wondering if you've had dinner yet. If you haven't, why don't you come over and eat a little something?"

"Is everyone still there?"

"Everyone left to go home and shower off the germs from the pool." That made us both crack up. Who would have thought taking a child into the pool could be that dangerous?

"Sure, I'll go over in a little bit, but let me give you your suit before I forget."

Donovan's suit. Delaney's dress. The two looked so good next to one another I didn't want to separate them. Before I left for Emily's I had put the cufflinks and the button covers into separate small felt bags and put them in the front pocket of his suit jacket. I was nervous he might discover them right away. I'd have no answer for him if he asked about the present.

"You stop by Bee's today?" he asked without emotion.

"Yeah, she needed me to try on one more dress so I stopped by to help. I really like your aunt."

"I see we have at least one thought in common," he answered briskly, took his suit off my hand and walked to the door. "Thanks for picking up my suit." This conversation quickly killed the whimsical dream I'd conjured in my head. *"Donovan and Laney—what a beautiful couple,"* everyone at the wedding would comment. I felt stupid for having bought him the gift. Once again, it was all in my head.

May 24-26, 2013
A Wedding And A Funeral

Friday was chaos at Emily's. It wasn't easy leaving for a trip with two little ones. My job was to occupy the kids while Emily got everything but the kitchen sink packed. Jake was busy at the hospital so we had a minivan pick us up, then we picked up Jake, and off we went to the airport. After an even more chaotic trip through check-in, we eventually settled in the plane. Ellie and James were hyper today. They itched to get out of their car seats and walk the aisle.

"They're a handful now, but wait till the plane starts rolling down the runway. They'll be asleep from the onset of the ascent."

Jake wasn't kidding. They both fell asleep instantly as the plane began taking off.

"Happens every time," Emily commented. "So...?" She faced me. "Did you give it to him?"

"I left it in a pouch in his jacket pocket. I was too chicken to give it to him, so I left it there for him to find."

"What if he doesn't find it?"

I shrugged my shoulders. "Oh well?"

"How will he know who gave it to him?"

I shrugged my shoulders again. "Who cares?" I said with a laugh.

The kids settled in nicely, and though many of the Reid and Taylor family were staying in the same hotel, we didn't run into anyone. Saturday was busy driving about an hour away to Emily's parents' gravesite. Jake was happy that Emily went to her parents with a smile. The twins loved playing hide and seek behind the tombstones while Emily talked to her parents. Seeing how well those two played together, I hoped twins ran in the Reid family.

Sunday, the kids were so tired from the day before, we stayed in the suite all day till it was time for the wedding.

"Laney, why don't you and Jake go ahead? I will join you at the reception after the kids get up."

"Emily, that's silly. I'm here to help you. I'll stay with the twins until they get up from their nap. Then I'll get them dressed and bring them to you. Or, I can stay here with them."

"Are you sure? Don't you want to get dressed up and enjoy the wedding?"

"No."

"You did bring a dress?" Emily gave me a funny look.

"Kind of," I said. "I have a dress, but I don't really know Ashley, and I'm sure she doesn't need wedding crashers. I can deliver the kids to you and come right back here. I'm sure with the family there, you won't need me."

"Laney," Jake answered while getting his bowtie on. "I rsvp'ed for all of us. Ashley's easy going, and one of Jane's best friends. She understood we would be a last minute add-on. So, I want you down in the ballroom with the kids, whenever."

"OK."

When Emily debuted her wedding attire, Jake couldn't hide his pleasure. Emily and Jake were perfection. What possessed me to think Donovan and I could look that good together? I sent off the happy couple and started tinkering with my make-up. To do Bee's dress justice, the make-up had to be on heavier and more seductively. My attempt at this combination was successful enough for me to be satisfied with the result.

The twins both woke up, and after a swig of their water bottle, I brushed Ellie's curls, put her pale pink flower girl-like dress on, and clipped the matching pin on her mass of curls. This beautifully vain little girl kept twirling, or at least attempting to twirl, in front of the full-length mirror. She knew she looked gorgeous.

James, too, looked gorgeous in his little suit and bowtie. He complained a bit when I got the dinner coat on him, but soon held my hand as we three walked into the elevator.

The doors to the reception hall were closed, and Ashley and her new husband, Jared, were waiting outside while the emcee spoke. As soon as the doors opened for their big introduction, Ellie stole the show by running in and shouting, "Mama! Looky-ME!" Then James, thinking this was a game, ran after her and yelled, "Mama!" The guests loved it, and clapped for the twins.

The bride and groom got another round of applause as they walked in.

"Well, hello there. I don't think we've met. You weren't at the wedding were you?"

"Hello." I greeted this very tall man. "No. I just got here."

"Are those two adorable ones yours?"

"No." I smiled.

"I'm Brent, the bride's brother."

"Hi Brent, the bride's brother, I'm Laney, the twins...au pair."

"Au pair?" He lifted one eyebrow, questioning the veracity of my statement. "I've never met such a stunning au pair."

"How many au pairs have you met?"

"None, but if you're the poster girl for them, I would've begged my parents for one, back when I was thirteen."

Brent made me laugh. "I've got to get in and watch the twins."

"So you're not kidding about this au pair business?" I shook my head no and began looking for the twins. "Wait," he held my arms gently and asked, "Are you here with a date?"

Thinking on my toes, I answered, "Yes. I'm here with James. See you later."

Brent pulled me back to him once again, and offered me his arm as an escort into the ballroom. I didn't want to take his arm, but it seemed rude not to take his arm. During my hesitation, he put my hand around him and walked me in.

"The twins are over there," I pointed to the left side of the room. Brent attempted to ask me a few questions, but I was distracted by the sheer number of people in the room, and truth be told, by the laughter coming from Donovan's table. He, Jane and Becky, along with the rest of their table were enjoying themselves immensely. He didn't notice me walk in, or he chose not to notice me.

"Here you are, my lady," Brent brought me to our table.

"Baby!" *Uh-oh*. It was Mrs. Taylor, and she didn't sound happy. "What are you doing in the arms of another man?"

"Hi, Mrs. Taylor."

"I thought I was 'Ma' to you now. Where's Donny? Has he seen how beautiful you look?"

"No. I just got here and this wonderful gentleman was walking me in." I took my hand out of his arm. "Thank you for escorting me. It was nice meeting you, Brent."

"The pleasure was all mine." He raised my hand up to his lips. Before he could kiss it, Mrs. Taylor came back—though I didn't know she'd left—with Donovan and pulled my hand away from Brent's.

"Look who's here, Baby. Donny, have you seen such an exquisite woman in your life? Why our Baby here is," she then proceeded to whisper, "even more beautiful than Ashley, the bride."

Donovan didn't look happy to see me. In fact, he looked livid. I wasn't sure why he was so angry with me.

Brent's interruption was a welcome distraction to the panic Donovan set in my heart.

He took my free hand, kissed it, and said, "Save me a dance, Au pair?" He left without hearing my answer.

"What was that?" Donovan asked in anger. "Do you fucking flirt with every guy who crosses your path? Don't you know how to say no to anyone?"

"Donovan!" Mrs. Taylor called out, shocked at his harsh words, and even harsher tone.

Donovan's words hurt so badly, I teared up immediately. I kept blinking my eyes hoping to push back the tears and the pain. With fortuitous timing, James took a fall and started crying, and without looking back, I raced over to him and let my mind forget my own pain.

Emily knew something wasn't right with me, so she let me take refuge in James. I held him and played with him till his spirits lifted. At least one of us had a smile.

"Hello, again."

"Hi Brent." I looked around, scared that Donovan might accuse me of being...I wasn't quite sure what he was accusing me of being.

"Who is this young fellow?"

"This is James. James," I addressed my little man, "can you say hi to Mr. Brent?"

James waved hello, but was more interested in the dessert spoons.

"So this is the infamous James? As in...your date?"

Brent actually brought out a laugh from me. "Yes, this is my favorite little man, James." James watched us talk briefly, then decided to wiggle off my lap and ran over to Jake who was motioning for him.

"If there's a favorite little man, is there a favorite big man?"

Yes. It's the same man who accused me of being a...

I was lost until I saw my father. "Why yes, there is." I stood up and greeted my father. "Hi Daddy." I hugged him like I used to when I was a little girl. I couldn't let go of him, or the pain.

"You all right, Laney?"

"Yes, Daddy." I answered with sadness.

"Hello, Chief. This is *your daughter*?"

"You don't remember her? Don't you remember how she spilled punch all over your science project when you were a freshman in high school?"

"Daddy. Not nice. Don't bring up the misdemeanors of my youth. I'm sure I have no idea what you are referring to right now."

"Jake, Donovan and Brent almost keeled over when you spilled red punch on their all white project." My dad let out a hearty laugh.

"Chief, where've you been hiding this beauty?"

"She's still where you last left her. Give up your practice in Texas and come work under me at General Hospital, if you want to see more of my daughter."

Brent rubbed the sides of his chin with his thumb and forefinger. "I may seriously take you up on that offer if you'll give me permission to date this stunning young lady."

"Delaney?" I stiffened with his voice. I refused to turn around and I hoped he'd go away if I ignored him.

"Daddy, let's dance." I pulled my father to the dance floor.

"You and Donovan get into a fight?"

I shook my head no.

"You look gorgeous, Baby. Where'd you get the dress?"

"It belongs to Bee. She wanted me to test try the dress and tell her what works and doesn't work."

"I guess one day you'll be the bride, and we'll be doing a father-daughter dance?" Daddy sighed.

I sighed too. "Maybe. I don't think anyone wants me, Daddy. I may never get married."

"From what I can see, too many men want you. You just need to be open to more than one person."

"Right now, I just want to leave, Daddy. I want to make new friends and live a new life."

"That's all fine as long as you don't settle down in England. My big fear is you'll meet someone on the plane and marry the first man who crosses your path."

"Chief, may I have this dance with Delaney?"

"No, Daddy. I don't want to dance with him," I whispered in my father's ear.

"What the hell did you do to my daughter?" My dad got angry with Donovan. "How dare you put this kind of fear in my daughter's voice? Listen to her quivering," Dad started scolding. "Next time I hear my daughter tell me she doesn't want to be near you, I'm going to kick your ass."

"Yes, Chief. I'm sorry." While the two of them carried on, I walked away, but Brent stopped my escape.

"Dance, now?"

"No, sorry. I'm headed back up to the room. I'll see you again."

Brent put his arms around my waist while I walked, and scooped me back to him.

"Hands off, Brent. Delaney and I need to talk."

"Doesn't look like the lady wants to talk to you." Brent was not helping this situation.

"Good night," I told both of them. Neither would let me go.

This was truly the worst night of my life. Stupid me thought we'd be at this wedding and have a fairytale-like time again. So much for the matching camellias.

"Both of you, get the hell out of my way!" I commanded.

Startled, they stepped aside, and I practically ran to the elevator. As soon as I got into my room, I took off the dress, put away all the accessories and scrubbed my face clean. *I am such an idiot. I'm the biggest moron on the face of this earth.*

"Laney?" I heard Emily walk in.

"Hey Emily. Let me help you with the kids."

"You want to talk?"

The tears came down like a monsoon. "Not now. It hurts too much," I whispered and helped the kids into their pjs. "I'm turning in for the night, OK?"

"Sure," I could tell Emily was worried, but I couldn't forget tonight fast enough.

"Hey, Donovan," I heard Emily whisper from the living room area. I tried my hardest to fall asleep, but I lay wide-awake.

"Hey, Emily. I was hoping to speak with Delaney. Is she here?" He sounded no different from his usual self—only quieter since he knew the babies were sleeping.

"She's already turned in for the night."

"How was she before she went to bed?"

"What do you want me to say?" Thank you, Emily, for not telling him that I was a blubbering mess.

"Love," Jake spoke, "I'm going down to the bar with Donovan."

"Sure. Should I wait up for you?"

"No, Love. This may take a while. You rest." I could hear Jake give Emily a kiss before leaving. "You," Jake stressed that word so I figured he was talking to Donovan, "better have a damn good reason for making my cousin cry. You're on my shit list right now."

"Jake..." Emily warned.

"I'm sorry, Emi. I'll be back soon. I love you." He kissed her again.

Closing my eyes shut, I begged for sleep to come so I could forget this day ever happened.

May 27, 2013
Breakfast Of Champions

*U*nlucky for me, we were having breakfast with Donovan. But lucky for me, the entire Reid and Taylor clan joined us. I sat next to Emily, Jake and the kids, and Donovan sat next to his sister, Al, and Jane. I did my best to blend in with the crowd and not attract any attention to myself. That worked well until of course friends and family of the bride joined us at breakfast. We practically took over the entire restaurant.

"Good morning, Au pair." Brent gave off a jovial vibe.

"Why do you keep calling Laney, Au pair?" Jane asked.

"Because when I asked her for her name, that's who she told me she was. I didn't realize that she was the chief's daughter till I saw her with her father."

My dad laughed at him. "Good one, Laney." He then addressed Brent again. "You coming back to California? I have a position with your name on it if you want to come and do an interview."

"Does that mean you'll let me date your daughter?"

"Who my daughter dates is not up to me, Brent. If you can impress her enough, she might consider dating you. Otherwise you'll stand in a long line of boys who want to date her."

"Uncle Henry," Jane complained, "I have Laney matched up with Josh, Max's brother. That's not cool to dangle your daughter as bait so you can get another surgeon in your hospital."

"I never dangled my daughter. My Laney has a mind of her own. She's not going to date anyone because I tell her to date him."

Jane continued. "I think she should date Josh and get to know him a little better. He's funny, charming, witty, good-looking...the list is endless."

"Speaking of dating," Brent interrupted Jane, "when do you leave, Laney?"

"We're all leaving after breakfast, Brent, so save your breath. She's gone in about an hour." Jake spoke up for me.

"I believe I was asking the lady? She seems to have quite a few spokes-people today."

"What do you say, Laney? Could we go have a cup of coffee without your entire family listening in on our conversation?"

I was so nervous that I didn't know what to say to him. I wasn't hesitating because I wanted to go have a cup of coffee with him; I was hesitating because I was afraid to see what Donovan's expression looked like. It was sad that Donovan's impression of me meant so much to me.

"Laney?" Brent asked again. "Is that a yes, but you're too shy to speak with everyone here?"

"No thank you, Brent. I haven't had a chance to talk to my mom all weekend. I'd like to catch up with her before this trip is done."

"But you see your mom all the time. A cup of coffee – that's all I ask."

"No thank you, Brent."

"Mrs. Reid?" Brent now was addressing my mom.

"She said no, Brent. Move along." Donovan spoke up this time.

Brett walked right up to me and whispered in my ear, "May I then have at least a phone number, email address, Twitter handle?"

That gave me a good chuckle. I took out a piece of paper and wrote, *"Good day, Brent. My heart belongs to another man."*

He laughed at what I'd written and tousled James' hair. "You're a lucky man," he spoke and went back to his seat.

"What did you write down?" Becky and Jane asked at the same time.

I was about to tell them the truth when Donovan angrily said, "You didn't give that asshole your number did you?" He once again assumed the worst of me.

I decided it was nobody's business what I wrote to Brent, and continued eating breakfast. Apparently, my non-answer wasn't a good enough answer as Donovan barked, "Outside, now! Let's talk!"

I stared at him wondering what I should do. I had no desire to go outside and talk to this man. Lucky for me, I didn't have to do anything. My dad and Jake took care of the situation, and told Donovan to sit and finish his breakfast.

On the plane I sat myself between each twin and made sure Donovan had no way of getting to me. And once we landed, I was in the clear as I ran into a car with Jake and Emily and the twins, and went straight home. As soon as we got on the cul-de-sac, I said my good-byes and I took the dress over to Bee's before possibly running into Donovan. Sure, I was being a chicken and avoiding confrontation, but I only had three days left, and I'd be in the clear for a year. And during that year, I'd find other interests and get rid of this stale one.

Today wasn't as bad of a day as yesterday, as long as I didn't think about what Donovan had said to me last night.

May 28, 2013
Camellia

By the end of this week, I'd be on an entirely different continent, experiencing a completely new life. My bags were packed, my good-byes were said, and after this past weekend, my heart knew its place in Donovan Taylor's life. The best I could, I wrote off that chapter of my life and looked toward the future with a reticent smile. I couldn't put into words what this last weekend did to my heart. I guess it was the nail I needed to close my coffin.

Dinner? Bee texted.
Sure. Where?
Sushi?
Yes!
I'll send over directions now. 7:30. Let's meet at the sushi bar.
Cool. See you then.

I was all ready to leave now. All the items that needed to be shipped were shipped, and my one carry-on suitcase was packed and ready to go.

I had accomplished a lot today. And the best part was, I accomplished it with my mom and with a (somewhat) happy heart.

At 7:30 sharp, I walked into the sushi bar excited to see Bee probably for the last time. I felt bad I hadn't told her that I was leaving on Thursday. I planned to rectify the situation tonight.

I stopped dead on my feet when I saw Donovan sitting at the sushi bar and unfortunately, Donovan saw me before I could turn around and leave. He got up and grabbed my hand before I could take another step toward the door.

"Don't go," he said it like he almost meant it.

"Please tell Bee that something came up and I had to leave," I whispered and tried to walk out.

Donovan pulled me even closer to him. In fact, he was holding me in his arms. "I'm sorry." His apology was like a plea. "Please stay. I have so much to say to you."

"I don't want to hurt anymore." I whispered back a plea.

"I won't hurt you anymore. I promise."

He let go of me and held my hand over to the sushi bar. Guests who stared at us probably thought we were a couple the way we clung to one another. Donovan was only feeling guilty, and I just couldn't walk away from his affection—even if it was only in the way of an apology.

"Hot or cold sake?" He started with the light-hearted conversation.

"Cold. I don't like hot sake."

"Cold it is. Anything you don't eat?"

"Nothing where the eyes are looking back at me."

"Got it," he smiled and put his hand on my face for a brief second.

"Where's Bee?"

"Not coming. I had her text you because this was the only way I could get you alone." Should I be happy he did this? Nope, I should've been scared.

"OK, I'm alone. Talk."

The server brought our sake, we toasted and Donovan began. "I'm sorry for getting upset with you and for what I said. Brent is the biggest asshole, and it pissed me off when I saw you walking in with him. How do you know Brent?"

"I don't know him, except for whatever I might remember now about my childhood. He was a stranger to me at the reception."

"Then why'd you walk in with him like he was your date?"

"I didn't. After Ellie usurped the bride's intro, I was trying to catch up to James, and Brent caught me off guard and placed my hand in his arm. By the time I realized what was happening, we were making an entrance and I didn't want to cause a scene."

"Well, you made quite a statement walking in with the brother of the bride."

"I didn't know that, and he had no idea who I was. I told him I was the twins' babysitter, and I also told him that I had a date when he asked if I was with anybody."

"Yeah?" Donovan's lips turned into a casual smile. "Who was your date?"

"James," I giggled realizing how silly that sounded.

"That kid gets all the chicks already." Donovan chuckled. "I'm going to have to learn from him."

"I'm sure he gets all his charm from his dad and godfather. There are no better teachers."

"Brent is a world-class asshole. To say that Jake and I don't like him is a mild statement. That doesn't excuse what I mouthed off to you when I saw you, but please take my word when I tell you that you don't want to go out with him. His sister, Ashley is sweet, but Brent is a dick."

"So noted," was really all I could say. I had no interest in Brent to begin with, so it didn't really matter what Donovan said about him.

"You'll cut off all communication?"

"There's none to cut off. We met, we talked, we separated. I highly doubt I'll ever have any contact with him, ever."

"Didn't you give him your number when you handed him that piece of paper?"

I shook my head no.

"Then what'd you write on there?" Donovan really had no reason to know. Moreover, I wanted him to suffer—if anything, to suffer out of curiosity. "Delaney...!" He pleaded.

"I don't think it's any of your business what I wrote on that piece of paper."

"All right. If you don't want to tell me, there's nothing I can do. Just know that it pissed me off to see that asshat smile the way he did after reading your note. That's why I slipped again and accused you of giving him your number."

"Look," giving off a heavier sigh than intended, I was unsure what I exactly wanted to say. "We've had this conversation before. I can forgive your overbearing big brother attitude, but I can't easily forgive you questioning my reputation. I've done nothing to have you or anyone question what I have and have not done with other men. As a matter of fact, yours was the first real..." Shit. I didn't mean to confess that part. How utterly embarrassing. I could feel myself turning red.

I caught Donovan's attention. He wasn't going to let this one go easily. "I was your first what?"

"Nothing." I tried to play it off.

It wasn't working. "Oh no you don't! You can't say something like that and not finish your statement. Give it up Delaney Reid!"

"No," I begged. "It's really embarrassing. I can't finish that statement. It shouldn't have even come out to begin with."

"Shit. There's no fucking way you are getting out of this one. I know how to get it out of you." He spoke with the server passing by, and she eventually produced a beautiful box. It looked like an old-fashioned hatbox, except it was square rather than round.

"What's this?"

He gave me that devilish grin that made his eyes look as shiny blue as Ian Somerhalder, his face as handsomely chiseled as David Beckham, his hair as stylishly unmanageable as Harry Styles, and his smile as gorgeous as Bradley Cooper. How could a man be this beautiful?

"It's a gift for you I had the hostess hold onto till we were done with dinner. This is yours in exchange for the rest of that sentence."

Was I going to make this deal? As much as I didn't want to, I knew I couldn't stand to leave this box unopened.

"Just agree. I know this is a weakness of yours. I've heard stories about you sneaking down early Christmas morning to open up, and then rewrap your gifts. Curiosity will kill you, Little Girl." He now laughed an evil laugh.

"That's mean!"

"No. You leaving me hanging to wonder what you were going to say is mean."

"All right. You've got a deal. BUT, I get to decide when I'm going to give you the rest of the information."

"No way. What if you reneg?"

"I promise I won't reneg. It'll take me a bit of time and courage to finish that sentence. It's embarrassing."

Donovan considered it briefly, then handed me the box. "I'm trusting you to keep your word."

Smiling big, I was like a little girl on Christmas morning, unwrapping the best looking present under the tree. The present inside far exceeded my expectation, and was a million times more beautiful than the timeless box. "What?" I couldn't finish the sentence, again.

"I'd never seen a more beautiful sight than that of you walking in wearing this dress. It was made for you."

"But Bee needs this for her spring collection. This was going to be her pièce de résistance. I can't take this."

"It's yours. No one can wear this like you can. I convinced Bee to give it up. She'll make a new one—in fact, that's probably what she's doing right now." He chuckled. "Look in the box, there's more."

I quickly looked back in, and waiting for me was a medium-sized black box with the word CHANEL written in white, right dab in the middle.

"Open it," he urged when I stopped.

Once the box was opened, a good-sized incredibly soft jewelry box was waiting for me. It had the signature quilted Chanel sheep-skin fabric with a short chained double-C as one zipper slider, and a tiny Chanel lock with key as the other zipper slider. I had no jewelry to place inside this beautiful box, but knowing it came from Donovan, I'd cherish it forever.

"It's gorgeous, but..." As much as I loved all that Donovan had given me, I didn't want anything out of guilt. No matter how desperate I was for this man's attention, I didn't want anything because he felt the need to make amends. "You don't have to buy me anything. You've bought me all those dresses already, and the shoes. I was hurt when you made that comment at the wedding, but this gesture isn't necessary."

"Unzip the jewelry case," he gently urged.

I did as he told me to do. Wrapped around a black cushioned-pillow that sat from one end of the jewelry case to the other was a modern-day version of the camellia necklace I wore to the wedding. He knew...he understood my intentions to match us, camellia for camellia, at the wedding. It was slightly embarrassing that he caught on to my childish pairing, but I was thrilled he paid enough attention to me to notice Gram's necklace.

I must have looked at him in awe. "Thank you for my button covers and cuff links."

"How'd you know it was me?"

"I didn't at first. When I found the gift in my pockets, I figured it was Bee being thoughtful. It was only when you turned away from me, with eyes full of tears, that I noticed the dramatic camellia dangling from your back. My big regret—among a myriad of regrets that night—was that we didn't get a picture together. We will have to go out again one night wearing the same outfits. We would've looked great next to one another."

"All these gifts are too much. I don't know what to say. I should return them to you, but to be honest, I want to keep them all; they're exquisite."

"They are all for you, Delaney."

"I guess what I'm trying to say is, you don't have to buy these for me because you feel guilty. All you had to do was apologize."

"These gifts were yours the moment I saw you walk in. I knew I'd convince Bee to let you have this dress. And the necklace—think of it as a thank you for my thoughtful gift." Whether or not we'd ever get to dress up in our matching outfits and spend an evening together, I'd cherish Donovan's thoughtfulness. "Will you excuse me? It's a client calling and I need to take this," Donovan said, looking at his ringing phone.

"Sure."

While he stepped out, I took out a pen and a piece of paper and scribbled,

Yours was my first real kiss. I will remember it, always.

Quickly folding the note, I stuffed it in Donovan's pocket again and hoped he would find this note long after I was gone.

"Shall we leave?"

It was late, and this was possibly my last meeting with Donovan till I got back home next year. Did I tell him I was leaving on Thursday? Would he really care? What would it accomplish for me to tell him I was leaving? What could he possibly say but, "oh," or "have a nice trip?" Tonight was a memory I wouldn't forget, no matter the passing of time. Rather than leaving one another on an awkward note, I thought it best to be able to flashback to such a wondrous time, for me.

"What's on your mind?" Donovan asked with a flashing of a devious smile. "Could it be how you are going to finish that one particular sentence?"

I laughed. "No. I've already figured out how to finish that sentence. You'll have to figure out where I've hidden it." I flashed back an equally devious smile, and got out of the car that was parked in my driveway. "I'll give you a hint. This car holds the rest of my sentence. If you can find it, it's yours to keep. If you can't, then I've held up my part of the bargain; you can't blame me if you're curious the rest of your life." I leaned over and kissed him on the cheek one last time. "Thank you," I whispered with much sadness. *I love you, and will remember tonight for a very long time.*

Donovan barely noticed me leaving as he furiously searched the car for my note. I saw him bend over and open the glove compartment. By the way he was moving his arms, it looked like he was dumping all the contents onto the passenger seat. Watching him from my window, frustration mounted with each minute, as he couldn't find the note. He gave up, sooner than I'd hoped, and pulled the car out of the driveway and left.

May 29, 2013
Confession

Tonight was it. My last night in LA, and my last chance to tell Donovan how I felt. I guess my feelings were the worst kept secret as just about everyone on this block seemed privy to my heart. I've been encouraged by Grandfather and Gram, Mom and Dad, Jake and Emily, and even Max, to reveal my hand and heart to Donovan. I feared rejection—though my life with Donovan Taylor had been nothing but...

"Won't you consider telling Donovan how you feel before leaving, tomorrow?" Jake encouraged me one last time.

I'd had a nice dinner with my parents and Doug, and we got through the meal without Mom crying about me leaving. I walked over to Emily and Jake's to spend a little more time with them before my graduation and move, tomorrow.

"I don't know, Jake. That's a tough one. I've held it in for so long...and I'm afraid of his reaction. If he laughs at me or rejects me outright, I'd be devastated. I like thinking that there's a miniscule possibility of him being interested in me. That gives me hope. Though, I'm leaving to get rid of all this hope."

"But Laney," Emily interjected. "That's not the only reason why you're leaving. When you first came up with the idea of moving away for a year, wasn't it to experience life abroad and to enjoy your year before starting another round of school? Donovan wasn't the main reason why you had decided to leave, was it?"

"Donovan wasn't the reason at all, initially, but as the days pass, it gets harder and harder to be near him and know that he doesn't return my feelings. I feel like an obsessed fan. He makes me so incredibly happy when I'm with him and he gives me attention, but I'm also so miserable when he doesn't find me interesting. I don't like what I've become, and I've got a golden opportunity to start fresh somewhere new."

"You may be surprised at Donovan's response if you tell him how you feel."

A part of me thought that maybe Jake knew something I didn't know. Perhaps his best friend had confided in him. Nevertheless, did I want to be the one to confess my feelings first, especially having no idea how the other person felt about me? There was no way I was going to take that chance.

"I'll think about it, Jake. But I'm not making any promises. I most likely won't get up the courage to tell him. He doesn't even know that I'm leaving tomorrow."

"He doesn't?" Emily was surprised to find out. "Why haven't you told him? What if he wants to stop you from leaving? For all you know, he may have feelings for you."

A bit confused as to why both Jake and Emily continually urged me to confess my feelings to Donovan, my hope grew. If anyone knew anything about Donovan's feelings, it would be these two. Were my eyes closed to some obvious feelings? Donovan had been hot and cold, but I always believed it had everything to do with him feeling like my older brother and protector, rather than a man interested in a woman.

Unable to sleep after such a conversation, I got up the courage to drive over to Donovan's. Sitting outside his house for a few minutes, I came up with several scenarios as to why I was here so late at night. I could tell him the truth and leave the ball in his court. I could tell him I was here to say good-bye. I could tell him...there were no other options but the first two. Either reveal my feelings or fall back on saying good-bye. I could do this!

"Hello, Laney. What brings you here at this hour?" Crushed to see a glamorous and smug Kate answering Donovan's door, I stuttered my way to asking about Donovan. "He's getting dressed. Give him a moment." She didn't ask me in. She had me stand outside as I heard footsteps racing to the door.

"Delaney, what a nice surprise." Donovan, who was buttoning up his shirt, looked pleased to see me, but was also somewhat preoccupied.

"I'm sorry to barge in on you at your home. Jake gave me your address and I wanted to..."

"Would you like to come in," Kate invited me into Donovan's home as though it was her own. As she stood next to Donovan in his home, at the front door, I was beyond devastated and embarrassed. Devastated that she was in his house at this time of night, and embarrassed that I'd intruded on their evening.

Was I crazy to want to confess my feelings to him? Why did Jake and Emily have to encourage me to talk to him? Obviously, they didn't know him as well as I thought they did. He was home, with his former girlfriend, at this late hour. There was no chance in hell that he thought of me as anything but a little sister.

But, I wanted to see him one last time. I wanted to talk to him one more time. I wanted to feel his affection for even a brief second, one last time.

"I'm sorry, Mr. Taylor. I came by to...never mind. It's not important. I'll get going."

"Wait, Delaney." He caught up to me as I approached my car. "Kate's leaving soon. I'll stop by and we'll talk?"

"You don't have to. It was nothing important."

He slowly pushed away my overgrown bangs and tucked them behind my ear. Perhaps that was the last image I'd have of him, and the very last sense of intimacy with that gesture. So very flippantly, my heart wanted to do what Emily and Jake had convinced me to do tonight, and tell him how much of my heart he unwittingly held.

"I have your graduation present, and I want to see your face when I hand it to you. Wait up for me? It might be a bit late to ring your doorbell, so wait for me on the swing on your front porch. I should be there soon."

That was the same swing where we were to meet when I asked him to marry me. Ten years later, he finally remembered and was obliging to my request.

"All right." I answered with renewed hope and unspeakable cheer. Regardless of his intention for meeting me tonight, regardless of his feelings for me, I'd reveal my heart and let him decide what to do with it.

Hurriedly, I sat on the swing hanging from my porch. This was my favorite place to be as a little girl, and swinging back and forth waiting for Donovan, took me back to the happy days of my youth. All kinds of nostalgic feelings traipsed through my mind and heart and a renewed happiness I hadn't felt in years engulfed me.

My future was beginning now.

The wait would not be much longer...

No different from Cinderella when her clock struck midnight, my life reverted to reality, and I was that same young woman whose tender heart got ensnared in this game of hope.

It was almost four in the morning, and for the second time in my life, I waited for this absent man to answer my love. No longer could I feel my fingers and toes, and little dots of water illuminated my head in this dark night. The searing pain that burned a hole in my heart numbed the shivers I experienced. Devastation continued.

This was a fitting end to a one-sided romance all conjured up in my head. I'd leave today and forget this man who never remembered me when it counted. Who was I kidding? He never remembered me at all.

May 30, 2013
Time To Say Goodbye...

*T*oday was it.

Graduation done.

Mom and Dad rejoiced at the announcement of my summa cum laude accolade and medical school acceptance.

A new year abroad started in a few hours.

And most importantly, this was my chance to let go.

"Mom, please don't cry. I'll be back in a year, I promise. I'm not going to London to live; I'm going just to visit. You can come visit me there whenever you want. We can see each other anytime."

"You're making a serious scene, Mom. Laney will be back sooner than you know it." My brother was a bit exasperated with Mom as we were eating a late breakfast together. "In fact, why don't you go with her and stay there for a few months, if it's that hard for you to separate from her?"

"Should I, Henry? Should I buy a ticket right now and fly to London with her?"

"Mom, give me a week or two and we'll see each other again? It'll be crazy once I land, and I really would like to get my bearing as soon as possible. Mrs. Haines, Gram's housekeeper, will help me once I get there."

"You call me daily!"

"I will. I promise. I have to get going, Mom. I want to say good-bye to a few people before I leave."

"All right. I'll miss you, my sweet child." Mom's tears started again.

"Good-bye, Daddy."

"Good-bye Baby. You made me so damn proud today." My dad kissed me on the forehead. "We will talk more about med school once you get to London. I love you."

"You can do your best to convince me." I smiled. "Bye Mom. Bye Daddy."

"Damn. What will they do when you get married?" Doug moaned as he put the car in drive and got us away from our parents who were both crying. "Where to?" Doug volunteered to drive me to the airport, but he knew I had to make a couple of stops, first.

"I need to say bye to Bee. Here's her address."

Just like a professional driver, he drove me to Bee's, but waited in the car.

"What brings you here at this hour?" Bee yawned a great big yawn.

"Bee. It's almost 11:00am. Did you work all night?"

"Yeah. I got to bed only an hour or so ago." She yawned again. "Nice dress, by the way."

I was wearing another one of Bee's creations. Her dresses were beautiful, but what made me feel beautiful was the knowledge that Donovan purchased them for me.

"I came by to say good-bye."

"What the hell? Good-bye for what?"

"I graduated today, and I leave for London in a few hours."

"You're seriously going? I thought it was something you were thinking about for sometime later in the future. You're leaving now?"

"Yes, now."

"You're pissing me off, Laney Reid. I thought we were friends." Bee wasn't kidding about being mad.

"Don't be mad. I tried to tell you a few times, but we kept getting interrupted and I...I'm sorry. I know it wasn't cool. On the one hand, I wanted to tell you all about what was going on with me, but on the other hand, I thought since we just met, and since you're so busy...I just felt kind of stupid explaining my life story to you."

"Did we not bond over your non-paying modeling gig?" She chuckled. "You even confessed to being in love with my nephew for half your life. Is that not close to bff status?" That made me chuckle.

"We did, and I'm really sorry. But, I assume you come to London and Paris often?"

"Not often, but I will be there in a couple of weeks. I have a buyer in London who wants to meet with me. This guy owns a chain of stores and is interested in possibly having my line in his stores."

"And I assume you'll stay with your almost bff in her grandmother's large home?"

"You betcha! It's going to cost me a fortune to ship out all the clothes ahead of time. Hey," the light bulb went off in her head. "I can ship all the clothes to your place and you can hold them for me till I get there."

"Of course I will. Whatever you need, Bee. I'm happy to help you. You see," I gave her a hug, "we'll see each other even more after I move to Europe. You can always stay with me."

"You know, I think you have my blessing now to leave."

"I'll miss you until we meet again in a couple of weeks. You have my number. Call me and let me know what you need me to do for you."

"All right," she hugged me back, tight. "I wish you a good trip."

With that good-bye done, I went off to Grandfather's office—and of course, Jane and Donovan's office as well. This visit, I dreaded. Though most likely we'd never run into one another, I didn't even want that remote chance.

After a warm conversation with Grandfather and Jane, they walked me to the elevator, and there I saw him one last time. Even after last night's fiasco, I still longed to see him. I didn't want my last memory of him, as a half-dressed, disheveled-looking man standing next to Kate. He was running a meeting with a conference room full of men and women, and all I could do was wave. I waved good-bye to the man who'd never see me for more than I was—a twenty-two-year-old college graduate, green to the world, inexperienced with life. This man ran in a cosmopolitan circle to which I didn't belong.

"You sure you want to leave?" Grandfather knew my heart's desire. How, I did not know, but he knew.

"Yes, Grandfather. I wish you and Gram good health," I whispered to my grandfather.

"Stay and tell him you love him," Grandfather whispered. "You may be surprised at his answer."

I held onto Grandfather, longer than necessary, and decided it was time to make my escape. I didn't need to break down in front of a group of strangers, and I didn't need a confrontation with Donovan.

"Bye," was my last word before getting into the elevator. I stayed as long as I reasonably could—but he still didn't come out to talk to me. There was only so much I could do without stripping my pride bare.

"Let's go." I choked out.

My brother looked concerned. "You all right?"

I nodded yes and explained, "Just a little sad, but I'll be OK."

A (New) Day

The way I met Michael was like a scene out of a Hollywood movie with Audrey Hepburn and her leading man Gregory Peck. After a harried escape from my parents, my family, my...Donovan, I sat on a plane for almost eleven hours squished between a large man, who started the ride with some form of a meat sandwich with raw onions, and a young girl whose hearing was probably shot from the loud music blaring through the earbuds glued in her ears. I say it was a harried escape because I wanted to leave before Mom shed any more tears, before Dad convinced me to stay home, and before I lost the chutzpah, hutzpah—whatever the word was—to set up a new life in a new town. Yes, it was a new day for me. As the saying went, "Out with the old, in with the new."

I was restless for a challenge. It was good to get away from living life outside the idyllic Reid cul-de-sac. All my life, my parents provided a solid education for their children, took us on no-expense-spared family vacations, and allowed us to experience college life to the fullest. Though they weren't crazy about me living in Japan as an exchange student, my parents allowed it. At twenty-two, it probably sounded obnoxious to travel through Europe for a year, but this was the life I envisioned after undergrad.

"Excuse me," I apologized as I ran my suitcase over a pair of shiny, just-got-polished, shoes. "Do your feet hurt? This suitcase probably weighs fifty pounds," I exaggerated.

A polished and dapper face smiled at me. "You can run over my shoes anytime." Of course, he had the most brilliant accent. "I wanted to say hello to you on the plane, but didn't have the guts to go over and introduce myself. Then, I waited for you at the exit, but somehow lost you. Who do I need to thank for this good fortune of getting my feet run over?"

"Why would you be waiting for me?"

"You walked by me on the plane and I couldn't help noticing you. I hoped you'd want to get to know me as I'd like to get to know you."

I couldn't come up with anything more unique than, "Oh!"

"I'm Michael Bennington, by the way."

"Laney Reid."

"A true pleasure," he answered as he took my hand that was resting by my side and kissed it.

Between the rugged good looks and the melt-my-insides English accent, I was mesmerized like a schoolgirl. Why was this man interested in me and who was he?

"Michael!" A girl called out—practically yelled out. "Let's go. Finneas is waiting for us."

"Ruby, come here. Meet my new friend, Laney Reid."

"Hello," she said politely, but was itching to leave the airport. "I'm usually not this rude but our driver is here and we really need to get going," she gritted her teeth and tried her best not to yell at Michael some more.

"We can leave if Laney here will catch a ride with us. Tell me you don't have a ride home. Say that you'll allow me to give you a lift to your place."

I didn't know how to answer this Michael person. Though the thought of catching a cab or the Underground in an unfamiliar city was a daunting one, did I want to be in a car with a complete stranger who expressed a surprising interest in me?

"Laney, I promise—my brother and I are not kidnappers, rapists, killers and the such. Some say my brother's a good bloke and perhaps you and I could become best friends one day, but none of this can happen if we don't get in that car. Finneas has the car parked in the double yellow lines right now, drinking the petrol. I'm sure the traffic warden's hot on

Finneas' tail right now or our lift has been clamped and towed away—in which case, we need to take the Underground. What's it gonna be?"

I was so confused. She spoke English, but her English was different from my American English, that's for sure. Seeing my hesitation, Michael decided for me, and grabbed my carry-on suitcase and walked with his sister.

"Wait!" I chased after them.

"Do you have more luggage?" I shook my head no. "Well, then come on. You heard my sis. She can be bloody ugly when she doesn't get her way."

This probably wasn't the best idea, but they both seemed like decent people, and I actually felt safe with Michael. We did what Ruby wanted us to do, and once we were comfortably ensconced in their car, Ruby relaxed and laughed.

"I was a bit of a nag, wasn't I?"

"Mental, would be a better word. We just met Laney and she's probably thinking we're both nutcases for forcing her into this car. What brings you to London, Laney?" Michael asked over Ruby as she ended up sitting between us.

"I'm going to live here for a year."

"Brill!" Michael showed a great big smile.

"You come to live in a new place for a year with one hand luggage? Do you plan on buying loads of clothes?"

"No, Ruby. The rest of my stuff has been shipped. I didn't want to get lost in the Underground with a cartful of suitcases."

"Tell me your story, Laney. Why's a stunning woman like yourself roaming around, alone, in this big city? Where are you from? Where are your parents? Are you married?"

"Give her some time to breathe, you fool. She looks like a frightened bunny."

"I'm well, Ruby. Thanks for the concern."

"Bugger off, Rubes and let me talk to Laney. Why don't you sit on the other side?" he whispered to her.

I smiled at Michael and Ruby who started arguing in British English, and I understood maybe a third of what they were saying. It also made me happy to see these two because they reminded me so much of my brother and myself.

"Why are you smiling, pretty lady?"

"You and your sister remind me of me and my brother. I'm twenty-two and my brother is twenty-four. We have the same cantankerous relationship."

"We four are the same age," Michael commented.

"It must be destiny," Ruby mimicked in a higher pitched voice.

My phone rang just in time to stop the two from arguing again.

"Hi Emily. Sorry I didn't call when I landed. It's been a little crazy here."

"Hi. How was your flight? Are you on your way to the flat or are you there already?"

"I've made some friends and they're giving me a ride to Gram's. The flight was long, but fine."

"Friends? Already?"

"I'll explain later."

"What will you do today? Is the weather dreary?"

"No, not at all, it's a nice day here today. Once I get to the flat, I'll get my bearings and maybe go explore a city a bit."

"Call me after you get settled?"

"Definitely. I'll call Mom and Dad tomorrow since I know it's late over there."

I heard a muffled sound in the background and Emily said quietly, "Donovan is still here and he'd like to talk to you."

"Please tell him I had to go. I don't think I can say good-bye." My heart hurt again thinking about the man I wouldn't see for a year.

"Good-bye. Take care of yourself, OK? Talk to you soon?"

"Yes and please give the twins a kiss for me."

"Will do."

Even before I hung up the phone, the questions came in a flurry. "Who's Emily? I assume Gram is your grandmother; will you be staying with her? I also assume these twins belong to Emily? If you must answer only one of these questions, I need to know who this man is that you're running away from."

On. The. Nose! But Michael didn't need to know that. "Emily is my cousin's wife and yes, she and Jake have the most beautiful twins. Here are pictures of them." I scrolled through all the pictures that I had.

"Wow! They are beautiful babies," both siblings commented.

"Gram is my English grandmother who has a home here, but currently lives in Los Angeles with her new husband and our family, and the man I'm 'running from?'" I smiled. "He's a family friend and I am not running from him. He's someone who's a tad bit upset with me because I didn't say my good-byes to him before I left. I'll talk to him when he gets over the snub." I tried to make light of my situation.

"So, he's not my competition?"

I laughed heartily this time. "There's no one competing for my heart or hand. I am single, newly graduated, my entire family lives in Southern California, and I'm just fortunate enough to be able to take some time off and enjoy this beautiful country for a year."

"Are you loaded?"

"Rubes, what a stupid question."

I laughed again. "With the cost of living here, I doubt I'll keep my head above water, but my grandmother is allowing me to stay in her flat, rent free for a year, so at least I'll have a roof over my head."

"Where does your grand mum live?"

"An area called Belgravia?"

"She is loaded!" Ruby exclaimed.

I cut Michael off before he got upset with his sister for the tenth time. "The home's been in my Gram's family for generations. I don't know if that means anything. By your expression, I take it Gram lives in a nice neighborhood?"

"I take it you haven't been there in a while?"

"It's been at least a decade since I've been to her home. I don't remember much of Gram's home except it's near the River Thames and Buckingham Palace."

"I'm happy to tell you that your Gram lives in a beautiful neighborhood, and that is also where we live. Welcome to the neighborhood. I suspect we will be seeing a lot of each other."

Was it good that I would be seeing a lot of Michael, or did it spell trouble? As of now, it seemed like a good prospect. The dynamic between he and his sister reminded me a lot of Doug and myself and they portrayed a fun relationship.

"Do you have parents? Do they live with you?"

"Yes our parents are alive, and they stay with us when they're in London, but most of the time they are out in the countryside." Michael smiled fondly speaking of his parents.

"Are you a close knit family?"

They both laughed and Michael explained, "Would it bother you if I said we practically live in each other's pockets?"

"I love close-knit families. We Reids are a tight lot as well. We all live on the same cul-de-sac back in LA."

"No kidding?" Ruby asked.

"No kidding. Before my grandparents had five sons, Grandpa Reid had the vision to buy an entire block and eventually each son got a lot. Once they earned enough money, they built their homes and all still own them, but now, only my family, Jake and Emily's family, and Jake's parents' family, along with my grandparents live there."

"We're at your Gram's home." Michael politely interrupted. "Rubes, why don't you take the car and go ahead, and I'll walk home after I make sure Laney is settled."

Ruby nodded her head in agreement, and Michael pushed me out of the car and didn't give me a choice in this matter. Michael picked up my suitcase, put his hand gently on my back, and led me to Gram's English home.

On a cobbled street with what looked like attached cookie cutter apartments next to and facing one another, I was transported to another world when I entered the home. A sweet older lady opened the door for me as I bumbled with the keys, and after describing herself as Gram's housekeeper, she gave us the grand tour of this stunning home.

Michael explained to me that it was normal to have four or even five levels to a home in this neighborhood. But Mrs. Haines explained that Gram pretty much stayed on the ground floor.

"This home is so grand. And what is a reception room and why is there one on every floor?"

Michael looked at me and that's when I first noticed him. He reminded me of baby James with wavy brown hair and green eyes, and he had a heavy five o'clock shadow from being on the plane all night. There was a slight scar on the side of his forehead, almost Harry Potter-like, and he was the Daniel Craig—rough and rugged looking I so admired. He wasn't a "wow" at first glance, but he grew on me in a comfortable way, and he was definitely handsome in his own right.

"You're staring at me. What's the verdict?"

"I find you comfortably handsome."

Disgruntled like a schoolboy he asked, "What does that mean?"

"How did you get that Harry Potter scar on your forehead?"

"You tell me I'm comfortably good-looking and then focus on the scar." Now he was pouting and that definitely reminded me of James.

"I like the scar. I think I'm attracted to imperfection."

"I'm imperfect, you're attracted to imperfection, so I'll deduce you're attracted to me?"

"We're all imperfect. If you use that kind of reasoning, then I'd be attracted to every man I meet." I could tell I was frustrating him, and he could tell I was enjoying it.

"What the hell does that mean?"

Luckily, I was saved by the bell. The phone rang and it was Doug, who was probably checking up on me, as that was part of an older brother's résumé.

"Hey, Doug. You're up late, or early," I answered happily.

"Delaney, it's Donovan." He didn't sound too happy. Could it be because I ignored all of his calls? There were several missed calls, texts and voicemails, which I deleted immediately. Moreover, I purposely pushed his calls over to voicemail.

"Hey Mr. Taylor, how are you?" I acted as if I had no idea why he was upset.

"I think you know damn well how I am."

"I don't, and I'm sure you want to spell it out for me, but I'm in the middle of getting a house tour, plus I'm entertaining a guest so can we talk about this later?"

"How the hell do you have a guest already, when you just arrived there? Who do you know in London already?"

"So now I'm an imperfect guest with the scar on his forehead that you are entertaining?"

That made me crack up.

"Who is that?" After what happened the night before I left, I didn't think he had any right to question whom I spent my time with.

"I told you I have a guest over. I need to call you back, OK?"

"Are you really going to call me back or are you just saying this to get me off the phone?" Now the cantankerous tone dissipated and Donovan's voice almost sounded insecure. Had I actually used the words insecure and Donovan in the same sentence? There was no way this man was insecure about anything.

"To be honest with you, Mr. Taylor, I don't know what I'm really going to do. This is the best I can give you for now. Good-bye." I hung up the phone abruptly.

"And ex-boyfriend? The one that you are running from?"

"No and no. He's just a friend, an *old* friend."

The house tour didn't take long and Michael finally went home so I could unpack and settle into my new abode. It was weird being at a strange home with no one else, but a once-a-week helper. For the first time, I'd be completely alone. In Tokyo, I was living in the dorms at the university so even though my family wasn't there, I had around-the-clock friends. Here, I was on my own spreading my wings and forging a new, if temporary, life.

As soon as the plane landed, my emotions were thrown into a tumultuous battle—fear vs. excitement, regret vs. satisfaction, sadness vs. happiness, and most importantly heartache vs. a chance for a new day, new life, and new beginnings. I had told myself that before the plane landed on English soil, I'd rid myself of the old life, old ways of looking at life, and give myself every opportunity to experience a life without feelings of dejection. Rather than constantly looking for another chance to see, talk, hope, and love—only to feel despondent when none of these happened – I would live life without the presupposed broken heart waiting for its daily curtain call. This year was my chance to live renewed and with confidence.

A knock on the door interrupted my self-help, self-esteem roll call.

"Michael. You're back…already." I laughed even before adding that last word.

"Ruby wants to invite you to tea, breakfast, lunch, brunch—whatever." Did I want this kind of attention already? Was Michael's attention part of this self-help, self-program or would this all eventually turn into regret? "Does it normally take you this long to come up with an answer?"

He brought out laughter from me again. "I guess I should say yes since I haven't eaten since yesterday. Although I think Mrs. Haines is cooking enough food for the entire month."

"May I walk you to our home?"

"Lead the way." Michael wasn't Donovan and he wasn't meant to be, but he was a fun distraction.

Michael and Ruby's home was not much different from Gram's. It, too, had four stories, six bedrooms, just as many bathrooms, two kitchens and a ballroom-like room on every floor. I didn't get that, or the two kitchens, but I didn't bother asking. I figured it was an English thing.

"Brill, Michael. You were able to convince her we weren't as loony as we looked?" Ruby gave me a friendly hug.

"Thank you for the invitation. I haven't eaten since lunch, yesterday."

"Gawd, blimey, don't they feed you in that cattle class?" Ruby took me to an intimate dining room and a flurry of people came out and set up the brunch table against the wall. They laid out enough food for about twenty people.

"Will that be all, Lady Alexandra?"

"Yes. This is wonderful, thank you," she answered someone who looked and sounded just like Mrs. Haines.

"Welcome home, Lady Alexandra."

"Thank you."

"Was what you said the equivalent of 'OMG, don't they feed you in coach?'"

Michael and Ruby died laughing. "Yeah. OMG, don't they feed you in coach?" Ruby repeated in a perfect American accent. Michael soon started talking American-English and they re-enacted some of the conversations between me and Michael.

"How do you do that so well? And why would you want to have an American accent when your accent is so beautiful? There are fewer things sexier on a man than an English accent."

Michael immediately changed his accent and went back to his indigenous roots. Ruby and I laughed at him.

"Shall we get lunch, then get to know one another a little better?" Michael accentuated his accent this time.

"Thank you," I answered and we piled up our plates with delicious English fare.

"So why are you really here in London?" Ruby was suspicious of me and quite curious, unnecessarily curious.

"I'll tell you all about myself if you'll explain why your brother calls you Ruby, but everyone else calls you Alexandra. Also, is Lady a formality, a term of endearment, or a title?"

"You first."

"There really isn't much else to tell. I wasn't lying when I said that I am just here for year to live the English life. I have a generous grandmother, parents who are OK with me putting off school for a year, and I just wanted to try something new."

"What do you mean put off school for a year?" Ruby asked.

"Nuh-uh! You're up. Also, I'm adding that I want you to teach me how to put on makeup the way you do because you are gorgeous." Ruby was stunning. She had red, full lips accentuated by her ruby red lipstick, deep brown eyes and straight, straight brown hair. There wasn't a flyaway anywhere. Her eyeliner was on perfectly, and wickedly close to the edge of her line, eye shadow had all the proper layers from the basecoat to the neutral colors, topped off by the darker colors. Her lashes were either generously God-given or false—and incredibly envy-worthy. Her makeup was perfection. "And by the way, where does the name Alexandra come from? Aren't you English?"

"Really? You find my sister gorgeous?"

"Yes. Don't you?"

"She's all right. You're the real beauty." Ruby groaned and rolled her eyes.

"OK, Ruby Alexandra. What's your story?"

Michael was the one who rolled his eyes this time, but allowed his sister to explain the story.

"My real name is Ruby Alexandra Bennington, but it was so boring I changed the spelling of my name to A-l-e-k rather than A-l-e-x. And to bring a little excitement into this blue-blooded English family, I tell everyone that I'm from Slovenia. Or at least that I'm part Slovenian—that I am the offspring of a love affair between my father and a Slovenian mistress."

"Seriously?"

Ruby, or Aleksandra, laughed at me.

"That's hilarious. What a great personality you have. I hope we can become friends."

"Isn't that what we are, already?"

"I guess we are." I thought about this odd and unexpected turn of events. I'd left home to get away from a man and here I was, courting the attention of another, incredibly sweet and down to earth man, with a sister who could be my new best friend. There was no pretense, no games, just pure humor and fun with these two.

"You're off in space again. Are you done with us? You want me to take you home?"

"No. I'll walk home on my own. I want to explore the neighborhood. Maybe I'll go over to the river and walk off this lunch."

"Would you like company?"

"Would it be the height of rudeness if I answered no?" By the downcast look on his face, I could tell I was being a bad friend.

"Laney," Aleksandra said between a fake cough, and all in one breath, "take my brother or he may shut himself in his room and cry till next Tuesday."

That made me crack up. I knew Aleksandra and I would definitely become good friends. "Well, we wouldn't want that." I winked at my new girlfriend. "Come on, tour guide. Make sure I don't get lost in this neighborhood where all the buildings look the same."

Michael was quiet all the way to the river. Perhaps I did offend him when I said no to his offer.

"I just wanted some time to think and get to know my surroundings. I'm not the best conversationalist when I'm tired and I feel like I've been up several days. I didn't mean to offend you in any way, especially after how generous you and Aleksandra have been to me."

"Huh?" Michael was in deep thought and hadn't listened to anything I'd said.

"I'm trying to say that I'm sorry if I offended you earlier." He only stared at me. I had no clue what he was thinking.

Though this silence made me slightly nervous, in the short time we'd known each other, I had to admit that this man made me feel...comfortable. That was the best way to describe him. We'd just met but he didn't seem like a stranger. Whether or not they knew it, both he and Aleksandra offered a diversion from the ritualistic angst I'd felt back at home. They brought humor and a new delight and vigor, in contrast to my usual dreariness.

"Do you believe in love at first sight?" His question made me want to laugh, but he was so serious, I didn't. "Well?" he asked as he came closer to me.

"I used to, but I gave that up two nights ago."

"Why?"

"Because I was once in love with someone at first sight, and eventually realized it was fanciful thinking that this person would return my love." My heart cried just a little again. "I struggled with what he thought of me, how I could make him notice me, and how I could possibly get him to return my love. When this turned into an obsession, I decided love at first sight didn't exist—that it was just a childhood fantasy. That's when I gave up on it."

"I hope I don't scare you when I tell you that the first time I saw you on the plane, walking back toward that bloody awful crowd of people with a disarming smile on your face, I knew this was what Adam must've felt when God made Eve out of the ribs of his body. Adam could do none other than exclaim, 'This is the bone of my bones, and flesh of my flesh.'

I cannot imagine how I existed before you, and how my life will continue to move on if I don't do my damned best to win your hand."

Somewhere in the middle of his beautiful profession, he had both my hands in his, brought them up to his lips, and delicately kissed them. Something about this moment turned off the crying faucet and persuaded me into believing that I'd made the right choice in coming to this new land.

"You know..." I lightened up this sweet, but uncomfortable situation. "I'm not into men who declare their intention within three hours of our meeting." I smiled genuinely.

He stared at his watch, waited a full minute, and started his speech again. "I hope I don't scare you..." I cracked up and put up my hand to signal for him to stop. "What? It's now officially three hours and one minute."

"Is that right? You've recorded exactly the time we met?"

He tapped his temple and uttered between a laugh, "It's all in here. I don't have a Harvard degree for nothing. If I learned anything in business school, it was to record the exact time my future began."

"Michael, I'm sorry but I can't and don't return your wonderfully romantic sentiment. I wish I did, but I barely know you. You don't know me either."

"My declaration must look disingenuous. You probably think I'm only interested in your body since I know you about as well as the last stranger Rubes and I picked up from the airport, and befriended..." I spotted a quick mischievous glint before he went back to Mr. Serious. "I just want a chance to court you. You can decide for yourself if you want me for my body as well."

"Considering I don't even know your middle name, how about if we become friends? I don't know anyone here, I'd love to get to know Aleksandra better, and if you happen to tag along here and there, I won't complain." I sported the same mischief during my speech. "And if I decide I want you for your body, I'll let you know."

"Deal." He put his hand on the small of my back and led me toward Gram's home. "My name is Michael Henry Montague Bennington,

Marquess of Salisbury, Earl of Warwick, 3rd in line to a dukedom, son of Michael Bennington, 1st Marquess of…"

"OK… perhaps I'll learn your parents' names and title in another lifetime, if I ever meet them."

"They'll be here today. Will you join us for dinner, tonight?"

"No thank you. I'll let you enjoy your family time without the intrusion of a stranger. Were you kidding me when you called out all your titles?"

"Nope. You wanted to know my name. I gave you my entire name, title, and family background, though you rudely interrupted me before I finished my family history."

"Well, I'll give you my family history next time we meet, from my four aunts and uncles to the many cousins to the twins. But until then, I bid you good-bye."

"Please join us for dinner?"

"No thank you, Michael. I'd like to rest and settle in. Plus, I'm sure I have loads to learn from Mrs. Haines."

Michael sighed seconds before his eyes lit up with what he probably thought were more bright ideas. I shook my head no before he suggested them.

"Tomorrow?"

I shrugged my shoulders to another bothered sigh.

"Good-bye."

He lifted my hand to his lips and kissed me adieu.

After a long enjoyable talk with Mrs. Haines who told me she'd be back next week, I went up to my room and lay in bed. I needed to sort my head about what had happened before I left home and throw out all that was unhealthy for my well-being.

"We will all miss you, so much, Laney. Why must you be gone for an entire year?"

"Don't cry, Emily. The kids are getting sad too. I came to say good-bye and to give my love to my favorite twins."

"Did you see Donovan last night?"

"I saw him…with Kate, and though he told me he'd come see me, he never did."

"Are you sure he didn't come by? Maybe it was too late and he left when he realized you weren't there?"

"I waited all night for him."

"Oh Laney..."

"I'm such a loser, huh? It's all right. That was a good way to end. There's no more hope. I'll keep in touch, regularly. Don't worry."

"You better, or the twins will forget their favorite godmother."

"James and Ellie? Don't you forget me the year that I'm gone. I'm sorry I won't be here to watch you grow, but I'm sure your godfather will love you doubly, in my stead. I love you."

"I love you, Laney. Be well."

"Thank you. I love you too, Emily."

The sound of the heavy knocker against an even heavier wood door woke me up from my daydream. Unaware how long my guest had been knocking, I ran downstairs to greet the person behind the persistence.

"Well it's about bloody time you answered the door. I'm freezing my bum off in this cold weather."

"Aleksandra. Don't you go through snowy winters here? How can you call this cold? I see the sun outside."

"This is what happens when you're used to sunny Southern California weather. You become a wimp to cold."

"Come in. Welcome to my temporary home." I showed her around Gram's palace.

"Too much home for one person, no?"

"It's only for a year."

"Not if my brother has anything to do with it. He has you settling down in England and having beautiful babies and future heirs to his dukedom, last I heard. He was prattling off his plans to all of us so bloody much that I decided to take refuge in your house."

I gave an uncomfortable smile.

"I take it you haven't thought of changing nappies and comparing the pros and cons of dummies vs. thumb sucking?"

That completely dissolved any uncomfortable feelings.

"Are you here to hang out with me till your family dinner time?"

"Yes. However, I've been tasked with the duty of bringing you home tonight. Mum is dying to meet you."

"I'd rather not, Aleksandra. I just met your brother and I made it clear to him that I was not interested in the same way. If I go tonight, he'll misunderstand, your parents will misunderstand, and eventually you and I won't be able to continue this friendship."

"Wow, you have this all figured out don't you?" She was being sarcastic. "I tell you what, come as my dinner guest tonight. You don't even have to talk to Michael if you don't want to. I'll introduce you to my parents as my friend." She pleaded. "Please come and satisfy my mother's curiosity."

"What is she so curious about?"

"Hello...! You are who she is curious about. Being a future duke, Michael has had his choice of just about every single girl in England, and maybe even Scotland and Ireland and all the other neighboring countries. And trust me, he's taken advantage of that future title one too many times for my comfort as a woman." She stopped her train of thought and shook her hands, repeatedly stating, "No no, I promise. It's nothing to be alarmed about. I just find it annoying when girls throw their bodies and their dignity away where my brother is concerned. Michael is no different from other men; he enjoys the attention."

"Your brother is quite a catch, though I've no idea what all the titles mean—not that it matters much."

"I think Michael finds that very refreshing about you. But then again you are American. You guys don't have peerage in your society. You are all a common lot so it doesn't really matter to you."

I gave her a *gee thanks a lot* look.

"I'm not trying to offend you. I'm just stating facts."

"Uh-huh..."

"In any case, if you stop interrupting me," she said while giving me her actress set-down stare, which only made me giggle. "Michael has never spoken of marriage. Yours is the only name associated with the future, spoken from the future duke, himself."

"Are we talking about your father, the future duke?"

"Don't get sassy with me, Commoner. My grandfather is on a first name basis with the Queen. Why I could have a girl like you thrown in prison for not curtsying to me properly." Aleksandra used her best grand-daughter of a duke voice.

"Well I suppose if you're going to throw me into prison for not giving you a proper greeting, I have no choice but to follow you to dinner."

"I knew this commoner had some brains in her. That's the spirit Laney. My parents don't bite. Mum is on the jolly side and my father is a bit of a stiff, but we'll all get along splendidly."

"Lead the way."

"Um...one more thing...dinner at our house is usually a more formal affair. Do you have any dresses you can wear?" Aleksandra was apologetic about their antiquated ways.

"I guess that decides it then. I don't have any dresses here as they've all been shipped. I guess I'll come over for dinner another day." Formal dinner attire sounded lame to me, so I was relieved I didn't have to go tonight.

"Wait! Before you think you're getting out of this dinner, we can make a pit stop. Lucky for you, we live right by Harvey Nics and I brought along Michael's credit card. Do you like to shop?"

"Am I a woman?"

"Let's go. Michael says if I can convince you to have dinner with us, I could even buy something for myself with this credit card."

"Michael looks like a brother who would let you use his credit card regardless."

"Don't tell him I said this, but he is fantastic. A sister could not ask for more in an older brother."

We went to Harvey Nichols department store and there was no doubt in my mind that I would find something I'd like to wear.

"Laney!" Michael pulled me into his body and I could feel genuine affection from the arms that swallowed me. At this immediate moment, I prayed God would teach me to return this kind of affection ten-fold.

"Laney is here with me...!" Aleksandra unraveled us.

I heard a jovial high-pitched voice walking our way. "Oh my darling!" I got another loving hug from a vivacious woman I assumed was Michael's mother. "You are beautiful! How divine to finally meet the girl who will give me cherubic grandchildren."

"Mum. We just met Laney today," Aleksandra spoke on my behalf. "She already believes we belong in the loony bin. Between you and Mikey, she'll shut her door and never come out."

"Always the actress, Rubes...don't be so dramatic..." Michael spoke to his sister with the same dramatic flair. He put an "O" to my mouth when he kissed my cheek, put his arms around my waist and pulled me toward his father. "Don't be afraid of The Stiff, Love. His austere voice," his own tone went super bass when he said the word 'voice' "is much worse than his bite. He's a pussycat deep inside."

"All right." I laughed. "I'll do my best not to be intimidated by the deep voice."

I'd never been in love before—well OK...outside of my one-sided love affair with Donovan Taylor, which was probably more infatuation than love. But if I were ever to fall in love, I wondered if it would feel like my heart did now. This golly geez wonder of "he likes me," or this feeling of fullness, and almost completeness. All these new flitting emotions were a welcome—even if they eventually turned into fleeting ones.

"What's that look?" Michael asked. "That's one I haven't seen before. I don't have that one committed to memory, yet." A man who wanted to know me in every possible way, even by way of a temporary visage...this man was like one from a fairy tale. "Well?"

"Wonder...appreciation...hope..."

"Cryptic, but positive," he said and kissed my cheek one more time, steps before reaching his dad.

"Father, I'd like to present to you Laney Reid. Laney, this is my father, Michael Bennington." I expected the title, rank, and serial number to be spelled out, but that's all I got. "Oh, and this is my mother, Elizabeth Montague Bennington."

"It's a pleasure to meet you, Mr. and Mrs. Bennington. Thank you for inviting me to your family dinner."

His mother was the first to speak. "You should call me Lizzy, and Michael goes by..." She thought about it for a while and said, "Michael." The whole family, but Mr. Bennington laughed.

Michael whispered in my ear, "I told you my father is a bit of a stiff. Don't let him frighten you. Once you get to know him, he's a top bloke. He just needs to thaw out a bit." Then he did it again and he kissed me, only this time it was a loud smack on my ear.

I returned his kiss with what must have been a not very complimentary look, because next thing I knew, Michael chuckled and took a half step away from me and whispered loudly, "Sorry. Couldn't resist."

"Laney, you are so darling. I am thrilled you are here tonight. Michael was down in the dumps earlier when he thought you wouldn't join us for supper. I see my daughter worked her magic."

"I'm happy to be here, Mrs. Bennington. I believe Aleksandra and I will become very good friends in the near future." I winked at my English friend. She winked back and went over to her father, put her arms around him, and gave him a kiss on the cheek.

"Daddy, please don't scare away my new friend with your scowl. I love everything about you and granddad except for your inherent scowls. Please do try to smile more tonight." She teased him.

I already loved the Bennington family dynamics. They were able to have fun with one another, tease one another, and laugh with one another. This was the English version of the Reid family.

"So Laney, where did you do your studies, and what will you be doing in the future? Michael tells me that you just finished at the Uni?"

"Yes I did Mr. Bennington. I graduated yesterday in fact and left for London right after. I am fortunate enough to spend a year here, and I hope to decide what to do about my future during this time."

Mr. Bennington's expression didn't change. He also didn't look very impressed with me either—not that I was an impressive person.

"What do you hope to accomplish while you're here for the year?"

"Daddy..." Aleksandra tried to argue but Mr. Bennington's hand went up and stopped her. It wasn't done in any mean way, nor was it intimidating, but Aleksandra respected her father's wishes.

"To be completely honest with you Mr. Bennington, I don't really have any plans this year. I needed, wanted, and asked for a year away from home. And...I got it." I asserted both myself and my decision.

Mr. Bennington's one eyebrow slightly lifted in disapproval. I could tell my assertion did absolutely nothing to put me in his favor. "That doesn't sound too productive. You are going to waste an entire year do-ing...nothing?" Once again, the disapproval was there.

I decided at this point that I didn't need to explain myself to Mr. Bennington or anybody else. This wasn't me trying to be rude or disre-spectful. I just didn't see the need to explain to everybody I came across, why I was here. It was really no one's business but my own. There wasn't only one way to live life and if people didn't want to give me the allowance to be myself, then I didn't need them in my life. No mold was going to hold me or shape me. I firmly believed in doing what made me feel com-fortable, of course not at anyone else's expense.

As it was, I was not in Mr. Bennington's favor, and of course, my cell phone rang loudly. But even this loud sound didn't cut through the strong hum of disapproval.

I opened my clutch and it was Dad. "Please forgive me for not having turned off my phone during dinner, but would you excuse me and allow me to speak with my father? I haven't talked to him since I left home and only now are we able to reach each other." I got the slightest of nods, which I think equaled an approval. I started to get up from my seat, but Michael held me down and gestured for me to take my phone call right here.

This had to have been the height of bad manners, and I could see Mr. Bennington's hard image turning into a block of cement. There was a slight sense of panic when Michael held onto me. I knew better than to answer a call at a dinner table, but every ring was keeping me further away from my father, whom I desperately wished to speak to tonight.

"It's all right, Love. Go ahead and talk to your dad." The phone was probably on its last ring before it went over to voicemail. Michael accepted the call and reassuringly put it to my ear.

"Hello?"

Hearing my dad's voice brought on a wave of emotion. If it was dif-ficult leaving my family yesterday, it was brutal talking to them today. Already, I wanted to give up and go back to the comforts of home.

"Hi, Daddy! Is your surgery done?"

"Laney! My beautiful baby! Daddy misses you so much already. How do we go a year without seeing each other?"

"I know Daddy. I feel the same way. I miss you, Mom, and the whole family too. It's going to be very hard."

"Come home, Baby. Just use your return ticket and we can have your belongings shipped right back. The house is too empty without you."

I got really emotional listening to my father's voice crack when he told me how empty the house felt. That same emptiness was in my heart as well.

"Daddy, we'll see each other at Christmas time. I want you, Mom and Doug to come visit me for Christmas."

"You're not coming home?" Dad was shocked to hear that I had no plans of going back to my old life until it was time to start school.

"No Daddy. But you, Mom and Doug can come visit me here."

My senses came alert when I heard Mr. Bennington clearing his throat with even greater disapproval. "Daddy I need to call you back. I met some friends at the airport and I'm having dinner with their family right now. I am behaving like an ill-mannered guest talking to you. But I wanted to hear your voice and tell you how much I love you and miss you."

"I love you too, Baby. Call me when your dinner is done?"

"Yes, Daddy. Bye."

As soon as I got off the phone, I looked around and four pairs of eyes were on me.

"Sorry," I whispered, unsure how many more notches I'd fallen with my five-year-old conversation with my father.

Mr. Bennington was again the first to speak. "You left your father when he is ill and had surgery?" Maybe it was time to clear the air and try to win Mr. Bennington's approval, somewhat. I could feel Michael's nervousness by the way he unconsciously tightened his hand around my shoulder or arm with every disapproving remark. He was nervous for me, for himself, for us....

For Michael and Aleksandra, who neither spoke a word against their father, but pleaded my cause with their body language, I decided to cooperate.

"My father is a surgeon and the Chief of Staff at the hospital. When I asked if he was done with surgery, it wasn't his surgery or better put, he is not the patient, but the doctor."

Comically, there was a collective sigh of relief from the three other Benningtons.

"So your father's a doctor?" Mr. Bennington asked with a teeny tiny bit of approval.

"Daddy, he's not just a doctor. He's a surgeon." Aleksandra stated with pride.

"And the Chief of Staff at the hospital." Mrs. Bennington tried to fast-forward my cause.

"And your mother?" The Q&A continued.

"She used to be an interior designer, but she decided to stay home and raise my brother and myself when we were born." Then I decided to give him my entire family's bio in a nutshell. "My father comes from a family of five boys, and he is second in the family. His brother above him, Uncle Robert, was also a doctor, but now he's retired. Uncle Robert's oldest son, Jake, is a heart surgeon and works at the same hospital as my dad. We all live on the same block and my three other uncles, who are businessmen, have homes on the same block as well. My brother is in his last year of business school, and after I spend an entire year lollygagging in London, I will go back to the States and either enter film school or med school." That was definitely a mouthful and an earful.

"Film school?"

"Med school?"

Of course the first question came from Alexandra, and the next was spoken by Michael.

Finally, Mrs. Bennington had a question. "How does one decide between film school and med school? Those are two very different schools."

I smiled at her because she had a smiling face. Mrs. Bennington had one of those "yes" faces that made me think of my own mother who also had a "yes" face. "I graduated with a double major in chemistry and English, and I couldn't decide which graduate school I wanted to go to, so I applied to both med school and film school."

"She's bloody brilliant, Daddy."

Michael was so excited that I had finally earned some points with his father, he was squeezing the circulation out of my arm. "Michael," I whispered. "You're hurting me," I said gently without giving him alarm.

"Sorry, Love. I wasn't aware that I was even touching you."

The rest of dinner was actually quite enjoyable. Michael regaled us with stories of trying to pack up Ruby's belongings before coming back home. Ruby had done her undergrad studies at a university not too far from my own and Michael had just finished his business degree at Harvard University of all places. Talk about brilliance, apparently he was the fourth generation of Harvard graduates from his family. Mr. Bennington seem to warm up to me once he realized I was a girl with somewhat of a future.

"May I offer you the car? Finneas can drive you home. After all the intimidating and personal questions I've asked, it's the least I can do for Aleksandra and Michael's new friend." Mr. Bennington said these words with a slight curve to his lips. It almost looked like a grin.

"Thank you for dinner. I enjoyed speaking with you and Mrs. Bennington, and I'd be happy to answer any more questions another day. For tonight, though, I think I'll walk back home. It's beautiful out and I live very close to your home."

"Then Michael, why don't you walk Laney home?" Mr. Bennington's voice had grown warmer throughout the night. Though he didn't have that loud and booming personality like my dad, I could feel the love and affection he had for his family. He was a good man.

"If it's all right with everyone, I'd like to walk home..." Michael's face fell, again. I didn't want to see him upset because I understood what it felt like to be continually disappointed, rejected, and hurt. "Thank you, Michael. I'd love it if you'd walk me home."

Michael steered me toward the river again. "Can I ask why your initial reaction to my offers is to turn them down?"

"When we get to know each other a little better, you'll see that I'm more of an independent person than I look. I think the blond hair and blue eyes already encourage everyone to believe that I can't think for my-self, or that I'm helpless. I don't like that stereotype and I'm constantly fighting against it."

"But you know that's not what I think of you. You're probably smarter than most of my business school mates."

"I like my freedom. And I like to be alone to think."

"To think? What do you think about? Or is it a whom…that you think about?"

"That would be telling…" I answered slyly. He frowned. "I just like to think. My head is full of happy thoughts, sad thoughts, funny anecdotes, creative fantasies, the next essay I have to edit, thoughts of friendships found, friendships lost…"

"Delaney, I'm sorry I didn't come see you last night. Really, I am sorry. I fell asleep and when I got up, it was already six in the morning and I knew you had to be at your graduation in a couple of hours so I didn't call. Why didn't you stop to talk to me when you dropped by the office this morning? I can't believe you didn't give me a second thought before you left for London. Don't I mean anything to you?"

Oh, Donovan…if you meant any more to me than you already do, I'd be at my last depth of despair. I didn't need to know that you fell asleep rather than coming to see me and I didn't want to know that you and Kate slept together.

"You're doing it again." Michael stood centimeters away from me. "You have a tendency to go off into your own world and forget those around you. Your face was intensely sad. What was going through that complicated mind of yours?"

"So sorry!" I put on a chipper face. "I was thinking about a voicemail I listened to from home. I guess all thoughts of home make me sad right now."

"What's on the calendar for you tomorrow?"

I had to think about that for a moment. This was the first time in years where I had nothing that needed my attention. "I've no idea. After I get caught up with sleep, I'll go out and explore the area, find my new coffee shop, shops for knick-knacks I need until my luggage arrives, maybe find a bookstore and thumb through books. Before I came here, I decided I'm going to enjoy myself this entire year. It's been a tough four years and an even tougher four plus years if I choose to go to med school. I want to enjoy myself."

"May I..." Michael stopped himself. I knew what he wanted to say and the uncertainty he felt. It was no fun being on the giving, but never receiving end.

Before he became completely discouraged, I asked, "Would you and Aleksandra want to go to an Indian restaurant with me tomorrow night? I've never had Indian food before and that's on my to-do list while I'm here."

"You are a wonderful person," Michael murmured while kissing me on the cheek. I understood what he was grateful about, and I didn't want him to feel like he was a second-class citizen around me.

"Michael?" He smiled. "Like I said earlier today, I want us to be friends, and possibly good ones at that. Please don't pressure me into anything and don't try and take random liberties with me." To make light of that last statement, I pointed to his lips, then to my cheek, and let him conclude the obvious.

"It's totally accidental, I assure you. My lips have a mind of their own." And he did it again and kissed me on the cheek. I could only laugh at this mischief.

"Good night." I waved.

"Till tomorrow."

Tomorrow turned out to be beautiful! Everyone warned me of London's gloomy weather but I thought it was just perfect. Sure there were clouds, sure it was colder than Los Angeles, but when I got up, I looked outside and saw hope and excitement. The only weird part about being in Gram's home was the solitude. This was something that would take me a while to get used to, as my life had always been full of family and noise.

I talked to Mom, Dad, Emily and Gram last night after I got home. Dad was home early so he and Mom put me on speakerphone, and the conversation mainly went in a circle between them wanting me to come home, and me telling them I'd be home in one year. Gram did her best to explain the house to me and who I could call if I should need help with the plumbing, electrical, the washing machine, the protocol of recycling and garbage pick-up, where to shop for food and clothes, and...she packed so much information in this one call, I had to start taking notes.

My favorite part of the night was the video chat I had with Emily. I didn't call in time to speak with the twins. I knew this was silly, but the one issue that almost kept me at home this year was James forgetting who I was in his life. He was only one, and the likelihood of him forgetting me was almost guaranteed. Thanks to Skype and FaceTime, I'd show my face as often as possible.

"So, who is this friend you made? I take it he's a boy?" Emily was able to talk freely once Jake and I finished our greetings.

"Michael and Aleksandra are their names, and I met them when we got off the plane. They gave me a ride home and invited me to their family dinner. It was a full day, yesterday. I'm surprised I got up this morning at all. I thought I may sleep all day."

"And what does this Michael do?"

"I'm not sure. He just graduated from Harvard business school and his sister recently graduated from undergrad."

"His family is nice?"

"His family is identical to ours. We are of the same age and order, the four of them have a great relationship, and both Michael and Aleksandra are warm, caring, and funny."

Emily turned introspective and stayed quiet. "Do you like this Michael?"

"Not yet, Emily. It's too soon. But he's asked to court me, and I told him I wasn't ready for anything of that sort."

"When you say, 'not yet,' that must mean he has an outside chance?"

"Maybe. I don't know. What I do know is that I understand his pain and frustration whenever I turn down any of his requests or proposals."

"You've lost me a bit."

"Every time Michael has wanted to do something with me, yesterday, I said no. And with each of those rejections, I saw his face fall. Maybe the best word to describe it is empathy. It bothers me to see him hurt."

"...because you like him enough to feel his hurt..." Emily paused, "...or because you're reliving your hurt from Donovan?" Emily's voice now got cautious and I could tell she wanted to give me a gentle warning. "Laney...I don't want you to mistake sympathy and empathy for affection and love. Those two are not even in the same ballpark. I know you're a kind-hearted soul, and I know Donovan did a number on your heart, but if you can't appropriately discourage Michael, then you'll do the same thing to him as Donovan has done to you."

I understood clearly what Emily was warning. "Thank you for the advice, but I do like this guy enough to want to get to know him. If it leads to something greater than friendship, I'll take it. If not, I'll leave it and we'll remain what we are now—friends."

After a heart-to-heart with Emily, I finally got around to walking the neighborhood at my leisure and pace. I found a welcoming coffee shop where I bought my morning pastry and jolt of caffeine. Then I went next door to buy a map and London travel guide. Of course everything could be done on the Internet and on my phone, but there was a quaint novelty to walking the neighborhood with a map in hand.

"Laney!" Aleksandra jumped me from behind and scared the hell out of me. "Fancy meeting you here. Mikey's been dying to call you but you never gave him your number." She cackled at her brother's frustration. "You need to thank me, my gal pal. If it wasn't for me, he would've been at your door at dawn's light."

"What are you doing here?"

"This is my favorite coffee shop. I stop here almost every morning when I'm home. Today's a late morning. I couldn't get myself together enough to get out here before all the scones were gone."

"Can you tell me if there's a drugstore around here where I can buy random household items?"

"Of course I can. Are we walking? Finneas is around the corner."

"Do you mind? It's so beautiful out and I love this neighborhood."

"I can do all this for you but I must call Michael. He'll be livid if he knew I was spending the morning with you."

"When you call him, can you ask him to pick the Indian restaurant for tonight? I'll meet you wherever you tell me to go. But..." I didn't know whether I'd offend Aleksandra by finishing my sentence.

"But you don't want to spend the whole day with him?"

"Is that rude?"

"It'll break his heart, but no, it's not rude." She laughed. "Hey Mikey…" She was already on the phone. "Guess who I ran into at my favorite coffee shop in South Kensington? Yes and no, you may not join me and my best gal pal till dinner tonight. She would like to have dinner with us. You can pick the time and place and she will be there." I heard a lot of uh-huhs, then she got off the phone.

"What did he say?"

"As you expected, he wasn't happy about not joining us, but he'll live. Dinner will be an early one at five. I suspect he wants to spend as much of the evening with you as possible. I have to warn you, as soon as I show you the store, I need to be on my way. I'm meeting some friends who are visiting from the States."

"I'll see you at dinner?" I hoped it wasn't going to be Michael and me alone.

"I'll see you at dinner," she reassured me.

After Aleksandra and I parted, I spent the rest of the morning purchasing odds and ends and I finished settling into this too-large-for-even-a-family-of-ten, home. I stared at my phone for a while knowing there was a message left for me from Donovan that I didn't pick up earlier this morning. I was still hurting from his last refusal to see me. Tears formed without warning when I thought about waiting for him on the swing all night. Why couldn't I have learned from all the times he pushed me away? Why did I think that there was always a small chance he may grow to love me? Embarrassingly enough, I'd cried more in the thirty-six hours away from Donovan than when I was back at home. All last night, I couldn't stop the tears from pouring. I realized it was finally over and I didn't want to let go, but had no choice.

"Delaney." The glutton that I was, I had left the message there long enough. I wanted to hear his voice and secretly, I wanted to hope, again. *"I miss you."* The tears were uncontrollable now. Why did he have to do this to me? Why tell me he missed me when his actions told me he could care less. *"I wish we could have said a few things to each other before you left. Then perhaps you might not have left me."* If he only knew how paramount it was for me to leave. *"I'm going to call you when I get up. Please answer your phone, Delaney. I need*

to talk to you and I want to figure some things out with you. I'm coming to London in a few days. We'll see each other then and talk, OK? I really miss you, Delaney. Talk to you soon?" With that last question, he understood that I was doing my damnedest to stay away from him. Why'd he have to sound sincere? I wanted that last biting memory of him and Kate. That was what was going to get me through the next few weeks as I put myself through withdrawal.

Mr. Taylor. I am well in London so no need to worry for me. I'd like to start a new life here and am trying to stand on my own two feet without anyone's help. I'd appreciate it if you didn't call or visit. Hope you are well. I'll see you when I come back next June.

That text would hopefully end our connection for a year and allow me to concentrate on myself. After pacing the house tirelessly, I decided to stop staring at the phone since it was still too early in LA for Donovan to have received the message. I left the phone on the bed and decided to hop on one of those double decker tour buses and a get an overview of the city.

After grabbing a quick lunch at the revolving sushi bar at Harvey Nics, I jumped on the bus in front of Harrods and spent long hours listening to the British man talk about everything from the Duke of Westminster owning most of Belgravia to the Shard being the tallest building in the European Union. I got off at one point and walked through Borough Market grabbing a quick drink. Then I traveled further to the Globe Theatre and purchased tickets for the next available show. It really didn't matter what and when the show was. I just needed a diversion from my heart that refused to begin the mending process.

When I finally arrived back at the flat, I tried to close my eyes to the obvious text waiting for me. I tried so hard, but I couldn't sever that connection between us, no matter how disgusted I was with myself.

How the hell am I supposed to be well when you tell me to stop communicating with you? What the hell is wrong with you? We need to meet and talk. I don't care what you've written in your text. I'll see you when I get to London.

Doing my best to ignore the text, I called my mother. "Hi Mom."

"Laney! How are you? Are you more settled, now?"

"I think I am all settled for now...until the rest of my stuff arrives. Then, it will be a crazy mess all over again."

"So tell me more about your new friends."

I was happy to share about Ruby and Michael. "They were on the same flight as me and they live around the corner from Gram's. Ruby is my age and Michael is Doug's age. I had dinner at their home with their parents last night and tonight, the three of us are going to an Indian place."

"I'm thrilled you've made friends already, and even more thrilled they live nearby. Are you sure you're doing OK?"

"I am, Mom. I'm glad I came here. It's been hard on the one hand, but I know it'll be a great year of exploration and growth. I'm also thinking about taking some courses at Oxford or Cambridge if they'll allow it."

"That's a splendid idea. Then you'll meet even more people your age."

"When would you like to visit, Mom?"

"I'll talk to your father and come out as soon as I can. The house isn't the same without you, Laney. The dinner table was like a funeral last night."

"I'm sure it wasn't that bad. It's no different than me having lived in the dorms or the apartments."

"Speaking of visiting, Donovan mentioned last night he was going to London very soon. Have you spoken with him? He was visibly upset you left without saying a word to him." I stayed silent, wondering how much to tell Mom. "Laney?" She approached, on tippy-toes.

"I answered his call thinking Doug was calling and spoke with him briefly. Then I texted this morning asking him not to call anymore or to visit."

"Laney..." Mom reprimanded carefully. "Why the drastic cut in communication?"

"Because it hurts to communicate with him." I had to stop talking because I didn't want Mom's heart breaking knowing my heart broke. "I went to see him late at night before graduation and Kate was the one who greeted me. That's when I should have bolted out of there, but I stayed and listened to what Donovan had to say. He asked me to wait for him on the swing because he was going to drop by with a graduation gift, but he never came, Mom." My voice became a whisper and the tears wouldn't stay away. "I waited all night." Now I was doing what I didn't want to do—bawling over the phone with my mother, who probably ached because there was nothing she could do for her daughter. "I don't want to do this anymore. I don't know why Donovan Taylor needs to speak with me, but I'm done."

"Laney. Your father and I thought that the way Donovan looked at you the past few months was not any different from the way you've been looking at him since you met him. Are you sure you want to be done now? I'm sure there was a good reason why Kate was over at his place and you need to ask him why he never came by, before being so upset with him. Who knows what happened?"

"Donovan and Kate most likely spent the night together and that's why he never came over. You know I've done this too long. I've waited, I've hoped, I've dreamed. I don't want to do it anymore."

"Laney…" Mom was at a loss for words.

"Mom, I think someone might be at the door. I hear knocking. Could I call you back?"

"Sure, Sweetheart. Take care of yourself."

"Bye, Mom. I love you."

"Love you, too."

I ran downstairs to greet my knocker.

"You're still here." There was a sweet-smiling Englishman at my door. "What's the matter with your face?" His perfect smile deflated into a not-so-perfect frown.

"What kind of a greeting is that? Do over," I said and closed the door on him.

He knocked on the door again and I opened.

What I expected was a, "Hello!" But what I got was a shocking kiss on the lips.

"You going to open your mouth so I can let you feel my tongue?" he asked with a grin. I shook my head no, wavering between laughing at Michael and giving him a cool set-down. "What's with the funny look on your face?"

"I'm wondering if I should laugh with you or slap you." I answered in all seriousness, just to freak him out.

"You should maybe consider kissing me back?" He took a giant step away, his eyes constantly monitoring my hands. I chose to laugh.

"You are a rascal, Michael Bennington. Stop stealing kisses from me!" I tried to sound stern, but it was impossible with a smile on my face. This man had a way of making me smile and turning a sour mood into a delightful one.

"I will not promise to stop stealing kisses, and I'm happy to be your rascal, chauffeur, tour guide, month-long lover...take your pick."

"Why only month-long?" I joined in the humor.

"When I say month-long, I mean all month long, as in we don't leave the house, month-long."

"Got it. Um...which one shall I choose...I think I'll have to choose the most desirable one, which would be…"

"...would be…?"

"The tour guide!" I pointed to an obvious taxi that was waiting for us, with the ticker going.

"Damn! I've wasted a lot of money on you, Ms. Reid. Let's go." He shooed me out the door and into the taxi.

"Why'd you stop by?" I'd forgotten to ask.

"What do you mean, why? I came by to take you to dinner, of course. I knew you wouldn't know how to get to the restaurant, and thought I'd take a chance on you being home. Now my turn to ask—why had you been crying?"

"Oh." I had forgotten about Donovan for a fun few minutes with Michael. "Mom," was all the information I was willing to offer.

"You miss your Mum?" He offered solace by scooting closer and putting his arm around me. I stared at his hand that had firmly grabbed onto the top of my arm. "What can I do to make you feel better?" His hand gently pushed my head down onto his shoulder and caressed my head.

"Michael." I warned. "You're doing it again."

"I'm only trying to make you feel better, Love." He chuckled and there was no choice but to join him.

The ride to the restaurant was only minutes from both our places. We got into the restaurant and were seated in a very private, very cozy booth, side-by-side.

"Where will Ruby sit if we're in such a small booth?"

"Well...hear me out." Michael pleaded. "Give me one night to talk to you and to have you get to know me and me get to know you. Once we are acquainted, you'll adore me and probably fall madly in love with me. I swear!" He spoke so fast I didn't know if I caught all his words correctly.

"So, if I give you one dinner, you'll try and impress me, and if I'm not impressed, I don't ever have to spend another minute with you, ever again?" I asked innocently.

"Well..."

"Which is it? You were confident that after tonight, I would want to continue to get to know you. If not, we're done. You want to put that much on the line?"

This time he didn't hesitate. "Yeah. I am that confident. Give me tonight, and I promise you we will become better friends, and possibly even lifelong best friends."

I liked the confidence. "Let's do it. You first." I let him speak.

"I grew up mostly in London and did my undergrad and graduate studies in the States."

"Is that how you speak such perfect American-English?"

"Yes. Your American-English grew on me and stuck. After getting an MBA, I am now about to jump into the family business."

"And what's the family business?"

"Our family holds a lot of land and property that my grandfather is too old to take care of, and my father would like to hand over to me. I need to bring everything up to date, so to speak."

"What does that mean?"

"Grandfather still uses ledgers for his P&L sheet, and we have too many properties that need updating. Much work needs to done, but here I am obsessed with getting to know a blonde American beauty." He smiled. "Tell me more about you."

"But I thought this was me getting to know you?" I teased.

"I'm dying to know more about you. We can stay up all night talking if you like, but I'd like to know where you're from, what you did for your eleventh birthday, what was your first pet—everything, give me everything about you."

His ardor was humbling. "I've lived in Los Angeles all my life. My dad is number two in a line of five boys, and he and my mom are brilliant in what they do."

"Your father, I know, is a surgeon, but what does your mother do?"

"She is non-paid professional party planner. My eleventh birthday, you asked—a huge water theme. Criss-cross water slides, a massive blow-up ten-foot water slide, all kinds of water guns, water balloons, anything water, it was there. My cake even floated on water."

"A floating cake?" He didn't believe me.

"Sound incredulous? Every party she plans is outrageous. My grandmother recently remarried, and she turned my uncle's regular grassy pool backyard into the most amazing English cottage backyard with ponds, and arches, and statues, and a wedding breakfast feast. For my cousin Jake's rehearsal dinner, she turned our backyard into a Moroccan Riad. Her parties are over the top and interactive. I think it was two Thanksgivings ago where we had to come dressed as Pilgrims and Indians."

"What did you dress as?"

"Pocahontas." I giggled. "I have a teeny-tiny fascination with Disney princesses."

"And you said you have a brother?"

"Yes. He's the same age as you, but he has one more year to go to finish his MBA."

"What will he do after school?"

"I don't know. He doesn't know either. My dad was hoping he'd go to med school, but it wasn't for Doug."

I was about to give more information on Doug when the devil himself rang my cell phone.

"Are you going to answer that?" Michael wondered why I just stared at the phone. He had no idea that the last time I answered a call that said Doug, it turned out to be Donovan. I was scared. Without asking my permission, Michael picked up the phone and answered, "Laney's Reid's phone." Then I heard him say, "May I ask who's calling?" Then a smile broke out. "Laney was just talking about her older brother. She said you were the kindest, most brilliant and handsome man she knew." Michael cracked up. "My name is Michael Bennington, and I'm a friend of your sister's. It's nice to meet you." I watched him listen to whatever Doug had to say. "She and I met at Heathrow when she ruined my favorite pair of dress shoes with her suitcase."

"I did not, you liar!" I accused.

"Or, it could have been that I purposely stuck out my foot so she would run over it." He laughed. "Will you be visiting Laney sometime soon?" Michael listened and nodded some more. "I wish." Michael looked at me while saying this. "Your sister gave me just this one night to convince her to want to get to know me better. If she decides I'm not interesting enough for her, she says she's never going to see me again."

"You make me sound so mean."

"You are, Love. I've got only one chance to prove that I'm worth your time."

"That's not true," I insisted.

"Then, tonight's not make it or break it, night? You're not giving me the ax, the boot, the noose, after tonight?"

"I see where Ruby gets her dramatic flair." I rolled my eyes.

"Oh, so sorry!" Michael chuckled. "Your brother would like to speak with you."

"Hey, Doug."

"You dating someone already?" My brother would always stay my older brother. *Groan!*

"I'm fine. How are you?" I ignored him.

"I'm calling to tell you that Mom is a bit of a basket case after talking to you earlier, so whatever it is that you said to her, undo it. She's been moping around the house."

"Sorry, Doug. I'll call her when I get home."

"Donovan know about Michael?"

"There's nothing to know, Doug." I needed to get off this topic, and fast. "Come visit with Mom and Dad, soon."

"I think Mom might have bought herself a ticket already." Doug bemoaned but laughed all the same. "Take care and don't get too close to Michael. You just met him."

"Yes, sir. Talk to you later."

"He sounds like a fine fellow, your brother."

"At times, he is. At times, I'd like to strangle him."

Dinner evolved into a budding friendship between the two of us, and in all honesty, I enjoyed Michael's company, immensely. After feasting on delicious Indian fare, Michael and I walked back home, and he introduced me to my very first Mr. Whippy with Flake. We shared the ice cream cone without a problem, but we fought hard for the flake. Who knew a stick of chocolate could taste so damn good!

"So...did I pass the test?" We were at my door, and it was cute how nervous he was.

"I tell you, it was a close one. Even after dinner, I had you on my drop-from-friend list, but you redeemed yourself and came back to square one after buying me a Mr. Whippy, and you finally passed when you let me have the last bite of the flake." I grinned.

"Shit, I'm calling Cadbury and sending you a crate full of them." He looked so relieved.

"No thank you! I don't need a crate full of chocolate. A Mr. Whippy with a double Flake will do from time to time."

"I'll send over the truck the next time you have a birthday party!"

I laughed. "Good night, Michael."

"You're not going to ask me in?" He gave me a sly smile that was endearing on this sweet-looking man.

"No. I'll see you again, soon."

He came in to kiss me again, but I put out my hand to stop him. "Am I pushing my luck?" He grinned.

"Just a tad...good night." I walked in and didn't look back.

I feared the evening when I first learned Ruby would not be joining us, but I was glad I stuck it out and got to know Michael. The more I learned about him and understood his temperament, the more I liked him. He was easy-going, kind, and humorous. In some ways, he never outgrew his childlike humor, but it wasn't annoying. It was cute.

Walking into my bedroom a text awaited me.

My plane lands around 4:00pm. Be nearby and ready to have dinner with me by six.

I would do my damnedest not to be home!

I was a flutter of nerves as I purposely left the house early in the afternoon. I had nowhere to be, nowhere to go, and without a cell phone, I was nervous about getting lost in this city. After wandering the British Museum, I couldn't say what I'd viewed. None of the rooms held any interest for me, so I left and walked aimlessly till I came upon the London Film School, which held my interest for a very brief while. When I could loiter no more, I grabbed a bite to eat and bought myself a ticket to watch *Matilda* at the Cambridge Theatre. I hated myself today for feeling so forlorn and for creating this unhappy afternoon. There was no reason why I couldn't have stayed home and faced Donovan. It was ridiculous to wander like the homeless. My cowardice was shameful and it was pissing me off. At intermission, I'd decided enough was enough. I'd go home and see what it was that Donovan wanted and why he was so desperate to get a hold of me.

The taxi turned into my street and nervously, I searched for an absent Donovan in front of Gram's home. My heart sank and my shoulders sagged. He wasn't there. Truly, I was the world's biggest moron! Why the hell was I sad and hurt that he didn't wait around for me? What the hell did I expect? It was 10:00pm! He wasn't going to sit around for four hours in hopes that I'd come running to him. But I missed him so badly, I wanted to cry. Being alone was hard on the willpower.

I'd left my phone on the entry hall table and missed copious calls, texts, and voicemails. There were almost an equal number from Michael and Ruby as there were from Donovan.

I called Ruby, first. "Hey. It's me." I put on a happy performance.

"Where the hell have you been all day? Michael's been frantic, and even I started worrying after the tenth unanswered call."

"Sorry. I went to tour Piccadilly and eventually ended up watching a show."

"By yourself?" Ruby thought I was nuts. "Why in bloody hell would you do that?"

"It wasn't planned, per se. One activity just led to another."

"You are one strange girl, Laney Reid. You have friends who would have joined you."

"I know." I tried to sound apologetic. "I just…" Truth wasn't an option at this point so I ended the conversation by saying, "Could you let Michael know I'm all right and I'll be turning in for the night?" Before Ruby could respond or make any other comments, I said, "Good night. Talk to you tomorrow," and hung up. That was done. Now, on to reading Donovan's texts.

4:13pm Just landed. See you in an hour.

5:41pm Where the hell are you? Why aren't you answering your phone?

5:48pm Dammit, Delaney. Answer your phone!

6:02pm You're really pissing me off.

6:23pm Delaney. What's going on? Why are you doing this to me? Why won't you see me?

Then, I listened to his voicemail. *"By the time you get this, I'll probably be back at my hotel."* There was a long pause in the message. *"What the hell do I have to do to get you to talk to me? Where did we go wrong? Why are you severing all ties with me? I'm hoping this is all a mistake and you'll give me a call when you get this message. I'm staying at The Berkeley Hotel. Call me no matter how late."*

I cried the entire night.

I never saw Donovan when he came here last week. Different from all his texts and voicemails, he never came back and he didn't contact me again during his stay in London. The weak girl that I was, I stayed home the next day and the next few days after that, waiting for him. Without a doubt, I'd give in the next time he showed his face or called me. Neither happened.

"Whatcha' been up to, Laney Reid?" A nice surprise sobered me up.

"Bee! How come it's taken you this long to call me?"

"And how come you've never called me? Are you not talking to anyone with the last name Taylor?"

I guess she and Donovan had been talking. "When are you coming here?" I decided no response was the best defense. "I would love to see a friendly face from home."

"Did my nephew not come with a friendly face? Was it only a scowl? Not to toot my own nephew, but even a scowl is striking on him." I guess I walked into that one.

"Are you calling to heckle me about not having seen Donovan last week? I wasn't here when he got here, OK? And he never came back like he said he would. As usual, I waited for him like the moron that I am, the entire next few days, but he never showed." I got angry at Bee for chastising me, with Donovan for being the jerk that he was, and with myself for being a fool!

"Easy, Girl. I'm just trying to relieve my nephew's frustration. You've done a number on him and his head is not on right."

"Good! He started this dance twelve years ago. My head's been on backwards since then. I'm glad someone else is suffering."

"My collection is done; I'm bringing it with me tomorrow. Will you meet me at Heathrow, or shall I try and navigate my way over to your 'hood?"

"I'll meet you!" I was so desperate for a friend right now. Ruby and I had been hanging out daily, with Michael in tow, but Ruby had gone to see her friends in Edinburgh, and I was wary about spending too much alone time with Michael. He continued to push more than I liked. "How long are you staying?"

"A few days, then I'm off to Paris. You could come with me if you have nothing else going on."

"Paris is a maybe, but if you send me your info, I'll bring Gram's Range Rover and pick you up in style!"

"Fab! See you soon."

I ran around getting the house ready and stocking an already stocked fridge for the arrival of my first guest. I practically jogged to the bakery to have some cupcakes ready for my guest.

"Well hello, Stranger! You didn't bring your phone out, again?"

"Michael! Hi. What brings you here?"

"Me mum has a craving." He sounded like a little boy.

"What does she want?"

"What else but cupcakes?"

"Let me choose some for her." I went about ordering a tray full of goodies for Mrs. Bennington and also for Bee and myself.

"You going to eat all that by yourself?" Michael looked worried.

"Why? You won't like me anymore if I get any bigger than I already am?" I squinted my eyes and gave him a seriously dubious look. He laughed at me and stole another kiss. Damn! I'd have to make sure not to say anything "cute" around him.

"Come have dinner with us." He somehow was holding my hand again. He had a way of catching me off guard.

"Looking like this?" I was in a summer dress of the un-fancy-kind. "I think even your staff is dressed more formally than I am."

Michael took out his phone and dialed. "Mother. I've run into Laney at the bakery and am trying to get her to dine with us tonight, but she says she can't because she's not properly dressed. What shall I do?"

After a few uh-huhs, a decision was made.

I chuckled. "What'd Mum say?"

"She told me to take you to Harrods and buy you whatever your heart desires."

"Damn! I like that Lizzy Bennington! And she has yet to know about my penchant for clothes."

"Or, she says she'd bring the duke-in-training out to meet us for dinner right now. I chose the latter option."

"But what about all these baked goods we just purchased?"

"We'll have Finneas take them home for us and you can pick them up later."

"What's for dinner?"

"There's a little French Bistro just a stone's throw from here. You want Finneas to drive us there, then go pick up my parents or you want to walk?"

"You seriously bothered your driver to bring you here?" I rolled my eyes.

"I don't know what you Americans think, but we English do not walk as much as you believe we do. Belgrave to South Kensington is not that close."

"My bad. You probably don't need it, but I need the exercise so let's walk to the restaurant."

Several times, this blackguard attempted to hold my hand. And every time I attempted a set-down, he'd send my attention elsewhere and have me laughing.

"What's so funny?" Mrs. Bennington inquired when she and the duke-in-training, as Michael called his father, approached us.

"Hello." I greeted them with a smile. "Your scoundrel of a son continues to take liberties with me." Not able to say this with a straight face, Michael held my face with both his hands and kissed my nose this time. "You see what I mean?" My appalled tone wasn't too appalled.

Mr. Bennington cracked a smile. "Son." He pulled out his duke-in-training voice. "You shall not take liberties with any woman who is unwilling to participate."

"But how will I know if she's unwilling unless I first try?" Michael asked in earnest.

Mr. Bennington was stumped, but not for long. "I guess you don't. You're doing just fine, Son. Keep up the good work." We all cracked-up and opened dinner with a good laugh.

"What have you done with your time since we last met?" Mr. Bennington asked.

"I've unpacked all the boxes that arrived from the States, seen a few shows, visited some museums, and walked a good portion of this city."

"What shows did you watch?" Lizzy asked.

"I saw *Matilda* at the Cambridge Theatre and *Macbeth* at the Globe."

"Did Michael and Ruby take you? Thanks to Grandpa Harry being a generous patron of the arts, we get good seats everywhere."

"No, Mum. This crazy girl went to all those places, alone." Michael was annoyed. "Not once did she invite her two English best friends."

"Why in heaven's name would you go watch a show alone? How dreadfully lonely."

As Lizzy Bennington said this, a dozen Hama Hama oysters came out and I was transported back to the beach where Donovan and I had kite-boarded and sat through a cozy meal. That day was the first day I thought, not wished, but thought, maybe Donovan had feelings for me. He'd taken me to his beach house, we'd learned a new sport together, had a meal to-gether, and after falling asleep at the movies, he told me I looked adorable when my brother thought I looked like I'd just woken up from the dead.

"You didn't have to bring me home. I could've jumped in the car with Doug."

"It seemed only right to bring you home after the day we spent together."

"Thank you for today. I loved the water and spending the afternoon learning a new water sport...with you...was...incredible."

"I had a great time too. And if I may...? Yesterday was a shit of a day for many reasons and Jane was also having a shit of a day with Max. We were two friends having drinks, consoling each other. It was nothing more, nothing less. Jane and I have become close friends and I like her as a person."

"All right..."

"Delaney. I don't know where you fit in my life right now. I'm conflicted in many ways, but I know whenever I'm with you, I can't help wondering when I'll be with you again."

"Laney?" Mr. Bennington was calling my name.

"Huh?" I was caught thinking about Donovan again. Shit. "I'm sorry. Since I was little, everyone told me that my head was in the clouds all the time. I guess it's a good thing I don't read and walk at the same time, any-more." This self-deprecating humor lightened the mood.

"As I was saying, we are taking our holidays soon and would love for you to join us."

"Where are you all going?"

"We will spend some time at my father's country home in Derbyshire, then we are thinking about maybe taking our holiday in the Seychelles. That's where all the fashionable people appear to go, so Lizzy and I thought you, Michael and Ruby might like it there too."

I was stunned at their generous heart. They'd met me once, and their children had known me for what the English would call a fortnight. The Benningtons wanting to take me on their family vacation humbled me.

"Without a doubt, I am honored you and Mrs. Bennington would offer to take me on your family vacation. May I think about your offer for a few days?" I hoped I didn't offend them by not jumping on their offer.

"Of course! We don't leave for the country house for another few weeks and the Seychelles won't be till August." Mrs. Bennington answered.

"Thank you. I'll let you know soon."

"My parents like you a great deal." Michael said while walking me home. We finished off a fun dinner with his parents, and Finneas had driven us back to the Benningtons so I could pick up my cupcakes, and Michael offered to walk me home. "I want you to know, neither Ruby nor I asked them to invite you on our summer holiday. I was going to invite you myself, but surprisingly my parents beat me to it."

"I like them very much too. They've gone out of their way to make me feel comfortable in a foreign land. I appreciate what they are doing in my parents' stead, and I promise to give it serious thought once my house guest leaves."

"What? You've got a guest already?"

"I do!" I was all smiles about seeing Bee again. I explained to Michael about Bee Taylor and how excited I was to have someone from home visiting me.

"Well, I'll help you pick her up."

"Michael. I'm sure you have better things to do than pick up my friend from the airport."

"Can you drive on the other side of the car and road?" He had a point there. "Are you confident you'll find your way to and from Heathrow?" Damn! Another fine point. "Do you know it's nearly impossible to park at Heathrow?"

"I guess I should actually beg you to help me pick up Bee?"

"That's the attitude, Laney Reid. What time is she landing?"

"Noon."

"I'll pick you up at ten, we'll go grab some coffee, then head out to meet your friend."

"Thank you, Michael. You and Ruby have become indispensable in my life these days."

"I like that, Laney. I hope to stay that way, and I hope one day you'll find me as endearing as I find you."

"In good time...I hope so too..."

Like an alarm clock, Michael rang the doorbell at ten and we were on our way to get coffee at half a minute past ten.

"Hello!"

"Well, hello to you, beautiful lady! That is a stunning dress. I wouldn't think a blonde could pull off a bright yellow dress, but you look like sunshine, today."

"What a compliment! Thank you. This is one of Bee's creations and my personal favorite." It had nothing to do with the fact that Donovan had purchased it for me and that he told me I looked beautiful the last time I wore it...

"What do you mean one of Bee's creations? Does she design clothes?"

"She does. She designs, makes, sells, she does everything! She's super talented is what she is."

"Can't wait to meet her."

We got to Heathrow and it was mayhem. Michael waited in the car while I ran in to collect my dear friend.

"BEE!" I yelled when I saw her with a cart-full of bags. We ran and hugged each other. "I'm so glad you're here. I've been so homesick and haven't been able to express this to anyone. Can you stay with me for a month?" I smiled to show her I was kidding.

"You trying to run my business to the ground? Some of us work for a living!" She tried to sound condescending but her laughing eyes made me feel like I was back at home. "Where are you parked? These bloody bags are damn heavy, even in a push cart." She stopped to pull out some money and handed it to a guy who was pushing her second cart! "Thank you." She called out then pointed for me to take the cart.

"You Taylors are all so damn pushy," I grumbled while pushing the heavy cart.

"Speaking of Taylors, they are all pissed with you right now—down to every last sister."

"Whatever. I can't worry about Mr. Taylor's bruised ego. He'll get over it in a week or so, trust me. He's only pissed because I won't follow his edicts."

"Laney." She stopped me at the curb. "Donovan's a mess right now. He's…"

"Laney! Over here." Michael waved from the back of the queue.

"Who's that handsome fellow?" Bee stared.

I laughed. "My friend. He offered to come pick you up because he didn't trust me to be able to drive on the wrong side of the car and road."

"I did wonder about that one myself, since you never seemed to like to drive even in LA."

We got to Michael's car and his eyes bugged out. "Do you Americans usually come with a Topshop-sized closet when you travel?"

"Michael, I'd like for you to meet Bee Taylor. Bee, this is Michael Bennington. He and his sister Ruby are my only two friends in this entire country."

"Very nice to meet you," Michael greeted and started loading up the car. "Good thing I decided on the bigger car."

After Bee and I helped Michael, we both got in the back and started chatting away. "So tell me what's going on back home. Nick?"

"Every Taylor is in mourning because the most important male Taylor is in mourning and as for Nick, nothing to tell."

"You're so full of shit. Spill it, Bee Taylor. What have you and my handsome cousin been up to lately?"

"Um…ladies?" Michael interrupted our fun. "Will both of you be sitting in the back and making me feel like the chauffeur? Should I have worn Finneas' uniform? You're going to ignore me the whole time?"

"Do you mind if we do?" Bee asked, point blank.

"As long as I get to spend time with two beautiful ladies, I suppose I don't mind at all. Where to, ladies? May I offer to take you both to lunch?"

"Michael, you don't have to do that. You can drop us off at Gram's. There's so much food at home Mrs. Haines has prepared, and I've yet to touch any of it."

"Does that mean I'm getting invited to lunch, too?" He looked like a kid waiting for his lost invitation.

I put my hand on his arm and answered, "You are always welcomed at our home for a meal. You and your sister have become very important people to me, and I thank you and your family for your friendship and kindness."

He grabbed my hand, but I gently got out of the embrace he was intending. Bee tilted her head and questioned what was going on. Lunch turned into unpacking and organizing all of Bee's clothes. One big box Bee brought with her was all her rolling racks disassembled. It was Michael's job to assemble the racks so we could hang and press the clothes that were to be shown to vendors.

"How the hell are you going to get all these clothes to the showroom?" Michael asked. "You brought a bloody lot of samples." Bee laughed at Michael as he was sweating, trying to screw on every last piece. "Doesn't your Gram have air conditioning in this palace of hers?"

Holding back a laugh, I brought a fan and directed it at Michael, only. "There's an air conditioner on every floor, but I don't know how expensive it will be for me to run it so I haven't turned it on, yet."

Michael got up, went straight to the controls, and blasted the cool air. Immediately, our room cooled down. "Have you been sleeping in this heat without the air on? It's hot and humid, Laney. Don't suffer."

"Damn!" Bee looked relieved. "I was about to pass out in here. I just thought you idiotic English didn't believe in air conditioners."

"It wasn't that bad." I tried to justify my frugality.

"I don't want you to be uncomfortable, Laney. Come stay with us if you don't want to run up the bill, but don't do that to yourself. As it is, it bothers me that you're in this big place by yourself. I worry about you."

Something in Michael's statement broke my heart, and it always led back to the man who broke my heart. Donovan's messages were always about how he was doing and what I was doing to him. Never once did he ask how I was faring in a foreign land. It would behoove me to fall in love with a man like Michael who cared for me every which way, but I needed to fall out of love first.

"Does she do this often?" Michael whispered to Bee. "She goes into a trance every time I see her, but she won't tell me what's going on in her head. We'll be having the most delightful conversation, and she'll turn into a hypnosis patient." By his chuckle, we all knew he was teasing me.

"Laney never did that back in the States, but I can tell you my nephew has been doing that a lot lately as well. Perhaps they caught some rare disease and they can only bring each other out of it." Of course, Michael had no idea who Bee's nephew was, and the two of them had a good time making fun of my many quirks.

"Laney always does and says the cutest things where she makes me want to kidnap her and keep her in my pocket so only I can play with her."

"That sounds very much like something a child molester would say…" Bee came over and pretended to protect me.

"He keeps stealing kisses from me, Bee," I complained jokingly.

We worked tirelessly to help Bee get ready for her showing tomorrow and after a simple dinner with the three of us, Michael left with the promise to be back in the morning to help us one more time.

"He's in love with you," Bee said in a warning tone while biting into a cupcake.

"He's not in love with me; it's more like a crush."

"Where'd you meet him?"

I told her the story of our first meeting and all the other times we'd spent together. Purposely, I left out the love at first sight conversation.

"Tell me about this buyer you're meeting tomorrow."

"I will, but I need to know about you and Donovan. I'm here on business and of course to see you, but I'm also here as the Taylor family ambassador. We are all worried about Donovan."

"Bee. There's nothing to worry about. I'll tell you why he's been trying to get a hold of me and why I've kept him at arm's length."

"OK. Do explain."

"The night before I left LA, I went to his house to confess everything. Jake and Emily finally convinced me I had nothing to lose. I figured he didn't return my feelings, at least I'd leave knowing it was all in my fancy-filled head."

"So did he reject you outright? Is that why you're not willing to see him?"

"No. I got to his place close to midnight and Kate opened the door. Then Donovan greeted me looking disheveled and told me to go back home and wait for him because he wanted to see me. Like the good little girl I've always been, as well as a freakin' idiot, I waited for him. And as it has always been in my life, he left me hanging. I didn't sleep a wink that night because I believed he was sincere in his wish to see me. That's how we left one another, and that's why he's been trying to make things up to me." My heart hurt so very much again. "And that's why I don't want to be a pawn in Donovan Taylor's chess board. I don't want to be sacrificed so he can conquer the queen."

"And you don't believe you are the queen?"

I laughed. "Did you know Donovan is attracted to my cousin Jane? And worse, Jane likes him back—even with Max in her life. How can I compete with Kate and Jane when he's put his hat in the ring for both of them and I've only been called 'a pain in the ass' by him? Would you want to put yourself out there, as I have so many times? I don't know what Donovan has told you, but he's only feeling guilty about that last night."

"Have you ever thought he might be in love with you too?"

"There were a few times I thought he might be interested. That night he took me to the observatory was like a page out of any fairytale. I was on such a high the next day. But you know what happened the moment he saw me after that night? He barely said hello and he never looked my way again."

"Maybe he's confused."

"Bee. When you like someone, you want to be with them, sit next to them, talk with them all night, get to know every last thing about them. You know that feeling. What I've seen of Donovan Taylor tells me he has not an iota of interest in me beyond a mild curiosity. Who he really wants is a toss-up between Kate and Jane. I think if Jane and Max were to break-up, Donovan would get right in there and swoop her up."

"What I saw was a hurt and confused man. My nephew's lost without you right now."

"I wish I could believe that, Bee, but I know it's not true. I heard him tell Jane that a chance to love her is what was keeping him from accepting Kate's proposal of marriage. Being rejected time and time again is not a fun feeling."

"No, I suppose not. I guess listening to Donovan's side of the story got me upset with you, but now that I know both sides, I don't know what to think."

"There's nothing to think about where we are concerned. He probably knows I'm interested in him, he was probably briefly curious, and that's it. I need to ask you not to reveal the depth of my feelings for him. It's embarrassing to have been in love with a man for so long when he has never once returned my feelings. What kind of self-respecting woman does that?"

"And Michael?"

I sighed not knowing what to say about Michael. "Michael is this fabulous man who waited to introduce himself to me when we got off the plane. He asked me the first night I met him if I believed in love at first sight. Michael is sweet, caring, funny, and has a wonderful relationship with his family. His parents are also kind and gracious. When I was out to dinner with them last night, his father asked me to go on their summer holiday with them. He and the Bennington family remind me of the Reids."

"Is there a but?"

"I don't love him. I can't love him."

"And why not?"

"Because I love Donovan Taylor and I don't know when my heart will allow me to let go of loving Donovan Taylor."

"Damn, woman, you have it bad for my nephew."

"Let's talk about happier topics. You been out with my cousin lately? I think there's more of a chance of us being related through you and Nick, than through me and Donovan."

"Fuck. Bring on the next topic. Nicholas Reid is on my shit list right now."

"And why's that?"

"Hell if he or I know why I'm so pissed with him. He just pisses me off."

Reaching for my phone, I called my cousin to try and weasel some information off him.

"Laney! What brings you to calling me when you seem to be avoiding the man you really want to talk to and who wants to talk to you?"

"Are there no secrets left in this world? How the hell do you know who I want to talk to right now?"

"Who the hell are you talking to?" Bee grabbed my phone. "Hello? Who's this?" I started busting up when she quickly hung up the phone. "That was hilarious!"

"You want to be on my shit list too? You want me to get Donovan Taylor on the phone for you?"

I sat up straight like I was back in grade school and shook my head no like a frightened little girl. Then I busted out laughing. "Please, teacher, no. Please don't beat me."

"Laney Reid. You can be a pain in the ass sometimes."

"Come on! There's a room with two single beds. Let's take up a pint of ice cream each and spill our woes to one another."

"I've got no woes to speak of." She tried to play it off.

"Bullshit!" I grabbed two spoons and two containers of ice cream and made her walk up three flights of stairs.

I was so happy to have Bee here with me; I played her non-paid assistant with a silly grin on my face the entire day. After Michael helped us transport the clothes to a makeshift showroom, I did everything she told me to do and acted as the docile employee. The industry people who came to see her clothes loved them. She sold just about every sample she'd brought with her, and when she got back home, she'd have to start immediately producing clothes to meet the demand. A proud mama, that's who I was whenever someone praised her creations.

"I don't know what I would have done without your help. Dinner is on me," Bee announced while we started packing things up. "Call out Michael."

"Here I am!" Michael walked in with Mr. Whippys and a box full of unopened Flakes.

"You, Michael Bennington, future duke of wherever, are the best!" I exclaimed and gave him a kiss on the cheek. "Try these." I handed a Mr. Whippy to Bee and jabbed three Flakes into the soft serve.

"Shit, what is this? This is even better than whatever we polished off last night."

"Did you bite into the chocolate? Heavenly, huh?" I was using the chocolate stick as a spoon.

"Let me have some more of those Flakes." Michael opened up a couple more and handed them to Bee who devoured them on the spot. "This combo might even be better than Haagen Dazs bars. I'm going to have to take a box of these home. You," she turned to Michael and also gave him a kiss on the cheek, "are a doll! I approve of you being Laney's friend."

"Would you approve of me being more than Laney's friend?"

Bee stopped eating and thought about his question. "Talk to me when I'm in Flake-coma. I may be in a good enough mood to say yes."

Michael took us first to a very cool East End thrift store where Bee searched through vintage frocks. Then Michael treated us to a trip to the Portobello Road Market where Bee went crazy again, looking through old clothes as well as creations from up and coming designers.

"This was thoughtful of you to bring Bee here, Michael. I am always in awe of your kindness and continue to find myself in your debt."

"This is what friends do for one another, isn't it?" He looked over at Bee. "Bee is soaking up this artistic vibe, huh?"

Bee was all over the place going from stall to stall. "She's loving it. Thank you." Many times Michael had attempted to capture my heart, and today, he finally succeeded. Bringing Bee on these excursions opened my eyes to a completely new man. This afternoon, I began to like him just a teeny-tiny bit, and took my first step toward where he was already waiting.

"You have a beautiful look on your face. What's the smile for?"

"For you…"

He gave me a similar smile and kissed my forehead. "I have one last place to take you ladies."

"More?"

349

"I'd give you a hundred more if you'd let me."

Maybe I'd learn to like this man the way he liked me. Maybe Donovan Taylor would be a distant past and my heart would make way for a new occupant.

"Let's just start with this more. Perhaps we'll discuss the other ninety-nine, day by day."

His smile explained that he knew I was leaning his way. "Hey Bee." Michael called to her attention. "If we don't get going, we're going to lose our reservation at a fashionista tea."

"Well, why didn't you say so earlier?" She hopped over to us with her bags of clothes.

When we got to tea, I was slightly shaken because this was the hotel Donovan stayed at last week. I didn't realize it was walking distance from my home. Trying not to dwell on Donovan when Michael had done every-thing and more to make this a great day for Bee and me, I reverted to my happy smile, and Bee and I ooh'ed and aah'ed over the delectable delights all in the shape of the Spring and Summer fashion collection. Along with delicious tea sandwiches, we ate a cake in the shape of Jason Wu's purse, a bikini cookie modeled after Tory Burch's collection, and a bumblebee yel-low Alexander McQueen inspired dress. When we were done with the first batch, we asked for another and stayed until we each had a full serving.

"We were such pigs." Bee laughed on our way home. "Did you see the server when I asked for one more of those Prada white chocolate bars?"

"That was so much fun. Have you been there before?"

"Believe it or not, I never even knew the tea existed. I put a question out there to a few of my friends and someone suggested I take you ladies over to the Berkeley."

"The food was yummy, the fruit tea I had was ingenious, and I loved the atmosphere. I'll have to go back there."

"If you liked it that much, I'll put in a standing reservation for us. I'm sure Ruby would love it, too. How about every Wednesday, in honor of Bee having dined with us today, a Wednesday?"

"That's kind of you but every Wednesday isn't necessary. Maybe we'll go once a month?"

"Once a month will do, too."

What was declared as once a month turned into a standing date every Wednesday afternoon. One week, Ruby, Michael and I went. The next week, Lizzy Bennington joined us, and the duke-in-training even joined us when we kept discussing this tea while at dinner with the Bennington family.

I'd decided to join the Benningtons on their summer holiday later in the summer, and Michael, Ruby and I became inseparable. We three dined together daily, Ruby came over at least once a week and spent the night at Gram's monstrous flat, and I saw Mr. and Mrs. Bennington almost as often as I saw Michael and Ruby. That small spark of interest that ignited when Bee was here grew by the week, but was still only a flicker. My love for Donovan wouldn't erase so easily.

Donovan had stopped by a few more times and the times Mrs. Haines was here, I asked her to let him know I wasn't here. Once he stayed for hours inside Gram's home and I was trapped in my room agonizing over whether or not I should go down and talk to him, wanting more than anything to hear him tell me that he loved me and wanted a relationship with me. The further the days separated the two of us, the more realistic I became about our so-called "relationship." I knew such a word didn't exist between us and I knew I didn't want to hurt anymore than I already did.

The last time Donovan stopped by, he left me a gigantic box, wrapped and with a large bow in the entry hall. Once he left, I ran down and unwrapped the box to find a pink golf bag with my name stitched in cursive and a set of pink golf clubs. Each club had my name etched and there were two notes attached. The first read, *Congratulations to the most brilliant girl. I am proud of you! Once vacation begins, I'll take you somewhere fun where we can golf and I can regain my title as king of the greens.* The second card read, *Delaney, I really don't understand where you and I went so wrong. I've come by numerous times in the month that you've been gone, and I can't believe you've gone to this length to avoid me. I guess it doesn't matter to you that I miss you. I guess you don't care about me and us anymore. I've heard through your family that you are well, and Bee tells me you've made some good friends. I'd like to hear about them from you. I was at the beach house this weekend and I felt empty there without you. Somehow, you put a mark on that place and I kept hearing your voice and seeing images of your laughing face. Please Delaney, call me. I want to hear your voice; I want to see your smiling face. I'm coming by early July. Please answer my calls!*

Today was early July and rereading Donovan's cards put me in a dour mood. If Donovan was being truthful about what he said in his second card, I, too, missed him. I, too, heard his voice everywhere I went. And I, too, was haunted by Donovan every hour of my day. I wished I could say there wasn't an hour that went by when he wasn't with me. With a monstrous sigh, I put on Bee's yellow dress that Donovan liked so much and sat outside thinking. I needed to be outside to get away from the quiet and solitude of Gram's home. I wished to be surrounded by my boisterous family and the twins, who could make me smile no matter my broken heart.

As I sat on the steps, I remembered our kiteboarding day and our dinner at the beach. I remembered our last "date" together at the sushi bar and as I felt the camellia that sat on my neck, I remembered his gentle embraces and the memories we created that night. If too many memories plagued me, I tortured myself even further by creating delusional fantasies about us.

I imagined Donovan telling me that he loved me. I imagined him getting on his knees, proposing marriage, and a future with lots of kids. I imagined a life with laughter and joy and more happiness than I ever dreamed possible. These imaginations alleviated the frustration that clogged up my heart. I yearned to see Donovan; I longed to feel his touch, even if for a brief moment.

Thinking of Donovan on the steps brought more solace than I imagined. Deciding these maudlin feelings were too much for a beautiful day, I got up to go back inside when I saw him. It was hard to mistake that handsome smile. It was him—Donovan Taylor—in a black taxi, turning the corner and I was thrilled! I would confess my heart to him. I'd tell him just how much I loved him and for how long I had loved him. I'd ask him what his feelings were for me and why he'd relentlessly pursued me while I stayed in London. We'd communicate honestly and maybe even try for a relationship. I knew this was it. Our time had finally come, and today would be a day of reckoning. The joy in my heart was indomitable!

"Laney!" An ecstatic voice greeted me and spun me around in the air like I was a little girl. "That smile you greeted me with was heart-stopping. Have I finally won you over? It's like a dream to see you look at me like I am the only man on earth who matters to you. You know you've been front and center in my heart since we met. And if that look in your eyes is genuine, then I'd like to tell you that you are the only woman I have considered as my future duchess. I know you're going to complain and say it's too soon, but I think I fell in love with you the moment I met you, and my thoughts were confirmed when you stood up to my father that first night at the dinner table. Tell me you feel the same way. Tell me you'll be my duchess!"

"Michael..." In the midst of the confusion and mistaken smile, I searched for the taxi that carried Donovan. I searched everywhere, but the taxi had disappeared and taken my dream with it. What had possessed me to believe Donovan was in that car, waiting to start a new life with me? How had I made such a careless error? Now I had to undo Michael's erroneous belief that I was meant to be his duchess.

"Laney?" Mrs. Haines called out. "Your cousin Jake is on the phone. Would you like to answer him, or shall I tell him you'll call him back?"

I looked at Michael. "Go answer your call. I stopped by in passing to say hello. I actually have a meeting to attend. Can we talk more later?"

I nodded yes, waved good-bye, and walked in to answer the phone. "Hello?"

"The contractions have begun. We have a new Reid on his or her way. I thought you'd like to know!" Jake sounded elated.

"I'm coming home to see the baby as soon as I can catch a flight. Same hospital?"

"Laney. You don't have to do that. I'll send you pictures."

"I'd like to see you and your family, Jake. I know I boasted that I wouldn't be back for a year, but I'm really homesick, and I need to be around my family. Will you keep my secret and allow me to come under the pretense that I wanted to see the baby being born?"

"Of course, Laney. You know you don't ever need an excuse to come home."

"I know, Jake. I thought I'd be stronger than this but I miss everyone so much."

"Your heart would feel that much better and lighter if you'd agree to see my buddy."

"Maybe I will when I come home…"

"See you soon, Auntie Laney."

"See you very soon."

There was a flight leaving in the evening, so I quickly grabbed a few necessities and flew out the door after explaining to Mrs. Haines where I was going, and also letting her know I wasn't sure when I'd be back. That would depend upon what Donovan Taylor had to say. This trip would be a day of reckoning for us. I needed to know where we stood and I needed to know why Donovan Taylor was all of a sudden so interested in seeing me. I'd be brutally honest and ask for the same kind of honesty from Donovan.

"Laney!" Mom practically dropped the cake stand she was dusting. "What are you doing here?"

I went over and hugged my mother whom I missed so dearly. "Jake called and said Emily was going into labor. I wanted to come see the birth of the baby."

"You tell your mother you won't come home for a year, but you rush over to see your cousin's wife having her baby?" Mom gave me a dubious stare. "No matter!" She hugged me again. "I'm just glad you're home."

"What happened with Emily? Jake didn't answer his phone."

"She had the baby!" Mom declared.

"Oh my gosh! I gotta go see. I'm going over there right now, OK?" I ran out the door with only my keys in hand and rushed to the hospital.

Coming home and running to the hospital was the worst mistake of my life. What I witnessed at the hospital before arriving at Emily's room was so devastating and destructive to my heart, I was confounded by grief and utterly lost. The scene in the hospital room next to Emily's room, jarred not only my fairytale outlook on life, but also crushed my self-esteem. Why was it never me? Why couldn't I ever be front and center in his life?

Several times, I pulled myself back together only to fall back into tears. This bathroom stall became my protection from the hurtful world outside. I sat and calmed myself so I could go back and live in reality again. Normally I did my damnedest to look at the brighter side of life but after today, I didn't know if a brighter side would ever exist for me. With every bone in my body telling me to go back to London, I fought that gut instinct and silently peeked into Emily's door, praying Donovan would not be the first person to greet me as I walked in. What did greet me was a whole other surprise I didn't expect today.

"Grandfather, she's the shine to my sun and the light to my moon. I would give up my future dukedom, if she would agree to spend the rest of her life with me."

"Are you insane boy? Do you know what you are saying? You can't just give up your dukedom for a woman."

There was a conversation going on between Michael, a man on the telephone whom I assumed was Michael's grandfather, and my grandfather who laughed loudly. "You hear that Harry, old boy, your grandson is willing to give up being a duke and all the land and fortune that goes with it, to live with my granddaughter. I guess I'll see you in America soon."

"When hell freezes over. I want to see this girl the minute you two land at Heathrow! You got that, Michael?"

"Yes, Sir. I'll bring her out to see you soon."

Having no idea why Michael was here and how he found Emily's hospital room when it took me two tries and a life-altering heartbreak, I tapped Michael on his back and whispered, "Hi. What are you doing here?"

"Laney," Michael said in the sweetest and gentlest way. "I'm so very sorry, my duchess. I didn't mean to scare you back in London. Please tell me you didn't leave after what I'd confessed." He held my hands as though they were his last lifeline and I closed my eyes, not so much because I was moved, but because Donovan stood right in front of me and I couldn't look at him without showing everyone my heartache.

"Michael, you didn't scare me." I said softly. This one man flew a dozen hours to clear up what he considered a misunderstanding, and that one man had kissed my cousin who was already dating a wonderful man.

"Then why did you leave so suddenly? I was so worried, I begged my grandfather to lend me his plane so I could come see you. I thought I had lost you forever. Thank God your mother answered your phone and told me where you were; otherwise I would not have been able to find you."

His distraught look was endearing. I felt bad that I had made him feel so terribly after our last conversation.

"I'm sorry you misunderstood and flew all the way over here, Michael. I came home because Emily was going to have her baby. I wanted to see the baby being born, so I left as soon as I got the call from Jake. It had nothing to do with our last conversation."

Michael's wrinkled face unwrinkled itself and he was finally smiling. He came over and hugged me. "Are you sure I didn't scare you? I know I came on too strong and I know you weren't ready to hear all that. I just can't help myself where you are concerned."

Everybody started clearing their throats to get our attention. I looked up over Michael's shoulder and saw the entire room staring at us. As much as I tried to hide it, I couldn't help but wipe the tears that filled my eyes once I saw Donovan and Jane again. I hoped my family would think I was tearing because I was happy for Jake and Emily, or because of Michael.

"Let me introduce you to everybody here, Michael. This is Emily, my dear cousin-in-law, and this is her husband Jake. This here must be their beautiful newborn, and these are the twins, Ellie and James." As soon as I mentioned James' name he looked up at me with a fabulous smile and put his arms out so I could pick him up. Oh, how I had missed this boy. "You seem to know my grandfather already, this is my brother Doug, my cousins Nick and Jane, and a family friend Donovan." I didn't look at Jane or Donovan when I mentioned their names. I just couldn't look at them anymore.

"Hello, it's nice to meet you all. I'm very sorry for the intrusion on your special occasion. Emily, please accept my apology for barging in on such a private moment."

"No apologies necessary. Any friend of Laney's is a friend of ours. We've spoken on the phone right after you and Laney met, haven't we? And Laney has spoken only great things about you."

"I'm honored you remember me, and that Laney has spoken to you about me." Michael was cute the way he spoke with Emily. He looked like a little boy trying to impress his new school teacher.

"Should I not remember you? You have something to hide?" Emily was now teasing him.

"Oh no! I'm thrilled Laney talked about me to her family. She talks about you, your children and your husband all the time. Why, I feel like I know the four of you as though you were my own family. In fact," he said turning toward Jake, "I need to get to know Jake better as Laney tells me that she wants to marry someone just like Jake. She has told me that the bar was set pretty high by your husband," he addressed Emily again.

"Oh brother," I heard Donovan lament. "Don't inflate his head any-more than it already is. He's going to use up all the oxygen in this room."

"You're always welcome to come take lessons from me, Donovan, old buddy. I won't even charge you." Everyone laughed. I looked away.

"Laney." Michael brought the attention back to me. "I'll get a room near your family home. I will stay here as long as you need to be with your family. But, will you promise to go home with me? I've got the plane at a hangar not far from here."

"Would you be OK with leaving now?" I asked quietly with high hopes that he'd agree.

"Now?" Everyone said together.

"But you just got here," Emily whispered. Her pleading eyes and the baby in my arms made me want to surround myself with the only love I was secure in—that of my family. But right now, this wasn't the place for me. Once I rescued my heart from his pain, I'd come back home with a smile.

I went and hugged the one person in this room who'd understand me and whispered, "I walked in on Donovan and Jane kissing just a minute ago. I can't stay. It hurts too much." I started crying again but I wiped the tear before anyone else noticed. "I'm sorry."

"I understand. I love you, Laney. Take care of yourself and be care-ful not to give your heart away too easily after what you saw today," she warned.

"I'm ready," I squeaked and put on the most genuine smile I could muster. "Bye, everyone. See you next June." Before I could leave, I stopped to kiss the top of Jake Jr's. head and to hug and kiss my favorite twins. "I'll miss you," I whispered and gave James and Ellie another kiss.

Michael opened the door for me and my body turned to Donovan one last time in hopes that he'd stop me from leaving. Especially now with Jane in his life, there was no reason for him to take another look at me, but I needed that hope to stay alive. When I saw him talking to Jane instead, the flicker was snuffed.

It was done.

Michael tried to hold my hand down the hallway, but I couldn't let him. I just wanted to find an empty room and cry my heart out.

"Delaney." I heard. I stopped. I breathed again. "May I speak to you, privately?"

"I'll hold the elevator for us," Michael said, while squeezing my arms in comfort.

"Thank you."

"Are you leaving early because of me and Jane? Because if you are…"

"I'm leaving because it's time I leave and let go. That was why I left in June, and today I realized for certain that there's no place for me here." *There's no place in your heart for me.*

"Delaney, what you saw wasn't what you're thinking," he tried to explain.

"It doesn't matter what I think. It never did." Those tears swelled again. "Thank you, Mr. Taylor. You've made my life that much brighter for knowing you. I've loved every moment of our…friendship." *I love you, Donovan Taylor.* "Bye," I said with a bright smile.

"But Delaney, you're not listening to me. Jane and I…" My next move wasn't what I had planned, but I leaned in and hugged him knowing this was the last physical contact I'd have with him, ever again.

"Good-bye…" I said aloud, but then whispered, "Donovan." I pulled away but he wouldn't let me go. The tears rolled down my cheeks.

"Don't leave me. I'll explain everything. It's not as it looked. I miss you. Don't do this to me."

I pulled away with a sad smile. Pursing my lips so I wouldn't cry any harder, I said, "Good-bye," one last time and ran into the elevator.

"You all right?" Michael's concern was evident, but he was gentleman enough to let me cry. I was a mess in the elevator and Michael, the kind man that he was, just let me be.

The trip back "home" was quick, luxurious, and quiet. I decided to try and sleep part of the time, and edit papers the other part of the time. Michael had copious amounts of paperwork to do for his father's estate, and he gave me space to work out the turmoil raging in my heart. During my "sleep," the image of Donovan and Jane kissing in the hospital wouldn't leave me.

"Hello. I'm looking for Emily Reid's room."
"Over there."
"Thank you."
"Stop, Donovan. You're tickling me. Stop making me laugh. I don't want to do this again."
"One more time, Jane. Let me try this one more time."

What he was trying "one more time" was holding my cousin in an intimate way and attempting to kiss her. His back was to me, but what I saw was unmistakable. He had his arms around her and was about to kiss her. Coming upon this scene, I was so shocked, I didn't know what to do. I just stared and kept telling myself to leave the room, and yet I couldn't help but stay and watch their affections unfold. Donovan and Jane saw me as I left them to their private act, but I didn't stay to hear their explanations – not that they needed an excuse for their actions. How could life be so cruel? The man I didn't want was willing to give up his entire future for me, and the man I wanted wasn't willing to give up anything for me.

"Laney?" Michael brought me back to the present. "Would you like fish or steak for dinner?" I was in such a deep reverie that I didn't even notice the flight attendant standing before me.

"Neither if that's OK? I'll just stick to water, thank you."

The flight attendant walked away. Michael put his work down, came over, and sat next to me.

"Are you ready to talk? Can we be honest with one another?"

"Sure," I agreed, it was time for honesty, and a decision-making time for me.

"When I first saw you in the hospital room, we could all tell that you'd been crying. No matter the beautiful smile you put on in front of your family, even I could tell you were heartbroken." Michael had me tearing again. "And since you had a talk with your family friend back at the hospital, you've been teary-eyed and hurting. What has you so sad, my duchess?" The last thing I wanted to do was a tell-all confessional. However, I knew I couldn't lie to him; I knew I didn't want to lie to him. If there was ever a chance that I could grow to like or even love this man, I needed to start today by being honest with him.

"I have been obsessed with, infatuated with, and in love with someone since I was ten years old."

"Was it the man who came out right before we got into the elevator and asked to talk to you?"

"Yes. His name is Donovan Taylor, and he is Jake's best friend since they were young. He's a decade older than I am, and he's known me all my life. When I was twelve, I was so in love with him, I actually asked him to marry me." I laughed at the thought.

Michael pretended to be heartbroken "You mean my proposal wasn't the first in your life?"

"Well, yours was the first proposal to me."

"Good to know. What did he say when you asked him to marry you?"

"Well I'm not exactly sure that he knew it was from me, though I'm pretty sure he knew but..."

"How does he not know who proposed to him? Did you blindfold him as you asked him?"

"No," I laughed. "I asked him to marry me in the form of a note in his pocket."

"Seriously?" Michael looked shocked. "You wrote him a note and asked him to marry you? How did you deliver this note to him?"

"We were all swimming one day at Jake's house and I shoved it in his pocket before leaving."

"So how was he to know who proposed to him? What if he wanted to accept your proposal? Where would he go find you?" Michael was finding this whole situation quite amusing. "I wish I had known you when you were younger. You are charming now; I can just imagine how much more adorable you would've been as a ten-year-old."

Michael was always a gentleman, and he had a way of making me feel special. It was a wonder why I couldn't give my heart to somebody like this, rather than somebody who always mangled it.

"I'm sure he knew it was me. I was always dropping notes in his pocket. I had such a big crush on him when I was little."

"So no one else had a crush on him? It was only you? For sure he knew that it was you who proposed to him?"

"I don't know… I guess it really doesn't matter. He never came to answer my proposal." I did my best not to sound too sad. I tried to look at the comical side of me as a twelve-year-old proposing to Donovan. "I had no chance with him then, and I have no chance with him now."

"I'm relieved to hear that you have no chance with him now, but may I ask why you believe you have no chance with him? If I were him and I knew you were interested, I would wake up and smell the tea, immediately."

"Right before I walked into Emily's hospital room I took a wrong turn and walked in on Donovan and my cousin Jane."

"What did you exactly walk in on?"

I laughed nervously. "This isn't something I want to keep reliving, but I have a feeling I don't have a choice but to tell you." I hoped Michael would let it go, but he sat next to me patiently waiting my answer. "You're going to make me spell it all out aren't you?"

He nodded yes. "Considering that I have asked you to marry me, and I have proclaimed in front of at least ten different people that I'm giving up my future dukedom for you if my grandfather disapproves, I would like there to be complete honesty between the two of us, if you don't mind."

"I walked in on them embracing...holding...kissing...."

"And that obviously broke your heart?"

"Was it that obvious?" Damn! I guess all those people were right. My face was too expressive to lie.

"You put on a good show for your family back in the hospital room, but I don't think anyone was fooled."

I smiled in response. "I don't know Michael. I don't know if it was the fact that he was kissing another woman, or the fact that he was kissing my cousin Jane, I don't know what broke my heart more."

"May I be honest this time?"

"Sure."

"I think perhaps that Donovan was a schoolgirl crush you have kept in your heart for so long, you believe you still love him, even today. Maybe since he's been in your life, for as long as you can remember, you've never had a chance not to love this man. But that was back when you were a little girl and now you are a woman. Perhaps it's time to shake off the old and bring in the new. You told me from day one that you were starting a new life. That means that there should be an absolute clean slate—especially in your heart. Could I be a part of this clean slate? Would you be willing to start new with me?"

It was at this moment I decided to give this man a chance. He was honest and openly refreshing. I appreciated the fact that he did not want to hide anything from me. He put everything out there for somebody like me and the least I could do was give him a chance. Who was I to make anyone tell his grandfather he'd give up his future?

"All right. A new beginning from here on out." I hoped.

"Splendid!" Michael showed off a brilliant smile. "And that new beginning starts at my grandfather's country home. He's dying to meet you, and I'm dying to show you off."

"Michael," I said cautiously, "I need you to take it slow with me. I know you're almost at the finish line already, but just remember we hardly know each other. We met a month ago, and I don't think I can accept anyone's proposal within a month. If you are in agreement with that then I am willing to meet your grandfather, re-introduce myself to your parents as your girlfriend, and start a new relationship with you."

Michael came closer and embraced me. I couldn't say that it felt bad to be embraced by Michael, but it wasn't quite right either. "Laney, you truly are the shine to my sun and the light to my moon. I will make you happy. I will convince you that I am the right man for you."

Once we got back to London, Michael went home to take care of our arrangements to his grandfather's home, and I went to Gram's to pack for the week we were staying. I was mentally and emotionally exhausted, but I felt bad the way I'd left things with Emily. And I also missed James and Ellie. While going through the motion of leaving for another trip, the phone rang.

"Hello?" I answered, surprised that anyone was calling me already.

"You got home safely?" Emily whispered.

"Yes." I whispered back. "Why are we whispering?"

"The baby's sleeping. He fell asleep while nursing, again. He's such a good baby, already. I am so in love again!" Emily sounded adorable talking about her new baby. "I worried that there wouldn't be enough love in me for this little one, but I was wrong. He's so sweet and such a darling." It was always beautiful hearing Emily talk about her kids. "This little one looks like a cross between the twins and reminds me very much of a male version of Ellie."

"So he reminds you of Jake?"

"I guess he does. But enough about me and the kids. How are you?"

"I'm all right. I felt terrible for leaving you so quickly, but I think I made the right decision."

"That Michael is quite the ardent suitor. You heard him, didn't you, when he told his grandfather that you meant the world to him?"

"Yeah. I did. We had a nice talk on the plane coming back to London."

"Yeah? What was the talk about?"

"I decided to try for a relationship with Michael."

"You did?" Emily sounded surprised and disappointed. "I was hoping you wouldn't jump into anything so soon. What you saw with Donovan and Jane wasn't what you were thinking. They explained it to me."

I didn't want to think about that scene again, but there didn't seem to be a choice.

"Emily. That scene at the hospital hurt, but what hurts most is the fact that Donovan is so flippant about what he wants. He doesn't care who becomes collateral damage. It's all about him and that's how he's always been. Finally, I've come to admit that's not what I want in a man. I want a man who's willing to make sacrifices for me, who'll love only me, and who'll always put me first."

"You think Michael will be that man for you?"

"I'm unsure, but I won't know till I try. All my life I have waited and put off relationships hoping Donovan might notice me…that he might come to love me. Those were childish and foolish dreams. I don't want to dream anymore, and I don't want to live in my own world anymore. I want to live in reality."

"But your hopes and dreams are what make you so special, Laney. Why do you want to give those up?"

"I don't know Emily," I hesitated to explain myself. "I feel like if I don't give those up, I'm forever going to hope that somebody who doesn't want me will want me one day. And I'll never be able to move on. There's no knight in shining armor. There's no Prince Charming. I have to live in reality."

Emily was silent for a comfortable while. "I want you to always understand that Jake and I love you, and we still believe your Prince Charming is out there. He just hasn't woken up from his slumber."

The baby was up and demanding his meal again. It was time to say good-bye.

"I'll let you go. Talk to you again, soon?"

"Absolutely. Take care."

Our conversation made me wonder if I had given up too soon on my knight in shining armor, but thinking back to the kissing scene, I knew I'd made the right decision.

Michael's grandfather's summer home was so vast, I couldn't tear my eyes away from the picture before me.

"*That's* your grandfather's home?" I pointed like a little girl going on her first outing.

"It is." Michael answered nonchalantly. "Does it impress you enough to want to be the owner of that property one day?" He tried to hold back a sly grin.

"Well..." I decided to act sly, myself. "A girl can't be so easy and say yes after one measly proposal on the steps of my grandmother's home. I've got to check out the inside of the palace before I can come to any sort of a conclusion on how vast my future husband's earnings and holdings must be."

"Indeed!" Michael declared and laughed at me. "You do that Laney Reid, because if a P&L sheet is all you're looking for, you've come to the right place!"

"So you think, Michael Bennington...there are plenty of rich men in America." I laughed with him.

"Yeah, but are any of them titled and on a first name basis with the future king?"

"Oh my gosh! You know the Prince? Can you introduce me to him and Duchess Catherine?" I started fan-girling on the English royal family. "I think she's so beautiful. That'd be so cool if I could meet her." Michael only shook his head at me.

The car pulled up the never-ending driveway, and an unexpected surprise awaited me. Even before the car came to a full stop, I opened the door and hugged my grandfather, who stood next to a disapproving and haughty face.

"Laney. It relieves my worries to see your smiling face." Grandfather kissed my forehead like I was a five-year-old.

"What are you doing here? How...why..." I wasn't sure what was happening, but I knew enough to stop talking to Grandfather Roland and to get myself in good graces with this man whose scowl could ruin my entire week. "Hello. I apologize for my bad manners in not introducing myself." I addressed the man whom I assumed was His Grace, Harry Michael Bennington. "I'm Laney Reid, granddaughter of Sir Roland Ascot."

"Unfortunately, I know all about you." Not the answer I was expecting at all.

"Grandfather." Michael wasn't happy.

"Don't you dare treat my granddaughter with anything but respect."

"And for what reason would I respect this girl? What has she done to prove herself worthy of my grandson's affections?"

"Grandfather!" Now Michael was upset. "Laney is my girlfriend and my guest. I will not have you intimidating her or treating her poorly. You have taught us to be kind and accepting of everyone; I hope you will practice what you preach."

"What the hell has she done to turn you into such a love-sick fool, already? Do you know anything about this girl or her family? Do you know if she's worthy of becoming a Bennington? How dare you disrespect your grandfather because of some girl!"

I wanted to say something, but my own grandfather held me back.

"After twenty-six years of learning under you and Father, if you cannot trust me to make decisions for myself and for the good of the Bennington family, I have learned nothing. You and Father have taught me to be open to the world around me and to trust my instincts. My instincts are telling me that I am in love with this woman who stands here with me. This is the woman I want with me when I am happy, when I am troubled, when I disagree with family members, when I am old and gray, and living a beautiful life with many children and grandchildren. This is my decision, Grandfather. I would like for you to respect it and come to accept it with open arms."

Harry Bennington snorted in disgust. "You can kiss your inheritance and title good-bye if you decide to marry this American girl. She's not good enough for you or our family."

Grandfather was about to have a word or two with His Grace, but Michael beat him to it. "Fine! I gladly let go of my inheritance, *your* title, and everything else that comes with being a Duke. But I won't let go of this chance to possibly make this woman my wife. If you are so against this relationship, we will leave right now." Michael grabbed my hand and pulled me away from my grandfather.

"Wait!" I stopped the war of words between Michael and his grandfather. "Michael." I addressed the more reasonable person, first. "Regardless of what your grandfather says to you, or how unreasonably he may act toward you, you may not be an *ass* in return." Michael broke into a smile and my grandfather blatantly laughed aloud. "He's family. I'm not. You can't sever your ties with family, no matter the person or situation you're defending." Then I spoke to the unreasonable man staring at me. "Your Grace, I don't know why you're so pissed with me when you hardly know me. Perhaps it's my blonde-haired, blue-eyed looks that offend you, or it's my American manners that appall you. And in all honesty, I wouldn't normally give a damn, but since you're Michael's grandfather, I will do my best to try and get along with you."

"Shit." I heard the duke grumble. "She sounds too much like someone else I know."

"You're in trouble now, Harry." My grandfather slapped the duke on his back. "Give up the pretense and let's go have dinner. I'm starving."

"Don't turn out your grandson because he does one thing you're not fond of, and don't judge a situation even before anything really happens. Michael and I are more friends than anything else and if it develops into something more serious than you like, then let's talk."

"Duchess, we can leave if you don't feel comfortable. We don't have to stay."

"Michael. My grandfather is here all the way from America. I am staying and enjoying the night with him. If the duke does not wish for me to be here, then I will leave with my grandfather. What will it be, Your Grace?"

"Are you sure about her, Michael? She's a demanding little thing. She might make you feel like you're walking on water now, but she could also make you feel like you're drowning in the deepest ocean if things go wrong."

"I'd like to take my chances, Grandfather." I returned Michael's smile and affectionate touch.

"Young kids these days…" was my welcome into the beautiful home.

Dinner consisted of too many courses that were impossible to finish. After greeting Michael's parents and having a mini love-fest with Ruby, I sat between Michael and my grandfather. As soon as dinner was over, His Grace wanted drinks and dessert, out in the garden so we moved our party to suit his whims.

"Will you all excuse us?" Grandfather motioned for me to get up. "I'd like to take a stroll with Laney." Everyone understood his clear meaning that we would be taking a walk alone.

"What brings you all the way out here, Grandfather?" I asked, while strolling hand in hand with this wonderful man.

"You, my granddaughter."

"Me?" Was I in trouble of some sort?

"Your Gram and I are very worried about you. The way you left that hospital broke our hearts. What exactly happened?"

The tears fell unexpectedly and heavily. "You didn't have to fly all the way here. What a waste of your time and energy." I tried to make light of the situation, but the tears fell continually.

"What happened?" he asked gently and pulled out his handkerchief before sitting me on a bench. "One minute I'm sitting in the hospital room admiring my newest great-grandson. The next minute Donovan runs in frantically looking for you. Then finally, you walk in with sadness and heartache written all over your face. Jake gave us a short and not so sweet version of what he thought happened. Your Gram and I were heartbroken for you when we heard."

I did my best to stop the unnecessary tears but it took a long while— much longer than expected.

Sighing, I explained, "I walked into the wrong room at the hospital and found Donovan and Jane kissing." With this confession, I started bawling harder than I did in the bathroom. Something about my grand-parents taking my side and wanting to comfort me gave me the nod to let out all my grief.

Grandfather hugged me when I calmed down to a semi-normal state. "So that pushed you into Michael's arms when you're in love with Donovan?"

"I decided that there's no hope with Donovan, and if that's the case, I need to open my heart to other people. Michael makes me feel special, and I like that. It's not something I'm used to, but it sure does feel nice, Grandfather."

"But is that fair to Michael?"

"I've told Michael about Donovan, and he knows I am not where he wants us to be. He's willing to see where this goes and so am I."

"But Laney, your feelings for Donovan won't go away so readily."

"They may, they may not, but I won't know unless I try. All my life I pushed away any man who held an interest in me because he wasn't Donovan Taylor. There were some men I thought I might like, but in the end I decided to hold off on the off chance that Donovan might grow to love me. I know I sound dumb and naïve, but that's how I've lived my life. No more, Grandfather. I'm done waiting, hoping, and dreaming. I choose to live in the present."

"May I suggest you take things very slowly with Michael? I have a feeling letting go of Donovan Taylor is not going to be as seamless as you believe, my darling granddaughter. You may have a fight on your hands from both men."

"I thank you for coming all the way here to make me feel better, and I love you for caring so much about me. Please reassure Gram that this is only a small setback in the grand scheme of life for me. I won't disappoint her, and I won't embarrass the Reid family."

"We have no doubt about that. You are a phenomenal young lady. I am proud to call you my granddaughter."

I kissed my grandfather on the cheek and pulled him up so we could rejoin the party.

Ruby and I shared a room in this mansion of a summer home and Grandfather left for London after an early breakfast with me and the Benningtons. He said he had business in the London office and needed to stop by the flat to pick up some of Gram's belongings. The Benningtons and I went back and forth on what we should do to occupy the day.

"Well, there are lots of forests and gardens and nature trails here." Lizzy Bennington said while sipping her tea.

"There are a few theatres with live productions and movies," Mr. Bennington added. "Oh, and there's that beautiful old opera house. I'm sure they're playing something wonderful."

"Father," Ruby interjected. "The theatres play movies that debuted in the States half a year ago, and I find opera dreadfully boring!"

"There's so much greenery here, I wish I'd brought my golf clubs. I assume there are lots of golf courses here?" I asked anyone in general.

"Golf?" Michael asked. "You speak golf?"

"I breathe it, speak it, and play it." The duke looked mighty interested. Up until now, he didn't say much more than a good-morning to me. Apparently, I had his attention now.

"What do you say, Grandfather?" His Grace gave Michael a doubtful stare. Michael quickly walked away and didn't come back for a good ten minutes. "I found a lady's set for Laney. Let's go golf," he told everyone.

Ruby explained to me that golf was an obsession for the Bennington family, especially the duke. Lizzy Bennington had no choice but to learn to play after she married into the family, or else, she'd be the only one sitting at home alone, while the entire family went out and played all day.

"Is there a course nearby?" I asked.

Ruby cackled away. "I'd say it's pretty nearby. Let's change and I'll take you to the course."

Ruby wasn't kidding when she mentioned how close the course was. This summer home sat on more acres than one could feasibly count, and about ten years ago, the backyard was turned into a nine-hole golf course.

"You've got to be freaking kidding me!"

"I am *not* kidding you." Ruby took us out on the golf cart over to the first tee.

When we arrived, I took a picture of the course and texted it to my father with the words, *My friend's grandfather's backyard* written below the picture.

"You willing to bet a little something, Ms. Reid?"

"I am, Your Grace. What would you like to bet?" I answered confidently.

"How about if you lose, you stop seeing my grandson?"

"Grandfather!" Both Michael and Ruby called out.

"Oh Harry, give the girl a break." Lizzy defended me. "We all like her very much. You're being unnecessarily bullish right now. That's neither gentlemanly nor very duke-like. You're usually kind to all around you. What has poor Laney done to get you so riled? I must ask you to stop this ugly and brutish behavior. You're upsetting my son, the *future duke.*"

"How about if I beat you, you stop being such a bully?" I challenged Michael's grandfather. "If I lose, I don't promise to stop seeing your grandson, but I promise to leave your home and go back to Belgravia as soon as possible so I will not be in your way." I had to admit, though I sounded tough, my feelings were hurt. After having been soundly rejected by Donovan, it hurt to have someone dislike me. I decided whether or not

I won this round, I'd pack up and go home. In truth, no matter how good Michael and the Benningtons were to me, my heart continued to hurt from what I witnessed in LA. I wanted to go home and talk to my mother and cry to my heart's content. I wanted to let out all this heartache and start fresh with Michael. Some time to decompress from my LA trip was sorely needed and coming straight here didn't allow me to straighten out my head.

Michael rode in a cart with his grandfather, Mr. and Mrs. Bennington paired up, and Ruby and I spent a fun day together. All of the Benningtons were excellent golfers. Even Lizzy, who picked up the sport late in life, played beautifully. When we got to the ninth and final hole, I was up on everyone. The duke wasn't far behind and I contemplated letting him win so I could leave without a fuss, but the competitor in me wouldn't allow it. I won fair and square, and the disgruntled duke huffed off the golf course.

"You are fantastic." Michael came over to me and Ruby. "I assume you've played all your life?"

"Your family was fantastic! I was in awe of your mother and how skilled she was even though she picked it up only ten years ago."

"That's what happens when all you do is play golf every day it doesn't rain." Ruby lamented. "Mum's obsessed."

"I thought you all were great out there. That was fun!" I turned to Michael to give him the bad news. "Michael?"

"Yes, Love." His term of endearment made me wince inside.

"Please don't take this the wrong way, but I'd like to get back to London today. Do you think there will be trains running at this hour?"

"Love. You don't have to leave. If it's because of Grandfather, I'll have a talk with him."

"It's not entirely because of your grandfather. There are unsettled matters I'd like to take care of back in London, and I need some time to talk to my mother. She's upset that I left so abruptly and in all honesty, I'd like to spend a little more time with my grandfather before he leaves. I don't know when I'll see anyone from home again."

Michael debated what to do. Ruby was a dear to be on my side. "Mikey, let her go. We're only here for a few days, anyhow. You'll be with her again, soon."

"Then let me drive you back to London."

"Please, no," I begged. "Stay with your family and I'll see you when you get back. The train will take me right into St. Pancras and I promise to take a taxi back to the flat."

"I feel like you're running away from me." My heart dropped upon hearing Michael's words.

"I'm not running away, but I do need a little time to make heads or tails out of all that's happened in the last few days. Will you give me some alone time?"

"You promise you're not running away?"

"Not running away, just walking to a corner for a time-out." I smiled to reassure him.

After saying a quick good-bye to everyone, Michael drove me to the train station. Luckily, there was a train departing within the hour so my good-byes had to be quick. The duke looked neither happy nor upset to see me go, but I reassured him that it wasn't him who was pushing me out. I also made Michael promise not to be upset with his grandfather.

During the more than three-hour train ride home, I wrote an email to Max. It wasn't my intention to get Jane into trouble, and it wasn't my intention to hurt Max, but when looking for solace in this situation, Max was the only person I felt I could turn to at this moment. The email explained what I'd been doing up until now and I told him about my quick trip to Los Angeles and how sorry I was that I didn't get to stop by and say hello to him. I told him that I missed him and I encouraged him to visit when Josh moved across the Atlantic and settled in his new home.

After sending off the email, I opened up a student thesis that needed correcting and I averted my attention to something that wouldn't make me sad. No sooner had I opened the file, a phone call came in. The number was one I'd never seen before. It made me nervous that it might possibly be Donovan calling. I wavered between picking up and letting it go to voicemail, but of course, I had to pick it up. On the slim chance that it might be Donovan, no matter how much I didn't want to face him, I still desired to have some contact with him.

"Hello?" I answered, scared of the caller on the other side.

"Laney." A not too cheerful voice greeted me.

"Max?"

"Yes, it's me, Max. How are you?"

"I'm all right." I said while holding back the tears. "How are you? Whose number is this?"

"It's my friend's number. I'm down in Mexico with the hospital and I didn't bring my phone so I'm calling you from his phone."

"Is it that time already? I thought you were going to Mexico later in the summer."

"It just happened that there was an opening and I took it." Max didn't sound like himself. Funny, but he and I sounded identical to one another. We were two lost souls on the phone trying to commiserate without revealing what we were commiserating about. "Is something the matter? Your email read like a river of tears."

"It's just homesickness."

"But you just went home. What's the matter, Laney?"

How could I tell him what was the matter? If I revealed my real pain, I'd end up hurting this good man who seemed to be in pain himself.

"Did I mention in the email that I'm dating someone?" This was an unusual way of deflecting unwanted attention on me by bringing up an even crazier topic about myself.

"You are? How did that happen?"

"It just did. His name is Michael and he's a good guy. I'd love for you to meet him one day."

"I'd like to meet him. I'm sure he's a better guy than the last one you were stuck on." Max was so bitter. This was probably a good time to get off the phone so we wouldn't have to talk about Donovan and I wouldn't have to do the courteous asking about Jane business.

"When you are done in Mexico, please come visit me. I'd love to see you."

"I'll keep that in mind, Laney. We'll talk again, soon?"

"Definitely."

That was a bizarre conversation between the two of us, but I was glad it happened. The next conversation I needed to have was with my mother. This was not going to be a happy one.

"Hi Mom." Mom had picked up on the first ring. Scary!

"What is the matter with you? You drop in without a word, then you leave within the same day without much of an explanation. What the hell did I miss?"

"I'm sorry, Mom. I'm sorry that I didn't let you know I was coming. And I'm even sorrier that I picked up my bags and left without giving you the whole story. I just couldn't tell you what happened at the hospital when I saw you. I didn't want you to see me cry."

"Oh my God. What happened? Are you crying right now? What's the matter?"

"I'm hurting so much right now, Mom. I don't know what to do with my heart." I tried my best not to cry, but I couldn't help it. My shattered heart broke some more talking to her.

"What's the matter, Baby?" Now Mom was crying with me.

"When I got to the hospital, I walked in on Donovan and Jane kissing. That's why I couldn't stay. I can't get the picture of the two of them out of my head. What do I do?"

"I'm coming to see you right now. I'll book myself a flight to London as soon as we get off the phone."

I loved my mother. This was what family was all about. "Los Angeles to London is far, Mom. You don't have to come. Your voice alone soothes my heart."

"Laney. Let me come to you. When you hurt, I hurt even more. I need to see you and make sure you're all right."

"I tell you what." I came up with this brilliant idea. "How about I meet you halfway?"

"New York?"

"Yeah. I have a huge thesis I'm editing, and that'll bring in enough money to buy me a roundtrip ticket from London to New York. Let's meet there, watch a show, drink fine wine and enjoy ourselves."

"You silly girl. You don't have to worry about money! Did you really think your father would cut off your allowance when you're thousands of miles away from us? Check your bank account. If I know your father, he's probably doubled your allowance so you wouldn't suffer out in London by yourself."

"How soon can you meet me, Mom?"

"Tomorrow?"

"Yes! Once I get home, I'll pack and book myself a flight. Where shall we stay?"

"I know just the place to relax and soothe your soul. You leave the details to me. Send me your flight info as soon as you make plans and I'll let you know where we are staying."

"Thanks, Mom. I love you."

"I love you too, sweet girl. See you soon."

Talking to Mom gave me the wings to attempt another flight. Visiting with Grandfather helped ease the pain, but knowing I'd be with Mom gave me new life. As soon as I got to the flat, I booked myself an open-ended flight to New York, checked my bank account and laughed at the fact that Mom was only partially correct. Dad had put so much money in my account, I double-checked to make sure I hadn't accidentally hacked into someone else's account. I turned on my phone to send Mom my flight info when I came upon the name Donovan Taylor, again. He had sent more text messages than there was space in my phone. Without reading a word, aside from his name, I deleted every single message. For the first time in days, I felt the cloud lifting. I didn't need Donovan messing up my life again.

I tried calling Grandfather but he didn't answer his phone, so I called Michael to let him know I had arrived safely.

"Hello, Duchess." Another term of endearment that made me wince. One day soon, I'd let him know how uncomfortable I felt, but for now, I needed to let him know where I was headed. "Are you home?"

"I am home for now but will be heading out to New York tomorrow."

"New York?" I could tell Michael was unhappy with my revelation.

"Mom and I are meeting out there. We just decided this and I thought I'd let you know."

"Is this all part of your time-out? Rather than walking to your corner, you're flying to one end of America?"

I chose to take that as a joke. "Yes, Michael." I answered in good spirit. "This is the fancy way of taking a time-out. Mom wanted to come into London but I thought it'd be easier on her if I met her halfway. Mom's a bit peeved with me that I left so soon."

"What will you do for me? I, too, am peeved that you left my grand-father's so soon."

I laughed. "I don't know what I'll do for you, but it'll be a few days before I can make anything up to you. I'll see you when I get back?"

"Of course, Love. I'll be waiting for you."

"Tell Ruby to hold off on the trip to Rome."

"What trip to Rome?"

"She thought it'd be fun for the three of us to visit. But I forgot that in about a month, I have a friend who'll move there for a year. I'd like for you to meet him."

"I'd go anywhere and meet anyone if you're there with me."

I didn't know how to respond. All of Michael's sweet words were having the opposite effect on me. I'd have to talk to Mom and reevaluate our situation.

Just like Emily, I loved New York! The flight landed midday, and I arrived at a very chic hotel in Tribeca. Always up to date on the coolest places, Mom had picked this ultra glamorous, ultra serene lodging that felt more like our comfortable home than a hotel. Feeling nothing but happiness knowing I'd be with my mother, I sent Emily a picture of our hotel with a hashtag that read, #wishyouwerehere! Of course, I got a quick call in response.

"You're in New York? How did that happen?"

"Mom and I talked yesterday and we thought a girls' trip to New York would be fun. If you didn't have three babies under eighteen months, I'd have invited you to join us."

"Once I realized I was pregnant with JR, I did wonder when we'd ever get back to our New York apartment. Where are you and Aunt Babs staying? You could've stayed at our place."

"I think I need a clean break from your part of the Reid family." I giggled.

"Ha ha ha." Emily didn't giggle back. "Have you spoken with Donovan?"

"Nope, and I don't plan to speak with him. Nothing good comes of being anywhere near that man." If I didn't make light of my situation, I'd go back into heartbreak mode, and that was the last thing I needed.

"Last I heard, he flew to London just to see you."

"Don't care and don't want to know. I know I sound like a brat right now, but I'm going to see Mom soon and I don't want her to see me crying. When I talked to her the other day, she was bawling on the phone because I was bawling on the phone. She shouldn't hurt because I can't let go of one Donovan Taylor."

"Laney." Emily had that disapproving voice. "If you gave him a chance, he'd be able to explain what's going on and that the kiss between…"

I cut Emily off. I didn't need the visual. I didn't want the visual. "I see Mom, Emily. I'll call you again. Bye." I hung up even before Emily returned my good-bye.

"Laney!" Mom ran as fast as her heels would bring her to me.

"Mom!" I greeted her with the same amount of enthusiasm. "I'm so happy you're here!" We hugged and kissed then hugged some more.

After leisurely putting our clothes away, we went to the lantern-lit swimming pool housed under a 250 year-old reconstructed wood and bamboo farmhouse. Lounging in that kind of beauty alone would have been fabulous enough, but Mom booked us treatments in the Japanese bathing room with tubs used for traditional bathing rituals. We got a couple's massage after our soak in the tub and after a light dinner at the hotel, we were whisked off by a hotel car to watch *Cinderella*, the musical.

"I loved the modern twist on this storyline!" I was feeling mighty empowered after watching this show. "I know I should be impressed with Cinderella's politically progressive ideas, but I loved the fact that she gave him back the glass slipper. She didn't wait for her knight in shining armor – she simply created her own destiny. I love her strength and self-confidence."

"I knew you'd like the show. Did you notice the costumes?"

"How could you not? They were stunning!" I gushed. "And how on earth did they do those magical *Bibbibi-Bobbidi-Boo* costume changes?"

"Who knows? This musical is going to be hard to beat."

"Are we watching another one?"

"Tomorrow night, we're watching *Wicked*."

"I like! This was such a good idea, Mom." I linked my arm in hers as we walked out to a late night snack at a chicken and rice food cart.

"I feel like I'm back in college, eating so late."

"This is so spicy, but so good." I couldn't stop adding more hot sauce to the mayo/yogurt sauce drizzled all over the chicken and rice.

"Where shall we go after this?"

"Oh my gosh. You want to go somewhere from here? I thought we'd go back and enjoy our hotel room."

"That is true. Your dad did give me the evil eye when I showed him where we were staying. I was never more glad he had to stay behind."

"Dad wanted to come?"

"Of course he wanted to come. He missed seeing you when you popped into LA."

"What a bad daughter I am. I haven't called him at all since I came and left," I answered between bites. "I didn't know how to explain what had happened."

"I gave your father the little you told me, and he was pissed!" Mom started laughing. "He called Donovan the moment I explained what happened."

"Oh no! Please tell me Daddy didn't go all 'Chief of Staff' on him." How embarrassing to have one's father berating a man who holds no interest in his daughter.

"No. Lucky for Donovan, he didn't answer his phone. In fact, Jake told me Donovan had come into London to see you right after you left. You didn't see him?" Mom cautiously brought up his name.

"No. And I'll explain why I didn't see him after I make this call to Daddy."

I called my father and he picked up immediately. "Hello, Baby!"

"Hi, Daddy. How are you?"

"Pissed." He chuckled.

"Who, what, when, where, and why?"

"I'm pissed that I have to work while the two loves of my life are having a ball in New York, and I'm pissed that my beautiful daughter is shedding tears over an ass who doesn't know his head from his tail."

"Ah. I see. Well, as for your first point of discontent, I say come join us. Leave the hospital for a few days. They'll survive without you."

"I wish I could, Baby. But we are short-staffed as it is and Jake's on a quick leave because of JR."

"That's a bummer."

"Are you feeling any better?"

"I am feeling a thousand times better, and as for Donovan Taylor, I don't want you to call him and say anything to him."

"You still sticking up for that jerk?"

"I am not sticking up for him; I am just trying not to embarrass myself. What could you possibly say to him that will not make me look like a lovesick fool? You going to berate him because he broke your little girl's heart?"

"Hell yes!"

"No Daddy. Whatever he chooses to do and whomever he chooses to do it with, I am not a part of that equation. Let's not bring to light my schoolgirl crush."

"Damn! I so wanted to kick his ass."

"How about saving that energy for when you visit me in London, once Jake comes back to the hospital?"

"All right, Baby. You have a great time with your mother."

"Thank you, Daddy. I will."

"Your father able to make it to New York?" Mom asked doubtfully.

"No. He's gotta work, but he says he'll try and come see me in London."

Mom was careful not to bring up the topic of Donovan Taylor and I didn't feel the need to mention him, either. We were enjoying ourselves dining, shopping and taking in a third show after *Cinderella* and *Wicked*. Even during the romantic musical, *Once*, I was fine, loving the time I had with my mother. I watched, listened, and marveled at the clever set changes and the beauty of the music.

It was when we got to our frozen hot chocolate dessert place I broke down like a fool over a song. While waiting for our dessert, I heard a part of a song in which Romeo kneels to the ground and proposes to Juliet, and this is what made me lose it. The picture of Donovan asking Jane to marry him flashed in my mind. Seeing the two of them happy and in love was too much for my feeble heart.

"Laney!" I had startled my mother. "What's the matter?"

"How am I going to watch Donovan and Jane together at family functions? Will I need to stay away from the family till I can get rid of this hurt?" I did my best to whisper in a crowded restaurant. To say Mom was alarmed would've been an understatement.

"Before I came here, I had a long talk with Jake and Emily and they were both under the impression that Donovan was in love with you. They told me that what happened between Donovan and Jane was a mistake and the two of them have corrected their ways since you last saw them."

"How can you be in love with someone and makeout with another person? Jake and Emily have been my champions and they want Donovan to be in love with me. But he's in love with Jane. I saw it with my own two eyes."

It was at this point that I decided enough was enough. I was sick of crying and I was damn sick of feeling sad. The hurt wasn't gone, but being with my mother in this lively city was a blessing, and having a man like Michael treat me like a queen was also another blessing. Rather than focusing on what didn't happen for me, or what went wrong, I would focus on the positives.

"What can I do for you, my sweet daughter? How can I take away the pain?"

"All is good now, Mom." Mom gave me the strangest look. I think my quick turnabout was too much for her. "I decided at this very moment that I'm going to change my attitude. I'm sick of feeling sorry for myself. If Jane and Donovan end up getting married and having a busload of kids, then so be it. I don't give a damn! If she is who he chooses, then more power to the both of them." Mom was seriously scared for me, now. "I wish them well and I'll see them at family functions with a smile on my face."

"All righty…" That's all Mom could say. I chuckled.

"Did I tell you I have a boyfriend named Michael?"

That's when Mom lost it and laughed all the way back to the hotel.

"Tell me about Michael." She said while lying on her side of the extra wide king-sized bed. "Where on earth did he come from and why haven't I heard about him till now?"

"I think I told you about Michael, his sister Ruby Aleksandra and the rest of the Bennington family. They're the ones I met off the plane, the day I landed in Heathrow."

"I remember you telling me about them, but how did that progress to Michael becoming your first boyfriend?"

Mom didn't bat an eye when I gave her the silly story of what happened while I was outside daydreaming about Donovan. But she was floored when I told her that Michael proposed. "He wants me to be his Duchess."

"Is that an English term of endearment?"

"Probably for most, but in the case of Michael, it's a title. His grandfather is an actual duke. He has a seat in Derbyshire."

"Oh." Mom paid more attention than before. "And what does Michael do?"

"He just got his MBA from Harvard and he'll go into the family business of managing their estate."

"Is it a large estate?"

"I assume. I've no idea." Shrugging my shoulders while laying on my side wasn't easy. "But his grandfather's summer home looks like one of those English castles."

"When have you seen this castle?"

"Michael took me straight to his grandfather's after I came back to London. That's why I didn't see Donovan if he stopped by."

"I see."

"What do you think?" I could tell by mom's lack of enthusiasm that there wasn't the approval I sought.

"I'm not crazy about the timing, but if you like this Michael and if he's good to you, I say enjoy yourself. He must be a wonderful young man if you chose him as your first boyfriend."

"He is wonderful." There wasn't the enthusiasm one would expect when talking about one's boyfriend, but I didn't want to lie to my mother. "Michael isn't Donovan in my heart, but he treats me like a duchess... maybe even a queen."

"That's all a mother could ask for in her daughter's boyfriend."

Mom and I ended up staying in New York for a week. During that time, I spoke to Michael several times, avoided all of Donovan's calls and messages, and had the time of my life with Mom. By the time we parted, I had convinced Mom that I was strong enough to live alone in a foreign land again.

"Welcome home, Duchess." Michael greeted me at the airport. "I trust you are refreshed and ready to start a new life with me?"

"Yes and no." Michael frowned. "Buy me dinner and I'll tell you all that's on my mind." My smiling face earned me a kiss that didn't last long with all the airport goers pushing us along.

"You want a summer Pimm's?" Michael asked when I couldn't figure out what to drink.

"What's that?"

He thought about it briefly and said, "Think of it as an English sangria."

"Sounds delish!"

"Now that the important part is decided, should we talk?"

"Yes. Let me start by saying Mom was impressed with you the few times you both spoke. Mom and Dad worry about my naïveté and the fact that you're my first boyfriend. After talking to you, Mom was reassured you wouldn't take advantage of my lack of experience." I laughed to alleviate the embarrassment.

"Oh." I laughed even harder at Michael's reaction. "I would have never guessed."

"Donovan Taylor has had a stronghold on my life since I was ten. I built a castle, a fortress, and a moat, keeping everyone out until Prince Taylor rode in as my knight in shining armor."

"OK..."

"And then I met you. You became my first friend, you made me laugh, and beyond question, you treated me like the princess I am not. While I appreciate your devotion and even adoration, my heart is still partly keeping a lookout from the tower of the castle. That hope hasn't died."

"And so..."

"I guess what I'm trying to say is that my selfish heart would like to believe I can stay in the tower and enjoy other suitors who come my way professing their love and adoration, while still staying on the lookout for the one suitor who's not ever coming. But I know it's not fair to a gallant suitor like you when I can't promise you my entire heart. You told me on the plane that my feelings for Donovan were a schoolgirl crush. I don't want to lie to you and say it's that simple. I was in love with Donovan, and to a great degree, I still am in love with him. Closure will take a while and you'll be caught in the middle. And I don't want to do that to you."

Now Michael laughed. "First of all, do you always talk in allegories and metaphors?"

I giggled in response. "Sorry, it's the drama queen in me coming out."

"While it doesn't make me happy to know that this man has such a stronghold over your heart, I don't think I can pass up the chance to get to know you better. You make my day brighter, you make me smile all the time, and I already love the little I know of you. My family enjoys spending time with you and believe it or not, Grandfather sent out another invitation to you in the form of a golf rematch."

"Well, I am honored." It made me happy to know Michael's grandfather didn't hate me. "Tell him I accept."

"If you haven't changed your mind, I'd like for us to date. I'd like to get to know everything about you and I think when you get to know all there is to know about me, you won't be able to stop yourself from falling insanely in love with me."

"Is that right?" I questioned with a chuckle. "Insanely in love? A bold statement there, Michael Bennington."

"A correct statement, Laney Reid."

"You know neither your title nor future wealth excites me at all. Though I have to admit your grandfather's golf course might sway me a little more your way."

"I knew placating that old man would have its advantages. Are we in agreement, Laney Reid? Should we date and see where this takes us?"

"Only if you are absolutely clear where I stand. I am not in love with you..."

"Yet," he interrupted me.

"And I need to walk at my own pace."

"Agreed!"

Dinner was a lot of questions and answers about me and the Reid family, and when we were done, we called out Ruby to join us for a late movie.

"Aren't you just the jet-setter these days," Ruby teased. "Los Angeles, New York, London – all within a couple of weeks. What's next?"

"I don't know. Should the three of us go somewhere?"

"Where should we go?" Ruby loved the idea. "How about somewhere exotic like Bangkok or the Amazon?"

"Rubes. Some of us have to start working. Let's stick to this part of the world if we want to take a long weekend."

"You don't have to come. Laney and I are free to roam about for a year." She had not a care in the world.

"What will you do after this year, Ruby?"

"To the chagrin of the entire family, I may go back to LA and start acting school. The life of a movie star suits me." Ruby used her most dramatic voice to prove her point.

She continued to show us her acting skills when she grabbed hold of a call I refused to answer. "Hello?" She answered in a sultry voice that made us laugh. "Laney's phone, but Ruby Aleksandra speaking."

"Who does she get that from? Your mother?" I asked Michael, who nodded yes.

"Um yes." All of a sudden, Ruby sounded like a little girl. "Hold on, please." Michael and I died laughing.

Ruby handed me the phone. "Hello?" I answered between laughs.

"Hey there, Cousin. How's life?"

"Hi, Jake." I felt like I was home again talking to my favorite cousin. "Life here is bearable," I winked at Michael after saying this. "How are you and your ever growing family? The babies are all well?"

"The babies are beautiful, my wife is absolutely beautiful, and we have some big news. I thought you should be the first one to hear."

"Oh my God! Not another baby, already?"

Jake started busting up! "I'm sure that's not the last time I'll hear that question when I tell everyone I have big news. But, no. Number four is not on the way."

"You don't know how huge my sigh of relief was, Jake. So what's up?"

"I have this opportunity to teach at two medical schools in and around London and work at their corresponding hospitals in the fall. Emily is encouraging me to uproot our family and live with you in Belgravia from August to December. Would you be willing to have us as guests in your home for a few months?"

"YES!" I answered so loudly Michael and Ruby jumped. "When do you arrive?"

"I don't think we'll get there any earlier than mid-August. It's not easy to round up three little ones and move. We've got so much of their crap to sort out."

"I am over the moon that you guys will come live with me! What can I do to help?"

"Gram will be calling you with instructions on how you can help. Are you sure you don't mind us invading your privacy?"

"Jake, that house is so big, you guys could move in and I may still not see you for days. I can't wait, Jake. You think maybe I can carpool with you on the days you teach and audit some classes? I'm itching to go back to school."

"I don't see why not. I'd love the company and as long as you're willing to pay, I'm sure the school would love the tuition. I'll call again soon with more concrete information."

"Sounds great!"

I would be lonely no more!

The next few weeks passed by in a blur. The first thing that happened was Donovan. He had stopped by again, and this time he didn't leave for almost an entire night. While out running errands for Jake, I got a call from Mrs. Haines who told me that Donovan was waiting for me. I stayed out later than necessary and waited for him to leave. Mrs. Haines left the flat after it got dark, and she told me Donovan was still in the library waiting for my return. Scared to face him, I spent the night in a hotel and went back home only after I had Mrs. Haines check the house for me the next morning. A few days after, Michael and Ruby took me up to the duke's summer home for our golf rematch. The duke actually had a smirk on his face, which I chose to consider a smile.

We played twenty-seven holes and after beating him two out of three, he finally spoke. "Where the hell did you learn to golf?"

"My father. He wanted to play in the PGA and was good enough as a scratch golfer, but not quite PGA material. Plus, medical school and life as a surgeon didn't give him much time to golf. So as soon as my brother and I were old enough to hold clubs, he had us out with him practicing."

"Damn, you're good. When's your father coming to visit? Have him come out and play with me."

"He would love that, Your Grace. In fact, the first time I came here, I took a picture of your backyard and my dad said it was the most beautiful backyard he's ever seen. He would jump at the chance of playing here."

"What are your intentions toward my grandson, young lady?"

"Are you worried you'll have an ill-mannered American for a granddaughter-in-law?" I teased.

"I am worried you will hurt my grandson. He is in love with you already and thinks of you as part of his future." The duke was in his serious mood again.

"I know, Your Grace. I can't say that I'm in love with Michael, but I have been honest with him from the beginning and I have told him that I am not thinking of marriage."

"This is one of the reasons why I don't want you dating him. You'll eventually break his heart. And I don't want to see my grandson hurt."

"I think it's wonderful how much you love Michael, but I can't give you any guarantees. The Bennington family reminds me a lot of the Reid family. It warms my heart whenever I see your family dynamics. Though, you're a little pricklier than both my grandfathers." I laughed. That didn't bring out the same kind of laughter from the duke.

"Tell me about your grandfather. What was he like?" I found this to be an odd question especially coming from a man who showed no interest in getting to know me.

"I assume it's Grandpa Jerry you want to know about since you already seem to know Grandfather Roland?"

"Tell me about both. Tell me what you think of both men."

"My Grandpa Jerry reminds me a lot of my father. He was playful, had a great sense of humor and always looked at the brighter side of life. He worked very hard and provided a great life for his children and grandchildren. Even with so many grandchildren, he made each and every one of us feel special. Though he and Gram both favored my cousin Jake, we all felt loved by our grandparents."

"He and your grandmother, I assume, got along well?"

This was another odd question, but I figured I would humor the duke and answer everything he asked of me.

"My grandfather adored my grandmother. He loved her till his very last breath. There was no doubt in any of our minds who was first in his life."

"He sounds like a good man. Your grandmother was a lucky woman."

"He was a great man. My grandmother could not have picked a better husband. My grandfather loved his wife, was generous to us all, and he left behind a legacy that none of us will ever surpass. That's how special he was."

"And Roland?"

"You probably know my grandfather Roland better than I do. I don't know him very well because I only recently met him, but I can tell you that he loves my grandmother as much as my grandfather Jerry did. And from what I have experienced so far, he treats us like his own grandchildren. But in the end, if he loves my grandmother and treats her well, that's all I can hope for."

"So he's good to your grandmother as well?"

"He is as ideal as my Grandpa Jerry." I was curious to ask him why he wanted so many answers concerning my grandparents, but we were getting along so well I didn't want to push my luck with him.

After twenty-seven holes, I was exhausted. Michael had to drive back home, so we finished up a quick dinner, said our good-byes and left with the promise that we would be back next weekend. As much as Michael enjoyed seeing me hanging out with his family, I knew he was frustrated with the lack of intimacy between us. We hadn't spent much alone time, and I did everything in my power not to be too physically close with him. Aside from kisses here and there, I just couldn't bear to let another man touch me. It felt somehow like I was betraying Donovan. Perhaps this alone should've been reason enough to end my relationship with Michael, but I enjoyed Michael's company and I enjoyed his family very much.

"Can we spend any time just the two of us?" Michael asked with bitterness. He knew my reservation, and he was done with it. I was at a loss for words. "I won't push you into anything you don't want to do, but I'd like to do a little more than hold your hand at my grandfather's home."

"Can you give me a little more time? Let me think about us and I'll let you know what I've decided when we go on our holiday?"

Michael wasn't satisfied. "You're more comfortable being alone with my grandfather than you are with me. I feel like you're holding me at arm's length, but I can't complain because you have no qualms about breaking up with me." What he was saying was absolutely true. I didn't realize that a relationship was so tough. And I didn't think that it would take me this long to let go of a man who had been in my heart since I was ten.

"Everything you say is true. I'm not going to pretend we are where we should be for two people dating. You've been nothing but patient." I wanted to raise the white flag and give up. Apparently, I wasn't cut out for a relationship. Friendships were my forté.

A frustrated Michael said, "I'm going hunting in Scotland with my uni friends. How about we continue this conversation after I get back?"

"Sure." This was as close to a pink slip a girl could get from her boyfriend, and I didn't feel as relieved as I thought I might. It hurt. I guess any form of rejection didn't feel good. "When do you leave?"

"I leave in a couple of days and come back on August 8th. It's a quick trip. We can head to Grandfather's as soon as I'm back, then we'll go straight to Seychelles from there. Be ready."

"All right." I did my best not to sigh.

Michael left without a proper good-bye and today I wished I had a swing on my front porch to chase away my blues. Since I didn't, I walked my neighborhood instead and compartmentalized the hopelessness.

Today was the eleventh day I hadn't heard from Donovan. It was hypocritical of me to search my phone for messages when I didn't read any of them, but I still did it. Today was also the day Michael called me out on another one of my hypocrisies. I accepted the position of being his girlfriend, but I wanted nothing beyond friendship. I spent time with everyone else, so I wouldn't have to spend quality time with Michael. He knew it, he called it, and I had to own it. Today, it felt like I had lost both men.

"Where the bloody hell have you been?"

"Hi Ruby." I found Ruby sitting on my steps annoyed. "With all the construction happening, it was too noisy to stay home, so I went to our local library and did some work."

"Who goes to a library nowadays?"

"What's wrong with the library? It has comfy chairs, free wi-fi and a bathroom. What else can a girl ask for when she's displaced?"

"How about calling your boyfriend or your boyfriend's sister and asking if you could spend a day at their house instead of roaming like the homeless? Honestly, Laney, you are an oddball at times. Why would you go sit at a library all day when your boyfriend's home is closer and much more inviting?"

"Maybe I don't feel very invited right now." All day I had done a good job of letting go of the emotions and finishing all the late projects. I stopped thinking about the fact that Donovan hadn't reached out in twelve days and that Michael was angry because I was selfish and had used him to fill my need for a friend and a substitute family. I got all my work done and hoped to curl up to a good book tonight and forget my woes. Ruby had other thoughts.

"Come with me," she demanded. "Why don't we go back to my house and spend the night there with me?"

"I don't think I should, Ruby. Michael and I are taking some time reevaluating us."

"Laney!" Her exasperation wasn't mild. "I think it's only you who is doing any reevaluating."

"You could spend the night here." I hoped she would take my offer. "I would love to have some company."

She looked like she was about to accept but she rolled her eyes and said, "I would but I think I've just been kicked out of your house." She motioned for me to turn around and that's when I saw a grinning Michael walking toward us. "I guess this is a good-bye for now. I'll see you later." She waved and walked toward her brother and beyond.

"Hi Michael." I half whispered.

"Hello Duchess."

"Are you here to say good-bye?"

He pulled me into his body. "I'm here to reassure you that I love you. I know you don't love me in return, but I had this crazy urge to refresh your memory. I felt like an ass after I left your house yesterday and I haven't been able to focus all day because I left us with so many question marks. There's no doubt in my mind where you belong in my life. I will wait for you."

"I don't want you to wait for me. No, let me rephrase that, I don't want you to have to wait for me. It's not fair to you. Trust me when I say, I'm not worth the wait. I'm afraid you'll be disappointed if and when I finally come around."

Michael wouldn't let go of me. "I know I won't be disappointed. I leave at the crack of dawn tomorrow and I needed to let you know this before I left you for a few days."

"What's the date today Michael?" I had a strange feeling I was forget-ting something.

"Today's the fifth."

"Oh my gosh! I forgot to call Max. Give me a second." I turned on my phone and gave Max a ring.

"Why hello there, Laney. You've been at the forefront of my mind the past few days. It's nice of you to call."

"Hi Max. Happy birthday!"

"Thank you. How do you know it's my birthday?"

"I spoke with Josh not too long ago, and he told me your birthday was coming up so I jotted it down. What are you doing today? I hope you have a fun day planned?"

"I'm in New York with Jane, and I have a dinner later tonight with some members of your family."

"New York? Jane?" Perhaps I shouldn't have questioned why Jane was there. As far as I knew, she *was* still his girlfriend – regardless of what I saw in the hospital room.

Max quietly chuckled. "Yes my girlfriend Jane is here. Were you expecting someone else?" He was teasing me and I didn't quite understand his reason.

"No, no. I don't know why I asked that silly question. I was caught off guard because you said you were in New York. I was just in New York with Mom not too long ago."

"I heard. You had a good time with your mother?"

"It was a wonderful time. So are you in New York celebrating your birthday?"

"It's a really long story and too long to explain over the course of one phone call, Laney. I'll tell you when I see you in person."

I was happy at the thought of seeing Max. "Does that mean you're coming to London sometime soon?"

"Laney, I think you've got a lot of surprises coming your way very soon."

"What does that mean, Max? Now you've got me curious."

"Surprises are never fun when you know ahead of time. When it happens, it'll catch you off guard, that's for sure."

"You're being terribly unfair Max."

"You still seeing that same guy?" There was slight disapproval in Max's tone.

"Yes. I'm still seeing Michael." That's when Michael could wait no longer and asked me to hand over the phone. I did as requested since it was such an unusual request.

"Hello this is Michael Bennington. I thought I should introduce myself to you since you seem to know who I am, already. I'm also curious to know what Laney has told you about me."

Max and Michael immediately hit it off over the telephone. Maybe the sense of disapproval was only in my head. Michael explained briefly how we met and a few of the things that we had been up to lately, and he also explained to Max about his hunting trip and how he would like for us to meet when he got back.

"We are off to my grandfather's once I get back and then to Seychelles. Perhaps we can see you when we come into London briefly before our trip to Seychelles, or I will see you after our holiday."

From the sound of it, Max agreed to meet with Michael. I didn't know whether that meant it would be the four of us, Jane included. I had no thoughts of seeing Jane for at least another year.

"He would like to say good-bye to you." Michael handed the phone back to me.

"Hello?"

"He sounds like a good guy, Laney. I can't wait to meet him if the occasion arises."

"Yeah, Max. I can't wait to see you too."

"I believe you have a birthday coming up soon? Let me be the first to say I hope all your dreams come true on that day, Laney. Because of all the people I know, you deserve everything you have ever wished for, and more."

His sweet sentiment made me feel homesick again. "Thank you, Max. I'll see you soon."

"What a top bloke!" Somehow talking to Max gave Michael a boost to his self-confidence. I didn't know what conversation had taken place between the two men, but Michael was happier now than when he arrived.

"He is one of the best guys out there." I agreed.

"I'll see you in a few days?"

"I'll see you in a few days!"

(K)night

What a way to spend a birthday. It was raining, but hot and muggy, again. This gloomy weather came and left without any rhyme or reason. Michael was still on a hunting trip with his buddies somewhere in Scotland. I didn't think it would bother me that no one was around on my birthday, but it did.

This flu that hit me in the wee hours of the morning didn't help, either. I could feel the ache down to my bones. I hadn't been this ill in a long time. Normally, an illness never bothered me, but being so far away from home and my family, I was feeling more homesick than ever.

Ding dong.

Ding dong.

Who could it be at this hour? I took my time getting downstairs hoping this person would go away before I made it to the door. I just wanted to crawl back to bed.

Ding dong.

Ding dong.

All right! "Who is it?"

No one answered. Why didn't this heavy wooden door have a peephole? I needed to see about getting a peephole as soon as possible.

"Can I help you?" I asked annoyed, only slightly opening the door. "Donovan…." I whispered in surprise.

"What are you doing opening the door at this hour for a stranger in only your pajamas? Where is everyone? Are you alone?"

No hellos. No, *how have you been, Delaney?* Only a scolding. I proceeded to turn around and head back to my room.

"Where the hell are you going?" He tugged on my hand. "I came halfway across the world to see you."

"Now that you've seen me, good-bye. Please close the door properly on your way out."

"Delaney," he pleaded in a tone I'd never heard before. I stopped to try and make heads or tails out of that tone. Coming from another man, I might have thought it an endearing, affectionate tone. But on this man, I had no idea what to make of it, so I continued to walk. "You Reids are all going to make me do my penance, aren't you?"

"Mr. Taylor, please go back to your hotel and let's talk again tomorrow. It's early, I've got the flu, and you're making me even more homesick."

"You're ill? Let me see." He came over and measured my temperature with his hand, looked over my face, touched my neck. I had to laugh. "Why are you laughing?"

"I have the flu. I wouldn't get too close if I were you."

"Let's go," he pulled my hand and took me to the first bedroom. "This isn't it. Which one is yours?"

I pointed to my room.

He took me to my room, had me get in bed, made himself comfortable by taking off his shoes, jacket and tie, and got in my bed with me. I just stared at him as though he were crazy.

"Why are you here, Mr. Taylor?"

"First of all, no more Mr. Taylor. You called out my name when you first saw me, so now that I know you can pronounce it, use it."

Who did he think he was coming here and making demands of me? "Mr..."

"I mean it, Delaney. Don't test me." He responded in a most menacing way, so I decided not to address him at all.

"What brings you to London?" I said without calling out his name. I wanted to stick out my tongue and show him that he was not the boss of me.

"I've moved here."

What? "You've moved here? But why?"

"I came here to court a lady who will soon be my wife."

I don't know why but the thought of Donovan marrying someone brought a flood of tears to my eyes. Uncontrollable tears poured down my face at the thought of Donovan Taylor courting another girl. Why did he have to come here and tell me his wonderful news?

"What's the matter? Are those tears of joy, of sadness, or of....you lost me, Little Girl. I was told by your entire family that you don't cry in front of anyone. Even when you fell off trees, you went into the confines of your own home to deal with the pain. Why the tears? Are you in pain?"

He seriously had no clue. *Yes, MORON! You're hurting me again.* Instead of yelling at him, I just shook my head and walked into the bathroom. I turned on the shower so he couldn't hear my wracking sobs.

"Delaney. What's the matter?" Donovan pounded on the door.

I cleaned myself up and walked outside and tried to act as normal as possible. "I'm sorry. I guess I'm feeling more homesick than I thought. Seeing you reminds me of my family." I tried to smile. "So when's the wedding?"

"I don't know. That all depends on you."

"Why me?"

"Because, Princess. You're the lady I'll be courting."

"Delaney, I really do want to let you sleep a little longer, but we have to get going." Donovan was still here. This flu had hit me so hard I didn't know whether I was hallucinating when he first showed up at my door.

"Where are we going?"

"Amsterdam."

"Why? What's in Amsterdam?"

"It's a surprise for your birthday," he whispered in my ear and gently coaxed me up. "Happy 23rd birthday, by the way." He then kissed me on my cheek, right by the ear his lips were speaking into.

"I can't go anywhere. Michael is taking me to his grandfather's home tomorrow. I'll disappoint his entire family if I don't show up."

"The hell you are," Donovan got angry. "You are not to see Michael anymore. I don't know what your status is with him, but I will not tolerate you getting friendly with any other man."

Was he for real? "Who the hell made you God, again?" I bit-off. "I don't remember needing your permission to date anyone. Did Dad give up his paternal rights to you?"

"In the olden days, a woman was the property of her father, then her husband."

"What the hell? Am I now a piece of cattle to you?"

He got frustrated. He scratched his beautiful head with both hands and harrumphed. "We are getting married, so yeah! You're mine and only mine."

"Mr. Taylor!"

"I told you to stop calling me that!" Now he was really mad. I had to say, I was kind of enjoying his frustration with our role reversal. "Call me by my damn name! I hate it when you call me Mr. Taylor. It feels like there's so much distance between us."

Had I not been feeling like shit, I would've enjoyed irritating him more, but this time I just gave in. "All right, Donovan."

Like a patient in a bipolar clinic, Donovan quickly went from pissed off to elated. He picked me up and swung me around—which was not good for the vertigo already in place. "Say my name again. That was so damn sexy."

"If you don't put me down, I'm going to make like that time at my grandmother's pool twelve years ago, and throw up on you."

"You are so sweet. You were adorable as a child; you are irresistible as a woman." He tried to kiss my lips but I pulled back.

"Um…I remember you resisting me many a time, Donovan Taylor. Why the change of heart?"

"I'll give you all the details in Amsterdam. But for now, I really have to get you to the airport."

"Give me one good reason why I should break my promise to the Bennington family and follow you to Amsterdam."

"I'll give you two. Because you love me and because you have family waiting for you in Amsterdam."

"I don't love you!" I denied. "And who's here to see me? Is Grandfather here, again? He and Gram are in Amsterdam?"

"You do love me, and I return your love so let's go. I won't tell you who, but I'll tell you two Reids have just landed at Schipol airport. You will regret not seeing them, and they will be sorely disappointed not seeing you."

"You're not lying to me are you?"

He was starting to get upset again. I supposed he had no reason to lie, especially since he had no way of getting out of the lie. "All right. You win. Let me leave a message for Michael."

"Do it later. I have a car waiting for us. Is that your going-away bag?" He pointed to my suitcase. Good thing I'd packed a couple of nights ago.

"Yes. Let me freshen up and we can leave."

Still feeling like death was knocking on my door, I let Donovan hold my hand and lead me through the airport till we were comfortably seated on the airplane. From there, I fell asleep again, not to speak with him until we landed.

"I told you once before that you'll never know if the man you're with is your knight in shining armor if you keep falling asleep on him." I could feel the chuckle in my ear. "Your chariot awaits, Princess."

We had another car waiting for us at Schipol airport, and in thirty minutes, we were in the heart of the city.

"Where are we?" I asked in awe. "This is so incredibly beautiful." It genuinely was the most incredible sight I'd ever seen.

"We are at your grandfather's home in Amsterdam."

"How old is this building? It's gorgeous. And the canal...absolutely breathtaking!"

"Your innocent look of awe is breathtaking and gorgeous. You, Miss Delaney Reid are a beautiful sight. I've missed you." Donovan leaned in to kiss me again, and I stepped away once more.

"Donovan," I gently chided. "I'm seeing Michael. Please don't..." I didn't believe this statement wholeheartedly myself at this very moment, but I needed to set parameters before I got myself into a situation of falling in love with this man again.

"Before this is over," Donovan gently chided me, "you and I will be man and wife. Michael will be a friend in passing. Don't push me away. I've missed you too much to be kept at a distance." He didn't kiss me again, but he held my wrist and led me into my grandfather's home.

"This place is indescribable. Look at the view of the canal from all the windows. How utterly charming! I could live here."

"Princess, I'm sure Roland would allow us to live here if we asked. We could even set up house before we got married." He gave me his rascally smile.

"Explain, Donovan Taylor. Why the change of heart? How did I go from pariah to princess in the course of a few months?"

"You were never a pariah," he chuckled. "It just took a bit for me to realize you were my princess."

A knock at the door interrupted our conversation. "My surprise?" I asked in a whisper.

Donovan flashed the most brilliant smile and walked with me to the door.

"Baby!" Four voices called out at the same time.

"Mom! Dad! Mr. Taylor? Mrs. Taylor?" What a surprise! I hugged my parents. "What are you doing here?"

"Your father had a last minute speaking engagement in Amsterdam, and Donovan was brilliant enough to suggest we all come out and celebrate your birthday with you. How are you, Laney?" Mom was all over me, making sure I was in one piece. "Why are you so hot?" She sounded upset.

"I have the flu, but Donovan still forced me out here with the enticement of seeing family. He didn't tell me who was here. I thought it might be Gram and Grandfather, but am I glad it's you." I went into my father's arms. I had missed my parents! "How long are you here for, and are you coming to England with me?"

"How about a greeting for us, Baby?" Mr. Taylor put out his arms. I looked over to Donovan for direction, and he motioned for me to go give his dad a hug; and so I did. "How have you been, beautiful girl? Your Ma and I have missed you." He kissed me on my forehead and sent me over to "Ma" who did the same. It was sweet the way the Taylors were greeting me.

"Why don't we go out for an early dinner and we can give Delaney all the details of what's happening? There's a great cafe right down the street from here. We can eat along the canal."

We shuffled out two by two, and Donovan quickly put his hand around my waist. I tried to give him a look of warning, but he didn't take it.

"You holding up?" he whispered in my ear, then kissed me where he'd just spoken. "It's good to have you next to me, Delaney. Don't leave me again," he pleaded.

"Hey, Lovebirds! You need to keep up. We don't know where we're going. You two can't take your sweet time canoodling." Mr. Taylor embarrassingly called us out in the middle of the street.

"Let's go." No matter how I resisted, Donovan held my hand or some part of my body all the way to the restaurant. Once at dinner, I quickly sat between my parents so this man wouldn't befuddle my senses any more than they already were. What on earth had happened since I left? Why was this man now giving me the attention I so craved when I was home? This had to be some crazy joke to have Donovan Taylor telling me I was to be his bride.

"Laney?"

"Yes, Mom?"

"Is Estelle's home ready for Jake's family?"

"Yes. It just finished the other day."

"You know there's a plane full of people coming?"

"No, I didn't know."

"Jake and his family, Robert and Sandy, Estelle, Nick, Doug, Josh, and Garret will be on the plane as well. And I think Donovan said that Jane and Max were headed to London, too."

What had happened to bring everyone this way? I wasn't complaining, but there were more changes than I could comprehend. Michael and Aleksandra had done a marvelous job keeping me busy, but I was still terribly homesick. And Jane…last I saw her, she was in Donovan's arms, lip-locked. What was I to do with that fact? I decided to let go of that for now.

"How long are you in town, Mom?"

"We are here for five days. Then we will go to London. I'm staying indefinitely, but your father has to leave soon."

"I can head back to London with you when you leave."

Donovan looked upset as soon as I made this statement. "I can't head back there, yet. I have business in other cities to attend to before reaching London. I was hoping you'd stay with me."

Truly, I didn't know what to say. What the hell had happened since I was gone?

"That can all be decided later, Donovan." Mom broke our stare-down.

"Are you staying at Grandfather's?" I changed subjects.

"No. The hospital put us up in a beautiful hotel very close to you and Donovan. We are just steps away."

"What do you mean, me and Donovan? I'm not staying with the two of you?" My parents were agreeing to let me spend the night with a man, when they were just a canal away?

"You and Donovan!" Mrs. Taylor exclaimed. "You're getting married soon and will be a Taylor!" Now she was getting really excited. "Scottie, can you believe our Donny is finally getting married?"

"And to such a gorgeous and sweet gal!" Mr. Taylor smiled. "Henry," he addressed my dad, "I promise to love Laney just as much as my other four girls."

"Like you have a choice," my dad stated matter-of-factly. "Look at her! How can you not love her?"

"Daddy," I shook my head and addressed everyone at the table. "I'm unsure what happened back in America while I was gone, but Donovan and I are not getting married."

The gasps began.

"In fact," I continued, "I've been seeing someone since I got here."

"No!" both Taylors gasped even louder. "We told you not to let her go, Donny!" They got upset with their son.

I could tell Dad didn't approve. "You're still seeing this Duke of England?"

I laughed. "Daddy, he's not the Duke of England. His grandfather is a duke of an area in England and one day, Michael will inherit his dukedom."

"Can you be a duchess even if you're an American citizen if you marry him?"

"I don't know, Mom. We're not at that point in our relationship. We are taking things slowly."

I looked over at Donovan who was seriously pissed.

"We can talk about the wedding another day," Mrs. Taylor brushed off the last five minutes of our conversation as if she hadn't heard a word I said. "Laney looks tired. Let's let her get some rest."

"That's a good idea," Dad said with disapproval in his eyes.

I walked next to my father and held us back a little so I could talk to him and see why he was upset with me. "Daddy. Michael's a great guy. I wish you wouldn't disapprove so much."

"Baby, it's not Michael that makes me unhappy. What I don't like is the thought of you living in England if you were to marry this guy. We'd see each other just a few days out of the year if that happened. I was hoping you'd get married and live on the cul-de-sac, like Jake and Emily."

I hadn't thought of that… "Daddy." I tried to assuage his worried heart. "Michael and I are not anywhere near that point in our relationship. We are just getting to know one another. You don't need to worry about me living a ten-hour plane ride away from you."

"What happened to your feelings for Donovan?" This question put me in a state of shock. "Since you were a little girl, you've been in love with him. How did that fall away so easily? Is it Michael?"

How did I answer this question? Answering my father would be admitting to myself that no one had replaced Donovan Taylor, and as hard as I tried to hide away my love for him, it never stayed hidden for long.

"How did you know, Daddy?"

"Sweetheart. I'm your father. You didn't think I saw the love in your eyes whenever Donovan came around? I saw the love, the joy, the hurt; your mother and I saw and felt your every emotion. When Donovan finally came around and admitted he had feelings for you, I thought this was done. I'd gain a son and still keep my daughter."

"I still love Donovan Taylor, but there is a mountain of issues we need to resolve before we can progress. I also can't trust that he has actually come around to noticing me, much less that he loves me. Do you understand?"

"Keep an open mind and heart because I think he's finally opened his mind and heart."

"All right, Daddy."

"Here we are," Donovan announced. "We will see you senior citizens tomorrow morning?"

"Who the hell are you calling a senior citizen?" Dad bellowed.

"Good night. We will see you in the morning." Donovan tried to push me into the house.

"You both are really going to let me be with Donovan...alone?"

"Donovan knows I'll kick his ass if he tries anything on you tonight or any other night." Dad said with a smile. "Do not worry, Baby."

I proceeded to be hugged and kissed by everyone, twice.

"Let's go in before my parents decide to take you home with them." Donovan, too, got his round of hugs and kisses.

"Which room do you want?" I asked. "I'm so tired from pretending to feel well. I need sleep right now."

"You don't want to talk?" Donovan spoke with caution. "We have a lot to talk about and I need to clear up a big misunderstanding concerning me and Jane."

He and Jane... "Let's not tonight. I really don't feel well. I didn't want to worry my parents or yours so I kept up the act, but I could collapse right now if you'd tell me which bed I can sleep in."

"You don't want to sleep with me tonight?" He was now tiptoeing around me. What I would have done to hear that question just a few months ago.

Rather than giving him a false answer, I chose a bed and literally collapsed.

"Delaney." A worried Donovan was wiping off the cold sweat from my face. "Take some medicine." He tried to get me up.

"My head is so hot and it hurts so much, but my body is freezing cold, Donovan. Help me." I croaked.

"Take this. I went out and got some medicine for you." I swallowed the pills he gave me and tried to get up, but couldn't. "You want me to call your mom?"

I shook my head no. "Don't do that. My parents will be worried. Let them sleep. Daddy has to speak tomorrow morning."

Donovan crawled into bed with me and held my shivering body. "Princess, you're piping hot. You want to take a shower or a bath and cool down your body?"

"No," I cried. "I know I'm hot, but I feel so cold. Am I going to die?" I was being what Mom would call, melo, but I needed the attention.

"You and I just started loving each other and have a life-long journey of unraveling this love. You are not dying on me till you're a very old grandma." Donovan chuckled.

It could only be the fever that was making me hallucinate and confess what I'd confessed. "Maybe you just started loving me, but I've been in love with you since I was ten. I was so desperate for your attention all those years. I got sick of feeling unwanted, and I got even sicker of watching you waver between every woman but me. I decided to come to London right after we were reintroduced, but I would have given up moving here had you shown me an ounce of interest. You, Donovan Taylor are my ideal man. You are the reason I never dated. You are the reason I almost gave up on finding my happily ever after. You are the reason my heart is so wary of love and weary from loving. My heart won't let Michael in because it refuses to forget you." I was like a drunken woman rambling. I had to stop myself.

I wasn't exactly sure what had happened last night, but I woke up feeling much better, and I woke up to Donovan Taylor's body surrounding my own. I was sprawled partially over his beautifully bare chest and both his arms wrapped tightly around me. I knew this was wrong of me to be in this position with him, but it felt so very wonderful, I decided to stay and willed myself back to sleep.

"Good morning, Princess." I heard as I stirred awake again. "How are you feeling?"

"Much, much better." I slowly got myself up. "How did we end up in bed together?"

"You don't remember begging me to hold you last night?" Donovan smiled the most beautiful smile.

"I did not beg you for anything last night," I argued, trying to get away.

"I see you're feeling better if you have the energy to argue with me." He brought me back down to his chest. "You don't remember confessing your undying love for me last night?" He questioned with mirth.

"I did not!" I yelped. "I don't love you!" I lied.

"Let's go grab a bite to eat because I need to drop you off with our mothers and get to work. Unlike you, I have to work for a living. Knowing your spending habits, I need to bill more hours." He kissed the top of my head and hopped in the shower.

I, too, got ready for whatever the day would hold. By what Donovan had intimated, it sounded as though the day consisted of the women socializing and the men working.

"What do you want to eat, Princess?" Donovan walked out in only a towel, and I didn't know where to look.

"I need a strong cup of coffee," I murmured, and decided to hop in the shower myself.

Mom and "Ma" were waiting for me at the cafe. "Good morning!" They both had a huge smile on their faces. "You feel better? Did Donny nurse you back to health?"

"Don't embarrass her, Ma. I'll leave my Princess in your care?" Donovan addressed both ladies. "I need to get to work before Roland fires me." He walked over, kissed each mother on the cheek, and said his good-bye. Then he came and put his arms around my waist. "I'll see you tonight?"

"What are you doing?" I tried to push him away. "I told you I'm seeing someone already."

He came over and whispered in my ear, "Last night you told me your heart wouldn't let Michael in because it can't forget me. I'm right here, Princess. You don't ever have to try to forget me. After dinner with the family tonight, we talk, OK?" Before I could answer, he kissed me lightly at first, then a full, open-mouth one in front of both moms. "Tonight…"

"Everything is going well?" Mom asked after Donovan left, with a smirk in her eyes.

"Mom. Nothing is as it seems. Donovan is pushing his cause, but I am still dating Michael."

"That kiss didn't look like you were with any other man but my son," Mrs. Taylor giggled. "He's a charmer, huh? He gets that from his father. My Scottie charmed the pants, the underwear, my entire outfit off of me, practically on the first date." We all laughed. "Wasn't Henry the same way?"

"Hell yes, he was, and he still is."

"OK, Ladies! That was way too much information for my virgin ears. Why don't we enjoy the exhibit instead of talking about the men in our lives?"

"Is she still a virgin?" I heard Mrs. Taylor ask my mom. "Do those still exist?"

Mom only laughed.

Dad had gone early in the morning to speak at his conference, and Mr. Taylor, who was also a retired doctor like Uncle Bobby, went with Dad. We, three ladies decided to spend our day visiting the Van Gogh *and* Rijk museums. Between a full day at two museums, lunch, and shopping, I thought I might collapse from fatigue. I could learn a thing or two from these moms. They were still going strong when we got in a cab to have dinner with the men at another beautiful restaurant. This time, we were slightly out of city center, eating at a botanical garden restaurant. The room was open, bright, and surrounded by homegrown food. I walked the garden while the two ladies chose to sit and drink their cocktails.

"Princess." Donovan walked over to me with a gorgeous smile. "You and the moms had a fun day, I assume?" I stepped away when it looked like he was going to kiss me again.

"We had a fun, but exhausting day – though I seem to be the only one worn out. How was your day?"

"Very productive. The client I met with liked all I proposed and decided to have our firm take care of his company's merger. Your grandfather showed up today, too. He's here right now."

"He is?" I started walking back into the restaurant.

"First," he pulled me back, "I need to hear you tell me that you missed me today." Though he spoke confidently, there was insecurity in his eyes.

"Mr. Taylor, every moment I'm not with you, I miss you." I didn't know what possessed me to confess again, but there it was. "Shit!" I added.

Donovan laughed loudly, proudly, and annoyingly. "I missed you too, I love you too, and I can't wait to hear your entire confession. I have a feeling it's going to be a hell of a story."

"There will be no more confessions, Donovan Taylor!" I answered adamantly. "Last I looked, I was dating Michael and you were making out with my cousin. I don't know what that was about, but those two facts are going to be difficult to overcome—regardless of what I once felt for you!"

"Shit!" Donovan agreed.

I walked into the restaurant with a genuine smile but had to pretend that all was well physically. If it hadn't been for my family, I would have gone straight home and slept. In fact, I probably wouldn't have come out at all, today. But I hadn't seen my family in months and it was a joy to have them here.

"Hi Daddy! Your conference went well?"

"Of course it did. You going to come hear me speak tomorrow?"

"I sure will. Last night, I wasn't feeling too well, but I feel much better today."

"Scott, did I tell you my brilliant daughter got into med school as well as film school?"

"No!" Mr. and Mrs. Taylor called out. "You mean our baby is not only gorgeous and sweet, but she's also a genius? We've got another doctor in the family?"

"I haven't decided on med school, yet, Mr. Taylor."

"Pa! I keep telling you, call me Pa!"

"Pa," I whispered at his insistence.

"So when will you get married if you go to med school?" Mrs. Taylor asked with much concern.

"I haven't decided to go to med school, and last I checked, I don't have any plans to get married in the near future."

"Don't you worry about a thing, Laney. When you and Donny decide on the wedding date, your mom and I will take care of everything. You can go to med school, film school, or don't do anything at all. My Donny will take care of you. You don't have to work if you don't want to work."

This conversation was going in circles and I couldn't convince anyone that I was dating Michael and that Donovan and I didn't exist.

"Hello, Grandfather." I kissed my wonderful grandfather on the cheek and chose to sit next to him. Thanks to my dad who scooted down a seat, Donovan placed himself right next to me. "Your home in Amsterdam is breathtaking. I don't think I've seen a more beautiful sight than that of the canal from your bedroom window. I could sit there for hours and read or write."

"You and Donovan can base yourselves here if you like, while Donovan works in Europe. I trust you've given Michael his eviction notice?" With a wicked smile, my grandfather was putting me in a difficult position.

"No, Grandfather. Michael is still very much in the picture. As soon as I get back to London, I'll go see the Bennington family in the countryside."

"Donovan?" Grandfather questioned. "What the hell's happened? You promised to bring Laney back to us."

"I've only been with her for a short two days. After we talk tonight, all will be where it should be." Donovan spoke confidently, but I could tell by his shifting around that he didn't wholly believe what he'd said.

Dinner was an elegant but simple three-course meal. Dad discussed his conference with "Pa," Donovan talked shop with Grandfather, and Mom and "Ma" were actually talking wedding—as in *my* wedding.

"How do you feel?" Donovan whispered.

"Tired. I'm still not recovered, and both moms really wore me out today. I love being with my family, but I need to sleep."

"Roland, will you be joining us at your home tonight?" Donovan asked.

"I'm going back home tonight to my wife. We will all be back very soon, though, and residing in Belgravia."

"Would you all excuse us and allow me to take Delaney back home? She's still not a hundred percent well."

"Oh no! Go. Take her home." Mom and Ma began fussing, and Donovan smoothly excused us before it became severe.

"Donovan, will you give me some more of the medicine from last night? I'm really beginning to feel ill again."

"Of course, Princess. You're not using this as an excuse to get out of talking to me, are you?"

"No." I gave him my most exasperated-sounding tone.

"Will you let me sleep with you again?" I looked up at him with a dubious stare. "You know, just in case you get delirious again?" He smiled a most delicious smile. "Your tongue gets awfully loose when you're delirious," he teased.

"You may...*NOT* sleep with me and I'm not sure what my tongue confessed, but delete it from your memory. I claim no responsibility for what was said while hallucinating."

"You know damn well what you professed, and I know you meant every word of it. You want me to recite point by point what you said?"

"Um...NO!" And once again, I was saved by the bell. I picked up my phone. "Hey, Michael."

"Duchess! I'm so glad I finally got a hold of you. I was in a remote area where I couldn't call, and we were delayed getting home. What's this about you being in Amsterdam?"

"My parents are here."

"They are? That's wonderful. Should I come out and meet them? Then we can go to Grandfather's together."

"Well...it's a little more complicated than that, Michael. I'll just meet you at your grandfather's as soon as I can."

"Like hell you will." A furious Donovan spit out.

"Who was that?"

"That was the complication I was mentioning..."

"Do I get an explanation?" Michael sounded worried. This was what I didn't want happening. I didn't want to make this good man wary and insecure.

410

"I am in Amsterdam with not only my parents, but also with Donovan and his parents." I wanted to give Michael the simple and honest truth.

"How did that happen, Duchess? Should I worry that you're with Donovan?"

"Donovan came to pick me up in London and he brought me here to my parents. You don't need to worry. I'll be here a few more days, and then I'll come back to you." I could feel Donovan's wrath as I said this. He adjusted and readjusted in his seat in the car, and he was close to throwing my phone out the window. "Michael, why don't I call you in the morning? I'm not all that well and we're back at my grandfather's apartment."

"What's wrong, Duchess?"

"I have the flu, but I feel much better now. I'll talk to you..." That was all Donovan could take. He took the phone from my hand and threw it in the canal. "You did NOT just do that!" I yelled at him.

"I did..." he trailed and walked into the house. I ran after him.

"What the fuck, Donovan Taylor! What gives you the right to cut off my conversation with *my boyfriend!*"

"You cannot have a boyfriend when you're about to marry me." He yelled back.

"At this point in my life, I'm closer to marrying Michael than I am to you."

"The hell you are!" He *ROARED*. "We are getting married, Delaney Reid. That's why I gave up everything and moved my life here."

"What the fuck do you know about giving up anything for anybody? Michael stood up to his grandfather and told him he'd give up his future title, land, money, and practically his family to be with me. What the hell did you give up?" Now I was roaring. "What, you gave up Kate? You gave up Jane? What did you give up for me? Last time I saw you, you were lip-locked with my cousin." Now, my heart was breaking and my voice weakened. "A woman who has a boyfriend, a woman who's related to me—is that what you gave up?"

I didn't wait for a response. I slammed the door to my room and threw myself on the bed and sobbed. The only picture in my mind was that of Donovan and Jane laughing in each other's arms. That picture had haunted me every night since I returned to the UK.

"Delaney." Donovan perched himself on my side of the bed and gently pulled me off the pillow and into his arms. "I have nothing to say but I'm sorry. What you saw that day wasn't exactly as it appeared, but what you didn't see with me and Jane in Chicago is a confession I need to make. When you are ready to let go of what happened in the hospital room and hear me out, I want to explain everything to you."

"I don't think I can take any confessions from you concerning Jane."

"It's not what you're thinking. We talked everything over and realized we weren't attracted to each other. Jane and I are just friends. She and Max were broken up at the time, and now they're back together, stronger than ever." I looked up at him, doubtful. "I promise. Those two are very much together and very much in love."

"Beautiful," I heard a tickle in my ear. "I would like for us to stay here cuddled together for years to come, but I have a meeting to attend and you have a father and future father-in-law waiting for you at a conference."

Last I remembered, Donovan and I were yelling at each other, but somehow it was morning and we were playing "limbo" in bed, again. "You slept with me again."

"I couldn't get away even if I wanted to," he laughed. "One minute you were screaming bloody murder at me, and the next second, you were asleep in my arms."

"Shut up. You're such a liar." I knew he was telling the truth, but I didn't want to give him an excuse for sleeping with me again.

He guffawed to a point where he was snorting. "You were calling me every name in the book, crying, nose-running everywhere—then next thing I know, you're knocked out. It was like a scene out of a horror movie. I thought you might have died. No lie, I checked for breathing."

There was no choice but to laugh with him. "It wasn't that dramatic."

"Princess, you were such dead weight on my body, I couldn't change either of us out of our clothes from yesterday. I would have done everything in my power to strip you of your clothes and see you naked before putting a nightgown on you."

I laughed some more. "You sound like a dirty old man."

"Trust me, any man, young or old would give half his fortune to see you naked. Our godson knew what was up when he latched onto you."

"Oh, I miss James and Ellie."

"And they miss you too. Right before I left, I saw James kissing your picture."

"I want to see them!"

"You will, real soon. They'll be here in a few days." Donovan took out his phone and started dialing. "Hey," he called out. "Babies sleeping?"

"Is it nighttime?" Jake appeared out of nowhere and asked. "Hey, Cousin. I see you two are in bed, together? All is well?" He gave us an innocent smile that was anything but innocent.

"Hi Jake. All is not well, and somehow your best friend keeps invading my space."

"How else is he supposed to get close to you if he doesn't invade your space? You think Emily and I got together by me giving her all the space in the world?" He winked at me.

"But Jake, I have a boyfriend."

"Laney, I think we all know who will eventually be your husband. It'll be most kind of you to let Michael go and accept the inevitable."

"God, I think I'm man-crushing on you right now! I knew there was a reason why I loved you since we were little." Donovan was acting silly, and Jake let out an aw-shucks kind of guffaw. "Where's Emily?"

"Right here." Emily jumped into our FaceTime. "Hello, Donovan. Hi Laney."

"Hi Emily." I sounded all mopey. "The kids are well?"

"The kids are beautiful and James was very happy when I told him we were going to go see Auntie Ne Ne. Ellie could care less, sorry to report."

"I can't wait to play with those two. It'll be so neat to live together. Your floor is all ready. The workers came in and did a spotless job."

"Great. Thank you for taking care of that for us. I can't wait to see the place, again, and it'll be fun to have everyone living under one roof. Will you be taking up residence in Belgravia, Donovan?"

"I'll be taking up residence wherever Delaney will be. She can stay at the company apartment with me, or I can stay at Gram's with her."

"Nobody invited you to stay with us."

"Your grandmother sent me an invitation in the form of a text. You want to read it?"

"NO! She did not ask you to move in with all of us."

He nodded his head in the affirmative. "She told me I could room with you if I liked."

"She did NOT tell you we could live in sin, especially knowing I have a boyfriend."

"I told you to stop calling him that. We are getting married soon. If anyone is your boyfriend, it's me!" Yet once again, he was getting upset.

"I see you two are working out your differences and strengthening the relationship." Jake chuckled while giving his wife a smooch on her temple.

"Do you know what this man did, yesterday? I was talking to Michael on the phone, and in the middle of our conversation, he grabbed the phone out of my hand and threw it in the canal."

Emily and Jake busted up. "Ah, young love!" Jake called out. "Were we ever that rash and stupid, Love?"

"Never!" Emily shook her head. "Laney, just don't find yourself in the Grand Canyon without a ride home." Emily started howling while Jake looked horrified.

"Emi! Not cool to bring that up."

"I've got to show you that you're human too, just like Donovan." She gave her husband a peck on the lips. "Mr. Donovan Taylor, godfather of my children, soon to be Laney's husband…"

"Yes, Ma'am!"

"Take good care of my cousin. I love her and Jane as though they were my sisters."

"I'll cherish this beautiful lady as though she were my last breath. See you two, later. I've got to get to work."

"Good-bye!" Jake and Emily called out in unison.

"You heard your cousins, it's inevitable. We will get married, so send Michael back to where he came from and look only at me. I can't stand you being with another man." *What about all the times when your heart was with other women?* "I know what you're thinking right now, Miss Delaney Reid. I can't change the mistakes of my past. I can only try and make perfect our present and future. Give me a chance to love you." With this, he put both his arms around me and held onto me, looking for an answer, looking for love. "Let's get ready."

"Hi Daddy. Hi Pa." I whispered the last two words.

"Oh, my God! Donny, I think I'm in love with your future wife." Pa pretended to faint then kissed me smack on the lips.

"Easy, old man. Stay away from the lips. That's my property." Donovan chuckled and brought me back into his body. "Good morning, Chief. I can entrust you with my Princess, today?"

"Impudent boy, she's been in my *entrusted* care for the past twenty-three years. What, in the course of a couple of days, you think you've usurped my position?"

"Just checking, Chief. Just checking..." Donovan gave me his mega-watt smile. "I'll see you tonight?"

I nodded yes. "Have a good day."

Donovan wouldn't leave. He had a hard time letting go of my hand.

"Can we talk, tonight? Will you give me a chance to come clean so we can start this courtship on the right foot?"

"Let's see tonight. At the rate I've been going, I may fall asleep in the middle of dinner."

"I forgot to ask how you're feeling this morning."

"I feel decent, but not well. Whatever this bug is, it's got me good. I just hope I don't doze off in the middle of my dad's seminar."

Donovan cupped the side of my face and came in for a kiss. I didn't refuse him. "Every moment I'm not with you, I miss you, too. I love you, Princess."

"Go to work before Grandfather fires you." I let out an unintended giggle.

"You two look beautiful, together, Baby. I trust everything is going well?"

I watched Donovan walk out with his father before answering. "Daddy. Can I trust this twist of fate? Can I really believe that the man I crushed on since I was ten has finally noticed me and wants to marry me?"

"I think you can. Donovan had a tough time dealing with your absence, but I honestly believe he fell in love with you while you were still in the States. All those days you spent together, your mother and I thought we saw fireworks from the start."

"I don't know, Daddy."

"What will you do about Michael?"

"I'm going to call him today and break up with him. Though I'm unsure where things will go between Donovan and me, I don't feel right being officially with one man, and unofficially with another. Can I ask you to keep this information a secret from everyone? Of course you can tell Mom."

"Sure, Baby. You do what you think is best for you. Your mother and I will support your every decision."

"Thank you, Daddy."

My father's seminar was a huge hit! I couldn't believe the number of people who came to hear him speak. I stayed with Mr. Taylor for most of the day while Dad was entertaining questions and guests, and my time with my possible future father-in-law was a sweet one.

"You know your Ma and I adore you, Laney Reid?" Pa Taylor formed his statement into a question.

"And I, too, think you and Ma are wonderful people."

"You love my Donny?"

"I believe I do."

"Then what's the matter? Why won't you accept his proposal?"

"Well, there hasn't been a proposal to accept, and we have many things to talk over."

"So I just need to get my son to propose and you'll accept? Your Ma and I can't wait for you to become better acquainted with our girls. Do you remember them?"

"I remember Kelley the best since she was with Jake when I was hopelessly in love with your son." I smiled.

"You've been lusting after my Donny since you were a little girl?" Mr. Taylor said that loudly enough for our entire lunch table to look up from their meals and conversations.

"Pa," I admonished. "I was only ten. Ten-year-olds don't lust. We crush."

"Whatevah! Lust, crush—all the same!"

I laughed. "I'll tell you a secret if you'll keep it to yourself." Now, this was the wine combined with medication, talking. I was getting loose-tongued again. Pa Taylor nodded his head feverishly. "I asked your son to marry me when I was a little girl, but he never had the courtesy to answer me."

"Shit! That moron of a son of mine could've been with you since you were in grade school?" Now Pa was just plain making fun of me. "You could've had a dozen kids by now."

"Oh my gosh, that's just wrong. I was twelve when I asked him to marry me in the form of a letter. Plus, that moron of a son of yours told me that he was going to ask Kate to marry him the same day I asked him to marry me!"

"Stupid! He's just stupid at times. He gets that from Jamie's side of the family." I saw Pa take out his phone and start texting.

"What are you doing?" I asked in horror.

"I'm telling my son that he's an idiot!"

"You promised to keep my secret," I cried.

"Don't you worry, my sweet Laney. I'll keep your secret."

Lunch with Pa Taylor was a hoot, and it was wonderful to see the close relationship my dad had with Scott Taylor. This was what family was all about—enjoying one another, loving one another, and supporting one another every way we could. I knew if Donovan and I could work through his issues with all the other women in his life, our marriage would be an easy one where all the pieces of the puzzle already fit together. We only needed two more pieces to finish the Reid-Taylor puzzle—those two pieces being Donovan and me.

"Will you excuse me, Pa? I have a phone call to make."

"Sure, Baby. I'll be right here if you want to divulge any more secrets to your Pa."

I laughed while walking away.

It was time. I wasn't sure where Donovan and I would end up, but I knew for sure where Michael and I were headed.

"Duchess!"

"Hi Michael. How are you?"

"I was worried about you when our call got cut off. Whose number is this?"

"This is my father's temporary phone while he's in Europe. My phone ended up in the canal, unfortunately."

"Canal?"

"Long story, Michael."

"How much longer are you in Amsterdam? When can we expect you at Grandfather's?"

"A couple more days, and I wanted to talk to you about us."

"Shit! I knew it wouldn't be long before that Donovan Taylor figured out what he was missing. Duchess, I don't want you to say what you're about to say. We need to see each other. When we're together and you can tell me the same words you're about to utter, then I'll consider it."

"But Michael, this isn't fair to you. I don't think I ever fell out of love with Donovan. He's here and he wants us to get married. His parents, my parents, my grandparents, my cousins—everyone is championing our cause. I haven't admitted anything to Donovan, yet, but I know I still care for him."

"And you don't care for me?" Michael was sad asking me this question and I was sad for him. I should never have gotten together with him. I knew it would only end in a broken heart.

"I do, Michael. You are the kindest and most caring person I've ever met. You and Ruby have made my adjustment to a new country so painless. I appreciate you and like you very much."

"But...you don't love me."

"Michael, I've been honest with you from the start. You knew my feelings for you weren't that strong, yet."

"Duchess, I need to see you. I can't come to any resolution till we meet face to face and you tell me that you can't ever grow to love me."

"Michael..." *Aargh!* When did my life get this complicated? "I should be in London soon. I'll call you when I leave Amsterdam and we can meet. But, Michael?"

"Yes, Duchess?"

"I don't think I can meet you at your grandfather's. That's going to make this situation even harder to resolve."

"I'll come to London to see you. Just *please*," he pleaded, "don't make any decisions before we get a chance to see each other. I love you, Duchess. Don't forget that."

I sighed quietly. "I'll see you soon."

As soon as the call was done, I sighed loudly. I should have listened to my gut instinct and never started a relationship with a man I knew wasn't my forever. What a mess I had created.

"Delaney...Delaney!"

"Huh?" After my call with Michael, I'd been a space cadet with Donovan and my family. I blamed it on the flu, but I knew what was ailing me.

"Bee's on the phone and she wants to talk to you."

"Bee?" I gladly answered the phone. "Hello, Stranger. What's going on?"

"I've got an unusual situation, and I need your help."

"Ok...how can I help you?"

"You know about my fashion show in a couple of days?"

"Is this where a few American designers based in Paris wanted you to join their mini fashion show in Paris?"

"Yes. I had a model drop out at the last minute, and I need you to model some of the clothes for me."

"NO WAY!" I almost shouted. "I'll come support you, I'll sit in the front row, I'll even buy a dress or two, but there's no freakin' way I'm modeling anything in public!"

"Come on, Laney! I've seen you strut your stuff. You're a natural. There's a catwalk coach here who'll walk you through the steps. I need you to model just a few items. I promise! I won't put you out on the catwalk more than twice."

"Bee...!" I complained. "Why would you want me as your model? I'm fatter, older, and uglier than the girls who do this for a living. I'll be *the* laughingstock."

"You're stunning," Donovan whispered into the other ear that wasn't occupied by the phone.

"Come to Paris tonight. There's a speed train that leaves Amsterdam Centraal and arrives in Paris in three hours. I'll send you tickets. Puleez! I'm in a bind."

"You are a pain in the ass is what you are, Bee Taylor! Hold on." I put Bee on hold and talked to everyone at my table. "Actually, let me call you back, Bee."

"You're coming?" She had a smile on the other end.

"I'll call you back!" I tried to sound annoyed, but couldn't.

"What's our agenda here in Amsterdam?" I asked Donovan, first.

"I'm done here. I need to visit clients in Paris, Rome, and then back to London, and it needs to be in that order."

"What about you?" I addressed the collective group of parents.

Dad was first to speak. "I have one more seminar tomorrow, and after that I'm done."

"The rest of us are free to do as we please, and go wherever we please." Mr. Taylor spoke for the rest of the members at the table.

"Bee needs my help in Paris. She wants me to take the Thalys train down to Paris tonight. I'd like to spend more time with you," I looked at my parents, "but Bee is in a bind and I want to help her."

"I guess we're going to Paris!" Mrs. Taylor announced. "I can spend more time with my future daughter-in-law and see if I can be of help to my sister-in-law."

"I haven't seen Paris in years. Why don't your father and I join you, tomorrow, after his last seminar is done?"

"Are you sure? If you want to go back to London, I'll go back with you, Mom."

"Honey, it doesn't matter where we go. We just wanted to spend time with you."

"Does Grandfather have a place in Paris that we can stay in for the time being, or do I need to get rooms at a hotel?"

"Your grandfather has the most stunning penthouse apartment with a 360 degree view of Paris. You can see the Eiffel Tower, the Seine, the rooftops of every major building on a clear day. I believe it has four bedrooms, which is enough for all of us to have a room. Does that meet with your approval?"

"That sounds marvelous!" I gushed. "I guess we're moving this party to Paris?"

I called Bee right away and told her the good news while Donovan got our arrangements taken care of so we could be on the next train to Paris.

"So Bee actually wants you to model her clothes?" Donovan had booked a semi-private "salon" with four seats so I could lay down during our three-and-a-half hour trip if I started feeling worse. It was sweet of him to put such thought into my comfort.

"Yes. Isn't that crazy? I've never modeled before. I can't do it. She's nuts if she thinks I can."

"Oh, I don't know. You got a little swagger in you. You might be able to pull it off."

"Really?" I gave him a doubtful look. "And when have you come upon this swagger?" I laughed.

"Princess. You've got a knock-out body. Most of those models have those waif thin boy figures. Now you, you've got curves in all the right places. Might I be able to sample these curves at some point in this relationship?" he asked with confidence.

I laughed some more. "What relationship are we talking about? Or better yet, whose relationship are we talking about? Last I checked, you and I were just friends. And friends do not *sample* each other—at least my friends and I never did."

Donovan easily placed his lips on mine and kissed me passionately. I didn't stop him, though it was wrong not to—I couldn't help it. I just hoped I was kissing him properly. "Let's talk about this 'relationship.'"

"Donovan." I whispered after catching my breath. "I'm still with Michael. You and I can't keep doing this. It makes me a bad person because essentially, I'm cheating on a good man."

"Let's talk about this *good* man. Do you love him?"

I was slow to answer. "Not yet."

"Can you see yourself with him in twenty years?"

"I don't know," was what I said, but I knew I couldn't see us married with a houseful of children.

"Is it his title that makes him attractive to you?"

I couldn't believe Donovan was asking me this question. "Don't be an ass. You know that's not what I'm looking for in a man. I've told you in the past. All I want is to love and be loved. I don't need a castle."

"If you don't love him and you can't see yourself with him in twenty years, why can't you let him go?"

I tried to let him go today. I didn't think Donovan needed to know this fact. His ego was grand enough. "He loves me and he's been good to me."

"Well, I love you and I know I'll be good to you, too."

"Why now, Donovan? I've tried since I was ten to get your attention. Why are you interested now? Is it one of those situations where now you want me because you can't have me?"

"I want you because I realize now that I love you. All those sweet days we spent together. The softball games, our dates to the beach, our unintended overnights—did you not feel our love grow?"

My laugh turned into a cynical cackle. "Mr. Taylor. My love for you got beaten up like a losing boxer, bruised like a kid falling off a bicycle, shattered like a broken window, shredded like a slip of paper in a paper shredder, during those *sweet* days. Should I come up with more metaphors if you don't get it?"

He gave me his ultra sexy smile and tried to kiss me again. This time I was quicker than he. "You are exaggerating. I've never beaten, bruised, shattered, or shredded this heart of yours," he put his hand on my heart while speaking in a seductive voice.

"Are you doing what I think you're doing?"

"And what's that, Princess?" His voice was still silky smooth.

"That big hand of yours is moving," I warned. "You may not feel me up, Mr. Taylor!" I laughed when it wasn't appropriate to laugh. I should have been sterner with this man whose hand kept roaming around my chest, heading to one side, about to grab my breast. "Get your hand off my property." My feeble attempt to pull his hand off my breasts didn't work till I demanded, "Hand off the merchandise!"

He laughed and quickly stole a kiss from me. "Damn! You're definitely on the opposite end of the spectrum from easy."

"Really? Last I remember, you accused me several times of being easy."

"I did not!" He feigned a gasp.

"Josh and Brent easily come to mind. I have never cried so much as I did that Sunday night in Austin when you accused me of being a slut." The tears started forming in my eyes. "I'd saved myself for you all these years. I never really dated because of you. I almost missed my high school prom because of you. I never even kissed a man until you came along in Hawaii, and there you were, accusing me of...who the hell knows what you were accusing me of when you saw me with Brent." Donovan's face fell penitent. "I know you never asked anything of me, and I know there were no promises spoken, but that's how much I loved you all those years. You beat me up when I saw you with Kate at the Montage Hotel, you bruised my heart when I heard you confess to Jane that you wanted a relationship with her, you shattered me with your accusations of flirting with your clients in Hawaii, and the shredding was complete when you told me that I wasn't in your league. After all this, what would make me believe that you all of a sudden love me and want to marry me?" I flicked the forming tears off my eyes and calmed myself.

"Hell and damnation." Donovan scratched his head as he usually did when he was frustrated. "You can't continually use my past sins against me. I was an idiot. I was an asshole. My head wasn't on straight, and I should've noticed you..." he stopped, abruptly got up and searched through his briefcase. He pulled out a bunch of folded pieces of paper of all sizes, colors, and shapes. I knew exactly what he had laid on the table.

"You still have these?" I asked in wonder. "You've kept them all this time?"

"Does this maybe make you believe that you've meant something to me all these years?"

I proceeded to open up and read each and every note. I laughed at some, I shook my head at others, and I groaned with a few. "Good God! I was such an obnoxious child!"

"You were an adorable child. You've been leaving me notes in my pocket for as long as I can remember." Donovan began searching through all the notes I'd written to him since I was ten years old. This was a game of mine to leave Donovan a slip of paper in one of his pockets, whenever I wanted to tell him something but didn't have the guts to say it to his face. These messages brought back such good memories.

You are so handsome!

You are even more handsome than my cousin, Jake.

Donovan, I truly hope you will one day help my New Year's resolution come true. See you again in 11 years.

Where have you been?

Who is this woman you keep hanging out with, and why have you forgotten me?

If you're going to forget me, I'm going to forget you, too.

Donovan, you me? If so, me at swing pm.

Yours was my very first kiss. I will remember it always.

I waited all night for you, but obviously you had Kate to keep you occupied. I wish things could have been different for us. Good-bye.

"Do I get any brownie points for keeping these?"

"Why do you still have them?"

"I'd like to tell you I kept them so I could woo you back to me, but in actuality, every time I got a note from you, I threw them in a drawer. Before I came here, I picked them all up so I could reread them and give myself the courage to woo you."

"I can't believe my first note to you was, *You are so handsome,*" I groaned. "I'm sure that did your ego a lot of good to know a minor was mooning over you."

Donovan picked up the New Year's resolution note and asked, "What did you want me to do to help your New Year's resolution come true? What was your resolution?"

I turned red and shook my head no. "This isn't Embarrass Delaney, Day. I think I'll take a nap right now." I got up to move to the other two empty chairs.

"Oh no you don't." Donovan pulled me onto his lap. "Explain, or I'm going to force my lips on you till you're ready to speak."

Did he really think that was a threat? He could tell by my silly half-smile that I'd welcome his kiss. And that's just what he did. His kiss started as light pecks on my lips. Then he just sucked on parts of my lips, savoring the feel and taste. Soon, he placed his mouth on mine and searched for an entry. I opened my mouth to give him full access. What was it about two tongues mating that made my heart sing and my body rejoice?

Donovan pulled away before I was ready to let go. "Had you really never kissed anyone till I kissed you in Hawaii?"

I shook my head no. "I told you back in Grandfather's car I have never been in a serious relationship with anyone. Where would I have gotten my make out sessions if I haven't had a boyfriend?"

There was a look on Donovan's face I couldn't decipher. "Is this good or bad that you and Emily seem to have this virgin thing in common?"

"*If* you were my boyfriend, it would be fantastic for you because you'd be the one to teach me the Kama Sutra ropes. In addition, I don't have a mother who made me promise to stay a virgin till I got married. *BUT,* you're *not* my boyfriend, so it shouldn't matter either way." I got up and sat across from him.

"Shit." He chuckled. "That's a challenge if I ever heard one." He got up, perched himself on the seat next to me and held my hand. "When are you going to break up with Michael?"

I hesitated but decided to be honest with Donovan. "I tried earlier today, but he wants a face-to-face before any decision is made. I need to go back to London as soon as possible. It isn't fair to Michael that there's so much uncertainty in the air." Donovan smiled and kissed the hand he held. "But that doesn't mean you and I are in the clear. I still don't believe your intentions and you have a few more confessions to make, I believe."

"I will confess only if you will confess what your New Year's resolution was back when you were eleven. Why were you and I to meet again in eleven years?"

"Now that I think about it, I guess we did meet again in eleven years, huh?"

"Fess up, Princess."

"Oh, all right!" I huffed. "I was resolute that one cold morning to become your wife in eleven years and that's why we were to meet again."

I giggled to myself. "One day I'll show you my notebook filled with Delaney Taylor signatures. So embarrassing!" I had to cover my blushing face.

"I've really missed out, huh?" His face gentled as he put his hand on my head and brought me into his chest. Donovan's affection—something I could never refuse. "All those years of searching and you were right there on the cul-de-sac, waiting. You think the Chief would have let me date you when you were in high school?"

"Hell no! You can't be a twenty-six year old perving on a sixteen year old!"

"Sleep, Princess. It's going to be a long day, tomorrow." And that's just what I did, in Donovan Taylor's arms.

"You're here!" Bee rammed her happy body into mine.

"Careful, Bee. Delaney's recovering from the flu."

"I got it, Nephew," she answered condescendingly. "I'll take good care of your woman." Bee looked at me. "I assume you're his woman now, and not Michael's?"

"Nope. Still with Michael." I answered matter-of-factly.

"Not for long..." Donovan sang. "I've got to go meet some clients. Don't overwork my princess," he warned his aunt.

"Whatever! Go work and get out of our business. Laney's already late meeting with the catwalk teacher."

"When will you be done with her? I want to take her somewhere later this afternoon."

"We should be done by lunch."

"I'll be back around one."

I smiled and waved good-bye. He came in for a kiss, and after last night, I didn't refuse him. We'd gotten in to Paris late at night, took a cab to Grandfather's spectacular penthouse apartment and slept in each other's arms. After last night, I was determined to end what Michael and I had and to figure out whether or not Donovan and I could work. Who was I kidding? As soon as Donovan knocked on Gram's door, my fate was sealed. I'd date this man; run away with this man; live in sin with this man...anything was possible with this man!

"Earth to Laney!" Bee woke me up from my fanciful thoughts about our "limbo" in bed last night. "What's going on with you and my nephew? Good thing I finished the wedding dress Donovan asked me to design."

"What? Donovan asked you for a wedding dress?"

"Before he moved to London, he stopped by and told me to start designing a dress."

I let out a forced cackle. "Oh, I'm not letting Donovan slither back into my life that easily. Aside from the mound of issues facing us, even if I was willing to overlook everything, I'm not going to make life that easy for him. Do you know how long I waited for him to notice me?" Now my voice was getting louder and higher. "Do you know how much he hurt me? There's no way in hell I'm letting him off that easily!"

Bee snorted. "You go, Girl! But first, go right to the catwalk master."

"Bee! Please! I can't do this."

"Yes. You. Can!"

I absolutely sucked at strutting like a model! And the catwalk-meister thought I was way too fat to be a model. He didn't have to say it; it was written all over his face. No model had big breasts like I had, and none of the models I saw had child-bearing hips, either. There was no way I was going to do this until I saw the dress!

"Bee! That's stunning!" Bee had recreated my midnight blue dress—the one I wore to Ashley's wedding reception—in fire-engine red. Between the colors and the Swarovski crystals, this dress was a standout!

"That's gorgeous, Auntie!" Donovan whistled with appreciation at Bee's masterpiece.

"You're back, already." I walked over to Donovan to greet him.

He put one arm around me and gave me a light peck on the lips. "I finished up as soon as I could and pushed to tomorrow what I could. Can we leave? Are you done?"

"I would love for Laney to try this on so I can see if it needs alterations. You don't by chance have your Grandmother's necklace, do you? The same one you wore to the wedding?"

"I don't have that one, but I have this." I unbuttoned the neckline of the shirt I was wearing and showed off the Chanel camellia necklace, compliments of Donovan Taylor.

"That's a bit fancy for the outfit you're wearing, no? Did I tell you about this dress? Is that how you knew to wear this necklace today, or do you just wear a fancy Chanel necklace wherever and whenever?" Bee questioned.

"I haven't taken this off since the night your nephew put it on me," I confessed quietly hoping Donovan wouldn't hear.

He touched the camellias on my neck and gazed at me with adoration in his eyes. I gazed back only partly, embarrassed that I couldn't ever hide my love for Donovan. He didn't say a word, but his smile said it all. He was pleased.

"OK, then!" Bee broke our locked eyes. "You," she pointed to me, "go try on the dress, and you," she pointed to her nephew, "hang out here with me till your *Princess* is back."

It didn't take me long to put on the dress, and I got appreciative claps and whistles on my way back to the two Taylors.

"Stunning!" Donovan declared.

"I think you are absolutely dead-on, Nephew. Let me put a few pins on this dress so I know where to do minor alterations, and you two love-birds can leave."

As hard as I tried to convince Bee to join us for the rest of the day, Donovan tried equally hard to convince his aunt that she wasn't invited. In the end, Donovan won. The two of us got in a car and were driven out of Paris to a location unknown.

"Are we going to Versailles?"

"Nope. We are going somewhere sweeter, smaller, and a lot more romantic."

"No clues?"

"Maybe I'll give you a clue if you'll clue me in on why you wear the camellia necklace everyday and why I've only now seen the 'D' charm on you."

"So it was you!" I happily declared. "Those were all from you – the clutch, the shoes, and the charm?"

"They were," he grinned smugly.

"Why?" I truly had no idea what would have possessed Donovan to go on such a shopping spree for me back in Hawaii. "And why didn't you give it to me yourself? Why hide behind Emily?"

"You first. Why the camellia around your neck every day?"

I shrugged my shoulders, embarrassed again to have to confess my weakness for him. "Because...it felt like you were with me, close to my heart, everywhere I went. I missed you horribly when I left you back in the States. That necklace was my only physical connection to you that I could have on me at all times, and I thought maybe if I kept that close to my heart, somehow it would connect us emotionally, too." I put my face in my hands. "I'm such a serious loser!" I now shook my head at the frivolity of my actions.

"I'm the loser for not having admitted how much you meant to me before you left for London." He took the hands off my face and held them instead. "There were many times I asked myself if I had feelings for you, and I always passed it off as lust. You are beautiful, funny, and you have an insanely tempting body. I kept telling myself it was wrong to lust after you—not ever understanding that it wasn't just lust. I think all those times we were together, I was falling in love with you. But I had convinced myself that it wrong to have feelings for you."

"Why?"

"Because you are the Chief's daughter, Jake's cousin, Doug's younger sister, the little girl who pushed me in the ocean when I was wearing my brand new Calvin Klein suit." We got a chuckle out of that Easter memory. "You were always a little girl to me, and then one day, I see you at Jake's wedding and you were this goddess, a nymph, my houri. I couldn't take my eyes off you until Jake informed me that you were the little girl who used to drop notes in my pocket, and I was horrified to be attracted to a girl I once wished was my little sister."

"Is that why you didn't speak to me that day? I so hoped you'd notice me and acknowledge me."

"Oh, I noticed you. Trust me, my entire body noticed you, and it did not make my date happy to see me staring at you."

"You did not stare at me! Every time I looked at you, you were turned away from me."

"I turned away, but I still couldn't take my eyes off you. I thought about calling you after that night but decided it wasn't prudent since you were only a sophomore in college. I probably would have freaked you out if I had asked you out at age thirty, when you were only twenty."

"Donovan," I giggled. "I would have gone out with you in a heartbeat and married you all within that same month, if that were an option."

He laughed with me. "Once I saw you again at my office, dressed like Coco Chanel, I knew I couldn't stay away for long."

"Then where does Jane fit into all this?"

He thought about it for a while and said, "Could I give you that explanation a bit later? Could we finish up this conversation about your gifts from Hawaii?"

"Sure."

"When we went shopping in Hawaii with Jake and Emily, I saw that look of longing in your eyes when Jake took Emily into the jewelry shop. I knew it wasn't any type of jealousy, but you just had this forlorn look that tugged at my heart. Then that look almost turned desperate, or maybe despondent is a better word, when Jake was changing out Emily's shoes. Your lost look didn't sit well with me, and I wanted to reach out to you. The only feasible way to reach out to you was to buy you those gifts."

"When I saw my cousin and his wife at that shoe store, it hit me that I'd never have that kind of intimacy and bond with anybody as you never noticed me, and I refused to notice anyone else. I guess I mourned a life that was never to be mine. You were right. I was so lost that day, not able to get myself out of that haze."

"I could tell when we met up again. That's when I decided I wanted to fill your void and returned to the mall after dropping you three off at the hotel. But why haven't you worn the charm till now?"

"Well...I don't have any necklaces, so I couldn't place the charm anywhere. And I also wanted to wear it on the camellia necklace because I liked pretending that it came from you."

"You've had this necklace on since that night at the sushi bar?"

"Yes, except when I knew I was going to see you. I didn't want you to think I was some loony stalker-girl wearing a crazy expensive necklace with shorts and a t-shirt." I laughed.

"You loved me that much?" He was confounded by how much of an obsessed loser I was.

I nodded. "And I still love you that much. That's why I'm scared of you. I'm scared to get hurt. I'm scared to believe. You never showed me an ounce of interest, and now you want to marry me. Would you believe you?"

"Princess, if you are honest with yourself, I showed plenty of interest in you. You were the first and only person I took up to my beach house. I didn't want to be apart from you that night we babysat the twins, so I picked you up when you were sleeping and brought you into my bed."

"That was you?" I was shocked!

"How else do you think you got from the twins' room to the guest room?"

"I thought the loser that I was, I walked over to you in my sleep."

Donovan almost died laughing. "It was all me."

"But then you ignored me the next morning and went to meet up with Kate."

"I was embarrassed. I figured you knew what I had done so I tried to play it off."

We had so many more things to resolve, but we got to our destination and Donovan took my hand and slowly led me to the water lilies of Monet's Garden. We were in Giverny exploring the beauty called Nympheas that inspired Monet to draw some of his most famous paintings.

"This is incredible," I whispered.

"Of all the places in the house and the gardens, this is my favorite spot." Obviously he had been here before. As for whom he visited this romantic landscape with, I would not ask, and I worked hard not to wonder.

Personally, I loved the long branches of the huge weeping willows that outlined the water lilies on the pond. This was the picture I envisioned when I thought of a Monet painting. We strolled hand-in-hand to another familiar picture in my head—the Japanese Bridge.

"Donovan, it's so beautiful here. I thought Amsterdam was gorgeous; I think this might just beat the canals."

"You want to spend the night here in a true French château?"

"Can we?" I asked with much too much eagerness. "Don't you have to get back? Shoot, I have to be back by noon, too."

"I'll push my meeting for noon. Then we can have a leisurely breakfast and head back into the city."

"I don't have a change of clothes."

"You can sleep naked tonight, then wear the same clothes tomorrow," this squirrely man suggested.

"Obviously, we are getting separate bedrooms?"

"Hell no! We haven't slept apart since I got to London. I'm not starting now." He kissed the hand he was holding. "We can buy what we need for tonight and just re-wear what we have on for tomorrow. We'll get back to Paris early enough to change."

"Can you give me a moment to call Michael?" Donovan didn't look happy. "I need to do this. It's unfair to Michael."

"You're breaking up with him?" That question was more like a demand.

"Yes," I answered, exasperated with his mother hen-like clucking.

He dug his phone out of his pocket and sighed, "Go. Do what you have to do."

"Thank you," I tried to give him a kiss on the cheek but he turned around and immediately we were in an amorous clinch on the picturesque Japanese bridge with violet wisteria as our overhang. This would have made an idyllic picture of the two of us—something I would have liked to frame.

"Let me get this done so I can decide with a clear conscience what to do with you." I pulled away much to both our chagrin.

He gave me his usual megawatt smile and let me walk away.

I, on the other hand, did not feel happy about the call I had to make. "Hi Michael."

"Laney." He sounded excited and reserved at the same time. "Duchess. How's Amsterdam?"

"Well, we are now in Paris because Bee needs my help." Michael was quieter than usual. "You remember Bee?"

"Yes. I do. What kind of help did she need?"

"One of her models dropped out at the last minute and she's coerced me to step in and model two outfits."

"Model?"

"I know! Crazy, huh? I can barely put my right foot in front of the left."

"You'll be stunning, as always."

"How are you?" I asked with caution. "I assume you're at your grandfather's?"

"Yes, I'm here. The weather is gloomy, I am gloomy, and my whole family is upset with me that I couldn't persuade you to be here." I flinched at the thought of disappointing the Bennington family. How would I break up with this man?

"Michael," I whispered. "I'm sorry. Back when you convinced me that a relationship could work, I was selfish. I knew deep in my heart it wouldn't last forever, but I really liked you. I enjoyed your company, I loved your family, and you were and are about as perfect as they come."

"But..." he said it first to spare me the pain.

"No buts, Michael. I enjoyed our time together, you have been the utmost gentleman to me, and you accepted all my foibles. You are too good for me."

"Spare me the condescension, Laney," he answered with much bitterness.

"Michael..." His acrimony caught me off guard, and all I could think was to get away from this conversation for now. "Maybe we should talk again, later."

"Yeah. I think that would be best." And he hung up on me.

I stood in place, numb from what had transpired.

"What's the matter, Princess? Do *not* tell me you didn't break up with him, again!" Now this man was biting my head off. What the hell did I do wrong to court the ire of two men, when normally no man paid any attention to me? "Well?"

My shoulders drooped, and immediately Donovan put his arms around me and apologized. I accepted the apology and explained our conversation. "He's so angry with me, Donovan. What have I done? It was all selfishness on my part. I shouldn't have toyed with his emotions all this time."

"Princess," he rubbed my back and kissed my head, "you weren't playing with his emotions. He was probably good to you, and you liked him as a person."

"And not as a man?" I asked for kicks.

"Of course, not as a man. Why the hell would you look at another man when I was always hovering?"

"Why the hell would I?" I imitated his voice.

Donovan had quickly turned this into a lighthearted conversation. "He'll get over you faster than you would like to believe."

"I hope so. I don't want him hurt. That's not a feeling I wish upon anyone."

"Is this your roundabout way of telling me I was an asshole to you all these years?"

I giggled. "Not my intention, but if the shoe fits..."

"The only one who found her lost shoe is you, my princess. You are my Cinderella and I plan to be your prince. Make a clean break from Michael and let's start our future, today."

"I'll call him tomorrow and try again. In the meanwhile, let's see the rest of Monet's garden."

The dining room was almost entirely yellow with accents of blue stemming from the dinnerware. And like most artists of his time, he had collected Japanese prints and covered the walls. The kitchen was decorated in shades of blue with copper accents coming from the sink and all the cookware.

"What a fabulous stove!" I declared. "The French make everything so beautiful, huh?"

"You want one? I can put one in my kitchen right now if you'll come live with me. You cook, Princess?"

I didn't answer the first question, but I was more than happy to answer the next one. "Nope. I don't cook, but I can reheat."

"You clean?" he asked dubiously.

"Nope. And I'm a serious packrat, too."

"You...you do anything that most housewives do?"

I had to think about this for a while. "Maybe you should stay home and take care of the house and kids *if* I choose to go down that path with you."

"You're going to be my sugar mama? Hell, yes! I'd stay home for that option." He laughed and kissed me again. "But we'd need a nanny for the kids and a housekeeper for the house."

"What the hell are you good for, then?"

"I was going to ask you the same thing. You don't cook, you don't clean...I guess as long as you pop out babies, we can hire people for the rest. Seeing you with the twins, I know you'll be a fantastic mother."

"You're getting ahead of yourself, Mr. Taylor."

"I don't think so, Ms. Reid. You love me, I love you, the rest is easy."

"Are you going to ever tell me about you and Jane? Whenever I'm with you, I forget all my woes and live in this giddy fantasy world where everything is perfect. But when I'm not with you, I still see images of you and Jane in that hospital room."

"Damn!" he sighed. "Let's go to dinner and I'll tell you everything."

Donovan took us to a house that looked like an extension of Monet's house. The restaurant was housed in an English Tudor with French overtone building. It was the wooden slats, painted in blue, that gave off the Monet vibe.

"Have you been here before? This neighborhood tops our cul-de-sac in the charming category."

"I believe this restaurant is fairly new. I haven't eaten here before, but yes, I've been to this area of Vernon and Giverny before."

"Oh," was all I could muster as I felt my face falling with the disappointment that I'd never be this man's first in anything.

"Maybe I should explain Kate, before explaining Jane?" He understood my discontent.

"Will Kate always be our shadow?"

He chuckled. "I hope not. Let's go in so I can have some sustenance before I explain the last ten years."

"Ten years...with Kate..." I droned. *That's how long I've loved you while you loved another woman.*

"Don't." He stopped me from delving deeper into my melo mood. "I wasn't committed to Kate the entire ten years. We were off more than we were on. It's not as serious as you're making it out to be."

I just nodded. We walked into the pristine restaurant and were startled to find a group of people waiting for us.

"Laney! Oh my gosh, it that you?"

"Kelley? What are you doing here in France?"

"Hi Laney." Becky and Al were here, as well as a man I assumed was Kelley's husband.

Kelley and I had a love-fest reunion as she and I hadn't seen one another in many years.

"You're so tall, now. Last I saw you, you were this tiny girl in pigtails and braces."

"I'll never outgrow that image, huh?" I laughed with Kelley. It was good to see her again. She never wavered in her support for me whenever I got into trouble as a youth. I was sorry she and Jake didn't work out, but seeing Jake and Emily as a couple, I knew he'd made the right decision.

"What the hell are you four doing here?" Donovan's exasperated pretense fooled no one.

"How about a hello for me, Laney?"

I walked over and gave Al a great big hug, but Donovan pulled me back immediately.

"Now I know why Jake does this anytime Emily touches another man."

"Bro'," Al teased. "We're family. Family members hug one another and even give each other loving kisses."

Donovan shook his head and muttered, "Stick to Becky!"

We all sat and the explanations began. "Al and I wanted one last getaway before this baby arrived, and Mom called to say she and Dad were going to Paris the same day my OB gave me clearance to fly. And since Al was already coming here for work, I tagged along."

"And you, Kelley?" Donovan inquired.

"Becky called me to tell me she and Al were headed to Paris. I complained to Noah that we hadn't gone away since the boys were born. Noah's parents offered to take the kids for a week, so here we are."

436

"You decided to fly all the way here on a whim?" Donovan didn't believe his sisters.

"Were you listening, *Donny*?" Becky spoke sarcastically. "Al was headed to Europe so I tagged along, and Kelley and Noah needed a vacation so they came to Paris."

"How did you know we were here?" I asked.

"Donny called Pa, and Ma told us where you'd be. I thought this reunion would be a nice surprise." Kelley was the one talking now.

"It's a wonderful surprise. I'm glad you're here Kelley. It's really been a long time, huh?"

"Yes, Laney Reid. I knew from when you were little you had a crush on my brother, but never did I think this was going to happen." Kelley pointed back and forth to me and Donovan.

"This is way beyond my imagination, too." Becky joined our conversation. "I thought after seeing Donovan with Jane in Chicago, he'd end up with my best friend." As soon as Becky spoke, Al nudged her, Donovan groaned and Becky apologized. "So sorry, Laney. I'm just caught by surprise."

"How could you not have seen the attraction between these two when we were in LA for Mother's Day? Your brother was mad for this young lady, but comically, he had no clue he was in love with her. That's why he was such an asshole to her in LA and in Austin, because he didn't have an answer for his feelings."

"Thank you, Brother." Donovan gave an appreciative nod to Al who was doing his best to make up for his wife. "Next bottle of wine is on me."

"So then..." Becky held back only long enough to be polite. "Why Jane? What was with the let's-have-sex, plane tickets?"

What?

"Shit, Becky. Really? Do you have no filter?" Donovan got angry with her.

"Shit," Becky replied. "I'm so sorry. That's not what I meant. Laney. They didn't have sex...right, Donovan? I mean when she spent the night at the Peninsula with you, everything was platonic...right?"

"Dear?" Al put a piece of tomato on his fork and shoved it in Becky's mouth. "Shut up and eat this, instead."

"Damn you, Becky!" Donovan cursed while I put my head down and ate my salad.

There were no words for the pain I felt hearing about Donovan and Jane. They were obviously more seriously involved than I'd imagined and that hurt more than all the painful memories combined. This was what I'd feared about Donovan's recent interest in me. This crushing pain he could so readily put in my heart was what I wanted to avoid. But no past heartbreak could have prepared me for the one I was feeling right now.

"It's not what you're thinking. Becky doesn't know what she's talking about, Princess. Jane and I were not involved like that. I mean...we were in Chicago together, but...I can explain it all. Please, don't let what you just heard put a wedge between us." Donovan begged pretty soundly, but what I heard and what I felt couldn't be helped. Otherwise, I would have tuned it out immediately.

The rest of dinner was Becky and Kelley talking about their other two sisters, Rachel and Amanda. They told me where they lived, how many kids they had, and who their husbands were. There wasn't anything I could add to their conversation until Kelley asked me about Jake and Emily.

"Jake and Emily had another boy, first week of July, and they just arrived in London. Jake is teaching at a few hospitals and their corresponding medical schools and the family will take up residence in Gram's flat for a few months."

"Is that where you're staying?" She continued to bring me into the conversation.

I wasn't much up for conversation so I gave her a simple "Yes."

"What will you do in London this next year?" Al asked.

"I was thinking about following Jake when he went to Oxford and Cambridge and auditing some classes. I don't know if that's done in England, but I'd like to take some literature classes. Or maybe I'll sit in one of Jake's med school classes."

"That's right. I remember Donovan telling me you were part genius." Al's smile forced a weak smile out of me. He was trying so hard to cover for his wife, who obviously wasn't happy with me as her brother's love interest, and for his brother-in-law, who would have a hard time recovering from this revelation. "You're going to med school next fall?"

"Possibly. I haven't decided between med school and film school."

"Oh, Laney! How wonderful. You're going to be a doctor just like your dad?" Kelley let out a great big smile.

"Maybe," I smiled back, minus the great and the big.

"How about if we retire for the evening?" Al suggested. "The four of us got in today and we are exhausted."

"Where are you staying?" Donovan spoke for the first time since he got upset with Becky. "You going back to Paris tonight?"

"No, we got rooms at the château you and Laney are lodging in. We borrowed a true *mini*van and drove out here for the night, so the six of us should fit, barely."

"Why'd you get a minivan in Paris?"

Al clearly stated his displeasure. "Because your sister insists that she needs ample space. She can't stand being crowded these days. Another quirk of pregnancy, I'm supposed to accept, I'm told."

Kelley and Noah laughed at Al's resigned face.

Though it was supposed to be a quick drive, we got lost due to the lack of signage. But when we came upon the château, we were all in awe of the property. The exterior red brick building reminded me of the Crawley's family home in Downton Abbey. This château was so spectacular it took my breath away, until a blinding disappointment walloped me back to reality. In all likelihood, Donovan and Kate had spent their nights here. From what Kelley mentioned, there were only four rooms in this surreal bed and breakfast and the thought of Donovan and me possibly being in the same room that Donovan and Kate had once been in, made me ill.

"What's wrong? You went from looking amazed to offended," Donovan whispered.

I didn't answer him. How could he read me so effortlessly, and yet have no idea when he was opening up an old wound?

When we checked-in, I didn't fight the same room situation. Donovan had booked us the largest one, and without argument, I followed him into the magnificent room. Everything about it was French, minus the gilded rococo feel. I felt like Marie Antoinette with her baroque-red canopied bed, the chandeliers in the sitting room, and green-marbled bathroom. The original 1800 decorative moldings were as breathtaking as the French doors leading in and out of every room. Had I not been in such a crappy mood, I would have enjoyed this château a lot more.

"You ready to talk?" Donovan carefully approached me.

"No. I don't want to talk. It's been a long day and I'm tired. Since we left London, I haven't had a day of rest. Could we push this off for another day?"

"Delaney. We can't progress if we don't talk."

"I don't know if we should progress. The more I hear, the more disturbed I am, and I don't know if I'll ever get over whatever *progressed* between you and my cousin."

"Nothing happened between us. I mean, nothing of importance happened. My idiotic sister spoke rashly."

"So you didn't give Jane *'let's-have-sex'* plane tickets?"

"No, I mean yes, I mean...SHIT! Sit down. Let me explain."

"Donovan, I don't want to know anymore. I told you earlier that I was afraid of you. This wasn't an exaggeration. Your past, your words, your actions can hurt me so profoundly. I don't want that kind of pain anymore and it isn't healthy for me. Coming to London, I thought I got away from it all. But you brought it all with you, and with a vengeance. What I'm feeling right now is exponentially worse than what I felt in LA. If you truly love me, stop hurting me."

With that, I picked up a jacket and walked the serene grounds. No matter the situation, there was always a pro and a con to it. Why couldn't life just give me the lemonade already squeezed, stirred, and made? I always got the bruised, hard and dirty lemons that made me scratch my head and wonder what I was to do with the delinquent batch. After walking the surroundings for a very long while, I did the usual and let logic guide me. There was always a rainbow at the end of a thunderstorm and a light at the end of a tunnel. If Donovan and I didn't work out, I'd know what it felt like to be loved by this man. My curiosity would be satiated and hopefully I could move on and learn to love someone else. Michael and I were done, but I was only twenty-three. There were ample years to love and be loved. If at worse, I could end up like Gram and find my second love sixty years later.

"Hello, Laney Reid." Al and Noah were sitting outside having a glass of wine. "We have here a fabulous bottle of Cabernet I just billed to the man you aren't speaking to right now. Would you like to join us?"

Al always had a way of making me laugh. He must be the sweet to the acidity in that relationship. "I think I will."

"You had a quirky look on your face before you answered. What were you thinking?"

"You speak!" I embarrassed Noah with that statement. "I'm sorry! That was obnoxious. Perhaps I caught the Becky syndrome."

"Ohhh!" I got cackles all around. "The tigress fights back," Noah raised his glass, and I clinked it before drinking what Al declared to be a fabulous Cabernet.

"Let me be the first to apologize for Becky's lack of discretion and also the first to say that nothing happened between our brother-in-law and your cousin."

"Do you know for sure?" I challenged.

Noah added, "Perhaps what Al is trying to say is that though he's not positive what happened between those two, we can tell that our brother-in-law is finally in love and shitting in his pants right now because you are pissed."

"Yep! That's what I meant to say. My wife is very uncomfortable in this pregnancy and every little thing gets on her last nerve. That doesn't mean you got on her nerve, but she just wanted some answers from her brother and it came out the wrong way."

Sighing very loudly, I said, "I don't blame Becky. Though tact doesn't seem to be her middle name, there'd be no issues if Mr. Taylor hadn't been such a Lothario."

"Do you remember me asking you to take it easy on Donovan, back in May? That he had never been in love before and that he had no clue what he was doing?"

I nodded yes but argued, "He asked a woman to marry him when he was my age. I think you can count that as having been in love, Al."

"He was infatuated with Kate. I'm sure he loved her to some degree, but what I see in him right now is the kind of love we men only find once in our lives. It's that knock-my-socks-off, blow-me-down, shit-woman-where've-you-been-all-my-life, kind of love. Donovan is in love and is lost because he doesn't know if you will accept him."

"Damn, Al. Is this how you won over your wife? You can be poetic in your own rudimentary way."

Noah almost coughed his wine back up, laughing at my comment. "You are one witty young lady. I can see why our brother-in-law can't take his eyes off of you."

"Was this bottle of wine bribery from Donovan? Did he ask you to come out here and put on this amateur production praising Donovan Taylor?"

Both men were now dying of laughter. "Hell!" Al was choking on his wine. "Donovan is in for the challenge of his life."

"Mr. Lothario has no idea the hell that awaits from a woman scorned," Noah agreed.

"Delaney."

"You're off the clock now," I whispered to the two men. "The star is ready for his monologue."

"Shit, Bro'. I thought Becky and Kelley were tough chicks. You got yourself the smartest, wittiest, and quite possibly the most entertaining woman of all the Taylor women," Al declared, getting up with Noah.

"Good night, Tigress!" Noah gave me a kiss on the cheek as support.

"Go easy on him. If we counted against us all the mistakes we've made in the past, who would have a future?"

"Go wax lyrical to your wife, Al. She obviously needs a little patting down, smoothing over, whatever you do to keep her happy." I waved good-bye.

"Can I join you in a glass?" Donovan asked hesitantly.

"You might as well. Those two men just billed this bottle to you, I was told."

"Assholes," he said with a grin and poured some in his glass, and topped off mine with the rest. "Is it good?"

"It's all right. Not the best, but not bad."

"How do you feel?"

"My body feels like a patient recovering from the flu and my heart feels like a recovering alcoholic at Oktoberfest."

Donovan cracked up. "What the hell does that mean, Delaney Reid? You were always so entertaining with your words. Remember your list of euphemisms? Jake, your uncle, and I had never laughed as much as we did that night in your bedroom. You are hysterically funny."

"I'm glad someone is finding humor in all this."

"Pick up your glass and let's walk back to our room. We'll talk on the way." I did as he asked and he underhandedly curled his fingers into mine. "What did you mean about being a recovering alcoholic at Oktoberfest?"

"My heart is like that of a recovering alcoholic at the *biergarten*. It knows it's dangerous to be around you, and yet it can't say no. You are temptation at its worst. Every time I see you, I desperately want you to see me back. Every time I talk to you, I long to hear you say a kind word to me. And every time my heart falls deeper in love with you, I search for a sign that you might return even an inkling of that love. That's what makes you so lethal and me so weak."

"Delaney." He tried to counter.

"There's more. Let me finish. There's a part of me that wants to know the good, the bad, the ugly about Donovan Taylor, but like I told you earlier, you have an enormous amount of power over my heart and I don't like it. I think I've decided during my walk that I am satisfied knowing you loved me at one point in my life. If it all ended tonight, my curiosity would be filled and I'd eventually find a man who loved me just as much as I loved him." All these words were spoken with confidence but why was my heart so sad?

"Delaney Reid," he said sweetly. "If you like, I will give you the entire trilogy on Donovan Taylor, the unabridged version. And you are not the only one hurting right now. I hurt knowing I've done this to you, and I fear wondering if you'll ever forgive me for all that's happened in the past few months. I am not satisfied with you knowing that I loved you for this brief a period, and we will not end tonight, nor any other night till one of us dies. As I uncover daily the endless layers of your love, I can confidently say, I will return these layers—in multifold—if you'll give me a chance. This probably won't be the first time I'll disappoint you and break your heart. I haven't even begun the unabridged version of my life. But bear with me and continue to love me?"

"How do you do this to me all the time?" I laughed and teared at the same time. "You have this freakin' gift, or curse, of making me happy and sad all within the same sentence. Who the hell taught you to play with people's emotions?" I tried to pull away as he put his arms tightly around me. "Don't spill wine on my only dress, Donovan Taylor," I warned in jest and broke our mood.

"Let's go to bed, Princess. Each and every day with you is a blessedly long one."

"Was that a backhanded compliment?"

"You take it any which way you like."

I woke up to the smell of a wonderfully strong cup of coffee and the buttery scent of French croissants. Donovan held onto a large tray of food while I sat up and readjusted my position in bed.

"My gosh, that smells delicious," I declared then took a sip of the strong coffee. "Oh, that's good."

"Wait till you try the jam and butter on these croissants." He tore off a piece, lathered it with both accoutrements, and fed it to me.

"That's heavenly, Donovan."

"That smile on your face is heavenly," he commented and then made up another bite for me and fed me again.

"You shouldn't spoil me like this. I may decide this is the life I want, and you'll be stuck."

"I'd gladly feed you every morning if this is what you ask of me."

"Sure, Donovan Taylor." I shook my head to show him I didn't believe him. "You say that now, but once I've decided to give in to your charms, I wonder if you'll be singing the same tune?"

"Why, Princess, I have no idea what you are talking about. You are already under my spell as I am under yours."

"Smooth, Mr. Taylor. Now stop with the yapping and feed me another bite," I demanded with a smile.

We left the château earlier than we wanted because Donovan couldn't rearrange his morning meeting. Without saying good-bye to anyone, we got into Paris in plenty of time for us to shower (separately) and change for a new day. Donovan dropped me off at the convention center before going to work, so I could give Bee a much-needed hand for her show.

"I'm going to do my best to make it to the show, but it all depends upon this lunch client." Donovan apologized.

"Donovan, you are not here on vacation. Put work first. It would be great if you could support Bee, but your parents and my parents will be here, and hopefully your siblings and their spouses will make it down in time to watch Bee's creations."

"Beautiful, it's you I want to see strut down that catwalk, not the clothes. I'll do my best to be here."

"All right." I smiled in his arms. "Have a productive day."

"Are we good?" His voice softened and his confidence weakened.

"We are good till the next round of drama," I gave him a lighthearted answer.

He wasn't satisfied. "When can we sit down and lay everything out on the table?"

"I've no idea. We are all supposed to have a family dinner at some bistro in Saint-Germaine-des-Prés after the show."

"Damn. I love my family and yours, but they're seriously cutting into our personal life."

"We will talk soon. But for now, all is right in my world—though it shouldn't be."

"I love you Delaney Reid," he said in all seriousness.

"Donovan Taylor. I have waited my entire life to hear those five words from you and to be able to tell you that I love you too."

He showed his cocky, self-assured and knowing grins, again. "One last kiss," he barely finished those words before capturing my mouth in his. Every one of these kisses stirred my senses and I honestly couldn't wait till we could get all our issues cleared—Kate, Jane, Michael—so we could move on in the physical sense of our relationship. I knew Donovan was itching to get there. Every night I could feel Donovan's hands roaming my body when he thought I was asleep.

It wasn't like he was molesting me in my sleep, but he roamed as much as was "proper" for him to touch a girl who technically had a boyfriend. Featherlike kisses generally came hand in hand with the roaming hands and there were times when I wanted to pop my eyes open and have him finish the job because I felt like I was on fire. Even if it killed us tonight, we'd get everything out in the open. I'd do my darnedest to let go of his past, and we'd move on to loving each other completely.

"Break it up! You're in public." Bee slapped her nephew on the shoulder and surprised the both of us. "Have you no decency even on the streets of Paris?" she asked with a quirky smile. "Let me take my future niece in with me, lest you molest her in public."

"Auntie..." Donovan pretended to whine. "We were just getting started." He grinned and looked so beautiful.

"Have you two not been spending every night together since you reunited? Must you do this in public and make us single people mourn being single and celibate?" she kidded.

"You mean you've haven't been molested by a Reid, lately?" I posed this question as a dare.

Bee laughed loudly, and I mean—LOUDLY—and walked away.

I asked Donovan, "What do you think that laugh means?"

He shrugged his shoulders. "Don't know, don't want to know! Nick is in London right now, so who knows if those two have made time for each other?"

"Have they been together all this time?"

"I don't think so, but Bee hasn't been forthcoming with her information."

"You better get going. I don't want a call from Grandfather telling me I'm a bad influence on you."

"Good-bye, Princess. I love you."

"Good-bye, my prince. I love you too."

"You two seriously depress the entire single population."

"Why?"

"Laney Reid, you really don't know?" she asked with aplomb.

"Bee Taylor, I really don't know!" I answered with equal aplomb.

"You're both gorgeous. Donovan is at the top of the food chain in looks, profession, and charm. You are equally gorgeous, a genuinely nice person, and brains to match that stunning body of yours. And now, you're both off the market. I think I hear the cries of every single man and woman mourning your loss."

"Stop, Bee. You are a hoot. When this is all over, I want info about you and Nick."

"Yeah, don't hold your breath on that one."

"You know he's in London?" I stared at her to get some sort of reaction. She was like a robot where her emotions for Nick were concerned. "I assume you two have met already, or will be meeting once this show is done?"

"You know what they say about the word assume?" I shook my head no. "It makes an 'ass' out of 'u' and 'me.'"

"Ha, ha," I answered sarcastically and asked Bee if I could borrow her phone. "Hello, Cousin!" I smiled devilishly and stepped away from Bee who was about to maim me with her long, sharp scissors.

"Laney?" Nick asked. "Isn't this Bee's phone?"

"It is. Whatcha' up to today?"

"I'm helping with these critters while Emily and Jake get settled."

"Who's there with you?"

"Everyone—your brother, Max, Jane, Garret, and your wanna-be boyfriend, Josh."

"Can you get away today?"

"NO!" I heard Bee crying from the other end of the room. Obviously, she was listening to our conversation.

"Well, you see, I'm in this fashion show in Paris, thanks to a designer friend of mine. You might know her? Donovan's aunt, Bee Taylor?" The pretense of coyness was causing a chuckle on the other end of the phone line. "Do you know her?"

"I might..."

"It only takes two hours on the Eurotunnel to come into Paris, and I was hoping you might want to come watch me on the catwalk."

"So then, should I bring the whole family?"

"Oh, no, Nick!" I kept up the pretense. "Then who would help Jake and Emily? Since I got you on the phone, why don't you come and represent the Reid family?"

"And what's in it for me if I spend all that money and time to get into Paris?"

"You'll see me, Donovan, and both our families. It'll be fun! Say you'll come," I begged.

"Will there be a place to stay if I come into Paris?"

"Grandfather's apartment is completely full with the six of us staying there, but Bee told me you could stay with her." I saw Bee crossing her arms and making a huge X to signal a big, fat "NO!" but I turned my body and pretended I didn't see her.

"Really?" He knew I was lying, but kept up the farce. "I'll think about it, Laney. Things going well with you and Casanova?" he chuckled.

"It depends on the day and time you ask. About twelve hours ago, I thought I might castrate Casanova, but right now, things are beautiful. I'll tell you all about it when I see you soon in Paris?"

"See you soon in Paris," he confirmed.

Doing my catwalk swagger all the way back to Bee, I gave her the Cheshire cat smile.

"You are so busted, Laney Taylor. I'm going to have you model some lingerie now in retaliation."

That was a horrifying thought! "You are NOT! My parents will be here, Donovan's parents will be here. There is no way I am modeling lingerie!"

"I think you are," she said confidently, but quickly added, "Come on, Laney. It looks so good on you. My lingerie is meant for women with tits and ass—and not these skinny-ass models who look like boys."

"I resent the tits and ass statement, but in any case, no."

"Yes!" she argued, so I used Bee's phone again and got Donovan on speakerphone.

"Hello?"

"Hi Donovan. Am I bothering you?"

"You can bother me anytime, Princess. What's up?"

"You auntie here is threatening to make me wear lingerie in the fashion show. I keep telling her that I won't wear it, but she won't listen to me."

"Hell NO! Bee! Delaney is not showing her body to anyone."

"She'll be a knockout, Donovan. The audience will love it."

"I do not want men ogling her and Ma and Pa will be there as well as her parents, Kelley, Becky and their husbands."

"Come on. They're all family and the men in the audience are mostly gay. If they ogle anyone, it won't be your princess."

"Bee." Donovan used his most convincing lawyer voice. "Delaney has never shown her body to any other man. I plan to keep it that way."

"Seriously?" she asked me and I nodded yes. "You're shitting me." She didn't believe me.

"Seriously!" Donovan confirmed. "I need to get back to my meeting. I'll see you both in a few hours. Bye Bee, and love you, Princess."

Bee rolled her eyes and hung up the phone before I could respond. "Oh, all right!" She conceded. "But I do have one more dress I want you to wear tonight. This is the outfit that will close the show."

"What dress is that? I didn't know you had another one."

"I didn't think I'd get it done in time, but it's finished and no one has seen it but me. You'll see it right before you go on."

"Ooh, sounds exciting. I can't wait."

The rest of the morning was a blur. Mom and Ma came early to help Bee with what they could and of course, Mom ended up helping the set designer more than Bee. Ma was quite handy with the sewing machine, so she helped Bee make last minute adjustments. I...really could do nothing but simple errands for Bee. I picked up lunches, went on latte runs, and soon sat to hair and makeup before it was time to put on the gown.

Bee's collection would start from casual day dresses, to bathing suits, to evening wear to lingerie to her final surprise, whatever that might be. Originally, I was to model a casual dress, then an evening dress, but Bee decided to have me come out only in the end.

"Hi, Daddy. Hi, Pa." I greeted the two men who comically sat in the front row of this show.

"Hello, Sweetheart." My father greeted me with a hug and a kiss. Pa greeted me with the same affection. "You ready for your fifteen minutes of fame?"

"I am praying that I will not make a fool of myself and of Bee's clothes. I have this fear I'll fall flat on my face."

"You'll be beautiful, no matter what happens," Pa encouraged.

"I've got to get back, but I wanted to pop out and say hello to the both of you." I patted both men on their shoulders and walked away.

"How are you going to let her go, Henry? She's a doll," I heard Pa say.

"I was hoping I'd have her with me for at least another five years..." Dad sounded sad making this statement. I knew regardless of when I married, our families would always live close to one another and practically in each other's pockets.

The show began and Bee's early creations were well received. I peeked out into the audience and saw everyone, Nick included, but no Donovan. It was unreasonable for me to want him there, late afternoon on a workday. Nevertheless, I was bummed.

"Laney," Bee called. "There's a change in the line-up. You're going on at the very end, one gown only."

"So no red dress?"

"No red dress. Go back to hair and makeup. They need to change a few things."

I did as I was told and the hairstylist put my hair up in a glamorous, messy-with-intent chignon. The front of my hair was slicked to the side with tons of gel and hairspray and the back of my head was a blob of hair all rolled into one. It looked messy and yet so cool. My natural curls rioted in just the right places and though the front looked like it was styled, the back looked as casual as if I was talented enough to whip it up. Once the makeup gal made me look like more of a model than a wanna-be model, I was ready to put on the last dress.

"Um...why are you blindfolding me?" I asked the gal who was supposed to help me get dressed.

"Because you're not to see the dress till the very last moment. Bee needs that element of surprise from you. She says your expressive face will put everyone in the right mood for this last number."

"OK..." Who was I to question? I did as instructed.

Embarrassingly, the gal undressed me completely—thank God we were in a private dressing room—and put one of Bee's lingerie pieces on me. Then she had me step into a dress that was strapless, tight on the body, and very sheer. I could feel something similar to sequins, thought it wasn't sequins, circling the dress every few inches, from top to bottom. It was a long dress and by the way air blew into parts of my legs that weren't covered by the lingerie, I knew Donovan would not be happy with this dress.

"Um, I have to ask, is this dress completely see-through?"

"It is, but you're covered in all the right areas," she said while snapping a belt on the dress.

"My parents and possible future in-laws are in the front row. Will I mortify my parents and horrify the in-laws?"

The gal chuckled. "Not at all. You look positively stunning. You'll put everyone in awe. I promise."

"I don't care about putting anyone in awe, I just don't want parts of my body playing peek-a-boo in this dress."

"I promise, you won't be embarrassed to be seen in it. Can you stay here a second? There's one other part to this dress I need to get."

"Sure," I answered casually, wondering where she thought I would go since I was blindfolded.

She came back in a flash and snapped a big piece of fabric all around my hips. Once again, feeling the fabric for information, I could tell it was layers of tulle wrapped around my bodice. The part right on top of my hips felt like tulle had been folded over and given a wavy, multi-layered look. Who knew if I was correct? For all I knew, I could be walking out there with only a slip over the lingerie. I trusted Bee would not embarrass me or Donovan in this way.

"It's done and it's the most beautiful piece tonight, by far!" The gal exclaimed. She held my hand and carefully took me to an area where I was to sit and wait for my next instruction. But before she left, she placed what I was sure was a tiara on my head. Now I was truly confused as to what I looked like.

Not long after, the music began and if memory served me correctly, it was the tune that Cinderella sang before the morning gong forced her out of bed to do the work of those nasty stepsisters and mother. I started softly humming to *"a dream is a wish your heart makes..."* when I felt a door of some kind open, a hand gently grabbing mine, and the audience gasping.

"I believe this is our ball?" An amused and familiar voice called out as he undid my blindfold.

Donovan! My Prince!

Taking in my surroundings, I noticed I was in a "makeshift" carriage. It was technically a picture of a carriage drawn on a large wooden board. The door was partially cut out so it could be opened from the outside and my seat was just a large chair on the other side of the board.

While I was still seated in my "carriage," Donovan kneeled and put the "missing" Swarovski glass slipper on my left foot. In all the craziness of the blindfolding, I didn't even realize I had walked barefoot and while the tiara was being placed, another person had put only one shoe on me. Donovan...glass slipper...Cinderella music...my Prince...all of this was over-the-moon, around-the-galaxy, to-infinity-and-beyond, romantic. We could hear the women sigh.

As the music changed to *Bibbibi-Bobbidi-Boo*, Donovan helped me out of my seat, lifted my hand and placed a gentlemanly kiss on it. I was in such a daze, it took me this long to realize Donovan was in a suit that looked like Cinderella's prince at their wedding. He had on a long dark yellow half coat with blue emblems and tassels as accents, and red pants with double dark yellow stripes on the side.

"Never in my wildest dreams would I have believed that primary colors could look so good on a man."

He gave me an adorable grin and whispered, "Enjoy it now, my princess. You'll never see these colors on me again."

I giggled and as soon as the song changed to, *So This Is Love*, the song Cinderella and her prince danced to at the ball, Donovan brought me close to him, and we danced for the audience.

"Was this part of the script?"

"No. I thought I'd make my aunt happy since she did such a stunning job on this wedding dress."

Wedding dress? I stopped and took a good look at myself. Oh. My. God! It was a very fancy party dress by itself, but with the addition of the wedding dress-like tulle around my hips, and the tiara that also had a short veil flung to the back, I was in a wedding gown.

The music changed again and once Wagner's wedding march played, Donovan placed my hand on his arm and now we were the bride and groom walking down the aisle.

"This is the path we are meant to take, Princess. No matter the obstacles that come our way, we will end up in each other's arms, pledging our love for one another in front of family and friends. Just think of tonight as practice."

I focused very hard on not crying happy tears.

I only realized we were at the end of the catwalk when everyone stood to give us—or better stated, Bee's creations—a standing ovation. Donovan took this opportunity to take his wedding kiss and kissed me in front of the entire audience. Various hoots, hollers, and whistles ensued as Donovan's kiss went longer than was expected or appropriate.

"I love you," he professed when we came up for air and kissed me one more time. This kiss was only half the length of the first one.

"That was the most romantic show we've ever had!" Donovan and I got congratulated by throngs of people as we headed to the dressing room to get changed. *"You were beautiful together." "Would you consider modeling for us?" "Bee, your creations are genius."* Those were just some of the repetitive questions and comments from other designers and staff. Donovan and I were thrilled for Bee. She deserved every adulation as her edgy creations wowed everyone in the house.

"Can we change now, Bee?" I asked.

"Sure. Take that room over there." She pointed. "And Donovan, your suit should be in there for you to change back into."

We got into the dressing room and Donovan took his sweet time unzipping me from this dress.

"Donovan." I tried to muster some sense of exasperation. "Everyone is waiting for us. Your sister, Becky, will get all pissy with me again if

I keep her from dinner. She already told me several times that she was hungry."

"I don't care." Donovan said between kisses. "Do we need to wait till our wedding night to make love? Because if that's the case, we're going down to city hall right now and getting hitched." He couldn't stop touching me.

"Um...we don't have to wait till our wedding night, but I think we should wait till I can break up with the man who's technically still my boyfriend, and figure out if I want to get into a relationship with the man who's fondling me right now." The giggling wouldn't abate no matter the seriousness of this situation.

"I'm on such a high right now, I may just take you back to the empty apartment and show you the proper ways of fondling a princess."

"How about you show me some other time? I promise to wear the lingerie, tiara, and high heels when that happens, but for now, we need to get to dinner."

"You're not helping, Princess. You don't understand how aroused I am by the sight of you in the lingerie under that dress."

I laughed before saying, "I don't know if that Hot-dog-on-a-Stick suit of yours does it for me, but let's talk about it tonight. We need to get going." I literally pushed Donovan away, stepped out of the dress and quickly put on another dress over the lingerie.

"You going to keep that on tonight?" he groaned.

I nodded yes. "Bee said I could take it with me."

"And how am I supposed to concentrate on dinner knowing you have on a garter belt that's holding up your equally sexy stockings?"

"Change!" I commanded and left the dressing room.

"You're out of the room," Nick gave me a rascally smile.

"Of course I'm out of the room. What kind of question is that, Nicholas Reid?"

"Just saying..." He grinned his sweet know-it-all grin. "You and Donovan looked good out there."

"Thank you, and I'm glad to see you here to support Bee."

"Bee? I thought I was here to support you?" he kidded.

"You coming to dinner?" Donovan came out quicker than I thought and joined our conversation.

He gave a lazy shrug of the shoulders. "I'll see what your aunt needs me to do around here. If we're done at a decent hour, we'll join you. But," he added, "I wouldn't expect us."

"Any chance we'll see you tomorrow?"

"Doubt it. I was told to get back first thing in the morning because you all are going somewhere?"

"Where?" I asked Donovan.

"Surprise." He pulled me along after patting Nick on the back. "See you again soon."

"Yeah. See ya." He answered in his lazy way, again.

"We can't leave without saying good-bye to Bee." I complained.

"She's busy. Let's get this dinner over with so I can get the lingerie, tiara and high-heeled princess tonight."

Just to get him riled up even more, I stopped and gave him a full, open-mouthed kiss before we got outside. "I can't wait to show you the naughty princess."

"Hell," he said under his breath, "you are not helping my cause. You better walk in front of me at all times or everyone in that restaurant will know what I'm thinking right now."

Purposefully swaying my hips like a cat-walker, I exaggerated my movements and got in the car. Donovan's groan became more pronounced.

The eating was in full swing when we entered the restaurant. Our family clapped for us and had us sit to a toast.

"To my beautiful daughter and her equally handsome soon-to-be husband. We can't wait to join our two families!"

"Cheers!" Everyone toasted.

"I guess it's a foregone conclusion in everyone's minds? I don't have a say in this matter?"

"If I remember correctly, *you* picked *me*. *I* don't have a say in this matter," he whispered and placed his hand on my thigh.

"My father is sitting next to me and your father is next to you. Please don't embarrass me," I pleaded.

"All right, Princess." He grinned and kissed me one last time to tide him over.

"Laney, you looked absolutely stunning tonight."

"Thank you, Kelley. It wasn't me so much as it was Bee's creation. She's so talented."

"When we were in middle school," Becky giggled, "she used to sew all of our Halloween costumes. We were too old for the store bought ones, but not creative enough to come up with our own costumes so we used to beg Bee to design something for us."

"Remember that year when Donovan was the hotdog and bun and we were all the condiments?" Kelley laughed.

"What about the year when he was John Bosley and you were Charlie's Angels?" Ma started cracking up. "Poor Rachel. She was too young to be an Angel so she was dressed as the speaker box that Charlie spoke into."

Pa said, "My favorite year was when all the kids dressed up as the Village People."

"Didn't they all have their shirts off or unbuttoned?" I inquired.

Donovan chuckled. "All the girls wore a beige shirt underneath the outfit. It was quite decent."

"Which one were you? I assume you went bare-chested?"

"That was the plan until Ma saw me and told me to put on the same shirt as all the girls. I was mortified wearing a girly shirt under my Village People costume."

"I'm sure you were adorable, regardless." I whispered.

"What's on the agenda for tomorrow?" Noah asked everyone. "I have never been to Paris before so Kelley and I would like to do the usual tourist jaunts—Eiffel Tower, Louvre, Musee D'Orsay, you know..."

"I have to work tomorrow so maybe you can take Becky with you?" Al asked.

"Sorry, but we are out of here first thing tomorrow morning." Donovan announced. "I know you wanted to spend time with your daughter, but..." He wouldn't continue and we were all curious.

"I got the message yesterday." My dad acquiesced. "We'll see the both of you back in London."

"Where are we going?" I asked.

"It's a surprise, Princess. Just know, it's something over-the-top spectacular."

"Come on, Donovan. Let us know, too," Becky begged.

"The Chief will tell you when we are out of here." He pulled me up from the table. "And we are out of here right now. Are you four staying with us at Roland's?"

"Hell yes, we are!" Dad exclaimed. "I noticed one of the rooms is completely empty and one room had both your bags. What is that all about?"

"Dad..." I groaned.

"We are out of here," Donovan repeated and pulled me from the restaurant. "I need you alone in that apartment before the senior citizens put the kibosh on our evening plans."

"And what's on the agenda for tonight?"

"Words can't do justice to what I want to do to you. I'll show you."

"That sounds scary."

"Nothing scary, my princess. Just think love and pleasure."

"Donovan." I pulled back from his amorous quest. "You know I'm not experienced at all. I have no idea what to do..." At this very moment, I had never felt so jejune, so unsophisticated, so primeval in matters of life and love. Why, I was almost embarrassed for myself.

"Princess, you don't need to do anything tonight, but feel and enjoy. I want to love you tonight."

Nervous, freaking-out, considering moving into my parents' room—these were some of the thoughts going through my head during our ride to my grandfather's apartment. Donovan went on about something I didn't care to listen to and I was in such a daze, the car had stopped and I still sat, looking out the window.

"Princess. We're here."

"Oh!"

We walked hand-in-hand and he led me straight to "our" bedroom. He began kissing me while we were still standing and I must not have participated because Donovan stopped mid-kiss and chuckled.

"I know I said I'd do all the work, tonight, but I can't kiss myself."

"What?"

"Come here," he looked amused and had us lay in bed. "Talk to me. What makes you so nervous?"

"I told you. I've never done any of this before. How do I know if I'm doing this correctly and if I'm pleasing you at all?" *GAAWWDD!* I just wanted to go lock myself in a room and sit in the dark for the next few millennia. How stupid did I sound just now?

Donovan tried hard not to laugh. "All right. Let's start with what you like and don't like."

"I don't know what the hell I like and don't like. And I have such jumbled up information on sex and whether or not I'll like it, or whether or not I'll have an orgasm—and if it even feels good." OH MY GOD! I couldn't believe I'd just spilled all that info to Donovan. I groaned, put my head on my perched-up knee, and put my hand on my head. Had we not been sitting on the comforter, I would have pulled the comforter over my entire body to hide my shame. "I can't believe I just told you all that. I feel like a teenager having the sex talk again with my parents for the twelfth time."

Now, Donovan tried his damnedest not to laugh at me. "I promise you, sex is good, you'll like it, and yes, you will have an orgasm." He kind of snorted while talking, trying to hold back his laughter. "And as for an orgasm feeling good...it feels...how can I explain the...wait a minute! What do you mean what does an orgasm feel like? You've never felt one?"

Now I just got pissed. "How many times do I have to tell you, I've *never* been with any other man?"

"But, but..." he sputtered. "You've never had one, solo?" I shook my head no. "How can that be? Is that normal for girls to not..." he left it at that.

This was a secret I thought I'd take to my grave, but in light of this situation, I had to spill the beans—apologies to my brother in advance! "When Doug was in his early teens, I heard my parents tell him that if he kept touching himself, he'd go blind. And I didn't want to go blind, so I never started."

That's when Donovan lost it. He howled so loudly and so violently, I thought he might choke on his own saliva. It took him a good long while to calm himself down, and once the tears were finally gone, he took out his phone and called someone. Perhaps he was calling Jake to verify this blindness theory?

"Hello, future brother-in-law!" Donovan smirked.

"Noooooo!" I yelled and tried to grab the phone.

"I heard your vision isn't too good."

"Stop it!" I slapped his arm and tried to grab the phone, again.

"I got an interesting tidbit about you possibly going blind when you were a teenager, but your parents saving you just in the nick of time."

I could hear my brother yelling, "*LANEY!*" on the other end.

"...no, you may not speak with my bride-to-be, and you definitely may not yell at her..."

I couldn't have been more mortified than I was right now. I tried to get up and move to the other bedroom, but Donovan quickly said his good-byes to my brother and stopped me.

"That was *not* cool. It was not information for you to use against me, and it was not meant to be a tool to embarrass me and my brother."

"Princess, I wasn't trying to embarrass you, and I wasn't using this information against you. Your brother and I were having a good laugh over his teenage years."

"I think you were the only one laughing."

"Come here!" His command was quite...demanding and startling enough for me to submissively obey.

No sooner had he barked out that order, than we were in bed fully engaged. To my chagrin, Donovan undid my garter belts instantly and both hands began to roam. It wasn't because he was going so fast. I was saddened that he could so quickly and expertly undo the snaps on the garter belt that usually took me a while to accomplish with both hands, and with my eyes open. When would this shadow disappear from our relationship? As much as I didn't want to, I couldn't stop picturing him and Kate together.

"What's the matter?" He stopped and stared at me.

"Nothing," I whispered.

He thought only briefly about it, then placed both hands on my breasts and practically revered them. "God, I've been dying to touch these since I saw you at Jake and Emily's wedding in that low-cut dress." It seemed like all he was doing was massaging and squeezing my breasts, but it felt so damn good. I didn't realize I could get so much pleasure from two parts of my body I always found annoying when I played sports. "Then when I saw you in that Chanel outfit with the thigh high boots, I thought I might explode from desire." He said this while distending my nipple with his thumb and forefinger. Truly, I thought *I* might explode right here and now from desire. "But tonight, I'm going to give you your first orgasm."

As soon as he said this, I knew I was finally going to have sex. This would be it! I would get to experience what I'd only heard about from all my girlfriends. I didn't understand why Donovan was going down the bed, but I was mentally preparing myself for the discomfort I'd heard about from some girls, the outright pain other girls spoke of, or the intense pleasure most girls liked to brag about. What I didn't expect was for Donovan to put his tongue on me. That feeling of his warm tongue on my most intimate part almost made *me* go half-blind.

It was as all that the romance authors explained. *"The leg stiffening," "teeth clenching," "heart beat racing," "skin heating," "toe-curling,"* sense of ecstasy building up to what I presumed would be the eventual climax. But, as I looked down and saw the top of Donovan's wavy head, to me it was so much more. A cynic could say it was oral sex. Men and women perform it, it's a part of sexual congress, it's mutually satisfying. And though with every *"tip of his tongue swirling about the sensitive bud,"* or *"lapping delicately into the heated channel,"* I thought I might die from either the absolute pleasure, or the utter embarrassment of being spread wide for the first time by the man I'd dreamed of for so long; the sheer intimacy of our closeness made me fall in love with him all over again. I could only have this done to me by, and reciprocate to, a man I loved, respected, and saw my happily ever after with. Without a doubt, I would give everything of myself to this man—that's how much I loved him.

"Princess," I heard soft breathing in my ear. "Princess," he said one more time but this time with a chuckle.

Huh? I got up from bed completely in a daze. "What time is it?"

"7:00a.m."

"Why am I sleeping?"

Donovan began to laugh. "Should I be insulted that you fell asleep before we were completely finished, or cocky that it was so good I knocked you into oblivion for the next ten hours?"

I thought about what he'd said. We went to the fashion show. Donovan showed up unexpectedly as my prince. We had dinner with our families. We came back to an empty apartment. "Shit!" I popped out of bed and Donovan laughed even harder. "What the hell happened to me?"

"You had the full French experience in Paris." I gave him a what-the-hell look. "*La petite mort* or the little death."

"Yes, I speak enough French to know what that means. But what the hell are you talking about?"

"It's a French idiom or *euphemism* for orgasm." He then searched something up on his phone. "Wikipedia says, 'it can refer to the spiritual release that comes with orgasm or to a short period of transcendence as a result of the life force which is caused by the release of oxytocin in the brain after the occurrence of orgasm.' Or in laymen's terms, you had your first orgasm and you passed out—immediately!" The smartass recited to me.

I threw a pillow at him. "Are you making fun of me?" Turning fire engine red; I was mortified!

"If the orgasm fits," he laughed and walked in the shower.

GAAWWDD!! How could I be so unsophisticated as to have a man goes down on me and not fully remember what happened? Obviously it was good, or else I wouldn't have passed out, but how could I have gone from being on the brink of dying from pleasure, to comatose? I would not, could not, ever live this down. I didn't know whether to cry from the embarrassment, or laugh from the ridiculousness of it all.

I couldn't face Donovan right now. I hurriedly washed my makeup-ridden face, got dressed, figuring I could shower after Donovan left for work, and started walking out to...SHIT! What if my parents and his parents knew what happened? Did I make a lot of noise last night? I didn't think I did, but...SHIT, SHIT, SHIT! What the hell was wrong with me? I was standing in the hallway wondering which was the lesser of two evils. Should I go back in the room with Donovan and live the ridicule, or sit in the breakfast room with two sets of parents and live the shame? Damn!

With Donovan, I knew there was a one hundred percent chance he would tease me. But with the parents, there was a fifty-fifty chance they had no idea what occurred last night. Going into the breakfast room was the better option.

"Good morning!" I cheerfully exclaimed.

"Good morning, Laney, Baby, Sweetheart," were all the greetings I got in return. Covertly looking at each parent, each acted absolutely normal. No one seemed the wiser. I broke into a relieved smile and started talking to them about their day.

"What will you do today?"

Mom said, "We are going antique shopping. Emily mentioned a wonderful antique area she and Jake visited when they were here a few years ago."

"That sounds like fun," I agreed. "What about you, Ma?"

"We are going with the girls and Noah to tour Paris. I wish you and Donny could join us but your dad told us what you are doing today and it sounds heavenly. I wish we could join *you*, instead."

"What are we doing, Ma?"

"I can't tell," she sounded absolutely and artificially flabbergasted.

OK...if she wasn't going to tell me, I'd ask the weaker link in this chain. "Pa?" I placed my head on his shoulder, and he returned my affection. "What does Donovan have planned for me?"

Pa hesitated only briefly, then said, "You, Donny, your cousins, and..."

"PA!" Donovan the party-pooper came in the breakfast room looking delicious, but intent on keeping this a secret from me. "What are you doing? This is supposed to be a surprise!"

"I can't help it. She's so adorable." Pa kissed me on the head and said, "You almost got me into a shitload of trouble with my son, young lady."

"Sorry, Pa." I gave him a peck on the cheek as an apology.

We were having a sweet breakfast, the six of us, when the buzzer signaled that someone was at the apartment at this early hour. Dad got up and buzzed the person into the building without asking who it was, and we went back to our conversation until Dad got up again and opened the door for this very early visitor.

"Donovan," Dad called. "You have a visitor."

In to the breakfast room walked a stunning Kate Beauvais, all confident in her stride and attitude. To say I was shocked to see her, and to see her at my grandfather's apartment, would be the understatement of the year.

"Kate," was Donovan's response.

"What the hell," was Ma's response.

"Jamie," was Pa's response.

"What is she doing here?" was Mom's question.

Except for Donovan, everyone spoke under their breaths, but it was still loud enough for all to hear.

"Hello," Kate still oozed confidence even though the five of us gave her a what-the-hell-are-you-doing-here, look. "Donovan," she flat out ignored our stares and turned to him. "I'm sorry to intrude, but your phone was off. I've been trying to get a hold of you."

"I guess I forgot to turn it back on after the fashion show. What's up?"

"Monsieur Montaigne is not happy about what we wrote up in the proposal."

"I thought he agreed to everything."

"He did, but now he wants everything changed. You need to come into the office right now and help me resolve this issue."

"Shit. Delaney and I are off to Florence this morning."

"Donovan." The tone in which she used to call my...boyfriend..? fiancé..? future husband..? pissed me off. It was too intimate of a tone, a pleading tone, a this-is-how-I-used-to-get-all-I-wanted-from-you-in-the-past, tone.

"OK," he agreed. "But I need to be done by noon. Let me get ready and I'll head into the office with you," he looked at me warily while talking to Kate. "Do you want a cup of coffee while you wait?" He tried to get her a cup, but she walked to the cupboard like she'd done this a million times before and picked-up the finest piece of china in the house.

Seeing her know her way around the sideboard of my grandfather's house completely deflated whatever high or embarrassment I was on from last night. A large crack in our intimate bond appeared as soon as Kate paraded her knowledge of her ex-lover in front of his parents, my parents, and me. At this very moment, I felt like a teenager again, seeing her in all her glory at one of our family functions. I felt inadequate, unpolished, and juvenile.

"Will you excuse us?" Donovan didn't wait for an answer as he held my hand and led us into our room. "You don't mind leaving a little later?" I didn't know how to react. Rather than explaining why Kate was here, or how she knew where to come, or how the fuck she knew where the china was in this house, Donovan wondered if I cared that our flight would be delayed. What the fuck. "I'll take all my stuff with me just in case I end up meeting you at the airport. I won't know how bad the situation is till I get to the office."

"Fine," I answered.

"What?" he had the stupidity to ask. I shook my head and kept my mouth shut. If he found nothing wrong with this situation, I wouldn't explain it to him. "It's nothing but work. You knew she worked for your grandfather."

"Yep. I knew." I had no freaking clue she was here in France, and maybe she was in Amsterdam, too, and I had no fucking clue. I just went around passing out after an orgasm, dead to the world, dead to any goings-on about Donovan and Kate. Yep. Stupid me!

"I'll see you in a couple of hours, all right?" He kissed my lips but got no response. "I'm a little unsure why you're so upset, but I have to go if we want to get to Florence in time. I'll answer any and all questions on the plane."

"Sure."

I let him go with her and didn't look back, didn't flinch, and didn't act perturbed. Our brilliant parents didn't ask any questions, and they got ready for their day. After a brief but loving good-bye from each set, I was alone.

To be honest, alone was not a good place to be right now. It gave me too much room to think, too much time to jump to conclusions, too much anxiety to enjoy our upcoming trip to Florence. I packed my travel bag and walked the neighborhood to clear my mind. I may not have showed it on the outside, but on the inside, I was an absolute mess.

I thought back to Grandfather's apartment in Amsterdam and wondered if they had shared the same bed over there as Donovan and I had.

Then the château in Vernon came to mind, and I couldn't help but think that he had recycled the same places but with a different woman. Seeing how familiar she was with this apartment, it killed me to know that I would always come after her. And though it was me sleeping in Donovan's bed right now, I could have been any other woman.

Feeling restless and sad, I went back to the apartment not knowing what I needed to do next. I got in just as the phone rang.

"Hello?"

"Where've you been? I've been calling you the last half hour."

"I'm here now. What is it?"

"I'm going to have to meet you at the airport. Can you take a cab or do you want me to send you a car to take you to the airport?"

"I'll just take the metro to the airport. Should I just wait for you at the gate?"

"Yeah. I'll get there soon. I've got to go." He hung up without even a good-bye.

Looking at my ticket, I had a couple hours to get to the airport, and as lost as I felt without Donovan, I decided to get to my destination and wait. When we sat on the airplane, I'd tell him how I felt and hear his explanation, rather than creating drama in my head.

I sat at the gate listening to the attendant call us onto the airplane. Donovan was not at the gate by the second call, so after cursing him for throwing my phone in the canal, I went to the payphone and called his cell phone. All three times calls went straight to voicemail. If I'd known the office number, I would've called there as well, and though I could have called Grandfather and gotten all the information, I decided I didn't want to go through the trouble. Without him, I got on the plane with no idea where I was to go in Florence.

The first thing I did when I landed was to get myself a cell phone. I called Grandfather to inquire about his possible home in Florence, and he was very surprised to hear from me.

"Laney? What's going on? Why are you calling me and asking me for directions to my villa? Where's Donovan?"

"I think Donovan is still in Paris, Grandfather. I don't know." I answered.

"What do you mean you don't know?" Grandfather was not only worried about me, but he was also getting angry.

"It's a bit of a long story, Grandfather, but I'm here and I'd like to get somewhere familiar."

"I'll text you the address. I believe Jake and Emily have either just arrived or they will be there soon."

It was such a relief knowing that Jake and Emily were going to be at my grandfather's. I needed some advice and I needed a friendly face.

"Laney!" Emily hugged me dearly. "I'm so happy to see you." And she genuinely was happy to see me. "Where's Donovan?" She looked about trying to figure out this change of events.

"Hey Laney. You had a nice flight?"

"Yeah."

"Where's your other half?"

I shrugged my shoulders.

They both wanted and required an answer, but Jake got a phone call and a baby, whom I assumed was JR, started crying, so I was left to my own devices while they went to take care of their own matters.

I assumed I was staying here tonight, so I took up residence in one of the rooms and took out the clothes from my suitcase. Not having done laundry for almost a week, I searched out a washer and dryer in the villa and put in all my clothes. Then I searched through the refrigerator, fixed myself a very late lunch, and did what I should have done yesterday.

"Hello?"

"Hi Michael."

"God! Duchess! You're calling me back. I'm sorry I was such an asshole to you the other day. I was so afraid you wouldn't ever call back." Why couldn't I just love this uncomplicated man? A man who loved me with no strings attached, a man who was willing to give up his entire future for me? Why did I have to reach for the unattainable and so very complicated?

"I don't blame you Michael for getting upset with me. What I'm doing right now with you and Donovan is inexcusable. And I'm truly sorry for hurting you. That was never my intention."

"Where are you now? Are you still in Paris? Can I come to see you there? I'm back in London. I can come to you within a few hours."

"I'm with Jake and Emily in Florence."

"Florence? You sure are covering a lot of countries this week. You're with your cousins only?"

I knew what he was getting at; I wanted to give him an honest answer. "Donovan is supposed to be here but I'm unsure if he'll make it."

"Can we talk today? Can you tell me where you'll be in about four hours? I'll come to you."

"Michael, today's not a good day. Jake has something planned for us, but he won't say what, so I'm unsure of my schedule. Really, I'm not trying to avoid you. I don't want to see you come all the way here and for us not to be able to talk."

"Stay in Florence. I'm getting on the next flight available."

"Michael," I complained.

"Is this your new phone number? It's a UK number."

"Yeah. I got a new phone today and figured I'd get a home number."

"I'll see you soon, Duchess."

"*Aargh!*" I sighed loudly after getting off the phone.

"Donovan?" Jake asked.

"Michael."

"Oh Laney. Your life has become complicated, huh?"

"It's been a nightmare and a dream all rolled into one," I answered with a weak smile. "What's the big surprise today, Jake?"

"Can't tell." He smiled. "All I can say is Max and Jane will be here, as well, and it's a surprise for you ladies."

"OK." I answered without much enthusiasm. At this point, it didn't really matter what we were doing. I had no idea whether I would be attending with or without Donovan.

"I just tried calling Donovan and couldn't get a hold of him. Where is he? Why did you come alone?"

"Jake, last I saw him, he was walking out of Grandfather's apartment with Kate to go back to work."

"Damn." I heard Emily utter as she walked into the kitchen. Jake was not happy, either.

"I'm sure it was just work, Laney," he reassured me.

"Oh I'm sure it was just work," I answered with sarcasm. "Sorry. You didn't need to hear that tone."

"You know she doesn't mean anything to him, right?" Jake was now adamant about pleading for Donovan. "You are the only one in his heart. He hasn't talked about Kate since you've reentered his life."

I gave my cousin a skeptical look.

Emily chimed in. "I think Jake is correct. I've heard Donovan talk about you more often than he ever spoke of Kate."

I decided to explain what was bothering me. "How would you feel if you had a ten-year-old shadow? Donovan showed me around Giverny, and he knew Giverny well enough to make me believe he and Kate must have been there often. Then we stayed at a beautiful four-bedroom château in Vernon and one of my initial thoughts was whether he had stayed in that same room, that same bed with Kate. Then this morning, Kate shows up at Grandfather's Paris apartment to tell Donovan he needs to get back to the office. Not only did she know where we were, when Donovan offered her a cup of coffee, she went to the sideboard and knew exactly where the cups, saucers, and spoons were. She was so familiar with the breakfast room, I had to wonder how much more familiar she was with the bedroom. I just feel like he's replaced one body for another. Everything we've done seems recycled." I let out another pitiful sigh.

"Oh Laney." Emily came and put her arms around me. "Is that why Donovan isn't here right now? You got into a fight?"

"No. The stupid man has no idea I'm upset. He called me earlier, barked an order for me to meet him at the airport, then never showed up for the flight." Jake was about to counter, but I beat him to it. "I called his cell phone three times and would have called the office if I had the number. In the end, I got on the plane without knowing what the hell I was doing."

"He didn't even call you?" Emily asked, astounded.

"Oh, that's another shitty story." Now I was getting pissed rather than being sad. "While I was talking to Michael in Amsterdam, trying to break up with him, Donovan didn't like the little he overheard, so he chucked my phone into the canal. I just got a phone when I landed in Florence."

Jake and Emily tried really hard not to laugh.

"All of this will only make your relationship stronger. Just make sure to talk to him and to let him know everything you are feeling. Don't keep anything in." Emily advised.

"Oh, don't you worry. He'll get an earful from me if he ever shows up."

JR slept the whole time I was keeping myself busy doing laundry and getting some summer editing done. I was hoping to see him and play with him but no such luck. I was also told that the twins were hanging out with their uncle and honorary uncles today. Their grandparents would take over babysitting duties tonight and tomorrow till Jake and Emily got back to London. Grudgingly, Jake agreed to take me back to London with him tomorrow after our surprise was done.

We took a still sleeping JR into a restaurant for an early dinner. Jake ordered for six people and said we needed to have a quick dinner so we could catch the 7:00pm bus to our destination. Emily and I were having a nice conversation when I heard an angry, "What the hell were you thinking getting on that plane without me? And did it occur to you to let me know you were getting on the plane before taking off?"

I looked up at an irate and disheveled Donovan and just blinked. I didn't know what to say, so I didn't say anything at all and tried to continue my conversation with Emily. This damn man was actually angry with *me*. What an idiot. What would have been a mole hill for him to climb had his explanation about Kate been a reasonable one, turned into Mount Vesuvius, now.

"Buddy, why don't you take a seat next to Laney and calm yourself before we get an explanation on what happened?" He did just that. He sat next to me, poured himself some Chianti and took a big gulp.

Emily started the conversation in her usual calm way. "Donovan, you want to tell us what happened to you, first?"

"I was working!" He looked at me and complained. "I couldn't get to the airport on time and had no way of reaching Delaney. Common sense would have told her to either wait for me at the airport, or to call me and leave me a message as to her whereabouts. I get to the airport, can't find her, can't locate her at all within the airport, and can't get a hold of anyone to give me some answers."

"I guess we were all en route when you called." Emily explained. "That's probably why you couldn't reach us."

"I only figured out what happened when a pissed off Roland called me to ask why I'd abandoned his granddaughter in Florence."

"Laney? You want to answer?"

As matter-of-factly as I could, I said, "You told me to go to the airport. You handed me a plane ticket in the morning and told me we were going to Florence. I called your cell phone *three* times but couldn't get a hold of you. Waiting for you while you were with Kate seemed too reminiscent of my pathetic days back in the States, so I took my plane ticket and left. You're a smart man. If you didn't see me at the airport, where else would I have gone?"

"Why the fuck didn't you leave a message? Do you know how worried I was about you?"

"Why the fuck didn't you answer your phone when it came close to take-off time? You knew I'd call you if you didn't call me first. Do you know how worried I was about you?"

"Dammit Delaney! You did this on purpose to punish me, and I have no fucking clue why you're so upset with me. You know Kate and I work together. You know Kate and I have had an on-and-off relationship for ten years. None of this is new to you. What the hell don't you get?"

"I don't know a damn thing because you haven't explained any of it to me. You've yet to tell me about Kate and your ten years. I'm told I'll see Jane in a few minutes and I still don't know why the hell you two were making out in that hospital room when she had a boyfriend, or where the 'let's have sex' plane tickets fall into this whole story. I don't know anything!" Immediately, Donovan's demeanor changed. He backed down and reached out to touch me, with no success. We could all see *busted!* written across his face.

"Oh my gosh!" Jane cried as she and Max walked into the restaurant and interrupted our argument. "What are you all doing here?" Jane looked good, though that went without saying. And Jane looked happy.

I looked over at Max, and he looked happy too. Max either had no idea that anything had happened between Jane and Donovan, or she confessed and he chose to forgive her. I didn't have any answers and I was in such a dilemma of my own, I didn't have the energy to try and figure it out.

Being her usual charismatic self, Jane gave everyone a warm greeting—even me, which was a first. She smiled at Donovan, and he smiled back with ease. Even Max gave Donovan a warm greeting and now, I was just plain confused. With another sigh, I decided to focus on tonight's dinner and activity.

"Bad day?" Max whispered as he came to greet me.

I stood up and returned his hug. "The worst, yet."

"I promise, it'll get better. He's a good man, and Jake and I believe he loves you and his intentions are good."

"I'm glad someone believes in him."

Max chuckled and gave me a kiss on the cheek before he let me go.

Laney, where in Florence are you right now? My phone buzzed this text from Michael.

I am in a restaurant in Piazza della Signoria.

What is the restaurant called?

Michael...please...I'm here with five other people. Donovan is here, too.

Duchess, I need to see you and talk to you.

I held off giving the location as long as I could but Michael wouldn't be put off. He called on the phone and I walked outside to try and convince him not to come.

"Michael," I answered.

"I'm near you. I just need an exact location. Please don't make me look for you in every restaurant in the piazza."

After this comment, I had no choice but to tell him where I was. This day started in purgatory, then went straight to hell.

"You all right?" Donovan asked with much concern.

I didn't need to try and explain this situation to Donovan so I deflected my sorrows to the beautiful baby who finally woke up.

"May I hold JR?" I practically begged Emily. She handed him over to me and was so precious he took my breath away. His head showed signs of being blond and his eyes looked hazel in color. With one blink, they were brown, and with another, they were green. He stared up at me and eventually fisted his hand and tried to suck on his balled fist. I loved the slurping, sucking sounds this little one made. I leaned down and kissed his forehead. No matter my status with Donovan, I couldn't wait to hold my own baby.

"Duchess!" My heart sank when I heard my moniker. Michael's presence got me so nervous, I began shaking and feared for JR's safety. Immediately I got up and handed the baby back to his momma.

"No, don't go." This time, it was more a plea than a demand from Donovan.

"I need to talk to Michael. This has gone on too long. Let me go, Donovan." Now I did the demanding.

"You'll come right back here after you talk to him?" Donovan's anxious voice made me realize for the first time that he feared losing me maybe as much as I feared losing him. Perhaps this wasn't as one-sided as I always believed.

Feeling slightly more self-confident about us, I made a shallow attempt at a joke. "Yes. I won't let Michael drag me away to some foreign country like some people I know." A miniscule sense of relief showed on Donovan's face, and I left him to take care of my situation with Michael.

"Duchess!" Michael took two huge steps, met me halfway and threw his arms around me.

Shit! This was not part of the plan. I could feel Donovan's angry presence behind me. Before a scuffle of any sort ensued, I took Michael outside.

"You came."

"Did you doubt I would? If you hadn't been so evasive, I would have come the day you and I lost contact."

"Michael..." I didn't care for his accusation, but I accepted it knowing that as hard as it was right now, it would be worse in a few minutes.

"I'm sorry, Duchess. That wasn't what I meant." He held my hand in his. "What I meant to say was that I would have fought for you from the moment Donovan showed up on your doorstep, had I known. What bloody bad fortune to leave for Scotland when I did."

"Michael. I know your sweet intentions, and they've always been for my benefit. But now, I need to stop being selfish and let you go."

"No." He countered immediately. "I won't let you go. I can't..."

Tears welled up in my eyes as I understood the love this man had for me. He was good to me and for me, but I wasn't good for him. "Michael, you have been a true friend and an ideal boyfriend. You were the only man I wanted to give my heart to and try for a relationship, in all my life, outside of Donovan. I tell you this to try and explain that's how much I adore you, and that's how much you mean to me."

"Don't do this, Laney," he begged.

I started crying hard. "I need to let you go to find your love, your future. It's not with me."

Michael hugged me with passion, but I could tell he knew it was time to let go. "You'll let me know if anything changes with Donovan?" he whispered.

"No. I won't, but one day soon, I hope you'll forgive me and accept me as a friend. I'll miss your friendship, Michael."

He let me go and walked away.

I sat on the narrow sidewalk and cried. I felt horrible for breaking Michael's heart. I didn't deserve to break anyone's heart. Our friendship, I'd never regret, but the hope I gave Michael the moment we entered into a relationship, I'd have a hard time forgiving myself for that selfishness. It was my sincerest hope that Michael would find his true love soon.

However, I had a family function to attend and a man to find a resolution with before this night was over.

"Delaney." Donovan rushed over to me immediately.

"Hi," I croaked and tried to pretend as if everything was normal.

He looked beyond worried, but he didn't probe. He gave me emotional space, but physically, he stuck right by me. With his hand never leaving my body, his touch soothed my weary mind, body and soul.

"Are you all right?" Emily asked, her forehead creased with concern. "How can I help you, Laney?"

That made me want to cry again. "I'll be OK," was the best I could muster.

"And Michael?"

I didn't know whether Emily was asking if Michael was all right, but I chose to play dumb and said, "He left."

Jake, too, looked concerned. "How did he know where you were?"

I didn't want to talk right now but I knew everyone was concerned for me and I knew they were curious. It was only human nature to want to know what happened after seeing this stupid love triangle.

I answered, "I had let Michael know daily where I was, and he called me earlier today asking exactly where I would be. I told him, not believing he was really coming here for me."

Donovan looked like he had a million questions; but aside from holding onto me, he let me be.

At least that's what I thought. Once we left the restaurant, Donovan couldn't hold it in any longer. "What happened?"

"Do I really have to explain right now?"

"When I see my woman walking out in the arms of another man, then coming back in with tears in her eyes...yeah, I'd say you really have to explain everything right now."

Long gone was the sensitive man! As if he didn't have enough negative adjectives working against him, he was probing me for information, *now!*

"Can you let me deal with what just happened? I'll tell you all about it later."

"No!" He actually had the gall to say. "Give me the truncated version — just a sentence or two so you can put me out of my misery. I don't like seeing you mourn another man. I don't like knowing that you loved this guy enough to cry as much as you obviously did. You *never* cry. I don't think I've ever seen you cry over me when we were back in the States."

What the hell did I ever see in this surly man?

Obviously he wanted a fight. I had no choice but to give him one. "Never in the days that we dated could I say I loved Michael. But I have always liked him and liked him very much. *YOU,* I have loved half my life, but right now, I do *NOT* like you very much. You think I've never cried over you? Since we met back in January, I've been crying a river from discontent and heartache. I once told you that just because you don't see it on the outside does not mean that I'm not black and blue on the inside. You can do more damage to me than anyone I know, outside of my immediate family. Don't use that against me."

Shit. Now, I was crying because of Donovan. I was such a blubbering mess.

"I'm sorry." He finally said the words that would have put everything to right the moment he saw me in the restaurant. "I don't want to hurt you, Delaney. That was the last thing I was trying to do. *Fuck!*" I heard him whisper. "What have I done?"

Assuming all of those were rhetorical statements and questions, I sat on the bus and begged for sleep to come. Ideally, I would have liked to sit next to Emily, but with JR, Jake needed to be with them and help where he could.

Emily kept turning around to make sure I was doing OK. At one point I closed my eyes and faked sleep. Donovan tried several times to curl my body into his, but I kept myself against the side of the bus.

"This morning was all work, Princess. You know that don't you? Kate doesn't mean anything to me, and she hasn't for a very long time. In fact it was Kate who pointed out to me that I was in love with you back when we were in Hawaii. That's why she and I had such a rocky relationship out there. Not that we were in a relationship back then."

I was dying to ask, *"So you just sleep with women you're not involved with?"* but decided not to, for the sake of my splitting head. This long ride was not helping the headache that followed me from Paris to Florence.

After an hour and a half, we had arrived. We arrived to an Andrea Bocelli concert in his hometown of Lajatico, Italy, to cross off one of Emily's bucket list items. The perfect husband that he would forever be, Jake got Emily tickets to her dream concert. The rest of us just happened to be in the right country at the right time.

"Isn't this great, Laney?" I heard Jane ask with over-exuberance.

"It is." I tried to answer this enthusiasm with a little of my own. It was a pathetic attempt but at least I showed an effort.

Poor Donovan was trying his damnedest to show me affection, but I just wasn't feeling it. Honestly, it was an effort to be in this incredible setting and be happy for Emily. What a brat I was. But, for now, I just couldn't help it.

"Can I hold him for you?" I just needed a break from everyone's attention. Emily understood and handed over her precious baby.

"My godbaby is beautiful, huh? He may even beat yours in the looks department when he grows a little older." Max taunted.

"Oh, I don't think so!" I got defensive about my little James. "Though, you are a gorgeous little thing." I kissed the top of his head and smelled him. I loved the way newborns smelled.

"I assume you broke up with the English duke?"

I laughed. "Yes, I broke up with the English duke."

"How did he take it? I was told he thought of you as his duchess."

"Not well. Why is life so complicated, Max?"

"Because your brilliant mind would be bored if everything sailed smoothly."

"Everything going well with you and Jane?" I treaded cautiously just in case he had no idea what had happened between her and Donovan.

Max gave me one of those side hugs and kissed my head like an older brother would. "Jane and I are better than ever. We've finally worked out every kink and I think our love is that much stronger because of our trials. Give him a chance. Jake and I wouldn't allow him to get near you if we didn't believe in him."

What Max said began melting away the mountain of frustration. Or, it could have been what Donovan said right before the concert started. "I can't wait to start crossing off some of your bucket list items." That alone would have been sufficient, but he added, "Shit, right now, I'd give an arm just to know what your bucket list items are."

He knew he'd won when he felt my light chuckle. Instantly, he brought my body into his and didn't let go. The practical girl that I was, I figured there was no good dwelling on the negative.

"I love you," Donovan whispered and kissed me in the temple. "And I'm sorry about today. But I want you to know, if it wasn't for Max holding me back, I would have beaten the shit out of Michael for touching you."

"Perhaps he might have beaten the shit out of you for taking his girlfriend out of the country and playing keep away."

Donovan pulled away and looked at me very seriously. "You didn't break-up with him?" He spoke a tad bit louder than proper. "You're still his girlfriend?"

Just to piss him off and make him stew a little longer, I ignored him and paid attention to the concert, instead.

"Delaney Reid." This time, every concertgoer within three rows of us looked our way. "Answer me!" he demanded even louder.

Since everyone was shushing us, I turned, grabbed his face and kissed him as long, as he was loud. "I am not a witness you are cross-examining." I whispered in his ear after the delicious kiss. "The good people of Italy would like to listen to their favorite tenor. You are disturbing them. Pay attention to the concert." He smiled like the cat that got the canary and brought me even closer into his body. I, too, decided to be satisfied until we got to our discussion tonight.

"You want a glass of Chianti?" Donovan asked as the lights went up for intermission.

"No. Not enough flavor. How about anything but Chianti?"

"What blasphemy, Ms. Reid. You are in Italy."

"So sue me." That almost earned me a kiss till Jane purposely interrupted him and put in her order.

"Talk to *your* man." Donovan tried to sound annoyed.

"Jake, will you take the baby? I think I'll use the restroom."

"I'll come with you." I jumped up.

"Me too!" Jane joined in.

"Do women always go to the bathroom in groups?" I heard Donovan ask, and saw Max shrug his shoulders while grinning. They both made a handsome pair.

"Everything good with you and Donovan, now?" Jane asked.

"Nope. We've got a long ways to go before we can be all good."

"What's the problem now?"

"What's not the problem? There are so many, I can't even begin to explain." Even my very own cousin was a part of the problem. One day very soon, we would get to talk over and resolve every issue.

"Oh, I hear someone talking." Emily hurried us. "Maybe the concert's beginning. Let's hurry."

"How does it feel to have a husband whose only desire is to fulfill all your dreams?" I asked dreamily. Jake would always be up there with my dad as the most special man.

"Laney, your Donovan will be the same way, and so will Max, Jane." She addressed the both of us.

"I don't know, Jake is pretty hard to beat," I answered and Jane agreed.

"Who would have thought that my brother would be the ultimate romantic?"

"Hi." Donovan walked over and met us.

"You see?" Emily whispered.

"Ah, young love..." Jane joked wistfully and walked over to her love.

Donovan was about to say something to me when the emcee scared us all by speaking to Jake. The spotlight was mostly on the emcee and Jake, but we took on part of it as well. I stepped behind Donovan and out of the limelight.

"Buonasera, Sir." The emcee brought his entourage with him to our party.

"Buonasera," Jake answered with his casual grin.

"I see you are here with a beautiful woman whom I assume is your wife, and your baby."

"Yes this gorgeous woman is my wife, and yes we are here as a family."

"Tell us what brings you here, and tell us a little bit about your relationship and any romantic stories you might have had during your courtship." Since romance was Jake's forte, there was a chance he'd wax lyrical all night about his relationship with Emily.

"When my wife and I were dating, I asked her to make a bucket list of all the things she wanted to do, and hearing Andrea Bocelli in Italy was one of them. It was our anniversary about six weeks ago, and she had just had a baby, so with this concert I am able to give her an anniversary present and cross off one of her bucket list items."

Everyone adored the story and my cousin Jake. I was proud of him and proud to be his cousin.

The emcee asked about Jake and Emily's courtship, and Emily was hesitant to talk about the two of them in any detail, but Jake answered all the questions posed to him.

"Your cousin is such a ham and an attention-monger."

"He's as ideal as they come. You could learn a thing or two from him." I whispered back to Donovan, who squeezed my hand tighter than I appreciated. "You're hurting my hand."

"Good. I'm trying to hurt it." He chuckled and loosened it immediately.

We were having our own conversation until I heard something about an ex-boyfriend proposing marriage and causing a break-up. That's when I paid attention again. Jake was obviously recounting *his* story of what happened.

"That's quite a story," the emcee said with very little satisfaction. "But what I really want to know is why you looked over to this gentleman over here when you said those words. What does this gentleman have to do with your separation?" 'This gentleman' in question was Max, and the emcee obviously knew the answer. Jane didn't look happy that he had discovered the love triangle between Jake, Emily, and Max. "If I were a betting man, and trust me I'm a betting man, I'd say this guy is the infamous ex-boyfriend who proposed to a girl who already had a boyfriend." When the emcee pointed to Max, Jane was *un*happy!

All of a sudden, someone yelled out something in Italian, the emcee called out some woman's name and "Sophia" came from nowhere and started speaking in Italian for a long while. The entire audience gasped when she was done.

"The audience is interested in your story so I called Sophia to translate for them. Now, where were we?" Yep, he was about as genuine as a three-dollar bill. "Ah, yes. You were about to tell us about your relationship. Did I win the bet?"

Max had no choice but to concede his loss. The audience loved it.

Then, the emcee, who was more like a private investigator, went up to Jane and asked where she belonged in this whole relationship. The revelation that Jane was Jake's sister and Max's girlfriend was so shocking to everyone that the concert was put on hold so Mr. Emcee could finish.

"Now for you," Mr. Investigator came our way. Shit. Now I knew what Jane felt. "Now if I was a betting man, and trust me I'm a betting man," he said again, "I am going to bet that you two have an interesting story as well, and it's somehow related to the four of them." He pointed his finger back to the original four.

I said nothing and fell back another step behind Donovan. This man and I were already on thin ice. No one needed to know of all our troubles and I didn't need to be embarrassed in front of all of Tuscany. Surprisingly, my lawyer kept mum, too. The impatient emcee couldn't get anything out of us, so he asked Jake, instead. The only information Jake let out was who Donovan and I were in relation to him.

"Laney?" The emcee asked and I saw myself blown up on the huge screen. "At some point in your life, did you date him?" He pointed to Max and I quickly shook my head no.

He was definitely not pleased with my answer. Truly, this was like an ugly, ugly episode of *The Bachelor* and *The Bachelorette*, combined.

"There's got to be some connection here. Did you," he returned to Emily, "date your husband's best friend?" Emily died laughing and answered in the negative.

"Then the only other possibility is...you and you dated at some point." This stranger figured out the sorest and most painful spot in my heart and poked at it when he pointed to Donovan and Jane. I could feel my heart break and the tears forming one more time. I had witnessed the kiss. Becky had mentioned the 'let's have sex' plane tickets, and now tonight I learned about these two dating. What more had happened between my cousin and Donovan and when would these surprise revelations end? Today had to have been a record day of public display of ugly emotions for me.

"Aha! I knew it." Mr. Emcee had hit the jackpot. "You all have quite an incestuous relationship going on. Did you know, or did we just out these two?" I was grateful he was questioning Max and not me. I took one more step back trying to disappear from this situation. Donovan didn't notice the tears glistening in my eyes or the pain in my heart making my entire body ache.

"I knew," Max gave a resigned answer.

"Now did you date Jane while you were with Laney?"

"No." Donovan's lightning fast answer didn't make me feel any better. "And we didn't really date. It was one date while both of us were technically single."

"Technically single..." The emcee wasn't convinced. "Is that correct, Laney? Was he not a part of your life when he dated your cousin? You know, the camera zoomed in on your face when it was mentioned that the man you're standing next to dated your cousin..."

"It was only one date!" Donovan kept clarifying.

"As I was saying, you looked shocked and hurt when you heard about these two. We all want to know what you're thinking. You're the only one who hasn't weighed in on this soap opera."

Shit. What I feared had happened. The camera deadpanned into my deer-in-headlight face and I knew I couldn't hide the answer any longer. In order to get out of this situation and this vicinity altogether, I gave him the answer he wanted.

"I just broke up with a good man who told me once that he started living the moment we met, for a man I've been in love with since I was ten, only to find out that he recently dated my cousin while pursuing me. Yeah...I'd say I'm shocked and hurt."

That was all I could take without crying in front of 15,000 people. I exited the camera space in haste and just got away. Every time I thought life between us might work, something crept back up to hurt me. These exposés on Donovan and my cousin were the worst.

"Delaney." Donovan called to me but looked frightened. I put out my hand like a stop sign so he would know I didn't want anything from him and continued to walk away. "Please," he begged but I didn't listen. "Please, let me explain."

"Loving you has been nothing but painful, Donovan. I don't think I want to do this anymore. I hurt so much and knowing about you and my cousin almost kills me. If you're going to add to my pain, please don't. Honestly, I can't take anymore. Because I've given in to you habitually, you might think I'm capable of taking on more of your bullshit lies. Well, I can't any longer. Let's just call it quits here."

Donovan didn't hesitate to put both his arms around me and hold me tight. He wouldn't let me move. "I'm sorry doesn't mean much when someone says it too many times. I know that's all I've been doing with you. The morning of Jane's birthday, I gave her two plane tickets and asked her to go away with me. The asshole that I was, I told her I didn't care what she told Max, I just wanted a weekend with her to explore the chemistry between us." And here, I started bawling. I remembered the day of Jane's birthday, and I remembered thinking that I saw Donovan in a cab and being so happy to finally run into him again. I was going to tell him how much I loved him. I was going to bare my soul to him and pray that he would accept all I had to give. While I was dreaming about him, he was asking Jane to go away with him. My fantasy never matched up with my reality. But it was Donovan who fed my fantasy when he waited for me all those hours on the steps of Gram's home. More times than I could count, I wanted so much to go out to him and to tell him everything. Each time he left, I thought if he had stayed even five minutes longer, I would have confessed everything and started the relationship he appeared to want to try with me. I just couldn't reconcile why he would wait for me all those days, all those hours, when the person he wanted was Jane. What kind of sick man played these kinds of games with women? "I know you're hurt because it looks like I was with Jane while pursuing you. And partially, that is true. I won't deny it."

This pain that came with loving someone was something I didn't equate into a relationship, and I wasn't convinced it was worth the possible happiness. Donovan continued to explain but we were interrupted by a loud gasp. Instinctively, both of us looked at the giant TV monitors and saw Max on one knee proposing to his love. The beautiful look on Jane's face somewhat settled my disturbed heart. Though Donovan and I had much to work through, if Max and Jane could forgive each other's iniquities and wanted to spend the rest of their lives together, I saw a small hope for us, too.

"Let's table our issues and go congratulate Max and Jane." I pushed Donovan away and started walking, but he grabbed my hand and apologized one more time.

There was a huge celebration going on around our seats. All the gracious concertgoers were enjoying the revelry.

"Congratulations!" I hugged Jane first, then Max. "I'm very happy for you." I truly hoped that though my splotchy face looked sad, I conveyed my love and good wishes for the both of them.

"You and Donovan will get here, too. Don't give up, Laney."

I knew at that moment, there were tears of sadness in my eyes, but I still smiled at Max, who was kind enough to comfort me.

"What can I do to make your heart not hurt so much?" Emily whispered as she came in for a group hug with Max.

"Laney." Max spoke in all seriousness. "After four years of being with this wonderful woman, I gave her up and didn't ever think I'd find someone as special. Then out of nowhere, I meet this high-spirited woman who kept me on toes the entirety of our relationship. She is beautiful, she is a lot of work, but she is worth every heartache and tear. She might be that much more special because I thought I might have lost her at one point. Don't lose hope. Once all your kinks are straightened, your love now will feel like puppy love compared to what's to come."

"Thank you, Max," was really all I could say because I didn't and couldn't believe him. I knew Max wasn't lying about any of his feelings. I just didn't believe that what had happened to him and Jane would happen with Donovan and me.

The trip back home was a long one. During some part of the ride, I must have fallen asleep because I found myself in Donovan's arms again. He didn't say much after the concert, and we all quietly disbanded to our rooms. It was disappointing to see Donovan's stuff in another room, but he came into mine and wanted to talk.

"You up for talking some more, or do you want to go to sleep?"

Was I up for talking? This needed to be done so we could both get on with our lives one way or the other. "Sure."

We made our way to the kitchen table, Donovan uncorked a bottle of wine, poured two glasses, then went right back to his story.

"I made that shitty proposal to Jane and went off to London to take care of some business and to hopefully talk to you to understand why I was so frustrated and yet so obsessed with you. It pissed me off that I couldn't get you off my mind. Jake and Al kept telling me I was in love with you, but I denied it and wanted answers. I wanted an answer concerning you, and I wanted an answer concerning Jane."

He stared at me with a funny look so I asked, "What?"

"You gonna say anything?"

"Is that a requirement in this conversation?"

That brought out a darling chuckle from this man. "No. I thought you might have a choice word or two for me, so I was waiting for it to begin."

"No comment."

He stared a while longer and was lost for a few more seconds, then continued.

"I went to see you at Gram's, and you were sitting on the steps looking beautiful in Bee's yellow bumble bee dress. You don't know how happy I was to finally see you and get a hold of you. All those times I stopped by, you were never home."

"Oh, I was home..." I briefly interrupted.

Donovan stopped his flow of conversation and looked like he might get pissed about me being home, but he only said, "We'll talk about that later."

"Later..." I repeated in a childish way.

"So," he said a little loudly to catch my attention back to his story—like my attention ever went anywhere else—"as I was saying, you were waiting and I thought you saw me because your face broke into the most stunning smile. Between your dress and your sweet smile, I thought I was being blinded by a ray of sunshine. But as soon as I took my eyes off you to tell the cab driver to stop, Michael had come and swept you into his arms. It looked like he caught you by surprise, but you looked happy. And I think that was the day everything changed for me."

"So that was you..." I said softly and sadly.

"Huh? What does that mean, Delaney?"

"That day, I sat on my steps for a very long time imagining and dreaming of you sitting next to me. I missed you so much I sat there and pretended you had come to tell me you were madly in love with me and couldn't live without me. I conjured up scenarios of us talking about our future and talking about how many kids we'd have, and in the midst of dreaming, I thought I spotted you in a black cab. It was like my dream had come true, and it brought me such elation. Clearly, I remember that day and how relieved I felt to be able to tell you and have you maybe under-stand and accept my heart. But at the blink of an eye, Michael was in front of me and you had vanished." I laughed sadly. "Poor Michael thought my smile was all for him and that made his day. Because of that smile, he proposed to me and asked me to be his future duchess. I guess Jane and I both got over-the-top proposals that day."

Donovan only scratched his head in frustration. "After I saw you and Michael, I flew into Chicago when Becky called to say Jane was there and in trouble. And when I got to Chicago, I learned that I had fucked things up for Jane, and Max had left her for his Mexico trip a month earlier than planned."

"How did Max find out?"

"Just my luck, he was outside her door. He had arrived right after me and left as soon as I was done."

"Poor Max." I didn't hurt for him as much as I thought I might, since everything worked out well for him and Jane. As Max said, they were stronger than ever, possibly thanks to their troubles.

"Jane was a mess, and to make a long story short, she and I went out on one date. We saw a show, had dinner, and shared one kiss." This was where the hurt came back and the tears I tried so hard to keep inside started rolling down my cheeks. "It was one kiss. And it was the most disgusting, incestuous kiss that ever occurred between two people. Jane and I were both repelled with one another and horrified that we'd hurt everyone around us to satisfy our curiosity. Also, what you saw at the hospital, it wasn't what you thought. I pulled Jane in and asked her to allow me to kiss her one more time. After seeing you with Michael and experiencing that kiss with Jane, I knew what Jake and Al had been telling me all this time was true. I'd been in love with you, but had denied it. So I asked Jane for one more kiss just to be clear once and for all on the issue of her and me. *BUT,* we came to the conclusion that it wasn't necessary. And as karma the bitch would have it, you walked in right when we were about to untangle from one another."

I wiped the tears from my eyes and said, "OK." To be completely honest, I didn't know what to feel at this point. The practical me put this whole scenario into focus, and I weeded out what mattered and what I needed to let go.

"OK? Um... is there more to that? Do you have any questions? Multi-word comments? A four-letter word or two?"

"The more I think about this situation, I suppose I have no right to be upset with you. You were not my boyfriend at the time. There were no promises made between us before I left. And I even had a boyfriend. I could be upset with the fact that you hurt Max, but since he got over all that's happened and felt sure enough to propose, whatever indignity I felt for him is moot. I can't exactly be on Jane's side, either, since she was just as guilty as you were. The only issue I can raise is the fact that I am alarmed by your selfishness. Just because you're curious about a woman does not give you the right to take her away from another man."

"You are absolutely right. That was the worst thing I've ever done in my life; every day I live with the guilt. I am grateful Max and Jane were able to work out their problems and get engaged."

"Donovan, I really don't know what to say. Yes, I'm hurt. Yes, that emcee caught me by surprise. But I don't know if I can cry foul anymore over something that happened, unrelated to me. As you pointed out, you and Jane were technically single."

"Delaney, don't do that. Don't go apathetic on me. Cry, yell, scream, do whatever you like, but don't make me think you don't care."

"You know I care. The problem is that I care too much and have always cared too much for you."

Donovan brought his chair right in front of me and had us face one another. "Tell me what went wrong this morning. If you don't want to talk about Jane anymore, we don't have to. We can bring that up later again if you want, or ask more questions if you have them. But tell me what happened this morning?"

I sighed heavily. "Maybe this, too, is a moot point. I was upset with how familiar and casually intimate Kate was with you, still."

"You've lost me. Give me an example."

Was he clueless or playing clueless? "Here are the questions that went through my mind while you were with Kate. How did she know where to reach you? How the hell did she know where to get a coffee cup and spoon from that Paris apartment? Has she stayed with you in Grandfather's apartment? Did you and I share one of the most intimate acts on the same bed you and she had slept in? Had all the beds we shared up until now been recycled? I know I'm being unfair to you since you were with her for so long, but I just can't get rid of her shadow—or perhaps I'm the shadow." He placed both his hands on my face and his forehead eventually leaned into mine. "I'm sorry for being so young and inexperienced in life and love. I probably sound stupid and juvenile to you. I can't ever be your first anything...I know. I just don't like coming in second place all the time."

"Princess," he softly spoke and placed his mouth on mine. It was the sweetest kiss he'd ever given me. That kiss touched every part of me that hurt and was like a soothing balm. "*You* are second to no one, and I don't want you ever thinking you are anyone's shadow. Kate has been to Roland's before on business, but I wasn't there. Her company has hired our firm in the past and she and Roland have worked together many times. That's why he hired her the minute he knew she was available." Well, now I felt kinda dumb for jumping the gun on that conclusion. "What we did that night in Paris was as intimate and beautiful to me as it was for you. I missed out on giving you some of my firsts, but I hope to be your first and only in every way."

"Did I totally go overboard in the drama department, again?" I was so embarrassed now for having jumped to all these conclusions. I dropped my head on his shoulder so I wouldn't have to look into his eyes.

He snickered, a little. "No bed has been recycled, but if you want to visit some of the European landmarks, then most likely I've been there with my family. My parents took us all on our first major European trip, so Eiffel Tower, the Sistine Chapel, the Louvre...been there, done that." Now he was just plain teasing me.

I giggled. "Well, I've been to all those places already, too. You won't be my first at any of those places, either."

"Is that right?" He pulled my face up to his and placed tender, sweet kisses all over me. "Then I suppose," he kissed my forehead, "we will have to," he kissed my nose, "create as many firsts as we can," he kissed both cheeks, "while your grandfather's firm is paying for these trips." He had me in a full-blown kiss. "Do I need to explain my years with Kate, now?" He interrupted our sweet kiss with that sour question.

"I'm thinking we will save her for another day. It's late and I'm tired."

"I am too, Princess."

"Hey." We both jumped when we heard another voice in this kitchen. "You guys haven't gone to bed yet?"

Jane appeared as if she had just woken up, and she looked dazed.

"Not yet. We've been talking." Donovan put his hand on my cheek again and smiled.

"Any chance I could talk to Laney for a bit?"

"She's tired, Jane." This protective stuff was cute.

"I know, Donovan," Jane rolled her eyes at him. "I won't keep her long. But I'd like for you to leave."

He obliged and kissed me one more time. "Come see me before you go to bed?"

Um...are we not in the same bed? "OK."

Jane watched Donovan leave and asked, "Everything copacetic between you two?"

"Not wholly yet, but we're getting there. We both have a lot to work through, and Donovan has a past that keeps creeping up on him."

"About Donovan's past...I've been waiting for you to come back to London so we could talk. I'm glad we got to meet up before I went back home. I've got a lot of apologizing to do."

"You don't have to apologize to me. As long as you and Max have worked out your relationship, I'm happy for you. Max is up there with Jake in my eyes. He's perfect for you."

"And Donovan is perfect for you." Jane paused and made us both a bit uncomfortable. "I've always been jealous of you, ever since we were young."

That statement almost knocked me off my chair. "Why would you be jealous of *me?* You're the smart one, the beautiful one, everyone's favorite—well, after Jake of course..."

"Of course! No one could beat my brother in that category."

"I've never harbored any ill will against you—well, maybe I did a little when I saw you and Donovan kissing—but I've always believed you had everything going for you. Your personality commanded attention while people thought mine was 'unique.' Your looks are exotic while mine are everyday Americana. You oozed intelligence while I always got the dumb blonde looks. What on earth would make you jealous of me?" Was Jane joking?

"Laney, you graduated summa cum laude, got into med school and film school, men adore you at every turn, and I don't know anyone who doesn't think you have an adorable personality. Aside from all that, what I always admired and envied about you was your independent spirit. Whatever you want to do, learn, experience—you go for it. Students generally don't leave the comforts of a very comfortable home just because they want to experience a new culture. Students also don't take classes in either spectrum of majors, just because they like it. You're unconventional and that makes you unique." Wow! Never in a million years did I see this conversation ever happening between us.

"I think odd is a more fitting term." That brought out the girly giggles. "But it's not like you couldn't have done all that."

"But I didn't. I found safety in the conventional. What makes you truly special is your unconditional love for everyone around you. Even in a difficult situation, you find the good in everybody. Donovan is head over heels in love with you for all those reasons. When I think back, he's always given you more attention than the rest of us—and that was another source of envy for me."

"Donovan..." I smiled like I was the luckiest girl, alive. "Perhaps he's the root of all evil." I'd have to let him know I said that when I went up to sleep in his arms.

"He's not, and he loves you. I'm sorry I was selfish all this time. It bothered me whenever I thought he had feelings for you and that selfishness almost cost me my relationship with Max." She groaned. "I was stupid—beyond stupid. I wanted to be the center of everyone's world, rather than enjoying my relationship with Max. You believe me when I say Donovan and I were really never anything more than friends?"

"I believe I do. Donovan explained it all to me, and I'm not upset with you. I still have some unresolved issues with Donovan's selfishness, but I meant it when I said I wish you and Max only the best."

"Thank you for understanding, and I wish you and Donovan this kind of happiness as well."

"I appreciate the talk and let me know if I can help you in any way when you prepare for your wedding. I'm sure your mom, as well as mine, will be thrilled with the news."

"I actually do have one thing you can help me with if you don't mind."

"Of course I don't mind." *Though I am a little tired.*

"Across the street from this villa, there was a motorcycle Max was drooling over. Since he got me this," she showed me her sparkly ring, "I thought I'd get him that. Only problem, I don't speak motorcycle so I don't know what *that* is."

"*That's* easy. It's a Ducati. They're made very close to here and they are beautiful, powerful, and fast. Max would love it! What a great idea, Jane."

"Is it safe?" she worried.

"Jane. It's a motorcycle. It's as safe as the driver and the crazy cars the driver comes in contact with. But Max should be fine. It's not like this would be his first motorcycle."

"Can you help me pick one out?" She was hesitant, but willing to do it for his sake.

I was happy to help! "Bring down your laptop. Let's order one now!"

Patting myself on the back for picking out the coolest Ducati, I got ready for bed and slipped into Donovan's room. It was tempting to put on one of Bee's lingerie outfits, but it was almost four in the morning, and I was too tired to see anything through tonight.

Donovan was knocked out and snoring softly. I snuggled into his body and put his arm around my waist while we spooned (with our pajamas on).

"Huh?" Donovan woke up startled to find himself hugging me.

"Why'd you get your own room?" I asked, baffled.

"What do you mean?" He even sounded sexy with a hoarse and scratchy voice.

"I'm in the room next door."

He answered groggily. "I thought you were in this room when I put my stuff down."

"Didn't you see all my stuff in the other room?"

"No, didn't pay any attention."

"Can we talk about what happened last night in Paris?" I was somewhat embarrassed, but I had a few questions for him.

"No." He cut me off.

What? "Why not?"

"Because if we talk about it right now, I'll get horny and want to do something about it, and it's late. I'm tired and so are you."

"I just have a few questions."

"Princess, I have a meeting in Rome later today and I'm unprepared because you scared the hell out of me today when I lost you. I need to get up in a few hours and get some work done before we head into Rome. Get some sleep!" He went all Mr. Commander on me again.

"I sort of booked a ticket back to London tomorrow morning. I'm supposed to leave with Jake's family."

"Like hell you are. Go to sleep!"

"All right." I closed my eyes but something seemed amiss. "Donovan?" I asked one last time.

"What...!?!" He was now annoyed with me.

"I love you." Even though it was dark and I was facing away from him, I stuck my tongue out at him in response to his 'What...!?!'

He chuckled. "Go to sleep, Princess. We'll do a thorough Q&A tonight in Rome. And I love you too."

"One absolute last question?"

"Shit, Woman. Spit it all out!"

"Does Grandfather have a nice place in Rome, too?"

"I'm told it is but we're staying in a hotel until Max and Jane leave."

"We are? Why?"

"Because you'll have questions and I'll have answers, that's why." I had to think about that. "*Now* can I go to sleep?"

"Good night." And I think it was a good night. But as always, I was out within minutes.

"I trust you are not leaving with us this morning?" Jake chuckled at my disheveled state.

JR's cry made me pop out of bed, and after making myself presentable in Donovan's clothes since all my stuff was next door, I ran outside to say good-bye to my cousin and his family.

Giving Jake a guilty smile I answered, "Um...yeah...I may stay here with Donovan."

"You may...? Or you will?"

"I think I will, Jake," I answered abashedly. "You've always known that my heart belonged to your best friend. Now that he's finally returning the feelings, I think I'll regret not giving this a try." I didn't know why I felt so shy telling this to Jake, who's probably been our biggest supporter.

"He loves you, Laney. You deserve the best and I think you got the best." My cousin came in to give me a hug. "Give him some room to make mistakes because we men make a lot of mistakes."

"Thank you for always watching out for me and taking care of me. Next to my dad, I think you are the coolest guy around."

"How come we were left out of this love-fest?" Emily walked into the hallway with JR and came and hugged us.

"I'll see you very soon," I cooed to the baby. "You give your brother and sister a hug and kiss for me," I said but decided to keep JR in my arms.

"Let's go have some breakfast." Emily led the way.

"You're up, already." Donovan came over and gave me a kiss on the lips and JR a kiss on top of his head. "Did I ever tell you that you are most beautiful when you have a child in your arms?" He whispered in my ear. "I can't wait to get you pregnant with our baby."

Damn! That statement gave me chills that ran up and down my body. His words put these tingles on the back of my neck, and I was so aroused I almost pulled Donovan back into our room to finish what was started in Paris.

"Will I enjoy the act of procreating?" I teased him with a whisper of my own.

"With the way you screamed with pleasure the other night, I have no doubt." He breathed into my ear.

Those tingles went everywhere, but mostly south. There was no time to be embarrassed with Donovan's comment. I was raring to go and scream some more. With every kiss he placed on my neck, I was shivering with pleasure.

"Hey. You two. Stop making out in the corner over there. We are trying to have breakfast."

"Jane, Jane, Jane..." Donovan spoke. "You always were the party pooper."

"Shut up and come have breakfast. Max and I walked to the bakery this morning and got all these freshly baked pastries."

"Can I make anyone some coffee?" I offered, once JR was safely back in his mother's arms. "I love this coffee machine. All you have to do is touch one button and voila, you have an espresso, or a latte, or a cappuccino. Grandfather must like this machine, because he has one at each of his homes. We don't have one in Belgravia. I think I'll buy one for all of us. It'll be cheaper than what I've been doing, getting it from the local cafe."

"Princess, I think that machine runs in the thousands. You can buy yourself a year's worth of coffee and still come away cheaper."

"Oh. Sorry, Emily. I take back my offer. We won't have one of these in Belgravia, but I'll introduce you to the great bakery I found not too far from us."

Emily laughed. "When will you come back to us?"

"Well..." I thought about that for a long while. "I don't know? Mr. Taylor?" I deferred to him.

"We will be in Rome tonight, then we have the weekend free to stay there or go wherever your heart desires. I need to be back in London by Monday for a meeting, and Tuesday for a firm function. You are to be my arm candy that night."

"Arm candy, huh?" I raised my eyebrow. "Will your glamorous ex be in attendance?"

Now *he* was raising his eyes at me.

"I have to ask you two," Emily chimed in, "was Kate always that glamorous? Even when you knew her in your younger days, did she never have a hair out of place?"

"Did I ever tell you I used to call her Sea-foam Goddess because when I first saw her at the Montage, she had just come out of the pool and she looked like Aphrodite coming out of her shell?" Jane laughed to herself.

"Damn, she makes every woman around her feel insignificant. I don't envy you coming after someone like that, Laney."

"It's all right. I've got something huge that she doesn't have." I answered with much confidence.

Donovan chuckled. "Yeah? What's that?"

"Youth!" I giggled. Donovan pulled me down onto his lap and kissed my cheek like he would a little girl.

"Laney," Max called out, "you have a clearer idea of your future after having been an unemployed college grad for a few months?"

"Funny you ask..." I looked at Donovan and spoke more to him than anyone else in the room. "I was thinking I might go to med school rather than film school."

"That's wonderful." He gave me a genuine smile with his answer. "But you can do whatever you like, you know that, right?"

"I know, and that's what my parents keep telling me, though I know Daddy wants me to go to med school. After hearing my dad speak at the conference in Amsterdam, I thought it would be a waste not to be under the tutelage of two brilliant surgeons on the cul-de-sac." I gave Jake a nod. "But I'm torn between having kids soon, and being in school and residency for so many years. Jane, what will you do about your pending marriage and kids?"

"Max and I will most likely get married as soon as his schooling is done. And maybe we'll get married right here in Tuscany?" She asked Max that general question and he shrugged his shoulders as though he didn't care where he got married as long as they got married. "As for kids, I don't know, either. I'd like to pop them out sooner than later, but it may be a few years."

"Ladies, you have many years before you have to have kids." Emily was the voice of reason for us. "I wouldn't trade my three for anything in this world but I will tell you, once they arrive, there's no sending them back. Do what you want to do, accomplish your goals, then you can decide when it's time to have kids. You don't have to do everything at once and all at the same time."

"I guess we'll just have to spoil our godchildren in the meanwhile," I answered Emily and kissed JR's head again.

Breakfast was perfect. The six of us got along beautifully, and Max would make a great addition to our family. He had become another member of the Reid family and I loved that he was so easy going. We all got ready for our respective trips. Jake, Emily, and JR left first for the airport. And soon after, the four of us left for Santa Maria Novella train station.

"I need to do a little work on the train, OK?" Donovan was warning me even before we got on.

"You do what you need to do. I talked to Daddy this morning and he says if I get married before I start med school, my husband is paying for it."

Donovan stopped everything and thought through what I'd just said. It kinda hurt my feelings that he looked like he was trying to decide if it was worth it to marry me right away.

"So you're finally admitting that we're getting married?"

Huh? So he wasn't weighing me vs. tuition? Shoot, I had to get out of this one. Considering this man hadn't proposed, he'd only told me we were getting married, I wasn't giving in. "I never admitted to *us* getting married. I was just telling you what Daddy said."

"Why do you keep refusing to marry me?"

"If you knew me at all, you'd know." Let him figure that one out! My cousin Jake proposed to his girlfriend in Paris, his sister Jane was proposed to in the middle of an Andrea Bocelli concert in the rolling hills of Tuscany, and all I get is *"you're marrying me."* That was no proposal in my book.

"Women!" He muttered and took out his laptop and started typing away. I watched a movie on my tablet and Max and Jane were just super cute together, talking about their impending wedding.

"Have you talked to my mom yet?" I interrupted Jane.

"Your mom was with my mom when I called to tell them about the proposal. My parents already knew it was happening, and your mom was going through a list of wedding themes."

"Oh, Jane. Will you really get married in Tuscany? How very romantic."

"That sounds really good to me. We can have the twins be our flower girl and ring bearer and maybe Gimpy knows of an owner of a winery nearby his home. We could rent a winery, get married and have a party there."

"What a dream to get married in a winery in Italy."

"What about you? I'm sure you picked out your wedding dress when you were five years old."

I let out a guffaw. "You know I was always partial toward Sleeping Beauty when I was younger."

"I know!" Jane groaned. "But why? Why her?"

"Because her dress was pink."

"Shit! Seriously?" Jane looked annoyed. "I looked terrible in pink and you kept making me put her dress on."

"Jane, you look good in any color—then and now. You just didn't like her because I liked her."

Jane also broke into a guffaw. "Well, there was some of that."

"But soon after, I grew into a Cinderella fan. I always thought my prince would come meet me at a ball, fall madly in love with me, and propose on the spot."

"Oh brother!" Max moaned. "You women really think like that?"

"Max!" I complained. "I was only like seven when I thought this."

"Then where did Donovan Taylor fit into your plan?"

Now I really let out a giggle. "I saw him for the first time when I was ten, in Aunt Sandy's kitchen, and I thought he was the most handsome man, ever. Even though he and Jake had been best friends since birth, that was the first time I registered who he was and let me tell you, Donovan Taylor was it. He was the cat's meow, the greatest thing since sliced bread, the absolute bomb!" I peeked over at Donovan, who was trying hard to type away, with a stupid grin on his face.

The phone rang before I could return to my story so I excused myself and picked it up.

"Hello?"

"Baby!"

"Hi Pa. How are you?"

"Is she talking to your dad?" I heard Jane whisper over to Donovan. He reached out and lovingly squeeze my hand while nodding yes to Jane.

"Where are you and Donny now?"

"We are on a train heading into Rome."

"Was the concert good?"

"Oh, Pa. It was wonderful. And did you hear the good news? Jane and Max are engaged."

"Yes. When am I going to hear this same good news about you and Donny?" he asked in earnest.

"I don't know, Pa. That's up to Donny." I answered with equal amount of sincerity. "What are you and Ma doing today? Are you still in Paris?"

"We are all heading into Rome, too, and wondered if we should meet up for dinner."

"Hold on, let me ask."

"The Taylors are all heading into Rome and would like to know if we can meet up for dinner with them tonight."

Donovan decided to answer his dad for us. "Pa, I have a meeting that will most likely turn into a dinner. And I think Delaney is hanging out with Max and Jane today. We can see you tomorrow if you like. Uh-huh. OK. Talk to you later."

"What did he say, and why did you saddle me with Max and Jane? They may be busy today."

"We've seen enough of my family on this trip. We'll see them next time."

"I like your family."

"I do too but once they get a hold of you, I won't see you till late tonight and I shouldn't be too late." He leaned over and whispered, "We have our unfinished Q&A."

Giddy, I turned to Max and Jane and said, "Don't feel the need to entertain me. You do what you need to do."

"We were going to help Josh set up his new apartment. You can join us," Jane invited.

"Oh, I'd love to help."

Grandfather's apartment in Rome was in the most fabulous location, in the heart of the city. He and Josh resided within minutes of one another, but most likely their apartments were as different as Cinderella and her stepsisters. Grandfather's apartment was nowhere as big as the Paris apartment, but it was still grand.

"I love having a rich grandfather," I squealed while looking through the beautiful building. The antiquity and beauty of Europe never ceased to amaze me.

Donovan looked amused. "Yeah. I love you having a rich grandfather, too. Just don't get too comfortable here; we are staying in a hotel, tonight."

"But it's so beautiful here and it's free. Why spend money on a hotel?"

His loving and most handsome face appeared. "If you are true about not making me wait till our wedding night, then I'm making love to you tonight. *But*, before that happens, let us clarify a few things."

"What do we need clarified?"

"You have broken up with Michael?"

"Michael...shoot! I need to give him a call and make sure he's OK," I digressed.

"Delaney!" Donovan brought me back to him.

"Yes. Michael and I broke up. It was such a terrible thing, Donovan. Who am I to break his heart? He was very hurt when he left. I don't think I could stand that kind of pain if you broke up with me." I spoke with much insecurity knowing if this happiness were taken away from me, I'd be utterly devastated and lost.

"This happiness will go on till death-do-us-part, assuming...we are getting married?"

Was *"We are getting married?"* close enough to a marriage proposal? At least it wasn't a demand. "Maybe." I held back the giggle.

Now, the disgruntled, but still very handsome face came out. "You drive me nuts," he declared. "What am I missing here? You've been in love with me for most of your life, I return this love, you have no boyfriend, why no marriage?"

"Like I said before, you're a smart man, Donovan Taylor. Figure it out."

"You, me, tonight—you got it?"

"Yes." I smiled and gave him a kiss. "You look incredibly dapper, Mr. Taylor. Go to work so you can pay my medical school tuition, *if* we get married."

"I would pay that bill and more if you'd be my wife." That was a sweet sentiment.

"Would you still be saying that if I told you my tuition would be free if I stayed a Reid?" I got his undivided attention, which amused me. "Daddy says since he works for the University as a surgeon as well as a professor, I get free med school tuition like I got free undergrad tuition. That's all part of the perks of working at a university. Do you still want me, right now?"

He didn't even blink. "We could take Jane and Max as witnesses, walk to city hall right now, and become man and wife. The choice is yours. I'll take you, medical tuition and all."

I truly loved this man. "Since it would kill my mother not to throw me a wedding, I think I'll have to say no to your idea of a city hall wedding. Go to work, Mr. Taylor. I'll see you tonight."

"I love you."

"I love you, too."

Max, Jane and I walked a few minutes to Josh's new place. None of us could believe he had found such a reasonably priced apartment in this posh neighborhood. Once we got inside, we understood why the rent was so cheap.

"Laney!" Josh came up and hugged me.

"Hello there, fellow unemployed college grad. How was your trip over here?"

"It was a dream in that private plane of your grandfather's. Then, I couldn't believe how nice your grandmother's place in London was. And then I come here to find this spacious place." He pointed to all of maybe 250 square feet.

"Wow. I think this apartment might just be big enough to serve as Donovan's closet." Jane and Max cracked-up.

"I still think it would still be too small. Between your wardrobe and Donovan's, you two will have to get a bigger house."

"So...Donovan?" Josh inquired.

"Yeah..." I answered with an apologetic-smile. Josh and I had had this talk a while back about us being better off as friends, but I guess it didn't hurt to say it one more time. "He returns my love and we are together now."

Josh came over and gave me a hug. "I'm happy for you, Laney. It took the idiot long enough to notice you."

"You tell him that when you see him."

"I will."

"OK," Jane broke us up. "I'm getting claustrophobic watching you two hug in this tiny quarter; let's go out and buy Josh what he needs for this matchbox-sized apartment."

The afternoon was all about buying as little as possible, but still making sure Josh stayed comfortable so far away from home.

"You know I'm only a flight away. You will always be welcomed in Belgravia if you get tired of all this luxury." I pointed to his sparse living quarters.

"Thanks, Laney. I think I may drop in more often than not. I kind of miss those twins already, though they were a handful when I was babysitting them."

"Kids have a way of doing that to you. Emily will enjoy having you with us, so come visit often."

We headed to a late lunch when my *boyfriend* called. That gave me goose bumps realizing he was now my *boyfriend*.

"Is this my deliciously handsome boyfriend calling?" Of course, I strayed from the others before making this forward comment. I could practically see his grin.

"Would my equally delicious and definitely more beautiful girlfriend like to join me and my clients for dinner? It has turned into a couples' dinner, and I'd be awfully alone without you."

"What time is dinner? We are about to eat a late lunch right now."

"8:00pm. Since I'll be in a meeting up until then, I'll have a car pick you up."

"Sure. I guess I'll have something light to tide me over. How should I dress?"

"We're at the only three Michelin-starred restaurant in Rome, at the Waldorf. You decide. Also, bring our suitcases because that's where we're staying tonight."

"Isn't that a little expensive? Does the firm usually put you up in such posh places? I'm going to have to tell Grandfather they are spending way too much money seeing to your comforts."

"Princess, I've yet to use any of the hotel money I've been allotted since we've stayed at Roland's everytime I've been working. I've got lots of credit built up."

"Well then...I guess we'll have to get a suite with all the bells and whistles, tonight!" I kidded.

"Nothing but the best for you, Princess. I'll see you tonight."

"Can't wait. Love you."

"Love you too."

I was so excited; I was practically bursting out of my skin.

"Donovan?" Jane had no need for any other words.

"Donovan." I answered.

Once lunch was done, the men headed to their respective rooms to take a siesta, and I convinced Jane to go shopping with me. Via Condotti was located in Grandfather's backyard, and I decided it was time Jane and I bonded over our favorite pastime.

"What's the occasion?"

" A client dinner at the Waldorf, with significant others. How should I dress?"

"Many of those women will come pretty dressed up because they can afford to look good."

"Shoot. What should I wear, then?"

"How about we get you a sexy little number?"

"Sounds fab!"

Our hours of shopping resulted in one super sexy, but also femininely flirty little black dress. With a jeweled neckline, a twirl-worthy skirt—slightly shorter and bunched in the front, longer and with a tie-back sash in the back, and no sleeves, I felt ready to take on these executive wives. I matched the dress with the same black heels Donovan presented me with when we went to the observatory, my favorite Chanel necklace, and my clutch from Hawaii. I felt enormously giddy knowing Donovan had gifted me all these accessories.

"Damn! You look good, Cousin."

"You think?" I felt shy now that Jane was commenting on my looks.

"I may have to come over and borrow that entire outfit from you one day."

"You are more than welcome to. It'll probably look better on your thin frame."

"You have no idea how good you look, Laney. Your curves are what make you look so feminine. And where, may I ask, did the necklace, clutch and shoes come from?"

I beamed. "If you can believe it, they were all from Donovan even before we started dating."

"What? Explain."

"These shoes came with a dress when he took me to the observatory one night, the clutch he bought for me when we were in Hawaii, but I was led to believe until recently that it was a gift from Jake and Emily, and the necklace that came in an adorable matching jewelry case, was an apology gift after Ashley's wedding."

"What the hell happened at that wedding between you two? I can't believe I was there and missed all the action."

"*LONG* story. I'll tell you one day when we have a lot of time." I looked upon my cousin with regret and sadness. "I guess this is good-bye for a while?" We had bonded over the past few days, and I would miss not being with her.

"Stupid me. We could've had this when we were younger. I always envied your friendship with Sam, but I thought I was too old for you two. I should've swallowed my stupid pride and joined you and Sam."

"We have the rest of our lives to become good friends. And there's Emily to be our referee if it gets ugly." We both laughed and hugged. "Have a safe trip back to London, then home. I'll miss both you and Max."

"We will miss you, too."

Max walked me out to the car that arrived after Jane and I had said good-bye. After putting our suitcases in the trunk, Max came around and gave me his easy-going grin.

"You happy?" he asked sweetly.

"Are you?"

"I couldn't be happier."

"Me neither and I have you to thank."

"Really?" He sounded surprised. "Why me?"

"Part of the reason why I decided to let go of Donovan's past, was after seeing you and Jane get engaged. I figured if you could forgive and work through your differences, who was I to hold a grudge? It wasn't like we were even together at the time. And to tell you the truth, I'm glad Donovan and I resolved everything and so quickly. He makes me incredibly happy."

Max gave me a big-brother hug. "He's a lucky man, but don't make it too easy for him. He needs to pay for some of his sins."

"Amen, Brother!" I agreed.

I got to our hotel room earlier than planned, hung up our clothes, and checked out the posh digs. He did get us a suite. There was soft music playing when I walked in and a huge vase of roses, almost blood orange in color, that sat in our bedroom. After a touch up to my make-up, I walked to the restaurant, excited to see my boyfriend.

To my horror, I realized I was the last one to arrive. Shit! How had that happened? All the men followed Donovan's example and stood up when I arrived. "I don't know how I could be the last one here when it took me less than two minutes to come from my room. I apologize!" I spoke hoping I didn't start the evening on the wrong foot.

"Hello, Princess. You look stunning." He kissed me lightly on the lips.

"Thank you." I did my absolute best not to look like a giddy teenager.

"New dress?" he whispered.

"Uh-huh! Jane and I decided to explore the 'hood."

Now he was doing his best not to look like a silly teenager in love.

"You two have to be either newlyweds or newly-dating," one of the ladies commented.

I looked at her in surprise. "How did you know?"

"You both have that *I'd rather be in a hotel bedroom rather than a hotel dining room* vibe."

The entire table laughed and though I laughed with them, I could feel my cheeks getting red.

"Hello. I'm Laney Reid."

"Reid?" One of the gentlemen asked, "Any relationship to Estelle?"

"She's my grandmother."

"You're dating the boss' granddaughter? Smart man!" All the men chuckled.

"Do all your client dinners last that long?" There was no way I was getting into the negligee I bought earlier today. All the wine and food weighed me down. "And what's with the meal lasting till almost midnight?"

"Italians like to start their dinners late, and it goes a good three hours. It was a bit heavy, huh?"

"I'm warning you now, there's not a chance in hell I'm wearing anything sexy to bed tonight. All that alcohol and salt have got me so bloated. I'm wearing my boyfriend sweats to bed."

"You actually own something sexy to wear to bed?"

When Donovan came to me in London, my go-to wear were those sweats, again. "I might have bought a piece or two...or three...or four..." I let it hang and went to brush my teeth and wash my face. The decision was made. I could not have sex tonight when I felt so unsexy. Tomorrow, I'd only eat a salad and drink water all day.

"Let me see what you bought."

"What for? I'm not wearing it. I feel about as sexy as a hippopotamus. We are not doing anything but sleeping tonight."

"The hell we aren't. I've had a semi hard-on all day today thinking about making love to you. Put on whatever it is that you bought today, or just strip and let's get started."

"That was so unromantic. You understand, this is my first time. This isn't like let's-get-it-over-with-in-the-back-seat-of-a-car."

"Princess, I booked a suite in one of Rome's finest hotels for you. A backseat romp was hardly my intention. Can I at least see what it is that I'm not getting tonight?"

Now I always thought of myself a smart girl, but somehow, I felt this man was duping me at this very moment. I took the bag of clothes and locked myself in the bathroom. While Jane went over to Josh's to drop something off this afternoon, I popped into the lingerie shop and the sales gal convinced me to buy four different possibilities for tonight. There was the black, barely there, split open in the front, come-hither one with lacy underwear. Then there was the pink, tight, hoochie-mama looking one. And then there were two white ones. The first white one was a pretty, romantic, Victorian looking one with lots of lace but very little cleavage, and then there was the white one with ruched straps, holding up a short, thin babydoll-looking dress. My large boobs made the dress even shorter but I thought this would be the one. All the sales gals voted for the black one, but given my status tonight, I went with the white babydoll one.

"Tonight..." he lamented.

Just for that comment, I decided to put on the hotel bathrobe over my negligee.

"OK, I'm ready for bed."

"Well?"

"Well what?" I played dumb.

"Why the hell are you wearing that robe? Let's see what's under it."

"You know," I said, "Max told me before he left, not to make life so easy for you, and I think he was right. After all the heartache you put me through, I think I gave in to you too easily. I was a floozy for always chasing after you and telling you how much I loved you."

"That bastard! I'm going to kick his ass for putting ideas into your head. Come on, Princess. Let's see what's under the robe." His begging soon turned into a threat, "Don't make me come over there and disrobe you."

"No. I think I'll sleep with this robe on tonight."

"Shit." he muttered and walked toward me. The suite was big enough for me to run away. I ran into the open balcony knowing I could come in through the living room. Donovan started giving chase.

"Aaah!" I screamed like a girl and ran as fast as I could, but our place wasn't exactly a football field.

"Gotcha!" Donovan tackled me onto the bed and I couldn't stop laughing. Before I could protest, I was divested of the robe, though I still lay on it, and Donovan gave an appreciative look-over.

"You like?" I asked in a breathy voice.

"I like." His approving hands roamed everywhere. "Can I see the other three tonight as well?"

"If you're a good boy, I may consider it."

"Model the other ones for me and I'll tell you which one is my favorite."

"And what will you do for me?"

"Everything." Now he was breathing hard and speaking of hard, I could feel him growing harder on me. It was exciting and scary at the same time.

Following his wishes, I tried on the other white one and Donovan said, "You're beautiful in it, but not for tonight. I need more skin."

When I wore the black one, he was speechless and the tenting in his pants was becoming even more pronounced, so I decided silence equaled approval.

The pink one got this reaction. "You can play the slut after I've turned you into one. Get back in the first one. You chose well."

As soon as I changed back into the first negligee, he pulled me onto the bed. With the way he was going to town on my neck after a brief but seriously hot kiss, I was glad we wouldn't see anyone this weekend. I'd have nips and bites all over.

"Um...Donovan...?"

"Hmmm?"

"It's too hot for a scarf and I'd like to leave the room before next week. Could you try not to leave too many dark marks on me?"

His lips went flat against my neck, and I could tell he was laughing. "Can I leave it in areas that can't be seen by others?"

"Uh-huh," I squealed as I felt his lips travel south.

He pulled the babydoll negligee over my head and now I was only in my lace underwear. The lights were completely on in the room and I was feeling totally self-conscious.

"You're gorgeous," he murmured right before he put a nipple in his mouth and started playing with it like I'd seen the twins playing with the nipple on their bottles. I would never be able to look at a nursing baby again without thinking of this man who was now suckling on my right nipple. He was soon trying his damnedest to swallow my breast—which was not happening unless you had the mouth of Jaws—and the feeling was insanely good.

"Is this supposed to feel this good?" The once squeal turned into a loud moan. The noises that came out of my mouth were foreign ones to me; ones I'd heard only in movies. I never thought they'd come from my own mouth.

"Uh-huh..." His voice trailed off as his mouth explored the left side.

"Uh...could we turn off a light or two or all?"

"Nope. I wanna see your body and watch your expressions."

So much for modesty. I figured at this point, I was just going to relax and enjoy. As much as it bothered me that this man knew exactly what he was doing, I suppose I was glad for it. He'd lead me in the right way.

His one hand moved down my body and began exploring me from over the lace underwear. His middle finger stroked right down my center, and it was embarrassing how soaked through I was. Feebly, I tried to push his hand away (though I had no idea why I did this). It felt like the right thing to do as Donovan kept assaulting every sense I had.

"Don't fight it. Just enjoy, Princess."

He was now watching me, and I had to turn away. I couldn't look him in the eye once the underwear came off and he really started stroking me.

"Love, look at me."

I shook my head no and closed my eyes.

Donovan placed his mouth over mine and I tightly grabbed onto his arms as he put one finger inside me.

"How does that feel?" He whispered in my ear, seconds before sucking it.

"So good," I moaned. "Everything feels so good, Donovan. I want more." I begged.

"More?" he teased while he took turns rubbing my clitoris then inserting that same finger inside me. I didn't know if this was normal practice but Donovan was going so slowly, it drove me completely wild.

"Faster!" I panted. "Faster, please..." I begged again. He smiled at my tortured expression and sped up just enough to get me moaning even louder and begging more frequently. "Donovan." I was crying without the tears. I'd never felt such frustration of wanting to reach a peak I could see right ahead of me, but kept disappearing like a mirage.

"Is this what you want?"

"AH!" My hips lifted off the bed when he put his finger in deeper. All this time I had no idea his finger wasn't even completely inside me. His finger gliding so easily all the way in and out felt glorious. The peak was that much closer; I could almost touch it.

"Perhaps this is what you want?" Donovan inserted another finger and all I could do was close my eyes and let death overtake me. This was pleasure and pain at its best. He then kept up the pressure of both fingers inserting in and out, and began stroking me with his thumb. I was at the absolute brink of exploding.

Whether it was the tenderness in his eyes, or the three-finger dexterity that made me break, but an orgasm ripped through me. I was lost. One moment, I was high-strung and tense from want, like an arrow on a bow waiting to be shot. Then in a split second, I was that wild and reckless arrow released into oblivion, not knowing where I was headed, not caring where I landed. My mind was blank of all thoughts but the pleasure that sluiced through my body, time and time again.

It wasn't until I let out a hard breath that I noticed I'd held my breath for the latter part of this orgasmic experience. When I returned to earth, Donovan was smiling wide and I turned red from all the noise and commotion I'd made.

"You enjoyed yourself?" He was kissing me lightly all over my face.

"Donovan, that was beautiful." I sighed with pleasure.

"How do you feel?" He had a smug, very satisfied look on his face.

"Boneless? Content? Thoroughly loved? Pick your favorite answer." I smiled, pushed him on his back and lay on top of him. "Why are you still dressed when I am totally naked?"

"I wanted to see you fall apart before I really got going. This is only the beginning, Princess. We've got all weekend." We began kissing again and as Donovan said, I could've done this with him all weekend if it were physically possible. "You are incredibly beautiful. I don't think I've seen a more beautiful woman than you, Princess."

Totally breaking the mood, I had to say, "You're so full of shit." I laughed to show him that I wasn't upset. I was only calling him on his sweet attempt at a lie.

"Did you just call me a liar?" His fingers went all over my naked body and tickled me till tears were spilling over. "Why would you think I was lying?" He asked in mock horror.

"Because you were with Kate all those years. Remember her? Ms. Glamorous? Then you crushed on Jane, Ms. Stunning. After those two ladies, I place a distant third."

"You, my precious lady will be first in my heart, forever." Now that was beautiful! "There's no denying Kate's beauty, but she's always made up. She's like one of those gorgeous look-but-don't-touch jewels." I didn't quite like how appreciative he was of her beauty. I guess I'd do best not to bring up other woman in the midst of making love, next time. "And Jane," *shit*, I guess I asked for this. "It's really her *I don't give a shit* attitude on the outside, but in actuality, *I do care* attitude on the inside that makes her endearing." The fact that he knew my cousin better than I thought he should was not sitting well with me. Here I was, naked and practically mounted on him, and he was waxing poetic about other women. *Sigh!*

"Are you done?" He understood my annoyance and his eyes crinkled in mirth.

"Nope. I'm not done."

"You'd rather talk when you have me naked and willing?"

"Nope. But since you brought it up, I need to clarify myself before someone jumps to unnecessary conclusions and we have an all out war, again."

"You're so melo..." That earned me a slap on the rear end.

"What makes you beautiful is your I-look-weak-on-the-outside-but-I'm-tougher-than-a-WWF-fighter-on-the-inside."

"Oh, that was really romantic." I used as much sarcasm as possible when saying this. Donovan chuckled.

"You're beautiful when you have absolutely no make-up on and your hair is in a pony tail, you're utterly irresistible when you're holding a baby, you're a knock-out in a bikini, and you're indescribable when you get dolled up for an evening. You are all that and so much more, Princess. And that's just the beginning of the beauty you are to me."

"Mr., after *that* kind of declaration, you can do whatever you want with me." I made my own declaration.

"Oh I plan to, Ms. Reid."

While Donovan was under me, I slowly undid his shirt buttons and opened him up, kissing his chest. Since I enjoyed his mouth on my nipple so very much, I'd return the favor.

"Fuck! That feels good," he groaned when my mouth landed on his chest and proceeded to play. Back and forth, back and forth, I went from one side of his chest to the other. His chest wasn't hairy like I imagined. In fact, it wasn't hairy at all. It was silky smooth and I couldn't stop touching it with my hand and mouth. Though Donovan was tall, his frame was on the thinner side. He was muscular, but not bulky and his abs were nice to feel and look at, but not ripped like an athlete. The picture that came to mind was David Beckham in the H&M underwear billboard, minus the tattoos. Damn! I was a lucky girl.

And to be perfectly honest, his body was second fiddle compared to how good-looking he was. My favorite look on my man was the one right now, with the overgrown stubble on his face, his wavy hair gone wild, and his eyes so full of love. All those times I'd wished for this man to notice me, someone up above was listening and had finally granted me my dearest wish.

"I love you," I spoke softly and continued going down his body. Clumsily, I undid his belt, then had a difficult time with all the buttons—outside and inside—but had no difficulty with the zipper. Once all his clothes were off, it seemed most natural for me to reciprocate orally. I had to pause, wondering if it was too forward of me to be so intimate. "Donovan?" I spoke quietly, again. "I don't know if I should do what I'd like to do." Super vague, super stupid—that's how I felt.

"You don't have to do anything you feel uncomfortable with, Princess. Come here and let me love you."

"I'd like to try on you what you did to me in Paris, but I'm unsure if I'll do it right."

"Just don't bite, that's all I ask."

That brought out the giggles, and I opened my mouth to take him in when the phone rang and startled me. Thank God, he wasn't in my mouth yet...

"Are you going to answer that?"

"Are you going to continue?"

"Not till you answer. When someone calls this late, it's usually not a good sign. Answer it."

"Fuck!" He swore soundly and picked up the phone, pissed. "What is it, Becky?" he asked, annoyed with his sister.

"Donovan!" I admonished.

"You have got to be fucking kidding me. Go back to your damn hotel. How'd you find me?"

I pulled the phone away from this irate man. "Hello? Becky?" I answered, worried. "What's wrong?"

"Laney." She was crying. "Can you please tell me which room you're in? I'm at the lobby in your hotel."

"We're in room 832. Come on up."

"Thank you."

"How can you yell at your pregnant sister like that? She's in the lobby, crying. Have you no heart?"

"She and Al got into another stupid argument."

"But she's crying." I defended Becky.

"What about me? My girlfriend was about to give me our first blowjob and my silly-ass sister interrupted us. I feel like crying, too." He pouted. I kissed this pouty mouth.

"We'll finish once Becky leaves."

"Don't let her reel you in with her drama or she'll never leave," he warned as we both got up to look decent.

Donovan put on a pair of pajamas and grudgingly greeted his sister while I went to assess the damage. Damn. This man had done a thorough job of leaving hickeys all over my upper body. Most could be covered with clothes, but the one right below my ear and the other one at the base of my neck and top of my shoulder were dark and obvious. I'd have to scold him later. For now, I threw on one of Donovan's nightshirts and put the plush hotel robe on, praying that it would cover most of the hickeys on my neck.

"Becky." I tried to appear kind and sympathetic to her situation, but I wasn't happy, either. Of course, I didn't want anything to be wrong with her or Al, or the baby, but my poor boyfriend was suffering. "What's the matter?"

"Laney..." Becky ran over to me, held me tight and began bawling. Donovan was behind her furiously shaking his head no.

"What's wrong, Becky? It's late. You and the baby should be in bed." *Like we were...*

"Al and I had the biggest fight." She was tugging on my robe while crying. I kept trying to pull it up around my neck, but Becky's weight wasn't helping the situation. Donovan, who noticed the dark mark on my neck, only laughed. I shot him a nasty look.

"What was the fight about?" I was having a verbal conversation with Becky and a silent one with Donovan yelling at him to stop making lewd faces at me. I was trying hard to empathize with his sister, and he was trying his best to get me to laugh.

"Al doesn't love me like he used to, Laney. He used to be so romantic before I got pregnant. Now he thinks I'm fat, and he doesn't want to court me like before." She wailed and Donovan rolled his eyes. "Don't you dare call him!" Becky bit off her brother's head when he took out his cell phone.

"He'll worry."

"No he won't. He doesn't care anymore."

"Don't be an idiot." Donovan's lost patience caused his sister to cry even harder.

"Now my brother doesn't love me anymore, either." She wailed loudly!

While Donovan whispered, "I need you the hell out of here." I consoled Becky while Donovan dialed his phone. *"Come pick up your wife!"* he demanded. *"Room 832. NOW!"*

"What could Al have possibly done? He's such a nice guy. Why he's as nice as my cousin Jake, or maybe even Max."

"He's not!" She insisted. "He never takes me out anymore because he's always tired. When I was first pregnant, he used to run to the market whenever I had a craving, or he used to rub my feet when I was tired. Now, he comes home from a trip and all he does is sleep."

"Your husband travels and works hard. You freaking stay home all day and eat bon-bons. You should be the one massaging his feet!" Donovan yelled at his sister, again.

"Why can't you be more like Jake? He's always looking out for Jane."

"Jane!" Donovan lit up like a Christmas tree. "Why the hell are you here with us when Jane is in town? She's staying at Roland's. Why don't you go and give her your woes?"

"Donovan," I admonished. "Not nice."

"You better watch out, Laney. Men are all like that. Once they get in your pants, they know they don't have to work that hard anymore. Don't let him in, Laney. Stay strong! Keep him chasing you."

"Are you drunk?"

"What the fuck do you think? I'm pregnant! Do you think I'd risk my child's life and get drunk, you moron?"

Now, this was getting ugly. "Donovan." I harped. "Sit over there and keep your mouth shut." Surprisingly, he did exactly as I told him to do. "Becky." I harped at her too. "It's close to sunrise. What you're doing is not considerate to your baby. Whatever issues you have going on with Al, don't take it out on your child. He or she needs rest, and so do you."

It was as though Becky needed my permission, because as soon as I was done talking, her head nodded onto my chest and she was gone.

"Did she just fall asleep on me while I was yelling at her?" I leaned Becky back so I could look at her face. "Shit, did I just yell at your sister?"

Donovan helped me get her settled comfortably on the sofa, and we brought out a pillow and blanket for her.

"Where the hell is Al?" Donovan muttered.

"Maybe you should try carrying her into our bedroom and have her sleep on our bed." I suggested.

"Hell no! Do you think I can carry her? She's a house, already. She's definitely been eating too many bon-bons."

"Donovan..." I lamented, but soon started laughing. Becky was quite big for being six months pregnant.

"Knock-knock?" Al walked in. I guess we had never properly closed the door.

"Where the hell have you been while your wife went off on a drunken rampage?"

"Have you tried catching a cab at this hour?"

"Hi, Al." I smiled, and closed my robe tighter and closer up my neck.

"Hey, Laney. I hope Becky didn't bother you too badly at this hour."

"Oh, no she wasn't much of a bother. We had nothing special going on." I tried to play it off like I didn't have two massive hickeys on my neck.

"Like hell we didn't!" Donovan huffed and puffed. "What was the issue tonight?"

"Becky wanted to go have dinner, but I had a dinner meeting. She's normally not this high strung," he tried to explain to me. "The baby has been sitting on her sciatic nerve and doesn't seem to want to get off it, so she's been in a lot of pain." It was sweet the way Al was protecting his wife.

"You don't have to explain, Al. I'm sure all women handle pregnancies differently. You want to sit and have a drink? You look like you could use one."

"Don't invite him, too. We're stuck with Becky, tonight." Donovan complained.

"Stop." I whispered and kissed his pouty mouth, again. "You're not being hospitable and this is family. I don't know how you Taylors roll, but we Reids never turn out a family member," I teased. "Al, why don't you stay the night? Both those sofas pull out into a bed. Once we get one open, you men can transfer Becky onto the bed and you can squeeze in there with her."

"Thanks, Laney. I'll forego the drink, but I welcome sleep. Come on, Bro'. Help me transfer your sister."

A good ten minutes later, Al and Becky were settled and we walked back into our bedroom, happy to be alone.

"Blow job?" was the first word out of Donovan's mouth.

"Not on your life with Al and Becky a wall away."

"Shit!" was the only other word I heard before we fell asleep.

"Hello?" I heard Donovan groan as he picked up his phone. "Yeah. No, Pa. We don't want to. We are tired. No...Pa! Good morning, Ma. No. No. No!"

Donovan was getting so cantankerous on the phone, I pulled it away from him. "Good morning, Ma. What's the matter?"

"Your Pa and I are trying to get the family together one last time for breakfast because Kelley and Noah are leaving today and Donny isn't being cooperative. You'll have breakfast with us?"

"We'd love to, Ma. It'll probably take us an hour or so. Would you like to come our way? Then we can meet you in half an hour."

"You're brilliant, Baby. We'll come to your hotel. I have to call Becky, now. I'll see you later."

"Ma?"

"What, honey?"

"Becky is right here. We will let her know. You get yourself here, safely."

"What the hell is Becky doing in your hotel room?"

"I'm sure she'll love explaining everything at breakfast. Bye, Ma."

"Bye, Baby!"

"Why the hell did you agree to have breakfast with everyone?"

"Because your sister and brother-in-law are leaving, and your parents want to get their children together."

"I'm getting us out of here after breakfast. I need to go someplace where I can't find a Taylor or a Reid."

We decided to get ready first and let Becky sleep in as long as possible. I was cursing Donovan Taylor to hell and back when I couldn't hide the hickeys on my neck. The best I could do was put a ton of mineral powder all over my neck, and a simple summer scarf to try and hide the prominent one at the base of my neck.

"Damn you for making these dark marks. I told you only in areas where they can't be seen."

Donovan grinned wide and kissed the other side of the neck that didn't have any marks. "I was putting a stamp on my woman."

"What am I, cattle? You're branding me with your mouth?"

"You didn't seem to mind when I was sucking on your neck and finger fucking you at the same time."

His sexy words made me instantly horny. In the craziest move known to Delaney Reid, I took off Donovan's towel and went straight to my knees. "You better pray your sister and brother-in-law stay asleep."

Before Donovan knew what hit him, I took him all the way in my mouth. My initial thought was to suck only on the tip, but I was fueled with pure unadulterated lust.

"Shit!" He groaned and put both hands on my head. Not having a clue between correct and incorrect, I took him in and treated him like my favorite popsicle. "Fuck," he whispered, "slow down." I did as he begged. With this being new to me, I sucked slowly and methodically, making sure I wasn't missing anything. "Shit, faster. Go faster." This man was even bossy while getting a blow job. There were too many damn instructions.

Donovan's face looked part pleasured, part pained, and with a sudden soft knock at our bedroom door, he cursed one last time and spilled into my not-ready-for-his-release mouth. My face crinkled into a this-is-freaking-gross look, but luckily, Donovan didn't catch it. He quickly donned a robe and went to address whoever was at the door. I didn't envy the person who had to contend with the ugly-fire-breathing-Donovan. While he took care of our visitor, I didn't know what the hell to do with the stuff in my mouth. Was I to swallow it? (Eew!) Was it rude to spit it out in the sink or the toilet? Before this taste stayed on my tongue any longer, I spit it into the sink and brushed my teeth, again.

Breakfast was a lively affair, but anytime you had Ma and Pa at a table, it was lively and fun. Becky explained why she and Al slept in our room, and Donovan added all the missing drama.

"You act like you're the youngest of the five. What is wrong with you?" Kelley scolded.

"I'm sorry. As much as I love this baby inside of me, I can't wait for him or her to come out. I'm in so much pain all the time."

"Maybe you shouldn't have flown all the way out here," Ma worried.

"The pain is the same no matter where I am." Becky answered sheepishly and looked at Al. "I'm sorry for yelling at you. I know you're working hard to provide for us."

"What about us?" Donovan butted into their private moment so I pinched him wherever I could grab some extra skin.

"Laney, I'm very sorry for barging in at that hour. And thank you for allowing us to sleep in the living room. I heard my brother wanted to kick us out in the middle of the night but it was you who suggested we sleep on the pull-out." Becky gave her brother a not very nice look.

"It wasn't a big deal."

"Donny, you and Laney want to…"

"Nope. We're leaving after breakfast, Ma."

"Where are you going?"

"Where you, Pa and anybody with the last names Taylor or Reid cannot find us."

I could see the disappointment on Ma's face. "Donovan. Can't we stay for just…"

"Nope," he cut me off. "Tickets are purchased. We leave in ninety minutes. The car will be here in forty-five."

"Sorry," I whispered to Ma and put my hand over hers. "Sorry, Pa." I reached over and patted his hand as well.

"Laney, when are you two getting married?" Pa asked. "You two are getting married?" This time, his question came out strained and uncertain.

"I don't know, Pa."

"You don't know when you're getting married or whether or not you're getting married?" He continued as the Taylor family spokesperson.

"Both. The answers lie with your son."

"She speaks in riddles, Pa. I've told her repeatedly that we're getting married, but she keeps thwarting me. She tells me I'm doing something wrong and I have no damn clue what it is that I'm doing wrong."

"Don't you want to marry our Donny? You told me you've been lusting after him since you were a little girl. Why you even asked him to marry you."

"Pa!" Blood was thicker than water, no matter the situation. "You promised to keep my secret! I can't believe you just blurted that out."

"We're family. There are no secrets." Pa answered nonchalantly. "And you," he turned to his son. "You big moron. Why didn't you accept her proposal and be done with? You could have had a dozen kids by now." Those mimosas were getting to Pa Taylor. Between the two big hickeys the family most likely noticed but was playing dumb about, and Pa's revelation of me lusting after Donovan since birth, my angelic reputation was shot.

"Why are you such a brat to your family?" Donovan and I were seated comfortably on a train headed back to Florence. Donovan explained there were a couple of things he wanted me to experience, and since no one would be there to interrupt us, we decided to go back to Grandfather's villa.

"They were driving me crazy. I moved my life to London so I could woo you, and they all follow me out here and disrupt my attempts to love you."

"If I recall correctly, it was thanks to our parents that you got me out of London and away from Michael."

"Smooth move, huh? That was all my idea."

"What do you mean?"

"Jake told me about this conference in Amsterdam so I convinced your dad to do his seminar—actually, I begged him because I knew I needed the help getting you away from Michael. That's when your mom and my parents offered to tag along and 'help.'"

"You are so devious."

"And you love me for it." He kissed me briefly. "Speaking of devious, what the hell was my father talking about at the breakfast table? You were very lucky to have had that awkward conversation deflected on Becky and her I-think-I'm-having-a-contraction-but-it-was-only-gas-pains. I hope you're not going to be such a pain in the ass when you're pregnant with our baby."

"And if I am?" I challenged.

Donovan shrugged like he could care less, but soon smiled. "I would love you no matter what." That made me smile with him. "Now talk. When did you ask me to marry you? Was this recent?"

"No." I answered without enthusiasm. I knew this conversation would not be to my benefit, and I had no idea how I was going to get out of it.

"Talk, Delaney Reid!" Now he was impatient.

"The summer I turned twelve," I stopped and dug out my notes from his briefcase. "Read this." I gave him my proposal note.

"Donovan, you   me? If so,   me at   swing   pm." He had a blank look. "What the hell is it supposed to say?"

"Didn't you read this eleven years ago when I put it in your pocket? It said, *'Donovan, will you marry me? If so, meet me at my swing at 11:00pm.'*"

This note, which was written with a red marker, had watermarks that bled through some of the words. Donovan kept looking at the note and I could see a whole lot of nothing going through his head.

"It's bugging me that I don't remember ever reading this note. I definitely would have remembered an offer of marriage had I read it. Why the hell do I not remember this one?"

"Maybe I'll help jog your memory. One summer day right after my twelfth birthday, you and Jake came to his house and swam with us. I shoved this note in your pocket when you weren't looking, then swam with you as you proceeded to tell me you were going off to law school in New York. If that wasn't devastating enough for a twelve-year-old who had missed you when you stopped coming around, you nearly put me in my grave when you told me you were going to propose to Kate the same day I proposed to you."

"Now I remember. I remember what happened that day and I have a perfectly good explanation why I never got this proposal. But I want to hear the rest of your story first. So what happened after I told you that I was going to propose to Kate? And why the hell did I tell a twelve-year-old that I was going to propose to my girlfriend?"

"I asked you point-blank whether or not you were going to marry this woman. I caught you off guard and you answered me truthfully."

"You always did have a way of throwing me off kilter—even as a young child."

"You must've known I had the biggest crush on you when I was little, didn't you?"

"Yeah I knew you had a crush on me, but so did the rest of your cousins. It was nothing new to have one of you Reid girls following me around trying to get my attention." His cocky grin was one of his sexiest expressions.

"Cocky Bastard!" That earned me a spine-chilling kiss on the base of my neck again. I had all kinds of images of us from last night, once he started sucking on my neck. "Decorum, please." I called out in a hoarse voice. "We're not the only ones on the train, Donovan." Now I was begging because Donovan refused to stop and I could feel his hand on my thigh. "Please," I moaned and panted.

He placed one last chaste kiss on my neck and returned to that cocky grin. "So that night, Jake and I stopped by our fraternity party, and we weren't there long, when some drunk bumped into me and spilled his beer on the front of my khaki pants. Not realizing you had placed a note in my pocket—a note written in *red*—I thought my dick or balls were bleeding because the front of my pants went red, everywhere. I kept looking for the cause of the blood. I kept trying to feel the pain but I couldn't figure it out until I went to the bathroom and found your note." He pulled out the note again. "And as you can see, beer had bled through the key words so I had no idea what this said."

"While you were partying it up at the frat house, I went home and cried myself to sleep after you told me about proposing to Kate. Mom woke me up to tempt me down to dinner, but I stayed in my room until everyone had gone to bed. Right before 11:00pm, I snuck down-stairs and waited for you on my swing. I cried a lot on my swing, you know."

"You did?" He sweetly brought me to him.

"Whenever I was sad because of you, I sat on that swing, and some-thing about that rocking motion helped me chase the blues away."

"You may have been crying, but I was seriously worried about my posterity when I saw what I thought was blood, everywhere."

We both laughed. Eleven years removed, that was quite funny.

"What did you do when you realized it wasn't blood, but my silly letter?"

"I almost went to your house to tell you never to write to me in red, again."

"So..." I contemplated whether I needed this bit of information in my life, but being the masochist that I was, I *had* to know. "What happened when you asked Kate to marry you? How did you propose?" Why was I such a glutton for punishment?

Donovan was a smart man. He carefully thought this over before opening his mouth.

"You sure you want to do this?"

"Yeah. I don't know if I'll ever understand you and Kate, but since we're on the topic of proposals, I'd like to know."

"With Kate being older and much wealthier than I, our relationship was always in her favor. I was her..."

"...boy toy...?"

Donovan busted up. "Yeah. For a lack of a better word, 'boy toy.' Her sophistication, her glamour, her power—those were all aphrodisiacs for a young man in his 20's. She took me to Europe, introduced me to power-ful lawyers, wined and dined me. In short, I was star-struck and Kate was very generous to me."

"Before leaving for law school, I proposed to her, our last night to-gether at the Montage, and she took my proposal and laughed at me. She said she had no thoughts of settling down, she had *no* desire to have kids, and she told me I needed to become somebody before she could consider marrying me."

"Ouch." I rubbed his arm, feeling his rejection.

"At the time it was an ouch, but after I went off to New York and re-covered from the kick in the pants, I realized it was a good thing she didn't accept. My parents didn't like her. My sisters thought I was crazy for dating her. Jake liked her as a friend, but never thought she was the right one for me. And what put the nail on the coffin was the fact that she didn't want kids. Coming from a family of five, I always knew I wanted a houseful of kids—and that was *not* for Kate. So in actuality, I was really only with Kate for less than two years."

"Then where does this ten-year hashtag come from?"

"If she and I were anywhere in the near vicinity, we usually hooked up if we weren't seeing other people." He said this super fast but there was no misunderstanding what he meant.

"And...when did this hook up finally end?"

"After the Montage when you Reids surprised me with your presence at dinner. After I saw you at the office back in January, when you didn't recognize me..."

"Oh, I knew who you were," I corrected him.

"Were you fucking with my mind, even back then? You knew who I was but pretended you didn't know me?" He had that flabbergasted look and his voice went up half an octave.

"Did you or did you not pretend not to know me at Jake and Emily's wedding when you showed up with that bimbo?"

"I can't ever win an argument with you." He chuckled and gave me an open mouth kiss. "Do you know why I didn't talk to you at Jake's wedding?"

"Because you were busy ogling other women, Jane included?"

"Damn. You gonna bust my balls every time another woman is involved in our conversation?" He chuckled some more.

"Maybe..." I gave a non-committal answer.

"I ignored you because when I asked Jake about the blonde bombshell sitting at the family table, he informed me that it was the little girl I considered a fifth sister. I didn't know which would kill me first, the heart attack or the boner coming on. You were breathtaking and all grown-up. I didn't think I could go up and talk to you without stumbling over my words like an idiot."

"You're so full of shit. I don't believe you."

His eyes bugged-out at my accusation. "Why do you keep calling me a liar? I am wounded, Princess."

"You never gave me a second look at the wedding. I kept hoping to catch your eye so I could go over and say hello, but you kept busy with everyone at the reception but me."

"I swear, I did my utmost not to look at you because of the constant hard-on I had from ogling your body. Now you tell me why you pretended not to know me when we met again that winter morning."

"I was still pissed that I had slept outside on the front porch for a man who never showed up to answer my proposal."

"What do you mean you slept outside? Why would you do that?"

"Because, Mr. Taylor. I waited for you to either call and say you weren't coming, or for you to come and tell me we were or were not getting married." I spoke a little louder than necessary. "Then, I fell asleep on the swing and my family thought I got kidnapped in the middle of the night. Dad finally found me outside, and I almost got the scolding of my life until I explained that I was supposed to meet someone who *never showed up!*" I laughed at my own silliness. "I said those last few words with such conviction, Dad laughed at me. You know what I told him when he warned me never to sleep outside, ever again?"

"What, Princess?"

"I told him, *'I won't ever do this again because no one is ever coming for me.'* I was such a melodramatic child, huh? I hope I don't have a daughter just like me." I groaned.

"I can't wait to fill our home with a gaggle of girls just like you. Although, they may put me into an early grave, huh?" He now turned serious on me. "I came back for you. I love you. And I want to start a life with you. Why don't you want to marry me?"

"You still don't get it?" I was disappointed that he continually demanded a marriage rather than proposing one.

"No. Will you clue me in one of these days?"

"Perhaps you should check your pockets, daily, for a note written in red?"

"Smart ass!" He laughed and kissed me again.

After dropping off our suitcases at the villa, our driver took us north to Bologna. Donovan gave me no clue what we were doing, except for telling me that I would love what we were about to experience.

He blindfolded me as we got close to our destination and carefully led me into a noisy machine-filled room.

"Enjoy, Princess. This afternoon is for you..." The blindfold came off and once my vision came back to 20/20, I observed my surroundings and found myself at the Ducati factory. I let out a small squeal, and followed the tour guide as she led us through the entire factory. We were actually in the production line watching factory workers assemble these gorgeous motorcycles. Interspersed with the tour was the history of Ducati and what made these bikes so special. After the tour, we went through the museum and I read every bit of information given, as well as drooled over all original, priceless, and soon-to-be released bikes.

"I love this. Thank you." I kissed my boyfriend in appreciation.

"What will you offer me if I offer you a test drive on the bike of your choice?"

"My virginity?" I giggled.

His smile was bright and *WIDE*. "If you're done here, get back in the car."

The driver led us to a test track near the Ferrari museum, and we were offered not only a chance to ride the Ducati motorcycles, but also to test drive Ferraris and Lamborghinis. Oh. My. Gaawwdd! What a thrill.

We picked different motorcycles, got brief instructions, put on our helmets, and were given free rein to ride the bikes around the track. Contrary to what was visible to the eye, the "track" was not what I considered a test track—going round and round in circles. We rode through the streets of Emilia Romagna, overlooking the mountains nearby Modena. The wind through my hair recharged the high I had been on since Donovan professed his love for me. What was supposed to be a ten-minute ride ended up being half an hour as our guide was cool enough to take us through streets not normally used for test drives. When we were done with the bikes, Donovan hopped into a Ferrari, I got into a Lamborghini and we went a different route from our bike route. I loved fast cars, but nothing felt as good as a fast bike.

When we got off our thrill rides, I felt punchy and almost skittish from the natural high. "That was so freaking cool! That beats everything we've done so far."

"You're a speed demon, Princess. I always knew you were a daredevil, but damn, you're a monster out on the road with a motorcycle. Pick a bike, Princess. I'll buy you which ever bike you want."

"Aaahhh!" I screamed. "You know my dream is to buy a Harley, but after test driving this Ducati, I might have changed my mind. But I don't think I should get a bike, yet. I don't want you to buy me one."

"Why not?"

"Because I can't ride it in London with all that crazy traffic and I eventually will have to take it back to the States. Let's hold off on getting it. But thank you for the generous offer." I gave him an innocent kiss on the cheek.

"Where did you learn to ride a bike?"

"A friend from college taught me. He had a Triumph, and I salivated over it enough for him to offer me a ride, and eventually lessons on that bike."

"He was probably salivating over you."

"We were just friends." I corrected him. "Did I tell you Max is getting a Ducati?"

"Doesn't he already have a bike?"

"He does. He has that beautiful Harley. Remember when Jane asked to talk to me the other night in Florence?"

"Yeah."

"Well, after we talked about you, she asked me to help her order a bike for Max. I picked out the bike I test-drove today. I can't wait to hear what Max thinks."

"Well, I offered you a test drive in exchange for your virginity," he announced smugly. "Let's go make good on your offer."

"How about dinner, first?"

"You better not complain you're too full to do anything tonight."

I laughed! "All right. After you feed me, I'll lay there and let you do whatever you want with me."

"Deal!"

Dinner was a simple and very quick couple bowls of pasta and a bottle of wine. We were both still coming off the high of the fast rides and eager to get home.

"Donovan?" He looked at me in response. "Would it bother you very much if I called Michael just to make sure he's OK? I texted him a few times but haven't gotten a response, and his sister Ruby also hasn't been responding back to me. It's really bothering me."

"If you must..." He didn't like my request at all. I had considered not asking Donovan, but thought for the good of the relationship, I should ask.

"You know, I'd like to eventually return to being good friends with Michael if he'll have me as a friend." Now I was getting the surly face. "Michael and Ruby were incredibly good to me when I landed in England, and they've become dear friends. I like them and I like him as a person very much."

"Just don't get angry with me when I stay friends with Kate."

Perhaps I was being a hypocrite, but what he just said pissed me off. "You cannot equate me and Michael with you and Kate!"

"Why not?" Did he really have no idea or was he trying to goad me into a fight?

"Because I wasn't in love with Michael. I didn't want to marry him. And I wasn't with him for ten years!"

"Well, it's been a long time since I've been in love with Kate. It's also been a long time since I've wanted to marry Kate. And I told you, we weren't together for ten years. Whomever you choose to stay friends with is your choice, but you need to give me the same courtesy."

"Fine!"

Later, I'd probably think this wasn't the best idea, but being the hot-headed woman that I was sometimes, I decided to call Michael right here, right then.

"Hello?" He actually answered my call.

"Hi Michael." I said, with some trepidation. "How are you?"

"All right, and you?"

"A little worried you may yell at me or hang up on me. I was surprised you picked up my call." I could feel Donovan's wrath from the other seat so I turned myself around and talked out the window.

"Are you back in London?"

"No. I'm back in Florence but I'll be back in London tomorrow. Can we meet?" Once again, I was tentative in asking and sitting on very thin ice with Donovan. I could feel the fire emanating from his skin. "Tea at the Berkeley? Your favorite?"

That brought out a small laughter from Michael, which made me feel a thousand times better. "Sure. The hostess should keep our standing reservation, even after one missed tea. Wednesday?"

I smiled. "Wednesday it is. Will you bring Ruby with you? I know she's mad at me, too, but please tell her I miss her as I've missed you."

And, that was the straw that broke the camel's back. Donovan grabbed my phone and threw it out of the car and into a flat, empty plot of land in the middle of Tuscany.

"What the hell was that?" I yelled really loudly, really angrily. Donovan and I were both caught off guard by my belligerence. "Why do you keep doing that?"

"Why the fuck are you missing this guy?" Now Donovan was angry. "You really miss him that much? You want me to disappear so you can get back together with him? Is that what you want? Shit, if I'd known how impossible you'd be, I wouldn't have started this chase. I've never had to work so hard for anything in my life and I'm sick of it. Stop playing these fucking games with me."

I was frozen from his anger, his acrimony, and his accusation. What I thought was one friend missing another friend, Donovan considered inappropriate. What I considered wooing, he considered it a difficult chase. And what I believed was playfulness, he had considered it a mind game. We were on complete opposite spectrums of thought.

Keeping to myself the rest of the ride, we got back to Grandfather's and I was absolutely lost. I didn't know what to do, where to go, and to whom I was supposed to turn to for comfort. I could feel my stomach knotting and my chest tingling in pain so I decided to do some work, lest the tears fell.

"I'm going to sleep," was all Donovan muttered before going upstairs.

I nodded and stared at my laptop.

Half an hour later, I was still staring at the screen, unable to move away from this feeling of abandonment. It was late, but I decided to call my mom from my laptop.

"Hello?"

"Hi Mom."

"Laney. Where are you, Sweetheart?"

"I'm back in Florence."

"What are you doing back there?"

"Donovan took me to the Ducati factory and museum and we test drove a Ducati, a Ferrari, and a Lamborghini."

"That Donovan is spoiling you rotten. He didn't buy you a motorcycle did he?" Mom never liked the idea of me on that dangerous vehicle.

"He offered, but I didn't take him up on it."

"Good! Tell him I don't approve."

A weak laugh escaped me. "How long will you be here?"

"As long as you need me. Your dad left already. He needed to get back to the hospital."

"I know. He called me from the airport."

"What's wrong, Honey?"

"Nothing." I knew Mom was too smart to fall for my lie, but I didn't want to admit that after all these years of loving a single man, I couldn't make it work for more than a week.

Mom was silent on her part and waited for me to talk. I didn't say anything to the contrary.

"What should you and I do before I go back home?" Mom tried to make small talk.

"I'd like to take you to watch a play at the Globe Theatre. I'd also like to see Stonehenge with you. You can make notes of the decor and placement of the rocks." Mom laughed. "And maybe you and I can visit Scotland and Ireland. I'll take advantage of your deep pockets and let you pay. Will you schedule those trips for us?"

"Sure. When do you want to go?"

"I'm supposed to meet Michael on Wednesday. I'll see if we can meet Monday, instead. How about if we leave Tuesday?"

"What about Donovan?" Mom treaded lightly. She knew there was something wrong with us. "Your Gram tells me there's a very important office function on Tuesday. Even she's attending. Won't you be attending with him?"

"I don't think he needs me there." *And I don't think he wants me there or anywhere else for that matter.*

"You sure you're doing all right?"

"I'm fine, Mom." I did my best to sound cheerful. "I'll see you tomorrow?"

"I'll be here. I love you, Laney."

"Love you too."

That conversation did nothing to alter my mood, so this time I called Dad. It was early in Los Angeles, but I knew Dad would be awake.

"Hello?" Dad answered as cheerfully as ever.

"Hi Daddy."

"Laney! Where is my globe-trotting daughter, now?"

"I'm back in Florence. Are you at the hospital, already?"

"My sweet daughter, I've been here since 4:30am, operated on a patient already, and am now enjoying my second cup of coffee."

I giggled. "Who made your scrambled eggs today?"

"Nobody." He pretended to be disgruntled. "I need my baby home to scramble my eggs for me."

"Daddy?"

"Yes, Baby?"

"I think I've decided to go to med school."

"I knew it! You made the right decision, Baby. You're going to make a phenomenal doctor."

"I think I want to be a heart surgeon like you and Jake."

"Damn! You have just made my day. You're a brilliant girl. You'll make a fine surgeon."

"But I'm a little worried, Daddy."

"What worries you?"

I sighed. "It takes so long to become a surgeon, and I'm already starting a year late. When will I get married and have kids? And how will I raise these kids if I'm working all the time? Although..."

"Although what?"

"Remember how I've always told you I didn't think anyone ever wanted me? How I thought I'd never get married?"

"Yeah..."

"I think my life is a series of self-fulfilled prophecies."

"If that's the case, you would have been married to that man of yours since you were ten." My father laughed. "You've always known what you wanted and were determined to work hard for it. Nothing has been handed to you, my sweet child. You are a going to be a great success in life because you are level-headed, logical, and you have your parents' work ethics. Don't worry about the future. Be content with the present, Laney."

"Do you think I should come back home and start med school this year? Should I start it out here? Can you and Jake help me get into a med school here, then transfer back home?"

"If you're sure you want to start now, come home. There's nothing keeping you in London anymore. I'll talk to the dean and get you enrolled."

"Give me a couple of days to think about it? I'll let you know soon. Thank you, Daddy."

"Sweet dreams, Laney."

"Bye, Daddy. I love you."

Another conversation done, and I felt a little better, but nothing would take away this sour mood. I wanted to change out of these jeans but doing that would require me to go into the bedroom and I didn't have the fortitude for that just now. I sat on the couch, streaming a scary movie and sleeping on and off.

As I saw the sun rising, I decided to get off the couch and visit that bakery Max and Jane had been to last time we were here. It was gorgeous outside. The way the sun was hitting the hills in all shades of reds and oranges and yellows, I could stare at the setting all morning. Grabbing some pastries and a cup of coffee, I walked the neighborhood and enjoyed the quiet.

When I finally got back in, Donovan was nowhere to be seen so I left his pastry right by the coffee machine and left him a note saying I was going out for a ride on the Vespa.

When we were last here and I was keeping myself busy before the Bocelli concert, my exploration of the house led me to the garage and the twin Vespas collecting dust. I cleaned off the years of dust on the scooter and went out for a long ride. My conversation with my dad last night was foremost on my mind. Maybe it was a good idea to go back home and to start med school this year. Regardless of what might happen between me and Donovan, I had a life to live and a future to secure. When I got back to my computer, I'd ask my father to help me enroll this year and work my way toward becoming a doctor.

While I was glad to have figured out a major part of my life, somewhere during the ride, I took a wrong turn and kind of got lost. Turning the scooter around, I did my best to backtrack and to remember buildings and signs that I may have passed. Unfortunately, there were no signs anywhere and I was so intent on figuring out my future, I couldn't remember seeing any buildings along the way. And one olive grove looked the same as all the others, and one vineyard was really no different from the rest.

It was too early for any places to be open, and in reality, there were no shops along this road. It was all farmland. I was screwed. As time passed, a few people came along the road so I asked about the bakery I'd visited this morning. Finally, a local showed me how to get back to the bakery and from there I was able to get back to the villa. I was never so happy to see a familiar place.

"Where the hell have you been?" Donovan lunged at me with his body and wouldn't let go of me. "I've been so worried."

"I got a little lost." I didn't expect this kind of welcome.

"A little lost? You've been gone for hours!" He made me wince when he raised his voice. "I thought you had left me, again."

"I haven't been gone that long. I don't know...I thought I was riding straight and was going to come back the same way, but I must have turned somewhere and all the roads look the same and..."

"Don't leave me again, Delaney." He implored while still holding me. "I'm sorry I was such an asshole last night. It puts me in a shit mood when I think about you having shared your affection with another man. If I had admitted to myself that I was in love with you before you left, you would never have been with Michael. It drives me insane whenever I think of my mistake."

I pulled away and looked at this man whose expression was broken. Weaving my fingers through his unruly hair, I smiled thinking of the last time I did this back at Jake's house while Donovan was sleeping. It was back then that I had wished him a happy life with another woman. "Maybe you were right, Donovan. This," I pointed to me and him, "was all a thrill of the chase for you. You may think otherwise, but I've never played games with you because I know I'll always lose, and losing hurts." I pushed away the falling tears with my hand. "As much as I dreamed you to be the perfect man for me, I don't think I'm the perfect girl for you. You don't have to try and make this work with me. I know Jake and my family, as well as your parents have pushed you to come find me. It may hurt for a while, but I'll be all right without you. Go and find your special lady." No matter how hard I tried, I couldn't stop crying because I knew deep in my heart, Donovan would be my one and only special man. There would be no other.

"Are you done?" he asked with a silly grin. With tears still falling, I nodded yes. "*You* are not getting away from me that easily. You may be all right without me, but I won't be all right without you. You are my one and only special lady, and you're not the only one who hurts when things go wrong. I love you, Delaney Reid. That's not going to change, no matter your melo mood and speech."

As usual, Donovan had me laughing and crying at the same time. "So what are you trying to say?" *Like I didn't know...*

"I love you. I know you're not playing games with me, though it's still a riddle why you won't marry me. Even if it takes an eternity, I'll win your hand and make beautiful babies with you."

"I might be too old to have kids if it's going to take you an eternity to get this right," I joked.

"Then we'll just have them out of wedlock," he joked right back. "Princess. Let's not fight. And if we do, let's resolve it immediately. I was so miserable last night without you. I kept waiting for you to come up so I could apologize but you never came up, and like a moron, I fell asleep. When I woke up this morning, I was a little crazed I couldn't find you."

"I left you a note."

"I read it but didn't know what to think when you didn't come back for this long."

"Where would I go?"

"Who the hell knows? Last time you left, I was minding my own business, trying to make a living when you disappeared on me."

"It wasn't that dramatic."

"Tell me, Princess. Why did you leave without saying good-bye the first time?"

"I tried to say good-bye and to confess my heart to you but you didn't come to me. I stayed up all night waiting for you on my swing...again." The tears came back. "And when I saw you at your office, Grandfather kept urging me to tell you how I felt and I couldn't stay there any longer without breaking down, so I left abruptly."

"That night..." At this point, Donovan led me by the hand and took me over to the sofa so we could finish our conversation. "Every fucking thing that could have gone wrong that night went wrong. Let me explain."

"Can I have you hold that thought while I get another cup of coffee? It was cold riding so early in the morning."

"Stay here. I'll get it for you."

"Latte..."

"Half the milk, no sugar. I know." He kissed me lightly and went to be my barista.

"This is perfect!" I said after the first sip. "OK. Tell me what happened after our epic date at the sushi bar where I got more gifts in one night than a girl could ever dream. You know, I slept with your necklace on every night and the jewelry case used to sit on the pillow next to me."

"So I've been sleeping next to you for all these months?"

"Theoretically, yes."

"After our epic date, I went home and searched my car inside and out looking for your note. I hadn't received one of your notes in so long, I forgot about looking in my pocket. It was when the dry cleaning service came by then next morning and checked through my pockets before taking my suits, that I came upon that sweet note saying my kiss was your very first."

"How embarrassing!" I briefly covered my face with both hands.

"At first I thought you were bullshitting me, and I was going to call you that morning, but then I thought it would be awfully awkward if this was the truth. So, I figured I'd stop by and see you that night and get to the bottom of that message. I don't know when it happened, but at some point, I started feeling lonely when you weren't with me. My days were made better knowing I'd see you at some point in the day, and I would make up excuses to be with you."

"With the way you treated me sometimes, I would never have thought that."

"*Anyhow,*" he was slightly irritated with me, "knowing I was going to stop by that night, I picked up your graduation gift and waited till my dinner meeting was over. I assume you got my graduation gift which I dropped off at Gram's."

I put one hand around his neck and came in to kiss him. "Thank you. That was a most thoughtful gift. I love it."

"I'll take you golfing up in Scotland soon. There are some gorgeous courses up there."

"Oh my gosh! I need to call Mom and cancel our trip...or maybe I'll keep it?" Shoot! Me and my big mouth! I couldn't have just waited to see where this relationship would take me, but instead, I had doomed us from the start and booked a trip with my mother.

"Already canceled."

"What?"

"I heard you talking to your mother last night and I called her immediately after you hung up and told her I'd take her up there with us the following weekend."

"Should I be annoyed you change my plans without consulting me, or happy that you want to travel with my mother?"

"Deliriously happy," he winked.

I gave him an obligatory smile. "All right. You get a pass because my graduation golf clubs are beautiful. The pink bag that came with the clubs is even more beautiful. And I can't believe each club has my name on it."

"You're welcome. Now back to my story. We had a dinner meeting with some difficult clients and during the course of dinner, they changed everything we had agreed upon, plus added exclusions and clauses. It was a nightmare. As it was, dinner ended late and we still had work to do in order to get them what they wanted by the following morning."

"So you brought Kate back to your house?" This time, I quirked my eyebrow in disapproval.

"It was that, or go to her hotel room."

That changed my tune immediately. "Good choice."

"What you didn't see were the two male associates who had also come back to my place. We were working when you made your unexpected visit."

"And of course, glamorous Kate opened your door and you came running over looking disheveled. That woman told me you were getting dressed and she actually invited me in to *your* house."

Donovan tried hard not to laugh at my annoyance. "What basically ended my 'ten-year' relationship with Kate was you, and Kate was not happy. Kate and I saw each other here and there whenever she came back to Southern California, and this time, she wanted to settle down and get married. She asked if my marriage offer still stood and told me she wanted us to have the Jake and Emily life with the house, the kids, the perfection..."

"And you told her no because you wanted to explore life with Jane." I punched him hard in the arm.

"Damn, Woman. You look so cuddly, but you're so damn strong. That hurt."

"That is what I told Jane, but..." he thought through what he wanted to say next and chose his words carefully. "It was you who brought me out of the Montage to play a game of softball seventy miles away, in traffic, and it was you, *not Jane*, Kate accused me of being in love with."

"What the hell was that all about? I barely ever saw her. What could she have noticed that I didn't notice?"

"Apparently, everyone noticed but us. It became a running joke with Jake and Emily. They'd take turns calling me and terrorizing me about getting an intervention group together if I didn't admit to my feelings soon. And if it wasn't the power couple, Al would call me and ask about you after having met you on Mother's Day. And who could forget my Aunt Bee? Damn. She was a force to reckon with."

"Anyhow, back to the story of why you didn't come see me on the swing when it was *you* who initiated the meeting."

"After you left, I got frustrated with how slowly everything was going and dumped the work on the associates and ended our work session. They left, Kate got pissed and eventually accused me of cheating on her in Hawaii with you."

"Were you together with her in Hawaii?"

"Kind of? It's hard to explain our dynamic. We're so used to being together that if we're in the same vicinity as one another and we are not in a relationship, we end up behaving like a couple. *However*, she and I have never approached one another if either one of us was in a relationship. That was not done."

"So it was no big deal to have sex with one another as long as you were both single?" This concept of a hook up confounded me. "You must have still loved her, even just a few months ago."

"Honest. I haven't been in love with Kate in a very long time." I looked at him dead in the eye and tried to find the lie—but I couldn't.

"How can you have sex without love? Am I just being naive, again? I can't reconcile the two."

"Come here." He led me to our bedroom and slowly undressed me and himself. All those nights I thought we were going to consummate our relationship, it didn't happen for one reason or another. But now, after the ordeal I went through last night and early this morning, I hadn't prepared my mind, heart and body for this. I was so freaking nervous, goose bumps appeared up and down my body and I started shaking. "Cold?"

I shook my head no. "Nervous."

He lowered us onto the bed and we began kissing.

"Before we go on, I want to know what you want to do in terms of birth control. I assume you don't want a child in nine months?"

"No. Children weren't in my immediate future. What do you normally do?"

"I've always used a condom, and I want you to know I'm healthy. I haven't been with as many women as you might think, and I've been careful."

"Is this conversation normal protocol?" He was making me even more nervous. I just wanted him to get on with it and be done. It was crazy embarrassing to be lying naked in broad daylight talking about birth control and sexually transmitted diseases.

Donovan smiled at my question and he tried his best to ease *my* unease. "Normally, the women I am with are not virgins, and I don't give them a choice in birth control. Whether they are protected or not, I won't have sex without a condom." OMG! Was this conversation *really* necessary? Perhaps we should have talked about this before we were lying naked. "But, if you are by chance on some form of birth control, I'd love to try this with you without a condom. I don't want any barriers between us." He spoke very cautiously.

"I've been on the pill since I was sixteen, so..."

That was all that needed to be said. His libido shot off and took me along for the ride. He began making love to every part of my body. It started with sweet tender kisses from my face down to my neck. His mouth soon suckled on my breast and we were both catapulted into an insatiable surge of lust.

"That feels so good, Donovan."

"I can't wait to get inside you. I've been dreaming of this for months. Let me get you ready for me."

Without warning, he put two fingers inside me and I was mortified at how wet I was. I was practically dripping down his fingers and I couldn't stop the lyrical noises flowing from me.

"More. Donovan. More," I panted.

I could feel his lips turning into a smile when he stopped suckling and soon after, his tongue replaced the thumb that was teasing my clitoris and I immediately climaxed.

"AH!" I screamed. "Donovan! Please. Stop. No..." I begged when he went from licking to sucking my clit. The sensation that tore through me over and over again was indescribable. It was like an ocean wave pounding into the sea, without ceasing. I was mired in sensation, and completely lost.

"I think you're ready, Princess," was what finally woke me back to the reality that Donovan hovered above me. "I love you," he said as he entered me in one thrust.

The initial pain of his thrust offset the high of the orgasm. He stayed motionless until I became restless with anticipation. Very soon, it felt wonderful to be joined with him. Staring into eyes filled with love, I decided there was truly no more a beautiful sight and feeling than to be joined with this man as one. This act of being filled by him, loved by him, and to know that one day I would have kids with him, brought me to tears.

"Are you all right? I'm sorry, Princess. I shouldn't have been so eager. I couldn't wait. Did I hurt you?" He looked apologetic and darling.

"You didn't hurt me at all. It feels amazing." I tried to move around somewhat and meet his slow thrust.

"Princess, don't move. You're going to unman me if you keep doing that."

"Am I doing something wrong?" Shit! How was I to know what was right and what was wrong?

"Princess. My dick has never been without a condom. You are unbelievably tight. I can feel every last sensation."

"Is that good?" Damn! I should have asked Emily or Jane for some instructions before we did the deed.

He chuckled lightly. "You feel better than good. I've never felt so much pleasure in my life—ever."

"Well then..." My answer was filled with conceit. "I guess I'll have to keep up the good work."

To my chagrin, Donovan pulled out and I felt the loss and yearned for his quick return. Even after one joining, I knew we were meant for each other, and there would be no better fit than ours.

"Wrap your legs around my waist," he said in a hoarse voice and began our ride.

He carefully eased in and out of me until he registered my body's lusty response. With every downward push, I effortlessly rose to meet him. I couldn't get enough of this fullness inside of me. The pleasure was borderline unbearable, his satisfied groans were unspeakable, and the height that we would reach together was undeniable.

"Donovan," I groaned when he plunged into my deepest core, "I don't know what to do."

"Come with me, Princess. I can't hold out much longer." He rammed into me harder and faster and I could feel myself wanting to spiral out of control, but I couldn't let go.

I whimpered in fervor and frustration until he leaned heavily onto one arm, and took his other arm and slid it between our bodies. His finger was slick against my clit, and it only took a few rubs for me to lose control again. I fell apart under him, and Donovan followed with the sounds of my explosion. My body convulsed as the pleasure rolled through me, and with one last push, Donovan finished his pleasure and stilled inside me.

This pleasure lasted long—much longer than I'd expected. I couldn't help but love the weight of Donovan's body on me. Something about his heavy body covering me in entirety made me feel secure.

We continued to breathe hard.

"I love you." I whispered in his ear.

"I love you, too, Princess." He placed butterfly kisses all over my face and neck. "You know that you have to marry me, now. In the olden days, if a man took the girl's maidenhood, he was honor-bound to marry her."

I cracked-up. "Really, Mr. Taylor?"

"Yes. Ms. Reid."

"Does she come with a herd of cattle as her dowry?"

"And a chest full of gold."

"Uh-huh. I'll let my father know that since my maidenhood has been taken, he needs to get the sheep, goats, cows, and gold ready."

"Your father will kick my ass if you say a word about me taking anything from you. He told me to keep you pure."

"You know he's got a chest full of rifles, rather than a chest full of gold?" I kidded.

"Shit, I forgot." He chuckled. "We're not doing this again till we get married."

"OK..." I agreed.

He gave me one last kiss on the nose and pulled out. Though this whole act of making love didn't last very long, I felt so alone, almost abandoned, when he pulled out. There was still a throbbing that wouldn't abate and there was also this... "Eew!" I unknowingly said, aloud.

"What?"

"There's all this gook that just came out of me," I cringed.

"Hold on," Donovan chuckled and walked to the bathroom. He came back with a warm towel and rather than handing it to me, he tenderly and thoroughly wiped me clean. I was so touched by what he did, there were tears in my eyes again. "What's the matter now?"

"This intimacy between you and me...just a few weeks ago, it was unimaginable. And now you're here...making love to me...I just don't know how to process all that's happened in the last few days."

"I'm here for good. No longer do you have to keep this camellia necklace on you as a substitute for my affection and touch. I've found my way and I won't let either of us get lost again. If you're ready, I'd like to take you somewhere before we leave for London."

"I haven't showered yet. Do I have time for a quick shower?"

"Princess, I think we have time for a quickie in the shower."

We packed up our bags and took everything with us in the car so we could run some errands in town, eat a meal, then get on the plane to go back home. We didn't end up having a quickie in the shower because European showers weren't meant for anything but showers. We were so cramped in there, we washed what needed to be washed, fooled around just a teeny-tiny bit and got ready for the day.

"Where are we going?"

"I want to buy you something for your birthday."

"Donovan. You've taken me through a quarter of Europe this week. I think that's birthday present, enough."

"It's something small. I really want to get it for you." And I couldn't stop him even if I tried. Donovan took me to a jewelry shop and bought me a simple gold chain for the D charm he had purchased for me back in Hawaii. "It bothers me that you have to add this to the back of your camellia necklace because you don't have a chain."

"Thank you." I smiled and had him help me change out necklaces. "I'll have to put this in the jewelry case and bring it out only for special occasions."

"Will you wear the camellias on Tuesday with your blue dress? I'll put on my matching button covers and cuff links."

"Of course, I will. What exactly is happening on Tuesday?"

"Well, your grandfather is thinking about selling off the European half of Ascot, Ascot, and Pemberley."

Whoa! That was big news. "When did this happen?"

"You're not supposed to know this yet, but since I'm honor-bound to marry you now, I'll have to let you in on the secret." He winked.

"So, do tell." We sat down at a little restaurant off the main piazza for lunch.

"Roland realizes that with all of Gram's family deeply rooted in Los Angeles, he doesn't want to work out here anymore. When I asked Roland to move offices, part of my new job description was to court buyers. I'm taking care of clients, too, but I'm not very familiar with all the different

European laws so I'm mainly here to find serious buyers and get them in touch with Roland."

"So Tuesday is..."

"Tuesday is an open invitation to anyone who is interested in learning about our firm. It could be potential buyers, potential clients, potential lawyers who may want to join the firm. The firm sponsors several charities, so these charities along with the firm will be highlighted. It's an all-purpose event. And you, my beauty, need to be my arm candy for the night."

"And will..." Did I want to go there, again?

"Yes, she will be there. She is in Paris, headed to London just like us. As long as Kate is with the firm, she and I will be in contact with one another. You need not be insecure or upset when she's around. She's just another colleague. All right?"

"Will you continue to stay friends with her when you and she are no longer colleagues?" Donovan gave me a disgruntled look, and I knew exactly what he was thinking—my friendship with Michael. "I'm not asking you to cut off your friendship with her; I'm asking if you'll continue to seek her out as a friend when she leaves the firm." He didn't look any less disgruntled. "Fine. I'll let it go. I've told you I wanted to stay friends with Michael, and it's only fair I don't tell you who you can and cannot be friends with since I've made my stand. Let me state for the record that Kate makes me insecure. If it isn't bad enough that she'd probably make Miss America insecure, she's had your heart for as long as I've known you. That's neither easily erased nor forgotten."

Donovan reached over from across the table, held my hand, and shared with me a tender look. "Why did you have tears in your eyes when we started making love? What were you thinking that made you cry?"

"I was just overwhelmed with the act, the emotions, the love...I don't know if I could term them as happy tears, but it wasn't anything associated with sadness. Like I said earlier, I've longed to be with you and never believed it was going to happen. It still feels like a dream, and possibly a nightmare if it all ends." I could feel my mood shift from buoyancy to drowning. "Right now, I've climbed to the very top of heaven, but in the recesses of my mind, I still believe there's a chance I could go right back to the depths of hell. And especially after having experienced all these emotions with you, it would be the absolute deepest depth of hell if we were to separate now."

He now moved over and sat next to me in our very crowded two-person booth. The person in the booth next to us wasn't happy Donovan had encroached upon his space. "I am no Swami with a crystal ball. I cannot tell you what will happen the rest of our lives. What I can promise you is that I love you and wish to spend my life with you. I want to make babies with you, and lots of them. I want to spend our weekdays working, raising our kids, dealing with homework and school projects. And I want to spend our weekends hanging out on the cul-de-sac with all the cousins, surfing at the beach house, and sending the kids off to Grandma Taylor's or Grandma Reid's so we can have some alone time. We'll take the kids to Europe for the summer and stay in one of Roland's homes, or at our beach house so they can learn to surf like their mother. I plan to live an unbelievably fun life with you and our brood. That much, I can promise you."

"Sounds nice. I think I might be able to clear out my calendar for that kind of a promise." I whispered and kissed him lightly.

"So back to this whole issue of Kate and Michael. I don't have a problem with you and Michael's sister, but I can't say I'm happy with you meeting Michael. Since you have made plans already, I'll not stop you. And as for Kate, you remember when you asked me how I could have sex without love?"

"Yeah..."

"Leaving out the emotional part of sex, how did it feel?"

"Incredible."

"That's something men can desire without having their emotions all tangled up in the act. I know it sounds cold, but it's just something that we do, and that's what Kate and I've done when we've met up from time to time."

"You mean to tell me there were no feelings involved? I can't believe that."

He sighed with slight frustration. "It's not that there are absolutely no feelings. I like Kate—scratch that, I *liked* Kate—but neither of us was in love the last eight years or so. We always got along well, had mutual respect for one another, and were physically attracted to each other. That's been what's fueled our libido for a long time, not love. Do you understand?"

"Not really, but I'll believe what you say."

"*But* I want to tell you what I thought and felt when we made love this morning. We didn't have the proper pillow talk after our first time, and I need to make amends for it."

"OK..." I had no idea what he was talking about.

"Physically, having sex with you was like no other. Being with you, without anything to desensitize me was without a doubt, the best sex I've ever experienced. Emotionally, seeing you under me—the woman I know I'll be making love to the rest of my life, a woman who's gifting me with her first, and the woman I'll be making babies with...I have no words that could describe my feelings. Incredible? Unbelievable? Extraordinary? None of these words comes close to what I felt. Truly, making love to you has been the greatest gift. To add to my beautiful gift, your uninhibited response to our lovemaking drove me wild. You are one hellcat in bed." I could feel my entire body get hot and turn beet red. "You don't believe me?" I didn't realize I'd said anything to contradict his statement. "Your face is telling me I've embarrassed you and that you have no clue what I'm talking about."

"Well...I don't know how other women react, but I didn't think I said or did anything unusual, did I?" Now I was super self-conscious.

"Princess, do you know how loud and verbal you are when you're aroused?"

Shit! "No...I didn't even know I said anything during our lovemaking." I whispered now since he accused me of being loud.

"Babe," he whispered back and in a sinfully sexy voice, "I almost came with you both times I made you come with my mouth and fingers because you expressed your pleasure so clearly. In fact, you're quite a demanding little wench in bed."

"I am not." Now I was just plain mortified at my sluttiness. "And speaking of demanding, you're the demanding one...or is it that I just didn't know what I was doing?"

"What do you mean?"

"You know...in the bathroom in Rome...when I..." In this situation, I couldn't say the word blowjob. "You had so many instructions and so many do's and don'ts. I thought I was doing it totally wrong."

He grinned pretty huge and kissed the base of my neck. "I'll tell you another secret. In all my years of being sexually active, I've never been given a blowjob before."

"You are so bullshitting me. You expect me to believe that?" There was no freaking way.

"I've never had luck in that department. All the women I've been with have never wanted oral sex—give or take."

"So I was the first girl you...you know..."

"Well, no." That extinguished my joy immediately. "Sorry. I should have explained. I've tried it in order to receive it, but none of my partners liked it enough to want to reciprocate. You're my first and seeing you on your knees with your eager mouth, I was just trying to make it last." He laughed at himself. "I thought I could hold off my release if I had you suck me slower, but that was even more arousing to watch your puckered mouth go up and down, so carefully, so methodically. Shit," he placed his lips on the back of my neck and started lightly sucking. "I'm horny as hell again. You do that to me all the time. You did that to me when we were just friends, and I thought I was going mad with lust whenever we spent time together."

"I would never have guessed. You never showed any interest in me whatsoever. If anything, you were always mad at me about everything. I didn't think I could ever do anything right in your eyes."

"I'm sorry, Princess. It was more a case where I was angry with myself for being so physically attracted to someone I once considered a little sister."

"Boy, if we equated the depths of your anger with the depths of your love, then buddy, you were madly in love with me all these months."

He laughed. "I think I was madly in love with you all this time."

"So everything I did back in Rome was OK?"

"Babe. It was beyond OK. You spoke of intimacy earlier, and that was the most intimate I'd been with any woman. It was beautiful and I thank you for loving me enough to try something that was probably not high on your to-do list."

"Um, could I ask one more question about that morning in Rome?"

"Anything."

"OK, so you came much sooner than I expected and was...I...supposed to...you know..." damn, this was hard, "was I supposed to have you stay inside my mouth when you came and if so, what the hell am I to do with all that stuff in my mouth?"

Donovan tried really, really hard not to laugh at me, but couldn't hold it in. Shit, I wanted to kick his ass for making fun of me. As soon as he saw my pissed off expression, he schooled his laughter. "I'm sorry." He showed penance but not enough. There was still a lot of laughter in his eyes.

"It's time to leave." I changed the subject and got up from the other side of the booth. "Do you have a company apartment, or were you planning on staying at Gram's."

"Princess..." He dragged out my nickname. "Come here," he pulled me back down and into his body. "I'm sorry. I've been dying to talk to you about the blowjob you gave me but I didn't know how to bring it up. I was laughing more at myself than anything else. In all honesty, I don't know what's correct protocol, and I was horrified that I came in your mouth. That's why I ran away after it happened and haven't brought it up since. You can do whatever is comfortable for you. But, if I may add, I couldn't tell you what was more arousing—seeing you on your knees, or seeing you suck me off. If you had kept me in your mouth, I may have spilled a second round."

"Is that even possible?"

"Usually not, but with you I'm gonna bet it might be." Now, I didn't know whether I was more embarrassed or aroused. "If we're done, shall we go?"

I waited till the plane took off and we had our drinks in hand before I started with the questions again. Though I'd known this man for many years, I still had so many questions I wanted answered. "Donovan, will you tell me about your sisters?" I'd been curious about the sisters since Becky and Kelley showed up in Paris. I thought I'd get to know the four ladies who might eventually be my sisters. "Are you busy? If you need to work, we can talk about them another day."

"I'm never too busy for you." He pulled up the armrest and had me lean into him, my back to his chest. "Start with Amanda?"

"Sure."

"Amanda is the oldest and a mother hen. She's thirty-five now, and being the oldest of five, much of the responsibility fell upon her to make sure we were safe. She used to boss me around especially, because Mom and Dad put her in charge of me whenever they weren't available."

"Poor Amanda. You were probably a pain in the ass, and your head was probably bigger than the globe Atlas carried on his shoulders."

Donovan laughed. "I was a pain, and I did believe I was king of the house."

"King of the world."

"Which would make you my queen," he suggested.

"Queen or slave?"

"Depends on what position you're in," he *suggestively* suggested.

I had to shush him. "No sex talk on the plane." I placed my hand on his inner thigh. "By the way, where will you be sleeping tonight?"

"Um, right next to you."

"You can't sleep with me at my grandmother's house! My mother is there and so are my grandparents and Jake and Emily's family."

"So? Your grandparents are probably more sexually active than we are, since they're newlyweds."

"Oh, Donovan. That's gross."

"But true." He laughed. "And you don't think your parents know that we're in bed together?"

"Oh my gosh! No!! They know I've been pure all this time."

"Yeah. *Have been*, being the operative word. And Jake and Emily have seen us in bed already so no surprise there."

"I really can't have you sleeping in my bed in Belgravia, especially not while my mother is next door."

"Fine. Then you can sleep with me at the company apartment."

It would be hard to stay away, but I had to resist. "I'm going to have to work up to that."

"Whatever. The bed at your Gram's or the bed at my apartment, you can decide which one you want to sleep in when we get to London."

"All right I'll think about it till then."

Donovan shook his head as though I was crazy. "So next oldest in my family is Kelley."

"I never understood how Kelley was older than you, but still in the same grade."

"Kelley and I both have nebulous birthdays on the school calendar where she was held back a year and I went to school a year earlier. That's how we ended up in the same grade. Plus, she's only eleven months older than I am."

"Tell me about her husband, Noah. He seems like a great guy. Oh, and you didn't tell me about Amanda's husband and kids."

"Amanda and Robert live in Maine with their two boys, Richie and Ronnie. The boys are nine and six and full of energy. Robert comes from a family full of fishermen and they own a pretty big fish and seafood company."

"What are Robert, Richie and Ronnie like?"

"Robert is on the quiet side, and he needs to be because Amanda talks so much. Richie and Ronnie are good boys who look like their father, but act like their mother."

"I don't think I remember Amanda at all."

"She might have been on the East Coast already when you and I first met. Kelley was only around because she and Jake dated for so long."

"Was Kelley bummed when she and Jake finally broke up?"

"Not at the time. She and Jake needed their freedom. They had been bosom buddies since they were young and slated to get married in the eyes of our parents. They needed to go out and date other people."

"Where did Kelley and Noah meet?"

"In Chicago when Kelley was doing her MBA. Noah's a police officer, and it was a classic case of him pulling her over for a speeding ticket and her weaseling out of the ticket because he was attracted to her and wanted her number."

"How cute is that?" I marveled. "What a sweet love story they must have to tell."

"I don't know about their love story, but they got married soon after they met. And now they have three boys ages six, four, and two."

"They must be darling if they look anything like their parents."

"They are really cute. Though I shouldn't have favorites as an uncle, I think those three are my favorite."

"I can't wait to meet them one day."

"You'll meet them at Thanksgiving or maybe Christmas."

"Maybe the Taylors can join the Reids for Thanksgiving. You know Mom throws the most elaborate Thanksgiving dinner and party."

Donovan looked pleased. "I can't wait for my sisters to meet you. I've told them all about you."

"You have?"

"Of course I have. I talk to my sisters quite often. Amanda, the mother hen, is most anxious to see who has captured my heart."

"So Noah, Kelley, and the three boys live in Chicago now?"

"They live outside of the city in a suburb. Kelly quit her job when she had Brandon, the youngest, but before she quit her job, they bought a small home and moved out into the suburbs where the schools are good."

"Did she quit so she can raise her boys?"

"Yeah. By the time she had three kids, it wasn't worth it for her to work, with the money she was paying in childcare. Though she was a successful ad executive, Noah is a cop so they always budgeted, and they were able to purchase a very small home. Their house is probably only a bedroom larger than my beach house. But Kelley's done a good job of turning the house into a warm and cozy home."

"It must have been an adjustment for her to go from living in your parents' big home to something small."

"I think it's tougher on my parents to see her living off a policeman's salary. That's why outside of coming to LA to see family, she and Noah haven't been anywhere since their honeymoon. It was huge for them to come to Paris."

"Oh Donovan. We should have hung out with them more. *I* should have hung out with them more."

"You did what you could. It wasn't like you were on your own schedule. You were following my work schedule."

"What does Kelley think of Emily? I always believed she and Jake would get married."

"I think that's what we all thought. Kelley was out here for Christmas, and she and Noah spent some time at Jake and Emily's. I think Kelley was a bit taken aback...maybe that's not the right word." He thought about it some more. "Maybe I should say that she envied Emily's home for all of half a second when she first saw it, but before the night was over, she and Emily became fast friends. How could you not like Emily?"

"She and Noah appear to be happy."

"They are and he's a good match for her and a great dad to Dylan, Steve and Brandon."

All of a sudden, Donovan started busting up.

"What's so funny?"

"Her boys were named after those three guys on Beverly Hills 90210. Kelley loved that show growing up, and with her name being Kelley, she thought it funny to name her boys after the main characters."

"I don't remember a Dylan, Steve, or Brandon. I only remember a Dixon, Ethan, and George." I answered without much thought.

"Is this what's called a generation gap?" Donovan couldn't help the continued laughter. I had no clue what he was talking about, so I pushed him along with his story.

"So what's the deal with Becky? How come she doesn't like me?"

"Becky and I have always had a cantankerous relationship. She's a couple of years younger than I am, and she's the one I mostly fought with when I was younger."

"Now too, it looks like."

"Only when she gets in my way of seeing some action." He gave me a sexy grin and kissed my cheek. "Though it looks like you and your brother do your share of fighting at your ripe old age of twenty-three."

"Only when he gets in my way of seeing some action," I repeated his words.

"Oh?" He purposely held me tighter. "And what action were you planning on seeing in Hawaii in that skimpy teal bikini of yours?"

"I had on a rash guard," I complained and defended myself.

"And then you didn't. I about had a heart attack when you stripped bare and showed all of Hawaii your tits." He briefly grabbed my breasts and the quick teasing ignited both our lust. "Adam from the Garden of Eden had nothing on me where temptation was concerned, when I first saw these." Donovan now placed his hands right below my breast and methodically stroked with his index fingers. I was getting so aroused I had to grab his hands and bring them around my waist, instead.

"I did not show anyone my tits." I whispered so the entire cabin was not privy to our conversation. "I was well covered."

"Woman, I had a hard-on all day after seeing you. I was never more glad that I had a rash guard that covered the protrusion in my swim trunks. I wanted so badly to suck on these." His hands traveled back up and rolled my nipples.

"Donovan," I leaned further back and whispered in his ear. "You've got to stop or I may strip bare on this flight because I need you to suck on my tits." Thank God we were sitting in the very front of the cabin. My face had to have been bright red.

"You and I are making a pit stop at the apartment before heading to Belgravia. We are going to have crazy sex before dinner."

"But then we're going to be late to the family dinner." Stupidly, I put out that complaint.

"The bathroom here or back at my place. Once again, your choice." We kissed briefly before the flight attendant came back.

"OK!" I sat upright in my seat and put the divider between us. "Becky. Continue with why she doesn't like me." We needed to get back to talking because anytime we started talking about anything sexual, the PDA was beyond inappropriate.

"She likes you. Her actions in Vernon had nothing to do with you. She's badgered me about what happened between me and Jane, and I've never told her. Obviously Jane hasn't told her either so that was her poor attempt at getting some answers from me."

"I think Jane told me at some point that Becky and Al met in college?"

"They did. They got married after graduate school and five years into being married, she finally got pregnant. Becky worked for the same pharmaceutical company Al works for, but is on a disability leave. This baby is doing a number on her and she's been in pain the past month. But her OB tells her the baby is fine and everything is moving along, so she tries to be pleasant where she can."

"And Al? He travels a lot? He's not home to help her?"

"Al got a promotion recently and has been traveling to Europe more than usual. It's uncertain if the travels will continue."

"I like him. He's got a great sense of humor, and he adores your sister."

"Of all the brothers-in-law, he and I are the closest. He does have a wicked sense of humor, and after he met you in May, he became one of your biggest fans."

"Really? How sweet."

"There was this one night in London when you refused to see me, and I got shit-face drunk with Al. He listened to me drone on like a girl."

"Drone on like a girl, huh?"

He showed a lot of teeth when he smiled an apologetic smile.

"And last but not least, Rachel. She's the youngest, but doesn't act like the youngest."

"How come I don't remember her, either? If she's the youngest, she's only like a year or so older than I am, where was she all these years?"

"I'm not sure why you and Rachel didn't strike up a friendship like Jane and Becky. It could be the fact that my parents hung out more with Jake's parents than yours. You only saw me and my sister because of Jake. Do you remember seeing my parents, much, when you were growing up?"

I shook my head no. "I just remember that Christmas when your mom was in the kitchen while my mom was busting my chops about purchasing a dress with her credit card."

Donovan started choking on his drink, laughing. "You always had a penchant for being a bad girl, didn't you?"

The way he said that made me want to be a bad girl!

Shit! And I was such a bad, bad girl. I was cringing in the cab thinking about what we'd just done.

"You're bright red and it's dark in this cab," said the man with the biggest, most satisfied mug on his face. "Could it be because of the call I answered while you were straddling me, banging the life out of me?"

"Oh my gosh! Could you shut up? The cab driver can hear you!" I practically yelled at him.

Now he spoke softly to the backside of my ear while kissing me here and there. "I hope your mother didn't hear your moans when I told her we were going to be late to dinner." I shivered with that comment. "The sight of your tits bobbing up and down when you were riding me is now my absolute favorite picture of you. That, and your intoxicated, drunk with pleasure look when you come."

"Donovan," I pleaded.

In the course of a few days, I had become a tramp. Never did I think I could act so wanton. With all the foreplay on the plane, we took a cab from Heathrow straight to Donovan's apartment and practically started having sex in the glass elevator that led up to the twenty-sixth floor of his residence at a very high end hotel. He pulled out the shirt that was neatly tucked into my pencil skirt and began unbuttoning – *in public*! The front clasp bra got unhooked within seconds and his mouth sucked hungrily on my breast. The floozy that I was, I didn't stop him in the least. All I could think about was why I wore such a freaking tight skirt where there was no way he could get a hand under it without ripping it, all the while cursing the damn elevator for moving too slowly.

As soon as the elevator dinged, Donovan did up a few buttons and we ran to his place with our rolling suitcases in hand. Comically, Donovan hadn't been to his place, yet, so we ran left, and of course had to turn around when we realized his apartment was on the opposite side. Once we arrived, Donovan punched in a few numbers and voila, privacy!

Neither of us made note of the luxurious, fully furnished apartment, nor the stunning view. All we wanted to do was rip each other's clothes off and get busy.

"You know," he said very faintly, "I had no idea I could go another round after you sucked me off so thoroughly to start. Though once I saw that you wanted to go on top, I couldn't help but get big again. If I didn't know any better, I would have thought you'd done this a time or two or twenty. Are there any other positions you want to try, tonight?"

After we had sex, our conversations always led to more arousal or gross embarrassment.

"After only having had sex with you once, I can't believe how forceful I was about what I wanted. Gaawwdd! I've become a strumpet!"

"Dominatrix would be the word for tonight." He had the most complacent smile. "I love how uninhibited you become in and out of bed. I'm going to start calling you my Jezebel from now on."

"Oh my gosh!" I groaned. "I'm a fallen woman."

"You're late." Jake gave me a knowing smile when he opened the door for us. "But please, spare me any details." He and Donovan laughed while I cringed some more. "Everyone just sat down to dinner."

"The twins?"

"...waited and waited for their aunt Ne Ne to show up, but in the end, I had to tell them she had more pressing to-do's on her agenda and that she would see them another day."

"Oh my gosh!" I groaned again. "It's not what you think, Jake."

"Hell ya it is...and then some!" Donovan declared to his best bud.

"What did you tell Jake?" I whispered only to Donovan and slapped him on the arm.

"We don't kiss and tell, Laney." Jake eyes crinkled with laughter.

"Gaawwdd!" I screamed and ran into the dining room. Even though I was ahead of the two men, their laughter resonated up and down the hallway.

"Laney!" I got a warm greeting from everyone.

"Hi Gram." I went over and hugged her from behind her seat, and proceeded to greet everyone in the same manner.

"How was your jaunt through Europe? I heard you saw Roland in Amsterdam?"

"Oh, Gram! Grandfather has the most beautiful homes in Europe. I'd just like to stop time and go live in each of these places for a couple of years."

"What's stopping you?" Gram wondered. "You're a young woman, unmarried, and without kids. The world is your oyster. Go. Live. Experience."

"Don't give her unnecessary ideas, Gram." Donovan came in the dining room and greeted everyone. Except for Grandfather and Uncle

Robert, everyone got a warm hug and big kisses from this man. "I only just convinced her to break up with this English boyfriend and start a relationship with me. I can't have her moving from country to country on a whim."

"And why not?" Gram challenged Donovan.

"Because, my sweet Gram, Delaney and I will settle down somewhere, build a home, build a family, and give Jake and Emily's kids cousins to play with in the near future."

"But my granddaughter is still young. I'm told she's decided to go to med school. If you tie her down now, when will she get to experience life?"

I thought Donovan would get exasperated by Gram's goading questions and comments, but he answered her with courtesy and affection. "I will promise you and Roland and..." he stopped and looked over at Mom. "What do I call you, now? Aunt Babs seems awfully inappropriate."

"Well, since your parents have insisted on being called Ma and Pa, I suppose you should call me Mom like my kids call me."

He let out a brilliant smile. "Mom," he spoke and she had a brilliant smile of her own, "I promise to aid Delaney in her endeavors to become a doctor, to live life to the fullest, and to experience whatever country her heart desires. But, all of this will be done with me." He made his statement, staked his claim, and in essence, put a ring on it.

"So you're telling us that you've succeeded in getting Laney to agree to marry you?" Gram first spoke to Donovan, but then asked me, "Is that true Laney? Did you agree to marry Donovan? I think you're too young and too beautiful to settle down already. You just graduated from college. Date around, love other men, and after you've done this for a while, if Donovan Taylor and you are meant to be, you can get married. You've been stuck on this man since you were little. You need not marry the first man you loved."

Gram was doing her best to play devil's advocate tonight. I held Donovan's hand before he fell for Gram's obvious bullying. Everyone at this table knew Gram adored Donovan. She always had, and I knew she was thrilled for me.

"Gram. I thank you for your advice. I respect you and all you've accomplished, and would be thrilled if I could be half the woman you are when I am your age. I think everyone here at the dinner table has known about my childhood crush on this man since I met him more than a decade ago. Never in all those years did I see myself with anyone but Donovan. Now that we are finally on the same page, I want to give this a try, Gram. I will love, live, experience—and I'll do it with Donovan." I stood my ground and let Gram and everyone at this table know that my life and Donovan's life would operate as one.

"So the wedding date is set?" Gram smirked at my quiet but forceful statement.

"Nope." I answered without hesitation. "Love, live and experience do not necessarily lead to forever."

Gram let out a loud, "Ha!" and cackled. Roland chuckled. Mom shook her head with a quizzical smile. Jake and Emily looked at Donovan with a sympathetic one.

"I can't believe after the declaration of love I made to your family, you just told them we're not getting married. What the hell am I still not getting?" He looked at my mother. "Mom? Do you know why she won't marry me?"

She was baffled too. "Sorry, Donovan. I don't know."

"Gram?"

"No idea, but I like the spirit, Laney Reid. I always liked that *I don't give a damn what you think, I'm going to do it my way* attitude about you. You give in to a man too easily, he'll walk all over you."

Grandfather snorted. "Like you know anything about giving in too easily. Damn woman made me wait sixty years to sleep next to her."

"But you finally got there, didn't you?" Gram gave Grandfather a peck on the lips. "Wasn't it worth the wait?"

Grandfather could only smile. They were adorable together.

"Donovan?" Mom asked. "Where's your company apartment?"

"In the financial district."

"Nice place, huh?" I didn't think Grandfather said this to embarrass me in any way, but I turned red again when Donovan couldn't answer.

Neither of us took the time to check out any part of the apartment. We couldn't even recall the color of the duvet cover.

"Can I report back to you next time? We were in a bit of a rush, so we didn't exactly check out the decor." This idiotic man gave off a silly grin that pretty much confessed our sins.

"What exactly did you do all that time while you were late to dinner?" Grandfather queried with the utmost intent.

That boyfriend of mine was so busted tonight. I could do nothing to wipe off that stupid smirk.

"Is that the baby?" Emily bounced out of her seat. "Laney you want to come and help me?" I would *forever* be grateful to Emily for this false interruption.

We walked out of the dining room, ran up the stairs and started laughing hard once we got into my room. Emily and her family were on the fourth floor, and there was no way Emily could hear them from where she was sitting. Plus, her kids, once asleep, rarely got up.

"Thank you, Emily! That Donovan Taylor is sleeping by himself tonight after what he did to me!"

"I take it you two have consummated your relationship?"

My eyes quickly looked at everything in my room but Emily. "I've become a wanton woman, Emily. I couldn't hold myself back."

Emily giggled. "Laney. You and Donovan love each other and you will be married, soon...won't you?" Even Emily was fooled by my grand speech during dinner. "What's with you declining Donovan's proposal?" And now she just downright wondered what the hell was wrong with me.

"There's nothing to decline since he hasn't proposed! All this time he's *told* me we're getting married. Never once did he get on his knee and propose."

"Ah...I see!"

"You got a beautiful and thoughtful proposal in Paris, all of Tuscany witnessed Max's proposal to Jane and all I get is, *'we're getting married.'* Is it wrong of me to expect a little more? I'm not asking for anything but a heartfelt declaration of love and a question asking me to spend the rest of my days with him."

"You're not asking for too much, but I don't think Donovan has any idea what's bothering you. Do you want to maybe clue him in?"

"No way! And you have to promise me that you and Jake will not clue him in, either. This is something he needs to figure out on his own. I'm not going to beg for a proposal."

Emily laughed. "I'll hold back the best I can, as long as he's good to you."

"Oh Emily, he's a dream. I couldn't be happier." The severe gushing was over the top. "In all my days of dreaming about Donovan, I never could have imagined this kind of joy."

"I know, Laney. That's what I think every morning when I get up and see my husband. He brings that crazy, happy contentment to my heart. Wait till you have kids with Donovan. You'll see them with facial expressions and little quirks that remind you of your husband and that wonderful sense of love and pride will fill your heart every time. You'll love that they are mini-me's of the both of you."

"I can't wait. I know Donovan really wants kids. He talks about having a house full of them constantly. Whenever he talks to me about the future, undoubtedly, kids will be at the top of his list."

"Does this mean you'll have kids right away? What about med school? Your dad was over the moon when you told him you wanted to be a surgeon."

"I don't know." I bemoaned my dilemma. "Donovan says he doesn't mind having kids later, but he's at that age where he wants kids now. All his friends have kids and he's itching to settle down. I've thought of copious options, and I think the best one might be to get married, sooner than later, and have kids right away. I'll raise them for a few years, and then reapply for med school."

"Won't it be hard to get back into school after taking that much time off?"

"Probably, but I feel like this is the best option. I haven't told Donovan, yet. I'll let him know once he proposes and we get our life started."

"I'm sure you'll come up with a novel idea. Since I used the excuse of the babies, why don't we go check up on them, before going back?"

When we got back to dinner, everyone was discussing a trip to Scotland this weekend.

"Babies all right?" Jake welcomed his wife back with a loving caress.

"They're beautiful." She smiled and surprisingly kissed Jake on the lips in front of all of us.

Donovan reached over, linked his fingers through mine, and whispered, "When are you dropping a note in my pocket to let me know where I'm going wrong? Why don't you want to marry me?" There was a hint of sadness in that question that I didn't like.

"I'll have to come up with some clever way of letting you know. In the meanwhile, we'll just have to practice the act of having wild, uninhibited sex, so we can get it right on our wedding night." My comment brought back Donovan's sexy smile, and he brought his lips close to mine until we heard an *ahem* from the grandparents for having bad table manners.

"So back to Scotland?" Gram brought the attention to Donovan.

"I wanted to take Delaney golfing this weekend at St. Andrews since there are several courses along the North Sea. Originally, I was going to take Delaney and Mom and stay at the resort, but I thought I'd see if you all wanted to join us? Roland, you still play golf?"

Grandfather chuckled. "Not as well as my granddaughter, but better than you."

Donovan laughed with him. "You may be my boss, but I won't go easy. And for the record, Delaney has only beaten me twice."

"How many times have you played her?" Jake outed his best friend.

"Twice." We all laughed at his confession. "I plan to bring my A game this weekend. You ready?" he asked me.

"Bring it on." I shrugged off his challenge.

Donovan squeezed my hand in affection and asked Grandfather, "I assume you're coming with us?"

"I'll get the plane ready. Let's all go and spend a long weekend there. Jake, can you make it?"

"Yes. School doesn't officially start until next week. I can go." He then asked Emily, "Are you OK traveling with our babies?"

"With our wonderful family, it'll be easy," she agreed.

"Who's golfing?"

"Dad, did you want to golf?"

Uncle Bobby grinned and confessed, "I haven't touched a golf club in years. But I suppose I will. I think Henry was thinking of coming back out here. He misses his family."

Grandfather then asked, "Any of you ladies, aside from Laney, want to golf?"

"Why golf when you can go to the spa?" Mom asked. "We'll take turns watching the kids and doing spa treatments."

"I assume you have connections to get us into the Old Course?"

"What's the Old Course, Donovan?"

"The Old Course at St. Andrews is considered to be the 'home of golf' because they first played the game of golf on these links back in the early 1400s. It's a public course but impossible to get a tee time. This course is supposed to be fabulous and unique in many ways."

"How so?" I asked.

"Roland, jump in and correct me if my information is wrong, but I believe they have these large double greens where several holes share one green?"

That was totally confusing. "You mean to tell me I could be playing on the 5th hole, and then the 9th hole, but I may be sinking the ball into the same green?"

"Exactly, Princess. There are also over 100 bunkers each with its own name and historical tale and I don't know how this happens, but this course can be played clockwise and counter-clockwise, depending upon the day of the week. I can't wait to see your attempts of getting out of some of those wicked bunkers."

"I just won't get my ball into the bunkers, then," I answered with confidence.

"I'll take care of tee times and hire caddies. Along with pointers, we can get a fine history lesson of the city and its golf courses from them. The only question is, where do we want to stay?" Grandfather was really asking this question to his wife.

"Do you have a castle up there, Grandfather?" That would have been an ideal scenario to play golf during the day, and to sleep in a castle with my prince at night.

"I don't but Harry the duke has one. Should I ask him to borrow his home for the weekend?"

"Roland! Not nice," Gram scolded with a chuckle. "I doubt he'll want to see or hear from anymore Reids. Why don't we just stay at the hotel on the Old Course? It'll be easier on Jake and Emily."

"Fine. I'll have my assistant take care of everything. Shall we separate so we men can go have a drink and smoke a cigar without offending any of you ladies?"

"Grandfather," I interrupted. "You know the two doctors here won't smoke with you."

"But your man will. See you later, Ladies." All the men followed Grandfather's lead.

I pulled Donovan down and whispered quickly in his ear. "There will be no mouth to mouth contact if you smoke a cigar tonight."

"Your mouth is not the only wet place my mouth enjoys sucking." He placed a chaste kiss on my ear and left the room.

Damn man got me all hot and bothered, again.

"So tell me, Granddaughter. After lusting after this man since you were in grade school, why did you tell me you may not marry him?"

"Gram!" I complained. "I didn't lust after him. I was in fourth grade. I crushed on him."

"Whatever!"

"As I told Emily earlier, Donovan hasn't proposed. He's mandated, and after all the years of thinking that he was my prince, I can't marry a man who commands and demands. I want my proposal!"

"Damn right!" Gram called out as if she was saying, "Amen!" at a church service on Sunday. "Babs, you've done a good job of raising this one. I always thought Jane was the only strong one, but I think this blonde-haired, blue-eyed beauty might even be tougher than her older cousin."

"Jane looks strong on the outside, but she's softhearted on the inside, always looking for approval from those around her. Being the middle child, she's learned to fight back, but she gets hurt easily." Aunt Sandy spoke.

"Jane's a smart girl and she snagged herself a bloody brilliant young man. He's damn good with her, and he compensates her selfish nature. Jake better watch out...I may have a new favorite."

"No way, Gram. Jake can do absolutely no wrong in your eyes. You and Grandfather shamelessly adored your oldest grandchild and paraded him as though he was your *only* grandchild."

"You have an issue with that?" Gram challenged.

"I think I might..." I answered back formidably.

Gram only laughed at me. "You always were a surreptitiously headstrong child. I think I'll retire for the night. Granddaughter?" She addressed me in a challenging way, again. "Will you walk me to my room?"

"I'd be honored."

I settled Gram in her sitting area and got us some tea and biscuits. Last time we sat to tea, I was down in the dumps because Donovan had ignored me the entirety of Emily's birthday, and I wondered what I'd do in London. Who knew back then that I'd be living here with my family, and Donovan?

"Only pour me half a cup, Laney. My bladder isn't what it used to be."

"Can I ask you a question, Gram?"

"Sure."

"Is it weird to sleep next to Grandfather Roland, after having lived with Grandpa Jerry for so long?"

"Only the first night. It was weirder to have someone in my bed again after having slept alone. I was getting used to not having to share a blanket."

"Is Grandfather Roland much different from Grandpa Jerry?"

"Actually, the two men are similar in nature. I must have a type." She laughed. "They are both strong, self-assured and smart men. Though I chose Jerry over Roland, I'm blessed to have a second chance with this good man."

"And he loves you so very much."

Gram looked dreamy. "That he does. You sure about Donovan?"

"You don't approve?" I knew this wasn't the case, but I needed to make sure.

"That scoundrel stole my heart as soon as he learned to talk. He was always the charmer. He and Jake made quite the dynamic duo." Gram reached out and held my hand. "And while I haven't been around you enough to have seen this crush begin, I think I know you well enough to know that once you set your mind to something, you don't turn back until the work is done. Are you sure you love Donovan enough to marry him? You don't want to continue dating other men like Michael?"

"Do you think Donovan and I don't suit? Do you think I'm too young for him or not worldly enough for him?" Insecurity and doubt began creeping in. Gram had lived a long life, in a world filled with glamour and sophistication. Perhaps she saw something I didn't see.

"Darling. It's not Donovan who worries me. I worry about you not having experienced life. From what your mother told me, Donovan is the first boy you gave your heart, soul, and body to, and we both wondered if you should date and get to know other men. There's no room for regret once you're married. This is your chance to explore."

"Gram. Since I was a little girl, I've dreamed of marrying Donovan Taylor. No, I didn't really date and yes, Donovan is the only boy I've given myself to, but I know I won't regret not having known other men. The few months I dated Michael, I enjoyed his company, but never did I feel this heart-racing, heart-thumping, and even heart-breaking kind of excitement. I have to confess, Gram, I'd rather live in complete heartbreak having once been with Donovan Taylor, than a mediocre happiness with any other man. I love him that much, Gram. I can't walk away unless he walks away first."

"Oh, you headstrong girl. Why must you be so black and white? As much as I adore that suitor of yours, I was hoping you'd find happiness with Michael. He's an upstanding young man with a good family background and wealth beyond imagination. You needn't marry Michael. I just wanted you to date him enough for you to know what it was like not to love Donovan Taylor."

"I don't remember what it's like not to love Donovan." I answered her in full truth. "I desire your blessing Gram, but even if you don't bless our relationship, this is something I have to try."

Gram came over, and I got up to meet her embrace. "He's a lucky man, Laney. If he doesn't treat you like the princess that you are, you come and let your grandparents know and we'll give him a good kick in the arse for you."

"Thank you, Gram."

A light knock on the door interrupted our embrace.

"You ladies done in here?" Grandfather walked in like he owned this place, and Donovan trailed right behind him. In reality, Grandfather Roland walked into any room as though he were royalty. His confidence cowered the average man. "May I have my wife back?"

"Of course, Grandfather."

"Where do you want to stay tonight?" Donovan asked aloud. This was not a conversation I wanted to be having with my grandparents in the room.

"I think I'll stay here and spend some time with Mom. Why don't you go back to your apartment?" I wasn't sure of what I'd just uttered.

Disappointment, annoyance, resignation, and resistance all showed on his face. My grandparents didn't hide their enjoyment, watching this entertaining drama unfolding before them.

"Go back and take a good look at your apartment this time, now that your girlfriend won't be there with you."

"Keep quiet, Roland. Let the two converse."

"Good night!" Donovan spoke for the both of us and pulled us out of their bedroom.

He walked upstairs to my room, shut the door, and put his arms around me. Face to face, he started his physical attack. "Princess," the kiss we couldn't share at the dinner table was about to happen now. "I can't sleep apart from you anymore." What I thought might be a devouring of my mouth, ended up as butterfly kisses starting from my lips, my nose, my eyes...this was an even bolder attack on my senses than a full-blown kiss. "Either we need to be together on this tiny bed, or you need to come back to my place. What's it going to be?" I felt a thousand needles pricking my body, thrilling my senses.

"Your kisses are making me want to ride you, again. You have to stop. There are too many people in this house."

He wouldn't stop. His fingers lightly played on my back, then caressed my rear end. "If you don't want people to know what's happening, then let's go back to my place."

I couldn't just receive these butterfly kisses any longer. I flung my arms around Donovan's neck and decided to devour his mouth instead. There was always something incredibly electrifying the first couple of seconds our tongues mated. My hormones were inflamed and I needed more than just kissing.

As Donovan was about to pick me up and take me to bed, a light knock interrupted us.

"Sorry to interrupt." Emily blushed, as she was wise to our hanky-panky actions. "Donovan," she addressed my boyfriend. "All your belongings arrived here so I organized them the best I could without opening any boxes. They're in the room down the hall. I thought you might like to use the room with the bigger bed," was all she said and gave us our privacy, again.

"Gotta love that Emily!" Donovan exclaimed. "You see, your entire family assumes I'm staying here. Why are you the only one who's pushing me away?"

This man just didn't get it. "Donovan, I've gone from a twenty-three-year-old virgin to a total floozy in the course of a week. I can't just shamelessly cohabitate with you. This is going to be too shocking for everyone who knows me. Bringing a boy home isn't me. I've never even brought a date home."

"What's the big deal? You and I cohabitated all throughout Europe. It's not like your parents didn't know we were sleeping together. Don't be a hypocrite."

"Can't you understand?"

"No. I can't understand." I had upset him again. "I don't understand why you'll talk about the future with me but won't marry me, and I don't understand why you'll sleep with me in one place, but not another. If you don't want to be under your family's nose, we can go back to my place."

"Donovan," I pleaded. "Just...give me a little time. I just can't tell my mom and grandmother I'm moving in with you after a week of dating."

"We're not just dating!" He waved his hand and turned around to leave. "Good-bye. I'll see you tomorrow if Your Highness will allow me, otherwise, see you on Tuesday at the company function."

"Donovan..." He paid no attention to my supplication.

"Why did Donovan leave?" Mom came into my room as soon as she saw Donovan go out the front door. "He didn't look happy."

"He wasn't happy." I bemoaned. "Is having a relationship always this difficult? I think we've had three arguments in a week—that's every other day. Maybe we aren't meant to be?"

Mom sat us down on my bed. "Relationships are hard no matter how many years you've been together."

"But everyone makes it look so easy. You and Dad never argue. Jake and Emily are always in sync with each other. This is all so new for me. I have no idea what I'm doing."

"Your father and I argue, plenty. And Jake and Emily have their issues, too. It's just a matter of compromise. You can't always have it your way, and you don't want to always give in and get pushed around, either. What was the matter, tonight?"

Now, I got bashful. I'd have to spell out for my mother what she probably already knew. "He wanted to stay here." This was my best attempt to be honest, but vague.

"And...?"

"And...I told him he couldn't."

"Why not?"

"Mom!" I groaned. "Do I need to confess everything?" I was dying of shame, and my mother was breaking into a fit of laughter. "OK, Mother. I confess I am no longer a virgin. I have lost my virginity to Donovan Taylor, and I had absolutely no qualms about giving it up. I did make sure all of our issues were ironed out before the act happened, but now I am a fallen woman." My head fell in shame. Did girls really have these kinds of conversations with their mothers?

"Was he considerate...? Was he gentle?" Mom asked awkwardly. She was concerned for me, but did not want too much information.

"Mom, it was perfect. And I am so glad my first was with Donovan."
Was I *really* having this conversation with my mother?

"So if you two have had sex already," Mom was trying to understand,
"what's the problem? Why did he leave upset?"

"I just didn't feel right having him stay here with me while you, Gram,
and Grandfather are here. It's very embarrassing for me to know that you
all know what I'm doing."

Mom died laughing. "You always were so prim and proper. I think
you're the most conservative person in the entire Reid family."

"I never told you that your father and I lived together before we got
married?"

"Oh my gosh Mom, you did? You never told me this!"

"I thought I told you. And trust me, your Gram was no angel either.
We all know you and Donovan will get married soon. We welcome him
here, so bring him back."

"But it's weird mom and so awkward. We will be living in sin."

"Then tell Donovan what's bothering you and have him propose to
you. Then you won't be living in sin because you'll be married. He looked
awfully upset, leaving. Call him right now and tell him to come back here."

"What kind of mother are you, encouraging me to live in sin with the
man I just started dating a week ago?" This was highly odd. I never realized she was so liberal.

"Donovan is not some guy you just started dating a week ago. I've
known him longer than I've known you, and I've watched him grow into a
fine young man. Knowing how much you love him, your father and I consider him a part of the family now. So no, I'm not some crazy mother telling her daughter to live in sin. I'm just trying to fast forward to the future."

"Are you sure you're OK with me having Donovan here? You sure
Gram and Grandfather will be OK as well?"

"We are all fine with it. It was actually me and your Gram who picked
out Donovan's room since it's quieter and bigger than yours."

"All right. I'll organize all his stuff for him in his new room and surprise him tomorrow."

Mom placed both her hands on my cheek and gave me a puckered
kiss. "Good night my sweet daughter. I am overjoyed for you. I love seeing

your beautiful face break into a constant smile. Your grandma and I were saying that we feel like we're falling in love again for the first time whenever we watch you. That sweet innocence of a first love gets lost when you're our age. It's beautiful to see on you and Donovan."

"Thank you, Mom."

After our talk, I felt confident that I could bring Donovan to Belgravia without feeling like a Jezebel. With a smile on my face, I went into his room and started unpacking his clothes. His suits came neatly packed on a hanger, in tall wardrobe boxes. This crazy man had something close to thirty suits. He was such a clotheshorse. Jane wasn't wrong when she said we'd need a separate room just for all of our clothes.

The bedding in this room was a bit on the old side, so I decided I would go to the department store tomorrow and pick up new bedding for us. I brought in some of my clothes to lay out in the dresser, but there was no way I could bring any hanging objects. The closet was full of suits. I also brought in my toiletries and placed them in the large bathroom. I'd have to remember to get a toothbrush holder for us, as well as a few containers to place our toiletries in a neat and orderly way. I was enjoying setting up our room. It felt like a honeymoon suite.

My phone dinged signaling a text.

What are you doing right now?

Even though you were mean and left without giving me a proper good-bye, I am arranging a surprise for you right now.

I would see how he would answer that kind of statement.

I can't fall asleep. I miss you. I need you next to me in bed.

Are you normally this needy? I added a smiley face next to that question so he wouldn't get upset with me.

Where you are concerned, yes.

It'll do you good to sleep without me tonight. You'll appreciate me more when we meet again.

Come over. I'll show you how much I appreciate you, tonight.

I can't. I'm slaving away getting your present ready.

I don't need any gifts from you. I just need you.

I loved this man who loved me.

Oh but trust me, you'll want this present.

I can't tempt you to join me tonight? I'll come pick you up.

Let me get this done for you, Donovan. I want to see your face when you get your present. Are you very busy tomorrow?

Probably. Roland and I have to clean house in London and get it in tiptop shape to sell. What are your plans?

I'm thinking of going to Oxford with Jake in the morning.

My phone rang and scared the shit out of me.

"Why the hell are we texting when we can talk?"

"Don't know. You started the thread."

"What will you do in Oxford?"

"I've been thinking, Donovan." I was going to tell him about starting med school this year, but decided against it. I was still unsure and I wanted to talk to him in person when bringing up such an important topic. "Never mind. I'll tell you tomorrow."

"You really won't come over?"

"It's not a won't. It's a can't. I love you and I'll see you tomorrow after work?"

"Yeah." He answered, unhappy. "I'll follow Roland straight to Belgravia after work."

That's all he would say, so I repeated myself. "I love you Donovan Taylor. I thank God you've found your way to me. Had you not loved me, I probably would've lived a spinster life with cats, and dogs, and maybe even a bird."

He still didn't answer but I knew he was smiling. "I miss you, Princess. I wish you were here with me in bed." That was all he would concede for the night.

"Me, too. Bye."

Monday started with two beautiful little toddlers greeting me at the breakfast table.

"Ne Ne!" James showed his gorgeous smile with two new teeth.

"James!" I ran over, picked him up from the high chair—oatmealed-face and all—and hugged this dear little boy. "Oh, I missed you." I kissed him where I could without eating his breakfast. James gave me a toothy grin and kissed my cheek and got cold oatmeal on me.

"Me too!" said the little girl who grew more and more beautiful by the day.

"Hello, my beautiful girl. You've grown so much." I crouched down with James in my arm and gave Ellie a kiss.

"Pick me. Pick me." She held out her arms. Emily walked over and took James from me, and I picked up Ellie and gave her another hug.

"I'm so very happy to be living in the same house as you two." I held out my arm and Emily gave James back to me. Feeling precarious, I chose to sit and have the two on my lap. "Are you done with your breakfast?"

"Yesh." They both answered.

"Should I help you get changed, then go play?"

"Yesh!" Who knew how much they understood, but I did what I advertised.

"What shall we play today?"

"Book." James answered and brought over his favorite.

"One fish, two fish, red fish, blue fish..." I proceeded to read and ended up reading it three times over.

"Laney?" Jake walked in. "Donovan is on the line." He handed me the phone while the kids called out, "More!"

"Hi." I greeted him with enthusiasm.

"Good morning, Princess. Sleep well?"

"No. I assume you slept well? You're definitely happier with me this morning than you were last night."

He chuckled. "You want to come out and have lunch with me today?"

"Yes, but are you sure you can spare the time?"

"I've been here since six. There's more work to do than I believed, but I gotta have lunch, and I'd like to have it with you, my beauty."

"All right. I was going to follow Jake to Oxford today, but maybe I'll go with him on Wednesday?" I queried and Jake nodded his head, yes, while reading the book one more time for the twins.

"What will you do this morning?"

"I was thinking of taking Emily and the twins to my favorite coffee shop and then maybe to Hyde Park. I also need to make some purchases at Harrods and Harvey Nics."

"Shit. You won't ever see me if that's how you roll, Babe. I'll have to bill all hours of the day and night. What the hell do you need to buy?"

"For your information, it's something for you! I'm not your little woman asking you for pin money, so you need not worry. If you are done lecturing, let me know what time you want to have lunch, and if I'm available, I'll pencil you in."

I could tell Donovan was grinning. "I'd do anything, give you everything, to have you as mine. Isn't that enough for you to want to marry me?"

"Mr. Taylor, you sound like a cheesy Valentine's Day card. I have to finish playing with the twins if I want to meet you for lunch. See you soon."

"With that kind of answer, I don't know if I'll be calling you for lunch." I'd say he was a tad upset, again.

"Your loss. Love you. Bye." I hung up.

"You're not giving him much wiggle room there, are you?" Jake was feeling sorry for his best friend.

"I assume Emily told you what I want from Donovan?"

"She did." Jake got up and handed James to me so we could walk downstairs together. "You sure I can't drop a hint?"

"Don't! Please, Jake. I need nothing from Donovan. No expensive ring, no fancy wedding – all I want is a heartfelt proposal asking me to be his wife."

"Damn! Why are you women all so difficult?"

Emily loved the bakery I introduced her to, and we hung out at the park with the twins and JR until it was naptime. We hit the jackpot when all three of them fell asleep in their strollers, because it gave us a chance to shop. However, with a double stroller and one Rolls Royce-sized pram, it wasn't easy getting around.

We started at the most expensive department store in London, and maybe even the world, where I purchased our bedding and towels. It was an absolute fortune! I couldn't believe how much I'd spent. As soon as we left the store, I wanted to go back and return everything I'd bought. Emily convinced me to keep the items and said I'd appreciate it every night when I used them. I hoped she was right because I'd spent a sizable chunk of my savings.

With the kids still asleep, we ventured to Harvey Nichols department store and Emily bought specialty food items and we sat at one of the tables on the top floor and had lattes and a couple of slices of cake.

"No call from Donovan, yet?"

"Nope. He must really be mad at me. Should we just eat lunch here? There are a plethora of choices."

"Why don't you text Donovan and make sure."

"It's already past one. I'm sure he's had lunch already. He has reasons to be upset. I was a brat to him this morning. I'll text to say I'm sorry. He's a busy man. No need to have him stewing over our conversation from last night and this morning."

I'm sorry I was a total brat this morning. Will you forgive me?

He didn't answer back.

"He's probably very busy with work."

"Yeah. I'm sure he is." That's what I told myself and Emily, but I was hurt. "Let's have a bite to eat before the twins get up."

"How about if we do take away, as the British would call it, and take lunch back home for the ladies?"

I put out a brave smile. "Sounds great."

We took the leisurely walk back to Gram's and my down-in-the-dumps mood brightened when I felt my phone signal a text.

"I think Donovan is getting back to me."

"I knew he would." Emily was happy for me.

I cannot meet on Wednesday. Any chance you can have tea now?
Michael sent a surprising text.

Yes, I can meet you today but I'm walking back home from Harrods with Emily and the kids. It'll take me another half an hour to meet you.

I'll pick you up at your house?

Perfect.

"Donovan?"

"No. Michael. He and I were supposed to meet for tea on Wednesday, but he needs to switch it to today, and right now. So I agreed to meet him."

"And Donovan knows you're meeting Michael?"

"He knew I was meeting him on Wednesday. I'll let him know later about today."

We had arrived at home and Aunt Sandy came out to help with the sleeping twins.

"Mom," Emily said, "Why don't we leave them in the stroller? They're wiped out from the park and it's too hard to transfer them to the fourth floor."

"All right. I'll leave the stroller in the library and keep the door open."

"You need help?" Mom came to us with Gram following.

"We're OK." Aunt Sandy called.

"Duch..." Michael started calling me by his term of endearment for me, then stopped. "Laney." He greeted me with a sweet smile.

Meeting him halfway, I gave him a big hug. "Hi Michael. I'm glad we can meet today."

"Me too."

"Michael Bennington, I presume?" Gram interrupted us.

"Sorry, Gram. Let me introduce Michael to everyone." I started with Gram. "This is my grandmother, Estelle Reid Ascot, my mom, Barbara Reid, and my aunt, Sandy Reid, and you've met Emily."

Everyone greeted each other.

"I believe you know my grandfather, Harry Bennington?" Michael spoke to Gram.

"We sure do know each other." Gram had a devilish glint.

"He said you were one unforgettable woman." Michael had that same playful tone.

Gram cackled. "You tell that Harry to come and say hello when he's back in Belgravia. I assume His Grace is out at his summer home?"

"He is and you would be most welcomed to visit...preferably without Sir Ascot." Michael and Gram both laughed. Obviously there was something going on here that the rest of us were not privy to at this very moment.

"It's good to meet you, Michael. I'm glad to see that you've grown into a fine young man. You tell your grandfather to call me personally if he wants to see me."

"I will. It was wonderful meeting you, too." Michael finished with Gram and spoke to Mom. "Your daughter has been a fabulous friend to me and my sister and I'm heartbroken we are no longer together. I'm hoping to change my status back from friend to boyfriend." His elfin grin was back.

"Let's go." I dragged him away from my family. "We are off to tea. I'll see you all in a few hours."

Before I left, Emily asked, "You want me to ask Mrs. Haines to take care of your purchases?"

"Can you just ask her to start the wash and I'll finish it?"

"Sure. Good-bye, Michael."

"Nice to see you again, Emily."

The initial few minutes of our walk were uncomfortable, but if we were to be friends again, we needed to start somewhere.

"What was that about my grandmother and your grandfather?"

Michael chuckled. "Grandfather finally confessed that the reasons he didn't like you in the beginning wasn't so much because you were American, but because you were Estelle's granddaughter. He said it was history repeating itself."

"Explain."

"Future Duke, Harry Bennington, was wildly in love with a young Estelle Cowper and courted her with zeal. My grandfather knew he'd found his duchess. Your great grandfather and my great grandfather had practically set the wedding date when a nobody named Jerry Reid came along and snagged your grandmother's heart. Grandfather was heartbroken, but worse, his pride was hurt, so he just sat and ignored the situation.

Harry Bennington, being the pompous man that he was, refused to chase after your grandmother. He figured once her fanciful dreaming was done, his Estelle would come back to reality and become his duchess. But alas, she never did, and he never forgave or forgot her."

This story was a little too reminiscent of our triangle right now. "My grandmother was quite a popular lady. Look at her and Grandfather Roland."

"Ah yes. We can't forget Sir Roland. After your grandfather passed away, Harry Bennington decided to court Estelle Cowper Reid, but once again, he was too late. He waited too long to come around to forgiving your grandmother for leaving him the first time. By the time he swallowed his pride, your grandmother was already seeing Sir Roland."

I giggled. "So that's why he took an immediate dislike to me. When did he tell you this story?"

"Right after you broke up with me in Florence. Our stories are eerily alike, don't you think?"

"They are, and I need you to know that even if my relationship with Donovan fails, I won't come back to you." Shoot! By the look on his face, I'd hurt Michael again. "I know this sounds like a cliché, but it's not you, Michael. It's all me."

"Laney. I don't want to hold onto the same regrets my grandfather has had his entire life. I need to give it my best effort to win you back, and if I fail, then so be it. At least I won't have any regrets when I'm eighty."

"Michael." Perhaps Donovan was right. This get-together with Michael wasn't a good choice. "Don't waste your time on me. There is someone out there who will make you the most wonderful duchess. I'm sorry I gave you false hope the past couple of months. It wasn't fair to you, and I feel terribly toward your family because they've been so good to me. Though I'm sad that Ruby has chosen not to be my friend anymore, I understand."

"Oh. Bloody hell. Rubes told me to tell you she's not upset."

"What? How come she hasn't answered any of my calls and texts?"

"She kind of ended up on this crazy cruise to the Arctic and didn't take her phone. Between not having phone reception and you changing your number, she hasn't been able to get a hold of you. She comes home soon. She'll call you when she's home."

"Why didn't you tell me this sooner? I was so sad."

"You were sad that you would no longer be with my sister, but it doesn't faze you not to be with me?"

"Of course it does. I can't begin to tell you how much it hurts me to see you hurt. There's no good reason for me to do this to you."

"Then don't do this." He pleaded. "Come back. Let's try again and see where this may lead. If in a few months time, you can't forget Donovan, I'll let you go. Please, Duchess. Help me not regret the rest of my life. I can't let you go."

"Michael." My mind ran back and forth trying to figure out how best to tell him that Donovan was my forever and only love. "It's been thirteen years and I haven't forgotten Donovan. I don't think a few months will make a difference...even with you. I'm sorry."

Michael was hurt, yet he didn't look defeated.

The rest of tea was talk of his time at his grandfather's home, and what he was planning on doing with some of their estate renovations. Michael walked me back home and we said our good-byes in front of the flat.

"I'll see you again when Rubes gets here?"

"We can see each other again, as *friends.*"

"Good-bye, Duchess." He smiled and playfully stole a kiss from me.

I started laughing at his mischievousness until I heard someone yelling, "What the fuck!" Then I cringed because I knew who this someone was, and why he was yelling.

SHIT! Why me and why now?

"Why the fuck is Michael kissing you, and why the fuck did you let him?" I got angry-Donovan, again.

"It was done in jest, Donovan. He didn't mean anything by it and he took me by surprise. I didn't know he was going to do that, and it wasn't like I kissed him back." I sighed. This jealousy bit was cute at first, but now it was getting old.

"What would you have done if Kate had kissed me?"

With the most serious face I could produce, I answered, "Beat the shit out of her."

Donovan didn't know how to respond to my answer; he was dumbfounded. Then he busted up in the middle of the street and had to hold on to the railing to keep from falling like a drunken man.

"You!" He pulled my body into his. "You are in serious trouble with me for..."

"For...?" I challenged him.

"A) Going out with another man. B) Allowing another man to kiss you. C) Being a smart-ass with me. Are those good enough reasons?"

"Whatcha' gonna do with me?" This time, I tried my best devil-may-care attitude.

"Oh-ho! Now role-playing a sassy girl?" This playful, teasing-Donovan was one of my favorites. "We'll have to try a few more roles, tonight, or whenever I can get off work."

"Why are you here in the middle of the afternoon?"

"Well, my girlfriend wouldn't answer her phone so I had to leave the office to come find her."

"I guess I left my phone in the shopping bag."

"Have you had lunch?" he asked apologetically.

"Yeah." I grumbled. "I was so hungry for a lunch date, I took the first invitation that came my way. I did text and apologize for my attitude this morning."

Donovan started kissing me on the street – nothing extreme. "I got it, and I'm sorry about lunch and the lack of response. I was in a meeting and couldn't exactly ask these potential buyers to stop talking so I could answer my girlfriend's text."

"I figured you were either being your usual petty self and were pissed with me, or busy. The former was a more likely explanation." I giggled.

"You're in a hell of a cheeky mood today. What's got you so brazen, and what can I do with this smart mouth of yours?"

"I don't know what you'll do, but let me show you where you can do it." The saucy attitude continued.

I quickly rushed him up two flights of stairs and took him to our new bedroom. Of course he had no idea what he was looking at since none of his belongings were evident. Mrs. Haines, or Emily, had already washed our bedding and placed it on the bed and the new towels were laid out in the bathroom.

I dragged a bewildered Donovan to the closet and had him open it.

"Voila!" I announced proudly and happily.

"Are these all mine?" The crazy man actually doubted.

"You know any other man, not royalty, with 100 designer suits? Eleanor Estes could write a novel about you."

"So…" He was still a bit unsure. I didn't know why. It was as clear as day that I had set up this room for him. "You made a room for me on the same floor as you?"

Ah. I now figured out where his mind was going. I opened up a few of the dresser drawers that had his clothes on one side and mine on the other, then I walked him into the bathroom where our toiletries were beautifully laid out next to one another. Finally! That sexy smile resurfaced.

"This is what I was doing last night when I couldn't come over and spend the night with you, you surly man. And this," I pointed to our bedding and towels, "was what I purchased at Harrods today. It cost me a bloody fortune to buy our bedding and towels. That's why there are very few towels. I hope you do laundry because we will have to do it often." Sadly, I wasn't kidding. I could not buy a spare set of anything at those prices.

"My God, I love you."

"I know," I answered egotistically.

He perched himself on the bed and bounced around a little, then explored the high thread count sheets under the duvet. "This feels really good. It'll feel even better when we're both naked." He pulled me onto the bed with him and we fell back. "I'll give you my credit card before I leave. Go back to Harrods and buy another set or two of everything."

"No thank you."

"Why not?" Now he perched himself on top of me.

"Because, Mr. Taylor, they will let not me use your credit card first of all, and secondly, I am not your mistress where you go around setting up accounts for her to go shopping. I'm sure that happened plenty in old England, but nowadays we don't do that kind of stuff for our girlfriends. Plus, I feel cheap and easy." I giggled.

"Princess, there ain't anything cheap or easy about you. And soon you'll be my wife, and we'll be sharing accounts anyhow. You'll just start a little earlier."

"I'll just go and get cheaper bed and bathroom paraphernalia somewhere else. There must be a Target or Bed Bath and Beyond equivalent here. I just wanted our first night here to be extra special."

"Any night with you is special." Donovan pulled me on top of him, and I laid my head in the crook of his neck and shoulder. His arms wrapped around me. "I love being with you."

"Me too." I mused.

"This feels like we're married, though we are *not*! I've thought through you and me and us and I still don't know what the hell I'm doing wrong. You love me, I love you. You've asked me to marry you. *Shit!* I got it. I need to answer you. That's the answer. I need to say, '*YES!*' Is that why you refuse to marry me?" Donovan shook me a little. "You asleep there?"

"No." I answered dreamily. "I was building castles in the sky with you as my prince and me as the princess. What were you saying?"

"Finally, I have the answer to why you won't marry me."

Putting my chin on the hands that were resting on Donovan's chest, I asked, "What's the answer?"

"Yes, I will marry you," he announced proudly.

"I know you'll marry me." I answered pragmatically.

"You weren't waiting for me to answer your proposal?"

My head bobbed on his chest as I laughed. "No...guess again." I practically sang.

"All right, back to the drawing board on that one." He kissed the top of my head. "What happened here? Why all of a sudden are we living together?"

"You complaining?" I was still in a very relaxed and lost-in-beautiful-thought kind of mood.

"No way. I just need to know who to thank for this fantastic surprise."

"You can thank my crazy mother who thought it was fine for her daughter to live in sin with a man she's been dating for only a week."

"We've been together longer than a week." He joined my good mood. "It's been like ten days, though when you get obstinate, it feels like ten years."

"Funny. You're lucky I'm feeling so good right now. I think I could stay like this forever."

Donovan continued rubbing my back until we heard an "Unca!" That high-pitched yell could only mean one thing. Elizabeth Reid. "Ne Ne. No!" She chided me as she tried her best to climb up our tall bed. I rolled off Donovan as he picked up his goddaughter. James was not far behind.

"Come here, James." Donovan picked him up too and handed him to me.

James busily played with his robot while Ellie chatted away with her "Unca." Donovan was enamored with the way she called out to him.

"Ellie, my beautiful goddaughter. You and I will see each other every day for a while from now on. Are you happy about that?"

"Yesh!" She had no clue what he said but from the smile on Donovan's face, she knew it was something good. This Ellie Reid was definitely life smarter than I ever was.

"Should Uncle Donovan and Auntie Laney take you and James to the aquarium next week?"

"Yesh!" This time the twins answered simultaneously.

"They've been to the aquarium already, so they know what you're talking about." I clued Donovan in.

"Do you love your Uncle Donovan?"

"Yesh!"

"Do you love your Auntie Laney?"

"Yesh." James answered.

"No!" Ellie responded firmly. "My Unca!" She admonished with her index finger.

"You are too smart for your own good." I tickled Ellie and kissed her cheek.

"No, Ne Ne! No kiss."

Donovan was loving Ellie's brattiness. "As much as your uncle would like to play with you, I need to get back to work."

"Really? I thought you were home for the night."

Donovan leaned over and kissed me tenderly. "I'll be *home* as soon as I can."

"No kiss!" Ellie didn't like the attention I was getting from her 'Unca.'

We brought both kids downstairs and Donovan said his good-byes to everyone.

"Donovan."

"Yes, Gram?"

"There are cars downstairs in the garage. You may drive any one of them."

"Grandpa Jerry still have the Jaguar E-Type?"

"You boys are all the same." Gram answered. "It's in the mews, turned garage, unless Jake took it out today. Have Laney show you where the keys are and drive what you like."

"Thank you, Gram." He smiled wide and kissed all the ladies good-bye, again.

The Jag was taken already so Donovan hopped into the Range Rover and said his last good-byes to me. "Most likely it'll be late when I get back. We've a mound of work to do and I spent too much time this afternoon with the woman I love madly."

"I'll stay up and wait for you in my old room till you get home. Call me later."

"No going out with Michael, or any other man who asks you to a meal."

"Yes, Sir." That earned me another kiss.

Donovan never made it home last night, and he was still at the office when I got a call from him in the early afternoon.

"Hi!" I missed not being with him last night, but understood he had played too much with me last week.

"Hi, Princess. You still helping feed the kids?"

"No. I'm getting ready to take Gram to the beauty salon. She told me that we are both to get our skins pampered and our hairs coiffed for tonight's event."

"I can't wait to see the result, though you look gorgeous with no makeup and your hair tied back. Extra pampering might bring more attention to you."

"I doubt it. It's Gram who will command attention with her flawless skin and striking presence."

Donovan agreed. "Babe. I'm calling because I don't think I can make it home before tonight's function. Can you get my suit and everything that goes with it and send it with a delivery service to the office?"

"Where will you shower and change?"

"Roland's office. I will also have to meet you at the event. We are working till the last minute."

"You must be so tired. Have you slept at all?"

"For about an hour. This is how much I usually work when it's busy."

"You never seemed this busy all those months I saw you back in the States."

"That's because I made time to see you. What you didn't see was me going back to the office after I dropped you off, or bringing work home. You see how much I loved you even back then?"

I didn't fall for that one. "Whatever. When Gram and I go out, I'll bring you everything you need. Are we still going with the camellia theme, tonight?"

"Yep."

"I'm wearing this under my dress tonight." I sent him a picture of a low cut lace bustier with matching lace panties, and lace-up front garter with straps to hold up the silky thigh-high stockings.

"Ah shit! Babe you can't do this to me mid-day. I don't need to walk around the office with a boner."

"And I bought a matching bra that has a flimsy tie in the front, though I won't wear the bra tonight."

"Princess. I need to get some work done," Donovan whined.

"OK. Once last thing..." I then sent him a selfie of me in a black nightie, similar to the French-laced garter and panties.

"You're killing me!" He groaned aloud. "I'm going to require you to come up and relieve me when you drop off the suit."

"But Gram will be waiting in the car," I answered with innocence. "I'll relieve you plenty when you come home. I've yet to try out our bed."

"Damn. Now I'm going to look at this picture the rest of the day and be horny. When are you stopping by?"

"Soon."

"Be ready for a quickie in my office."

Damn. Talk about getting horny. The thought of having sex in his office was making me pulsate. "Oh, no, Donovan," I coyly answered, "I can't have sex with you in the office, but I'll give you a preview of the new teal and hot pink bra and thong I picked up at Harvey Nics." I took a barely-there, peak-a-boo snapshot of the thong I was wearing and sent one last picture. "See you soon." I hung up before he responded, very satisfied with myself.

I got all of Donovan's clothes ready, and Gram and I left for the office. Knowing I didn't like driving on the wrong side of the car and road, but most likely because Donovan wanted me in his office, ASAP, he sent us the company car.

"Gram, would you like to come in and say hello to Grandfather? I won't take long dropping this off if you prefer to wait."

"I'll wait. You go ahead. If you see your grandfather, give him a kiss for me."

"Will do."

I was all smiles walking into the building. Of course the first person I ran into when stepping off the elevator was none other than Kate Beauvais, but I didn't give a shit. Smiling and waving only, I walked off before I had to talk to her.

"Knock, knock." I called out to my boyfriend who was hard at work. "You look awfully dapper for a man who hardly slept last night. And where did that suit come from, considering you didn't come home to change?" My attempt at a disapproving look probably failed miserably since a smile wouldn't leave my face.

The pulsing resumed as soon as this handsome man greeted me with a you-are-the-love-of-my-life, look. He frosted his office windows and slithered over to me like I was his prey and he was the captor. Once his clothes were out of my hands and carelessly thrown onto the sofa, he asked, "Are you the one they sent to remedy my ailment?" His lips grazed my bare shoulders without his hands ever touching me. It was incredibly arousing.

"Oh no, Sir. I'm no doctor, yet. I can't cure any afflictions." I boldly put my hand on his erection and asked a question of my own. "Is this where it hurts?" I couldn't believe that little ole me had become such a hussy.

Donovan turned me around, pushed me up against his desk and lifted up my skirt.

"Donovan, Gram is waiting outside. I won't be able to face her if I'm here even a minute longer."

"Then you shouldn't have sent me those pictures. Plus, you promised to show me your underwear and bra." He caressed from the outside of the silky underwear.

"I need to go," I panted a complaint.

His hand came around to the front of my thong and was about to go inside when a knock on the door made me frantically readjust my outfit. Donovan gave me one last lingering kiss and answered, "Come in."

"Our meeting is about to start."

"I'll be right there."

"Does Kate play your PA before every meeting?" I was more annoyed with myself for being the jealous girlfriend, than with Kate who purposely interrupted us.

"No, but you can role-play my PA tonight." Donovan suggested. "Tonight!" He promised and threatened with a slap to my rear end.

We walked out together, and I went over and hugged and kissed my grandfather who was walking toward us.

"Do you greet every man with such enthusiasm?"

"Only the handsome ones, Grandfather." Then I added one more kiss. "And that was from your wife. Have a productive meeting." I waved good-bye and walked into the sunset.

Gram indulged the both of us in a facial, massage, and hair and make-up treatments. When we got home, all we had to do was put on our gowns and get in the car.

"You look beautiful, Gram!" At her age, my grandmother was a knockout. Out of all the grandchildren, Jane most resembled her. Gram, too, had the dark hair, thanks to coloring magic, bright blue eyes, and a fair complexion. Gram, Jane, and Ellie in a portrait would be stunning.

"Thank you, Dear. You look beautiful as well. Donovan won't be able to concentrate tonight."

"And neither will Grandfather."

The firm function was a rooftop party on their building. Initially, I dreaded being outside in the heat and humidity, but tonight turned out to be a beautiful night. My grandmother caused quite a commotion as she walked in as though she owned the place. She was Queen Estelle and commanded attention without uttering a word. I'd do well to learn this trait from her.

All the sycophants came over in droves as soon as we entered the party. Gram was beseeched with praise and adoration.

"Hello, Sexy." A deep, husky voice greeted me with a kiss on my neck from behind with his hand placed scandalously low on my hips.

"Um, excuse me Sir, but I'm meeting the love of my life here. I ask you to kindly take your hands and lips off me." I continued this role-play.

"This love of your life is a lucky man." His kissing turned into devouring. I could feel myself heating up.

"He sure is," I answered with false innocence.

"Won't you come downstairs to my empty office and lay on my desk while I pleasure you?"

I prayed no one saw me quiver and practically buckle at the knees after that indecent offer. Turning around to face him, I placed my arms around him and answered him with an incendiary kiss. "Good evening, Mr. Taylor."

"You look stunning, my love."

"Thank you. It's all thanks to my grandmother whose motto is 'a girl can't have too many diamonds, too much lingerie, and never leave the house without make-up.' I don't have diamonds, I don't always wear make-up, but I'm working to build up the lingerie collection."

He smiled and kissed me one more time.

"This is a work event, Donovan." Grandfather broke us up in jest.

"Laney, you look almost as beautiful as my wife, tonight."

"Thank you, Grandfather. I think if you were fifty years younger, you'd definitely be the front runner in the handsome category."

"I knew there was a reason why I liked you." Grandfather indulged me in a kiss.

"Like, but still not a favorite with anyone." My hurt expression fooled no one. "Jake will forever be Gram's favorite, and Jane will forever be yours."

"I see why you're such a fool in love, Donovan. She reminds me of Estelle when I first met her in Paris. Beautiful, playful, bust-your-balls tough if you cross her. She's a keeper."

"She sure is, Roland." As Gram said earlier, Donovan only had eyes for me. "Babe," he whispered, "I need to go say hello to a potential client. Do you want to greet him with me?"

"Can I help you in a few minutes after I go fix my lipstick? I'm sure that flagrant kiss earlier is making my lips look like Bobo the Clown."

"I'd make out with Bobo the Clown any day if he looked like you."

"See you soon."

Dazed from feeling so loved, I practically waltzed into the bathroom, but stopped dead in my tracks when I heard, "You know Donovan is only dating her because she's Roland's wife's granddaughter." I had no idea of the identity of the woman who just spoke.

"I was told he's to inherit a big part of the company if he marries her. That's why he's lavishing so much attention on her. Back when we were together, I couldn't figure out why he was so interested in her. Now I get it." This voice, I knew all too well.

"It's not like she's got anything going for her. She's just living off her grandparents' wealth. Don't worry, Kate. Donovan has always come back to you. Ten years is a long time to love someone. That's not simply forgotten. Not even for a piece of a law firm. And it's not like you haven't amassed your own fortune."

"Oh, I'm not worried. I know he'll come back. He always has."

Hurrying away from the bathroom, I kept telling myself that Kate was a spiteful bitch and I had nothing to worry about where Donovan's love was concerned. Obviously, the fact that Donovan wanted to marry me instead of Kate pissed her off enough to try and spread lies and rumors. Still, what I had heard was unsettling. No one had informed me that I came with a law firm dowry, not my grandparents, parents, or Donovan.

"You all right?" Donovan reached out and brought me closer to him.

"Yeah." I answered and tried to put on a happy face for the clients.

I "worked" the party the best I could, laughing where required, and answering questions where needed. The evening was a long one and smiling, when it didn't reach my heart, wore me out.

"Donovan, Gram looks tired. Are you or Grandfather able to leave?"

"I need to stay till the end, but you take your grandmother home. It is quite late."

"I'll see you soon?" was my only good-bye to him.

" Princess." He pulled me into his body and forced me to look him in the eye. "I don't know how soon you will see me, but I do know you haven't been yourself most of the evening. I don't know what could have gone wrong in the bathroom, or what I could've done to piss you off, but you're brooding with a smile."

This man was more in tune with my body than I believed. "We'll talk tonight."

"Are you upset with me? Did I do something wrong?"

"I don't think so...I don't know. You know I'm not one to hold back my feelings. When we have some privacy, you'll hear *all* about what's bothering me."

"Should I be scared?" He kidded. "Maybe I should stay at the apartment tonight?"

"You should be as scared as your conscience tells you to be. And if you choose to stay at the apartment tonight, you'll miss out on picture number two." My sense of humor partly returned.

Without missing a beat, he placed his mouth over mine and kissed me long and hard – tongue and all. This kiss soothed my unsettled heart.

"I love you." He said, catching his breath. "And Princess," I brought his lips next to my ear, "sleep in our bed tonight, but lose the nightie. I want to see you naked when I come home."

I walked away, unable to keep the smile at bay.

My eyes popped open at a body that curled into mine from behind. "Donovan?" I whispered.

"Were you expecting someone else?" He readjusted us slightly and without warning, entered me in one push.

"Ah." I squealed because it hurt and felt good at the same time. "What are you doing?"

"Making love to the woman who's teased me all day and night with this sexy body."

"But, I'm not ready." I complained weakly.

"You will be soon, and you need to keep your voice down. I know this is a big house but at four in the morning, everyone can hear you."

He placed his hands at my hipbone and rocked in and out of me slowly till I woke up and started participating like this was my very last night on earth. We'd never been in this spooning position before, and I loved how his body completely outlined my own. I also loved the feel of his hands gripping me as he lost control in me, feverishly pumping in and out.

I tried my damnedest but couldn't keep from moaning. I turned my head into the pillow, but the whole idea of trying to keep quiet so others couldn't hear, turned-me on even more. Amazingly, Donovan sensed when I was about to climax and placed his hand over my mouth in perfect timing. What would have been a cry, calling out my boyfriend's name, turned out to be a mumble-jumble of muffled sounds. Donovan came right behind me and we both attempted to regain our senses after the orgasm died down.

"I'm thinking we should move into the apartment."

"I hate the thought of leaving my family, but I think you're right. Maybe we'll go back and forth and only have sex when we're at the apartment."

"I plan on fucking you every night so that's not going to work. We'll figure something out."

"Just don't attack me in the middle of the night when the house is in dead silence."

"Got it." He laughed.

"You got home late. You must be exhausted."

"I am but I'm willing to listen to what you have to say before I crash for a couple of hours."

"Why just a couple of hours?"

"I have an 8:00am meeting."

"Geez, you work hard."

"And so will you when you when you become a surgeon."

"Hmmm. At this hour, that doesn't sound too appealing."

"You'll love it, Princess, and you'll save hundreds of lives."

"Go to sleep, Donovan. I know you're tired."

"Speak, Princess, or I'll attack you one more time."

"Is that why you haven't pulled out yet?"

"You complaining?"

"No. I like this feeling of us being joined."

"I do too." He kissed me by the ear and asked again, "What was wrong, tonight?"

"When I went to the restroom, I heard, I mean I..." Earlier, I had thought over how I was going to ask him this question at least fifty times, but it still wasn't coming out correctly. "All right. How about if I ask you this. What do you get if you marry me?"

There was some pause and but eventually he answered, "I get a beautiful, sexy, passionate, and caring woman *when* we get married."

Obviously, I didn't ask the question correctly. So I tried it another way. "What do you get financially if we get married?"

Once again, another pause. "I get a quarter of a million dollars in medical school bills, plus whatever credit card bills you may carry?"

"No." I was now frustrated. "That's not what I meant. And plus, I don't have any credit card bills; I don't spend money I don't have."

"Hallelujah!" he interrupted.

"And Daddy is looking into getting me into med school this year so you won't have to pay for it because I'm still a Reid."

"Wait, what? When did this happen? Why didn't you tell me you were headed back to school?"

Now we were totally off tangent. Because I needed to see his eyes, I pulled away and turned myself to face him. "I heard Kate and some woman talking in the restroom earlier tonight, and they were saying that you were only dating me because you'll inherit a part of the law firm if you marry me. While I don't believe everything these bitches said, I am disgruntled that no one told me about this million dollar dowry of mine. Why haven't you mentioned any of this?"

"Because I was just told this information the day before I landed in London. Supposedly, Roland set up his will to divide the company amongst your uncles, Jake, Jane, and me, by marriage through you. And if by some hell-freezes-over chance we don't get married, I can buy into this stake."

"And...?"

"And that's it. Jane and I will get bigger shares because we are the working partners and your uncles are technically silent partners."

"There's nothing more to this?"

"Babe. What I told you is all I know. I've no idea how much of the company we will receive. Roland never offered that information, and I'm not about to wonder. You and I will be fine with my income alone, even if you chose not to work. Plus I don't care to work to death so I can have more money than I can spend. I've told you before, I want to raise a family with you. I want to travel with you. We don't need hoards of money to do this," Donovan chuckled, "especially since your grandparents have laid the groundwork for us to live in their homes."

"So with my new-found wealth, perhaps I'll go to law school instead and put myself in the will instead of you."

Donovan fell back and laughed. "Babe. I believe it's you who's in the will. I'm just your worker bee. But if you want to work and support me, I'm all for that. So is this explanation to your satisfaction?"

"I guess so. It wasn't that I was mad at you. It was just weird hearing private family matters from two strangers. I swear, if we weren't at yours and grandfather's company function, I would have dropkicked both those bitches. Do you know what that middle-aged ex of yours said?"

"What?" Donovan couldn't keep from howling.

"She said you'd come back to her after we broke up because you always came back to her. *Bitch!*"

"Remind me never to cross you."

"It doesn't piss you off that Kate's going around saying those things about you and me?" I whined.

"Not really. What's there to be mad about? I love you. We're getting married, and that's that. Now you tell me what's going on with med school. What's this talk about your dad getting you into school this year?"

"I was thinking that maybe wasting a year isn't a good idea now with you in the picture. When I contemplate going to school for four years, then doing my residency for another four years, I wondered when I would have kids and how this was all going to work out."

"Explain."

"If we were to get married, you're at a stage in your life where you want kids, a family, the Jake and Emily life. I am only starting my life now, a year late at that, so I won't be able to give you any of that for eight years at the earliest. If that is the case, then it seems not very prudent to push off the inevitable by messing around in Europe. So I asked Dad to see if I could possibly enroll in med school in a couple of weeks. I was going to tell you, but we just never had the time to sit and talk about this."

"Delaney, I appreciate what you were doing, but I don't want you to do this for me. In fact, I want you to keep this year open so we can travel while I'm based here in Europe. Once you start school, once we create a family, we will never be able to do this as freely, again. This year is a gift most people don't ever receive. Let's make the most of our situation and enjoy life."

"Are you sure? You're going to be kind of old when you have your first child."

"Is this an admission that we are getting married?"

"Donovan, I'd marry you today if only you understood…" I sighed deeply.

"What am I doing wrong? Is it the lack of a ring? I know I haven't picked out your ring yet. I thought you might want to do it together."

"It's not a ring. I don't need one."

He looked at me in total frustration. "Have you changed your mind? You don't want to marry me anymore?"

"I've wanted this since I was ten. My heart's the same. Nothing's changed." Seeing this man so bewildered and frustrated, I decided to give up my wish for a proposal and agreed in my heart to marry him. "Never mind. I don't need you to do anything. You're all that I need. I'll tell Mom later today to start the prepar..."

"Wait." Donovan put a finger on my lips and shut me up. "Don't say anymore." He was thinking through something and didn't say a word to me. When he was done, he flashed a blinding smile. "I was talking to Jane today..." he cryptically stopped again.

"And...? What did Jane say?"

"Um, she and I talked about..." He kept searching for the right words. "We talked about the firm and how originally I was to stay out here for a year, try and win you over, then she would work here while Max did his residency in London."

"Is there a but to that?"

"With Roland deciding to sell the European side of the firm, neither of us will ever have to live away from our families. As principle owners, we wouldn't have a choice in the matter. Now, the furthest we have to travel to is New York. We could both be based in LA."

"That's fantastic."

"It is. Roland told me he never had much luck with large families. His parents had two boys, but lived only long enough to see them married. Then his wife, Lauren passed on from cancer in her early thirties, and they never had kids due to her illness. He and his brother were close but he died a few years back from natural causes leaving behind a wife and a daughter."

"Where are his niece and sister-in-law?"

"I'm unsure. I think they are somewhere in Europe. Roland set them up nicely for the rest of their lives and purchased his brother's share of the firm. He did the same for his other partner, William Pemberley when he died. So in essence, your grandfather probably owns ninety to ninety-five percent of this massive firm."

"That sounds impressive but it doesn't mean anything to me. Is that a lot of money?"

"It's an insane amount of money."

"And the largest share is coming to me and Jane?" I asked in a high-pitched voice, pretending to be interested in the money.

"Um...no. I get first dibs on buying those shares if we don't get married, so it all boils down to you needing to marry me, not the other way around."

We both laughed. "I'm glad Grandfather Roland married Gram. He's finally found his family."

"That's exactly what he said to me when we talked back in LA. He loves all of you like his own children and grandchildren, and he will gladly divide his wealth to everyone when the time comes."

"So Jane must be happy she doesn't have to move."

"She is, and we talked about sharing responsibilities so neither of us has to be away from our families for too long, or too often. I'm thankful she and I have stayed good friends, despite our stupidity and selfishness. We work well together."

"And I'm glad you and Jane have each other. It's always easier to share the burden." I wondered if I should be the one helping Donovan, and not Jane. This wasn't because I was jealous of Donovan and Jane's camaraderie. I just wondered if this was what wives did for their husbands. "You think I should go to law school, instead? Then I can help you, too. You think I'll get in?" Perhaps my mind didn't work in the analytical, argumentative kind of way.

"From what I can tell, your heart is set on becoming a doctor. I thank you the beautiful offer, but I am here to help *you* achieve your dream. You are brilliant enough to do whatever you want to do in life. But don't do it for someone else—not even for me."

"Thank you, Donovan. And I love you." I yawned while expressing my love for him.

I cringed at the mess I created on my bedding, but I was too tired to get up and do anything about it. Laundry would be high priority, later in the morning.

"Princess." I heard Donovan whispering in my ear. "I'm leaving for the day and I probably won't be home till very late again." I felt like I had just closed my eyes. He kissed my cheek and took his weight off the bed.

"Wait." I croaked. Quickly, I ran to the bathroom, got myself presentable and put on a robe. "Didn't we just get to bed?"

"We did." He smiled and kissed my lips. "You don't have to get up with me. I just didn't want to leave without saying good-bye to you. Go back to sleep."

"I'll walk you out. Have you had anything to eat?"

He chuckled. "Will you be the type of wife to get up and make me coffee and breakfast every morning?"

"Probably not." I chuckled with him. "Most likely, you'll have to take care of me in the mornings."

"It would be my dream to take care of you anytime of the day."

"Don't be so sweet and sappy first thing in the morning. As it is, I don't want you to go. I don't like being apart from you." Those words got mumbled and jumbled, similar to my moaning climax this morning. I felt embarrassed confessing such weakness to him.

"I don't like being apart from you either, but if we are to have three free days up in Scotland, I need to get some work done." We walked hand in hand down the stairs. "By the way, I found a castle we could stay at up in Scotland. I thought I'd rent a room just for us. What do you think?"

"That sounds glorious, but I don't think we should be away from the family. It looks like my dad and your dad are coming back to London on Thursday. It'll be another family extravaganza."

"Why are they both coming back and how do you know?"

"Mom says that Dad claims he needs to be here to help Jake settle into his first week at the new school and hospital. But she thinks he's lonely without us."

"I was lonely, too, when you had left me for London."

"Good one." I squeezed his hand and giggled. "And Ma says your dad doesn't want to go to Chicago with her to hang out with a whining Becky, so he's coming here from Italy. That decision was of course made once my dad told him we were golfing at St. Andrews."

"So another boisterous family affair?"

"Yep."

"Shit. Maybe I should rent that room in the castle for us. We're not going to have any privacy."

"Don't do that. Grandfather already booked us all rooms at the resort on the golf course. Let's not deviate from family plans."

"Do I have a choice?"

"Nope." I squeezed his hand once more in affection. "You have time for a cup of coffee with me? I can make you one."

"I thought there was no coffee maker here."

"Oh...but there is..." A sly grin came upon my face. "I bought one of those coffee machines I liked so much at the villa."

"Where is all this money coming from?" Donovan gave me a semi-disapproving look.

"I got two big fat paychecks the other day from editing senior theses. It was big enough to buy our bedding, a few bathroom paraphernalia, the lingerie I've yet to model for you, and the coffee machine."

"That must have been some check."

"Times, *two!*"

Donovan laughed at me. "All right. Let's go try out this new machine you bought."

"UNCA!" We both jumped back at the screaming welcome Donovan got when we walked into the breakfast room. "UNCA!" she yelled, again.

"You better say hello to my daughter before she blows the house down."

"Hello, beautiful girl." Even in his nice suit, he picked up his god-daughter and gave her a loving hug and kiss. After he put her back in her high chair, he went over to James and gave him equal attention. "Hi James."

"Ne Ne." James pointed to me, and I walked over and kissed him on both cheeks, times two, or maybe even three, while he was still in Donovan's arms.

"Good morning, Ellie," I went over to try and kiss her.

Ellie once again pointed at me and said, "No! No kiss."

"Ellie," Emily gave a stern warning. "Do not point your finger at anyone. You're not being very nice. What do you have to say to Auntie Laney?"

"Thowry." Ellie's head went down with the reprimand, but she fooled no one with her pretend "thowry." She quickly bounced back from being penitent to prattling on about who knew what. She babbled to herself, to her brother, and to anyone who might be looking at her.

"She just doesn't like me anywhere near her favorite uncle. As long as Donovan and I are not in the same room, she's fine," I let a worried Emily know.

"You're going to make some poor fella feel awfully loved, or awfully trapped." Donovan placed James back in his chair and kissed Ellie one more time. "Ellie, can I have some of your oatmeal?" Donovan pretended to pick up her spoon.

Of course her answer was, "No! Lellie oatme."

"Wow, her use of words is coming along. I can't believe the way she can put together two, three word sentences already."

Jake shook his head in forced exasperation. "I just hope she doesn't talk our ears off in six months."

"Where's the baby?" Donovan asked.

"JR is not a morning baby. He likes to sleep in," Emily answered while cleaning up the two who were done with their meals.

"He's the smart one in the family." Grandfather spoke. "Good morning, my sweet granddaughter. I thank you for buying a Jura for the flat."

"I bought it just for you, Grandfather. You had one in every home I visited."

He motioned for us to sit down once our coffees were made. Contrary to my promise, it was Donovan who went over and got us a cup of coffee and some baked goods from the sideboard.

"What did you think of the Eggleston group last night, Donovan?"

"Well, if they are as interested as they appeared, I think a sale is imminent, Roland."

"That's the feeling I got."

"What does it mean to sell a law firm?" I asked.

My grandfather spoke first. "There are two options. We could technically merge two firms, with full disclosure that our firm will be eventually bought out by the other firm. This merger will allow our clients to acclimate themselves with the new firm and get comfortable. When all is settled, we will bow out of the picture completely."

"The second option," Donovan spoke, "is to sell the company outright."

"What are the pros and cons of both?" I asked again.

"Merging would take longer because we'd have to make sure everyone is settled, but would make us more money." Donovan continued to speak. "Selling outright, if all goes well legally, would be quicker, but we couldn't ask as much because there are risks that clients may bolt on the new firm."

"And so your job is to," I started.

"It is two-fold. I need to court serious buyers, and I need to assure current clients that their expected level of service and legal competency won't be compromised with a sale or merger. Rumors are rampant right now. That's why I've been going from city to city visiting top clients."

"I think I finally get it." I smiled at my boyfriend.

"And if this all goes well, your boyfriend, soon-to-be husband" Grandfather gave me a baffled and unhappy grimace, "I still don't know why you won't marry the guy," he grumbled some more. "You're too much like your grandmother, Laney. Put the guy out of his misery and marry the damn man."

"Grandfather," I put on my sassy hat again. "I can't marry someone because you or my parents tell me to marry him. I have to be absolutely certain that this is the man I want to love forever." I feigned surprise that my grandfather would even bring up this topic, much less chastise me for my actions. "I love you for being concerned for me and Donovan, but I need to make my own decisions." I walked over and kissed him on the cheek to let him know I wasn't upset with his comment.

"You are undoubtedly no push over. Jane may be the spitting image of your grandmother, but you are the split personality of Estelle."

"Why thank you, Grandfather." I walked back over to my boyfriend and leaned into his open arms. "You were saying?" I asked Grandfather.

He thought back to what he was saying and repeated, "If this all goes well, Donovan stands to get a significant bonus for selling the firm. That'll start you two off very handsomely as newlyweds."

"I'll take him rich or poor, Grandfather – as long as he comes with a latte machine." And that was the last chuckle for the day.

The next few days passed in a flurry of activities. I followed Jake to both Oxford and Cambridge and to their corresponding hospitals. I played his assistant in the office—cleaning, putting his books away, and answering calls. At the hospital, I just watched in amazement at the technology and procedures described by fellow doctors. Jake would make a great addition as a guest lecturer and doctor, and he in turn would bring back valuable information and experience to his home base.

Donovan continued to come home at an hour where I was in deep sleep. He would wake me up, we'd make frenzied love, then fall asleep. We didn't have time to talk during the day, but we had the most intense sex every night to make up for our lack of communication.

"Hello?" Speak of the devil, Donovan called late, the night before our trip.

"Princess," he crooned. "What are you doing?"

"Stripping bare so I can be ready for you when you get home at some insane hour."

"You do have a way of getting me horny every time I get you on the phone."

"On the phone, only?"

"The sexting does not help my cause, especially when I'm sitting in a meeting."

"Should I send visuals, instead? Perhaps another selfie?" I giggled and clicked on the picture button so it'd make that picture-taking sound.

"No!" He begged. "Please, no pictures. Those are the worst. My pants will tent and I won't be able to concentrate."

"That's making me horny thinking of your pants tenting."

"Princess. Focus and stop talking dirty."

"OK...what's up?"

"I won't make it home tonight. Will you pack for me and come pick me up an hour before we have to get to the airport?"

"Really?" I didn't like it when I slept alone.

"I know how you feel. I don't like being apart from you but, I need to finish this so we won't be bothered this weekend."

"No problem. I'll be the good little woman and pack your stuff."

"Thank you. I'll see you in the morning?"

"Try and stop me!"

Friday we all got up extra early and seamlessly got ready to leave with the three kids. With so many adult-helping hands, we had no issues leaving the house. I got out a little earlier than everyone else and took a separate car to pick up Donovan.

"I'm here." It was very tempting to go up and see Kate and her bff, and show them that Donovan and I were *not* breaking up, *ever*, but I decided to call instead.

A knock on the car window made me jump. "Hey." Donovan hopped in and kissed me, open-mouthed in the taxi. "I've missed you."

"Me, too." I whispered. "Ready for our trip?"

"Can't wait." He grinned. "Everyone on their way to the plane?"

"Yeah. Your dad and mine took our suitcases and golf clubs. I was surprised you brought your clubs with you to London."

"Why would you be surprised? I knew I'd end up golfing with you here."

"You came better prepared than I thought you would."

"Princess, I came prepared with all the arsenals needed to win you over."

"Stupid me. I gave in after one kiss. I should have read up on the art of playing hard to get."

"You get me hard all the time," he whispered and got me cackling our way to the airport.

We arrived at the beautifully lush golf course and resort. After a "quick" meal, as quick as it could be with eleven adults and three little ones, we all changed into our golf attire ready to compete.

"Oh Donovan," I was in a daze with the gorgeous surroundings and the happiness of being with everyone I loved. "Every place you take me to is more beautiful than the last."

"You think this is beautiful, wait till I take you to Vienna next week."

"You have to '*work*' out there next week?"

"Yes, I have to '*work.*' You know how hard I work don't you?"

"Of course I do. I was only kidding."

"You like it here?"

"I don't know if it's because you are with me, but everywhere we go, it's magical." This dreamy mood continued.

"Shall we go kick ass in golf?" He smacked me in the ass.

"You just worry about your own ass being kicked." I slapped him back. "Shall we play for something?"

"How about loser is the winner's sex slave for the weekend?" he suggested with a wickedly beautiful smile.

"Is that a punishment or a reward?" I copied that same smile, but mine wasn't as beautiful or as wicked.

He kissed me until we were both out of breath and said, "Let's go before I pull up that orange golf dress of yours and fuck you against this wall."

Damn! That sounded divine to me. *"The hell with golf,"* I wanted to say.

We were the last ones to arrive and I thought I heard a "Duchess" from the crowd.

"No fucking way," Donovan spit out. "Is that your English duke?"

I looked carefully and tried to make sense of the blob of people milling around the pro shop.

"Duchess."

What the hell?

"Laney Reid. You owe me a game of golf."

The duke was here, too. Shit. *Awkward!*

"Hi Michael." I went over to give him a side hug, but Michael took advantage of my proximity and he gave me an amorous-type hug and light kiss on the lips.

Donovan exploded in anger. "Keep your fucking hands and lips off my girlfriend."

The duke cackled at his grandson's prankish move, and I quickly admonished, "Not cool, Michael," before walking away. He shrugged and his laissez-faire grin made me let out a small laugh while shaking my head no. "I've told you where I stand, Michael. Please respect my decision."

"And I've told you where I stand, Duchess. I'm not living in regret the rest of my life."

Jake could only hold back Donovan for so long. I let that statement go and calmed Donovan before fisticuffs happened at the golf course.

"Don't, Donovan. It was just a greeting, and he didn't mean to do that."

"Like hell he didn't." Donovan was still angry.

"I sure as hell did." Michael joined our conversation.

Jake and I blocked Donovan from moving in Michael's direction.

"Michael." I warned and Michael put up his hand in defeat and walked to his grandfather and another man standing next to the duke. "Donovan?" I turned my attention to this furious man. "I'll be more careful next time I see him. Please don't be angry. We have our families here, and your ire will only make this situation more awkward. I love you." I declared in front of everyone and smiled. "Enough of this. Let's go kick some ass."

"What are we playing and how are we pairing up?" My dad who'd been watching and waiting to break-up a fight got us back in the right mood.

"What the hell are you and your grandsons doing here?" I heard Grandfather talking to the duke.

"What the hell do you think we're doing? We're here to play golf." The duke was no pushover.

"Why aren't you at your fancy club?"

"We thought we'd play with you commoners for a change." This was getting ugly.

"Grandfather, you want to pair up with me? We're playing the Pinehurst System."

"I thought we were playing as a team?" Donovan grabbed my hand and pulled me back to him.

"Tomorrow?" I pleaded and promised at the same time. "I'll pair up with Grandfather but we'll be in a foursome with you and your partner."

"Tomorrow," he pledged. "Jake, you want to pair up?"

"We are teeing off soon," the duke answered. "Why don't you all join us? We can go in three groups of four. Miss Reid, I believe, owes me a round of golf."

"The hell she does." Grandfather spoke before Donovan could say anything rude. "She's playing with me. If you want to join us, you better control your older grandson and have him stay far away from my grand-daughter. Otherwise, we're going to have problems."

"Michael. Can you keep your hands and lips off Laney for a few hours?" The duke asked sarcastically.

"I shall try." Michael answered with a false resignation.

I could tell Donovan wanted to protest, but he was mindful of my grandfather's position in this family and respected his decision. It helped that my dad, his dad, and Jake were doing an intervention in the corner.

It turned out that Grandfather and I paired up with the duke and my dad. Jake and Donovan paired up with Michael and his cousin Niles. Pa and Uncle Bobby played on their own.

"Please don't get into a scuffle with Michael." I begged Donovan as we headed out to the first tee. While Grandfather and the duke rode in a cart, or a buggy as they called it here, the rest of us walked with a couple of caddies per foursome. "Jake," I pleaded with my cousin, also. "Please keep Donovan and Michael apart."

"Don't worry, Laney." Jake reassured me looking at both men, but I knew trouble was brewing.

From the first shot, I played terribly. The fairway was wider than an airport landing strip and I couldn't hit onto it. Grandfather rescued us from total disaster as I got my ball into an ugly bunker when I took my second swing with Grandfather's ball. The format of this game had both players shooting their own balls at first. Then we played each other's ball on the second shot, and for the third shot, we picked the better-shot ball. From here on, we played alternate shots till the ball got in the hole. Luckily, Grandfather's second shot was a good one and he saved me with his great alternate shots.

"Losing your touch, Laney Reid? Was that beginner's luck the first time we played?" The duke was playfully harassing me.

I couldn't concentrate on the game as I kept my eyes on Donovan's group more so than my own.

"They'll be all right, Laney. They're grown men. You don't have to worry," Dad reassured me.

"Oh, Daddy. In my twenty-three years of life I've never really dat-ed anyone – until now, where I decided to date two guys within months of each other. What have I done so wrong where I ended up on a golf course with both of them in the same foursome?" I scratched my head in frustration.

My dad put his arm around me. "You found two men who love you. Consider yourself a lucky girl. That Michael wants to fight for what he lost. I respect that, and it puts Donovan on the defensive and offensive. He knows he can't take you for granted because he's replaceable."

"Daddy." My father was taking this all in from a father's perspective. I placed my head on my father's shoulder while we walked to hole two.

The next couple of holes were just as dismal. I heard a shout from behind us and if it hadn't been for my grandfather bringing my attention back to him with a poor attempt at a joke, I would have lost it. Worrying about Michael provoking Donovan had my nerves on edge. At one point, I almost broke down and cried. Before something ugly happened, I walked to the next hole by myself.

"Delaney." I turned around at the welcome voice.

"Donovan." I ran into his arms and started crying. "What are you doing here?"

"I saw you walking by yourself so I came after you. What's the matter? Why are you here, alone, and why are you crying?"

"I'm so miserable right now. This whole thing with Michael shouldn't have happened…I don't know how we ended up playing together…and you seemed so upset with everything…I'm sorry." I stayed in his shelter and cried some more. "You know Michael doesn't mean anything to me. You know I love you, right?"

"I know," Donovan's voice softened and his body relaxed. "I love you too, and I'm sorry I've made this difficult for you. I'll try and finish this game without troubling you, OK?"

I just nodded. "Maybe we shouldn't have come here. I can't get my head into the game without worrying about you."

"If you lose, you'll be my sex slave, so I'm all for you losing." That made me break into a smile. "Princess." He wiped away my tears and kissed me several times. "I should have realized earlier this would stress you out. Let's finish this game and go have a quiet evening in our room with no interruptions, all right?"

"That sounds wonderful," I tried to dry up the tears and calm myself down. "You know I love you, right? You know that's not why I haven't agreed to marry you? I decided the other night when we talked that I was being silly and selfish. I thought I needed a…" I didn't know why I needed to profess my love to him again, and I didn't know why it hurt to give up my dream of a proposal. But the more I thought about it, it was just a formality. It was childish of me to expect something Donovan didn't understand. "It doesn't matter anymore what I need. We love each other and there's no reason why we can't get…"

Donovan cut me off with a hard kiss and wouldn't let go until my father announced, "You're both going to get us all kicked off this course for indecent behavior." I was too embarrassed to look at my father when the three of us walked to meet our groups.

Apparently, all the groups had convened at our hole for a pow-wow. "We are all going to get along and finish this game like grown adults, you got it?" My grandfather addressed the two in question. "Stop being shit-heads and let me and my granddaughter kick your asses fair and square."

"Yes, Sir," both men answered.

"I'm sorry, Duchess."

Before Michael could finish his sentence, Donovan got angry again. "How many fucking times do I have to tell you she's not your duchess?"

"I don't see a fucking ring on her finger, which means she can still be my duchess."

"Cut it out!" The duke roared. "You two can duel at dawn when we're not around to see your moronic behaviors. Take out your anger on the golf course. Let's sweeten this game with a bet. With all this idiotic bluster, I think we need to put a little money on this game."

Great! Just what was needed on top of all this machismo—a wager to fuel their fire.

"In order to keep your heads in the game, shall we get a bet going?"

"Oh no Grandfather," Niles, the younger grandson grumbled, "most of us are not in the same betting league as you. We won't be able to pay the buy-in."

"Man up, Niles," his grandfather didn't even bat an eye when he said, "it won't be so bad. How about a thousand pounds per team?"

"Shit, Grandfather, we don't have that kind of money." Niles looked as though he were about to have an apoplectic fit. I, too, was a little freaked out with the large amount.

"What do you say?" It was as though the duke was challenging my family to pony up the money or go home.

Of course my grandfather, who would not be outdone by a duke, pulled out his wallet and counted ten 100£ notes. Then, every man pulled 500£ each without complaint, except for Niles. He had a hard time letting his money go. I didn't blame him.

"This is insane!" I voiced my displeasure. "We cannot play for this kind of money. That's 5000£ on the line."

"You scared of losing, Laney?" The duke challenged. "What do you care? Your grandfather put in your 500£."

His taunting pissed me off. "I'm just afraid you're going to be royally pissed when I take your money from you," I challenged back.

My grandfather squeezed my hand and was proud of my comment. Donovan looked over at me and winked.

"Game on, Princess. And don't forget our side bet," he whispered in my ear before giving me one last kiss.

Starting from hole three, it was truly game on. We took every shot, every stroke seriously and Grandfather and I strategized with our caddy, as did everyone else. At the end of the first nine holes Donovan and Jake had a significant lead over all of us.

"Laney, go distract your boyfriend any way you can. He's on fire," my grandfather urged.

We had all stopped before the 10th hole for a drink and a little sustenance to keep us going another nine holes. I did as I was told and walked over to Donovan and Jake to try and distract the both of them.

"You two were amazing out there."

"Laney, we, two, are amazing all the time," my cousin informed me. These men were high-fiving each other, way too happy with their progress up until hole nine.

"You got nine more holes to go," I reminded them. "I wouldn't be so self-assured already."

"Little Woman," Donovan said in the most condescending way, "just get ready to lose and be ready to pay up tonight."

Jake started laughing. I so didn't want to do this, but I knew I had to.

"I assume Emily, with the three kids, is OK by herself? I remember hearing that everyone else was going on a shopping spree in St Andrews. I think Emily decided to stay in the room with the babies. I hope she's all right." I said nothing else and walked very quickly away from the two men I knew I had done my job against Jake. And now it was time to rattle Donovan.

"I don't think I ever introduced myself." I approached Michael's cousin, Niles. "My name is Laney Reid. It's nice to meet you Niles."

"Hello, Laney Reid. You are quite the golfer out there. Grandfather is a little miffed that you are beating him right now."

"That's nothing new," I kidded with their grandfather who was standing right next to them. "Are you surprised that I'm beating you? You should be used to that by now." I laughed along with Michael and Niles.

"You, Laney Reid, are one sassy young lady. And I'm very unhappy and disappointed with you that you have chosen to break up with my grandson for that guy over there." He pointed over to Donovan. Donovan was watching us, unable to hear what we were saying, but concerned nonetheless.

"I know you are, Your Grace. I'm upset with myself for the way things turned out as well. I hope Michael and I will stay friends, and I hope you will forgive me one day for hurting your grandson. That was never my intention, and I know I'm not good enough to hurt anybody, but this is the way life seems to have worked out for all of us."

"What about that young man over there do you find better than my grandson? He's definitely not as handsome as my grandson, or as wealthy, or as good-hearted, from what I can see."

"Your Grace, Michael is as you say, handsome, will one day be extremely wealthy thanks to his grandfather, and he is as kind-hearted as they come. You are correct in your assessment. He is also one of the best men I have ever met and believe it or not, he was my first boyfriend. All these years, I have been in love with Donovan Taylor, and it wasn't until I met Michael that I ever thought I could learn to love anybody else."

"Then what's the problem?"

"The problem was, I was hasty in my decision with Michael. I knew deep down I couldn't forget Donovan. I was selfish. Michael was so good to me I thought I could return his affection in entirety...eventually...but it didn't happen."

"You never gave it a chance to happen, young lady." The duke was getting really upset with me.

"I know...and I'm sorry. I'm sorry I didn't realize sooner that Donovan Taylor could never be replaced in my heart. I'm very sorry that I let your entire family down because the Bennington family was like a second family to me when I came to London. And I am truly sorry I'll never get to know you as my grandfather, because underneath this gruff exterior, I know you're a soft teddy bear. My grandmother would never have loved a coldhearted man." That last comment softened this angry man.

"Anybody ever tell you you're just like your grandmother, Estelle?"

"That's what both my grandfathers have told me. And I consider it one of the highest compliments I could ever receive. I would have loved you as a grandfather, too." I said with a smile and kissed the duke on the cheek.

"Damn, Michael. I see now why you're pathetically in love with this girl. I've never seen anyone put a spell on Grandfather like she just did."

"Everything good?" Donovan walked over and grabbed my hand. "You all right?"

The duke answered for me. "You afraid we stole her from under your nose?" The duke scoffed. "We honorable English men don't do things like that, unlike you dishonorable Americans."

"Your Grace," I sounded my displeasure. "We've got a lot of money on the line here, let's go play."

Donovan walked me back to Grandfather. "I just want you to know, my conniving wench, that you've accomplished what you set out to do." Donovan attempted to look annoyed, but his silly grin gave him away.

"Oh?" I asked in all innocence. "And what is it that I tried to do?"

"My buddy over there is concerned now that his wife is struggling with the three kids while he's out having a grand time, and I'm concerned with the heart-to-heart I saw you having with the Bennington clan. *You* are one devious little tart." He came in to kiss me, but I stepped back.

"Oh, no you don't. Your kiss is going to befuddle me. If you think I played the wench and the tart earlier today, you ain't seen nothing yet. Wait till you get a glimpse of the outfit I brought with me." I pulled out my phone and sent him another naughty-nightie selfie, minus my face. "That'll give you some *hard* evidence of my *cunny*-ing ways."

I ran away and stood next to Grandfather.

"Damn you, Delaney Reid," we all heard Donovan grumble.

"Mission accomplished, Sir Roland."

Grandfather and I played as though our lives were on the line. We worked well as a team and in all honesty, lady luck was on our side. Dad and Michael's grandfather hit some great shots, but they fell in the Hell Bunker on the 14th hole and saw their dreams of winning the pot-o'-pounds go down the drain. Jake and Donovan were still two shots in the lead, and gloating, until they fell in the Road Hole Bunker on the 17th hole. It was good-bye, pot-o'-pounds for them as well. Grandfather and I leisurely and gleefully walked over the 700-year-old Swilcan Bridge leading to the last hole, and we played conservatively. That was good enough for us to win the 5000£!

"We did it!" Grandfather and I hugged each other.

"I'm going to have you partner with me in every tournament I play, Laney."

"I'd be honored to pair up with you." Jake and Donovan met us at the 18th hole, disgruntled they'd lost by one stroke.

"You, Laney Reid, did not play fair." Jake accused.

"I was told golf is a mentally challenging game, Jake. If you can't handle the pressure, don't open your wallet."

Jake shook his head and said, "She's all yours, Man. And I thought Max had it tough." Jake walked over and tousled my hair like I was some five-year-old. "I don't know what you did to my buddy, but he was hell to play with after you talked to him."

I motioned as if I had no idea what Jake was talking about.

"Daddy!" We heard Ellie's scream as she and James ran to their father. Jake crouched down to greet both kids.

"Were you a good girl for your momma today?" He asked Ellie, first.

"Yesh," she answered so child-like, and so unlike Elizabeth Reid.

"Were you a helpful boy to your momma today?" He talked to James, next.

"Yesh, Dada." James nodded his head feverishly.

Emily and JR walked into the patio of the clubhouse with the rest of the family. Jake went and greeted his wife with a sweet kiss. "You were fine with the three by yourself? I wouldn't have golfed if I knew you had no help." Jake apologized.

"I was fine. All three took an extra long nap after missing their morning nap. In fact, they just woke up." We could all see that Jake still felt guilty for leaving his wife by herself. "It was a good thing you golfed. If you had been around, I don't know that you would have let me nap the entire time the kids were down." Jake displayed a silly grin and kissed his wife again.

"James, you want to come to Auntie Laney?" I put out my hand so he could hop over to me. Donovan did the same for Ellie, so Jake could go show some love to the ever quiet, JR.

"Your momma tells me you were a good boy today, too." Jake cooed to his newborn.

"Your children are adorable." Michael, along with everyone else, appreciated the lovely picture Jake's family portrayed.

"Thank you, Michael." Emily answered.

"Estelle." The duke was first to acknowledge my grandmother who had only just walked in with Mom.

"Harry!" Gram looked surprised. "What brings you here?"

The duke didn't hesitate in embracing my Gram with a loving kiss on both cheeks. "You look as fetching today as the day we met."

"Oh brother," Grandfather bemoaned.

Gram laughed.

"You don't age, my English beauty."

"You always were the charmer, Harry. Are you here with your family? I was told you're staying at your summer home?"

"We're staying at the castle in Fife. You remember the place?" There was love and regret, nostalgia and sweetness in those last four words. The duke wore his heart on his sleeves with my grandmother. His grandsons kept looking at one another quizzically.

"I do remember it. That's one of those beautiful memories that will stay with me forever, Harry." She smiled and reached out to touch his hand. "I never told you how sorry I was to hear about the duchess. Did she suffer much?"

"No." The duke went grim. "It was quick. We lived a good long life together and she gave me my heir and a spare." Sadly, there was no mention of the love that existed between him and his wife. "I'd love for you and your family to dine with us, tonight or the next. What do you say, Estelle?"

Gram looked around at us, but mainly at Jake and Emily. "I suppose we could do it tomorrow night. But the babies go down early so we'd have to have an early dinner, if that's all right with you."

"We could do that. Or I could have the nursery opened up and they could sleep there while we have dinner." The duke had an enormous grin on his face.

"I think an early dinner would be fine. No need to open up any nurseries. I don't know that the twins will sleep there with their parents away. We will see you tomorrow?"

"Tomorrow." His Grace kissed Gram's cheeks once more and left with his grandsons.

I waved good-bye to all three men.

"You were more accommodating than I thought you might be." I whispered to my grandfather.

"He may be a Duke, but I married the only woman he wanted as his duchess. You," he spoke to Donovan, "ease up on Michael. You could've been Harry and Michael combined, had my granddaughter chosen to walk away from you."

"Yes, Sir." Donovan showed only a teeny tiny bit of remorse.

"Damn! I didn't think dinner was ever going to end." Donovan pushed me up against the wall, as threatened earlier, as soon as the door to our room closed. "I've wanted to do this to you since we got here." He pinned me against the wall and lifted me till our bodies were in sync. Twining my arms around his neck and my legs around his, I rubbed the sensitive notch between my legs against his erection, over and over finding pure pleasure even in this act, with all our clothes on.

"Bed, now!"

"No. Here." Donovan pushed me harder against the wall and with one hand under my butt and one hand deftly undoing his pants, he freed himself. I helped him by lifting my dress over my head and displaying the loosely tied underwear and bra. He ripped both off and unable to hold back any longer, placed himself at my opening, not holding out for an invitation.

I froze with the first push. Maybe because this was still new to me, whenever Donovan first entered me, my body registered shock first, pleasure, second. With each powerful thrust, I was pushed against the wall so hard, I knew I'd have a wall burn when this was all over. At one point, my head fell and my body sagged with pleasure insanely intense, as he impaled me repeatedly, without any sign of respite.

I grabbed onto his shirt and forced myself to give of the pleasure as much as I was partaking, while in my precarious state. What was first a self-conscious thought of being too heavy to be held up by this man, quickly turned to a violent lust and greed for more. Each push brought on a maddening sensitivity that led me one step closer to my peak. And each pull made me hunger and crave the next assault. Push and pull worked like cylinders to make my engine run.

"Babe," he moaned as he was close to his peak. "Come with me," he begged.

Something in his beseeching made me clench and grip him tighter than before. He lost himself in me and moaned my name so reverently; I couldn't help but get lost with him. A stand-up orgasm was as glorious as all the other ones.

Something about this position made it harder for us to get back to a standing heart rate. I still felt dull pulsations and my body spasmed gracelessly. His breathing was harsh and his body, too, let out random twitches and thrusts that were in comical harmony with my own.

"Is sex always this good?" I asked when my breathing returned to normal.

"It's never been this good, Babe. You bring out the crazed lust in me."

I didn't completely believe him, but I also didn't let him know what I thought.

Donovan gently pulled out of me and after cleaning up, we laid naked in bed.

"Tell me the truth." I treaded lightly. "Does sex always feel like you're pleased as hell to be falling off a cliff? I won't be mad with your answer. I just want to know if this is how it would have felt if I had had other partners."

Donovan's face went completely hard and I knew I'd said the wrong words. "Why the hell do you need to know about sex with other women and men right now?"

"I was just curious to know what it's like for others." Now I was feeling awkward about having brought up this topic. "It's always so fast paced and frenzied for us, whereas in the movies they always show couples making love like they had nothing else to do the rest of their lives." I turned onto my stomach and faced away from Donovan, hurt. "Sorry. I shouldn't have asked."

"Come here," he rolled me back to him. "I'm sorry for being a dick. When you mentioned hypothetical sex partners, it pissed me off to think of you with someone else."

"Don't be an idiot." I laughed. "I haven't been with anyone."

"I know, but the thought of you wondering what it would be like with someone else put me in a hellish mood." This was one of those incredulous scenarios that warranted no response. "Sex with you is really like no other. I'm not making this up. I've told you before—it's a combination of you being a virgin, you being my future bride, me not wearing a condom—I can't get enough. I keep thinking I can slow it down and make sweet love to my woman, but once we get going, it's a race to the finish line."

Donovan stopped apologizing with his words and used his mouth instead. And this time, he did his damnedest to make sweet love to me—his woman.

"Good morning." I was up first for a change, playing with his five o'clock shadow.

"What time is it? Are we late for anything?" Donovan grumbled into his pillow.

"It's late morning. We've missed the 5:30am tee time with the senior citizens, and I was told we were to show up for brunch at 10:30, which is in about ten minutes."

"Damn family won't leave us alone. Let's order room service and make love again."

"No." I slapped his perfectly formed ass. "We need to be downstairs in ten minutes. Let's not be late."

"Good morning," I greeted the family. "What's on the agenda for today?"

"We are going to take in the sights after the kids take their morning naps." Emily informed us.

"We are going shopping because dinner at the Bennington's is no casual affair." Gram announced.

"I agree. Even a regular dinner at their house is like a cocktail party. I better go buy something, too. Did you bring a dinner jacket?" I asked Donovan.

"Of course," he answered. "Gram?" She looked up from her coffee. "Are we *all* expected to attend?"

"Yes, Donovan. *You,* especially, must attend. I want you to see firsthand what my granddaughter is giving up, dating you instead of Michael."

"Gram," I complained. "You gave all of that up for Grandpa Jerry."

"Jerry was worth every castle and summer home."

"And so is Donovan." I defended him.

"Just don't get upset if I have a choice word or two if Michael comes on to your granddaughter."

"I expect you to be a complete gentleman, Donovan. We are guests in their home."

"When are we golfing, again?" My father asked. "Isn't that what we're here to do?"

"How about we golf after breakfast, Daddy?"

"Let's do it."

Everyone was in a good mood after another round of eighteen holes. I bailed after nine to go shopping with all the ladies. Grandfather gave us his winnings and told us to buy whatever we desired. We went into Edinburgh and did good damage on Prince Street and George Street. Gram, Mom, Aunt Sandy and Ma all picked out long formal wear. I picked out a slinky short number for Emily, who decided to go sightseeing with her family. Emily would complain about the sexy dress, but I was sure Jake would appreciate it. I, on the other hand was in a bind. I wanted something appealing for Donovan, but not so appealing for Michael. In the end, I got a fitted, stretch maxi dress that looked no different from a comfortable long dress, except for when I turned around. The back had what would be a very low cowl-type backless "neckline." I would cover the back with a shawl, but tease my boyfriend with what wasn't covered under the shawl.

We arrived at our hotel in plenty of time to get ready for dinner. Donovan was in the shower when I entered our room and quickly hopped in with him.

"Well, hello there."

"Hi." I was already breathing hard as he turned his attention to soaping me down.

"Good day shopping?"

"It's always a good day when I'm shopping."

"You pick out a sexy number?"

I shook my head no. "Seeing as how we'll be at the Bennington's, I thought I'd pick something understated and not draw any attention on me."

Donovan gave me an appreciative soaping, down there.

"What, may I ask, is this?" Donovan finally noticed the backless dress once we got into our cab and the shawl fell off my shoulder.

I played dumb. "Hmm?"

"You said this dress was understated and I thought it was, though it hugs your curves more than I'd like for Michael to see."

"It is understated. You see no skin except for my arms, toes, neck and face."

"Babe…" He groaned. "And what about this?" He placed his hand on the lowest part of the open back and slid his fingers lower into the dress. "Shit." He whispered and panted slightly in my ear. "Are you not wearing underwear?"

"It gave me panty lines so I had to ditch the underwear."

Then Donovan placed the shawl back on my shoulder and surreptitiously slid his hand to the side of my dress and felt the curve of my right breast. "Are you trying to kill me?"

"What?" I played dumb again, but he didn't buy it. "When I bought this dress, I figured I'd cover the back with a shawl and no one would be wiser, but you. What I didn't figure into the equation was the bra and panty situation. It was only when I actually put the dress on, I realized I was in trouble."

"Princess." Donovan ground his teeth. "I've been telling myself since morning that I'll be as aloof as possible where Michael is concerned, but now…" He was *un*happy! "Now, I'll not only have to worry about my hard-on the entire evening knowing that this slip of a dress is the only thing separating the proper you and the slutty you, but I'll also have to worry about whether or not Michael is wondering why there are no bra or panty lines!" He ground out each of the last four words.

"Michael is not going to be staring at me and wondering about bra lines and panty lines. You can be so dramatic." I played it off as though he was nuts.

The ride to the castle was a quick one and we got there at about the same time as the rest of the family. Donovan put the shawl around me, gripped his arms around the shawl and we walked down the beautiful walkway leading to the gorgeous old castle.

"Isn't this stunning? I feel like I'm at Pemberely from *Pride and Prejudice*."

"Me, too, Laney." Emily was in as much awe as me. "Michael's never brought you here before?"

"No," was all I could say because I was so dazed with my surroundings.

"You sure you're ready to give all this up for a small home and an even smaller hut in Southern California?" Emily teased an unhappy Donovan.

"I'd take the beach over this any day." Donovan muttered.

"And I'd take you over any piece of property, any day." I brought out his ridiculously cute smile. "No matter what happens tonight, no matter what is said, I want you to understand that I love you. For as long as I can remember, I've loved you and nothing—no matter the property, the money, the people—will change my mind."

"Thank you, Princess. Sometimes I know I don't deserve you."

"Only sometimes…?"

"Laney!" I heard a holler and saw a mad woman running down the steps to greet me.

Ruby Aleksandra Bennington hurled her body into mine and hugged me so fast and furious, we would have both fallen to the ground had Donovan not had a firm grip on my body.

"Ruby!" I hugged her back once I got my footing. "Where have you been?"

"Where have I been? I've been all over the freakin' Arctic, thanks to a bet I lost to my damn cousin. It was so damn cold, I couldn't wait to get back to the terrible summer heat and humidity in London." She hugged me again, but quickly halted to stare at Donovan. "Well, hello!" She looked him up and down, and then all over again. "I'd dump Michael for this guy, too." She whispered just loudly enough for all of the Reid and Bennington families to hear.

"Ahem!" The duke cleared his throat in displeasure. "Ruby," he warned.

"Sorry, Grandfather." Her apology was only a formality as her face giggled to all who could see.

"Good evening, everyone." The duke spoke to all of us, but only had eyes for Gram. "May I walk you in?" He put out his arm for Gram, but Grandfather had her locked in his arm already.

Resigned, Gram linked her arm around both men and walked up the stairs.

"May I walk you in?" Michael came down the steps and gave the same offer as his grandfather.

I looked to an unhappy Donovan, gave him a light peck on the cheek and said, "I'll see you inside. I thank you in advance for being so understanding. You shall be greatly rewarded tonight." He grinned stupidly, but still insanely handsomely, and decided to be a good sport.

Before Michael and I ascended the steps, I saw Ruby put out her arm for Donovan to hold. She was taking the lead, which made us all laugh.

"You look beautiful, Duchess." Michael looked at me with such love in his eyes, I knew another talk was necessary.

"Michael." I warned.

"Don't say it," he warned back. "I'm not going to listen. I'm not going to live in regret like my grandfather. Look at him, sixty years later, still regretting not having gone after your grandmother. There was no passion between the duke and duchess. I don't want to live like that."

"And you won't live like that. You will meet a woman who will return your love equally, who will give you that passion you so want and deserve."

"I have met that woman. That woman is you. I have told you before, and I'll say it again for the last time. I'm not giving up."

Confounded by his recalcitrant behavior, I walked away and greeted his parents instead, and brought my parents over to meet them.

"Mom, Dad, I want you to meet Michael's parents. They treated me like a member of their family."

"Thank you very much for taking care of our daughter. Laney has told us several times how good you have been to her. My wife and I appreciate all that you've done."

"It's our pleasure, Dr. Reid. We were just saddened by the fact that Laney will not be joining us in our family activities like she used to in the past."

"Please call me Henry."

"And you must call me Michael." The dads shook hands and the moms gave each other hugs. "I heard that Michael and Laney had a bit of a falling out?" Mr. Bennington asked all of us.

Dad only chuckled. Mom looked very apologetic to Michael's mother.

"Hello I'm Donovan Taylor." Donovan rescued us from the awkwardness by introducing himself and putting out his hand first to Mr.

Bennington, then to Mrs. Bennington. Even knowing who he was, they greeted him kindly.

"You look beautiful, Mom." Donovan gave mom a loving embrace that made Mom's heart melt almost as completely as mine.

"Son?" Dad asked with affection. "Will you get us a glass of wine?"

"White?"

"Sounds good."

"Can I get you anything, Princess?" I was loving and cringing at this love-fest.

"I'll take whatever Dad is having."

"Let me not see any skin on your back tonight," he whispered, "or those perky nipples I so love to roll around my tongue."

Damn man got my nipples so hard they were poking through the nipple "patch" I was wearing. Just to show him what he did to me, I lowered the shawl enough for him to go through the evening with an image of my backless dress and perky nipples.

When we all sat down, it was no surprise to any of us that Donovan and I were separated. He was at one end of the table while I was at the other end. And to make matters worse, we sat on the same side so we couldn't even look at one another. In the Bennington's defense, all couples were separated except for Jake and Emily. They stayed with each other thanks to JR. The twins were at a table in the kitchen with two collegians who were hired by Mrs. Bennington, to help. The twins loved them immediately as the collegians brought a chest full of toys with them.

"Laney?" Ruby had to shout since the table was so long. "You want to spend the night here tonight?"

"Absolutely not," Donovan answered her.

"I don't believe my sister was asking you."

"I don't give a damn what you believe. I'm telling your sister, no."

"How about you come over to Gram's when you get back to London?" I suggested. "We are here as a family. I should stay with them this weekend."

"I'll be back end of next week. When should we meet?" This was rude to speak over everyone but since she was sitting across from Donovan, we had very little choice.

"Donovan said we are going to Vienna next week." I told Ruby, and then asked Donovan, "When do we leave and when do we return?"

"We have a bit of a change of plans." He wouldn't expound.

"And they are?"

"You are going home with Mom and Dad and I am going on several quick trips throughout Europe. I'll meet you at home Friday or Saturday."

"Home as in Belgravia?" I asked because the way he said home was a bit suspect.

"Home as in our home in LA."

"LA? Why are we going there?"

"Many reasons." This man was being more circumspect than usual.

"And those reasons being...?"

"To make sure our home has a roof, the beach house is still standing, the cars run, the LA office is billing copious hours, to celebrate your father's 55th birthday, my parents' 37th wedding anniversary...need I give you more reasons?"

"Oh..." I knew Dad's birthday was coming up, but I didn't realize there would be a celebration. "Mom, are we having a party for Dad's birthday?"

"Of course we are. We always have parties for his birthday."

"And I'm going home with you and Dad instead of Donovan because..." *Would someone give me some answers?* I was getting pissed with these non-answer answers.

"We can't leave till Wednesday and I'll need your help getting the party together. We decided to combine parties, so it'll be a bigger production than I originally planned."

Since it was even ruder of me to only speak with my mother and Donovan, who were both far from me, I dropped the conversation and figured I'd get some answers back at the hotel.

Dinner was long. It was like, I-don't-know-how-many-courses-I've-eaten, long. Michael and his mother kept me apprised of the Bennington goings-on, and all was going well till Ruby asked, "Grandfather. Will you tell us about you and Laney's grandmum? Why didn't you marry her?"

Yikes. That was not a topic of conversation I thought would ever come up in this family.

The duke didn't look happy with the question, but surprisingly, he became a hell of a lot more loquacious than we could have ever imagined. We were done with dinner and moved to another room. Donovan was quick to nab me from the Bennington family and we sat in a comfortably small "love" seat. This is where Michael's grandfather began his tale.

"I met Estelle for the first time right after she turned eighteen. Her family came here to attend a weekend house party and I couldn't keep my eyes off her from the moment I met her. She was incredible."

Looking over at Grandpa Roland, I could tell he agreed with the duke. My grandmother was a loved woman.

"Is that when you decided she was your future Duchess?" Ruby asked.

His Grace looked over at Gram and answered, "Yes. I courted her for about a month, then brought her back up to this castle and proposed to her."

"How romantic," Mrs. Bennington sighed.

"She wouldn't say yes, but she also didn't say no. She told me it was too soon to know. Our parents had already talked and we were to be married by winter, had all gone well."

"So why didn't you say yes to the duke?" I asked Gram.

"It *was* too soon, and I didn't want to be like all the girls and get married so young. I wanted to go to the Uni and study more. I also wanted to study fashion. We were finally out of those stuffy dresses and into skirts that were knee-length and wearing pants had become more commonplace. Being a Duchess at eighteen was not what I wanted for myself."

"Also, your grandmother met Jerry at Oxford." Duke Harry Bennington spoke in a hard tone that let all of us know what he thought of Jerry Reid.

"I did." If a picture was worth a thousand words, the picture of Gram when Grandpa Jerry's name was mentioned was a thousand words of love. "Jerry told me the day he met me that we were destined to be married. I believed he was right. Once we decided to get married, I let Harry know that I couldn't be his duchess, but never would have believed we wouldn't speak again till now."

"You mean to tell me you've never kept in touch with Laney's grandmother till today?" Mrs. Bennington was shocked. "How can that be? She was the love of your life. Her Grace used to always say there was the ghost of Estelle Cowper haunting her every move."

Gram smiled and stated, "Harry kept in touch in his own sweet way."

"How?" All the ladies asked at the same time.

Gram smiled even wider. "Harry would send a large bouquet of Foxgloves whenever I celebrated a special occasion—every one of my birthdays, the birth of my five boys, Christmas, but never my wedding anniversary. I don't know how he knew I'd given birth, but no sooner had I arrived home from the hospital with a newborn, than there they were, the flowers I fell in love with when I first came to this castle. How on earth did you get those to me? I didn't think they had them in the States back then," she asked the duke.

"I had my ways," was all he'd divulge.

"So when you ran into Gram at the golf course, you hadn't seen her in more than sixty years?" I was amazed. "Why didn't you fight for my grandmother?" Maybe that wasn't the correct thing to say. Michael didn't need any further encouragement.

The duke answered with only a shrug. The rest of us wanted more, but we let it go and got up to say good night.

After thanking the Benningtons, we got in our taxis, but Gram took a few extra minutes talking to His Grace. None of us knew what she said, but Michael's grandfather uncharacteristically broke out of his stoic demeanor and embraced Gram with a grand smile. She returned the smile and the cuddle.

"Wasn't that a romantic story?" I nuzzled my head into Donovan's chest once we got back to the hotel.

"A little reminiscent of our own if you ask me," the grim-Donovan was here with me.

"That's what Michael told me on Monday, but he told me he wasn't going to live in regret like his grandfather and not chase after his future duchess," I confessed.

Donovan pushed me away just enough to look me eye to eye. "Are you shitting me? That's bastard thinks he's going to pursue you while you have a boyfriend?"

"Isn't that what you did? Pursued me while I was dating Michael?"

"Um...NO! You had been in love with me all your life. I was only re-claiming what was already mine."

"Do you hear yourself? I am not a piece of property to buy and sell."

"But if you were, I'd give my entire fortune and live the life a beggar for a chance to be with you." He covered his faux pas nicely. That de-served a kiss in many places, and not just his lips.

We golfed one last time with only our family and left for Belgravia after lunch. Donovan was busy preparing for his trip, so I kept myself busy helping Emily with the three kids, then preparing for my visit to LA.

"Why can't I come with you on your business trip this time?"

Donovan stopped himself and had to think of an answer. If I didn't know better, I'd think he didn't want me with him.

"I have to cover a lot of clients in all different cities. I won't be able to do anything fun with you, and I'll probably worry about you getting lost or kidnapped."

"You are so lame. I can take care of myself. You don't have to babysit me...I'd really like to be with you..." I put it out there hoping he'd change his mind.

"You are needed in LA. Your parents want you home with them for a while. It'll only be a few days, Princess. I'll be back on Saturday at the latest."

I knew it was all business, but it felt like he was trying to get rid of me, and that hurt. Then, the most God-awful thought occurred. "Will Kate be with you at all these meetings?"

Now I got exasperated-Donovan. "She will be at some, possibly all, depending upon how the meetings fare."

"Got it," was all I could muster before leaving the room and going out for a walk.

I knew I was being lame. I knew there was nothing inappropriate about Donovan and Kate working together. But we were only going on the third week of our relationship and I didn't want to separate from him.

Separating on Monday for almost a week about did me in. I couldn't say a proper good-bye Monday morning, and I purposely left the house before Donovan came to pick up his suitcase in the afternoon. As stupid as I felt, I couldn't let go of the hurt. Donovan cheerfully said his farewells in the morning, and wasn't fazed that we'd be apart for so many days. I didn't ask for an itinerary, and all I could say was that I'd see him in LA.

"Laney!" I heard a cheery voice when I returned to the flat.

"Ruby! What are you doing here?"

"I was commanded to come down here while your boyfriend was away. From now till Wednesday morning is 'Operation Laney.'"

"What are you talking about?"

"Come home with me." She dragged me all the way to her house without an explanation.

"Please tell me you're not taking me to your brother, Ruby. You're not helping him by trying to get us back together."

"He's not here, yet. But, I need for *you* to explain to me what happened."

We sat on the bed in her room like old times and I explained my entire saga from the day I met Donovan in Aunt Sandy's kitchen to the day he showed up in London. "After all those years of wanting to be with him, he finally wants to marry me. You see why I can't be with Michael?"

"But what if your relationship with Donovan fizzles? What then?"

"Then, I know what it is like to have loved and been loved and I move on—but not with Michael." I added.

"Why not with Michael?"

"Because it's not fair to him. I don't love Michael. From the start, I've been honest with you and your brother concerning my feelings for him. Love was not a part of our relationship."

"Not a part of yours, but Michael's been in love with you from day one."

"I know, and in all honesty, I'm sorry I encouraged it. We shouldn't have come this far. When I met you two at the airport, I was lonely, you were both genuinely nice and fun, and I was grateful for friends. The night before I came to London, Donovan and I were to talk and I was going to confess my feelings to him. He told me to wait for him on my swing in my front porch, but he never came. I waited all night and he never showed. After loving him for so many years, that's how we ended. So do you see why I was overjoyed to meet you and Michael?"

"Was I wrong thinking you liked Michael and were genuinely happy with him?"

"Not at all. He did make me happy..."

"But not Donovan happy?"

"Yeah," I answered sheepishly. "What's our plan tonight?"

"Dinner, a sleepover, and intervention throughout."

"All right. You can try your best, but I'm not budging."

"Let's go to dinner." I pushed her out the door hoping she would forget about her motive and just have a great time with me.

Dinner with Ruby Aleksandra never disappointed. She was the life of the party, and two of her uni friends had joined us at our table. During her tale of the Arctic, I got a phone call.

"Hello?"

"Hi Princess."

My heart dropped like it did on a rollercoaster ride. "Hi."

"I missed you at home. Where were you?"

"I'm with Ruby right now at dinner." I skimmed over the fact that I had purposely left the house because I still felt hurt about him leaving me behind.

"Ruby?"

"She's here, *alone*. I'm going to hang out with her tonight and spend the night at her place."

"No Michael?"

"No Michael."

"You know that I'm only going on a business trip?" He was trying to reassure my unstable heart.

"I know." I sounded like an insipid child.

"And you know I love you?"

"I know." My attitude didn't get any better.

"I'll see you soon."

Though it wasn't my intention, I sighed before answering. "I'll see you soon," and hung up.

Ruby kept me up all night, literally, and then forced me to breakfast as the sun came up.

"I'm ditching you after breakfast, Rubes. I need some sleep."

"I'm just getting you ready for your Pacific time zone."

I gave her a surly look, and we both laughed. We got to breakfast and Michael and his cousin Niles were seated and expecting us. I looked over at Ruby one more time but she wouldn't make eye contact with me.

"Hi Duchess." Michael stood up and greeted me with a kiss that would have landed on my lips had I not turned around.

"Hi," I answered curtly. "And hello, again, Niles."

"Hello, Michael's duchess," he kidded with a cute smile.

"What brings you both here? I thought you were staying up in Scotland?"

"Niles and I would like to see Stonehenge and thought you and Rubes should come along."

"I leave for LA, tomorrow, Michael."

"What time is your flight?"

"I think it's a morning one."

"Let's go for the day. We have a car, it only takes about ninety minutes from here to Stonehenge, then another thirty minutes to Bath. Let's spend the day sightseeing."

My face must have spoken hesitancy all over it because now everyone was trying to convince me.

"Laney." Niles added. "Believe it or not, I've never seen Stonehenge. My cousin is offering to spend a day playing my chauffeur and tour guide. This has never happened. Please make my dreams come true of bossing around this future duke. He's paying for all our meals."

"He even brought Grandfather's gaudy, but ultra-luxurious Bentley." Ruby nudged. "It's a convertible."

That last comment made me laugh. "Do I have a choice in this matter?"

Niles and Ruby simultaneously shook their heads and said, "No!"

It was decided. I'd spend the day with the three Benningtons.

Once breakfast was done and I let my family know where I'd be today, we got on our way for our road trip when the phone call happened.

"Hello?"

"Hello my sweet lady."

"Hi." I was feeling like a child caught in a naughty act.

"It's hard to see a beautiful place and not be reminded of my beautiful woman."

"Where are you?" The three Benningtons were listening in on my conversation.

"In Vienna. I start here, then go to Budapest for a dinner meeting, then to Prague for a breakfast meeting. I'll be in Germany all day Wednesday. You ready to leave for LA?"

"Yes. I packed my belongings when you packed yours. How long are we staying in LA?"

"Not sure, yet. Rachel and Derek are coming for the celebration, and Becky and Al, as well as Amanda and her family are contemplating coming. So we may hang out with the family till they all leave."

"You don't need to be back for work?"

"I have a few LA-based clients I need to check in with, so I'll still be working."

"Oh..." This was news to me. I guess this joint celebration was a bigger one than I'd imagined.

"Where are you and what are you up to?"

"I am on the road to Stonehenge with Ruby, Michael, and Niles. After that, Bath is next on the agenda before coming home."

Donovan went completely silent on me. Talk about awkward, it couldn't have been any more awkward than having three people listening to a conversation that wasn't happening.

"Delaney." He spoke to me as though I was ten and he was thirty.

"Don't." I warned back.

He sighed and sounded like he was going to let it go...but, he didn't. "If you can't do it for me, *your boyfriend*, then do it for the guy who can't seem to get it out of his brains that you are not his anymore, and let him go. You're not doing either of us a favor." Though I was seething, I didn't respond. This was another one of those cases where it was good for the relationship to just stay quiet. "I know you were pissed that I didn't bring you with me, but there was a good reason. Stop screwing around with Michael and with me."

And...that did it! He pissed me off with that last sentence. "Thank you for the unsolicited advice," I ground out in anger, "because it was so necessary. And now let me give you *my* response."

"Princess..." he called apologetically. He knew he was busted!

"I will no longer be your on-call travel partner. When I go back to LA on Wednesday, I will have most of my stuff packed and I will be attending medical school this fall. I am *not* attending medical school this year because of you, as previously stated, but because this sorry situation of mine as a lady-in-waiting is pissing me off. I will not wait around for your charity and I will not hope for you to take me places when it's convenient for you."

"Delaney!" He tried to interrupt. I was a force to reckon with right now, and he couldn't sway my anger.

"I understand you are working. But if you want me to put my life on hold so we can travel, I don't want to be left behind. And as for your unsolicited warning and lack of trust, I know what I will *not* be doing, but if you so choose to do so with Kate, be my guest. You have my permission! Good! Bye!"

"Shit." Niles whistled after the curse. "I don't think any of the duchesses had this kind of a temper. She'll whip all the staff and employees into shape. You are one smart-mouthed woman," he said to me. "You sure you want her as your duchess?" he asked Michael.

Before Michael could answer, I cut him off. "Michael. We are friends. We will stay friends and I will *not* be your duchess. If any of you mentions that word again, I'm going to take the bus back to Belgravia."

The three Benningtons laughed at me.

I got texts throughout the day from Donovan to which I didn't respond. Aside from those disturbances, today turned out to be a surprisingly enjoyable day.

"Are you truly leaving for Los Angeles for good or were you bluffing?" Michael sounded worried.

"I said it in haste, but it's been something that's been on my mind the past few weeks. As much fun as these few months have been, I'm getting restless. I need to do something, and that something is school. Eight years of schooling is a long time and to start a year late doesn't seem like the best idea."

"But what about Donovan? What will happen with your relationship?"

Reaching for Michael's hand, I hoped he would accept what I was going to say for the last time. "Michael. Donovan and I will get married. We might be in a tiff now, but unless Donovan calls it off, we will stay together for the rest of our lives. I'm sorry I led you to believe otherwise. I love Donovan."

Michael didn't have a rebuttal, and he had no answers. He kept to himself the rest of the day no matter how much we three tried to include him.

"Are you seriously leaving tomorrow?" Now it was Ruby's turn to be pissed. "You can't give us a little notice?"

"Yeah. I made the final decision while I was in the car without discussing it with anyone. Not too smart, huh?"

"But tomorrow?"

"Ruby." What a mess this had all become. "When I moved here, I had no idea what I wanted in life. Everything was a big question mark and that was one of the reasons I came here. I wanted time away from my life, and I wanted the space to think. Then Donovan showed up a couple months later and put everything into perspective for me. I want to marry Donovan. And watching my dad during his conference in Amsterdam made me decide med school was the right decision for me. Now that I have my answers, I'm itching to start. Even if Donovan has to stay out here for a while, I want to move onto that next phase. School's already begun and my dad is going to have to work overtime to get me in this year. But I know with his help, I can start my life right now."

"Damn you for coming into our lives and making us love you." Ruby started a chain of tears that I couldn't keep from joining.

"I'm sorry, but you and I will remain great friends even after we're both married. I can't apologize to Michael enough for all the heartache I've caused. Can you tell me what I can do to make him feel any better?"

"Dump that hottie boyfriend of yours and date my brother, again?" Ruby went from tearing to giggling.

"Will you comfort him?"

"Oh, he'll get over you...one day."

"You'll come visit me?"

"Does that hottie of yours have a brother?"

"No, but I do. And he's pretty cute, though nowhere near Donovan's cuteness."

"Laney, no one can touch your man in that category. He's incredible with his clothes on. I'm green with envy that you get to see him with his clothes off."

Now that made us giggle hysterically.

After giving Michael and Ruby much love and a fond farewell, I arrived at home to find the family waiting for me.

"May we speak with you in the morning room?" Mom called me over.

"What's up?"

"Donovan called, frantic that you were packing for home. What's this about?" Dad asked.

"I want to start school this year. My decision's been made. Once Donovan proposes, I'll marry him, but for now, if you'll help, I'd like to start med school ASAP."

"What about Donovan?" Grandfather asked.

I was unsure where this was going. "What about Donovan?"

"He moved his life here for you."

"He temporarily moved here to woo me and to sell your company. He would have moved back home in a year regardless of either result. I figure I'll start school, he'll do what needs to be done here, then he'll come back home."

"Don't you want this time to travel and spend days in beautiful cities with the man you love?" Gram questioned.

"This week's trip has convinced me I don't want to be one of those women who sit around waiting for her man to say jump. I know I've waited a long time for this man to love me, but that doesn't mean I stopped all aspects of my life for him. I studied, I prepared for a future, and I came here to live. You may all think I'll do whatever Donovan asks of me, but I want you to know, everything in my life has a purpose. If I give in to

Donovan's wishes, it's because I want to, and not just because he wants me to."

"Jake." Gram addressed a very quiet Jake and Emily. "You've just been replaced by Laney as my favorite grandchild."

"That can never be, Gram." Jake wasn't worried. "I've given you James and Ellie. Don't forget that Ellie is this spitting image of you in every way. She and I will always be your favorite."

I let out an evil laugh. "Until Donovan and I have kids..." That ended our discussion, and I went upstairs to pack.

Donovan must have been busy in Prague because he never called that night. I knew he was sorry for what he said, and I had forgiven him already, but we hadn't spoken since our fight.

"You ready?" Mom asked.

"Yes." I didn't end up taking back as much stuff as I'd originally intended. But I did pack up our bedding and towels to put in Donovan's home. Once school was situated, I'd have to make a trip back soon.

"Oh James." I was sad to be leaving this little one. "I'll come visit whenever I can, and in ten weeks, you'll be home." I hugged him and kissed him longingly. I'd miss him, again. "Ellie, Auntie Laney loves you even though you love Uncle Donovan more."

"My Unca!" she let me know.

"I know, Cutie!" I kissed her and hugged her as well.

"I guess this is good-bye again?" Emily hugged and kissed me. "But this time, it's a much happier good-bye."

"I'll see you in a few weeks. I'll be back here before you know it. Somebody's gotta pack up my stuff to bring back home. Please take care of Donovan for me when he's out here by himself."

"My buddy is not going to be happy."

"He'll just have to work harder to finish selling off this company. The sooner he's done, the sooner he can come home to me."

Jake asked, "Aren't you sad or upset that you're going to be separated from him after finally getting together with him?"

"If I can leave knowing that he doesn't love me, I can leave knowing that he does love me."

"Always the poet." Jake chuckled. "Have a safe flight home and do well in med school."

"I will. I can't wait to be in one of yours or Dad's classes. I expect an easy A."

He laughed even harder. "Just don't be a pain in my ass."

On my way to the airport I texted a silent Donovan.

Going to LA. Though you've yet to call, I've decided to forgive you for your lack of trust. And though I gave you a bye, I'm hoping you didn't take me up on it...

I put one of those sad face emoticons with the text and waited for a response. Nothing came.

Sitting on the plane, my heart reverted to the old days and felt that unwanted tingle. Donovan was most likely pissed that I had made a decision on school that was contrary to his own. I supposed one day we'd get this relationship stuff right.

"Laney?"

"Yes Dad?"

He handed me his phone.

"Hello?"

"How can you possibly think I could be with anyone else after having been with you, Princess?" The waterfall immediately began. "Thank you for forgiving my idiotic behavior. I love you and have a safe trip home."

"I love you too," I whispered. "And I'm sorry to have made you move your life to Europe. Once you came, everything fell into place for me, and knowing what I have to do, I need to start now."

"I'll be home soon. We'll talk then."

"OK. Bye."

"Bye, Princess."

From here on out, all was good, and I was all smiles till we got home. I got a warm welcome from my brother and Nick and a dinner invite from Max and Jane at their new home the next night.

I started school on Thursday, though I wasn't officially enrolled yet, and the amount of schoolwork I'd missed was scary. I ran into Max and Nick and we sat down to a fun lunch.

"Where's Donovan right now?" Max asked biting into his sandwich.

"He still stuck in Germany. He's been so busy, we've hardly had time to talk. We chatted briefly this morning."

"When are you two getting married now that you're back here and he's out there?" Nick had disapproval written all over his face. "You women are nuts. Why go all the way out to Europe, make a man follow you out there, then come back here within a couple of months? Are you out to purposely drive him mad?"

Max partly spit up his drink as he found what Nick had said to be comical. "And I thought Jane was the difficult one in the family. You are deceptively a pain in the ass, Laney Reid."

Dinner at Max and Jane's was postponed to next week after I caught my bearing with school and after Donovan came home. Though Donovan and I spoke briefly and texted here and there, we hadn't fully communicated much since I left Europe. And to make matters worse, Donovan wasn't coming home till Saturday. I missed him.

"Mom." I complained. "Could we ever have a get-together without making it such a big to-do?"

"And what would be the fun in that?" Mom looked at me as though I was crazy. "Get dressed. Everyone will be here soon."

I did just that and greeted all the Reids and Taylors who walked through the door. Every one of Donovan's sisters and family members came to the party—everyone but Donovan. Not liking this feeling of being apart from him, I went outside on the front porch and sat on the swing waiting for him.

So many memories were associated with this swing. I could still remember the heartache of a twelve-year-old who knew that her knight in shining armor was not coming for her. I remembered wondering if he was marrying Kate and why it was her and not me. Then there were the more current memories of hoping for graduation because I couldn't stand the pain any longer, the memory of Donovan coming to see me on this swing after his date with Jane, the memory of Donovan ignoring me all night, then coming here to tell me he'd play my tour guide in London. There were so many memories. I wondered what new memories we'd create on this swinging bench now that we were in love.

"Hey." That voice was here again. "What has you so deep in thought that you don't see the love of your life walking up your driveway?"

He was here! "Donovan!" I flung my body on this man who had kneeled in front of me to greet me. "When did you get here? Why'd you take so long? God, I missed you."

"Obviously, you didn't miss me enough not to pack your bags and start med school against my wishes."

"It was something I…"

He brought both hands on my face and kissed me longingly, lovingly, tenderly. "What were you thinking about so intensely?" he asked when we were done with our embrace.

He continued to sit with his knees on the ground, in front of me. I couldn't convince him to sit next to me. "I was thinking about all the times you broke my heart and I had to come here for solace, then my last thought was what kind of memories we'd make here now that we were in love."

"I remember the day I met a spunky ten-year-old, who looked like Goldilocks with her beautifully long blonde hair and piercing blue eyes. There was something special about this ten-year-old that made me think of her from time to time, and look forward to seeing her again. This was the same girl who threw up on me, pushed me in the ocean while we were both fully clothed, and the same girl who followed me around with her genius-sized vocabulary." He held my hands in his and kissed them fondly. "Then one day, I see that this girl was no longer a girl but a stunning woman who made my body stir and senses come alive. She was so beautiful, so sweet, and so caring. And I wanted so much to love her, but I was never honest with myself or courageous enough to try."

"You're going to make me cry, Donovan," I warned as he went even more sentimental on me.

"While I made this woman smile, and while I made this woman cry, I was falling in love with her but had no freakin' clue what these feelings were and what to do with them. Stupid me focused my energies on other women who didn't mean anything to me when compared to this brave and beautiful woman who cried too many tears over me. No more crying, my Princess. This swing is the most fitting place for me to tell you that I know now what it means to love a woman and I know now that you mean everything to me. My life, my breath, my all, I give to you. I can only be complete with you. Delaney Grace Reid. Will you marry me?"

I was so caught up in all he was saying, I'd barely noticed that he had switched positions, and was on one knee. And though I saw him put his hand in his jacket pocket, I didn't register what he was doing. He had just asked me to marry him. He knew. He'd figured it out. Oh, my gosh! I was going to marry Donovan Taylor! But, none of it was going to happen if I didn't answer his proposal.

"Yes." I whispered. "Yes I'll marry you because you have been my life, my breath, my all, for as long as I can remember. There's never been anyone else, and there never will be. I love you Donovan Taylor and can't wait to be your wife!"

He placed the ring on my finger and pulled me up for another heart-stirring kiss. We would have gone straight back to Donovan's had our families not come out to congratulate us.

"I love you," he whispered one last time before we were front and center at our engagement party.

"You all knew? That's why everyone's here?" I had no idea Donovan had worked so hard to get the family together to witness our engagement.

"Let me tell you, Fiancée. You did not make it easy for me this week."

"I'm sorry." I spoke quietly because I knew I had made Donovan's life difficult. "I promise to be good from now on." I teased.

"Yeah…" He shook his head in disbelief. "I need that in writing."

I was curious to know how this proposal came about, but didn't want to take away too much of the spotlight from my dad, who was celebrating his birthday, and Ma and Pa who were celebrating their anniversary with all their children and grandchildren. Amanda came over and hugged me like she'd found her lost sister. I was grateful to have found her and her family. As Donovan warned earlier, I did end up falling in absolute love with her and Kelley's boys. I also got to know Rachel and her husband.

They juggled a ten-month-old, who reminded me of James. I played with him and gave his parents a much-needed rest.

We made love the moment we came home and made up for the week's absence. Of course our first attempt lasted all of three minutes with the built-up tension. The next attempt was truly the most delicious lovemaking, as we took time to express our love and lust for one another.

"How did you finally figure out I wanted a proposal?" This question was on the tip of my tongue the entire night but I'd kept it in. I knew I wanted this to be our first topic of pillow talk. Of course nothing beat the intimacy of being joined as one with Donovan, but our pillow talk that happened after each act of intimacy, I cherished almost as much as the love making.

"After Max and Jane left for home, I happened to speak with her on the phone and she asked me how things were going between us. I told her that telling you we were getting married was like telling Ellie to do something. The only answer I ever got was a firm no. Jane suggested I ask rather than tell you we were getting married, and even then, it didn't fully dawn on me what you wanted."

"So how did you figure it out when you didn't know after Jane spelled it out for you?"

"It was that night after the firm party when I asked you if you didn't want to marry me anymore. I had said that more to get you to pity me, but the look of sad resignation I saw in your eyes when you told me that you didn't need anything from me, and that you'd get your mom to start preparations. It was then that I wondered what the hell was wrong with me. I should have known from the start that all you wanted was a confession of my heart and a proposal of marriage. You were always too fanciful and too headstrong to give in to a demand."

"That's why you wouldn't let me finish my sentence and you stuttered your way through that conversation?"

"Yes. That's why." He lifted up my ring finger. "You like the ring? It's not as big as I would have liked on your finger, but when I saw this diamond, I knew it was for you."

"I love it. When did you have the time to purchase a ring?"

"Oh, between doing your grandfather's bidding to sell the company, keeping one irate girlfriend from being too pissed with me for not taking her on this business trip, and looking for an elusive princess cut fancy pink diamond, this week has been hell. This," he kissed my ring finger, "was the reason why I didn't take you with me. It wouldn't have been a surprise if you knew I was searching for this diamond."

"I'm sorry!" I kept my head tucked in his neck in shame. "I went a bit overboard, huh?"

Donovan let out a loud, "Yeah! You can say that again."

"I really am sorry, but I'm not sorry I started med school. Especially now that we are getting married, I want to move on with my life so we can start a family. I want kids with you and seeing you with the twins, I know that's high priority for you too."

"We'll figure out this long distance engagement, somehow." Donovan kind of sighed which made me giggle. Poor guy...

"Can you tell me how this pink diamond came about?" I lifted up my left hand and stared at the gorgeous diamond staring back at me. "I've never seen a pink diamond before. It's stunning!"

"Back in Scotland I asked your parents and your grandparents for permission to propose to you. After they approved I started talking to Gram about possible diamonds for you. It was your grandfather who put the idea of a pink diamond in my head and I went all over Europe looking for *THE* one I thought was perfect for you. When I finally saw this one, I knew I'd found your ring."

"It's gorgeous. I couldn't have asked for a more perfect ring."

"It fits you. You were born to wear this ring. I want you to know, it's a good thing you enrolled in med school as a Reid. I think I used up half your tuition on this piece of jewelry."

"That's crazy! You could have taken one of my mom's small diamonds, and I would have been fine. Even a plain wedding band would have suited me. You know all I wanted was a proposal."

"I know. Your parents, Roland, and Gram all offered me anything I wanted from their collections, but this is what I wanted to get for you."

"I'll cherish it forever." I thanked him.

"Oh." He lit up. "I forgot to tell you that you got a ring named after you. The jewelry store I ended up purchasing this three carat pink fancy diamond from liked what they had created for you so much, they made another one just like it and called it the '*Delaney*.'"

"Are you kidding me?"

"I am not. Next time you go to Munich, you can walk in the store and tell them who you are."

"What a gift!"

...Forever...

"Shit! I'm late. How can that be?"

"You are late. Let's go!" Sam urged as she helped me into my wedding gown.

"Huh…? Oh, yeah. Let's get going."

As I talked to myself, I became worried and excited about what I thought might be happening.

"You've got to hurry. The ceremony's supposed to take place in thirty minutes and we've yet to leave for the church. I saw Donovan earlier and he looks so handsome, Laney."

"I know," I answered dreamily. "He's always devastatingly handsome, especially in a tuxedo."

"He is. I thought Jake and Max were handsome. I think your Donovan is off-the-chart on the handsome scale."

I smiled. "Thanks. I think so too."

After putting on the gown Gram sent me from London, and the Swarovski glass slippers I got from Grandfather's treasure chest, I carefully walked down the steps. Since Gram had purchased Emily's wedding gown, she decided to start a new Reid family tradition of taking all the future brides wedding dress shopping with her. During our three-month "separation," Gram had this gown made for me, and each time I visited Donovan I went in for my fittings. Somehow, even separated by all of America and the Atlantic Ocean, Donovan and I still saw each other at least once a month. I flew out to Europe whenever I had a random Monday or Friday off and took long weekends, or he came here whenever he had more than three days to spare. It wasn't ideal, but it worked.

Crazily enough, Gram and I never found the perfect gown in the stores, no matter how hard we tried. She eventually turned to a seamstress she'd used for decades and after we brainstormed ideas for a gown, we ended up copying Grace Kelly's wedding dress, minus all the lace over the actual bodice of the dress. Instead of the peau de soi and lace of Grace Kelly's dress, mine had a peau de soie and tiny crystals over the bodice of the dress. The crystals just seemed appropriate after all the dresses I had been in with Donovan. Plus, it matched my shoes. But, the big bummer was, I had to lose a bit of weight. Actually, it took more than a few pounds, to get that dramatic Grace Kelly waistline look when the taffeta cummerbund fused the top and bottom part of my dress together. Losing weight was painful, but once I put on the dress, I knew it was worth it. Donovan would be pleased.

"Let's go or we'll be late!" Sam resorted to nagging. "Everyone is there already."

"Oh, all right! I'm going as fast as I can. It's not easy moving in this dress and I think my circulation is cut off by the cummerbund."

"You look so beautiful, Laney. That's the most beautiful dress I've ever seen. I might want to borrow it when I get married."

"That's what I thought when I first saw Emily in her dress. But I'm sure Gram will come up with an even more stunning dress for you."

"I don't know what could beat your dress."

After inching down the steps, I finally got outside and found the first of my wedding surprises from my husband-to-be. It was an exact replica of Cinderella's carriage waiting for me.

"For you, Princess Laney." Sam was all smiles as she helped me step into the carriage.

"Where did this come from? And why aren't you getting in?"

"As for where? Ask the groom. And as for why? I was told you were the only one to be in this carriage. My carriage awaits in the form of my Volkswagen Beetle." She pointed to her car.

"That's silly. Get in with me." I urged.

"Oh no! Your fiancé told me that I was not to be in the carriage." She laughed and pretended to be offended. "Your husband-to-be had specific ideas of what this wedding is to be like for you. He wanted it to be your fairytale."

With that she shut the door and waved good-bye. I traveled down the lanes to the nearby church and waved to the few passersby who gawked wondering what nut was in Cinderella's pumpkin-shaped carriage on the streets of LA. They probably thought I was a star filming a movie.

When the carriage pulled up to the church, Doug, Nick, and Max were waiting for me, ready to be my escorts.

"You look beautiful, little sis." My brother actually paid me a compliment.

"The groom is waiting anxiously for you." Nick smiled.

"He was sweating bullets thinking you might not show. You're cutting it a bit close, aren't you? The ceremony starts in a few minutes." Max was the last to speak.

"Well, you try going to the bathroom after getting into layers and layers of clothes. And the carriage only goes like two miles per hour," I quipped in return. "It's not easy moving around right now."

"Now that your chariot has brought you here, your knight in shining armor awaits inside." Max held out an arm and I carefully walked up the steps and into the church.

"Oh, Baby!" Dad was almost in tears when he saw me. "You look stunning."

"Thank you, Daddy. I guess it's time, huh?" He was sadder than I had hoped. "You know I'll be around all the time. And it's not like Donovan and I will be far. We're just a few minutes away."

"I know, Baby. It'll just be different knowing I won't see you every day."

"Between med school and events on the cul-de-sac, I'm sure I'll see you just about daily. And don't forget our Sunday dinners."

"I know..." I did my best to stay chipper for a father who believed he was losing his daughter too soon.

We stepped closer to the closed door where Emily, along with the twins, was waiting for us. She gave me a radiant smile and whispered, "You look beautiful!"

I whispered back a "Thank you," and embraced the twins with a loving touch to their backs.

We decided to make the wedding party simple—Jake, Emily and the twins. Since the twins were younger than the usual flower girl and ring bearer, we thought Emily would walk in with them in tow.

The music began, and the doors opened to my matron of honor and her children. I was set back so I saw them enter, then the doors closed.

Next, the bridal march began, and my father placed my arm atop his as we stepped up to the door. When it opened, the only person I saw was my groom, so handsomely dressed in a black tuxedo, wearing the most incredible smile. I'd dreamed of this moment a thousand times, but never did I understand how heart stopping this moment would be. The imaginary figure I'd seen in my dreams walking down the aisle to meet Donovan at his wedding actually turned out to be me. I'd dreamed, but never believed in this dream. And now, it was no longer a fantasy but a reality.

The wave of tenderness on his face had me mindless. His evocative smile, his completely unguarded emotions wrapped around me like a silky cocoon to a moth, with promises of protection and care, and a brighter future. This man would help me transform from an egg to a chrysalis to an exquisite butterfly—free to fly, free to explore, and always safe in his love. My dream. My knight. My Donovan.

"Dazzling, Princess. Simply dazzling!" he whispered in my ear as he unlocked my arm from an unwilling father. "Thank you, Chief. I promise to take good care of her." Donovan reassured my dad.

The entire ceremony was a blur. I continued to remind myself that I was standing here with Donovan, and this was our wedding day.

At one point, Donovan had to lean over and whisper, "Princess. You need to say, 'I do' if you want to marry me." Embarrassed and startled to be caught daydreaming, by all our guests, I said, "I do," a little too loudly and got a rise out of the crowd. Donovan tried hard not to laugh.

"What has you in such a daze?" Donovan asked after he happily kissed the bride.

"You. Us. This wedding. The fact that I'm the bride." I made very little sense, but Donovan loved every word. He kissed me again and the guests stood up and cheered.

"Where did this fabulous carriage come from?" I still couldn't believe I was in Cinderella's carriage.

"Wait till you see what your mom's done with the house."

"What do you mean? The house looked the same when I left it a couple of hours ago."

"Princess, this is your fairytale and I am your prince today. Your mom and I are going to give you all your heart has ever desired."

Well, with that confession of love, I had to kiss him from the church to the house. Though distance-wise it wasn't far, it took a long time.

Somehow, during the ceremony and pictures at the church, Mom had turned our house into a Winter Wonderland. When we got back, there was snow all along the Reid cul-de-sac. Today being Christmas, lights were all sparkling white and *snow* decorated our entire neighborhood, especially our home.

"How did Mom do this? It's stunning."

"Wait till you walk in. I wanted everything to be perfect for you." He kissed me one more time and helped me out of the carriage.

We walked into a myriad of cheers, and before I could walk into the backyard, Bee met us.

"Congratulations, Niece. I guess we are finally family." We hugged. "I have a wedding present for you and it's upstairs, so come with me."

Donovan let me go, initially, then pulled me back into his arms and kissed me hungry...long... deep… "I love you, Delaney Taylor."

That moniker made me squeal. "It's finally come true! I knew my notebook wouldn't let me down."

His smile told me he thought I was the cutest girl in the whole wide world, before he let me go with Bee.

"You're happy?"

"I am!" I sighed with contentment. "I'm so happy to be your niece!" I fell into Bee with a hug.

"You're a nut," she said with a laugh. "Come on up. Your family is waiting."

Gram, Mom, all my aunts, Emily, Ellie, Jane, Ma, and my new sister-in-laws stood around to give me hugs, good cheers, and to watch me get into my new outfit.

"First," Bee said and pointed to my bathroom, "you're getting out of your wedding gown and dressing into your wedding reception gown."

"I have a wedding reception gown?" Could this get any better for a woman who loved clothes?

"Follow," she announced, helping me into the bathroom, out of my treasured wedding gown, and into her very own creation from the Paris fashion show. The only difference—the tulle was now a red tulle rather than the typical wedding white tulle.

"This is so Christmasy and festive."

"That's the plan."

I came out to many more oohs and aahs. Gram spoke, "Since we weren't able to give you a proper family bridal shower, we thought we might give you our wedding tradition presents here, but Donovan just asked us to come down and present it together with his rehearsal dinner gift. So, let's all go down."

What? There were so many things going on all at once, I didn't know how to respond.

"Just follow," Jane suggested. "Donovan's got the day planned. I've never seen such an involved groom." She rolled her eyes. "Max better be this interested in our wedding."

"How can Donovan be involved when he just got home last night? He barely made it to the wedding."

"Trust me." Now Mom and Ma both rolled their eyes. "He was plenty involved from Europe!"

I didn't ask.

My groom awaited me at the bottom of the steps and had that look of adoration, again. A girl could really get used to this kind of attention.

"This dress reminds me of our first night in Paris, ma petite mort," he announced, aloud, and with a rascally smile.

I pulled him away from a bunch of giggling women who understood the euphemism. "Are you kidding me? Did you need to brag in front of my family? That was *mort*ifying." I giggled at my own pun.

"You are always so good with your mouth." He pulled me into him and gave me another one of those rock-my-world, don't-give-a-damn-who's-at-my-party, we-are-so-going-to-our-honeymoon-suite-now! kind of kiss.

"Let's get the show on the road, Mr. Taylor!" Jane groaned at our amorous show.

"Don't mind her, Husband." I teased my cousin. "She's just upset that I got married before she did. She always did want whatever was mine." That earned me a swat on my backside by my cousin and much laughter among the three of us.

Donovan walked me into a tent where the party was hopping, and we got a grand ovation from all our family and friends. Mom cleverly planned a Christmas-themed wedding reception where everything appeared white, but silver and red somehow emerged from the white. There were hundreds of Christmas balls hanging like chandeliers with bright white lights in the balls, but here and there, a red light or two or ten sparkled among the white. On the tables were huge cylindrical vases filled with white, silver and red Christmas ornaments in water and floating white candles in the shape of balls. The light gave off the image of white, but silver and red popped from the vases. White flowers filled the tent, highlighted by red flowers, or even cranberries decorating the flower design. We were told to have "bites" of food because we needed to get on to the main event.

"Is dancing the main event?" I asked Hubby.

"Your gifts are the main event."

"Ooh, I like gifts! But first, I need to eat. Feed me, Husband." I commanded with the prettiest bridal smile.

Mom and the rest of the female commanders literally gave us five minutes to eat. They weren't kidding when they said we were getting "bites" of food. I shoved more food into my mouth as Gram took the microphone.

"As matriarch of the Reid family, nothing gives me more joy than watching one of my grandchildren get married, or have babies. I've been fortunate enough to see two weddings and three babies, and I'm hoping to see all my grandchildren at least married, before I die." Gram literally looked at every one of her grandkids in the tent and commanded them to get married soon. "Laney has always been the happiest of my grandchildren, always with her nose in a book, or her head up in the sky, dreaming. She had the brain power of two adults, even as a child, and no matter how docile and timid she looked, she was always a force to reckon with when you crossed her." The crowd laughed and cheered in agreement.

"One time, I told her fairies didn't exist and to prove me wrong, she put pixie dust all over my room and told me Tinkerbell had stopped by and left the fairy dust so I may become a believer." Doug stood up and gave that anecdote of my childhood.

"But Tinkerbell did come by," I argued with laughter.

"One time, I told Laney the worst color on the wheel was pink," Jane explained, "and next thing I know, she had ordered enough pink balloons to fill my entire bedroom. It took me so long to pop every one of those damn balloons."

"You would be pissy enough to pop the balloons rather than enjoy them." I yelled, as sweetly as possible, at her.

Gram took hold of the entire room again, just by lifting her hand. "Contrary to her sweet and easy-going appearance, this granddaughter of mine never followed the norm, didn't need someone to lead her, and told everyone to go to hell with a smile and a 'please.'"

"That's my girl." Dad called out with pride.

"She never needed anyone to play with her because her imagination was enough. She never needed anyone's approval because she was secure in herself. And she never loved any other man because she believed this one Donovan Taylor was her perfect man, and the hell with anyone who didn't agree with her. Back in London when Laney and Donovan first started dating, I encouraged her to date other men, love other men, experience life. In her delightful way, she told me that as much as she wanted my approval, she wouldn't give up on Donovan. He was the man for her and even if it didn't work out, she'd rather live in misery, having loved with Donovan, than in partial-contentment, never having known what it was like to be loved by this man."

My husband beamed as he leaned over and said, "Remind me to show you how much I appreciate you, later."

"If Gram speaks any longer, I may be asleep, later," I whispered back.

Donovan smirked and replied, "Yeah...like you're not ready and willing whenever my lips touch your lips...both lips." I shivered while he grinned. "Like I don't know that you're already wet right now remembering how I woke you up last night."

"Stop," I let out a weak complaint. "This dress is partially see-through and flimsy. I don't need people seeing spots since I'm not wearing any underwear."

That, plus my hand on his thigh, jolted Donovan in his seat. "Why the hell aren't you wearing underwear under this dress?"

I shrugged my shoulders. "The gal at the salon gave me a full wax this morning and I was feeling braver than usual." I gave a blasé, oh-I-do-this-no-underwear-business-all-the-time attitude.

"Is a full-wax what I think it is?"

I shrugged again and pointed his attention to my Gram.

"We have a tradition among the ladies where we gather around the bride and give her something old, something new, something borrowed, and something blue. This year, because of the unusual circumstance of the groom showing up the morning of his wedding, we decided to present her with these gifts at the reception." The crowd clapped for Gram. We all loved surprises, and we all loved gifts. "Normally, we'd start with something old, but today, we decided to start with something new. Taylor sisters, take it away..."

All four sisters walked up to the makeshift riser on the dance floor. Even Becky with her newborn stood up there and they all had wicked grins.

"Shit." Donovan didn't even bother whispering. "Brace yourself, Delaney. This could get ugly. Damn. What are my sisters up to?"

"When we were growing up, there were four girls and one boy in the family. You could say he was the king of the house, and he could get away with something as close to murder." Amanda started.

"That's a lie." Ma said with deep laughter. "We loved you girls just as much as Donny."

"Yeah. It's more like they loved the four of us combined as much as they loved their one and only Donny." Kelley joined her sister. "He was the first to eat, first to get a bath, first and only to get the remote."

"We treated you equally." Pa pretended to cry. "Don't do this and embarrass the family, girls." He wiped his non-existent tears. We all died laughing at Pa's performance.

"Being the child who came right after Donny, I got all his leftovers. I think one time, I even had to wear his hand-me-downs because even as a child, he tended toward the questionable colors. I mean, what teenager wore coral shorts and periwinkle button-downs?"

"Hey, I never wore those colors in combination. I had much better fashion sense than that." Donovan was now defending himself.

Rachel was the last, but not the least to speak. "Becky just had a baby, I was struggling with having a one-year-old and being pregnant with a second, but did Mom offer to help either one of us in our time of need? She chose to stay in LA and plan Donny's wedding with her new Baby! Even his bride has taken precedence over us." Rachel giggled those last few words.

"Ma and Pa offered to help you if you came to LA. They even offered to buy your plane tickets out here." I defended my "helpless" in-laws.

"Thank you, Baby," Ma called out. I blew her a kiss.

"Ingrates." Pa went up the riser and kissed every one of his daughters. "We promise to try and love all the grandchildren, equally." That earned him a groan as he ran to kiss me before he sat back in his seat.

"We four agreed that the worst part of being one of four girls was the fact that we never had anything of our own." Amanda was back at the helm. "We shared clothes, rooms, toys, boyfriends..." That got the loudest roar.

"Who shared boyfriends, and who was the lucky boy?" Nick asked.

The Taylor sisters only laughed, but stayed mum.

I looked at my husband, and he too kept his mouth shut.

"Well?" Nick kept at it.

Amanda barely let out, "We don't want our ex-boyfriend to get into trouble with his wife, do we, Kelley?" before she burst out into a fit of guffaw.

"No freakin' way." Nick howled. "Was it at the same time?" He made a blushing Jake even more uncomfortable.

I saw Jake whisper something in Emily's ears and he, too, made an appearance on stage. "I only tried it when Donovan made dating an older woman look so incredibly enticing."

"Asshole!" Donovan yelled at his best friend who had deflected the attention from him, back to the groom. Jake and my new sisters died laughing. Before Jake left the stage, he hugged and gave a peck on the cheek to both his exes.

"Sorry, Emily. I hope that doesn't cause any rift in the bedroom tonight." Amanda must've had a drink or two or five already.

Jake quickly darted back to his wife and kissed her passionately in front of everyone. "Two years, three kids, and possibly another one coming soon. All is good in the bedroom."

"What the hell? Again?" Nick turned to Jake and Emily. Emily shook her head vehemently and mouthed, "NO!"

"So back to something new," Amanda brought the attention front and center.

"Damn, at this rate, we're never getting on to the honeymoon." I said, maybe a little too loudly.

"We heard that, Laney Taylor." Rachel waggled her finger at me.

"Tonight?" I questioned with a grin.

"When we were growing up," Amanda didn't give a damn what I groaned about, "my sisters and I had a chest full of toys and Donovan had his own chest full of toys. While the four of us shared four Barbie dolls and four outfits, Donovan had ten of everything. So when my sisters and I thought through what we could get our newest sister for a bridal shower gift, we thought we'd get Laney her own chest full of toys."

This is when Al and Noah brought up a chest even bigger than Gimpy's chest the night before his wedding.

"Laney Taylor," Becky yelled like Bob Barker from the *Price is Right*, "Come on down!"

"Now this toy chest is filled with gifts from everyone. The Taylors and the Reids, as well as your girlfriends." Amanda did a slow reveal of what was inside. "This is a collection of all of our favorite toys."

SHIT! I turned as red as the fake pomegranate tree decorating the stage. "You have got to be kidding me." I said to my newfound sisters.

"We are not kidding you." Rachel answered me then told Donovan, "You're very welcome, Donny!"

"What the hell is in there?" Nick asked.

"Bee Taylor? You want to start us off?"

Bee sauntered onto our shared stage and began handing us each a lingerie. I followed my sisters and put it over our bodies, to the hoot and holler of all.

"Featuring, my new lingerie collection." Bee looked like one of Bob Barker's hand models, with all her gesticulations. "You remember the first time you saw her in this?" Aunt Bee asked her nephew. "You're welcome, Nephew." She hugged me before going off stage.

"Jane Reid, soon to be Davis. Come on down." Becky Bob Barker called out again.

Jane began her monologue. "I remember you as one who always loved to read and role play. You put me in those damn Maleficent costumes often enough. So to say thank you for the hundreds of times you made me wear pink, then black, I give you a Kindle with all the naughty books you might want to read alone...or with your husband and outfits that will allow you to role play some of the scenes from the books." Jane pulled out all kinds of outfits—nurse, candy-striper, doctor, teacher, student, cheerleader, waitress at Hooters, French maid, naughty Pocahontas, naughty Cinderella, and even a policewoman outfit complete with Raybans, handcuffs, and a vibrator made to look like a cane that she turned on for all to see and hear. "You're very welcome, Donovan Taylor!" She walked over and gave him a big kiss on the cheek before going back into her fiancé's arms.

"We Taylor girls put in a few favorite toys of our own. As to who picked which toys...?" Amanda's eyebrows lifted along with her shoulders, in the cutest way.

Rachel picked up a plastic dildo and put her hand to her mouth that formed into an "O." She made like she was shocked to see such an item in the chest and had me hold the base with one hand, and the phallic part with the other hand—lewd and crass! "This is just in case...my brother isn't the *big* brother I thought he was." Everyone howled, especially the men.

"And this one," Kelley picked up something that looked like a teething ring I'd seen the twins use, "this one is called an erection ring." She read the tag on the ring, then stuck it down my middle finger. "This is just in case our brother can't *stand up* to the demands of being a newlywed!" The sisters were putting on the show of a lifetime.

"In all seriousness, we are thrilled that our brother has found his soul mate. The four of us wholeheartedly agree that Laney is the perfect girl to handle our brother. You two are a match made in heaven, and we wish you as much happiness as we have found in our own marriages. Welcome to the Taylor family, Laney!" Amanda ended her speech and Donovan came up to hug his sisters with me.

Gram was back up as my newfound sisters were putting the toys back in the chest and Donovan and I sat back in our seats. "Where the hell were we?" She looked at Mom and Aunt Sandy for direction. "Those Taylor girls will fit right in with the Reid women. We'll have to lock the liquor cabinets before those girls arrive for the holidays." We all laughed in good cheer. "OK, I think we are onto something borrowed. And for that, Roland, take it away, my love."

Grandfather came up and kissed his wife, first and foremost, then addressed all of us. "For those of you who don't know, Estelle and I only recently married. I knew the Reid children through Estelle and her first husband, Jerry, but I never got a chance to know all the grandchildren until Estelle and I came back here and made our union final. I know grandparents aren't supposed to have favorites...."

"Yeah, Gram!" Doug called out in jest.

"But there are some kids who just call out to us. Jane was always that child for me. When I met her, she spoke to my heart, and I adored her."

"How come it's always Aunt Sandy's kids?" Sam complained.

"But after getting to know Laney the past few months, I have to say, you're very special to my heart as well, young lady."

"Thank you, Grandfather. I love you too." I spoke from my heart.

"I first met Donovan about ten years ago when Jake brought him to the LA office one of the months I was in town. Jake, being a good friend, thought he'd introduce us and let me know that his best friend was headed to law school. I liked Donovan instantly, as did all the other female staff in the LA office," Grandfather chuckled, "and made note to remember him when he came to interview for a job in three years. The thing about Donovan most of you don't know is that he's an absolute lion in the courtroom, the boardroom, and every M&A dealing that comes his way. He roars, but he's also fair in his dealings. Because of that, all the lawyers who work with him and against him respect him. It's rare in our business to be so successful, and so well liked. Donovan is one of those few people."

"Thank you, Roland." Donovan spoke. "But in all honesty, Grandfather here is exceptionally happy with me right now because I finished up the sale of his company to the highest bidder, plus an extra buck or two."

"Made you and your wife pretty rich, too," Grandfather smirked.

"All in a day's work." Donovan shrugged it off like it was nothing.

"As for his counterpart, if he's the lion, she's unequivocally his lioness. The day of Estelle and my wedding, I asked Laney why she chose the glass slippers she is currently wearing rather than a piece of jewelry. There were still quite a number of valuable items, but she chose these shoes, which incidentally, only fit her feet out of all the women in the room. And her answer?" Grandfather looked at me for an answer, so I repeated what I told him months ago.

"Some women, like my grandmother, have two princes in their lifetime who come and sweep them off their feet. Some women, like my mother, have one prince who fall at their feet from day one and love them forever. For me, I like to believe that though my prince has yet to even notice my feet, with such pretty shoes as these, I'll land on my two feet no matter the situation."

Grandfather chuckled along with the crowd at my explanation. "As much as Laney was already in love with a very dense Donovan Taylor, she understood that she would be all right, with or without him. I loved the tough-girl fairytale attitude."

"Did you really say that?" Donovan asked, surprised.

"I did. Why are you so surprised?"

"You truly would have been all right without me in your life?" His voice was slightly sad.

"I wouldn't have been all right, but I would have moved on with life and tried my damnedest to forget you, Mr. Taylor. You were nothing but heartache up until about two hours ago." I winked and gave him a kiss on the lips.

"Because your grandmother and I are so pleased with the both of you as individuals, and as a couple, we are happy to present you with a 'borrowed' plane for your honeymoon. Take the jet to your honeymoon destination. That, and a much needed time off, is yours for as long as you like."

We got up to thank our grandfather.

"That has to be the most generous offer. Thank you, Grandfather." I was speechless.

"Roland. That's extraordinarily thoughtful of you, but I have tickets purchased. You and Gram use the plane to go visit your homes in Europe."

"Your Gram wants to be nowhere but home with her family. We will be on this cul-de-sac till we die. Use the plane. You and Laney deserve it."

"Thank you." We were awestruck by their kindness.

As we walked back to our seats, we saw Jake and Emily walk up to the stage. Emily started the speech, first. "Everyone in this tent wanted to do something special for this couple, tonight. Jake and I fought to get one of the four traditions and something blue fell upon us after much begging. I first got to know Laney at my bridal shower and wedding, and my initial thought upon spending some time with her was, what a confident woman. We shared a similarity in that we had both just finished up our time in Japan. She went to study abroad whereas I went to mend a broken heart. I can't tell you how much my heart hurt watching her love a man who loved her in return, but had no clue that he did!" Emily was doing a little reprimand. "Donovan Taylor, you were as bad as Jake when…" That's when Jake took the microphone from her and brought his wife into his body.

"I'd like to tell you a story about two people who could not get each other off their minds no matter the number of years that went by. Young Laney Reid was smitten with an older Donovan Taylor, and she'd ask me to deliver notes to him in the form of dropping them in his pocket. I'd get specific instructions like, 'Now place this note in his front, right pants' pocket when he's not looking,' or 'Jake, can you slip this note in the inside pocket of his jacket?' Now in reality, Laney, how was I supposed to do this if he was wearing his pants or jacket?"

Everyone laughed.

"You mean to tell me all these years, you lied and said you did what I asked without really doing it?" I accused.

"Every note was placed in his right jacket pocket." Jake winked at me.

"How boring," I complained.

Jake only shrugged. "These two have also been giving each other gifts for as long as I could remember. Donovan." He got my husband's attention. "That brown messenger bag you take with you to work every day. Guess who gave that to you when you graduated from law school?"

"You?"

"Guess again."

"You?" He turned to me as I nodded yes.

"I take it you liked it?" I whispered.

"I used it every day. It's my go-to bag for everything." That made me smile.

"Yep. It was from a young Laney Reid who had to have saved up her money for a long time to be able to afford designer travel bags. Comically enough, as Laney asked me to give Donovan the present as a gift from me, Donovan gave me a gift, just a few weeks later, and told me to give it to Laney under the pretense that I had purchased it for her sixteenth birthday."

"You're the one who bought me that ring?"

"I saw it in Europe and thought of you, and I knew your sixteenth birthday was coming up."

"Why didn't you give it to me? It would have made me so happy."

"It seemed inappropriate at the time."

"And the gift giving went on." Jake continued his story. "Laney has given Donovan a birthday gift every year since her sixteenth birthday. Lucky for me, I never had to buy my best friend a gift because Laney did it for me." He got laughs from everyone. "And Donovan started showering

Laney with gifts once they re-met back in January, but those gifts always came from me and Emily."

It was at this point Emily took back the mic. "When we went to Hawaii, Jake and I saw Laney and Donovan's love blossom into something special. We could almost taste a wedding in the near future. It was there that we think these two truly fell in love, and it was there that Donovan opened his eyes to a Laney who wasn't so young anymore. In honor of something blue, Jake and I would like to recreate that trip for you. We have two plane tickets and a stay at the same resort, but not the same Presidential villa room." That got huge laughter from all who went to Hawaii with us.

"Thank you." We both embraced our best friends. Donovan and I were floored at our family's love and generosity. I would have cried, if the practical me didn't understand that running make-up on a bride was not a pretty sight.

Gram got back on stage. "We are almost done, but we need the groom up here to explain the something old part, as well as to present his wife with her wedding rehearsal gift."

Donovan kissed me again before taking center stage. He was truly the most handsome man on this earth. I'd never tire of looking at his face.

"I have a friend who's not only my best friend, but has been my biggest competition since birth. He was born earlier than I was, he's slightly taller than I am, and he's always gotten better grades. If I got an A, he got an A+, if I got a BMX bike, he got the BMX X-games bike. We were always competing—but in a friendly way...kind of…" Donovan gave a nod to his best friend. "Of course he got married before I did and thanks to an over-the-top grandma, his bride got a six-carat diamond. Now how the hell does any man compete with a six-carat rock? Well, you don't. You do something different and unexpected. So after much thinking about this something old gift, I thought I'd finally outdo my best friend." Donovan gave Jake an evil grin.

All of a sudden, we heard, "Let's keep it simple and sane," from Max in the background. Max, of course was the next one up and he knew it wasn't going to be easy to top Jake's diamond earrings.

"Just like my buddy, I also picked something old and something new, but unlike my buddy, I've got more than two diamonds to give to my wife." We could all hear Max groaning loudly! The other Reid men followed suit. "Delaney Taylor, come on down!" My husband, too, did a Bob Barker imitation.

"Diamonds, diamonds, diamonds…" All the ladies chanted.

"My beautiful bride," he turned me to him. "You are more beautiful than Aphrodite, possess the intelligence and wisdom of Athena, and are more desirable than Persephone. If I were Hades, I wouldn't ever let you leave me. Every goddess, every princess have one thing in common—a crown. Since you are my princess, my goddess, my all, I thought it fitting to get a crown made for you." Donovan pulled out a black square jewelry box and opened it for me. "This crown was made from the generosity of your grandmother, grandfather, aunts, and parents who gave you all their loose diamonds. And all the pink diamonds that dot the crown are from me. I love you, Princess."

This is where I lost it and cried. It wasn't the tiara that broke me, but the love bestowed upon the both of us from our entire family. There was no doubt the Reid family personified love, but tonight was another fine example of just how much.

"Thank you," was really all I could say to my thoughtful husband.

"Now, my Cinderella, I want you to recognize the practicality of this crown. If you wear it this way," he adjusted it to sit on my head, "it becomes a tiara. But if you wear it this way," he then readjusted it to lay flat on my head, "it becomes a fancy headband."

After kissing my husband, we walked to our parents and showed them our appreciation for all they'd done for us from birth until now.

The party kept on, but Donovan and I were both ready to leave. Next to Donovan's proposal, tonight was the most memorable night of my life. My family and Donovan had made sure everything went beautifully.

"Last surprise, Princess." Donovan handed me a present box as I headed upstairs to change into my going-away outfit.

"More?" I broke into a huge smile. "How will you ever top tonight?" I teased.

"You just stick around long enough to find out," he teased back.

Bee helped me up to my bedroom for the last time and out of the stunning reception dress.

"What on earth is this?" I asked pulling out a pair of faded jeans, a fitted t-shirt and a leather jacket. "Are we off to a concert somewhere?"

"I've no idea, Laney Taylor. Your husband went through great lengths and secrecy to make this night better than a fairytale."

"And he succeeded!" I changed without arguing and with the last zip of my killer crocodile leather boots, I walked down the steps to a crowd of people milling about my porch. As the crowd saw me, they slowly cleared the way like Moses parting the Red Sea, and in my driveway were two Ducati motorcycles! My husband sat on one and the other had my name on it. "No freaking way!"

"Yes, freaking way! Come on, Wife. This is part one of our honeymoon."

"What does that mean?" Donovan had also planned the honeymoon, so I had no idea where we were headed. Not surprisingly, he had purchased all my clothes for the honeymoon and had packed my suitcase as well.

"We are riding to the hotel, and tomorrow we ride to where the plane is waiting." That was all I was getting for now.

"Well then, let's go!" I ran through the showering of white grains of rice with, crazy enough, red and silver-dyed rice mixed in the batch. Mom had truly thought of everything.

As I got on and looked over the bike, the nagging sensation that started my day came back. I knew there was something that needed to be done before we started our honeymoon. Getting off the bike, I walked a short step over to Donovan and asked him to follow me to our first of two destinations. He did as asked.

"What are we doing back at our house?"

"Can you come in for just a minute? I promise, it won't take long." I ran upstairs to our bedroom and had him wait by the staircase. After what seemed like an eternity, I frantically called Donovan up to our bedroom.

"What's the matter?" He had made a mad dash up the steps. "What's wrong?"

"This…" I handed him my wedding gift for a lifetime.

"I can't believe we're back here." I mused, watching the canals from our bedroom window.

"And I can't believe the wedding gift you gave me!" Donovan was still in shock with what happened right after the wedding.

"What do you think I was going through during the wedding? I couldn't stop thinking about it. I am now a certifiable floozy."

"That you are, my little tramp." He had that look in his eyes again.

"Shit. Not again. We just had sex for like the tenth time since we got to Amsterdam. We haven't left the room. We haven't had a bite to eat. Your baby is starving."

"That's your fault for changing our honeymoon plans last minute. We could've been surfing in South Africa, but here we are lounging in Europe."

"I thought since this was the place that started it all, we should come back here. Plus, we'll see water in a few days. The Maldives idea was a good one. I can't wait to be on the water. You think I can do some water sports while I'm there?"

"Absolutely not!"

"Hell. I just want it stated for the record, it was all your fault. I told you we needed to wait or you needed to use something."

"Yeah, like after not seeing you for almost a month, I could hold back. Tell me again how this baby happened." *Yes! A baby, Our baby!*

"The baby was conceived that week we spent skiing in Switzerland, during Thanksgiving break."

Donovan and I hadn't seen each other in close to a month, and decided that rather than spending time with the family during Thanksgiving, we'd spend it alone. I had a week off from school and Donovan's last client was in Zurich, so we decided to meet in St. Moritz and ski for a week.

"That was a hell of a week, wasn't it?"

"It was!"

Donovan met me at the airport and we couldn't keep our hands and lips off each other. The built up foreplay from sexting and phone sex reached its climax as we made a mad dash to the hotel and literally locked ourselves in for two straight days. What I failed to mention to my fiancé during the two days of uninterrupted sex was the fact that I was coming off a nasty sinus infection and that I was still on strong antibiotics. The doctor had warned me that antibiotics could reverse the effects of the pill, but since I hadn't seen Donovan in a while, I figured it wouldn't be an issue. Well, obviously I was wrong because the day of the wedding, I realized I was late with my period, and that had me wondering if I was possibly pregnant.

"You know, I worked really hard to come up with details of our wedding that would make it memorable for you."

"And you did. Our modes of transportations were the best. How did you find that Cinderella carriage?"

"I have a buddy who works in the movie industry, and after a bit of research, he found the carriage and restored it for me."

"And the Ducatis?"

"I had Max go to the Ducati dealer and pick out two bikes for us."

"Imagine my surprise when I was told to put on jeans and a biker's jacket for my going-away outfit, and imagine my double surprise when I got outside and found two Ducatis waiting for me. All your wedding presents were perfect!"

"Well, your surprise beat mine by a longshot. When you had us stop by the drugstore, then back at the house before our road trip, I didn't know what to think."

"I'm sorry I ruined your original plans. Riding up the coast in our bikes, then flying to South Africa to surf sounded like a dream. I guess I won't be surfing any time soon, huh? By the way, what were you going to do with our bikes if we got on the plane from San Francisco?"

"I was going to put them on Roland's plane with us."

"Oh." I would have never thought of that.

"Now I have a question that was never answered, Mrs. Taylor."

"And what's that, Mr. Taylor?"

"Who the hell sent me that diary of yours? You know, that was the final straw on the camel's back. Although...why the hell did you put three locks on a diary? I could only read bits and pieces of that book. From those few excerpts, I convinced myself we could work, but it took a lot of convincing. Though, I adored the ones from your childhood. There was no sweeter child than you."

I cracked-up at him. "Pretty ingenious of me to add two more locks, huh? I battled with Doug and Nick all my youth trying to keep this diary a secret. They kept stealing it from me, no matter where I hid it and would read it and laugh at me. So I invented a way of locking portions of the book so even if they stole it, they couldn't read the latest pages."

"You are ingenious, my lovely bride. But who was it?"

"Who do you think it was?"

"My money is on Jake. He and his wife were our biggest supporters. But when I asked him, he acted like he had no idea."

"It wasn't Jake and it wasn't Emily. It was actually my mother."

"Seriously?" Donovan laughed. "She was the matchmaking mama?"

"Yep. It was actually both our mothers."

"What? How did Jamie Taylor get involved?"

"When I asked Mom about the diary, she explained that your mom had come over one day, lurking about..."

"Lurking...?" Donovan was amused.

"She had heard that I was dating Michael and she asked in a round-about way about my feelings for you."

"Once Mom caught on, she spilled the beans about my infatuation for you since I was a babe-in-arms, so to speak, and the moms started conspiring. Mom said that between the two of them, they came up with some crazy ideas to get me home, since they knew I wouldn't see you in London. It took awhile for them to come up with a plan to get us together, but once the idea was hatched, Mom said she searched high and low for my diary and gave it to your mom to leave in your mailbox."

"I always thought it was mailed to me. I guess I never took a good look at the envelope. Why didn't they just mail it?"

I cracked-up again. "I asked the same question, and Mom said they were worried it might possibly get lost. Since you wouldn't listen to your parents and come after me in London, the moms thought the diary was their only hope."

"Well, they were right. Though I was so frustrated with the lock, I almost took a hammer myself and broke it open."

"And what about my privacy?" I feigned horror.

"Your privacy be dammed. This book held the key to our future."

I snorted in feigned disgust. "Our future my ass. Curiosity was killing you and you were willing to invade my privacy for your satisfaction."

"I'll show you what I'd like to do with you for my satisfaction, right now!"

And food was in the distant future again...

"I cannot believe you are actually on campus right now." Nick came over and greeted me with a hug. "Let's see the little bugger." He peeked into the baby carrier and gently rubbed the back of his forefinger on Henry's cheeks. "He's a beautiful blend of you and your husband."

"Thank you, Uncle Nick. I think he's pretty terrific, myself," I announced proudly.

"What the hell are you doing here?"

"I'm here for the same reason you are. Today is the first day of classes."

"You are a freaking glutton for punishment, aren't you? You're going to finish med school?"

"Of course I am. Thank God Henry was a bit early. Otherwise, I would have had to put med school on hold."

"You look like one of those out-of-wedlock teen moms bringing their babies to school. You bringing him to class with you daily? The school is allowing this?"

"I've got a nursery set up in Dad's office, and both sets of parents are helping for the time being. You know the first two years are mostly lectures and heavy coursework. I think that can be accomplished with kids-in-tow. It just means I sleep even less than I'm sleeping now."

Nick grinned. "And what about when you start rotations next year?"

"Who the hell knows? Maybe Donovan can take some time off and raise the kids."

"Mr. All-Powerful Lawyer?"

"Yep. The one and only. Since Jane and Max just got married, they're not having a baby anytime soon. She can be at the helm of the company for a while."

"Last I heard, Max says they're going to try right away to have kids. My brother-in-law is a bit starry-eyed over your little ones. And speaking of little ones, where's Scottie?"

"Scottie's been fed and is sleeping in Dad's office. It's Henry who's temperamental and needs to be walked after he's fed. That's why I'm out here."

"Shit, Laney. You are a posterboard for birth control and maybe even abstinence."

I laughed, but not too loudly. This little one had finally gone down for his nap. "I'll see you later. The twins don't like to be separated for long. I've got to quickly put Henry down next to his brother in their travel crib before either child notices."

"Bye and good luck."

"See ya. Say hi to Aunt Bee for me."

More Author's Notes...

I can't thank enough all the friends who've made this book possible. I want to start by thanking S.N. who has tirelessly looked for every grammatical error committed by me. It's a tough job to look for the subject-verb agreements or to remember that Delaney said "this" in one chapter and didn't switch to "that" in the next. I also want to thank all my dear friends who were willing to read this story and find errors out of the goodness of their hearts. D.F. and my British expert, R.P., thank you from the bottom of *my* heart! And to J.M. and J.T., who despite their crazy schedules, pull through for me every time and provide valuable insight just listening to what I have to say, it's a comfort knowing you are there.

But the biggest thank you has to go to all my Reiders / Friends! Without you, these books would be a waste of time. I thank you for loving the Reid family and for giving me an identity. This is a late-found hobby and thanks to you, I see myself writing for years to come. I hope you enjoy reading as much as I enjoy writing.

As a sincere thank you, I've enclosed excerpts from two projects I am currently working on. First is from *Near Perfect Attraction – Donovan's Story*. Donovan has his say and we get to find out what was going through his mind when he had three women on his radar, simultaneously! Next is my new blog that will be featured in Nov. / Dec. 2013. It will chronicle the lives of Nick and Bee. This time, I'll do something a little differently and have Bee speak on Mondays and Nick speak on Thursdays. It should be another Mr. Toad's Wild Ride!

As always, you can reach me at:
http://www.dwcee.com/
dw@dwcee.com
Facebook: https://www.facebook.com/DWCee
Twitter: https://twitter.com/DWCee_
Smashwords: https://www.smashwords.com/profile/view/DWCee

Near Perfect Attraction

Donovan's Story

d. w. cee

Near Perfect Attraction: Prologue

"Jake, *who* is that stunning blonde laughing with your bride?"

"*That's* the little girl you called your fifth sister."

"Shut the fuck up! That is not Delaney Reid!"

"That is. She's all grown up, huh? While you were screwing around with Kate and all the other women in between, our Laney grew into quite a beauty."

"She was always beautiful, and bright, but was she always that well-endowed?"

"Hey. That's my little cousin you're talking about. Uncle Henry would kick your ass if he knew you were ogling his daughter in such a way."

"Speaking of kicking your ass, I see that Jane and your bride's ex have become an item. Shit, you knew I wanted to ask Jane out, and you wouldn't let me. What the hell?"

"Buddy, I've always told you. She's not the girl for you. I say this not just because she's my sister. You and she are too fickle, too alike, too selfish—the list is endless as to why it would never work. However, I think this match with Max is a good one. And Emily is thrilled with the two of them getting to know one another."

"When the hell did you become a matchmaking mama?"

"What's wrong with the woman you have in your arms right now?"

"Nothing's wrong. She's just not right."

"And Kate?"

"Kate and I are done. I'm tired of us."

"What happened to living in wedded bliss with her for the rest of your life?"

"That wedded bliss ended the moment I got out of my early twenties. I don't think I'll ever find my Emily."

"Don't look too far. She may be closer than you think."

Perhaps I had been looking on the wrong cul-de-sac.

Nick & Bee's Blog (unofficial title)

BEE: Nicholas Gerald Reid!

"Shit, Bee. We said we wouldn't do this again." With that good morning, this asshole flew out of my bed and nearly ran out the door until the realization struck—he was buck-naked.

"Last I checked my clothes didn't rip open on their own. Are you Reid men all that aggressive in bed?" That was my good morning to Nicholas.

He grinned. *Fuck.* He was good looking when he grinned. I was so screwed. What the hell, I'd admit he was good looking any which way and form. "I haven't asked the other Reid men what they do to woo their woman."

"Woo? You call ripping off my dress and doing me against the wall, wooing? Let me tell you, what you did ends in an 'ing', but begins with a 'fuck.'"

Now he was laughing hard. "Where the hell do you come from, Bee Taylor? I've never met anyone like you."

"Which part makes me so irresistible to you, Nicholas? Charming as your cousin Laney, part? Opinionated but beautiful like your sister Jane, part? Or is it the perfect-all-around like Emily, part? Because I know it isn't the tall and buxom part like your cousin, dark hair, sparkling blue-eye combo like your sister, or is it the flawless skin and never gain an ounce of weight like your sister-in-law."

"It's the bust-my-balls but still make my dick hard, part that makes you so charming." If I ever thought he was going to lie like a doormat, I had another thing coming.

"Where are we going with this, Nicholas? Are we back to being friends with benefits when it's convenient, are we trying for something steadier, or are you going to get the hell out of here for the fifth time and never see me again...till the next time?"

"Are you asking me to be your boyfriend?"

He laughed.

I laughed.

We both fell back on the bed laughing.

In truth, I wouldn't have minded having someone like Nick as a boyfriend. At almost thirty, I was no spring chicken but I didn't consider myself an old maid, either. I had a successful career, a great family, and cool friends who kept me busy. I didn't need a man to fill my calendar, but a man did keep the bed warm. It was also nice to have someone to talk to about life. However, Nick believed he was going to die a bachelor. A part of me didn't want to fight it, and the other part didn't want to ask him to change. If he didn't see my worth, then the hell with him.

"Why don't you go home?" I asked as nonchalantly as possible. I didn't want to admit to Nick or to myself that I was irritated.

"Are you kicking me out?"

"Weren't you the one who bolted out of here with his bare ass on display? I'm not stopping you from leaving if you're so revolted by us sleeping together."

"Bee..." He gave me this tone whenever he had no answer to our unresolved situation.

"I get it. You like fucking me, but you don't want to date me."

"What's going on today? You're not acting like your usual carefree self. Why the sudden rant about relationships?"

Rant? Did this asshole think I was ranting and begging him to be in a relationship with me? "Just go home, Nicholas. I still have to finish Donovan and Laney's wedding gifts."

Nick put his clothes back on but didn't take his eyes off me. I didn't know what he thought he was accomplishing by staring at me while his very erect figure hung.

Nicholas Gerald Reid—6' 4", dark hair, blue eyes, just like his siblings, but taller, better built, and a rascal. If Jake was the quintessential good-looking, jet-black hair, shiny blue-eyed man who made women stop and take a second look, Nick was the younger, don't-give-a-damn, just-wanna-enjoy-life, man. He charmed women with not only his good looks, but also with his carefree personality. Jake was the ideal Reid. Nick was the fun Reid. I liked this fun Reid but wondered if we'd had enough fun now, and I should ask for a commitment.

Watching my nephew Donovan fall in love and court his fiancée, Delaney, there were too many times where I'd wished for that kind of adoration. But, was I willing to give up the freedom of doing what I wanted to do without anyone getting on my case? This was always the dilemma for me—my freedom vs. the security of a relationship.

"What are you being so spacey about? You're zoning." Nick was done getting dressed but hadn't left.

"It's nothing." There was not a chance in hell I was going to tell Nick about my insecurities. "Make sure to close the door on your way out. I'm hopping in the shower." With that, I left him standing there and jumped in the cold shower to wake myself up from an unrealistic fantasy.

When I got downstairs to my kitchen, I was peeved, again, to find that Nick did leave. What made me think he'd stick around? My last words were for him to close the door on his way out. He hadn't left a note, started my coffee, or in the least, shouted out a good-bye while I was showering. Hell! I needed to get Nicholas Reid off my mind.

"What are you doing here at this hour?" I answered the door with very little enthusiasm.

"What kind of welcome is that for your soon-to-be niece who brings you presents?"

Delaney stopped by early this morning, but thankfully, right after Nick left.

"It's the kind of welcome for someone who doesn't call to let me know she's coming." I was still irritated by my morning interaction with Nick.

"Um...you get up on the wrong side of the bed?" Delaney giggled. "Is Nick here and you're trying to hide him from me? Should I come back later?"

"What the hell makes you think Nicholas was here?" Shit! That was said too emphatically for it to sound nonchalant.

"Nicholas, huh? Is Nicholas Gerald what you yell out right at the point of climax?" Donovan was rubbing off on her. She was being smug!

"Impudent child!" I admonished but laughed together with her. "How was Switzerland?"

"Don't know, but my fiancé was beautiful!"

Here it was...the fairy tale love story! "Please, spare me the details!"

"I think we skied once the entire time I was there. We didn't leave the hotel room for two days straight. We only had to leave when housekeeping was absolutely necessary."

"Damn you, Delaney Reid! I told you I didn't want any details!"

"Oh, Auntie! Your nephew is the most romantic man. I am so in love with him."

"Are you here to torture me with your gory tales of love and sex?" If I was irritated earlier, now, I was thoroughly pissed with her happy mood.

"I'm here to give you a gift!"

"And what are you gifting dear old aunt?"

"There are two seats left on Grandfather's plane bound for London in a few days. I've put your name and Nick's name down for those empty seats." This girl was smiling so much I thought her face would break.

"And why the hell would I go to London?"

"For many reasons...to see the sights, to get another Mr. Whippy cone, to buy more boxes of Flakes, to check in with your vendors, to help all of us move our stuff back home, because Nick will be there..."

"What the hell? You signed me up to be your mover?"

"Kind of? It'll be fun! Have you ever been on my grandfather's plane? Donovan says it's the ultimate luxury. Plus, there's a bunch of us going. We'll have a great time!"

"Does Nick know he's going?"

"He does. I just told him when I caught him leaving your building at this very early hour." There was the reason why she had that cat got the canary look since she got here. "Care to share any details?"

"No! Now get out. I have added work because you're forcing me to Europe as your hired hand."

"Donovan will be so happy with the news!"

"Whatever. Good-bye!" I literally pushed her out the door. She left with an even more self-satisfied smile.

London with Nick? Had potential.

www.ingramcontent.com/pod-product-compliance
Lightning Source LLC
Chambersburg PA
CBHW072006020726
47501CB00006B/1710